The Fourth
Cadfael Omnibus

Also by Ellis Peters

Ellis Peters

The Fourth Cadfael Omnibus

The Pilgrim of Hate
An Excellent Mystery
The Raven in the Foregate

WARNER FUTURA

A *Warner Futura* Book

First published in this omnibus edition in Great Britain in 1993 by
Warner Futura

THE PILGRIM OF HATE first published by Macmillan London in 1984 and
by Futura in paperback in 1985
Published by Warner Futura in 1992
Copyright © Ellis Peters 1984

AN EXCELLENT MYSTERY first published by Macmillan London in 1985
and by Futura in paperback in 1986
Published by Warner Futura in 1992
Copyright © Ellis Peters 1985

THE RAVEN IN THE FOREGATE first published by Macmillan London
in 1986 and by Futura in paperback in 1987
Published by Warner Futura in 1992
Copyright © Ellis Peters 1986

This omnibus edition copyright © Ellis Peters 1993

A CIP catalogue record for this book
is available from the British Library

ISBN 0 7515 0392 4

Photoset in North Wales by
Derek Doyle & Associates, Mold, Clwyd.
Printed and bound in Great Britain by
Hazell Books Limited, Aylesbury, Bucks.

Warner Books
A Division of
Little, Brown and Company (UK) Limited
165 Great Dover Street
London SE1 4YA

Contents

The Pilgrim of Hate

Chapter One

HEY WERE together in Brother Cadfael's hut in the herbarium, in the afternoon of the twenty-fifth day of May, and the talk was of high matters of state, of kings and empresses, and the unbalanced fortunes that plagued the irreconcilable contenders for thrones.

'Well, the lady is not crowned yet!' said Hugh Beringar, almost as firmly as if he saw a way of preventing it.

'She is not even in London yet,' agreed Cadfael, stirring carefully round the pot embedded in the coals of his brazier, to keep the brew from boiling up against the sides and burning. 'She cannot well be crowned until they let her in to Westminster. Which it seems, from all I gather, they are in no hurry to do.'

'Where the sun shines,' said Hugh ruefully, 'there whoever's felt the cold will gather. My cause, old friend, is out of the sun. When Henry of Blois shifts, all men shift with him, like starvelings huddled in one bed. He heaves the coverlet, and they go with him, clinging by the hems.'

'Not all,' objected Cadfael, briefly smiling as he stirred. 'Not you. Do you think you are the only one?'

'God forbid!' said Hugh, and suddenly laughed, shaking off his gloom. He came back from the open doorway, where the pure light spread a soft golden sheen over the bushes and beds of the herb-garden and the moist noon air drew up a heady languor of spiced and drunken odours, and plumped his slender person down again on the bench against the timber

3

wall, spreading his booted feet on the earth floor. A small man in one sense only, and even so trimly made. His modest stature and light weight had deceived many a man to his undoing. The sunshine from without, fretted by the breeze that swayed the bushes, was reflected from one of Cadfael's great glass flagons to illuminate by flashing glimpses a lean, tanned face, clean shaven, with a quirky mouth, and agile black eyebrows that could twist upward sceptically into cropped black hair. A face at once eloquent and inscrutable. Brother Cadfael was one of the few who knew how to read it. Doubtful if even Hugh's wife Aline understood him better. Cadfael was in his sixty-second year, and Hugh still a year or two short of thirty but, meeting thus in easy companionship in Cadfael's workshop among the herbs, they felt themselves contemporaries.

'No,' said Hugh, eyeing circumstances narrowly, and taking some cautious comfort, 'not all. There are a few of us yet, and not so badly placed to hold on to what we have. There's the queen in Kent with her army. Robert of Gloucester is not going to turn his back to come hunting us here while she hangs on the southern fringes of London. And with the Welsh of Gwynedd keeping our backs against the earl of Chester, we can hold this shire for King Stephen and wait out the time. Luck that turned once can turn again. And the empress is not queen of England yet.'

But for all that, thought Cadfael, mutely stirring his brew for Brother Aylwin's scouring calves, it began to look as though she very soon would be. Three years of civil war between cousins fighting for the sovereignty of England had done nothing to reconcile the factions, but much to sicken the general populace with insecurity, rapine and killing. The craftsman in the town, the cottar in the village, the serf on the demesne, would be only too glad of any monarch who could guarantee him a quiet and orderly country in which to carry on his modest business. But to a man like Hugh it was no such indifferent matter. He was King Stephen's liege man, and now King Stephen's sheriff of Shropshire, sworn to hold the shire for his cause. And his king was a prisoner in Bristol castle since the lost battle of Lincoln. A single February day of this year had seen a total reversal of the fortunes of the two claimants to the throne. The Empress Maud was up in the clouds, and Stephen, crowned and anointed though he might be, was down in the midden, close-bound and close-guarded, and his brother Henry of Blois, bishop of Winchester and papal legate, far the

4

most influential of the magnates and hitherto his brother's supporter, had found himself in a dilemma. He could either be a hero, and adhere loudly and firmly to his allegiance, thus incurring the formidable animosity of a lady who was in the ascendant and could be dangerous, or trim his sails and accommodate himself to the reverses of fortune by coming over to her side. Discreetly, of course, and with well-prepared arguments to render his about-face respectable. It was just possible, thought Cadfael, willing to do justice even to bishops, that Henry also had the cause of order and peace genuinely at heart, and was willing to back whichever contender could restore them.

'What frets me,' said Hugh restlessly, 'is that I can get no reliable news. Rumours enough and more than enough, every new one laying the last one dead, but nothing a man can grasp and put his trust in. I shall be main glad when Abbot Radulfus comes home.'

'So will every brother in this house,' agreed Cadfael fervently. 'Barring Jerome, perhaps, he's in high feather when Prior Robert is left in charge, and a fine time he's had of it all these weeks since the abbot was summoned to Winchester. But Robert's rule is less favoured by the rest of us, I can tell you.'

'How long is it he's been away now?' pondered Hugh. 'Seven or eight weeks! The legate's keeping his court well stocked with mitres all this time. Maintaining his own state no doubt gives him some aid in confronting hers. Not a man to let his dignity bow to princes, Henry, and he needs all the weight he can get at his back.'

'He's letting some of his cloth disperse now, however,' said Cadfael. 'By that token, he may have got a kind of settlement. Or he may be deceived into thinking he has. Father Abbot sent word from Reading. In a week he should be here. You'll hardly find a better witness.'

Bishop Henry had taken good care to keep the direction of events in his own hands. Calling all the prelates and mitred abbots to Winchester early in April, and firmly declaring the gathering a legatine council, no mere church assembly, had ensured his supremacy at the subsequent discussions, giving him precedence over Archbishop Theobald of Canterbury, who in purely English church matters was his superior. Just as well, perhaps. Cadfael doubted if Theobald had greatly minded being outflanked. In the circumstances a quiet, timorous man might be only too glad to lurk peaceably in the shadows, and let the legate bear the heat of the sun.

'I know it. Once let me hear his account of what's gone forward, down there in the south, and I can make my own dispositions. We're remote enough here, and the queen, God keep her, has gathered a very fair array, now she has the Flemings who escaped from Lincoln to add to her force. She'll move heaven and earth to get Stephen out of hold, by whatever means, fair or foul. She is,' said Hugh with conviction, 'a better soldier than her lord. Not a better fighter in the field – God knows you'd need to search Europe through to find such a one, I saw him at Lincoln – a marvel! But a better general, that she *is*. She holds to her purpose, where he tires and goes off after another quarry. They tell me, and I believe it, she's drawing her cordon closer and closer to London, south of the river. The nearer her rival comes to Westminster, the tighter that noose will be drawn.'

'And is it certain the Londoners have agreed to let the empress in? We hear they came late to the council, and made a faint plea for Stephen before they let themselves be tamed. It takes a very stout heart, I suppose, to stand up to Henry of Winchester face to face, and deny him,' allowed Cadfael, sighing.

'They've agreed to admit her, which is as good as acknowledging her. But they're arguing terms for her entry, as I heard it, and every delay is worth gold to me and to Stephen. If only,' said Hugh, the dancing light suddenly sharpening every line of his intent and eloquent face, 'if only I could get a good man into Bristol! There are ways into castles, even into the dungeons. Two or three good, secret men might do it. A fistful of gold to a malcontent gaoler ... Kings have been fetched off before now, even out of chains, and he's not chained. She has not gone so far, not yet. Cadfael, I dream! My work is here, and I am but barely equal to it. I have no means of carrying off Bristol, too.'

'Once loosed,' said Cadfael, 'your king is going to need this shire ready to his hand.'

He turned from the brazier, hoisting aside the pot and laying it to cool on a slab of stone he kept for the purpose. His back creaked a little as he straightened it. In small ways he was feeling his years, but once erect he was spry enough.

'I'm done here for this while,' he said, brushing his hands together to get rid of the hollow worn by the ladle. 'Come into the daylight, and see the flowers we're bringing on for the

6

festival of Saint Winifred. Father Abbot will be home in good time to preside over her reception from Saint Giles. And we shall have a houseful of pilgrims to care for.'

They had brought the reliquary of the Welsh saint four years previously from Gwytherin, where she lay buried, and installed it on the altar of the church at the hospital of Saint Giles, at the very edge of Shrewsbury's Foregate suburb, where the sick, the infected, the deformed, the lepers, who might not venture within the walls, were housed and cared for. And thence they had borne her casket in splendour to her altar in the abbey church, to be an ornament and a wonder, a means of healing and blessing to all who came reverently and in need. This year they had undertaken to repeat that last journey, to bring her from Saint Giles in procession, and open her altar to all who came with prayers and offerings. Every year she had drawn many pilgrims. This year they would be legion.

'A man might wonder,' said Hugh, standing spread-footed among the flower beds just beginning to burn from the soft, shy colours of spring into the blaze of summer, 'whether you were not rather preparing for a bridal.'

Hedges of hazel and may-blossom shed silver petals and dangled pale, silver-green catkins round the enclosure where they stood, cowslips were rearing in the grass of the meadow beyond, and irises were in tight, thrusting bud. Even the roses showed a harvest of buds, erect and ready to break and display the first colour. In the walled shelter of Cadfael's herb-garden there were fat globes of peonies, too, just cracking their green sheaths. Cadfael had medicinal uses for the seeds, and Brother Petrus, the abbot's cook, used them as spices in the kitchen.

'A man might not be so far out, at that,' said Cadfael, viewing the fruits of his labours complacently. 'A perpetual and pure bridal. This Welsh girl was virgin until the day of her death.'

'And you have married her off since?'

It was idly said, in revulsion from pondering matters of state. In such a garden a man could believe in peace, fruitfulness and amity. But it encountered suddenly so profound and pregnant a silence that Hugh pricked up his ears, and turned his head almost stealthily to study his friend, even before the unguarded answer came. Unguarded either from absence of mind, or of design, there was no telling.

'Not wedded,' said Cadfael, 'but certainly bedded. With a

7

good man, too, and her honest champion. He deserved his reward.'

Hugh raised quizzical brows, and cast a glance over his shoulder towards the long roof of the great abbey church, where reputedly the lady in question slept in a sealed reliquary on her own altar. An elegant coffin just long enough to contain a small and holy Welshwoman, with the neat, compact bones of her race.

'Hardly room within there for two,' he said mildly.

'Not two of our gross make, no, not there. There was space enough where we put them.' He knew he was listened to, now, and heard with sharp intelligence, if not yet understood.

'Are you telling me,' wondered Hugh no less mildly, 'that she is *not* there in that elaborate shrine of yours, where everyone else *knows* she is?'

'Can I tell? Many a time I've wished it could be possible to be in two places at once. A thing too hard for me, but for a saint, perhaps, possible? Three nights and three days she was in there, that I do know. She may well have left a morsel of her holiness within – if only by way of thanks to us who took her out again, and put her back where I still, and always shall, believe she wished to be. But for all that,' owned Cadfael, shaking his head, 'there's a trailing fringe of doubt that nags at me. How if I read her wrong?'

'Then your only resort is confession and penance,' said Hugh lightly.

'Not until Brother Mark is full-fledged a priest!' Young Mark was gone from his mother-house and from his flock at Saint Giles, gone to the household of the bishop of Lichfield, with Leoric Aspley's endowment to see him through his studies, and the goal of all his longings shining distant and clear before him, the priesthood for which God had designed him. 'I'm saving for him,' said Cadfael, 'all those sins I feel, perhaps mistakenly, to be no sins. He was my right hand and a piece of my heart for three years, and knows me better than any man living. Barring, it may be, yourself?' he added, and slanted a guileless glance at his friend. 'He will know the truth of me, and by his judgement and for his absolution I'll embrace any penance. You might deliver the judgement, Hugh, but you cannot deliver the absolution.'

'Nor the penance, neither,' said Hugh, and laughed freely. 'So tell it to me, and go free without penalty.'

The idea of confiding was unexpectedly pleasing and

acceptable. 'It's a long story,'* said Cadfael warningly.

'Then now's your time, for whatever I can do here is done, nothing is asked of me but watchfulness and patience, and why should I wait unentertained if there's a good story to be heard? And you are at leisure until Vespers. You may even get merit,' said Hugh, composing his face into priestly solemnity, 'by unburdening your soul to the secular arm. And I can be secret,' he said, 'as any confessional.'

'Wait, then,' said Cadfael, 'while I fetch a draught of that maturing wine, and come within to the bench under the north wall, where the afternoon sun falls. We may as well be at ease while I talk.'

'It was a year or so before I knew you,' said Cadfael, bracing his back comfortably against the warmed, stony roughness of the herb-garden wall. 'We were without a tame saint to our house, and somewhat envious of Wenlock, where the Cluny community had discovered their Saxon foundress Milburga, and were making great play with her. And we had certain signs that sent off an ailing brother of ours into Wales, to bathe at Holywell, where this girl Winifred died her first death, and brought forth her healing spring. There was her own patron, Saint Beuno, ready and able to bring her back to life, but the spring remained, and did wonders. So it came to Prior Robert that the lady could be persuaded to leave Gwytherin, where she died her second death and was buried, and come and bring her glory to us here in Shrewsbury. I was one of the party he took with him to deal with the parish there, and bring them to give up the saint's bones.'

'All of which,' said Hugh, warmed and attentive beside him, 'I know very well, since all men here know it.'

'Surely! But you do not know to the end what followed. There was one Welsh lord in Gwytherin who would not suffer the girl to be disturbed, and would not be persuaded or bribed or threatened into letting her go. And he died, Hugh – murdered. By one of us, a brother who came from high rank, and had his eyes already set on a mitre. And when we came near to accusing him, it was his life or a better. There were certain young people of that place put in peril by him, the dead lord's daughter and her lover. The boy lashed out in anger, with good reason, seeing his girl wounded and bleeding. He

*See *A Morbid Taste for Bones.*

9

was stronger than he knew. The murderer's neck was broken.'

'How many knew of this?' asked Hugh, his eyes narrowed thoughtfully upon the glossy-leaved rose-bushes.

'When it befell, only the lovers, the dead man and I. And Saint Winifred, who had been raised from her grave and laid in that casket of which you and all men know. *She* knew. She was there. From the moment I raised her,' said Cadfael, 'and by God, it was I who took her from the soil, and I who restored her – and still that makes me glad – from the moment I uncovered those slender bones, I felt in mine they wished only to be left in peace. It was so little and so wild and quiet a graveyard there, with the small church long out of use, meadow flowers growing over all, and the mounds so modest and green. And Welsh soil! The girl was Welsh, like me, her church was of the old persuasion, what did she know of this alien English shire? And I had those young things to keep. Who would have taken their word or mine against all the force of the church? They would have closed their ranks to bury the scandal, and bury the boy with it, and he guilty of nothing but defending his dear. So I took measures.'

Hugh's mobile lips twitched. 'Now indeed you amaze me! And what measures were those? With a dead brother to account for, and Prior Robert to keep sweet ...'

'Ah, well, Robert is a simpler soul than he supposes, and then I had a good deal of help from the dead brother himself. He'd been busy building himself such a reputation for sanctity, delivering messages from the saint herself – it was he told us she was offering the grave she'd left to the murdered man – and going into trance-sleeps, and praying to leave this world and be taken into bliss living ... So we did him that small favour. He'd been keeping a solitary night-watch in the old church, and in the morning when it ended, there were his habit and sandals fallen together at his prayer-stool, and the body of him lifted clean out of them, in sweet odours and a shower of may-blossom. That was how he claimed the saint had already visited him, why should not Robert recall it and believe? Certainly he was gone. Why look for him? Would a modest brother of our house be running through the Welsh woods mother-naked?'

'Are you telling me,' asked Hugh cautiously, 'that what you have there in the reliquary is *not* ... Then the casket had not yet been sealed?' His eyebrows were tangling with his black forelock, but his voice was soft and unsurprised.

10

'Well ...' Cadfael twitched his blunt brown nose bashfully between finger and thumb. 'Sealed it was, but there are ways of dealing with seals that leave them unblemished. It's one of the more dubious of my remembered skills, but for all that I was glad of it then.'

'And you put the lady back in the place that was hers, along with her champion?'

'He was a decent, good man, and had spoken up for her nobly. She would not grudge him house-room. I have always thought,' confided Cadfael, 'that she was not displeased with us. She has shown her power in Gwytherin since that time, by many miracles, so I cannot believe she is angry. But what a little troubles me is that she has not so far chosen to favour us with any great mark of her patronage here, to keep Robert happy, and set my mind at rest. Oh, a few little things, but nothing of unmistakable note. How if I have displeased her, after all? Well for me, who *know* what we have within there on the altar – and *mea culpa* if I did wrongly! But what of the innocents who do *not* know, and come in good faith, hoping for grace from her? What if I have been the means of their deprivation and loss?'

'I see,' said Hugh with sympathy, 'that Brother Mark had better make haste through the degrees of ordination, and come quickly to lift the load from you. Unless,' he added with a flashing sidelong smile, 'Saint Winifred takes pity on you first, and sends you a sign.'

'I still do not see,' mused Cadfael, 'what else I could have done. It was an ending that satisfied everyone, both here and there. The children were free to marry and be happy, the village still had its saint, and she had her own people round her. Robert had what he had gone to find – or thought he had, which is the same thing. And Shrewsbury abbey has its festival, with every hope of a full guest-hall, and glory and gain in good measure. If she would but just cast an indulgent look this way, and wink her eye, to let me know I understood her aright.'

'And you've never said word of this to anyone?'

'Never a word. But the whole village of Gwytherin knows it,' admitted Cadfael with a remembering grin. 'No one told, no one had to tell, but they knew. There wasn't a man missing when we took up the reliquary and set out for home. They helped to carry it, whipped together a little chariot to bear it. Robert thought he had them nicely tamed, even those who'd been most reluctant from the first. It was a great joy to him. A

11

simple soul at bottom! It would be great pity to undo him now, when he's busy writing his book about the saint's life, and how he brought her to Shrewsbury.'

'I would not have the heart to put him to such distress,' said Hugh. 'Least said, best for all. Thanks be to God, I have nothing to do with canon law, the common law of a land almost without law costs me enough pains.' No need to say that Cadfael could be sure of his secrecy, that was taken for granted on both sides. 'Well, you speak the lady's own tongue, no doubt she understood you well enough, with or without words. Who knows? When this festival of yours takes place – the twenty-second day of June, you say? – she may take pity on you, and send you a great miracle to set your mind at rest.'

And so she might, thought Cadfael an hour later, on his way to obey the summons of the Vesper bell. Not that he had deserved so signal an honour, but there surely must be one somewhere among the unceasing stream of pilgrims who did deserve it, and could not with justice be rejected. He would be perfectly and humbly and cheerfully content with that. What if she was eighty miles or so away, in what was left of her body? It had been a miraculous body in this life, once brutally dead and raised alive again, what limits of time or space could be set about such a being? If it so pleased her she could be both quiet and content in her grave with Rhisiart, lulled by bird-song in the hawthorn trees, and here attentive and incorporeal, a little flame of spirit in the coffin of unworthy Columbanus, who had killed not for her exaltation but for his own.

Brother Cadfael went to Vespers curiously relieved at having confided to his friend a secret from before the time when they had first known each other, in the beginning as potential antagonists stepping subtly to outwit each other, then discovering how much they had in common, the old man – alone with himself Cadfael admitted to being somewhat over the peak of a man's prime – and the young one, just setting out, exceedingly well-equipped in shrewdness and wit, to build his fortune and win his wife. And both he had done, for he was now undisputed sheriff of Shropshire, if under a powerless and captive king, and up there in the town, near St Mary's church, his wife and his year-old son made a nest for his private happiness when he shut the door on his public burdens.

Cadfael thought of his godson, the sturdy imp who already clutched his way lustily round the rooms of Hugh's town house, climbed unaided into a godfather's lap, and began to utter human sounds of approval, enquiry, indignation and affection. Every man asks of heaven a son. Hugh had his, as promising a sprig as ever budded from the stem. So, by proxy, had Cadfael, a son in God.

There was, after all, a great deal of human happiness in the world, even a world so torn and mangled with conflict, cruelty and greed. So it had always been, and always would be. And so be it, provided the indomitable spark of joy never went out.

In the refectory, after supper and grace, in the grateful warmth and lingering light of the end of May, when they were shuffling their benches to rise from table, Prior Robert Pennant rose first in his place, levering erect his more than six feet of lean, austere prelate, silver-tonsured and ivory-featured.

'Brothers, I have received a further message from Father Abbot. He has reached Warwick on his way home to us, and hopes to be with us by the fourth day of June or earlier. He bids us be diligent in making proper preparation for the celebration of Saint Winifred's translation, our most gracious patroness.' Perhaps the abbot had so instructed, in duty bound, but it was Robert himself who laid such stress on it, viewing himself, as he did, as the patron of their patroness. His large patrician eye swept round the refectory tables, settling upon those heads most deeply committed. 'Brother Anselm, you have the music already in hand?'

Brother Anselm the precentor, whose mind seldom left its neums and instruments for many seconds together, looked up vaguely, awoke to the question, and stared, wide-eyed. 'The entire order of procession and office is ready,' he said, in amiable surprise that anyone should feel it necessary to ask.

'And Brother Denis, you have made all the preparations necessary for stocking your halls to feed great numbers? For we shall surely need every cot and every dish we can muster.'

Brother Denis the hospitaller, accustomed to outer panics and secure ruler of his own domain, testified calmly that he had made the fullest provision he considered needful, and further, that he had reserves laid by to tap at need.

'There will also be many sick persons to be tended, for that reason they come.'

Brother Edmund the infirmarer, not waiting to be named, said crisply that he had taken into account the probable need, and was prepared for the demands that might be made on his

13

beds and medicines. He mentioned also, being on his feet, that Brother Cadfael had already provided stocks of all the remedies most likely to be wanted, and stood ready to meet any other needs that should arise.

'That is well,' said Prior Robert. 'Now, Father Abbot has yet a special request to make until he comes. He asks that prayers be made at every High Mass for the repose of the soul of a good man, treacherously slain in Winchester as he strove to keep the peace and reconcile faction with faction, in Christian duty.'

For a moment it seemed to Brother Cadfael, and perhaps to most of the others present, that the death of one man, far away in the south, hardly rated so solemn a mention and so signal a mark of respect, in a country where deaths had been commonplace for so long, from the field of Lincoln strewn with bodies to the sack of Worcester with its streets running blood, from the widespread baronial slaughters by disaffected earls to the sordid village banditries where law had broken down. Then he looked at it again, and with the abbot's measuring eyes. Here was a good man cut down in the very city where prelates and barons were parleying over matters of peace and sovereignty, killed in trying to keep one faction from the throat of the other. At the very feet, as it were, of the bishop-legate. As black a sacrilege as if he had been butchered on the steps of the altar. It was not one man's death, it was a bitter symbol of the abandonment of law and the rejection of hope and reconciliation. So Radulfus had seen it, and so he recorded it in the offices of his house. There was a solemn acknowledgement due to the dead man, a memorial lodged in heaven.

'We are asked,' said Prior Robert, 'to offer thanks for the just endeavour and prayers for the soul of one Rainald Bossard, a knight in the service of the Empress Maud.'

'One of the enemy,' said a young novice doubtfully, talking it over in the cloisters afterwards. So used were they, in this shire, to thinking of the king's cause as their own, since it had been his writ which had run here now in orderly fashion for four years, and kept off the worst of the chaos that troubled so much of England elsewhere.

'Not so,' said Brother Paul, the master of the novices, gently chiding. 'No good and honourable man is an enemy, though he may take the opposing side in this dissension. The fealty of this world is not for us, but we must bear it ever in mind as a true

14

value, as binding on those who owe it as our vows are on us. The claims of these two cousins are both in some sort valid. It is no reproach to have kept faith, whether with king or empress. And this was surely a worthy man, or Father Abbot would not thus have recommended him to our prayers.'

Brother Anselm, thoughtfully revolving the syllables of the name, and tapping the resultant rhythm on the stone of the bench on which he sat, repeated to himself softly: 'Rainald Bossard, Rainald Bossard ...'

The repeated iambic stayed in Brother Cadfael's ear and wormed its way into his mind. A name that meant nothing yet to anyone here, had neither form nor face, no age, no character; nothing but a name, which is either a soul without a body or a body without a soul. It went with him into his cell in the dortoir, as he made his last prayers and shook off his sandals before lying down to sleep. It may even have kept a rhythm in his sleeping mind, without the need of a dream to house it, for the first he knew of the thunderstorm was a silent double-gleam of lightning that spelled out the same iambic, and caused him to start awake with eyes still closed, and listen for the answering thunder. It did not come for so long that he thought he had dreamed it, and then he heard it, very distant, very quiet, and yet curiously ominous. Beyond his closed eyelids the quiet lightnings flared and died, and the echoes answered so late and so softly, from so far away ...

As far, perhaps, as that fabled city of Winchester, where momentous matters had been decided, a place Cadfael had never seen, and probably never would see. A threat from a town so distant could shake no foundations here, and no hearts, any more than such far-off thunders could bring down the walls of Shrewsbury. Yet the continuing murmur of disquiet was still in his ears as he fell asleep.

Chapter Two

BBOT RADULFUS rode back into his abbey of Saint Peter and Saint Paul on the third day of June, escorted by his chaplain and secretary, Brother Vitalis, and welcomed home by all the fifty-three brothers, seven novices and six schoolboys of his house, as well as all the lay stewards and servants.

The abbot was a long, lean, hard man in his fifties, with a gaunt, ascetic face and a shrewd, scholar's eye, so vigorous and able of body that he dismounted and went straight to preside at High Mass, before retiring to remove the stains of travel or take any refreshment after his long ride. Nor did he forget to offer the prayer he had enjoined upon his flock, for the repose of the soul of Rainald Bossard, slain in Winchester on the evening of Wednesday, the ninth day of April of this year of Our Lord 1141. Eight weeks dead, and half the length of England away, what meaning could Rainald Bossard have for this indifferent town of Shrewsbury, or the members of this far-distant Benedictine house?

Not until the next morning's chapter would the household hear its abbot's account of that momentous council held in the south to determine the future of England; but when Hugh Beringar waited upon Radulfus about mid-afternoon, and asked for audience, he was not kept waiting. Affairs demanded the close co-operation of the secular and the clerical powers, in defence of such order and law as survived in England.

The abbot's private parlour in his lodging was as austere as

16

its presiding father, plainly furnished, but with sunlight spilled across its flagged floor from two open lattices at this hour of the sun's zenith, and a view of gracious greenery and glowing flowers in the small walled garden without. Quiverings of radiance flashed and vanished and recoiled and collided over the dark panelling within, from the new-budded life and fresh breeze and exuberant light outside. Hugh sat in shadow, and watched the abbot's trenchant profile, clear, craggy and dark against a ground of shifting brightness.

'My allegiance is well known to you, Father,' said Hugh, admiring the stillness of the noble mask thus framed, 'as yours is to me. But there is much that we share. Whatever you can tell me of what passed in Winchester, I do greatly need to know.'

'And I to understand,' said Radulfus, with a tight and rueful smile. 'I went as summoned, by him who has a right to summon me, and I went knowing how matters then stood, the king a prisoner, the empress mistress of much of the south, and in due position to claim sovereignty by right of conquest. We knew, you and I both, what would be in debate down there. I can only give you my own account as I saw it. The first day that we gathered there, a Monday it was, the seventh of April, there was nothing done by way of business but the ceremonial of welcoming us all, and reading out – there were many of these! – the letters sent by way of excuse from those who remained absent. The empress had a lodging in the town then, though she made several moves about the region, to Reading and other places, while we debated. She did not attend. She has a measure of discretion.' His tone was dry. It was not clear whether he considered her measure of that commodity to be adequate or somewhat lacking. 'The second day ...' He fell silent, remembering what he had witnessed. Hugh waited attentively, not stirring.

'The second day, the eighth of April, the legate made his great speech ...'

It was no effort to imagine him. Henry of Blois, bishop of Winchester, papal legate, younger brother and hitherto partisan of King Stephen, impregnably ensconced in the chapter house of his own cathedral, secure master of the political pulse of England, the cleverest manipulator in the kingdom, and on his own chosen ground – and yet hounded on to the defensive, in so far as that could ever happen to so expert a practitioner. Hugh had never seen the man, never been near the region where he ruled, had only heard him described, and yet could see him now, presiding with imperious composure over his half-unwilling assembly. A difficult part he had to play, to extricate himself from his known allegiance to his brother, and yet preserve his face and his status and influence with those who had shared it. And with a tough, experienced woman narrowly observing his every word, and holding in reserve her own new powers to destroy or preserve, according to how he managed his ill-disciplined team in this heavy furrow.

'He spoke a tedious while,' said the abbot candidly, 'but he is a very able speaker. He put us in mind that we were met together to try to salvage England from chaos and ruin. He spoke of the late King Henry's time, when order and peace was kept throughout the land. And he reminded us how the old king, left without a son, commanded his barons to swear an oath of allegiance to his only remaining child, his daughter Maud the empress, now widowed, and wed again to the count of Anjou.'

And so those barons had done, almost all, not least this same Henry of Winchester. Hugh Beringar, who had never come to such a test until he was ready to choose for himself, curled a half-disdainful and half-commiserating lip, and nodded understanding. 'His lordship had somewhat to explain away.'

The abbot refrained from indicating, by word or look, agreement with the implied criticism of his brother cleric. 'He said that the long delay which might then have arisen from the empress's being in Normandy had given rise to natural concern for the well-being of the state. An interim of uncertainty was dangerous. And thus, he said, his brother Count Stephen was accepted when he offered himself, and became king by consent. His own part in this acceptance he admitted. For he it was who pledged his word to God and men that King Stephen would honour and revere the Holy Church, and maintain the good and just laws of the land. In which undertaking, said Henry, the king has shamefully failed. To his great chagrin and grief he declared it, having been his brother's guarantor to God.'

So that was the way round the humiliating change of course, thought Hugh. All was to be laid upon Stephen, who had so deceived his reverend brother and defaulted upon all his promises, that a man of God might well be driven to the end of his patience, and be brought to welcome a change of monarch with relief tempering his sorrow.

18

'In particular,' said Radulfus, 'he recalled how the king had hounded certain of his bishops to their ruin and death.'

There was more than a grain of truth in that, though the only death in question, of Robert of Salisbury, had resulted naturally from old age, bitterness and despair, because his power was gone.

'Therefore, *he said*,' continued the abbot with chill deliberation, 'the judgement of God had been manifested against the king, in delivering him up prisoner to his enemies. And he, devout in the service of the Holy Church, must choose between his devotion to his mortal brother and to his immortal father, and could not but bow to the edict of heaven. Therefore he had called us together, to ensure that a kingdom lopped of its head should not founder in utter ruin. And this very matter, he told the assembly, had been discussed most gravely on the day previous among the greater part of the clergy of England, who – *he said*! – had a prerogative surmounting others in the election and consecration of a king.'

There was something in the dry, measured voice that made Hugh prick up his ears. For this was a large and unprecedented claim, and by all the signs Abbot Radulfus found it more than suspect. The legate had his own face to save, and a well-oiled tongue with which to wind the protective mesh of words before it.

'Was there such a meeting? Were you present at such, Father?'

'There was a meeting,' said Radulfus, 'not prolonged, and by no means very clear in its course. The greater part of the talking was done by the legate. The empress had her partisans there.' He said it sedately and tolerantly, but clearly he had not been one. 'I do not recall that he then claimed this prerogative for us. Nor that there was ever a count taken.'

'Nor, as I guess, declared. It would not come to a numbering of heads or hands.' Too easy, then, to start a counter-count of one's own, and confound the reckoning.

'He continued,' said Radulfus coolly and drily, 'by saying that we had chosen as Lady of England the late king's daughter, the inheritor of his nobility and his will to peace. As the sire was unequalled in merit in our times, so might his daughter flourish and bring peace, as he did, to this troubled country, where we now offer her – *he said*! – our whole-hearted fealty.'

So the legate had extricated himself as adroitly as possible

19

from his predicament. But for all that, so resolute, courageous and vindictive a lady as the empress was going to look somewhat sidewise at a whole-hearted fealty which had already once been pledged to her, and turned its back nimbly under pressure, and might as nimbly do so again. If she was wise she would curb her resentment and take care to keep on the right side of the legate, as he was cautiously feeling his way to the right side of her; but she would not forget or forgive.

'And there was no man raised a word against it?' asked Hugh mildly.

'None. There was small opportunity, and even less inducement. And with that the bishop announced that he had invited a deputation from the city of London, and expected them to arrive that day, so that it was expedient we should adjourn our discussion until the morrow. Even so, the Londoners did not come until next day, and we met again somewhat later than on the days previous. Howbeit, they did come. With somewhat dour faces and stiff necks. They said that they represented the whole commune of London, into which many barons had also entered as members after Lincoln, and that they all, with no wish to challenge the legitimacy of our assembly, yet desired to put forward with one voice the request that the lord king should be set at liberty.'

'That was bold,' said Hugh with raised brows. 'How did his lordship counter it? Was he put out of countenance?'

'I think he was shaken, but not disastrously, not then. He made a long speech – it is a way of keeping others silent, at least for a time – reproving the city for taking into its membership men who had abandoned their king in war, after leading him astray by their evil advice, so grossly that he forsook God and right, and was brought to the judgement of defeat and captivity, from which the prayers of those same false friends could not now reprieve him. These men do but flatter and favour you now, he said, for their own advantage.'

'If he meant the Flemings who ran from Lincoln,' Hugh allowed, 'he told no more than truth there. But for what other end is the city ever flattered and wooed? What then? Had they the hardihood to stand their ground against him?'

'They were in some disarray as to what they should reply, and went apart to confer. And while there was quiet, a man suddenly stepped forward from among the clerks, and held out a parchment to Bishop Henry, asking him to read it aloud, so confidently that I wonder still he did not at once comply.

Instead, he opened and began to read it in silence, and in a moment more he was thundering in a great rage that the thing was an insult to the reverend company present, its matter disgraceful, its witnesses attainted enemies of Holy Church, and not a word of it would he read aloud to us in so sacred a place as his chapter house. Whereupon,' said the abbot grimly, 'the clerk snatched it back from him, and himself read it aloud in a great voice, riding above the bishop when he tried to silence him. It was a plea from Stephen's queen to all present, and to the legate in especial, own brother to the king, to return to fealty and restore the king to his own again from the base captivity into which traitors had betrayed him. And I, said the brave man who read, am a clerk in the service of Queen Matilda, and if any ask my name, it is Christian, and true Christian I am as any here, and true to my salt.'

'Brave, indeed!' said Hugh, and whistled softly. 'But I doubt it did him little good.'

'The legate replied to him in a tirade, much as he had spoken already to us the day before, but in a great passion, and so intimidated the men from London that they drew in their horns, and grudgingly agreed to report the council's election to their citizens, and support it as best they could. As for the man Christian, who had so angered Bishop Henry, he was attacked that same evening in the street, as he set out to return to the queen empty-handed. Four or five ruffians set on him in the dark, no one knows who, for they fled when one of the empress's knights and his men came to the rescue and beat them off, crying shame to use murder as argument in any cause, and against an honest man who had done his part fearlessly in the open. The clerk got no worse than a few bruises. It was the knight who got the knife between his ribs from behind and into the heart. He died in the gutter of a Winchester street. A shame to us all, who claim to be making peace and bringing enemies into amity.'

By the shadowed anger of his face it had gone deep with him, the single wanton act that denied all pretences of good will and justice and conciliation. To strike at a man for being honestly of the opposite persuasion, and then to strike again at the fair-minded and chivalrous who sought to prevent the outrage – very ill omens, these, for the future of the legate's peace.

'And no man taken for the killing?' demanded Hugh, frowning.

'No. They fled in the dark. If any creature knows name or hiding-place, he has spoken no word. Death is so common a matter now, even by stealth and treachery in the darkness, this will be forgotten with the rest. And the next day our council closed with sentence of excommunication against a great number of Stephen's men, and the legate pronounced all men blessed who would bless the empress, and accursed those who cursed her. And so dismissed us,' said Radulfus. 'But that we monastics were not dismissed, but kept to attend on him some weeks longer.'

'And the empress?'

'Withdrew to Oxford, while these long negotiations with the city of London went on, how and when she should be admitted within the gates, on what terms, what numbers she might bring in with her to Westminster. On all which points they have wrangled every step of the way. But in nine or ten days now she will be installed there, and soon thereafter crowned.' He lifted a long, muscular hand, and again let it fall into the lap of his habit. 'So, at least, it seems. What more can I tell you of her?'

'I meant, rather,' said Hugh, 'how is she bearing this slow recognition? How is she dealing with her newly converted barons? And how do they rub, one with another? It's no easy matter to hold together the old and the new liegemen, and keep them from each other's throats. A manor in dispute here and there, a few fields taken from one and given to another ... I think you know the way of it, Father, as well as I.'

'I would not say she is a wise woman,' said Radulfus carefully. 'She is all too well aware how many swore allegiance to her at her father's order, and then swung to King Stephen, and now as nimbly skip back to her because she is in the ascendant. I can well understand she might take pleasure in pricking into the quick where she can, among these. It is not wise, but it is human. But that she should become lofty and cold to those who never wavered – for there are some,' said the abbot with respectful wonder, 'who have been faithful throughout at their own great loss, and will not waver even now, whatever she may do. Great folly and great injustice to use them so high-handedly, who have been her right hand and her left all this while.'

You comfort me, thought Hugh, watching the lean, quiet face intently. The woman is out of her wits if she flouts even the like of Robert of Gloucester, now she feels herself so near the throne.

'She has greatly offended the bishop-legate,' said the abbot,

22

'by refusing to allow Stephen's son to receive the rights and titles of his father's honours of Boulogne and Mortain, now that his father is a prisoner. It would have been only justice. But no, she would not suffer it. Bishop Henry quit her court for some while, it took her considerable pains to lure him back again.'

Better and better, thought Hugh, assessing his position with care. If she is stubborn enough to drive away even Henry, she can undo everything he and others do for her. Put the crown in her hands and she may, not so much drop it, as hurl it at someone against whom she has a score to settle. He set himself to extract every detail of her subsequent behaviour, and was cautiously encouraged. She had taken land from some who held it and given it to others. She had received her naturally bashful new adherents with arrogance, and reminded them ominously of their past hostility. Some she had even repulsed with anger, recalling old injuries. Candidates for a disputed crown should be more accommodatingly forgetful. Let her alone, and pray! She, if anyone, could bring about her own ruin.

At the end of a long hour he rose to take his leave, with a very fair picture in his mind of the possibilities he had to face. Even empresses may learn, and she might yet inveigle herself safely into Westminster and assume the crown. It would not do to underestimate William of Normandy's grand-daughter and Henry the First's daughter. Yet that very stock might come to wreck on its own unforgiving strength.

He was never afterwards sure why he turned back at the last moment to ask: 'Father Abbot, this man Rainald Bossard, who died ... A knight of the empress, you said. In whose following?'

All that he had learned he confided to Brother Cadfael in the hut in the herb-garden, trying out upon his friend's unexcitable solidity his own impressions and doubts, like a man sharpening a scythe on a good memorial stone. Cadfael was fussing over a too-exuberant wine, and seemed not to be listening, but Hugh remained undeceived. His friend had a sharp ear cocked for every intonation, even turned a swift glance occasionally to confirm what his ear heard, and reckon up the double account.

'You'd best lean back, then,' said Cadfael finally, 'and watch what will follow. You might also, I suppose, have a good man take a look at Bristol? He is the only hostage she has. With the

23

king loosed, or Robert, or Brian FitzCount, or some other of sufficient note made prisoner to match him, you'd be on secure ground. God forgive me, why am I advising you, who have no prince in this world!' But he was none too sure about the truth of that, having had brief remembered dealings with Stephen himself, and liked the man, even at his ill-advised worst, when he had slaughtered the garrison of Shrewsbury castle, to regret it as long as his ebullient memory kept nudging him with the outrage. By now, in his dungeon in Bristol, he might well have forgotten the uncharacteristic savagery.

'And do you know,' asked Hugh with deliberation, 'whose man was this knight Rainald Bossard, left bleeding to death in the lanes of Winchester? He for whom your prayers have been demanded?'

Cadfael turned from his boisterously bubbling jar to narrow his eyes on his friend's face. 'The empress's man is all we've been told. But I see you're about to tell me more.'

'He was in the following of Laurence d'Angers.'

Cadfael straightened up with incautious haste, and grunted at the jolt to his ageing back. It was the name of a man neither of them had ever set eyes on, yet it started vivid memories for them both.

'Yes, *that* Laurence! A baron of Gloucestershire, and liegeman to the empress. One of the few who has not once turned his coat yet in this to-ing and fro-ing, and uncle to those two children you helped away from Bromfield to join him, when they went astray after the sack of Worcester. Do you still remember the cold of that winter? And the wind that scoured away hills of snow overnight, and laid them down in fresh places before morning? I still feel it, clean through flesh and bone ...'

There was nothing about that winter journey that Cadfael would ever forget.* It was hardly a year and a half past, the attack on the city of Worcester, the flight of brother and sister northwards towards Shrewsbury, through the worst weather for many a year. Laurence d'Angers had been but a name in the business, as he was now in this. An adherent of the Empress Maud, he had been denied leave to enter King Stephen's territory to search for his young kin, but he had sent a squire in secret to find and fetch them away. To have borne a hand in the escape of those three was something to remember

*See *The Virgin in the Ice.*

lifelong. All three arose living before Cadfael's mind's eye, the boy Yves, thirteen years old then, ingenuous and gallant and endearing, jutting a stubborn Norman chin at danger, his elder sister Ermina, newly shaken into womanhood and resolutely shouldering the consequences of her own follies. And the third …

'I have often wondered,' said Hugh thoughtfully, 'how they fared afterwards. I knew you would get them off safely, if I left it to you, but it was still a perilous road before them. I wonder if we shall ever get word. Some day the world will surely hear of Yves Hugonin.' At the thought of the boy he smiled with affectionate amusement. 'And that dark lad who fetched them away, he who dressed like a woodsman and fought like a paladin … I fancy you knew more of him than ever I got to know.'

Cadfael smiled into the glow of the brazier and did not deny it. 'So his lord is there in the empress's train, is he? And this knight who was killed was in d'Angers' service? That was a very ill thing, Hugh.'

'So Abbot Radulfus thinks,' said Hugh sombrely.

'In the dusk and in confusion – and all got clean away, even the one who used the knife. A foul thing, for surely that was no chance blow. The clerk Christian escaped out of their hands, yet one among them turned on the rescuer before he fled. It argues a deal of hate at being thwarted, to have ventured that last moment before running. And is it left so? And Winchester full of those who should most firmly stand for justice?'

'Why, some among them would surely have been well enough pleased if that bold clerk had spilled his blood in the gutter, as well as the knight. Some may well have set the hunt on him.'

'Well for the empress's good name,' said Cadfael, 'that there was one at least of her men stout enough to respect an honest opponent, and stand by him to the death. And shame if that death goes unpaid for.'

'Old friend,' said Hugh ruefully, rising to take his leave, 'England has had to swallow many such a shame these last years. It grows customary to sigh and shrug and forget. At which, as I know, you are a very poor hand. And I have seen you overturn custom more than once, and been glad of it. But not even you can do much now for Rainald Bossard, bar praying for his soul. It is a very long way from here to Winchester.'

'It is not so far,' said Cadfael, as much to himself as to his friend, 'not by many a mile, as it was an hour since.'

He went to Vespers, and to supper in the refectory, and thereafter to Collations and Compline, and all with one remembered face before his mind's eye, so that he paid but fractured attention to the readings, and had difficulty in concentrating his thoughts on prayer. Though it might have been a kind of prayer he was offering throughout, in gratitude and praise and humility.

So suave, so young, so dark and vital a face, startling in its beauty when he had first seen it over the girl's shoulder, the face of the young squire sent to bring away the Hugonin children to their uncle and guardian. A long, spare, wide-browed face, with a fine scimitar of a nose and a supple bow of a mouth, and the fierce, fearless, golden eyes of a hawk. A head capped closely with curving, blue-black hair, coiling crisply at his temples and clasping his cheeks like folded wings. So young and yet so formed a face, east and west at home in it, shaven clean like a Norman, olive-skinned like a Syrian, all his memories of the Holy Land in one human countenance. The favourite squire of Laurence d'Angers, come home with him from the Crusade. Olivier de Bretagne.

If his lord was here in the south with his following, in the empress's retinue, where else would Olivier be? The abbot might even have rubbed shoulders with him, unbeknown, or seen him ride past at his lord's elbow, and for one absent moment admired his beauty. Few such faces blaze out of the humble mass of our ordinariness, thought Cadfael, the finger of God cannot choose but mark them out for notice, and his officers here will be the first to recognise and own them.

And this Rainald Bossard who is dead, an honourable man doing right by an honourable opponent, was Olivier's comrade, owning the same lord and pledged to the same service. His death will be grief to Olivier. Grief to Olivier is grief to me, a wrong done to Olivier is a wrong done to me. As far away as Winchester may be, here am I left mourning in that dark street where a man died for a generous act, in which, by the same token, he did not fail, for the clerk Christian lived on to return to his lady, the queen, with his errand faithfully done.

The gentle rustlings and stirrings of the dortoir sighed into silence outside the frail partitions of Cadfael's cell long before he rose from his knees, and shook off his sandals. The little

26

lamp by the night stairs cast only the faintest gleam across the beams of the roof, a ceiling of pearly grey above the darkness of his cell, his home now for – was it eighteen years or nineteen? – he had difficulty in recalling. It was as if a part of him, heart, mind, soul, whatever that essence might be, had not so much retired as come home to take seisin of a heritage here, his from his birth. And yet he remembered and acknowledged with gratitude and joy the years of his sojourning in the world, the lusty childhood and venturous youth, the taking of the Cross and the passion of the Crusade, the women he had known and loved, the years of his sea-faring off the coast of the Holy Kingdom of Jerusalem, all that pilgrimage that had led him here at last to his chosen retreat. None of it wasted, however foolish and amiss, nothing lost, nothing vain, all of it somehow fitting him to the narrow niche where now he served and rested. God had given him a sign, he had no need to regret anything, only to lay all open and own it his. For God's viewing, not for man's.

He lay quiet in the darkness, straight and still like a man coffined, but easy, with his arms lax at his sides, and his half-closed eyes dreaming on the vault above him, where the faint light played among the beams.

There was no lightning that night, only a consort of steady rolls of thunder both before and after Matins and Lauds, so unalarming that many among the brothers failed to notice them. Cadfael heard them as he rose, and as he returned to his rest. They seemed to him a reminder and a reassurance that Winchester had indeed moved nearer to Shrewsbury, and consoled him that his grievance was not overlooked, but noted in heaven, and he might look to have his part yet in collecting the debt due to Rainald Bossard. Upon which warranty, he fell asleep.

Chapter Three

N THE seventeenth day of June Saint Winifred's elaborate oak coffin, silver-ornamented and lined with lead behind all its immaculate seals, was removed from its place of honour and carried with grave and subdued ceremony back to its temporary resting-place in the chapel of the hospital of Saint Giles, there to wait, as once before, for the auspicious day, the twenty-second of June. The weather was fair, sunny and still, barely a cloud in the sky, and yet cool enough for travelling, the best of weather for pilgrims. And by the eighteenth day the pilgrims began to arrive, a scattering of fore-runners before the full tide began to flow.

Brother Cadfael had watched the reliquary depart on its memorial journey with a slightly guilty mind, for all his honest declaration that he could hardly have done otherwise than he had done, there in the summer night in Gwytherin. So strongly had he felt, above all, her Welshness, the feeling she must have for the familiar tongue about her, and the tranquil flow of the seasons in her solitude, where she had slept so long and so well in her beatitude, and worked so many small, sweet miracles for her own people. No, he could not believe he had made a wrong choice there. If only she would glance his way, and smile, and say, well done!

The very first of the pilgrims came probing into the walled herb-garden, with Brother Denis's directions to guide him, in search of a colleague in his own mystery. Cadfael was busy weeding the close-planted beds of mint and thyme and sage late in the afternoon, a tedious, meticulous labour in the ripeness of a favourable June, after spring sun and shower had been nicely balanced, and growth was a green battlefield. He backed out of a cleansed bed, and backed into a solid form, rising startled from his knees to turn and face a rusty black brother shaped very much like himself, though probably fifteen years younger. They stood at gaze, two solid, squarely built brethren of the Order, eyeing each other in instant recognition and acknowledgement.

'You must be Brother Cadfael,' said the stranger-brother in a broad, melodious bass voice. 'Brother Hospitaller told me where to find you. My name is Adam, a brother of Reading. I have the very charge there that you bear here, and I have heard tell of you, even as far south as my house.'

His eye was roving, as he spoke, towards some of Cadfael's rarer treasures, the eastern poppies he had brought from the Holy Land and reared here with anxious care, the delicate fig that still contrived to thrive against the sheltering north wall, where the sun nursed it. Cadfael warmed to him for the quickening of his eye, and the mild greed that flushed the round, shaven face. A sturdy, stalwart man, who moved as if confident of his body, one who might prove a man of his hands if challenged. Well-weathered, too, a genuine outdoor man.

'You're more than welcome, brother,' said Cadfael heartily. 'You'll be here for the saint's feast? And have they found you a place in the dortoir? There are a few cells vacant, for any of our own who come, like you.'

'My abbot sent me from Reading with a mission to our daughter house of Leominster,' said Brother Adam, probing with an experimental toe into the rich, well-fed loam of Brother Cadfael's bed of mint, and raising an eyebrow respectfully at the quality he found. 'I asked if I might prolong the errand to attend on the translation of Saint Winifred, and I was given the needful permission. It's seldom I could hope to be sent so far north, and it would be pity to miss such an opportunity.'

'And they've found you a brother's bed?' Such a man, Benedictine, gardener and herbalist, could not be wasted on a bed in the guest-hall. Cadfael coveted him, marking the bright eye with which the newcomer singled out his best endeavours.

'Brother Hospitaller was so gracious. I am placed in a cell close to the novices.'

29

'We shall be near neighbours,' said Cadfael contentedly. 'Now come, I'll show you whatever we have here to show, for the main garden is on the far side of the Foregate, along the bank of the river. But here I keep my own herber. And if there should be anything here that can be safely carried to Reading, you may take cuttings most gladly before you leave us.'

They fell into a very pleasant and voluble discussion, perambulating all the walks of the closed garden, and comparing experiences in cultivation and use. Brother Adam of Reading had a sharp eye for rarities, and was likely to go home laden with spoils. He admired the neatness and order of Cadfael's workshop, the collection of rustling bunches of dried herbs hung from the roof-beams and under the eaves, and the array of bottles, jars and flagons along the shelves. He had hints and tips of his own to propound, too, and the amiable contest kept them happy all the afternoon. When they returned together to the great court before Vespers it was to a scene notably animated, as if the bustle of celebration was already beginning. There were horses being led down into the stableyard, and bundles being carried in at the guest-hall. A stout elderly man, well equipped for riding, paced across towards the church to pay his first respects on arrival, with a servant trotting at his heels.

Brother Paul's youngest charges, all eyes and curiosity, ringed the gatehouse to watch the early arrivals, and were shooed aside by Brother Jerome, very busy as usual with all the prior's errands. Though the boys did not go very far, and formed their ring again as soon as Jerome was out of sight. A few of the citizens of the Foregate had gathered in the street to watch, excited dogs running among their legs.

'Tomorrow,' said Cadfael, eyeing the scene, 'there will be many more. This is but the beginning. Now if the weather stays fair we shall have a very fine festival for our saint.'

And she will understand that all is in her honour, he thought privately, even if she does lie very far from here. And who knows whether she may not pay us a visit, out of the kindness of her heart? What is distance to a saint, who can be where she wills in the twinkling of an eye?

The guest-hall filled steadily on the morrow. All day long they came, some singly, some in groups as they had met and made comfortable acquaintance on the road, some afoot, some on ponies, some whole and hearty and on holiday, some who had

30

travelled only a few miles, some who came from far away, and among them a number who went on crutches, or were led along by better-sighted friends, or had grievous deformities or skin diseases, or debilitating illnesses; and all these hoping for relief.

Cadfael went about the regular duties of his day, divided between church and herbarium, but with an interested eye open for all there was to see whenever he crossed the great court, boiling now with activity. Every arriving figure, every face, engaged his notice, but as yet distantly, none being provided with a name, to make him individual. Such of them as needed his services for relief would be directed to him, such as came his way by chance would be entitled to his whole attention, freely offered.

It was the woman he noticed first, bustling across the court from the gatehouse to the guest-hall with a basket on her arm, fresh from the Foregate market with new-baked bread and little cakes, soon after Prime. A careful housewife, to be off marketing so early even on holiday, decided about what she wanted, and not content to rely on the abbey bakehouse to provide it. A sturdy, confident figure of a woman, perhaps fifty years of age but in full rosy bloom. Her dress was sober and plain, but of good material and proudly kept, her wimple snow-white beneath her head-cloth of brown linen. She was not tall, but so erect that she could pass for tall, and her face was round, wide-eyed and broad-cheeked, with a determined chin to it.

She vanished briskly into the guest-hall, and he caught but a glimpse of her, but she was positive enough to stay with him through the offices and duties of the morning, and as the worshippers left the church after Mass he caught sight of her again, arms spread like a hen-wife driving her birds, marshalling two chicks, it seemed, before her, both largely concealed beyond her ample width and bountiful skirts. Indeed she had a general largeness about her, her head-dress surely taller and broader than need, her hips bolstered by petticoats, the aura of bustle and command she bore about with her equally generous and ebullient. He felt a wave of warmth go out to her for her energy and vigour, while he spared a morsel of sympathy for the chicks she mothered, stowed thus away beneath such ample, smothering wings.

In the afternoon, busy about his small kingdom and putting together the medicaments he must take along the Foregate to

Saint Giles in the morning, to be sure they had provision enough over the feast, he was not thinking of her, nor of any of the inhabitants of the guest-hall, since none had as yet had occasion to call for his aid. He was packing lozenges into a small box, soothing tablets for scoured, dry throats, when a bulky shadow blocked the open door of his workshop, and a brisk, light voice said, 'Pray your pardon, brother, but Brother Denis advised me to come to you, and sent me here.'

And there she stood, filling the doorway, shoulders squared, hands folded at her waist, head braced and face full forward. Her eyes, wide and wide-set, were bright blue but meagrely supplied with pale lashes, yet very firm and fixed in their regard.

'It's my young nephew you see, brother,' she went on confidently, 'my sister's son, that was fool enough to go off and marry a roving Welshman from Builth, and now her man's gone, and so is she, poor lass, and left her two children orphan, and nobody to care for them but me. And me with my own husband dead, and all his craft fallen to me to manage, and never a chick of my own to be my comfort. Not but what I can do very well with the work and the journeymen, for I've learned these twenty years what was what in the weaving trade, but still I could have done with a son of my own. But it was not to be, and a sister's son is dearly welcome, so he is, whether he has his health or no, for he's the dearest lad ever you saw. And it's the pain, you see, brother. I don't like to see him in pain, though he doesn't complain. So I'm come to you.'

Cadfael made haste to wedge a toe into this first chink in her volubility, and insert a few words of his own into the gap.

'Come within, mistress, and welcome. Tell me what's the nature of your lad's pain, and what I can do for you and him I'll do. But best I should see him and speak with him, for he best knows where he hurts. Sit down and be easy, and tell me about him.'

She came in confidently enough, and settled herself with a determined spreading of ample skirts on the bench against the wall. Her gaze went round the laden shelves, the stored herbs dangling, the brazier and the pots and flasks, interested and curious, but in no way awed by Cadfael or his mysteries.

'I'm from the cloth country down by Campden, brother, Weaver by name and by trade was my man, and his father and grandfather before him, and Alice Weaver is my name, and I keep up the work just as he did. But this young sister of mine, she went off with a Welshman, and the pair of them are dead now, and the children I sent for to live with me. The girl is eighteen years old now, a good, hard-working maid, and I daresay we shall contrive to find a decent match for her in the end, though I shall miss her help, for she's grown very handy, and is strong and healthy, not like the lad. Named for some outlandish Welsh saint, she is, Melangell, if ever you heard the like!'

'I'm Welsh myself,' said Cadfael cheerfully. 'Our Welsh names do come hard on your English tongues, I know.'

'Ah well, the boy brought a name with him that's short and simple enough. Rhun, they named him. Sixteen he is now, two years younger than his sister, but wants her heartiness, poor soul. He's well-grown enough, and very comely, but from a child something went wrong with his right leg, it's twisted and feebled so he can put but the very toe of it to the ground at all, and even that turned on one side, and can lay no weight on it, but barely touch. He goes on two crutches. And I've brought him here in the hope good Saint Winifred will do something for him. But it's cost him dear to make the walk, even though we started out three weeks ago, and have taken it by easy shifts.'

'He walked the whole way?' asked Cadfael, dismayed.

'I'm not so prosperous I can afford a horse, more than the one they need for the business at home. Twice on the way a kind carter did give him a ride as far as he was bound, but the rest he's hobbled on his crutches. Many another at this feast, brother, will have done as much, in as bad case or worse. But he's here now, safe in the guest-hall, and if my prayers can do anything for him, he'll walk home again on two sound legs as ever held up a hale and hearty man. But now for these few days he suffers as bad as before.'

'You should have brought him here with you,' said Cadfael. 'What's the nature of his pain? Is it in moving, or when he lies still? Is it the bones of the leg that ache?'

'It's worst in his bed at night. At home I've often heard him weeping for pain in the night, though he tries to keep it so silent we need not be disturbed. Often he gets little or no sleep. His bones do ache, that's truth, but also the sinews of his calf knot into such cramps it makes him groan.'

'There can be something done about that,' said Cadfael, considering. 'At least we may try. And there are draughts can dull the pain and help him to a night's sleep, at any rate.'

'It isn't that I don't trust to the saint,' explained Mistress

33

Weaver anxiously. 'But while he waits for her, let him be at rest if he can, that's what I say. Why should not a suffering lad seek help from ordinary decent mortals, too, good men like you who have faith and knowledge both?'

'Why not, indeed!' agreed Cadfael. 'The least of us may be an instrument of grace, though not by his own deserving. Better let the boy come to me here, where we can be private together. The guest-hall will be busy and noisy, here we shall have quiet.'

She rose, satisfied, to take her leave, but she had plenty yet to say even in departing of the long, slow journey, the small kindnesses they had met with on the way, and the fellow pilgrims, some of whom had passed them and arrived here before them.

'There's more than one in there,' said she, wagging her head towards the lofty rear wall of the guest-hall, 'will be needing your help, besides my Rhun. There were two young fellows we came along with the last days, we could keep pace with them, for they were slowed much as we were. Oh, the one of them was hale and lusty enough, but would not stir a step ahead of his friend, and that poor soul had come barefoot more miles even than Rhun had come crippled, and his feet a sight for pity, but would he so much as bind them with rags? Not he! He said he was under vow to go unshod to his journey's end. And a great heavy cross on' a string round his neck, too, and he rubbed raw with the chafing of it, but that was part of his vow, too. I see no reason why a fine young fellow should choose such a torment of his own will, but there, folk do strange things, I daresay he hopes to win some great mercy for himself with his austerities. Still, I should think he might at least get some balm for his feet, while he's here at rest? Shall I bid him come to you? I'd gladly do a small service for that pair. The other one, Matthew, the sturdy one, he hefted my girl safe out of the way of harm when some mad horsemen in a hurry all but rode us down into the ditch, and he carried our bundles for her after, for she was well loaded, I being busy helping Rhun along. Truth to tell, I think the young man was taken with our Melangell, for he was very attentive to her once we joined company. More than to his friend, though indeed he never stirred a step away from him. A vow is a vow, I suppose, and if a man's taken all that suffering on himself of his own will, what can another do to prevent it? No more than bear him company, and that the lad is doing, faithfully, for he never leaves him.'

34

She was out of the door and spreading appreciative nostrils for the scent of the sunlit herbs, when she looked back to add: 'There's others among them may call themselves pilgrims as loud and often as they will, but I wouldn't trust one or two of them as far as I could throw them. I suppose rogues will make their way everywhere, even among the saints.'

'As long as the saints have money in their purses, or anything about them worth stealing,' agreed Cadfael wryly, 'rogues will never be far away.'

Whether Mistress Weaver did speak to her strange travelling companion or not, it was he who arrived at Cadfael's workshop within half an hour, before ever the boy Rhun showed his face. Cadfael was back at his weeding when he heard them come, or heard, rather, the slow, patient footsteps of the sturdy one stirring the gravel of his pathways. The other made no sound in walking, for he stepped tenderly and carefully in the grass border, which was cool and kind to his misused feet. If there was any sound to betray his coming it was the long, effortful sighing of his breath, the faint, indrawn hiss of pain. As soon as Cadfael straightened his back and turned his head, he knew who came.

They were much of an age, and even somewhat alike in build and colouring, above middle height but that the one stooped in his laboured progress, brown-haired and dark of eye, and perhaps twenty-five or twenty-six years old. Yet not so like that they could have been brothers or close kin. The hale one had the darker complexion, as though he had been more in the air and the sun, and broader bones of cheek and jaw, a stubborn, proud, secret face, disconcertingly still, confiding nothing. The sufferer's face was long, mobile and passionate, with high cheekbones and hollow cheeks beneath them, and a mouth tight-drawn, either with present pain or constant passion. Anger might be one of his customary companions, burning ardour another. The young man Matthew stalked at his heels mute and jealously watchful in attendance on him.

Mindful of Mistress Weaver's loquacious confidences, Cadfael looked from the scarred and swollen feet to the chafed neck. Within the collar of his plain dark coat the votary had wound a length of linen cloth, to alleviate the rubbing of the thin cord from which a heavy cross of iron, chaced in a leaf pattern with what looked like gold, hung down upon his breast. By the look of the seam of red that marked the linen, either this padding was new, or else it had not been effective. The cord was mercilessly thin, the cross certainly heavy. To what desperate end could a young man choose so to torture himself? And what pleasure did he think it could give to God or Saint Winifred to contemplate his discomfort?

Eyes feverishly bright scanned him. A low voice asked: 'You are Brother Cadfael? That is the name Brother Hospitaller gave me. He said you would have ointments and salves that could be of help to me. So far,' he added, eyeing Cadfael with glittering fixity, 'as there is any help anywhere for me.'

Cadfael gave him a considering look for that, but asked nothing until he had marshalled the pair of them into his workshop and sat the sufferer down to be inspected with due care. The young man Matthew took up his stand beside the open door, careful to avoid blocking the light, but would not come further within.

'You've come a fairish step unshod,' said Cadfael, on his knees to examine the damage. 'Was such cruelty needful?'

'It was. I do not hate myself so much as to bear this to no purpose.' The silent youth by the door stirred slightly, but said no word. 'I am under vow,' said his companion, 'and will not break it.' It seemed that he felt a need to account for himself, forestalling questioning. 'My name is Ciaran, I am of a Welsh mother, and I am going back to where I was born, there to end my life as I began it. You see the wounds on my feet, brother, but what most ails me does not show anywhere upon me. I have a fell disease, no threat to any other, but it must shortly end me.'

And it could be true, thought Cadfael, busy with a cleansing oil on the swollen soles, and the toes cut by gravel and stones. The feverish fire of the deep-set eyes might well mean an even fiercer fire within. True, the young body, now eased in repose, was well-made and had not lost flesh, but that was no sure proof of health. Ciaran's voice remained low, level and firm. If he knew he had his death, he had come to terms with it.

'So I am returning in penitential pilgrimage, for my soul's health, which is of greater import. Barefoot and burdened I shall walk to the house of canons at Aberdaron, so that after my death I may be buried on the holy isle of Ynys Enlli, where the soil is made up of the bones and dust of thousands upon thousands of saints.'

'I should have thought,' said Cadfael mildly, 'that such a privilege could be earned by going there shod and tranquil and

36

humble, like any other man.' But for all that, it was an understandable ambition for a devout man of Welsh extraction, knowing his end near. Aberdaron, at the tip of the Lleyn peninsula, fronting the wild sea and the holiest island of the Welsh church, had been the last resting place of many, and the hospitality of the canons of the house was never refused to any man. 'I would not cast doubt on your sacrifice, but self-imposed suffering seems to me a kind of arrogance, and not humility.'

'It may be so,' said Ciaran remotely. 'No help for it now, I am bound.'

'That is true,' said Matthew from his corner by the door. A measured and yet an abrupt voice, deeper than his companion's. 'Fast bound! So are we both, I no less than he.'

'Hardly by the same vows,' said Cadfael drily. For Matthew wore good, solid shoes, a little down at heel, but proof against the stones of the road.

'No, not the same. But no less binding. And I do not forget mine, any more than he forgets his.'

Cadfael laid down the foot he had anointed, setting a folded cloth under it, and lifted its fellow into his lap. 'God forbid I should tempt any man to break his oath. You will both do as you must do. But at least you may rest your feet here until after the feast, which will give you three days for healing, and here within the pale the ground is not so harsh. And once healed, I have a rough spirit that will help to harden your soles for when you take to the road again. Why not, unless you have forsworn all help from men? And since you came to me I take it you have not yet gone so far. There, sit a while longer, and let that dry.'

He rose from his knees, surveying his work critically, and turned his attention next to the linen wrapping about Ciaran's neck. He laid both hands gently on the cord by which the cross depended, and made to lift it over the young man's head.

'No, no, let be!' It was a soft, wild cry of alarm, and Ciaran clutched at cross and cord, one with either hand, and hugged his burden to him fiercely. 'Don't touch it! Let it be!'

'Surely,' said Cadfael, startled, 'you may lift it off while I dress the wound it's cost you? Hardly a moment's work, why not?'

'*No!*' Ciaran fastened both hands upon the cross and hugged it to his breast. 'No, never for a moment, night or day! No! Let it alone!'

37

'Lift it, then,' said Cadfael resignedly, 'and hold it while I dress this cut. No, never fear, I'll not cheat you. Only let me unwind this cloth, and see what damage you have there, hidden.'

'Yet he should doff it, and so I have prayed him constantly,' said Matthew softly. 'How else can he be truly rid of his pains?'

Cadfael unwound the linen, viewed the scored line of half-dried blood, still oozing, and went to work on it with a stinging lotion first to clean it of dust and fragments of frayed skin, and then with a healing ointment of cleavers. He refolded the cloth, and wound it carefully under the cord. 'There, you have not broken faith. Settle your load again. If you hold up the weight in your hands as you go, and loosen it in your bed, you'll be rid of your gash before you depart.'

It seemed to him that they were both of them in haste to leave him, for the one set his feet tenderly to ground as soon as he was released, holding up the weight of his cross obediently with both hands, and the other stepped out through the doorway into the sunlit garden, and waited on guard for his friend to emerge. The one owed no special thanks, the other offered only the merest acknowledgement.

'But I would remind you both,' said Cadfael, and with a thoughtful eye on both, 'that you are now present at the feast of a saint who has worked many miracles, even to the defiance of death. One who may have life itself within her gift,' he said strongly, 'even for a man already condemned to death. Bear it in mind, for she may be listening now!'

They said never a word, neither did they look at each other. They stared back at him from the scented brightness of the garden, with startled, wary eyes, and then they turned abruptly as one man, and limped and strode away.

Chapter Four

HERE WAS so short an interval, and so little weeding done, before the second pair appeared, that Cadfael could not choose but reason that the two couples must have met at the corner of his herber, and perhaps exchanged at least a friendly word or two, since they had travelled side by side the last miles of their road here.

The girl walked solicitously beside her brother, giving him the smoothest part of the path, and keeping a hand supportingly under his left elbow, ready to prop him at need, but barely touching. Her face was turned constantly towards him, eager and loving. If he was the tended darling, and she the healthy beast of burden, certainly she had no quarrel with the division. Though just once she did look back over her shoulder, with a different, a more tentative smile. She was neat and plain in her homespun country dress, her hair austerely braided, but her face was vivid and glowing as a rose, and her movements, even at her brother's pace, had a spring and grace to them that spoke of a high and ardent spirit. She was fair for a Welsh girl, her hair a coppery gold, her brows darker, arched hopefully above wide blue eyes. Mistress Weaver could not be far out in supposing that a young man who had hefted this neat little woman out of harm's way in his arms might well remember the experience with pleasure, and not be averse to repeating it. If he could take his eyes from his fellow-pilgrim long enough to attempt it!

The boy came leaning heavily on his crutches, his right leg

dangling inertly, turned with the toe twisted inward, and barely brushing the ground. If he could have stood erect he would have been a hand's-breadth taller than his sister, but thus hunched he looked even shorter. Yet the young body was beautifully proportioned, Cadfael judged, watching his approach with a thoughtful eye, wide-shouldered, slim-flanked, the one good leg long, vigorous and shapely. He carried little flesh, indeed he could have done with more, but if he spent his days habitually in pain it was unlikely he had much appetite.

Cadfael's study of him had begun at the twisted foot, and travelling upward, came last to the boy's face. He was fairer than the girl, wheat-gold of hair and brows, his thin, smooth face like ivory, and the eyes that met Cadfael's were a light, brilliant grey-blue, clear as crystal between long, dark lashes. It was a very still and tranquil face, one that had learned patient endurance, and expected to have need of it lifelong. It was clear to Cadfael, in that first exchange of glances, that Rhun did not look for any miraculous deliverance, whatever Mistress Weaver's hopes might be.

'If you please,' said the girl shyly, 'I have brought my brother, as my aunt said I should. And his name is Rhun, and mine is Melangell.'

'She has told me about you,' said Cadfael, beckoning them with him towards his workshop. 'A long journey you've had of it. Come within, and let's make you as easy as we may, while I take a look at this leg of yours. Was there ever an injury brought this on? A fall, or a kick from a horse? Or a bout of the bone-fever?' He settled the boy on the long bench, took the crutches from him and laid them aside, and turned him so that he could stretch out his legs at rest.

The boy, with grave eyes steady on Cadfael's face, slowly shook his head. 'No such accident,' he said in a man's low, clear voice. 'It came, I think, slowly, but I don't remember a time before it. They say I began to falter and fall when I was three or four years old.'

Melangell, hesitant in the doorway – strangely like Ciaran's attendant shadow, thought Cadfael – had her chin on her shoulder now, and turned almost hastily to say: 'Rhun will tell you all his case. He'll be better private with you. I'll come back later, and wait on the seat outside there until you need me.'

Rhun's light, bright eyes, transparent as sunlit ice, smiled at her warmly over Cadfael's shoulder. 'Do go,' he said. 'So fine and sunny a day, you should make good use of it, without me dangling about you.'

She gave him a long, anxious glance, but half her mind was already away; and satisfied that he was in good hands, she made her hasty reverence, and fled. They were left looking at each other, strangers still, and yet in tentative touch.

'She goes to find Matthew,' said Rhun simply, confident of being understood. 'He was good to her. And to me, also – once he carried me the last piece of the way to our night's lodging on his back. She likes him, and he would like her, if he could truly see her, but he seldom sees anyone but Ciaran.'

This blunt simplicity might well get him the reputation of an innocent, though that would be the world's mistake. What he saw, he said – provided, Cadfael hoped, he had already taken the measure of the person to whom he spoke – and he saw more than most, having so much more need to observe and record, to fill up the hours of his day.

'They were here?' asked Rhun, shifting obediently to allow Cadfael to strip down the long hose from his hips and his maimed leg.

'They were here. Yes, I know.'

'I would like her to be happy.'

'She has it in her to be very happy,' said Cadfael, answering in kind, almost without his will. The boy had a quality of dazzle about him that made unstudied answers natural, almost inevitable. There had been, he thought, the slightest of stresses on 'her'. Rhun had little enough expectation that he could ever be happy, but he wanted happiness for his sister. 'Now pay heed,' said Cadfael, bending to his own duties, 'for this is important. Close your eyes and be at ease as far as you can, and tell me where I find a spot that gives pain. First, thus at rest, is there any pain now?'

Docilely Rhun closed his eyes and waited, breathing softly. 'No, I am quite easy now.'

Good, for all his sinews lay loose and trustful, and at least in that state he felt no pain. Cadfael began to finger his way, at first very gently and soothingly, all down the thigh and calf of the helpless leg, probing and manipulating. Thus stretched out at rest, the twisted limb partially regained its proper alignment, and showed fairly formed, though much wasted by comparison with the left, and marred by the inturned toe and certain tight, bunched knots of sinew in the calf. He sought out these, and let his fingers dig deep there, wrestling with hard tissue.

41

'There I feel it,' said Rhun, breathing deep. 'It doesn't feel like pain – yes, it hurts, but not for crying. A good hurt ...'

Brother Cadfael oiled his hands, smoothed a palm over the shrunken calf, and went to work with firm fingertips, working tendons unexercised for years, beyond that tensed touch of toe upon ground. He was gentle and slow, feeling for the hard cores of resistance. There were unnatural tensions there, that would not melt to him yet. He let his fingers work softly, and his mind probed elsewhere.

'You were orphaned early. How long have you been with your Aunt Weaver?'

'Seven years now,' said Rhun almost drowsily, soothed by the circling fingers. 'I know we are a burden to her, but she never says it, nor she would never let any other say it. She has a good business, but small, it provides her needs and keeps two men at work, but she is not rich. Melangell works hard keeping the house and the kitchen, and earns her keep. I have learned to weave, but I am slow at it. I can neither stand for long nor sit for long, I am no profit to her. But she never speaks of it, for all she has an edge to her tongue when she pleases.'

'She would,' agreed Cadfael peacefully. 'A woman with many cares is liable to be short in her speech now and again, and no ill meant. She has brought you here for a miracle. You know that? Why else would you all three have walked all this way, measuring out the stages day by day at your pace? And yet I think you have no expectation of grace. Do you not believe Saint Winifred can do wonders?'

'I?' The boy was startled, he opened great eyes clearer than the clear waters Cadfael had navigated long ago, in the eastern fringes of the Midland Sea, over pale and glittering sand. 'Oh, you mistake me, I *do* believe. But why for me? In case like mine we come by our thousands, in worse case by the hundred. How dare I ask to be among the first? Besides, what I have I can bear. There are some who cannot bear what they have. The saint will know where to choose. There is no reason her choice should fall on me.'

'Then why did you consent to come?' Cadfael asked.

Rhun turned his head aside, and eyelids blue-veined like the petals of anemones veiled his eyes. 'They wished it, I did what they wanted. And there was Melangell ...'

Yes, Melangell who was altogether comely and bright and a charm to the eye, thought Cadfael. Her brother knew her dowryless, and wished her a little of joy and a decent marriage,

42

and there at home, working hard in house and kitchen, and known for a penniless niece, suitors there were none. A venture so far upon the roads, to mingle with so various a company, might bring forth who could tell what chances?

In moving Rhun had plucked at a nerve that gripped and twisted him, he eased himself back against the timber wall with aching care. Cadfael drew up the homespun hose over the boy's nakedness, knotted him decent, and gently drew down his feet, the sound and the crippled, to the beaten earth floor.

'Come again to me tomorrow, after High Mass, for I think I can help you, if only a little. Now sit until I see if that sister of yours is waiting, and if not, you may rest easy until she comes. And I'll give you a single draught to take this night when you go to your bed. It will ease your pain and help you to sleep.'

The girl was there, still and solitary against the sun-warmed wall, the brightness of her face clouded over, as though some eager expectation had turned into a grey disappointment; but at the sight of Rhun emerging she rose with a resolute smile for him, and her voice was as gay and heartening as ever as they moved slowly away.

He had an opportunity to study all of them next day at High Mass, when doubtless his mind should have been on higher things, but obstinately would not rise above the quivering crest of Mistress Weaver's head-cloth, and the curly dark crown of Matthew's thick crop of hair. Almost all the inhabitants of the guest-halls, the gentles who had separate apartments as well as the male and female pilgrims who shared the two common dortoirs, came in their best to this one office of the day, whatever they did with the rest of it. Mistress Weaver paid devout attention to every word of the office, and several times nudged Melangell sharply in the ribs to recall her to duty, for as often as not her head was turned sidewise, and her gaze directed rather at Matthew than at the altar. No question but her fancy, if not her whole heart, was deeply engaged there. As for Matthew, he stood at Ciaran's shoulder, always within touch. But twice at least he looked round, and his brooding eyes rested, with no change of countenance, upon Melangell. Yet on the one occasion when their glances met, it was Matthew who turned abruptly away.

That young man, thought Cadfael, aware of the broken encounter of eyes, has a thing to do which no girl must be allowed to hinder or spoil: to get his fellow safely to his

43

journey's end at Aberdaron.

He was already a celebrated figure in the enclave, this
Ciaran. There was nothing secret about him, he spoke freely
and humbly of himself. He had been intended for ordination,
but had not yet gone beyond the first step as sub-deacon, and
had not reached, and now never would reach, the tonsure.
Brother Jerome, always a man to insinuate himself as close as
might be to any sign of superlative virtue and holiness, had
cultivated and questioned him, and freely retailed what he had
learned to any of the brothers who would listen. The story of
Ciaran's mortal sickness and penitential pilgrimage home to
Aberdaron was known to all. The austerities he practised upon
himself made a great impression. Brother Jerome held that the
house was honoured in receiving such a man. And indeed that
lean, passionate face, burning-eyed beneath the uncropped
brown hair, had a vehement force and fervour.

Rhun could not kneel, but stood steady and stoical on his
crutches throughout the office, his eyes fixed, wide and bright,
upon the altar. In this soft, dim light within, already reflecting
from every stone surface the muted brightness of a cloudless
day outside, Cadfael saw that the boy was beautiful, the planes
of his face as suave and graceful as any girl's, the curving of his
fair hair round ears and cheeks angelically pure and chaste. If
the woman with no son of her own doted on him, and was
willing to forsake her living for a matter of weeks on the
off-chance of a miracle that would heal him, who could wonder
at her?

Since both his attention and his eyes were straying, Cadfael
gave up the struggle and let them stray at large over all those
devout heads, gathered in a close assembly and filling the nave
of the church. An important pilgrimage has much of the
atmosphere of a public fair about it, and brings along with it all
the hangers-on who frequent such occasions, the pickpockets,
the plausible salesmen of relics, sweetmeats, remedies, the
fortune-tellers, the gamblers, the swindlers and cheats of all
kinds. And some of these cultivate the most respectable of
appearances, and prefer to work from within the pale rather
than set up in the Foregate as at a market. It was always worth
running an eye over the ranks within, as Hugh's sergeants were
certainly doing along the ranks without, to mark down
probable sources of trouble before ever the trouble began.

This congregation certainly looked precisely what it
purported to be. Nevertheless, there were a few there worth a

second glance. Three modest, unobtrusive tradesmen who had arrived closely one after another and rapidly and openly made acquaintance, to all appearances until then strangers: Walter Bagot, glover; John Shure, tailor; William Hales, farrier. Small craftsmen making this their summer holiday, and modestly out to enjoy it. And why not? Except that Cadfael had noted the tailor's hands devoutly folded, and observed that he cultivated the long, well-tended nails of a fairground sharper, hardly suitable for a tailor's work. He made a mental note of their faces, the glover rounded and glossy, as if oiled with the same dressing he used on his leathers, the tailor lean-jowled and sedate, with lank hair curtaining a lugubrious face, the farrier square, brown and twinkling of eye, the picture of honest good-humour.

They might be what they claimed. They might not. Hugh would be on the watch, so would the careful tavern-keepers of the Foregate and the town, by no means eager to hold their doors open to the fleecers and skinners of their own neighbours and customers.

Cadfael went out from Mass with his brethren, very thoughtful, and found Rhun already waiting for him in the herbarium.

The boy sat passive and submitted himself to Cadfael's handling, saying no word beyond his respectful greeting. The rhythm of the questing fingers, patiently coaxing apart the rigid tissues that lamed him, had a soothing effect, even when they probed deeply enough to cause pain. He let his head lean back against the timbers of the wall, and his eyes gradually closed. The tension of his cheeks and lips showed that he was not sleeping, but Cadfael was able to study the boy's face closely as he worked on him, and note his pallor, and the dark rings round his eyes.

'Well, did you take the dose I gave you for the night?' asked Cadfael, guessing at the answer.

'No.' Rhun opened his eyes apprehensively, to see if he was to be reproved for it, but Cadfael's face showed neither surprise nor reproach.

'Why not?'

'I don't know. Suddenly I felt there was no need. I was happy,' said Rhun, his eyes again closed, the better to examine his own actions and motives. 'I had prayed. It's not that I doubt the saint's power. Suddenly it seemed to me that I need not even wish to be healed ... that I ought to offer up my lameness and pain freely, not as a price for favour. People bring offerings, and I have nothing else to offer. Do you think it might be acceptable? I meant it humbly.'

There could hardly be, thought Cadfael, among all her devotees, a more costly oblation. He has gone far along a difficult road who has come to the point of seeing that deprivation, pain and disability are of no consequence at all, beside the inward conviction of grace, and the secret peace of the soul. An acceptance which can only be made for a man's own self, never for any other. Another's grief is not to be tolerated, if there can be anything done to alleviate it.

'And did you sleep well?'

'No. But it didn't matter. I lay quiet all night long. I tried to bear it gladly. And I was not the only one there wakeful.' He slept in the common dormitory for the men, and there must be several among his fellows there afflicted in one way or another, besides the sick and possibly contagious whom Brother Edmund had isolated in the infirmary. 'Ciaran was restless, too,' said Rhun reflectively. 'When it was all silent, after Lauds, he got up very quietly from his cot, trying not to disturb anyone, and started towards the door. I thought then how strange it was that he took his belt and scrip with him ...'

Cadfael was listening intently enough by this time. Why, indeed, if a man merely needed relief for his body during the night, should he burden himself with carrying his possessions about with him? Though the habit of being wary of theft, in such shared accommodation, might persist even when half-asleep, and in monastic care into the bargain.

'Did he so, indeed? And what followed?'

'Matthew has his own pallet drawn close beside Ciaran's, even in the night he lies with a hand stretched out to touch. Besides, you know, he seems to know by instinct whatever ails Ciaran. He rose up in an instant, and reached out and took Ciaran by the arm. And Ciaran started and gasped, and blinked round at him, like a man startled awake suddenly, and whispered that he'd been asleep and dreaming, and had dreamed it was time to start out on the road again. So then Matthew took the scrip from him and laid it aside, and they both lay down in their beds again, and all was quiet as before. But I don't think Ciaran slept well, even after that, his dream had disturbed his mind too much, I heard him twisting and turning for a long time.'

46

'Did they know,' asked Cadfael, 'that you were also awake, and had heard what passed?'

'I can't tell. I made no pretence, and the pain was bad, I think they must have heard me shifting ... I couldn't help it. But of course I made no sign, it would have been discourteous.'

So it passed as a dream, perhaps for the benefit of Rhun, or any other who might be wakeful as he was. True enough, a sick man troubled by night might very well rise by stealth to leave his friend in peace, out of consideration. But then, if he needed ease, he would have been forced to explain himself and go, when his friend nevertheless started awake to restrain him. Instead, he had pleaded a deluding dream, and lain down again. And men rousing in dreams do move silently, almost as if by stealth. It could be, it must be, simply what it seemed.

'You travelled some miles of the way with those two, Rhun. How did you all fare together on the road? You must have got to know them as well as any here.'

'It was their being slow, like us, that kept us all together, after my sister was nearly ridden down, and Matthew ran and caught her up and leaped the ditch with her. They were just slowly overtaking us then, after that we went on all together for company. But I wouldn't say we got to know them – they are so rapt in each other. And then, Ciaran was in pain, and that kept him silent, though he did tell us where he was bound, and why. It's true Melangell and Matthew took to walking last, behind us, and he carried our few goods for her, having so little of his own to carry. I never wondered at Ciaran being so silent,' said Rhun simply, 'seeing what he had to bear. And my Aunt Alice can talk for two,' he ended guilelessly.

So she could, and no doubt did, all the rest of the way into Shrewsbury.

'That pair, Ciaran and Matthew,' said Cadfael, still delicately probing, 'they never told you how they came together? Whether they were kin, or friends, or had simply met and kept company on the road? For they're much of an age, even of a kind, young men of some schooling, I fancy, bred to clerking or squiring, and yet not kin, or don't acknowledge it, and after their fashion very differently made. A man wonders how they ever came to be embarked together on this journey. It was south of Warwick when you met them? I wonder from how far south they came.'

'They never spoke of such things,' owned Rhun, himself

considering them for the first time. 'It was good to have company on the way, one stout young man at least. The roads can be perilous for two women, with only a cripple like me. But now you speak of it, no, we did not learn much of where they came from, or what bound them together. Unless my sister knows more. There were days,' said Rhun, shifting to assist Brother Cadfael's probings into the sinews of his thigh, 'when she and Matthew grew quite easy and talkative behind us.'

Cadfael doubted whether the subject of their conversation then had been anything but their two selves, brushing sleeves pleasurably along the summer highways, she in constant recall of the moment when she was snatched up bodily and swung across the ditch against Matthew's heart, he in constant contemplation of the delectable creature dancing at his elbow, and recollection of the feel of her slight, warm, frightened weight on his breast.

'But he'll hardly look at her now,' said Rhun regretfully. 'He's too intent on Ciaran, and Melangell will come between. But it costs him a dear effort to turn away from her, all the same.'

Cadfael stroked down the misshapen leg, and rose to scrub his oily hands. 'There, that's enough for today. But sit quiet a while and rest before you go. And will you take the draught tonight? At least keep it by you, and do what you feel to be right and best. But remember it's a kindness sometimes to accept help, a kindness to the giver. Would you wilfully inflict torment on yourself as Ciaran does? No, not you, you are too modest by far to set yourself up for braver and more to be worshipped than other men. So never think you do wrong by sparing yourself discomfort. Yet it's your choice, make it as you see fit.'

When the boy took up his crutches again and tapped his way out along the path towards the great court, Cadfael followed him at a distance, to watch his progress without embarrassing him. He could mark no change as yet. The stretched toe still barely dared touch ground, and still turned inward. And yet the sinews, cramped as they were, had some small force in them, instead of being withered and atrophied as he would have expected. If I had him here long enough, he thought, I could bring back some ease and use into that leg. But he'll go as he came. In three days now all will be over, the festival ended for this year, the guest-hall emptying. Ciaran and his guardian shadow will pass on northwards and westwards into Wales, and Dame Weaver will take her chicks back home to Campden. And those two, who might very well have made a fair match if things had been otherwise, will go their separate ways, and never see each other again. It's in the nature of things that those who gather in great numbers for the feasts of the church should also disperse again to their various duties afterwards. Still they need not all go away unchanged.

Chapter Five

ROTHER ADAM of Reading, being lodged in the dortoir with the monks of the house, had had leisure to observe his fellow pilgrims of the guest-hall only at the offices of the church, and in their casual comings and goings about the precinct; and it happened that he came from the garden towards mid-afternoon, with Cadfael beside him, just as Ciaran and Matthew were crossing the court towards the cloister garth, there to sit in the sun for an hour or two before Vespers. There were plenty of others, monks, lay servants and guests, busy on their various occasions, but Ciaran's striking figure and painfully slow and careful gait marked him out for notice.

'Those two,' said Brother Adam, halting, 'I have seen before. At Abingdon, where I spent the first night after leaving Reading. They were lodged there the same night.'

'At Abingdon!' Cadfael echoed thoughtfully. 'So they came from far south. You did not cross them again after Abingdon, on the way here?'

'It was not likely. I was mounted. And then, I had my abbot's mission to Leominster, which took me out of the direct way. No, I saw no more of them, never until now. But they can hardly be mistaken, once seen.'

'In what sort of case were they at Abingdon?' asked Cadfael, his eyes following the two inseparable figures until they vanished into the cloister. 'Would you say they had been long on the road before that night's halt? The man is pledged to go barefoot to Aberdaron, it would not take many miles to leave the mark on him.'

'He was going somewhat lamely, even then. They had both the dust of the roads on them. It might have been their first day's walking that ended there, but I doubt it.'

'He came to me to have his feet tended, yesterday,' said Cadfael, 'and I must see him again before evening. Two or three days of rest will set him up for the next stage of his walk.' From more than a day's going south of Abingdon to the remotest tip of Wales, a long, long walk. 'A strange, even a mistaken, piety it seems to me, to take upon oneself ostentatious pains, when there are poor fellows enough in the world who are born to pain they have not chosen, and carry it with humility.'

'The simple believe it brings merit,' said Brother Adam tolerantly. 'It may be he has no other claim upon outstanding virtue, and clutches at this.'

'But he's no simple soul,' said Cadfael with conviction, 'whatever he may be. He has, he tells me, a mortal disease, and is going to end his days in blessedness and peace at Aberdaron, and have his bones laid in Ynys Enlli, which is a noble ambition in a man of Welsh blood. The voluntary assumption of pain beyond his doom may even be a pennon of defiance, a wag of the hand against death. That I could understand. But I would not approve it.'

'It's very natural you should frown on it,' agreed Adam, smiling indulgence upon his companion and himself alike, 'seeing you are schooled to the alleviation of pain, and feel it to be a violator and an enemy. By the very virtue of these plants we have learned to use.' He patted the leather scrip at his girdle, and the soft rustle of seeds within answered him. They had been sorting over Cadfael's clay saucers of new seed from this freshly ripening year, and he had helped himself to two or three not native in his own herbarium. 'It is as good a dragon to fight as any in this world, pain.'

They had gone some yards more towards the stone steps that led up to the main door of the guest-hall, in no hurry, and taking pleasure in the contemplation of so much bustle and motion, when Brother Adam checked abruptly and stood at gaze.

'Well, well, I think you may have got some of our southern sinners as well as our would-be saints!'

Cadfael, surprised, followed where Adam was gazing, and

stood to hear what further he would have to say, for the individual in question was the least remarkable of men at first glance. He stood close to the gatehouse, one of a small group constantly on hand there to watch the new arrivals and the general commerce of the day. A big man, but so neatly and squarely built that his size was not wholly apparent, he stood with his thumbs in the belt of his plain but ample gown, which was nicely cut and fashioned to show him no nobleman, and no commoner, either, but a solid, respectable, comfortably provided fellow of the middle kind, merchant or tradesman. One of those who form the backbone of many a township in England, and can afford the occasional pilgrimage by way of a well-earned holiday. He gazed benignly upon the activity around him from a plump, shrewd, well-shaven face, favouring the whole creation with a broad, contented smile.

'That,' said Cadfael, eyeing his companion with bright enquiry, 'is, or so I am informed, one Simeon Poer, a merchant of Guildford, come on pilgrimage for his soul's sake, and because the summer chances to be very fine and inviting. And why not? Do you know of a reason?'

'Simeon Poer may well be his name,' said Brother Adam, 'or he may have half a dozen more ready to trot forward at need. I never knew a name for him, but his face and form I do know. Father Abbot uses me a good deal on his business outside the cloister and I have occasion to know most of the fairs and markets in our shire and beyond. I've seen that fellow – not gowned like a provost, as he is now, I grant you, but by the look of him he's been doing well lately – round every fairground, cultivating the company of those young, green roisterers who frequent every such gathering. For the contents of their pockets, surely. Most likely, dice. Even more likely, loaded dice. Though I wouldn't say he might not pick a pocket here and there, if business was bad. A quicker means to the same end, if a riskier.'

So knowing and practical a brother Cadfael had not encountered for some years among the innocents. Plainly Brother Adam's frequent sallies out of the cloister on the abbot's business had broadened his horizons. Cadfael regarded him with respect and warmth, and turned to study the smiling, benevolent merchant more closely.

'You're sure of him?'

'Sure that he's the same man, yes. Sure enough of his practices to challenge him openly, no, hardly, since he has never yet been taken up but once, and then he proved so slippery he slithered through the bailiff's fingers. But keep a weather eye on him, and this may be where he'll make the slip every rogue makes in the end, and get his comeuppance.'

'If you're right,' said Cadfael, 'has he not strayed rather far from his own haunts? In my experience, from years back I own, his kind seldom left the region where they knew their way about better than the bailiffs. Has he made the south country so hot for him that he must run for a fresh territory? That argues something worse than cheating at dice.'

Brother Adam hoisted dubious shoulders. 'It could be. Some of our scum have found the disorders of faction very profitable, in their own way, just as their lords and masters have in theirs. Battles are not for them – far too dangerous to their own skins. But the brawls that blow up in towns where uneasy factions come together are meat and drink to them. Pockets to be picked, riots to be started – discreetly from the rear – unoffending elders who look prosperous to be knocked on the head or knifed from behind or have their purse-strings cut in the confusion ... Safer and easier than taking to the woods and living wild for prey, as their kind do in the country.'

Just such gatherings, thought Cadfael, as that at Winchester, where at least one man was knifed in the back and left dying. Might not the law in the south be searching for this man, to drive him so far from his usual hunting-grounds? For some worse offence than cheating silly young men of their money at dice? Something as black as murder itself?

'There are two or three others in the common guest-hall,' he said, 'about whom I have my doubts, but this man has had no truck with them so far as I've seen. But I'll bear it in mind, and keep a watchful eye open, and have Brother Denis do the same. And I'll mention what you say to Hugh Beringar, too, before this evening's out. Both he and the town provost will be glad to have fair warning.'

Since Ciaran was sitting quietly in the cloister garth, it seemed a pity he should be made to walk through the gardens to the herbarium, when Cadfael's broad brown feet were in excellent condition, and sensibly equipped with stout sandals. So Cadfael fetched the salve he had used on Ciaran's wounds and bruises, and the spirit that would brace and toughen his tender soles, and brought them to the cloister. It was pleasant there in the afternoon sun, and the turf was thick and springy and cool to bare feet. The roses were coming into full bloom, and their scent hung in the warm air like a benediction. But two such closed and sunless faces! Was the one truly condemned to an early death, and the other to lose and mourn so close a friend?

Ciaran was speaking as Cadfael approached, and did not at first notice him, but even when he was aware of the visitor bearing down on them he continued steadily to the end, ' ... you do but waste your time, for it will not happen. Nothing will be changed, don't look for it. Never! You might far better leave me and go home.'

Did the one of them believe in Saint Winifred's power, and pray and hope for a miracle? And was the other, the sick man, all too passionately of Rhun's mind, and set on offering his early death as an acceptable and willing sacrifice, rather than ask for healing?

Matthew had not yet noticed Cadfael's approach. His deep voice, measured and resolute, said just audibly, 'Save your breath! For I will go with you, step for step, to the very end.'

Then Cadfael was close, and they were both aware of him, and stirred defensively out of their private anguish, heaving in breath and schooling their faces to confront the outer world decently. They drew a little apart on the stone bench, welcoming Cadfael with somewhat strained smiles.

'I saw no need to make you come to me,' said Cadfael, dropping to his knees and opening his scrip in the bright green turf, 'when I am better able to come to you. So sit and be easy, and let me see how much work is yet to be done before you can go forth in good heart.'

'This is kind, brother,' said Ciaran, rousing himself with a sigh. 'Be assured that I do go in good heart, for my pilgrimage is short and my arrival assured.'

At the other end of the bench Matthew's voice said softly, 'Amen!'

After that it was all silence as Cadfael anointed the swollen soles, kneading spirit vigorously into the misused skin, surely heretofore accustomed always to going well shod, and soothed the ointment of cleavers into the healing grazes.

'There! Keep off your feet through tomorrow, but for such offices as you feel you must attend. Here there's no need to go far. And I'll come to you tomorrow and have you fit to stand somewhat longer the next day, when the saint is brought home.' When he spoke of her now, he hardly knew whether he was truly speaking of the mortal substance of Saint Winifred, which was generally believed to be in that silver-chaced

54

reliquary, or of some hopeful distillation of her spirit which could fill with sanctity even an empty coffin, even a casket containing pitiful, faulty human bones, unworthy of her charity but subject, like all mortality, to the capricious, smiling mercies of those above and beyond question. If you could reason by pure logic for the occurrence of miracles, they would not be miracles, would they?

He scrubbed his hands on a handful of wool, and rose from his knees. In some twenty minutes or so it would be time for Vespers.

He had taken his leave, and almost reached the archway into the great court, when he heard rapid steps at his heels, a hand reached deprecatingly for his sleeve, and Matthew's voice said in his ear, 'Brother Cadfael, you left this lying.'

It was his jar of ointment, of rough, greenish pottery, almost invisible in the grass. The young man held it out in the palm of a broad, strong, workmanlike hand, long-fingered and elegant. Dark eyes, reserved but earnestly curious, searched Cadfael's face.

Cadfael took the jar with thanks, and put it away in his scrip. Ciaran sat where Matthew had left him, his face and burning gaze turned towards them; they stood at a distance between him and the outer day, and he had, for one moment, the look of a soul abandoned to absolute solitude in a populous world.

Cadfael and Matthew stood gazing in speculation and uncertainty into each other's eyes. This was that able, ready young man who had leaped into action at need, upon whom Melangell had fixed her young, unpractised heart, and to whom Rhun had surely looked for a hopeful way out for his sister, whatever might become of himself. Good, cultivated stock, surely, bred of some small gentry and taught a little Latin as well as his schooling in arms. How, except by the compulsion of inordinate love, did this one come to be ranging the country like a penniless vagabond, without root or attachment but to a dying man?

'Tell me truth,' said Cadfael. 'Is it indeed true – is it *certain* – that Ciaran goes this way towards his death?'

There was a brief moment of silence, as Matthew's wide-set eyes grew larger and darker. Then he said very softly and deliberately, 'It is truth. He is already marked for death. Unless your saint has a miracle for us, there is nothing can save him. Or me!' he ended abruptly, and wrenched himself away to return to his devoted watch.

55

Cadfael turned his back on supper in the refectory, and set off instead along the Foregate towards the town. Over the bridge that spanned the Severn, in through the gate, and up the curving slope of the Wyle to Hugh Beringar's town house. There he sat and nursed his godson Giles, a large, comely self-willed child, fair like his mother, and long of limb, some day to dwarf his small, dark, sardonic father. Aline brought food and wine for her husband and his friend, and then sat down to her needlework, favouring her menfolk from time to time with a smiling glance of serene contentment. When her son fell asleep in Cadfael's lap she rose and lifted the boy away gently. He was heavy for her, but she had learned how to carry him lightly balanced on arm and shoulder. Cadfael watched her fondly as she bore the child away into the next room to his bed, and closed the door between.

'How is it possible that that girl can grow every day more radiant and lovely? I've known marriage rub the fine bloom off many a handsome maid. Yet it suits her as a halo does a saint.'

'Oh, there's something to be said for marriage,' said Hugh idly. 'Do I look so poorly on it? Though it's an odd study for a man of your habit, after all these years of celibacy ... And all the stravagings about the world before that! You can't have thought too highly of the wedded state, or you'd have ventured on it yourself. You took no vows until past forty, and you a well-set-up young fellow crusading all about the east with the best of them. How do I know you have not an Aline of your own locked away somewhere, somewhere in your re-membrance, as dear as mine is to me? Perhaps even a Giles of your own,' he added, whimsically smiling, 'a Giles God knows where, grown a man now ...'

Cadfael's silence and stillness, though perfectly easy and complacent, nevertheless sounded a mute warning in Hugh's perceptive senses. On the edge of drowsiness among his cushions after a long day out of doors, he opened a black, considering eye to train upon his friend's musing face, and withdrew delicately into practical business.

'Well, so this Simeon Poer is known in the south. I'm grateful to you and to Brother Adam for the nudge, though so far the man has set no foot wrong here. But these others you've pictured for me ... At Wat's tavern in the Foregate they've had practice in marking down strangers who come with a fair or a feast, and spread themselves large about the town. Wat tells my people he has a group moving in, very merry, some of them strangers. They could well be these you name. Some of them, of course, the usual young fellows of the town and the Foregate with more pence than sense. They've been drinking a great deal, and throwing dice. Wat does not like the way the dice fall.'

'It's as I supposed,' said Cadfael, nodding. 'For every Mass of ours they'll be celebrating the Gamblers' Mass elsewhere. And by all means let the fools throw their money after their sense, so the odds be fair. But Wat knows a loaded throw when he sees one.'

'He knows how to rid his house of the plague, too. He has hissed in the ears of one of the strangers that his tavern is watched, and they'd be wise to take their school out of there. And for tonight he has a lad on the watch, to find out where they'll meet. Tomorrow night we'll have at them, and rid you of them in good time for the feast day, if all goes well.'

Which would be a very welcome cleansing, thought Cadfael, making his way back across the bridge in the first limpid dusk, with the river swirling its coiled currents beneath him in gleams of reflected light, low summer water leaving the islands outlined in swathes of drowned, browning weed. But as yet there was nothing to shed light, even by reflected, phantom gleams, upon that death so far away in the south country, whence the merchant Simeon Poer had set out. On pilgrimage for his respectable soul? Or in flight from a law aroused too fiercely for his safety, by something graver than the cozening of fools? Though Cadfael felt too close to folly himself to be loftily complacent even about that, however much it might be argued that gamblers deserved all they got.

The great gate of the abbey was closed, but the wicket in it stood open, shedding sunset light through from the west. In the mild dazzle Cadfael brushed shoulders and sleeves with another entering, and was a little surprised to be hoisted deferentially through the wicket by a firm hand at his elbow.

'Give you goodnight, brother!' sang a mellow voice in his ear, as the returning guest stepped within on his heels. And the solid, powerful, woollen-gowned form of Simeon Poer, self-styled merchant of Guildford, rolled vigorously past him, and crossed the great court to the stone steps of the guest-hall.

Chapter Six

HEY WERE emerging from High Mass on the morning of the twenty-first day of June, the eve of Saint Winifred's translation, stepping out into a radiant morning, when the abbot's sedate progress towards his lodging was rudely disrupted by a sudden howl of dismay among the dispersing multitude of worshippers, a wild ripple of movement cleaving a path through their ranks, and the emergence of a frantic figure lurching forth on clumsy, naked feet to clutch at the abbot's robe, and appeal in a loud, indignant cry, 'Father Abbot, stand my friend and give me justice, for I am robbed! A thief, there is a thief among us!'

The abbot looked down in astonishment and concern into the face of Ciaran, convulsed and ablaze with resentment and distress.

'Father, I beg you, see justice done! I am helpless unless you help me!'

He awoke, somewhat late, to the unwarranted violence of his behaviour, and fell on his knees at the abbot's feet. 'Pardon, pardon! I am too loud and troublous, I hardly know what I say!'

The press of gossiping, festive worshippers just loosed from Mass had fallen quiet all in a moment, and instead of dispersing drew in about them to listen and stare, avidly curious. The monks of the house, hindered in their orderly departure, hovered in quiet deprecation. Cadfael looked beyond the kneeling, imploring figure of Ciaran for its inseparable twin, and found Matthew just shouldering his way forward out of the crowd, open-mouthed and wide-eyed in patent bewilderment, to stand and gaze a few paces apart, and frown helplessly from the abbot to Ciaran and back again, in search of the cause of this abrupt turmoil. Was it possible that something had happened to the one that the other of the matched pair did not know?

'Get up!' said Radulfus, erect and calm. 'No need to kneel. Speak out whatever you have to say, and you shall have right.'

The pervasive silence spread, grew, filled even the most distant reaches of the great court. Those who had already scattered to the far corners turned and crept unobtrusively back again, large-eyed and prick-eared, to hang upon the fringes of the crowd already assembled.

Ciaran clambered to his feet, voluble before he was erect. 'Father, I had a ring, the copy of one the lord bishop of Winchester keeps for his occasions, bearing his device and inscription. Such copies he uses to afford safe-conduct to those he sends forth on his business or with his blessing, to open doors to them and provide protection on the road. Father, the ring is gone!'

'This ring was given to you by Henry of Blois himself?' asked Radulfus.

'No, Father, not in person. I was in the service of the prior of Hyde Abbey, a lay clerk, when this mortal sickness came on me, and I took this vow of mine to spend my remaining days in the canonry of Aberdaron. My prior – you know that Hyde is without an abbot, and has been for some years – my prior asked the lord bishop, of his goodness, to give me what protection he could for my journey ...'

So that had been the starting point of this barefoot journey, thought Cadfael, enlightened. Winchester itself, or as near as made no matter, for the New Minster of that city, always a jealous rival of the Old, where Bishop Henry presided, had been forced to abandon its old home in the city thirty years ago, and banished to Hyde Mead, on the north-western outskirts. There was no love lost between Henry and the community at Hyde, for it was the bishop who had been instrumental in keeping them deprived of an abbot for so long, in pursuit of his own ambition of turning them into an episcopal monastery. The struggle had been going on for some time, the bishop deploying various schemes to get the house into his own hands, and the prior using every means to resist these manipulations. It seemed Henry had still the grace to show compassion even on a servant of the hostile house, when he fell under the threat of disease and death. The traveller over whom the bishop-legate spread his protecting hand would pass unmolested wherever law retained its validity. Only those irreclaimably outlaw already would dare interfere with him.

'Father, the ring is gone, stolen from me this very morning. See here, the slashed threads that held it!' Ciaran heaved forward the drab linen scrip that rode at his belt, and showed two dangling ends of cord, very cleanly severed. 'A sharp knife – someone here has such a dagger. And my ring is gone!'

Prior Robert was at the abbot's elbow by then, agitated out of his silvery composure. 'Father, what this man says is true. He showed me the ring. Given to ensure him aid and hospitality on his journey, which is of most sad and solemn import. If now it is lost, should not the gate be closed while we enquire?'

'Let it be so,' said Radulfus, and stood silent to see Brother Jerome, ever ready and assiduous on the prior's heels, run to see the order carried out. 'Now, take breath and thought, for your loss cannot be lost far. You did not wear the ring, then, but carried it knotted securely by this cord, within your scrip?'

'Yes, Father. It was beyond words precious to me.'

'And when did you last ascertain that it was still there, and safe?'

'Father, this very morning I know I had it. Such few things as I possess, here they lie before you. Could I fail to see if this cord had been cut in the night while I slept? It is not so. This morning all was as I left it last night. I have been bidden to rest, by reason of my barefoot vow. Today I ventured out only for Mass. Here in the very church, in this great press of worshippers, some malevolent has broken every ban, and slashed loose my ring from me.'

And indeed, thought Cadfael, running a considering eye round all the curious, watching faces, it would not be difficult, in such a press, to find the strings that anchored the hidden ring, flick it out from its hiding-place, cut the strings and make away with it, discreetly between crowding bodies, and never be seen by a soul or felt by the victim. A neat thing, done so privately and expertly that even Matthew, who missed nothing that touched his friend, had missed this impudent assault. For Matthew stood there staring, obviously taken by surprise, and unsure as yet how to take this turn of events. His face was

60

unreadable, closed and still, his eyes narrowed and bright, darting from face to face as Ciaran or abbot or prior spoke. Cadfael noted that Melangell had stolen forward close to him, and taken him hesitantly by the sleeve. He did not shake her off. By the slight lift of his head and widening of his eyes he knew who had touched him, and he let his hand feel for hers and clasp it, while his whole attention seemed to be fixed on Ciaran. Somewhere not far behind them Rhun leaned on his crutches, his fair face frowning in anxious dismay, Aunt Alice attendant at his shoulder, bright with curiosity. Here are we all, thought Cadfael, and not one of us knows what is in any other mind, or who has done what has been done, or what will come of it for any of those who look on and marvel.

'You cannot tell,' suggested Prior Robert, agitated and grieved, 'who stood close to you during the service? If indeed some ill-conditioned person has so misused the holy office as to commit theft in the very sacredness of the Mass ...'

'Father, I was intent only upon the altar.' Ciaran shook with fervour, holding the ravished scrip open before him with his sparse possessions bared to be seen. 'We were close pressed, so many people ... as is only seemly, in such a shrine ... Matthew was close at my back, but so he ever is. Who else there may have been by me, how can I say? There was no man or woman among us who was not hemmed in every way.'

'It is truth,' said Prior Robert, who had been much gratified at the large attendance. 'Father, the gate is now closed, we are all here who were present at Mass. And surely we all have a desire to see this wrong righted.'

'All, as I suppose,' said Radulfus drily, 'but one. One, who brought in here a knife or dagger sharp enough to slice through these tough cords cleanly. What other intents he brought in with him, I bid him consider and tremble for his soul. Robert, this ring must be found. All men of goodwill here will offer their aid, and show freely what they have. So will every guest who has not theft and sacrilege to hide. And see to it also that enquiry be made, whether other articles of value have not been missed. For one theft means one thief, here within.'

'It shall be seen to, Father,' said Robert fervently. 'No honest, devout pilgrim will grudge to offer his aid. How could he wish to share his lodgings here with a thief?'

There was a stir of agreement and support, perhaps slightly delayed, as every man and woman eyed a neighbour, and then in haste elected to speak first. They came from every direction, hitherto unknown to one another, mingling and forming friendships now with the abandon of holiday. But how did they know who was immaculate and who was suspect, now the world had probed a merciless finger within the fold?

'Father,' pleaded Ciaran, still sweating and shaking with distress, 'here I offer in this scrip all that I brought into this enclave. Examine it, show that I have indeed been robbed. Here I came without even shoes to my feet, my all is here in your hands. And my fellow Matthew will open to you his own scrip as freely, an example to all these others that they may deliver themselves pure of blame. What we offer, they will not refuse.'

Matthew had withdrawn his hand from Melangell's sharply at this word. He shifted the unbleached cloth scrip, very like Ciaran's, round upon his hip. Ciaran's meagre travelling equipment lay open in the prior's hands. Robert slid them back into the pouch from which they had come, and looked where Ciaran's distressed gaze guided him.

'Into your hands, Father, and willingly,' said Matthew, and stripped the bag from its buckles and held it forth.

Robert acknowledged the offering with a grave bow, and opened and probed it with delicate consideration. Most of what was there within he did not display, though he handled it. A spare shirt and linen drawers, crumpled from being carried so, and laundered on the way, probably more than once. The means of a gentleman's sparse toilet, razor, morsel of lye soap, a leather-bound breviary, a lean purse, a folded trophy of embroidered ribbon. Robert drew forth the only item he felt he must show, a sheathed dagger, such as any gentleman might carry at his right hip, barely longer than a man's hand.

'Yes, that is mine,' said Matthew, looking Abbot Radulfus straightly in the eyes. 'It has not slashed through those cords. Nor has it left my scrip since I entered your enclave, Father Abbot.'

Radulfus looked from the dagger to its owner, and briefly nodded. 'I well understand that no young man would set forth on these highroads today without the means of defending himself. All the more if he had another to defend, who carried no weapons. As I understand is your condition, my son. Yet within these walls you should not bear arms.'

'What, then, should I have done?' demanded Matthew, with a stiffening neck, and a note in his voice that just fell short of defiance.

'What you must do now,' said Radulfus firmly. 'Give it into the care of Brother Porter at the gatehouse, as others have done with their weapons. When you leave here you may reclaim it freely.'

There was nothing to be done but bow the head and give way gracefully, and Matthew managed it decently enough, but not gladly. 'I will do so, Father, and pray your pardon that I did not ask advice before.'

'But, Father,' Ciaran pleaded anxiously, 'my ring ... How shall I survive the way if I have not that safe-conduct to show?'

'Your ring shall be sought throughout this enclave, and every man who bears no guilt for its loss,' said the abbot, raising his voice to carry to the distant fringes of the silent crowd, 'will freely offer his own possessions for inspection. See to it, Robert!'

With that he proceeded on his way, and the crowd, after some moments of stillness as they watched him out of sight, dispersed in a sudden murmur of excited speculation. Prior Robert took Ciaran under his wing, and swept away with him towards the guest-hall, to recruit help from Brother Denis in his enquiries after the bishop's ring; and Matthew, not without one hesitant glance at Melangell, turned on his heel and went hastily after them.

A more innocent and co-operative company than the guests at Shrewsbury abbey that day it would have been impossible to find. Every man opened his bundle or box almost eagerly, in haste to demonstrate his immaculate virtue. The quest, conducted as delicately as possible, went on all the afternoon, but they found no trace of the ring. Moreover, one or two of the better-off inhabitants of the common dormitory, who had had no occasion to penetrate to the bottom of their baggage so far, made grievous discoveries when they were obliged to do so. A yeoman from Lichfield found his reserve purse lighter by half than when he had tucked it away. Master Simeon Poer, one of the first to fling open his possessions, and the loudest in condemning so blasphemous a crime, claimed to have been robbed of a silver chain he had intended to present at the altar next day. A poor parish priest, making this pilgrimage the one fulfilled dream of his life, was left lamenting the loss of a small casket, made by his own hands over more than a year, and decorated with inlays of silver and glass, in which he had hoped to carry back with him some memento of his visit, a dried

63

flower from the garden, even a thread or two drawn from the fringe of the altar-cloth under Saint Winifred's reliquary. A merchant from Worcester could not find his good leather belt to his best coat, saved up for the morrow. One or two others had a suspicion that their belongings had been fingered and scorned, which was worst of all.

It was all over, and fruitless, when Cadfael at last repaired to his workshop in time to await the coming of Rhun. The boy came prompt to his hour, great-eyed and thoughtful, and lay submissive and mute under Cadfael's ministrations, which probed every day a little deeper into his knotted and stubborn tissues.

'Brother,' he said at length, looking up, 'you did not find a dagger in any man's pouch, did you?'

'No, no such thing.' Though there had been, understandably, a number of small, homely knives, the kind a man needs to hack his bread and meat in lodgings along the way, or meals under a hedge. Many of them were sharp enough for most everyday purposes, but not sharp enough to leave stout cords sheared through without a twitch to betray the assault. 'But men who go shaven carry razors, too, and a blunt razor would be an abomination. Once a thief comes into the pale, child, it's hard for honest men to be a match for him. He who has no scruple has always the advantage of those who keep to rule. But you need not trouble your heart, you've done no wrong to any man. Never let this ill thing spoil tomorrow for you.'

'No,' agreed the boy, still preoccupied. 'But, brother, there *is* another dagger – one, at least. Sheath and all, a good length – I know, I was pressed close against him yesterday at Mass. You know I have to hold fast by my crutches to stand for long, and he had a big linen scrip on his belt, hard against my hand and arm, where we were crowded together. I felt the shape of it, cross-hilt and all. I know! But you did not find it.'

'And who was it,' asked Cadfael, still carefully working the tissues that resisted his fingers, 'who had his armoury about him at Mass?'

'It was that big merchant with the good gown – made from valley wool. I've learned to know cloth. They call him Simeon Poer. But you didn't find it. Perhaps he's handed it to Brother Porter, just as Matthew has had to do now.'

'Perhaps,' said Cadfael. 'When was it you discovered this? Yesterday? And what of today? Was he again close to you?'

'No, not today.'

No, today he had stood stolidly to watch the play, eyes and ears alert, ready to open his pouch there before all if need be, smiling complacently as the abbot directed the disarming of another man. He had certainly had no dagger on him then, however he had disposed of it in the meantime. There were hiding-places enough here within the walls, for a dagger and any amount of small, stolen valuables. To search was itself only a pretence, unless authority was prepared to keep the gates closed and the guests prisoned within until every yard of the gardens had been dug up, and every bed and bench in dortoir and hall pulled to pieces. The sinners have always the start of the honest men.

'It was not fair that Matthew should be made to surrender his dagger,' said Rhun, 'when another man had one still about him. And Ciaran already so terribly afraid to stir, not having his ring. He won't even come out of the dortoir until tomorrow. He is sick for loss of it.'

Yes, that seemed to be true. And how strange, thought Cadfael, pricked into realisation, to see a man sweating for fear, who has already calmly declared himself as one condemned to death? Then why fear? Fear should be dead.

Yet men are strange, he thought in revulsion. And a blessed and quiet death in Aberdaron, well-prepared, and surrounded by the prayers and compassion of like-minded votaries, may well seem a very different matter from crude slaughter by strangers and footpads somewhere in the wilder stretches of the road.

But this Simeon Poer – say he had such a dagger yesterday, and therefore may well have had it on him today, in the crowded array of the Mass. Then what did he do with it so quickly, before Ciaran discovered his loss? And how did he know he must perforce dispose of it quickly? Who had such fair warning of the need, if not the thief?

'Trouble your head no more,' said Cadfael, looking down at the boy's beautiful, vulnerable face, 'for Matthew nor for Ciaran, but think only of the morrow, when you approach the saint. Both she and God see you all, and have no need to be told of what your needs are. All you have to do is wait in quiet for whatever will be. For whatever it may be, it will not be wanton. Did you take your dose last night?'

Rhun's pale, brilliant eyes were startled wide open, sunlight and ice, blindingly clear. 'No. It was a good day, I wanted to give thanks. It isn't that I don't value what you can do for me.

Only I wished also to give something. And I did sleep, truly I slept well ...'

'So do tonight also,' said Cadfael gently, and slid an arm round the boy's body to hoist him steadily upright. 'Say your prayers, think quietly what you should do, do it, and sleep. There is no man living, neither king nor emperor, can do more or better, or trust in a better harvest.'

Ciaran did not stir from within the guest-hall again that day. Matthew did, against all precedent emerging from the arched doorway without his companion, and standing at the head of the stone staircase to the great court with hands spread to touch the courses of the deep doorway, and head drawn back to heave in great breaths of evening air. Supper was eaten, the milder evening stir of movement threaded the court, in the cool, grateful lull before Compline.

Brother Cadfael had left the chapter-house before the end of the readings, having a few things to attend to in the herbarium, and was crossing towards the garden when he caught sight of the young man standing there at the top of the steps, breathing in deeply and with evident pleasure. For some reason Matthew looked taller for being alone, and younger, his face closed but tranquil in the soft evening light. When he moved forward and began to descend to the court, Cadfael looked instinctively for the other figure that should have been close behind him, if not in its usual place a step before him, but no Ciaran emerged. Well, he had been urged to rest, and presumably was glad to comply, but never before had Matthew left his side, by night or day, resting or stirring. Not even to follow Melangell, except broodingly with his eye and against his will.

People, thought Cadfael, going on his way without haste, people are endlessly mysterious, and I am endlessly curious. A sin to be confessed, no doubt, and well worth a penance. As long as man is curious about his fellow-man, that appetite alone will keep him alive. Why do folk do the things they do? Why, if you know you are diseased and dying, and wish to reach a desired haven before the end, why do you condemn yourself to do the long journey barefoot, and burden yourself with a weight about your neck? How are you thus rendered more acceptable to God, when you might have lent a hand to someone on the road crippled not by perversity but from birth, like the boy Rhun? And why do you dedicate your youth and strength to following another man step by step the length of the

66

land, and why does he suffer you to be his shadow, when he should be composing his mind to peace, and taking a decent leave of his friends, not laying his own load upon them?

There he checked, rounding the corner of the yew hedge into the rose garden. It was not his fellow-man he beheld, sitting in the turf on the far side of the flower beds, gazing across the slope of the pease fields beyond and the low, stony, silvery summer waters of the Meole brook, but his fellow-woman, solitary and still, her knees drawn up under her chin and encircled closely by her folded arms. Aunt Alice Weaver, no doubt, was deep in talk with half a dozen worthy matrons of her own generation, and Rhun, surely, already in his bed. Melangell had stolen away alone to be quiet here in the garden and nurse her lame dreams and indomitable hopes. She was a small, dark shape, gold-haloed against the bright west. By the look of that sky tomorrow, Saint Winifred's day, would again be cloudless and beautiful.

The whole width of the rose garden was between them, and she did not hear him come and pass by on the grassy path to his final duties of the day in his workshop, seeing everything put away tidily, checking the stoppers of all his flagons and flasks, and making sure the brazier, which had been in service earlier, was safely quenched and cooled. Brother Oswin, young, enthusiastic and devoted, was nonetheless liable to overlook details, though he had now outlived his tendency to break things. Cadfael ran an eye over everything, and found it good. There was no hurry now, he had time before Compline to sit down here in the wood-scented dimness and think. Time for others to lose and find one another, and use or waste these closing moments of the day. For those three blameless tradesmen, Walter Bagot, glover; John Shure, tailor; William Hales, farrier; to betake themselves to wherever their dice school was to meet this night, and run their necks into Hugh's trap. Time for that more ambiguous character, Simeon Poer, to evade or trip into the same snare, or go the other way about some other nocturnal business of his own. Cadfael had seen two of the former three go out from the gatehouse, and the third follow some minutes later, and was sure in his own mind that the self-styled merchant of Guildford would not be long after them. Time, too, for that unaccountably solitary young man, somehow loosed off his chain, to range this whole territory suddenly opened to him, and happen upon the solitary girl.

67

Cadfael put up his feet on the wooden bench, and closed his eyes for a brief respite.

Matthew was there at her back before she knew it. The sudden rustle as he stepped into sun-dried long grass at the edge of the field startled her, and she swung round in alarm, scrambling to her knees and staring up into his face with dilated eyes, half-blinded by the blaze of the sunset into which she had been steadily staring. Her face was utterly open, vulnerable and childlike. She looked as she had looked when he had swept her up in his arms and leaped the ditch with her, clear of the galloping horses. Just so she had opened her eyes and looked up at him, still dazed and frightened, and just so had her fear melted away into wonder and pleasure, finding in him nothing but reassurance, kindness and admiration.

That pure, paired encounter of eyes did not last long. She blinked, and shook her head a little to clear her dazzled vision, and looked beyond him, searching, not believing he could be here alone.

'Ciaran …? Is there something you need for him?'

'No,' said Matthew shortly, and for a moment turned his head away. 'He's in his bed.'

'But you never leave his bed!' It was said in innocence, even in anxiety. Whatever she grudged to Ciaran, she still pitied and understood him.

'You see I have left it,' said Matthew harshly. 'I have needs, too … a breath of air. And he is very well where he is, and won't stir.'

'I was well sure,' she said with resigned bitterness, 'that you had not come out to look for me.' She made to rise, swiftly and gracefully enough, but he put out a hand, almost against his will, as it seemed, to take her under the wrist and lift her. It was withdrawn as abruptly when she evaded his touch, and rose to her feet unaided. 'But at least,' she said deliberately, 'you did not turn and run from me when you found me. I should be grateful, even for that.'

'I am not free,' he protested, stung. 'You know it better than any.'

'Then neither were you free when we kept pace along the road,' said Melangell fiercely, 'when you carried my burden, and walked beside me, and let Ciaran hobble along before, where he could not see how you smiled on me then and were gallant and cherished me when the road was rough, and spoke

68

softly, as if you took delight in being beside me. Why did you not give me warning then that you were not free? Or better, take him some other way, and leave us alone? Then I might have taken good heed in time, and in time forgotten you. As now I never shall! Never, to my life's end!'

All the flesh of his lips and cheeks shrank and tightened before her eyes, in a contortion of either rage or pain, she could not tell which. She was staring too close and too passionately to see very clearly. He turned his head sharply away, to evade her eyes.

'You charge me justly,' he said in a harsh whisper, 'I was at fault. I never should have believed there could be so clean and sweet a happiness for me. I should have left you, but I could not ... Oh, God! You think I could have turned him? He clung to you, to your good aunt ... Yet I should have been strong enough to hold off from you and let you alone ...' As rapidly as he had swung away from her he swung back again, reaching a hand to take her by the chin and hold her face to face with him, so ungently that she felt the pressure of his fingers bruising her flesh. 'Do you know how hard a thing you are asking? No! This countenance you never saw, did you, never but through someone else's eyes. Who would provide you a mirror to see yourself? Some pool, perhaps, if ever you had the leisure to lean over and look. How should you know what this face can do to a man already lost? And you marvel I took what I could get for water in a drought, when it walked beside me? I should rather have died than stay beside you, to trouble your peace. God forgive me!'

She was five years nearer childhood than he, even taking into account the two years or more a girl child has advantage over the boys of her own age. She stood entranced, a little frightened by his intensity, and inexpressibly moved by the anguish she felt emanating from him like a raw, drowning odour. The long-fingered hand that held her shook terribly, his whole body quivered. She put up her own hand gently and closed it over his, uplifted out of her own wretchedness by his greater and more inexplicable distress.

'I dare not speak for God,' she said steadily, 'but whatever there may be for me to forgive, that I dare. It is not your fault that I love you. All you ever did was be kinder to me than ever man was since I left Wales. And I did know, love, you did tell me, if I had heeded then, you did tell me you were a man under vow. What it was you never told me, but never grieve, oh, my own soul, never grieve so ...'

While they stood rapt, the sunset light had deepened, blazed and burned silently into glowing ash, and the first feathery shade of twilight, like the passing of a swift's wings, fled across their faces and melted into sudden pearly, radiant light. Her wide eyes were brimming with tears, almost the match of his. When he stooped to her, there was no way of knowing which of them had begun the kiss.

The little bell for Compline sounded clearly through the gardens on so limpid an evening, and stirred Brother Cadfael out of his half-doze at once. He was accustomed, in this refuge of his maturity as surely as in the warfaring of his youth, to awake fresh and alert, as he fell asleep, making the most of the twin worlds of night and day. He rose and went out into the earliest glowing image of evening, and closed the door after him.

It was but a few moments back to church through the herbarium and the rose garden. He went briskly, happy with the beauty of the evening and the promise for the morrow, and never knew why he should look aside to westward in passing, unless it was that the whole expanse of the sky on that side was delicate, pure and warming, like a girl's blush. And there they were, two clear shadows clasped together in silhouette against the fire of the west, outlined on the crest above the slope to the invisible brook. Matthew and Melangell, unmistakable, constrained still but in each other's arms, linked in a kiss that lasted while Brother Cadfael came, passed and slipped away to his different devotions, but with that image printed indelibly on his eyes, even in his prayers.

Chapter Seven

HE OUTRIDER of the bishop-legate's envoy – or should he rather be considered the empress's envoy? – arrived within the town and was directed through to the gatehouse of the castle in mid-evening of that same twenty-first day of June, to be presented to Hugh Beringar just as he was marshalling a half-dozen men to go down to the bridge and take an unpredicted part in the plans of Master Simeon Poer and his associates. Who would almost certainly be armed, being so far from home and in hitherto unexplored territory. Hugh found the visitor an unwelcome hindrance, but was too well aware of the many perils hemming the king's party on every side to dismiss the herald without ceremony. Whatever this embassage might be, he needed to know it, and make due preparation to deal with it.

In the gatehouse guard-room he found himself facing a stolid middle-aged squire, who delivered his errand word perfect.

'My lord sheriff, the Lady of the English and the lord bishop of Winchester entreat you to receive in peace their envoy, who comes to you with offerings of peace and good order in their name, and in their name asks your aid in resolving the griefs of the kingdom. I come before to announce him.'

So the empress had assumed the traditional title of a queen-elect before her coronation! The matter began to look final.

'The lord bishop's envoy will be welcome,' said Hugh, 'and shall be received with all honour here in Shrewsbury. I will lend an attentive ear to whatever he may have to say to me. As at this moment I have an affair in hand which will not wait. How far ahead of your lord do you ride?'

'A matter of two hours, perhaps,' said the squire, considering.

'Good, then I can set forward all necessary preparations for his reception, and still have time to clear up a small thing I have in hand. With how many attendants does he come?'

'Two men-at-arms only, my lord, and myself.'

'Then I will leave you in the hands of my deputy, who will have lodgings made ready for you and your two men here in the castle. As for your lord, he shall come to my own house, and my wife shall make him welcome. Hold me excused if I make small ceremony now, for this business is a twilight matter, and will not wait. Later I will see amends made.'

The messenger was well content to have his horse stabled and tended, and be led away by Alan Herbard to a comfortable lodging where he could shed his boots and leather coat, and be at his ease, and take his time and his pleasure over the meat and wine that was presently set before him. Hugh's young deputy would play the host very graciously. He was still new in office, and did everything committed to him with a flourish. Hugh left them to it, and took his half-dozen men briskly out through the town.

It was past Compline then, neither light nor dark, but hesitant between. By the time they reached the High Cross and turned down the steep curve of the Wyle they had their twilight eyes. In full darkness their quarry might have a better chance of eluding them, by daylight they would themselves have been too easily observed from afar. If these gamesters were experts they would have a lookout posted to give fair warning.

The Wyle, uncoiling eastward, brought them down to the town wall and the English gate, and there a thin, leggy child, shaggy-haired and bright-eyed, started out of the shadows under the gate to catch at Hugh's sleeve. Wat's boy, a sharp urchin of the Foregate, bursting with the importance of his errand and his own wit in managing it, had pinned down his quarry, and waited to inform and advise.

'My lord, they're met – all the four from the abbey, and a dozen or more from these parts, mostly from the town.' His note of scorn implied that they were sharper in the Foregate. 'You'd best leave the horses and go afoot. Riders out at this hour – they'd break and run as soon as you set hooves on the bridge. The sound carries.'

Good sense, that, if the meeting-place was close by. 'Where are they, then?' asked Hugh, dismounting.

'Under the far arch of the bridge, my lord – dry as a bone it is, and snug.' So it would be, with this low summer water. Only in full spate did the river prevent passage beneath that arch. In this fine season it would be a nest of dried-out grasses.

'They have a light, then?'

'A dark lantern. There's not a glimmer you'll see from either side unless you go down to the water, it sheds light only on the flat stone where they're throwing.'

Easily quenched, then, at the first alarm, and they would scatter like startled birds, every way. The fleecers would be the first and fleetest. The fleeced might well be netted in some numbers, but their offence was no more than being foolish at their own expense, not theft nor malpractice on any other.

'We leave the horses here,' said Hugh, making up his mind. 'You heard the boy. They're under the bridge, they'll have used the path that goes down to the Gaye, along the riverside. The other side of the arch is thick bushes, but that's the way they'll break. Three men to either slope, and I'll bear with the western three. And let our own young fools by, if you can pick them out, but hold fast the strangers.'

In this fashion they went to their raiding. They crossed the bridge by ones and twos, above the Severn water green with weedy shallows and shimmering with reflected light, and took their places on either side, spaced among the fringing bushes of the bank. By the time they were in place the afterglow had dissolved and faded into the western horizon, and the night came down like a velvet hand. Hugh drew off to westward along the by-road until at length he caught the faint glimmer of light beneath the stone arch. They were there. If in such numbers, perhaps he should have held them in better respect and brought more men. But he did not want the townsmen. By all means let them sneak away to their beds and think better of their dreams of milking cows likely to prove drier than sand. It was the cheats he wanted. Let the provost of the town deal with his civic idiots.

He let the sky darken somewhat before he took them in. The summer night settled, soft wings folding, and no moon. Then, at his whistle, they moved down from either flank.

It was the close-set bushes on the bank, rustling stealthily in a windless night, that betrayed their coming a moment too soon. Whoever was on watch, below there, had a sharp ear. There was a shrill whistle, suddenly muted. The lantern went out instantly, there was black dark under the solid stonework of the bridge. Down went Hugh and his men, abandoning stealth for speed. Bodies parted, collided, heaved and fled, with no sound but the panting and gasping of scared breath. Hugh's officers waded through bushes, closing down to seal the archway. Some of those thus penned beneath the bridge broke to left, some to right, not venturing to climb into waiting arms, but wading through the shallows and floundering even into deeper water. A few struck out for the opposite shore, local lads well acquainted with their river and its reaches, and water-borne, like its fish, almost from birth. Let them go, they were Shrewsbury born and bred. If they had lost money, more fools they, but let them get to their beds and repent in peace. If their wives would let them!

But there were those beneath the arch of the bridge who had not Severn water in their blood, and were less ready to wet more than their feet in even low water. And suddenly these had steel in their hands, and were weaving and slashing and stabbing their way through into the open as best they could, and without scruple. It did not last long. In the quaking dark, sprawled among the trampled grasses up the riverside, Hugh's six clung to such captives as they could grapple, and shook off trickles of blood from their own scratches and gashes. And diminishing in the darkness, the thresh and toss of bushes marked the flight of those who had got away. Unseen beneath the bridge, the deserted lantern and scattered dice, grave loss to a trickster who must now prepare a new set, lay waiting to be retrieved.

Hugh shook off a few drops of blood from a grazed arm, and went scrambling through the rough grass to the path leading up from the Gaye to the highroad and the bridge. Before him a shadowy body fled, cursing. Hugh launched a shout to reach the road ahead of them: 'Hold him! The law wants him!' Foregate and town might be on their way to bed, but there were always late strays, both lawful and unlawful, and some on both sides would joyfully take up such an invitation to mischief or justice, whichever way the mind happened to bend.

Above him, in the deep, soft summer night that now bore only a saffron thread along the west, an answering hail shrilled, startled and merry, and there were confused sounds of brief, breathless struggle. Hugh loped up to the highroad to see three

74

shadowy horsemen halted at the approach to the bridge, two of them closed in to flank the first, and that first leaning slightly from his saddle to grip in one hand the collar of a panting figure that leaned against his mount heaving in breath, and with small energy to attempt anything besides.

'I think, sir,' said the captor, eyeing Hugh's approach, 'this may be what you wanted. It seemed to me that the law cried out for him? Am I then addressing the law in these parts?'

It was a fine, ringing voice, unaccustomed to subduing its tone. The soft dark did not disclose his face clearly, but showed a body erect in the saddle, supple, shapely, unquestionably young. He shifted his grip on the prisoner, as though to surrender him to a better claim. Thus all but released, the fugitive did not break free and run for it, but spread his feet and stood his ground, half-defiant, eyeing Hugh dubiously.

'I'm in your debt for a minnow, it seems,' said Hugh, grinning as he recognised the man he had been chasing. 'But I doubt I've let all the salmon get clear away up-river. We were about breaking up a parcel of cheating rogues come here looking for prey, but this young gentleman you have by the coat turns out to be merely one of the simpletons, our worthy goldsmith out of the town. Master Daniel, I doubt there's more gold and silver to be lost than gained, in the company you've been keeping.'

'It's no crime to make a match at dice,' muttered the young man, shuffling his feet sullenly in the dust of the road. 'My luck would have turned ...'

'Not with the dice they brought with them. But true it's no crime to waste your evening and go home with empty pockets, and I've no charge to make against you, provided you go back now, and hand yourself over with the rest to my sergeant. Behave yourself prettily, and you'll be home by midnight.'

Master Daniel Aurifaber took his dismissal thankfully, and slouched back towards the bridge, to be gathered in among the captives. The sound of hooves crossing the bridge at a trot indicated that someone had run for the horses, and intended a hunt to westward, in the direction the birds of prey had taken. In less than a mile they would be safe in woodland, and it would take hounds to run them to earth. Small chance of hunting them down by night. On the morrow something might be attempted.

'This is hardly the welcome I intended for you,' said Hugh, peering up into the shadowy face above him. 'For you, I think,

75

must be the envoy sent from the Empress Maud and the bishop of Winchester. Your herald arrived little more than an hour ago, I did not expect you quite so soon. I had thought I should be done with this matter by the time you came. My name is Hugh Beringar, I stand here as sheriff for King Stephen. Your men are provided for at the castle, I'll send a guide with them. You, sir, are my own guest, if you will do my house that honour.'

'You're very gracious,' said the empress's messenger blithely, 'and with all my heart I will. But had you not better first make up your accounts with these townsmen of yours, and let them creep away to their beds? My business can well wait a little longer.'

'Not the most successful action ever I planned,' Hugh owned later to Cadfael. 'I under-estimated both their hardihood and the amount of cold steel they'd have about them.'

There were four guests missing from Brother Denis's halls that night: Master Simeon Poer, merchant of Guildford; Walter Bagot, glover; John Shure, tailor; William Hales, farrier. Of these, William Hales lay that night in a stone cell in Shrewsbury castle, along with a travelling pedlar who had touted for them in the town, but the other three had all broken safely away, bar a few scratches and bruises, into the woods to westward, the most northerly outlying spinneys of the Long Forest, there to bed down in the warm night and count their injuries and their gains, which were considerable. They could not now return to the abbey or the town; the traffic would in any case have stood only one more night at a profit. Three nights are the most to be reckoned on, after that some aggrieved wretch is sure to grow suspicious. Nor could they yet venture south again. But the man who lives on his wits must keep them well honed and adaptable, and there are more ways than one of making a dishonest living.

As for the young rufflers and simple tradesmen who had come out with visions of rattling their winnings on the way home to their wives, they were herded into the gatehouse to be chided, warned, and sent home chapfallen, with very little in their pockets.

And there the night's work would have ended, if the flare of the torch under the gateway had not caught the metal gleam of a ring on Daniel Aurifaber's right hand, flat silver with an oval bezel, for one instant sharply defined. Hugh saw it, and laid a hand on the goldsmith's arm to detain him.

'That ring – let me see it closer!'

Daniel handed it over with a hint of reluctance, though it

76

seemed to stem rather from bewilderment than from any feeling of guilt. It fitted closely, and passed over his knuckle with slight difficulty, but the finger bore no sign of having worn it regularly.

'Where did you get this?' asked Hugh, holding it under the flickering light to examine the device and inscription.

'I bought it honestly,' said Daniel defensively.

'That I need not doubt. But from whom? From one of those gamesters? Which one?'

'The merchant – Simeon Poer he called himself. He offered it, and it was a good piece of work. I paid well for it.'

'You have paid double for it, my friend,' said Hugh, 'for you bid fair to lose ring and money and all. Did it never enter your mind that it might be stolen?'

By the single nervous flutter of the goldsmith's eyelids the thought had certainly occurred to him, however hurriedly he had put it out of his mind again. 'No! Why should I think so? He seemed a stout, prosperous person, all he claimed to be ...'

'This very morning,' said Hugh, 'just such a ring was taken during Mass from a pilgrim at the abbey. Abbot Radulfus sent word up to the provost, after they had searched thoroughly within the pale, in case it should be offered for sale in the market. I had the description of it in turn from the provost. This is the device and inscription of the bishop of Winchester, and it was given to the bearer to secure him safe-conduct on the road.'

'But I bought it in good faith,' protested Daniel, dismayed. 'I paid the man what he asked, the ring is mine, honestly come by.'

'From a thief. Your misfortune, lad, and it may teach you to be more wary of sudden kind acquaintances in the future who offer you rings to buy – wasn't it so? – at somewhat less than you know to be their value? Travelling men rattling dice give nothing for nothing, but take whatever they can get. If they've emptied your purse for you, take warning for the next time. This must go back to the lord abbot in the morning. Let him deal with the owner.' He saw the goldsmith draw angry breath to complain of his deprivation, and shook his head to ward off the effort, not unkindly. 'You have no remedy. Bite your tongue, Daniel, and go make your peace with your wife.'

The empress's envoy rode gently up the Wyle in the deepening dark, keeping pace with Hugh's smaller mount. His own was a fine, tall beast, and the young man in the saddle was long of body and limb. Afoot, thought Hugh, studying him sidelong, he will top me by a head. Very much of an age with me, I might give him a year or two, hardly more.

'Were you ever in Shrewsbury before?'

'Never. Once, perhaps, I was just within the shire, I am not sure how the border runs. I was near Ludlow once. This abbey of yours, I marked it as I came by, a very fine, large enclosure. They keep the Benedictine Rule?'

'They do.' Hugh expected further questions, but they did not come. 'You have kinsmen in the Order?'

Even in the dark he was aware of his companion's grave, musing smile. 'In a manner of speaking, yes, I have. I think he would give me leave to call him so, though there is no blood-kinship. One who used me like a son. I keep a kindness for the habit, for his sake. And did I hear you say there are pilgrims here now? For some particular feast?'

'For the translation of Saint Winifred, who was brought here four years ago from Wales. Tomorrow is the day of her arrival.' Hugh had spoken by custom, quite forgetting what Cadfael had told him of that arrival, but the mention of it brought his friend's story back sharply to mind. 'I was not in Shrewsbury then,' he said, withholding judgement. 'I brought my manors to King Stephen's support the following year. My own country is the north of the shire.'

They had reached the top of the hill, and were turning towards Saint Mary's church. The great gate of Hugh's courtyard stood wide, with torches at the gateposts, waiting for them. His message had been faithfully delivered to Aline, and she was waiting for them with all due ceremony, the bed-chamber prepared, the meal ready to come to table. All rules, all times, bow to the coming of a guest, the duty and privilege of hospitality.

She met them at the door, opening it wide to welcome them in. They stepped into the hall, and into a flood of light from torches at the walls and candles on the table, and instinctively they turned to face each other, taking the first long look. It grew ever longer as their intent eyes grew wider. It was a question which of them groped towards recognition first. Memory pricked and realisation awoke almost stealthily. Aline stood smiling and wondering, but mute, eyeing first one, then the other, until they should stir and shed a clearer light.

'But I know you!' said Hugh. 'Now I see you, I do know you.'

'I have seen you before,' agreed the guest. 'I was never in this shire but the once, and yet …'

'It needed light to see you by,' said Hugh, 'for I never heard your voice but the once, and then no more than a few words. I doubt if you even remember them, but I do. Six words only. "Now have ado with a man!" you said. And your name, your name I never heard but in a manner I take as it was meant. You are Robert, the forester's son who fetched Yves Hugonin out of that robber fortress up on Titterstone Clee. And took him home with you, I think, and his sister with him.'

'And you are that officer who laid the siege that gave me the cover I needed,' cried the guest, gleaming. 'Forgive me that I hid from you then, but I had no warranty there in your territory. How glad I am to meet you honestly now, with no need to take to flight.'

'And no need now to be Robert, the forester's son,' said Hugh, elated and smiling. 'My name I have given you, and the freedom of this house I offer with it. Now may I know yours?'

'In Antioch, where I was born,' said the guest, 'I was called Daoud. But my father was an Englishman of Robert of Normandy's force, and among his comrades in arms I was baptised a Christian, and took the name of the priest who stood my godfather. Now I bear the name of Olivier de Bretagne.'

They sat late into the night together, savouring each other now face to face, after a year and a half of remembering and wondering. But first, as was due, they made short work of Olivier's errand here.

'I am sent,' he said seriously, 'to urge all sheriffs of shires to consider, whatever their previous fealty, whether they should not now accept the proffered peace under the Empress Maud, and take the oath of loyalty to her. This is the message of the bishop and the council: This land has all too long been torn between two factions, and suffered great damage and loss through their mutual enmity. And here *I* say that I lay no blame on that party which is not my own, for there are valid claims on both sides, and equally the blame falls on both for failing to come to some agreement to end these distresses. The fortune at Lincoln might just as well have fallen the opposing way, but it fell as it did, and England is left with a king made captive, and a queen-elect free and in the ascendant. Is it not time to call a halt? For the sake of order and peace and the sound regulation of the realm, and to have a government in command which can and must put down the many injustices and tyrannies which you know, as well as I, have set themselves up outside all law. Surely any strong rule is better than no rule at all. For the sake of peace and order, will you not accept the empress, and hold your county in allegiance to her? She is already in Westminster now, the preparations for her coronation go forward. There is a far better prospect of success if all sheriffs come in to strengthen her rule.'

'You are asking me,' said Hugh gently, 'to go back on my sworn fealty to King Stephen.'

'Yes,' agreed Olivier honestly, 'I am. For weighty reasons, and in no treasonous mind. You need not love, only forbear from hating. Think of it rather as keeping your fealty to the people of this county of yours, and this land.'

'That I can do as well or better on the side where I began,' said Hugh, smiling. 'It is what I am doing now, as best I can. It is what I will continue to do while I have breath. I am King Stephen's man, and I will not desert him.'

'Ah, well!' said Olivier, smiling and sighing in the same breath. 'To tell you truth, now I've met you, I expected nothing less. I would not go from my oath, either. My lord is the empress's man, and I am my lord's man, and if our positions were changed round, my answer would be the same as yours. Yet there is truth in what I have pleaded. How much can a people bear? Your labourer in the fields, your little townsman with a bare living to be looted from him, these would be glad to settle for Stephen or for Maud, only to be rid of the other. And I do what I am sent out to do, as well as I can.'

'I have no fault to find with the matter or the manner,' said Hugh. 'Where next do you go? Though I hope you will not go for a day or two, I would know you better, and we have a great deal to talk over, you and I.'

'From here north-east to Stafford, Derby, Nottingham, and back by the eastern parts. Some will come to terms, as some lords have done already. Some will hold to their own king, like you. And some will do as they have done before, go back and forth like a weather-cock with the wind, and put up their price at every change. No matter, we have done with that now.'

He leaned forward over the table, setting his wine-cup aside. 'I had – I have – another errand of my own, and I should be glad to stay with you a few days, until I have found what I'm seeking, or made certain it is not here to be found. Your mention of this flood of pilgrims for the feast gives me a morsel of hope. A man who wills to be lost could find cover among so many, all strangers to one another. I am looking for a young man called Luc Meverel. He has not, to your knowledge, made his way here?'

'Not by that name,' said Hugh, interested and curious. 'But a man who willed to be lost might choose to doff his own name. What's your need of him?'

'Not mine. It's a lady who wants him back. You may not have got word, this far north,' said Olivier, 'of everything that happened in Winchester during the council. There was a death there that came all too near to me. Did you hear of it? King Stephen's queen sent her clerk there with a bold challenge to the legate's authority, and the man was attacked for his audacity in the street by night, and got off with his life only at the cost of another life.'

'We have indeed heard of it,' said Hugh with kindling interest. 'Abbot Radulfus was there at the council, and brought back a full report. A knight by the name of Rainald Bossard, who came to the clerk's aid when he was set upon. One of those in the service of Laurence d'Angers, so we heard.'

'Who is my lord, also.'

'By your good service to his kin at Bromfield that was plain enough. I thought of you when the abbot spoke of d'Angers, though I had no name for you then. Then this man Bossard was well known to you?'

'Through a year of service in Palestine, and the voyage home together. A good man he was, and a good friend to me, and struck down in defending his honest opponent. I was not with him that night, I wish I had been, he might yet be alive. But he had only one or two of his own people, not in arms. There were five or six set on the clerk, it was a wretched business, confused and in the dark. The murderer got clean away, and has never been traced. Rainald's wife ... Juliana ... I did not know her until we came with our lord to Winchester, Rainald's chief manor is nearby. I have learned,' said Olivier very gravely, 'to hold her in the highest regard. She was her lord's true match, and no one could say more or better of any lady.'

'There is an heir?' asked Hugh. 'A man grown, or still a child?'

'No, they never had children. Rainald was nearly fifty, she

81

cannot be many years younger. And very beautiful,' said Olivier with solemn consideration, as one attempting not to praise, but to explain. 'Now she's widowed she'll have a hard fight on her hands to evade being married off again – for she'll want no other after Rainald. She has manors of her own to bestow. They had thought of the inheritance, the two of them together, that's why they took into their household this young man Luc Meverel, only a year ago. He is a distant cousin of Dame Juliana, twenty-four or twenty-five years old, I suppose, and landless. They meant to make him their heir.'

He fell silent for some minutes, frowning past the guttering candles, his chin in his palm. Hugh studied him, and waited. It was a face worth studying, clean-boned, olive-skinned, fiercely beautiful, even with the golden falcon's eyes thus hooded. The blue-black hair that clustered thickly about his head, clasping like folded wings, shot sullen bluish lights back from the candle's waverings. Daoud, born in Antioch, son of an English crusading soldier in Robert of Normandy's following, somehow blown across the world in the service of an Angevin baron, to fetch up here almost more Norman than the Normans ... The world, thought Hugh, is not so great, after all, but a man born to venture may bestride it.

'I have been three times in that household,' said Olivier, 'but I never knowingly set eyes on this Luc Meverel. All I know of him is what others have said, but among the others I take my choice which voice to believe. There is no one, man or woman, in that manor but agrees he was utterly devoted to Dame Juliana. But as to the manner of his devotion ... There are many who say he loved her far too well, by no means after the fashion of a son. Again, some say he was equally loyal to Rainald, but their voices are growing fainter now. Luc was one of those with his lord when Rainald was stabbed to death in the street. And two days later he vanished from his place, and has not been seen since.'

'Now I begin to see,' said Hugh, drawing in cautious breath. 'Have they gone so far as to say this man slew his lord in order to gain his lady?'

'It is being said now, since his flight. Who began the whisper there's no telling, but by this time it's grown into a bellow.'

'Then why should he run from the prize for which he had played? It makes poor sense. If he had stayed there need have been no such whispers.'

'Ah, but I think there would have been, whether he went or

stayed. There were those who grudged him his fortune, and would have welcomed any means of damaging him. They are finding two good reasons, now, why he should break and run. The first, pure guilt and remorse, too late to save any one of the three of them. The second, fear – fear that someone had got wind of his act, and meant to fetch out the truth at all costs. Either way, a man might break and take to his heels. What you kill for may seem even less attainable,' said Olivier with rueful shrewdness, 'once you have killed.'

'But you have not yet told me,' said Hugh, 'what the lady says of him. Hers is surely a voice that should be heeded.'

'She says that such a vile suspicion is impossible. She did, she does, value her young cousin, but not in the way of love, nor will she have it that he has ever entertained such thoughts of her. She says he would have died for his lord, and that it is his lord's death which has driven him away, sick with grief, a little mad – who knows how deluded and haunted? For he was there that night, he saw Rainald die. She is sure of him. She wants him found and brought back to her. She looks upon him as a son, and now more than ever she needs him.'

'And it's for her sake you're seeking him. But why look for him here, northwards? He may have gone south, west, across the sea by the Kentish ports. Why to the north?'

'Because we have just one word of him since he was lost from his place, and that was going north on the road to Newbury. I came by that same way, by Abingdon and Oxford, and I have enquired for him everywhere, a young man travelling alone. But I can only seek him by his own name, for I know no other for him. As you say, who knows what he may be calling himself now!'

'And you don't even know what he looks like – nothing but merely his age? You're hunting for a spectre!'

'What is lost can always be found, it needs only enough patience.' Olivier's hawk's face, beaked and passionate, did not suggest patience, but the set of his lips was stubborn and pure in absolute resolution.

'Well, at least,' said Hugh, considering, 'we may go down to see Saint Winifred brought home to her altar, tomorrow, and Brother Denis can run through the roster of his pilgrims for us, and point out any who are of the right age and kind, solitary or not. As for strangers here in the town, I fancy Provost Corviser should be able to put his finger on most of them. Every man knows every man in Shrewsbury. But the abbey is the more

83

likely refuge, if he's here at all.' He pondered, gnawing a thoughtful lip. 'I must send the ring down to the abbot at first light, and let him know what's happened to his truant guests, but before I may go down to the feast myself I must send out a dozen men and have them beat the near reaches of the woods to westward for our game birds. If they're over the border, so much the worse for Wales, and I can do no more, but I doubt if they intend to live wild any longer than they need. They may not go far. How if I should leave you with the provost, to pick his brains for your quarry here within the town, while I go hunting for mine? Then we'll go down together to see the brothers bring their saint home, and talk to Brother Denis concerning the list of his guests.'

'That would suit me well,' said Olivier gladly. 'I should like to pay my respects to the lord abbot, I do recall seeing him in Winchester, though he would not notice me. And there was a brother of that house, if you recall,' he said, his golden eyes veiled within long black lashes that swept his fine cheekbones, 'who was with you at Bromfield and up on Clee, that time … You must know him well. He is still here at the abbey?'

'He is. He'll be back in his bed now after Lauds. And you and I had better be thinking of seeking ours, if we're to be busy tomorrow.'

'He was good to my lord's young kinsfolk,' said Olivier. 'I should like to see him again.'

No need to ask for a name, thought Hugh, eyeing him with a musing smile. And indeed, should he know the name? He had not mentioned any, when he spoke of one who was no blood-kin, but who had used him like a son, one for whose sake he kept a kindness for the Benedictine habit.

'You shall!' said Hugh, and rose in high content to marshal his guest to the bedchamber prepared for him.

84

Chapter Eight

BBOT RADULFUS was up long before Prime on the festal morning, and so were his obedientiaries, all of whom had their important tasks in preparation for the procession. When Hugh's messenger presented himself at the abbot's lodging the dawn was still fresh, dewy and cool, the light lying brightly across the roofs while the great court lay in lilac-tinted shadow. In the gardens every tree and bush cast a long band of shade, striping the flower-beds like giant brush-strokes in some gilded illumination.

The abbot received the ring with astonished pleasure, relieved of one flaw that might have marred the splendour of the day. 'And you say these malefactors were guests in our halls, all four? We are well rid of them, but if they are armed, as you say, and have taken to the woods close by, we shall need to warn our travellers, when they leave us.'

'My lord Beringar has a company out beating the edges of the forest for them this moment,' said the messenger. 'There was nothing to gain by following them in the dark, once they were in cover. But by daylight we'll hope to trace them. One we have safe in hold, he may tell us more about them, where they're from, and what they have to answer for elsewhere. But at least now they can't hinder your festivities.'

'And for that I'm devoutly thankful. As this man Ciaran will certainly be for the recovery of his ring.' He added, with a glance aside at the breviary that lay on his desk, and a small frown for the load of ceremonial that lay before him for the next few hours: 'Shall we not see the lord sheriff here for Mass this morning?'

'Yes, Father, he does intend it, and he brings a guest also. He had first to set this hunt in motion, but before Mass they will be here.'

'He has a guest?'

'An envoy from the empress's court came last night, Father. A man of Laurence d'Angers' household, Olivier de Bretagne.'

The name that had meant nothing to Hugh meant as little to Radulfus, though he nodded recollection and understanding at mention of the young man's overlord. 'Then will you say to Hugh Beringar that I beg he and his guest will remain after Mass, and dine with me here. I should be glad to make the acquaintance of Messire de Bretagne, and hear his news.'

'I will so tell him, Father,' said the messenger, and forthwith took his leave.

Left alone in his parlour, Abbot Radulfus stood for a moment looking down thoughtfully at the ring in his palm. The sheltering hand of the bishop-legate would certainly be a powerful protection to any traveller so signally favoured, wherever there existed any order or respect for law, whether in England or Wales. Only those already outside the pale of law, with lives or liberty already forfeit if taken, would defy so strong a sanction. After this crowning day many of the guests here would be leaving again for home. He must not forget to give due warning, before they dispersed, that malefactors might be lurking at large in the woods to westward, and that they were armed, and all too handy at using their daggers. Best that the pilgrims should make sure of leaving in companies stout enough to discourage assault.

Meantime, there was satisfaction in returning to one pilgrim, at least, his particular armour.

The abbot rang the little bell that lay upon his desk, and in a few moments Brother Vitalis came to answer the summons.

'Will you enquire at the guest-hall, brother, for the man called Ciaran, and bid him here to speak with me?'

Brother Cadfael had also risen well before Prime, and gone to open his workshop and kindle his brazier into cautious and restrained life, in case it should be needed later to prepare tisanes for some ecstatic souls carried away by emotional

86

excitement, or warm applications for weaker vessels trampled in the crowd. He was used to the transports of simple souls caught up in far from simple raptures.

He had a few things to tend to, and was happy to deal with them alone. Young Oswin was entitled to his fill of sleep until the bell awoke him. Very soon now he would graduate to the hospital of Saint Giles, where the reliquary of Saint Winifred now lay, and the unfortunates who carried their contagion with them, and might not be admitted into the town, could find rest, care and shelter for as long as they needed it. Brother Mark, that dearly-missed disciple, was gone from there now, already ordained deacon, his eyes fixed ahead upon his steady goal of priesthood. If ever he cast a glance over his shoulder, he would find nothing but encouragement and affection, the proper harvest of the seed he had sown. Oswin might not be such another, but he was a good enough lad and would do honestly by the unfortunates who drifted into his care.

Cadfael went down to the banks of the Meole brook, the westward boundary of the enclave, where the pease-fields declined to the sunken summer water. The rays from the east were just being launched like lances over the high roofs of the monastic buildings, and piercing the scattered copses beyond the brook, and the grassy banks on the further side. This same water, drawn off much higher in its course, supplied the monastery fish-ponds, the hatchery, and the mill and millpond beyond, and was fed back into the brook just before it entered the Severn. It lay low enough now, an archipelago of shoals, half sand, half grass and weed, spreading smooth islands across its breadth. After this spell, thought Cadfael, we shall need plenty of rain. But let that wait a day or two.

He turned back to climb the slope again. The earlier field of pease had already been gleaned, the second would be about ready for harvesting after the festival. A couple of days, and all the excitement would be over, and the horarium of the house and the cycle of the seasons would resume their imperturbable progress, two enduring rhythms in the desperately variable fortunes of mankind. He turned along the path to his workshop, and there was Melangell hesitating before its closed door.

She heard his step in the gravel behind her, and looked round with a bright, expectant face. The pearly morning light became her, softened the coarseness of her linen gown, and smoothed cool lilac shadows round the childlike curves of her

87

face. She had gone to great pains to prepare herself fittingly for the day's solemnities. Her skirts were spotless, crisped out with care, her dark-gold hair, burning with coppery lustre, braided and coiled on her head in a bright crown, its tight plaits drawing up the skin of her temples and cheeks so strongly that her brows were pulled aslant, and the dark-lashed blue eyes elongated and made mysterious. But the radiance that shone from her came not from the sun's caresses, but from within. The blue of those eyes burned as brilliantly as the blue of the gentians Cadfael had seen long ago in the mountains of southern France, on his way to the east. The ivory and rose of her cheeks glowed. Melangell was in the highest state of hope, happiness and expectation.

She made him a very pretty reverence, flushing and smiling, and held out to him the little vial of poppy-syrup he had given to Rhun three days ago. Still unopened!

'If you please, Brother Cadfael, I have brought this back to you. And Rhun prays that it may serve some other who needs it more, and with the more force because he has endured without it.'

He took it from her gently and held it in his cupped hand, a crude little vial stopped with a wooden stopper and a membrane of very thin parchment tied with a waxed thread to seal it. All intact. The boy's third night here, and he had submitted to handling and been mild and biddable in all, but when the means of oblivion was put into his hand and left to his private use, he had preserved it, and with it some core of his own secret integrity, at his own chosen cost. God forbid, thought Cadfael, that I should meddle there. Nothing short of a saint should knock on that door.

'You are not angry with him?' asked Melangell anxiously, but smiling still, unable to believe that any shadow should touch the day, now that her love had clasped and kissed her. 'Because he did not drink it? It was not that he ever doubted *you*. He said so to me. He said – I never quite understand him! – he said it was a time for offering, and he had his offering prepared.'

Cadfael asked: 'Did he sleep?' To have deliverance in hand, even unopened, might well bring peace. 'Hush, now, no, how could I be angry! But *did* he sleep?'

'He says that he did. I think it must be true, he looks so fresh and young. I prayed hard for him.' With all the force of her new happiness, loaded with bliss she felt the need to pour out upon all those near to her. In the conveyance of blessedness by affection Cadfael firmly believed.

'You prayed well,' said Cadfael. 'Never doubt he has gained by it. I'll keep this for some soul in worse need, as Rhun says. It will have the virtue of his faith to strengthen it. I shall see you both during the day.'

She went away from him with a light, springing step and a head reared to breathe in the very space and light of the sky. And Cadfael went in to make sure he had everything ready to provide for a long and exhausting day.

So Rhun had arrived at the last frontier of belief, and fallen, or emerged, or soared into the region where the soul realises that pain is of no account, that to be within the secret of God is more than well being, and past the power of the tongue to utter. To embrace the decree of pain is to translate it, to shed it like a rain of blessing on others who have not yet understood.

Who am I, thought Cadfael, alone in the solitude of his workshop, that I should dare to ask for a sign? If he can endure and ask nothing, must not I be ashamed of doubting?

Melangell passed with a dancing step along the path from the herbarium. On her right hand the western sky soared, in such reflected if muted brightness that she could not forbear from turning to stare into it. A counter-tide of light flowed in here from the west, surging up the slope from the brook and spilling over the crest into the garden. Somewhere on the far side of the entire monastic enclave the two tides would meet, and the light of the west falter, pale and die before the onslaught from the east; but here the bulk of guest-hall and church cut off the newly-risen sun, and left the field to this hesitant and soft-treading antidawn.

There was someone labouring along the far border of the flower-garden, going delicately on still tender feet, watching where he trod. He was alone. No attendant shadow appeared at his back, yesterday's magic still held. She was staring at Ciaran, Ciaran without Matthew. That in itself was a minor miracle, to bring in this day made for miracles.

Melangell watched him begin to descend the slope towards the brook, and when he was no more than a head and shoulders black against the brightness, she suddenly turned and went after him. The path down to the water skirted the growing pease, keeping close to a hedge of thick bushes above the mill-pool. Halfway down the slope she halted, uncertain whether to intrude on his solitude. Ciaran had reached the waterside, and stood surveying what looked like a safe green floor, dappled here and there with the bleached islands of sand, and studded with a few embedded rocks that stood dry from three weeks of fine weather. He looked upstream and down, even stepped into the shallow water that barely covered his naked feet, and surely soothed and refreshed them. Yet how strange, that he should be here alone! Never, until yesterday, had she seen either of these two without the other, yet now they went apart.

She was on the point of stealing away to leave him undisturbed when she saw what he was doing. He had some tiny thing in his hand, into which he was threading a thin cord, and knotting the cord to hold it fast. When he raised both hands to make fast the end of his cord to the tether that held the cross about his neck, the small talisman swung free into the light and glimmered for an instant in silver, before he tucked it away within the neck of his shirt, out of sight against his breast. Then she knew what it was, and stirred in pure pleasure for him, and uttered a small, breathless sound. For Ciaran had his ring again, the safe-conduct that was to ensure him passage to his journey's end.

He had heard her, and swung about, startled and wary. She stood shaken and disconcerted, and then, knowing herself discovered, ran down the last slope of grass to his side. 'They've found it for you!' she said breathlessly, in haste to fill the silence between them and dispel her own uneasiness at having seemed to spy upon him. 'Oh, I am glad! Is the thief taken, then?'

'Melangell!' he said. 'You're early abroad, too? Yes, you see I am blessed, after all, I have it again. The lord abbot restored it to me only some minutes ago. But no, the thief is not caught, he and some fellow-rogues are fled into the woods, it seems. But I can go forth again without fear now.'

His dark eyes, deep-set under thick brows, opened wide upon her, smiling, holding her charmed in the abrupt discovery that he was, despite his disease, a young and comely man, who should have been in the fulness of his powers. Either she was imagining it, or he stood a little straighter, a little taller, than she had ever yet seen him, and the burning intensity of his face had mellowed into a brighter, more human ardour, as if some foreglow of the day's spiritual radiance had given him new hope.

'Melangell,' he said in a soft, vehement rush of words, 'you can't guess how glad I am of this meeting, it was God sent you here to me. I've long wanted to speak to you alone. Never think that because I myself am doomed, I can't see what's before my eyes concerning others who are dear to me. I have something to ask of you, to beg of you, most earnestly. Don't tell Matthew that I have my ring again!'

'Does he not know?' she asked, astray.

'No, he was not by when the abbot sent for me. He must not know! Keep my secret, if you love him – if you have some pity, at least for me. I have told no one, and you must not. The lord abbot is not likely to speak of it to any other, why should he? That he would leave to me. If you and I keep silent, there's no need for anyone else to find out.'

Melangell was lost. She saw him through a rainbow of starting tears, for very pity of his long face hollowed in shade, his eyes glowing like the quiet, living heart of a banked fire.

'But why? Why do you want to keep it from him?'

'For his sake and yours – yes, and mine! Do you think I have not understood long ago that he loves you? – that you feel as much also for him? Only I stand in the way! It's bitter to know it, and I would have it changed. My one wish now is that you and he should be happy together. If he loves me so faithfully, may not I also love him? You know him! He will sacrifice himself, and you, and all things beside, to finish what he has undertaken, and see me safe into Aberdaron. I don't accept his sacrifice, I won't endure it! Why should you both be wretched, when my one wish is to go to my rest in peace of mind and leave my friend happy? Now, while he feels secure that I dare not set out without the ring, for God's sake, girl, leave him in innocence. *And I will go*, and leave you both my blessing.'

Melangell stood quivering, like a leaf shaken by the soft, vehement wind of his words, uncertain even of her own heart. 'Then what must I do? What is it you want of me?'

'Keep my secret,' said Ciaran, 'and go with Matthew in this holy procession. Oh, he'll go with you, and be glad. He won't wonder that I should stay behind and wait the saint's coming here within the pale. And while you're gone, I'll go on my way. My feet are almost healed, I have my ring again, I shall reach my haven. You need not be afraid for me. Only keep him happy as long as you may, and even when my going is known, then use your arts, keep him, hold him fast. That's all I shall ever ask of you.'

91

'But he'll know,' she said, alert to dangers. 'The porter will tell him you're gone, as soon as he looks for you and asks.'

'No, for I shall go by this way, across the brook and out to the west, for Wales. The porter will not see me go. See, it's barely ankle-deep in this season. I have kinsmen in Wales, the first miles are nothing. And among so great a throng, if he does look for me, he'll hardly wonder at not finding me. Not for hours need he so much as think of me, if you do your part. You take care of Matthew, I will absolve both you and him of all care of me, for I shall do well enough. All the better for knowing I leave him safe with you. For you do love him,' said Ciaran softly.

'Yes,' said Melangell in a long sigh.

'Then take and hold him, and my blessing on you both. You may tell him – but well afterwards! – that it is what I designed and intended,' he said, and suddenly and briefly smiled at some unspoken thought he did not wish to share with her.

'You will really do this for him and for me? You mean it? You would go on alone for his sake … Oh, you are good!' she said passionately, and caught at his hand and pressed it to her heart for an instant, for he was giving her the whole world at his own sorrowful cost, and for selfless love of his friend, and there might never be any time but this one moment even to thank him. 'I'll never forget your goodness. All my life long I shall pray for you.'

'No,' said Ciaran, the same dark smile plucking at his lips as she released his hand, 'forget me, and help him to forget me. That is the best gift you can make me. And better you should not speak to me again. Go and find him. That's your part, and I depend on you.'

She drew back from him a few paces, her eyes still fixed on him in gratitude and worship, made him a strange little reverence with head and hands, and turned obediently to climb the field into the garden. By the time she reached level ground and began to thread the beds of the rose garden she was breaking into a joyous run.

They gathered in the great court as soon as everyone, monk, lay servant, guest and townsman, had broken his fast. Seldom had the court seen such a crowd, and outside the walls the Foregate was loud with voices, as the guildsmen of Shrewsbury, provost, elders and all, assembled to join the solemn procession that would set out for Saint Giles. Half of the choir monks, led by Prior Robert, were to go in procession to fetch home the reliquary, while the abbot and the remaining brothers waited to greet them with music and candles and flowers on their return. As for the devout of town and Foregate, and the pilgrims within the walls, they might form and follow Prior Robert, such of them as were able-bodied and eager, while the lame and feeble might wait with the abbot, and prove their devotion by labouring out at least a little way to welcome the saint on her return.

'I should so much like to go with them all the way,' said Melangell, flushed and excited among the chattering, elbowing crowd in the court. 'It is not far. But too far for Rhun – he could not keep pace.'

He was there beside her, very silent, very white, very fair, as though even his flaxen hair had turned paler at the immensity of this experience. He leaned on his crutches between his sister and Dame Alice, and his crystal eyes were very wide, and looked very far, as though he was not even aware of their solicitude hemming him in on either side. Yet he answered simply enough, 'I should like to go a little way, at least, until they leave me behind. But you need not wait for me.'

'As though I would leave you!' said Mistress Weaver, comfortably clucking. 'You and I will keep together and see the pilgrimage out to the best we can, and heaven will be content with that. But the girl has her legs, she may go all the way and put up a few prayers for you going and returning, and we'll none of us be the worse for it.'

She leaned to twitch the neck of his shirt and the collar of his coat into immaculate neatness, and to fuss over his extreme pallor, afraid he was coming down with illness from over-excitement, though he seemed tranquil as ivory, and serenely absent in spirit, gone somewhere she could not follow. Her hand, rough-fingered from weaving, smoothed his well-brushed hair, teasing every tendril back from his tall forehead.

'Run off, then, child,' she said to Melangell, without turning from the boy. 'But find someone we know. There'll be riffraff running alongside, I dare say – no escaping them. Stay by Mistress Glover, or the apothecary's widow ...'

'Matthew is going with them,' said Melangell, flushing and smiling at his very name. 'He told me so. I met him when we came from Prime.'

It was only half-true. She had rather confided boldly to him

93

that she wished to tread every step of the way, and at every step remember and intercede for the souls she most loved on earth. No need to name them. He, no doubt, thought with reflected tenderness of her brother; but she was thinking no less of this anguished pair whose fortunes she now carried delicately and fearfully in her hands. She had even said, greatly venturing, 'Ciaran cannot keep pace, poor soul, he must wait here, like Rhun. But can't we make our steps count for them?'

But for all that, Matthew had looked over his shoulder, and hesitated a sharp instant before he turned his face fully to her, and said abruptly: 'Yes, we'll go, you and I. Yes, let's go that short way together, surely I have the right, this once ... I'll make my prayers for Rhun every step of the way.'

'Trot and find him, then, girl,' said Dame Alice, satisfied. 'Matthew will take good care of you. See, they're forming up, you'd best hurry. We'll be here to watch you come in.'

Melangell fled, elated. Prior Robert had drawn up his choir, with Brother Anselm the precentor at their head, facing the gate. The shifting, murmuring, excited column of pilgrims formed up at his rear, twitching like a dragon's tail, a long, brightly-coloured, volatile train, brave with flowers, lighted tapers, offerings, crosses and banners. Matthew was waiting to reach out an eager hand to her and draw her in beside him. 'You have leave? She trusts you to me ...?'

'You're not troubled about Ciaran?' she could not forbear asking anxiously. 'He's right to stay here, he couldn't manage the walk.'

The choir monks before them began their processional psalm, Prior Robert led the way through the open gate, and after him went the brothers in their ordered pairs, and after them the notabilities of the town, and after them the long retinue of pilgrims, crowding forward eagerly, picking up the chant where they had knowledge of it or a sensitive ear, pouring out past the gatehouse and turning right towards Saint Giles.

Brother Cadfael went with Prior Robert's party, with Brother Adam of Reading walking beside him. Along the broad road by the enclave wall, past the great triangle of trodden grass at the horse-fair ground, and again bearing right with the road, between scattered houses and sun-bleached pastures and fields to the very edge of the suburb, where the squat tower of the hospital church, the roof of the hospice, and the long wattle fence of its garden showed dark against the bright eastern sky, slightly raised from the road on a gentle green mound. And all the way the long train of followers grew longer and more gaily-coloured, as the people of the Foregate in their best holiday clothes came out from their dwellings and joined the procession.

There was no room in the small, dark church for more than the brothers and the civic dignitaries of the town. The rest gathered all about the doorway, craning to get a glimpse of the proceedings within. With his lips moving almost soundlessly on the psalms and prayers, Cadfael watched the play of candle-light on the silver tracery that ornamented Saint Winifred's elegant oak coffin, elevated there on the altar as when they had first brought it from Gwytherin, four years earlier. He wondered whether his motive in securing for himself a place among the eight brothers who would bear her back to the abbey had been as pure as he had hoped. Had he been staking a proprietary claim on her, as one who had been at her first coming? Or had he meant it as a humble and penitential gesture? He was, after all, past sixty, and as he recalled, the oak casket was heavy, its edges sharp on a creaky shoulder, and the way back long enough to bring out all the potential discomforts. She might yet find a way of showing him whether she approved his proceedings or no, by striking him helpless with rheumatic pains!

The office ended. The eight chosen brothers, matched in height and pace, lifted the reliquary and settled it upon their shoulders. The prior stooped his lofty head through the low doorway into the mid-morning radiance, and the crowd clustered about the church opened to make way for the saint to ride to her triumph. The procession reformed, Prior Robert before with the brothers, the coffin with its bearers, flanked by crosses and banners and candles, and eager women bringing garlands of flowers. With measured pace, with music and solemn joy, Saint Winifred – or whatever represented her there in the sealed and secret place – was borne back to her own altar in the abbey church.

Curious, thought Cadfael, carefully keeping the step by numbers, it seems lighter than I remember. Is that possible? In only four years? He was familiar with the curious propensities of the body, dead or alive, he had once been led into a gallery of caverns in the desert where ancient Christians had lived and died, he knew what dry air can do to flesh, preserving the light

95

and shrivelled shell while the juice of life was drawn off into spirit. Whatever was there in the reliquary, it rode tranquilly upon his shoulder, like a light hand guiding him. It was not heavy at all!

Chapter Nine

OMETHING WONDERFUL happened along the way to Matthew and Melangell, hemmed in among the jostling, singing, jubilant train. Somewhere along that half-mile of road they were caught up in the fever and joy of the day, borne along on the tide of music and devotion, forgetting all others, forgetting even themselves, drawn into one without any word or motion of theirs. When they turned their heads to look at each other, they saw only mated eyes and a halo of sunshine. They did not speak at all, not once along the way. They had no need of speech. But when they had turned the corner of the precinct wall by the horse-fair, and drew near to the gatehouse, and heard and saw the abbot leading his own party out to meet them, splendidly vested and immensely tall under his mitre; when the two chants found their measure while yet some way apart, and met and married in a triumphant, soaring cry of worship, and all the ardent followers drew gasping breaths of exultation, Melangell heard beside her a broken breath drawn, like a soft sob, that turned as suddenly into a peal of laughter, out of pure, possessed joy. Not a loud sound, muted and short of breath because the throat that uttered it was clenched by emotion, and the mind and heart from which it came quite unaware of what it shed upon the world. It was a beautiful sound, or so Melangell thought, as she raised her head to stare at him with wide eyes and parted lips, in dazzled and dazzling delight. Matthew's wry and rare smile she had seen sometimes, and wondered and grieved at its brevity, but never before had she heard him laugh.

The two processions merged. The cross-bearers walked before, Abbot Radulfus, prior and choir monks came after, and Cadfael and his peers with their sacred burden followed, hemmed in on both sides by worshippers who reached and leaned to touch even the sleeve of a bearer's habit, or the polished oak of the reliquary as it passed. Brother Anselm, in secure command of his choir, raised his own fine voice in the lead as they turned in at the gatehouse, bringing Saint Winifred home.

Brother Cadfael, by then, was moving like a man in a dual dream, his body keeping pace and time with his fellows, in one confident rhythm, while his mind soared in another, carried aloft on the cushioned cloud of sounds, compounded of the eager footsteps, exalted murmurs and shrill acclamations of hundreds of people, with the chant borne above it, and the voice of Brother Anselm soaring over all. The great court was crowded with people to watch them enter, the way into the cloister, and so into the church, had to be cleared by slow, shuffling paces, the ranks pressing back to give them passage, Cadfael came to himself with some mild annoyance when the reliquary was halted in the court, to wait for a clear path ahead. He braced both feet almost aggressively into the familiar soil, and for the first time looked about him. He saw, beyond the throng already gathered, the saint's own retinue melting and flowing to find a place where eye might see all, and ear hear all. In this brief halt he saw Melangell and Matthew, hand in hand, hunt round the fringes of the crowd, and find a place to gaze.

They looked to Cadfael a little tipsy, like unaccustomed drinkers after strong wine. And why not? After long abstention he had felt the intoxication possessing his own feet, as they held the hypnotic rhythm, and his own mind, as it floated on the cadences of song. Those ecstasies were at once native and alien to him, he could both embrace and stand clear of them, feet firmly planted, gripping the homely earth, to keep his balance and stand erect.

They moved forward again into the nave of the church, and then to the right, towards the bared and waiting altar. The vast, dreaming, sun-warmed bulk of the church enclosed them, dim, silent and empty, since no other could enter until they had discharged their duty, lodged their patroness and retired to their own insignificant places. Then they came, led by abbot and prior, first the brothers to fill up their stalls in the choir, then the provost and guildsmen of the town and the notables of the shire, and then all that great concourse of people, flooding in from hot mid-morning sunlight to the cool dimness of stone, and from the excited clamour of festival to the great silence of worship, until all the space of the nave was filled with the colour and warmth and breath of humanity, and all as still as the candle-flames on the altar. Even the reflected gleams in the silver chacings of the casket were fixed and motionless as jewels.

Abbot Radulfus stood forth. The sobering solemnity of the Mass began.

For the very intensity of all that mortal emotion gathered thus between confining walls and beneath one roof, it was impossible to withdraw the eyes for an instant from the act of worship on which it was centred, or the mind from the words of the office. There had been times, through the years of his vocation, when Cadfael's thoughts had strayed during Mass to worrying at other problems, and working out other intents. It was not so now. Throughout, he was unaware of a single face in all that throng, only of the presence of humankind, in whom his own identity was lost; or, perhaps, into whom his own identity expanded like air, to fill every part of the whole. He forgot Melangell and Matthew, he forgot Ciaran and Rhun, he never looked round to see if Hugh had come. If there was a face before his mind's eye at all it was one he had never seen, though he well remembered the slight and fragile bones he had lifted with such care and awe out of the earth, and with so much better heart again laid beneath the same soil, there to resume her hawthorn-scented sleep under the sheltering trees. For some reason, though she had lived to a good old age, he could not imagine her older than seventeen or eighteen, as she had been when the king's son Cradoc pursued her. The slender little bones had cried out of youth, and the shadowy face he had imagined for her was fresh and eager and open, and very beautiful. But he saw it always half turned away from him. Now, if ever, she might at last look round, and show him fully that reassuring countenance.

At the end of Mass the abbot withdrew to his own stall, to the right of the entrance from nave to choir, round the parish altar, and with lifted voice and open arms bade the pilgrims advance to the saint's altar, where everyone who had a petition

99

to make might make it on his knees, and touch the reliquary with hand and lip. And in orderly and reverent silence they came. Prior Robert took his stand at the foot of the three steps that led up to the altar, ready to offer a hand to those who needed help to mount or kneel. Those who were in health and had no pressing requirements to advance came through from the nave on the other side, and found corners where they might stand and watch, and miss nothing of this memorable day. They had faces again, they spoke in whispers, they were as various as an hour since they had been one.

On his knees in his stall, Brother Cadfael looked on, knowing them one from another now as they came, kneeled and touched. The long file of petitioners was drawing near its end when he saw Rhun approaching. Dame Alice had a hand solicitously under his left elbow, Melangell nursed him along on his right, Matthew followed close, no less anxious than they. The boy advanced with his usual laborious gait, his dragging toe just scraping the tiles of the floor. His face was intensely pale, but with a brilliant pallor that almost dazzled the watching eyes, and the wide gaze he fixed steadily upon the reliquary shone translucent, like ice with a bright bluish light behind it. Dame Alice was whispering low, encouraging entreaties into one ear, Melangell into the other, but he was aware of nothing but the altar towards which he moved. When his turn came, he shook off his supporters, and for a moment seemed to hesitate before venturing to advance alone.

Prior Robert observed his condition, and held out a hand. 'You need not be abashed, my son, because you cannot kneel. God and the saint will know your goodwill.'

The softest whisper of a voice, though clearly audible in the waiting silence, said tremulously: 'But, Father, I can! I will!'

Rhun straightened up, taking his hands from his crutches, which slid from under his armpits and fell. That on the left crashed with an unnerving clatter upon the tiles, on the right Melangell started forward and dropped to her knees, catching the falling prop in her arms with a faint cry. And there she crouched, embracing the discarded thing desperately, while Rhun set his twisted foot to the ground and stood upright. He had but two or three paces to go to the foot of the altar steps. He took them slowly and steadily, his eyes fixed upon the reliquary. Once he lurched slightly, and Dame Alice made a trembling move to run after him, only to halt again in wonder and fear, while Prior Robert again extended his hand to offer aid. Rhun paid no attention to them or to anyone else, he did not seem to see or hear anything but his goal, and whatever voice it might be that called him forward. For he went with held breath, as a child learning to walk ventures across perilous distances to reach its mother's open arms and coaxing, praising blandishments that wooed it to the deed.

It was the twisted foot he set first on the lowest step, and now the twisted foot, though a little awkward and unpractised, was twisted no longer, and did not fail him, and the wasted leg, as he put his weight on it, seemed to have smoothed out into shapeliness, and bore him up bravely.

Only then did Cadfael become aware of the stillness and the silence, as if every soul present held his breath with the boy, spellbound, not yet ready, not yet permitted to acknowledge what they saw before their eyes. Even Prior Robert stood charmed into a tall, austere statue, frozen at gaze. Even Melangell, crouching with the crutch hugged to her breast, could not stir a finger to help or break the spell, but hung upon every deliberate step with agonised eyes, as though she were laying her heart under his feet as a voluntary sacrifice to buy off fate.

He had reached the third step, he sank to his knees with only the gentlest of manipulations, holding by the fringes of the altar frontal, and the cloth of gold that was draped under the reliquary. He lifted his joined hands and starry face, white and bright even with eyes now closed, and though there was hardly any sound they saw his lips moving upon whatever prayers he had made ready for her. Certainly they contained no request for his own healing. He had put himself simply in her hands, submissively and joyfully, and what had been done to him and for him surely she had done, of her own perfect will.

He had to hold by her draperies to rise, as babes hold by their mothers' skirts. No doubt but she had him under the arms to raise him. He bent his fair head and kissed the hem of her garment, rose erect and kissed the silver rim of the reliquary, in which, whether she lay or not, she alone commanded and had sovereignty. Then he withdrew from her, feeling his way backward down the three steps. Twisted foot and shrunken leg carried him securely. At the foot he made obeisance gravely, and then turned and went briskly, like any other healthy lad of sixteen, to smile reassurance on his trembling womenfolk, take up gently the crutches for which he had no further use, and carry them back to lay them tidily under the altar.

101

The spell broke, for the marvellous thing was done, and its absolute nature made manifest. A great, shuddering sigh went round nave, choir, transepts and all, wherever there were human creatures watching and listening. And after the sigh the quivering murmur of a gathering storm, whether of tears or laughter there was no telling, but the air shook with its passion. And then the outcry, the loosing of both tears and laughter, in a gale of wonder and praise. From stone walls and lofty, arched roof, from rood-loft and transept arcades, the echoes flew and rebounded, and the candles that had stood so still and tall shook and guttered in the gale. Melangell hung weak with weeping and joy in Matthew's arms, Dame Alice whirled from friend to friend, spouting tears like a fountain, and smiling like the most blessed of women. Prior Robert lifted his hands in vindicated stewardship, and his voice in the opening of a thanksgiving psalm, and Brother Anselm took up the chant.

A miracle, a miracle, a miracle …

And in the midst Rhun stood erect and still, even a little bewildered, braced sturdily on his two long, shapely legs, looking all about him at the shouting, weeping, exulting faces, letting the meaningless sounds wash over him in waves, wanting the quiet he had known when there had been no one here in this holy place but himself and his saint, who had told him, in how sweet and private conference, all that he had to do.

Brother Cadfael rose with his brothers after the church was cleared of all others, after all that jubilant, bubbling, boiling throng had gone forth to spill its feverish excitement in open summer air, to cry the miracle aloud, carry it out into the Foregate, beyond into the town, buffet it back and forth across the tables at dinner in the guest-hall, and return to extol it at Vespers with what breath was left. When they dispersed the word would go with them wherever they went, sounding Saint Winifred's praises, inspiring other souls to take to the roads and bring their troubles to Shrewsbury. Where healing was proven, and attested by hundreds of voices.

The brothers went to their modest, accustomed dinner in the refectory, and observed, whatever their own feelings were, the discipline of silence. They were very tired, which made silence welcome. They had risen early, worked hard, been through fire and flood body and soul, no wonder they ate humbly, thankfully, in silence.

Chapter Ten

T WAS not until dinner was almost over in the guest-hall that Matthew, seated at Melangell's side and still flushed and exalted from the morning's heady wonders, suddenly bethought him of sterner matters, and began to look back with a thoughtful frown which as yet only faintly dimmed the unaccustomed brightness of his face. Being in attendance on Mistress Weaver and her young people had made him a part, for a while, of their unshadowed joy, and caused him to forget everything else. But it could not last, though Rhun sat there half-lost in wonder still, with hardly a word to say, and felt no need of food or drink, and his womenfolk fawned on him unregarded. So far away had he been that the return took time.

'I haven't seen Ciaran,' said Matthew quietly in Melangell's ear, and he rose a little in his place to look round the crowded room. 'Did you catch ever a glimpse of him in the church?'

She, too, had forgotten until then, but at sight of his face she remembered all too sharply, with a sickening lurch of her heart. But she kept her countenance, and laid a persuasive hand on his arm to draw him down again beside her. 'Among so many? But he surely would be there. He must have been among the first, he stayed here, he would find a good place. We didn't see all those who went to the altar – we all stayed with Rhun, and his place was far back.' Such a mingling of truth and lies, but she kept her voice confident, and clung to her shaken hope.

'But where is he now? I don't see him within here.' Though there was so much excitement, so much moving about from table to table to talk with friends, that one man might easily avoid detection. 'I must find him,' said Matthew, not yet greatly troubled but wanting reassurance, and rose.

'No, sit down! You know he must be here somewhere. Let him alone, and he'll appear when he chooses. He may be resting on his bed, if he has to go forth again barefoot tomorrow. Why look for him now? Can you not do without him even one day? And such a day?'

Matthew looked down at her with a face from which all the openness and joy had faded, and freed his sleeve from her grasp gently enough, but decidedly. 'Still, I must find him. Stay here with Rhun, I'll come back. All I want is to see him, to be sure …'

He was away, slipping quietly out between the festive tables, looking sharply about him as he went. She was in two minds about following him, but then she thought better of it, for while he hunted time would be slipping softly away, and Ciaran would be dwindling into distance, as later she prayed he could fade even out of mind, and be forgotten. So she remained with the happy company, but not of it, and with every passing moment hesitated whether to grow more reassured or more uneasy. At last she could not bear the waiting any longer. She rose quietly and slipped away. Dame Alice was in full spate, torn between tears and smiles, sitting proudly by her prodigy, and surrounded by neighbours as happy and voluble as herself, and Rhun, still somehow apart though he was the centre of the group, sat withdrawn into his revelation, even as he answered eager questions, lamely enough but as well as he could. They had no need of Melangell, they would not miss her for a little while.

When she came out into the great court, into the brilliance of the noonday sun, it was the quietest hour, the pause after meat. There never was a time of day when there was no traffic about the court, no going and coming at the gatehouse, but now it moved at its gentlest and quietest. She went down almost fearfully into the cloister, and found no one there but a single copyist busy reviewing what he had done the previous day, and Brother Anselm in his workshop going over the music for Vespers; into the stable-yard, though there was no reason in the world why Matthew should be there, having no mount, and no expectation that his companion would or possibly could acquire one; into the gardens, where a couple of novices were clipping back the too exuberant shoots of a box hedge; even into the grange court, where the barns and storehouses were, and a few lay servants were taking their ease, and harrowing over the morning's marvel, like everyone else within the enclave, and most of Shrewsbury and the Foregate into the bargain. The abbot's garden was empty, neat, glowing with carefully-tended roses, his lodging showed an open door, and some ordered bustle of guests within.

She turned back towards the garden, now in deep anxiety. She was not good at lying, she had no practice, even for a good end she could not but botch the effort. And for all the to and fro of customary commerce within the pale, never without work to be done, she had seen nothing of Matthew. But he could not be gone, no, the porter could tell him nothing, Ciaran had not passed there; and she would not, never until she must, never until Matthew's too fond heart was reconciled to loss, and open and receptive to a better gain.

She turned back, rounding the box hedge and out of sight of the busy novices, and walked breast to breast into Matthew.

They met between the thick hedges, in a terrible privacy. She started back from him in a brief revulsion of guilt, for he looked more distant and alien than ever before, even as he recognised her, and acknowledged with a contortion of his troubled face her right to come out in search of him, and almost in the same instant frowned her off as irrelevant.

'He's gone!' he said in a chill and grating voice, and looked through her and far beyond. 'God keep you, Melangell, you must fend for yourself now, sorry as I am. He's gone – fled while my back was turned. I've looked for him everywhere, and never a trace of him. Nor has the porter seen him pass the gate, I've asked there. But he's gone! Alone! And I must go after him. God keep you, girl, as I cannot, and fare you well!'

And he was going so, with so few words and so cold and wild a face! He had turned on his heel and taken two long steps before she flung herself after him, caught him by the arms in both hands, and dragged him to a halt.

'No, no, *why*? What need has he of you, to match with my need? He's gone? Let him go! Do you think your life belongs to him? He doesn't want it! He wants you free, he wants you to live your own life, not die his death with him. He knows, he knows you love me! Dare you deny it? He knows I love you. He wants you happy! Why should not a friend want his friend

105

to be happy? Who are you to deny him his last wish?'

She knew by then that she had said too much, but never knew at what point the error had become mortal. He had turned fully to her again, and frozen where he stood, and his face was like chiselled marble. He tugged his sleeve out of her grasp this time with no gentleness at all.

'*He wants!*' hissed a voice she had never heard before, driven through narrowed lips. 'You've spoken with him! You speak *for* him! *You knew!* You knew he meant to go, and leave me here bewitched, damned, false to my oath. *You knew!* When? When did you speak with him?'

He had her by the wrists, he shook her mercilessly, and she cried out and fell to her knees.

'You knew he meant to go?' persisted Matthew, stooping over her in a cold frenzy.

'Yes – yes! This morning he told me … he wished it …'

'*He wished it!* How dared he wish it? How could he dare, robbed of his bishop's ring as he was? He dared not stir without it, he was terrified to set foot outside the pale …'

'He has the ring,' she cried, abandoning all deceit. 'The lord abbot gave it back to him this morning, you need not fret for him, he's safe enough, he has his protection … He doesn't need you!'

Matthew had fallen into a deadly stillness, stooping above her. '*He has the ring?* And you knew it, and never said word! If you know so much, how much more do you know. Speak! *Where is he?*'

'Gone,' she said in a trembling whisper, 'and wished you well, wished us both well … wished us to be happy … Oh, let him go, let him go, he sets you free!'

Something that was certainly a laugh convulsed Matthew, she heard it with her ears and felt it shiver through her flesh, but it was like no other laughter she had ever heard, it chilled her blood. '*He* sets *me* free! And you must be his confederate! Oh, God! He never passed the gate. If you know all, then tell all – how did he go?'

She faltered, weeping: 'He loved you, he willed you to live and forget him, and be happy …'

'*How did he go?*' repeated Matthew, in a voice so ill-supplied with breath it seemed he might strangle on the words.

'Across the brook,' she said in a broken whisper, 'making the quickest way for Wales. He said … he has kin there …'

106

He drew in hissing breath and took his hands from her, leaving her drooping forward on her face as he let go of her wrists. He had turned his back and flung away from her, all they had shared forgotten, his obsession plucking him away. She did not understand, there was no way she could come to terms so rapidly with all that had happened, but she knew she had loosed her hold of her love, and he was in merciless flight from her in pursuit of some incomprehensible duty in which she had no part and no right. She sprang up and ran after him, caught him by the arm, wound her own arms about him, lifted her imploring face to his stony, frantic stare, and prayed him passionately: 'Let him go! Oh, let him go! He wants to go alone and leave you to me ...'

Almost silently above her the terrible laughter, so opposed to that lovely sound as he followed the reliquary with her, boiled like some thick, choking syrup in his throat. He struggled to shake off her clinging hands, and when she fell to her knees again and hung upon him with all her despairing weight he tore loose his right hand, and struck her heavily in the face, sobbing, and so wrenched himself loose and fled, leaving her face-down on the ground.

In the abbot's lodging Radulfus and his guests sat long over their meal, for they had much to discuss. The topic which was on everyone's lips naturally came first.

'It would seem,' said the abbot, 'that we have been singularly favoured this morning. Certain motions of grace we have seen before, but never yet one so public and so persuasive, with so many witnesses. How do you say? I grow old in experience of wonders, some of which turn out to fall somewhat short of their promise. I know of human deception, not always deliberate, for sometimes the deceiver is himself deceived. If saints have power, so have demons. Yet this boy seems to me as crystal. I cannot think he either cheats or is cheated.'

'I have heard,' said Hugh, 'of cripples who discarded their crutches and walked without them, only to relapse when the fervour of the occasion was over. Time will prove whether this one takes to his crutches again.'

'I shall speak with him later,' said the abbot, 'after the excitement has cooled. I hear from Brother Edmund that Brother Cadfael has been treating the boy these three days he has been here. That may have eased his condition, but it can scarcely have brought about so sudden a cure. No, I must say it, I truly believe our house has been the happy scene of divine grace. I will speak also with Cadfael, who must know the boy's condition.'

Olivier sat quiet and deferential in the presence of so reverend a churchman as the abbot, but Hugh observed that his arched lids lifted and his eyes kindled at Cadfael's name. So he knew who it was he sought, and something more than a distant salute in action had passed between that strangely assorted pair.

'And now I should be glad,' said the abbot, 'to hear what news you bring from the south. Have you been in Westminster with the empress's court? For I hear she is now installed there.'

Olivier gave his account of affairs in London readily, and answered questions with goodwill. 'My lord has remained in Oxford, it was at his wish I undertook this errand. I was not in London, I set out from Winchester. But the empress is in the palace of Westminster, and the plans for her coronation go forward – admittedly very slowly. The city of London is well aware of its power, and means to exact due recognition of it, or so it seems to me.' He would go no nearer than that to voicing whatever qualms he felt about his liege lady's wisdom or want of it, but he jutted a dubious underlip, and momentarily frowned. 'Father, you were there at the council, you know all that happened. My lord lost a good knight there, and I a valued friend, struck down in the street.'

'Rainald Bossard,' said Radulfus sombrely. 'I have not forgotten.'

'Father, I have been telling the lord sheriff here what I should like to tell also to you. For I have a second errand to pursue, wherever I go on the business of the empress, an errand for Rainald's widow. Rainald had a young kinsman in his household, who was with him when he was killed, and after that death this young man left the lady's service without a word, secretly. She says he had grown closed and silent even before he vanished, and the only trace of him afterwards was on the road to Newbury, going north. Since then, nothing. So knowing I was bound north, she begged me to enquire for him wherever I came, for she values and trusts him, and needs him at her side. I may not deceive you, Father, there are those who say he has fled because he is guilty of Rainald's death. They claim he was besotted with Dame Juliana, and may have seized his chance in this brawl to widow her, and get her for himself, and then taken fright because these things were so soon being said. But *I* think they were not being said at all until after he had vanished. And Juliana, who surely knows him better than any, and looks upon him as a son, for want of children of her own, she is quite sure of him. She wants him home and vindicated, for whatever reason he left her as he did. And I have been asking at every lodging and monastery along the road for word of such a young man. May I also ask here? Brother Hospitaller will know the names of all his guests. Though a name,' he added ruefully, 'is almost all I have, for if ever I saw the man it was without knowing it was he. And the name he may have left behind him.'

'It is not much to go on,' said Abbot Radulfus with a smile, 'but certainly you may enquire. If he has done no wrong, I should be glad to help you to find him and bring him off without reproach. What is his name?'

'Luc Meverel. Twenty-four years old, they tell me, middling tall and well made, dark of hair and eye.'

'It could fit many hundreds of young men,' said the abbot, shaking his head, 'and the name I doubt he will have put off if he has anything to hide, or even if he fears it may be unfairly besmirched. Yet try. I grant you in such a gathering as we have here now a young man who wished to be lost might bury himself very thoroughly. Denis will know which of his guests is of the right age and quality. For clearly your Luc Meverel is well-born, and most likely tutored and lettered.'

'Certainly so,' said Olivier.

'Then by all means, and with my blessing, go freely to Brother Denis, and see what he can do to help you. He has an excellent memory, he will be able to tell you which, among the men here, is of suitable years, and gentle. You can but try.'

On leaving the lodging they went first, however, to look for Brother Cadfael. And Brother Cadfael was not so easily found. Hugh's first resort was the workshop in the herbarium, where they habitually compounded their affairs. But there was no Cadfael there. Nor was he with Brother Anselm in the cloister, where he might well have been debating some nice point in the evening's music. Nor checking the medicine cupboard in the infirmary, which must surely have been depleted during these last few days, but had clearly been restocked in the early hours of this day of glory. Brother Edmund said mildly: 'He was here. I had a poor soul who bled

109

from the mouth – too gorged, I think, with devotion. But he's quiet and sleeping now, the flux has stopped. Cadfael went away some while since.'

Brother Oswin, vigorously fighting weeds in the kitchen garden, had not seen his superior since dinner. 'But I think,' he said, blinking thoughtfully into the sun in the zenith, 'he may be in the church.'

Cadfael was on his knees at the foot of Saint Winifred's three-tread stairway to grace, his hands not lifted in prayer but folded in the lap of his habit, his eyes not closed in entreaty but wide open to absolution. He had been kneeling there for some time, he who was usually only too glad to rise from knees now perceptibly stiffening. He felt no pains, no griefs of any kind, nothing but an immense thankfulness in which he floated like a fish in an ocean. An ocean as pure and blue and drowningly deep and clear as that well-remembered eastern sea, the furthest extreme of the tideless midland sea of legend, at the end of which lay the holy city of Jerusalem, Our Lord's burial-place and hard-won kingdom. The saint who presided here, whether she lay here or no, had launched him into a shining infinity of hope. Her mercies might be whimsical, they were certainly magisterial. She had reached her hand to an innocent, well deserving her kindness. What had she intended towards this less innocent but no less needy being?

Behind him, approaching quietly from the nave, a known voice said softly: 'And are you demanding yet a second miracle?'

He withdrew his eyes reluctantly from the reflected gleams of silver along the reliquary, and turned to look towards the parish altar. He saw the expected shape of Hugh Beringar, the thin dark face smiling at him. But over Hugh's shoulder he saw a taller head and shoulders loom, emerging from dimness in suave, resplendent planes, the bright, jutting cheekbones, the olive cheeks smoothly hollowed below, the falcon's amber eyes beneath high-arched black brows, the long, supple lips tentatively smiling upon him.

It was not possible. Yet he beheld it. Olivier de Bretagne came out of the shadows and stepped unmistakable into the light of the altar candles. And that was the moment when Saint Winifred turned her head, looked fully into the face of her fallible but faithful servant, and also smiled.

A second miracle! Why not? When she gave she gave prodigally, with both hands.

110

Chapter Eleven

HEY WENT out into the cloister all three together, and that in itself was memorable and good, for they had never been together before. Those trusting intimacies which had once passed between Cadfael and Olivier, on a winter night in Bromfield priory, were unknown still to Hugh, and there was a mysterious constraint still that prevented Olivier from openly recalling them. The greetings they exchanged were warm but brief, only the reticence behind them was eloquent, and no doubt Hugh understood that well enough, and was willing to wait for enlightenment, or courteously to make do without it. For that there was no haste, but for Luc Meverel there might be.

'Our friend has a quest,' said Hugh, 'in which we mean to enlist Brother Denis's help, but we shall also be very glad of yours. He is looking for a young man by the name of Luc Meverel, strayed from his place and known to be travelling north. Tell him the way of it, Olivier.'

Olivier told the story over again, and was listened to with close attention. 'Very gladly,' said Cadfael then, 'would I do whatever man can do not only to bring off an innocent man from such a charge, but also to bring the charge home to the guilty. We know of this murder, and it sticks in every gullet that a decent man, protecting his honourable opponent, should be cut down by one of his own faction ...'

'Is that certain?' wondered Hugh sharply.

'As good as certain. Who else would so take exception to the man standing up for his lady and doing his errand without fear? All who still held to Stephen in their hearts would approve, even if they dared not applaud him. And as for a chance attack by sneak-thieves – why choose to prey on a mere clerk, with nothing of value on him but the simple needs of his journey, when the town was full of nobles, clerics and merchants far better worth robbing? Rainald died only because he came to the clerk's aid. No, an adherent of the empress, like Rainald himself but most unlike, committed that infamy.'

'That's good sense,' agreed Olivier. 'But my chief concern now is to find Luc, and send him home again if I can.'

'There must be twenty or more young fellows in that age here today,' said Cadfael, scrubbing thoughtfully at his blunt brown nose, 'but I dare wager most of them can be pricked out of the list as well known to some of their companions by their own right names, or by reason of their calling or condition. Solitaries may come, but they're few and far between. Pilgrims are like starlings, they thrive on company. We'd best go and talk to Brother Denis. He'll have sorted out most of them by now.'

Brother Denis had a retentive memory and an appetite for news and rumours that usually kept him the best-informed person in the enclave. The fuller his halls, the more pleasure he took in knowing everything that went on there, and the name and vocation of every guest. He also kept meticulous books to record the visitations.

They found him in the narrow cell where he kept his accounts and estimated his future needs, thoughtfully reckoning up what provisions he still had, and how rapidly the demands on them were likely to dwindle from the morrow. He took his mind from his store-book courteously in order to listen to what Brother Cadfael and the sheriff required of him, and produced answers with exemplary promptitude when asked to sieve out from his swollen household males of about twenty-five years, bred gentle or within modest reach of gentility, lettered, of dark colouring and medium tall build, answering to the very bare description of Luc Meverel. As his forefinger flew down the roster of his guests the numbers shrank remarkably. It seemed to be true that considerably more than half of those who went on pilgrimage were women, and that among the men the greater part were in their forties or fifties, and of those remaining, many would be in minor orders, either monastics or secular priests or would-be priests. And

Luc Meverel was none of these.

'Are there any here,' asked Hugh, viewing the final list, which was short enough, 'who came solitary?'

Brother Denis cocked his round, rosy, tonsured head aside and ran a sharp brown eye, very reminiscent of a robin's, down the list. 'Not one. Young squires of that age seldom go as pilgrims, unless with an exigent lord – or an equally exigent lady. In such a summer feast as this we might have young friends coming together, to take the fill of the time before they settle down to sterner disciplines. But alone ... Where would be the pastime in that?'

'Here are two, at any rate,' said Cadfael, 'who came together, but surely not for pastime. They have puzzled me, I own. Both are of the proper age, and such word as we have of the man we're looking for would fit either. You know them, Denis – that youngster who's on his way to Aberdaron, and his friend who bears him company. Both lettered, both bred to the manor. And certainly they came from the south, beyond Abingdon, according to Brother Adam of Reading, who lodged there the same night.'

'Ah, the barefoot traveller,' said Denis, and laid a finger on Ciaran in the shrunken toll of young men, 'and his keeper and worshipper. Yes, I would not put half a year beween them, and they have the build and colouring, but you needed only one.'

'We could at least look at two,' said Cadfael. 'If neither of them is what we're seeking, yet coming from that region they may have encountered such a single traveller somewhere on the road. If we have not the authority to question them closely about who they are and whence they come, and how and why thus linked, then Father Abbot has. And if they have no reason to court concealment, then they'll willingly declare to him what they might not as readily utter to us.'

'We may try it,' said Hugh, kindling. 'At least it's worth the asking, and if they have nothing to do with the man we are looking for, neither they nor we have lost more than half an hour of time, and surely they won't grudge us that.'

'Granted what is so far related of these two hardly fits the case,' Cadfael acknowledged doubtfully, 'for the one is said to be mortally ill and going to Aberdaron to die, and the other is resolute to keep him company to the end. But a young man who wishes to disappear may provide himself with a circumstantial story as easily as with a new name. And at all events, between Abingdon and Shrewsbury it's possible they

113

may have encountered Luc Meverel alone and under his own name.'

'But if one of these two, either of these two, should truly be the man I want,' said Olivier doubtfully, 'then who, in the name of God, is the other?'

'We ask each other questions,' said Hugh practically, 'which either of these two could answer in a moment. Come, let's leave Abbot Radulfus to call them in, and see what comes of it.'

It was not difficult to induce the abbot to have the two young men sent for. It was not so easy to find them and bring them to speak for themselves. The messenger, sent forth in expectation of prompt obedience, came back after a much longer time than had been expected, and reported ruefully that neither of the pair could be found within the abbey walls. True, the porter had not actually seen either of them pass the gatehouse. But what had satisfied him that the two were leaving was that the young man Matthew had come, no long time after dinner, to reclaim his dagger, and had left behind him a generous gift of money to the house, saying that he and his friend were already bound away on their journey, and desired to offer thanks for their lodging. And had he seemed – it was Cadfael who asked it, himself hardly knowing why – had he seemed as he always was, or in any way disturbed or alarmed or out of countenance and temper, when he came for his weapon and paid his and his friend's score?

The messenger shook his head, having asked no such question at the gate. Brother Porter, when enquiry was made direct by Cadfael himself, said positively: 'He was like a man on fire. Oh, as soft as ever in voice, and courteous, but pale and alight, you'd have said his hair stood on end. But what with every soul within here wandering in a dream, since this wonder, I never thought but here were some going forth with the news while the furnace was still white-hot.'

'Gone?' said Olivier, dismayed, when this word was brought back to the abbot's parlour. 'Now I begin to see better cause why one of these two, for all they come so strangely paired, and so strangely account for themselves, may be the man I'm seeking. For if I do not know Luc Meverel by sight, I have been two or three times his lord's guest recently, and he may well have taken note of me. How if he saw me come, today, and is gone hence thus in haste because he does not wish to be

114

found? He could hardly know I am sent to look for him, but he might, for all that, prefer to put himself clean out of sight. And an ailing companion on the way would be good cover for a man wanting a reason for his wanderings. I wish I might yet speak with these two. How long have they been gone?'

'It cannot have been more than an hour and a half after noon,' said Cadfael, 'according to when Matthew reclaimed his dagger.'

'And afoot!' Olivier kindled hopefully. 'And even unshod, the one of them! It should be no great labour to overtake them, if it's known what road they will have taken.'

'By far their best way is by the Oswestry road, and so across the dyke into Wales. According to Brother Denis, that was Ciaran's declared intent.'

'Then, Father Abbot,' said Olivier eagerly, 'with your leave I'll mount and ride after them, for they cannot have got far. It would be a pity to miss the chance, and even if they are not who I'm seeking, neither they nor I will have lost anything. But with or without my man, I shall return here.'

'I'll ride through the town with you,' said Hugh, 'and set you on your way, for this will be new country to you. But then I must be about my own business, and see if we've gathered any harvest from this morning's hunt. I doubt they've gone deeper into the forest, or I should have had word by now. We shall look for you back before night, Olivier. One more night at the least we mean to keep you and longer if we can.'

Olivier took his leave hastily but gracefully, made a dutiful reverence to the abbot, and turned upon Brother Cadfael a brief, radiant smile that shattered his preoccupation for an instant like a sunburst through clouds. 'I will not leave here,' he said in simple reassurance, 'without having quiet conference with you. But this I must see finished, if I can.'

They were gone away briskly to the stables, where they had left their horses before Mass. Abbot Radulfus looked after them with a very thoughtful face.

'Do you find it surprising, Cadfael, that these two young pilgrims should leave so soon, and so abruptly? Is it possible the coming of Messire de Bretagne can have driven them away?'

Cadfael considered, and shook his head. 'No, I think not. In the great press this morning, and the excitement, why should one man among the many be noticed, and one not looked for at all in these parts? But, yes, their going does greatly surprise

115

me. For the one, he should surely be only too glad of an extra day or two of rest before taking barefoot to the roads again. And for the other – Father, there is a girl he certainly admires and covets, whether he yet knows it to the full or no, and with her he spent this morning, following Saint Winifred home, and I am certain there was then no other thought in his mind but of her and her kin, and the greatness of this day. For she is sister to the boy Rhun, who came by so great a mercy and blessing before our eyes. It would take some very strong compulsion to drag him away suddenly like this.'

'The boy's sister, you say?' Abbot Radulfus recalled an intent which had been shelved in favour of Olivier's quest. 'There is still an hour or more before Vespers. I should like to talk with this youth. You have been treating his condition, Cadfael. Do you think your handling has had anything to do with what we witnessed today? Or could he – though I would not willingly attribute falsity to one so young – could he have made more of his distress than it was, in order to produce a prodigy?'

'No,' said Cadfael very decidedly. 'There is no deceit at all in him. And as for my poor skills, they might in a long time of perseverance have softened the tight cords that hampered the use of his limb, and made it possible to set a little weight on it – but straighten that foot and fill out the sinews of the leg – never! The greatest doctor in the world could not have done it. Father, on the day he came I gave him a draught that should have eased his pain and brought him sleep. After three nights he sent it back to me untouched. He saw no reason why he should expect to be singled out for healing, but he said that he offered his pain freely, who had nothing else to give. Not to buy grace, but of his goodwill to give and want nothing in return. And further, it seems that thus having accepted his pain out of love, his pain left him. After Mass we saw that deliverance completed.'

'Then it was well deserved,' said Radulfus, pleased and moved. 'I must indeed talk with this boy. Will you find him for me, Cadfael, and bring him here to me now?'

'Very gladly, Father,' said Cadfael, and departed on his errand. Dame Alice was sitting in the sunshine of the cloister garth, the centre of a voluble circle of other matrons, her face so bright with the joy of the day that it warmed the very air; but Rhun was not with them. Melangell had withdrawn into the shadow of the arcade, as though the light was too bright for her eyes, and kept her face averted over the mending of a frayed seam in a linen shirt which must belong to her brother. Even when Cadfael addressed her she looked up only very swiftly and timidly, and again stooped into shadow, but even in that glimpse he saw that the joy which had made her shine like a new rose in the morning was dimmed and pale now in the lengthening afternoon. And was he merely imagining that her left cheek showed the faint bluish tint of a bruise? But at the mention of Rhun's name she smiled, as though at the recollection of happiness rather than its presence.

'He said he was tired, and went away into the dortoir to rest. Aunt Weaver thinks he is lying down on his bed, but I think he wanted only to be left alone, to be quiet and not have to talk. He is tired by having to answer things he seems not to understand himself.'

'He speaks another tongue today from the rest of mankind,' said Cadfael. 'It may well be we who don't understand, and ask things that have no meaning for him.' He took her gently by the chin and turned her face up to the light, but she twisted nervously out of his hold. 'You have hurt yourself?' Certainly it was a bruise beginning there.

'It's nothing,' she said. 'My own fault. I was in the garden, I ran too fast and I fell. I know it's unsightly, but it doesn't hurt now.'

Her eyes were very calm, not reddened, only a little swollen as to the lids. Well, Matthew had gone, abandoned her to go with his friend, letting her fall only too disastrously after the heady running together of the morning hours. That could account for tears now past. But should it account for a bruised cheek? He hesitated whether to question further, but clearly she did not wish it. She had gone back doggedly to her work, and would not look up again.

Cadfael sighed, and went out across the great court to the guest-hall. Even a glorious day like this one must have its vein of bitter sadness.

In the men's dortoir Rhun sat alone on his bed, very still and content in his blissfully restored body. He was deep in his own rapt thoughts, but readily aware when Cadfael entered. He looked round and smiled.

'Brother, I was wishing to see you. You were there, you know. Perhaps you even heard … See, how I'm changed!' The leg once maimed stretched out perfect before him, he bent and stamped the boards of the floor. He flexed ankle and toes,

117

drew up his knee to his chin, and everything moved as smoothly and painlessly as his ready tongue. 'I am whole! I never asked it, how dared I? Even then, I was praying not for this, and yet this was given ...' He went away again for a moment into his tranced dream.

Cadfael sat down beside him, noting the exquisite fluency of those joints hitherto flawed and intransigent. The boy's beauty was perfected now.

'You were praying,' said Cadfael gently, 'for Melangell.'

'Yes. And Matthew, too. I truly thought ... But you see he is gone. They are both gone, gone together. Why could I not bring my sister into bliss? I would have gone on crutches all my life for that, but I couldn't prevail.'

'That is not yet determined,' said Cadfael firmly. 'Who goes may also return. And I think your prayers should have strong virtue, if you do not fall into doubt now, because heaven has need of a little time. Even miracles have their times. Half our lives in this world are spent in waiting. It is needful to wait with faith.'

Rhun sat listening with an absent smile, and at the end of it he said: 'Yes, surely, and I will wait. For see, one of them left this behind in his haste when he went away.'

He reached down between the close-set cots, and lifted to the bed between them a bulky but lightweight scrip of unbleached linen, with stout leather straps for the owner's belt. 'I found it dropped between the two beds they had, drawn close together. I don't know which of them owned this one, the two they carried were much alike. But one of them doesn't expect or want ever to come back, does he? Perhaps Matthew does, and has forgotten this, whether he meant it or no, as a pledge.'

Cadfael stared and wondered, but this was a heavy matter, and not for him. He said seriously: 'I think you should bring this with you, and give it into the keeping of Father Abbot. For he sent me to bring you to him. He wants to speak with you.'

'With me?' wavered Rhun, stricken into a wild and rustic child again. 'The lord abbot himself?'

'Surely, and why not? You are Christian soul as he is, and may speak with him as equal.'

The boy faltered: 'I should be afraid ...'

'No, you would not. You are not afraid of anything, nor need you ever be.'

Rhun sat for a moment with fists doubled into the blanket of

118

his bed; then he lifted his clear, ice-blue gaze and blanched, angelic face and smiled blindingly into Cadfael's eyes. 'No, I need not. I'll come.' And he hoisted the linen scrip and stood up stately on his two long, youthful legs, and led the way to the door.

'Stay with us,' said Abbot Radulfus, when Cadfael would have presented his charge and left the two of them together. 'I think he might be glad of you.' Also, said his eloquent, austere glance, your presence may be of value to me as witness. 'Rhun knows you. Me he does not yet know, but I trust he shall, hereafter.' He had the drab, brownish scrip on the desk before him, offered on entry with a word to account for it, until the time came to explore its possibilities further.

'Willingly, Father,' said Cadfael heartily, and took his seat apart on a stool withdrawn into a corner, out of the way of those two pairs of formidable eyes that met, and wondered, and probed with equal intensity across the small space of the parlour. Outside the windows the garden blossomed with drunken exuberance, in the burning colours of summer, and the blanched blue sky, at its loftiest in the late afternoon, showed the colour of Rhun's eyes, but without their crystal blaze. The day of wonders was drawing very slowly and radiantly towards its evening.

'Son,' said Radulfus at his gentlest, 'you have been the vessel for a great mercy poured out here. I know, as all know who were there, what we saw, what we felt. But I would know also what you passed through. I know you have lived long with pain, and have not complained. I dare guess in what mind you approached the saint's altar. Tell me, what was it happened to you then?'

Rhun sat with his empty hands clasped quietly in his lap, and his face at once remote and easy, looking beyond the walls of the room. All his timidity was lost.

'I was troubled,' he said carefully, 'because my sister and my Aunt Alice wanted so much for me, and I knew I needed nothing. I would have come, and prayed, and passed, and been content. But then I heard her call.'

'Saint Winifred spoke to you?' asked Radulfus softly.

'She called me to her,' said Rhun positively.

'In what words?'

'No words. What need had she of words? She called me to go to her, and I went. She told me, here is a step, and here, and

119

here, come, you know you can. And I knew I could, so I went. When she told me, kneel, for so you can, then I kneeled, and I could. Whatever she told me, that I did. And so I will still,' said Rhun, smiling into the opposing wall with eyes that paled the sun.

'Child,' said the abbot, watching him in solemn wonder and respect, 'I do believe it. What skills you have, what gifts to stead you in your future life, I scarcely know. I rejoice that you have to the full the blessing of your body, and the purity of your mind and spirit. I wish you whatever calling you may choose, and the virtue of your resolve to guide you in it. If there is anything you can ask of this house, to aid you after you go forth from here, it is yours.'

'Father,' said Rhun earnestly, withdrawing his blinding gaze into shadow and mortality, and becoming the child he was, 'need I go forth? She called me to her, how tenderly I have no words to tell. I desire to remain with her to my life's end. She called me to her, and I will never willingly leave her.'

Chapter Twelve

'ND WILL you keep him?' asked Cadfael, when the boy had been dismissed, made his deep reverence, and departed in his rapt, unwitting perfection.

'If his intent holds, yes, surely. He is the living proof of grace. But I will not let him take vows in haste, to regret them later. Now he is transported with joy and wonder, and would embrace celibacy and seclusion with delight. If his will is still the same in a month, then I will believe in it, and welcome him gladly. But he shall serve his full novitiate, even so. I will not let him close the door upon himself until he is sure. And now,' said the abbot, frowning down thoughtfully at the linen scrip that lay upon his desk, 'what is to be done with this? You say it was fallen between the two beds, and might have belonged to either?'

'So the boy said. But, Father, if you remember, when the bishop's ring was stolen, both those young men gave up their scrips to be examined. What each of them carried, apart from the dagger that was duly delivered over at the gatehouse, I cannot say with certainty, but Father Prior, who handled them, will know.'

'True, so he will. But for the present,' said Radulfus, 'I cannot think we have any right to probe into either man's possessions, nor is it of any great importance to discover to which of them this belongs. If Messire de Bretagne overtakes them, as he surely must, we shall learn more, he may even persuade them to return. We'll wait for his word first. In the meantime, leave it here with me. When we know more we'll take whatever steps we can to restore it.'

The day of wonders drew in to its evening as graciously as it had dawned, with a clear sky and soft, sweet air. Every soul within the enclave came dutifully to Vespers, and supper in the guest-hall as in the refectory was a devout and tranquil feast. The voices hasty and shrill with excitement at dinner had softened and eased into the grateful languor of fulfilment.

Brother Cadfael absented himself from Collations in the chapter house, and went out into the garden. On the gentle ridge where the gradual slope of the pease fields began he stood for a long while watching the sky. The declining sun had still an hour or more of its course to run before its rim dipped into the feathery tops of the copses across the brook. The west which had reflected the dawn as this day began triumphed now in pale gold, with no wisp of cloud to dye it deeper or mark its purity. The scent of the herbs within the walled garden rose in a heady cloud of sweetness and spice. A good place, a resplendent day – why should any man slip away and run from it?

A useless question. Why should any man do the things he does? Why should Ciaran submit himself to such hardship? Why should he profess such piety and devotion, and yet depart without leave-taking and without thanks in the middle of so auspicious a day? It was Matthew who had left a gift of money on departure. Why could not Matthew persuade his friend to stay and see out the day? And why should he, who had glowed with excited joy in the morning, and run hand in hand with Melangell, abandon her without remorse in the afternoon, and resume his harsh pilgrimage with Ciaran as if nothing had happened?

Were they two men or three, Ciaran, Matthew and Luc Meverel? What did he know of them, all three, if three they were? Luc Meverel had been seen for the last time south of Newbury, walking north towards that town, and alone. Ciaran and Matthew were first reported, by Brother Adam of Reading, coming from the south into Abingdon for their night's lodging, two together. If one of them was Luc Meverel, then where and why had he picked up his companion, and above all, *who was his companion*?

By this time, surely Olivier should have overhauled his quarry, and found the answers to some of these questions. And he had said he would return, that he would not leave Shrewsbury without having some converse with a man remembered as a good friend. Cadfael took that assurance to his heart, and was warmed.

It was not the need to tend any of his herbal potions or bubbling wines that drew him to walk on to his workshop, for Brother Oswin, now in the chapter house with his fellows, had tidied everything for the night, and seen the brazier safely out. There was flint and tinder there in a box, in case it should be necessary to light it again in the night or early in the morning. It was rather that Cadfael had grown accustomed to withdrawing to his own special solitude to do his best thinking, and this day had given him more than enough cause for thought, as for gratitude. For where were his qualms now? Miracles may be spent as frequently on the undeserving as on the deserving. What marvel that a saint should take the boy Rhun to her heart, and reach out her sustaining hand to him? But the second miracle was doubly miraculous, far beyond her sorry servant's asking, stunning in its generosity. To bring him back Olivier, whom he had resigned to God and the great world, and made himself content never to see again! And then Hugh's voice, unwitting herald of wonders, said out of the dim choir, 'And are you demanding yet a second miracle?' He had rather been humbling himself in wonder and thanks for one, demanding nothing more; but he had turned his head, and beheld Olivier.

The western sky was still limpid and bright, liquid gold, the sun still clear of the treetops, when he opened the door of his workshop and stepped within, into the timber-warm, herb-scented dimness. He thought and said afterwards that it was at that moment he saw the inseparable relationship between Ciaran and Matthew suddenly overturned, twisted into its opposite, and began, in some enclosed and detached part of his intelligence, to make sense of the whole matter, however dubious and flawed the revelation. But he had no time to catch and pin down the vision, for as his foot crossed the threshold there was a soft gasp somewhere in the shadowy corner of the hut, and a rustle of movement, as if some wild creature had been disturbed in its lair, and shrunk into the last fastness to defend itself.

He halted, and set the door wide open behind him for reassurance that there was a possibility of escape. 'Be easy!' he said mildly. 'May I not come into my own workshop without

123

leave? And should I be entering here to threaten any soul with harm?'

His eyes, growing accustomed rapidly to the dimness, which seemed dark only by contrast with the radiance outside, scanned the shelves, the bubbling jars of wine in a fat row, the swinging, rustling swathes of herbs dangling from the beams of the low roof. Everything took shape and emerged into view. Stretched along the broad wooden bench against the opposite wall, a huddle of tumbled skirts stirred slowly and reared itself upright, to show him the spilled ripe-corn gold of a girl's hair, and the tear-stained, swollen-lidded countenance of Melangell.

She said no word, but she did not drop blindly into her sheltering arms again. She was long past that, and past being afraid to show herself so to one secret, quiet creature whom she trusted. She set down her feet in their scuffed leather shoes to the floor, and sat back against the timbers of the wall, bracing slight shoulders to the solid contact. She heaved one enormous, draining sigh that was dragged up from her very heels, and left her weak and docile. When he crossed the beaten earth floor and sat down beside her, she did not flinch away.

'Now,' said Cadfael, settling himself with deliberation, to give her time to compose at least her voice. The soft light would spare her face. 'Now, child dear, there is no one here who can either save you or trouble you, and therefore you can speak freely, for everything you say is between us two only. But we two together need to take careful counsel. So what is it you know that I do not know?'

'Why should we take counsel?' she said in a small, drear voice from below his solid shoulder. 'He is gone.'

'What is gone may return. The roads lead always two ways, hither as well as yonder. What are you doing out here alone, when your brother walks erect on two sound feet, and has all he wants in this world, but for your absence?'

He did not look directly at her, but felt the stir of warmth and softness through her body, which must have been a smile, however flawed. 'I came away,' she said, very low, 'not to spoil his joy. I've borne most of the day. I think no one has noticed half my heart was gone out of me. Unless it was you,' she said, without blame, rather in resignation.

'I saw you when we came from Saint Giles,' said Cadfael, 'you and Matthew. Your heart was whole then, so was his. If yours is torn in two now, do you suppose his is preserved without wound? No! So what passed, afterwards? What was this sword that shore through your heart and his? You know! You may tell it now. They are gone, there is nothing left to spoil. There may yet be something to save.'

She turned her forehead into his shoulder and wept in silence for a little while. The light within the hut grew rather than dimming, now that his eyes were accustomed. She forgot to hide her forlorn and bloated face, he saw the bruise on her cheek darkening into purple. He laid an arm about her and drew her close for the comfort of the flesh. That of the spirit would need more of time and thought.

'He struck you?'

'I held him,' she said, quick in his defence. 'He could not get free.'

'And he was so frantic? He *must* go?'

'Yes, whatever it cost him or me. Oh, Brother Cadfael, why? I thought, I believed he loved me, as I do him. But see how he used me in his anger!'

'Anger?' said Cadfael sharply, and turned her by the shoulders to study her more intently. 'Whatever the compulsion on him to go with his friend, why should he be angry with you? The loss was yours, but surely no blame.'

'He blamed me for not telling him,' she said drearily. 'But I did only what Ciaran asked of me. For his sake and yours, he said, yes, and for mine, too, let me go, but hold him fast. Don't tell him I have the ring again, he said, and I will go. Forget me, he said, and help him to forget me. He wanted us to remain together and be happy ...'

'Are you telling me,' demanded Cadfael sharply, 'that *they did not go together*? That Ciaran made off without him?'

'It was not like that,' sighed Melangell. 'He meant well by us, that's why he stole away alone ...'

'When was this? When? When did you have speech with him? *When* did he go?'

'I was here at dawn, you'll remember. I met Ciaran by the brook ...' She drew a deep, desolate breath and loosed the whole flood of it, every word she could recall of that meeting in the early morning, while Cadfael gazed appalled, and the vague glimpse he had had of enlightenment awoke and stirred again in his mind, far clearer now.

'Go on! Tell me what followed between you and Matthew. You did as you were bidden, I know, you drew him with you, I doubt he ever gave a thought to Ciaran all those morning

125

hours, believing him still penned within doors, afraid to stir. When was it he found out?'

'After dinner it came into his mind that he had not seen him. He was very uneasy. He went to look for him everywhere ... He came to me here in the garden. "God keep you, Melangell," he said, "you must fend for yourself now, sorry as I am ..." ' Almost every word of that encounter she had by heart, she repeated them like a tired child repeating a lesson. 'I said too much, he knew I had spoken with Ciaran ... he knew that I knew he'd meant to go secretly ...'

'And then, after you had owned as much?'

'He laughed,' she said, and her very voice froze into a despairing whisper. 'I never heard him laugh until this morning, and then it was such a sweet sound. But this laughter was not so! Bitter and raging.' She stumbled through the rest of it, every word another fine line added to the reversed image that grew in Cadfael's mind, mocking his memory. '*He* sets *me* free!' And '*You* must be his confederate!' The words were so burned on her mind that she even reproduced the savagery of their utterance. And how few words it took, in the end, to transform everything, to turn devoted attendance into remorseless pursuit, selfless love into dedicated hatred, noble self-sacrifice into calculated flight, and the voluntary mortification of the flesh into body armour which must never be doffed.

He heard again, abruptly and piercingly, Ciaran's wild cry of alarm as he clutched his cross to him, and Matthew's voice saying softly: 'Yet he should doff it. How else can he truly be rid of his pains?'

How else, indeed! Cadfael recalled, too, how he had reminded them both that they were here to attend the feast of a saint who might have life itself within her gift – 'even for a man already condemned to death!' Oh Saint Winifred, stand by me now, stand by us all, with a third miracle to better the other two!

He took Melangell brusquely by the chin, and lifted her face to him. 'Girl, look to yourself now for a while, for I must leave you. Do up your hair and keep a brave face, and go back to your kin as soon as you can bear their eyes on you. Go into the church for a time, it will be quiet there now, and who will wonder if you give a longer time to your prayers? They will not even wonder at past tears, if you can smile now. Do as well as you can, for I have a thing I must do.'

There was nothing he could promise her, no sure hope he

126

could leave with her. He turned from her without another word, leaving her staring after him between dread and reassurance, and went striding in haste through the gardens and out across the court, to the abbot's lodging.

If Radulfus was surprised to have Cadfael ask audience again so soon, he gave no sign of it, but had him admitted at once, and put aside his book to give his full attention to whatever this fresh business might be. Plainly it was something very much to the current purpose and urgent.

'Father,' said Cadfael, making short work of explanations, 'there's a new twist here. Messire de Bretagne has gone off on a false trail. Those two young men did not leave by the Oswestry road, but crossed the Meole brook and set off due west to reach Wales the nearest way. Nor did they leave together. Ciaran slipped away during the morning, while his fellow was with us in the procession, and Matthew has followed him by the same way as soon as he learned of his going. And, Father, there's good cause to think that the sooner they're overtaken and halted, the better surely for one, and I believe for both. I beg you, let me take a horse and follow. And send word of this to Hugh Beringar in the town, to come after us on the same trail.'

Radulfus received all this with a grave but calm face, and asked no less shortly: 'How did you come by this word?'

'From the girl who spoke with Ciaran before he departed. No need to doubt it is all true. And, Father, one more thing before you bid me go. Open, I beg you, that scrip they left behind, let me see if it has anything more to tell us of this pair – at the least, of one of them.'

Without a word or an instant of hesitation, Radulfus dragged the linen scrip into the light of his candles, and unbuckled the fastening. The contents he drew out fully upon the desk, sparse enough, what the poor pilgrim would carry, having few possessions and desiring to travel light.

'You know, I think,' said the abbot, looking up sharply, 'to which of the two this belonged?'

'I do not know, but I guess. In my mind I am sure, but I am also fallible. Give me leave!'

With a sweep of his hand he spread the meagre belongings over the desk. The purse, thin enough when Prior Robert had handled it before, lay flat and empty now. The leather-bound breviary, well-used, worn but treasured, had been rolled into the folds of the shirt, and when Cadfael reached for it the shirt slid from the desk and fell to the floor. He let it lie as he opened the book. Within the cover was written, in a clerk's careful hand, the name of its owner: 'Juliana Bossard'. And below, in newer ink and a less practised hand: *Given to me, Luc Meverel, this Christmastide, 1140. God be with us all!*

'So I pray, too,' said Cadfael, and stooped to pick up the fallen shirt. He held it up to the light, and his eye caught the thread-like outline of a stain that rimmed the left shoulder. His eye followed the line over the shoulder, and found it continued down and round the left side of the breast. The linen, otherwise, was clean enough, bleached by several launderings from its original brownish natural colouring. He spread it open, breast up, on the desk. The thin brown line, sharp on its outer edge, slightly blurred within, hemmed a great space spanning the whole left part of the chest and the upper part of the left sleeve. The space within the outline had been washed clear of any stain, even the rim was pale, but it stood clear to be seen, and the scattered shadowings of colour within it preserved a faint hint of what had been there.

Radulfus, if he had not ventured as far afield in the world as Cadfael, had nevertheless stored up some experience of it. He viewed the extended evidence and said composedly, 'This was blood.'

'So it was,' said Cadfael, and rolled up the shirt.

'And whoever owned this scrip came from where a certain Juliana Bossard was chatelaine.' His deep eyes were steady and sombre on Cadfael's face. 'Have we entertained a murderer in our house?'

'I think we have,' said Cadfael, restoring the scattered fragments of a life to their modest lodging. A man's life, shorn of all expectation of continuance, even the last coin gone from the purse. 'But I think we may have time yet to prevent another killing – if you give me leave to go.'

'Take the best of what may be in the stable,' said the abbot simply, 'and I will send word to Hugh Beringar, and have him follow you, and not alone.'

Chapter Thirteen

EVERAL MILES north on the Oswestry road, Olivier drew rein by the roadside where a wiry, bright-eyed boy was grazing goats on the broad verge, lush in summer growth and coming into seed. The child twitched one of his long leads on his charges, to bring him along gently where the early evening light lay warm on the tall grass. He looked up at the rider without awe, half-Welsh and immune from servility. He smiled and gave an easy good evening.

The boy was handsome, bold, unafraid; so was the man. They looked at each other and liked what they saw.

'God be with you!' said Olivier. 'How long have you been pasturing your beasts along here? And have you in all that time seen a lame man and a well man go by, the pair of them much of my age, but afoot?'

'God be with you, master,' said the boy cheerfully. 'Here along this verge ever since noon, for I brought my bit of dinner with me. But I've seen none such pass. And I've had a word by the road with every soul that did go by, unless he were galloping.'

'Then I waste my hurrying,' said Olivier, and idled a while, his horse stooping to the tips of the grasses. 'They cannot be ahead of me, not by this road. See, now, supposing they wished to go earlier into Wales, how may I bear round to pick them up on the way? They went from Shrewsbury town ahead of me, and I have word to bring to them. Where can I turn west and fetch a circle about the town?'

The young herdsman accepted with open arms every exchange that refreshed his day's labour. He gave his mind to the best road offering, and delivered judgement: 'Turn back but a mile or more, back across the bridge at Montford, and then you'll find a well-used cart-track that bears off west, to your right hand it will be. Bear a piece west again where the paths first branch, it's no direct way, but it does go on. It skirts Shrewsbury a matter of above four miles outside the town, and threads the edges of the forest, but it cuts across every path out of Shrewsbury. You may catch your men yet. And I wish you may!'

'My thanks for that,' said Olivier, 'and for your advice also.' He stooped to the hand the boy had raised, not for alms but to caress the horse's chestnut shoulder with admiration and pleasure, and slipped a coin into the smooth palm. 'God be with you!' he said, and wheeled his mount and set off back along the road he had travelled.

'And go with you, master!' the boy called after him, and watched until a curve of the road took horse and rider out of sight beyond a stand of trees. The goats gathered closer; evening was near, and they were ready to turn homeward, knowing the hour by the sun as well as did their herd. The boy drew in their tethers, whistled to them cheerily, and moved on along the road to his homeward path through the fields.

Olivier came for the second time to the bridge over the Severn, one bank a steep, tree-clad escarpment, the other open, level meadow. Beyond the first plane of fields a winding track turned off to the right, between scattered stands of trees, bearing at this point rather south than west, but after a mile or more it brought him on to a better road that crossed his track left and right. He bore right into the sun, as he had been instructed, and at the next place where two dwindling paths divided he turned left, and keeping his course by the sinking sun on his right hand, now just resting upon the rim of the world and glimmering through the trees in sudden blinding glimpses, began to work his way gradually round the town of Shrewsbury. The tracks wound in and out of copses, the fringe woods of the northern tip of the Long Forest, sometimes in twilight among dense trees, sometimes in open heath and scrub, sometimes past islets of cultivated fields and glimpses of hamlets. He rode with ears pricked for any promising sound, pausing wherever his labyrinthine path crossed a track bearing

130

westward out of Shrewsbury, and wherever he met with cottage or assart he asked after his two travellers. No one had seen such a pair pass by. Olivier took heart. They had had some hours start of him, but if they had not passed westward by any of the roads he had yet crossed, they might still be within the circle he was drawing about the town. The barefoot one would not find these ways easy going, and might have been forced to take frequent rests. At the worst, even if he missed ·them in the end, this meandering route must bring him round at last to the highroad by which he had first approached Shrewsbury from the south-east, and he could ride back into the town to Hugh Beringar's welcome, none the worse for a little exercise in a fine evening.

Brother Cadfael had wasted no time in clambering into his boots, kilting his habit, and taking and saddling the best horse he could find in the stables. It was not often he had the chance to indulge himself with such half-forgotten delights, but he was not thinking of that now. He had left considered word with the messenger who was already hurrying across the bridge and into the town, to alert Hugh; and Hugh would ask no questions, as the abbot had asked none, recognising the grim urgency there was no leisure now to explain.

'Say to Hugh Beringar,' the order ran, 'that Ciaran will make for the Welsh border the nearest way, but avoiding the too open roads. I think he'll bear south a small way to the old road the Romans made, that we've been fools enough to let run wild, for it keeps a steady level and makes straight for the border north of Caus.'

That was drawing a bow at a venture, and he knew it, none better. Ciaran was not of these parts, though he might well have some knowledge of the borderland if he had kin on the Welsh side. But more than that, he had been here these three days past, and if he had been planning some such escape all that time, he could have picked the brains of brothers and guests, on easily plausible ground. Time pressed, and sound guessing was needed. Cadfael chose his way, and set about pursuing it.

He did not waste time in going decorously out at the gatehouse and round by the road to take up the chase westward, but led his horse at a trot through the gardens, to the blank astonishment of Brother Jerome, who happened to be crossing to the cloisters a good ten minutes early for

Compline. No doubt he would report, with a sense of outrage, to Prior Robert. Cadfael as promptly forgot him, leading the horse round the unharvested pease-field and down to the quiet green stretches of the brook, and across to the narrow meadow, where he mounted. The sun was dipping its rim beyond the crowns of the trees to westward. Into that half-shine half-shadow Cadfael spurred, and made good speed while the tracks were familiar to him as his own palm. Due west until he hit the road, a half-mile on the road at a canter, until it turned too far to the south, and then westward again for the setting sun. Ciaran had a long start, even of Matthew, let alone of all those who followed now. But Ciaran was lame, burdened and afraid. Almost he was to be pitied.

Half a mile further on, at an inconspicuous track which he knew, Cadfael again turned to bear south-west, and burrowed into deepest shade, and into the northernmost woodlands of the Long Forest. No more than a narrow forest ride, this, between sweeping branches, a fragment of ancient wood not worth clearing for an assart, being bedded on rock that broke surface here and there. This was not yet border country, but close kin to it, heaving into fretful outcrops that broke the thin soil, bearing heather and coarse upland grasses, scrub bushes and sparsity trees, then bringing forth prodigal life roofed by very old trees in every wet hollow. A little further on this course, and the close, dark woods began, tall top cover, heavy interweaving of middle growth, and a tangle of bush and bramble and ground-cover below. Undisturbed forest, though there were rare islands of tillage bright and open within it, every one an astonishment.

Then he came to the old, old road, that sliced like a knife across his path, heading due east, due west. He wondered about the men who had made it. It was shrunken now from a soldiers' road to a narrow ride, mostly under thin turf, but it ran as it had always run since it was made, true and straight as a lance, perfectly levelled where a level was possible, relentlessly climbing and descending where some hummock barred the way. Cadfael turned west into it, and rode straight for the golden upper arc of sun that still glowed between the branches.

In the parcel of old forest north and west of the hamlet of Hanwood there were groves where stray outlaws could find ample cover, provided they stayed clear of the few settlements within reach. Local people tended to fence their holdings and band together to protect their own small ground. The forest was for plundering, poaching, pasturing of swine, all with secure precautions. Travellers, though they might call on hospitality and aid where needed, must fend for themselves in the thicker coverts, if they cared to venture through them. By and large, safety here in Shropshire under Hugh Beringar was as good as anywhere in England, and encroachment by vagabonds could not survive long, but for brief occupation the cover was there, and unwanted tenants might take up occupation if pressed.

Several of the lesser manors in these border regions had declined by reason of their perilous location, and some were half-deserted, leaving their fields untilled. Until April of this year the border castle of Caus had been in Welsh hands, an added threat to peaceful occupation, and there had not yet been time since Hugh's reclamation of the castle for the depleted hamlets to re-establish themselves. Moreover, in this high summer it was no hardship to live wild, and skilful poaching and a little profitable thievery could keep two or three good fellows in meat while they allowed time for their exploits in the south to be forgotten, and made up their minds where best to pass the time until a return home seemed possible.

Master Simeon Poer, self-styled merchant of Guildford, was not at all ill-content with the pickings made in Shrewsbury. In three nights, which was the longest they dared reckon on operating unsuspected, they had taken a fair amount of money from the hopeful gamblers of the town and Foregate, besides the price Daniel Aurifaber had paid for the stolen ring, the various odds and ends William Hales had abstracted from market stalls, and the coins John Shure had used his long, smooth, waxed finger-nails to extract from pocket and purse in the crowds. It was a pity they had had to leave William Hales to his fate during the raid, but all in all they had done well to get out of it with no more than a bruise or two, and one man short. Bad luck for William, but it was the way the lot had fallen. Every man knew it could happen to him.

They had avoided the used tracks, refraining from meddling with any of the local people going about their business, and done their plundering by night and stealthily, after first making sure where there were dogs to be reckoned with. They even had a roof of sorts, for in the deepest thickets below the old road, overgrown and well-concealed, they had found the

133

remains of a hut, relic of a failed assart abandoned long ago. After a few days more of this easy living, or if the weather should change, they would set off to make their way somewhat south, to be well clear of Shrewsbury before moving across to the east, to shires where they were not yet known.

When the rare traveller came past on the road, it was almost always a local man, and they let him alone, for he would be missed all too soon, and the hunt would be up in a day. But they would not have been averse to waylaying any solitary who was clearly a stranger and on his way to more distant places, since he was unlikely to be missed at once, and further, he was likely to be better worth robbing, having on him the means to finance his journey, however modestly. In these woods and thickets, a man could vanish very neatly, and for ever.

They had made themselves comfortable that night outside their hut, with the embers of their fire safe in the clay-lined hollow they had made for it, and the grease of the stolen chicken still on their fingers. The sunset of the outer world was already twilight here, but they had their night eyes, and were wide awake and full of restless energy after an idle day. Walter Bagot was charged with keeping such watch as they thought needful, and had made his way in cover some distance along the narrow track towards the town. He came sliding back in haste, but shining with anticipation instead of alarm.

'Here's one coming we may safely pick off. The barefoot fellow from the abbey ... well back as yet, and lame as ever, he's been among the stones, surely. Not a soul will know where he went to.'

'He?' said Simeon Poer, surprised. 'Fool, he has always his shadow breathing down his neck. It would mean both – if one got away he'd raise the hunt on us.'

'He has not his shadow now,' said Bagot gleefully. 'Alone, I tell you, he's shaken him off, or else they've parted by consent. Who else cares a groat what becomes of him?'

'And a groat's his worth,' said Shure scornfully. 'Let him go. It's never worth it for his hose and shirt, and what else can he have on him?'

'Ah, but he has! Money, my friend!' said Bagot, glittering. 'Make no mistake, that one goes very well provided, if he takes good care not to let it be known. I know! I've felt my way about him every time I could get crowded against him in church, he has a solid, heavy purse belted about him inside coat, hose, shirt and all, but I never could get my fingers into it without using the knife, and that was too risky. He can pay his way wherever he goes. Come, rouse, he'll be an easy mark now.'

He was certain, and they were heartily willing to pick up an extra purse. They rose merrily, hands on daggers, worming their way quietly through the underbrush towards the thin thread of the track, above which the ribbon of clear sky showed pale and bright still. Shure and Bagot lurking invisible on the near side of the path, Simeon Poer across it, behind the lush screen of bushes that took advantage of the open light to grow leafy and tall. There were very old trees in their tract of forest, enormous beeches with trunks so gnarled and thick three men with arms outspread could hardly clip them. Old woodland was being cleared, assarted and turned into hunting-grounds in many places, but the Long Forest still preserved large tracts of virgin growth untouched. In the green dimness the three masterless men stood still as the trees, and waited.

Then they heard him. Dogged, steady, laborious steps that stirred the coarse grasses. In the turfed verge of a highroad he could have gone with less pain and covered twice the miles he had accomplished on these rough ways. They heard his heavy breathing while he was still twenty yards away from them, and saw his tall, dark figure stir the dimness, leaning forward on a long, knotty staff he had picked up somewhere from among the debris of the trees. It seemed that he favoured the right foot, though both trod with wincing tenderness, as though he had trodden askew on a sharp-edged stone, and either cut his sole or twisted his ankle-joint. He was piteous, if there had been anyone to pity him.

He went with ears pricked, and the very hairs of his skin erected, in as intense wariness as any of the small nocturnal creatures that crept and quaked in the underbrush around him. He had walked in fear every step of the miles he had gone in company, but now, cast loose to his own dreadful company, he was even more afraid. Escape was no escape at all.

It was the extremity of his fear that saved him. They had let him pass slowly by the first covert, so that Bagot might be behind him, and Poer and Shure one on either side before him. It was not so much his straining ears as the prickly sensitivity of his skin that sensed the sudden rushing presence at his back, the shifting of the cool evening air, and the weight of body and arm launched at him almost silently. He gave a muted shriek

135

and whirled about, sweeping the staff around him, and the knife that should have impaled him struck the branch and sliced a ribbon of bark and wood from it. Bagot reached with his left hand for a grip on sleeve or coat, and struck again as nimbly as a snake, but missed his hold as Ciaran leaped wildly back out of reach, and driven beyond himself by terror, turned and plunged away on his lacerated feet, aside from the path and into the deepest and thickest shadows among the tangled trees. He hissed and moaned with pain as he went, but he ran like a startled hare.

Who would have thought he could still move so fast, once pushed to extremes? But he could not keep it up long, the spur would not carry him far. The three of them went after, spreading out a little to hem him from three sides when he fell exhausted. They were giggling as they went, and in no special haste. The mingled sounds of his crashing passage through the bushes and his uncontrollable whining with the pain of it, rang unbelievably strangely in the twilit woods.

Branches and brambles lashed Ciaran's face. He ran blindly, sweeping the long staff before him, cutting a noisy swathe through the bushes and stumbling painfully in the thick ground-debris of dead branches and soft, treacherous pits of the leaves of many years. They followed at leisure, aware that he was slowing. The lean, agile tailor had drawn level with him, somewhat aside, and was bearing round to cut him off, still with breath enough to whistle to his fellows as they closed unhurriedly, like dogs herding a stray sheep. Ciaran fell out into a more open glade, where a huge old beech had preserved its own clearing, and with what was left of his failing breath he made a last dash to cross the open and vanish again into the thickets beyond. The dry silt of leaves among the roots betrayed him. His footing slid from under him, and fetched him down heavily against the bole of the tree. He had just time to drag himself up and set his back to the broad trunk before they were on him.

He flailed about him with the staff, screaming for aid, and never even knew on what name he was calling in his extremity.

'Help! Murder! Matthew, Matthew, help me!'

There was no answering shout, but there was an abrupt thrashing of branches, and something hurtled out of cover and across the grass, so suddenly that Bagot was shouldered aside and stumbled to his knees. A long arm swept Ciaran back hard against the solid bole of the tree, and Matthew stood braced beside him, his dagger naked in his hand. What remained of the western light showed his face roused and formidable, and gleamed along the blade.

'Oh, no!' he challenged loud and eager, lips drawn back from bared teeth. 'Keep your hands off! This man is mine!'

Chapter Fourteen

HE THREE attackers had drawn off instinctively, before they realised that this was but one man erupting in their midst, but they were quick to grasp it, and had not gone far. They stood, wary as beasts of prey but undeterred, weaving a little in a slow circle out of reach, but with no thought of withdrawing. They watched and considered, weighing up coldly these altered odds. Two men and a knife to reckon with now, and this second one they knew as well as the first. They had been some days frequenting the same enclave, using the same dortoir and refectory. They reasoned without dismay that they must be known as well as they knew their prey. The twilight made faces shadowy, but a man is recognised by more things than his face.

'I said it, did I not?' said Simeon Poer, exchanging glances with his henchmen, glances which were understood even in the dim light. 'I said he would not be far. No matter, two can lie as snug as one.'

Once having declared his claim and his rights, Matthew said nothing. The tree against which they braced themselves was so grown that they could not be attacked from close behind. He circled it steadily when Bagot edged round to the far side, keeping his face to the enemy. There were three to watch, and Ciaran was shaken and lame, and in no case to match any of the three if it came to action, though he kept his side of the trunk with his staff gripped and ready, and would fight if he must, tooth and claw, for his forfeit life. Matthew curled his lips in a bitter smile at the thought that he might be grateful yet for that strong appetite for living.

Round the bole of the tree, with his cheek against the bark, Ciaran said, low-voiced: 'You'd have done better not to follow me.'

'Did I not swear to go with you to the very end?' said Matthew as softly. 'I keep my vows. This one above all.'

'Yet you could still have crept away safely. Now we are two dead men.'

'Not yet! If you did not want me, why did you call me?'

There was a bewildered silence. Ciaran did not know he had uttered a name.

'We are grown used to each other,' said Matthew grimly. 'You claimed me, as I claim you. Do you think I'll let any other man have you?'

The three watchers had gathered in a shadowy group, conferring with heads together, and faces still turned towards their prey.

'Now they'll come,' said Ciaran in the dead voice of despair.

'No, they'll wait for darkness.'

They were in no hurry. They made no loose, threatening moves, wasted no breath on words. They bided their time as patiently as hunting animals. Silently they separated, spacing themselves round the clearing, and backing just far enough into cover to be barely visible, yet visible all the same, for their presence and stillness were meant to unnerve. Just so, motionless, relentless and alert, would a cat sit for hours outside a mousehole.

'This I cannot bear,' said Ciaran in a faint whisper, and drew sobbing breath.

'It is easily cured,' said Matthew through his teeth. 'You have only to lift off that cross from your neck, and you can be loosed from all your troubles.'

The light faded still. Their eyes, raking the smoky darkness of the bushes, were beginning to see movement where there was none, and strain in vain after it where it lurked and shifted to baffle them more. This waiting would not be long. The attackers circled in cover, watching for the unguarded moment when one or other of their victims would be caught unawares, staring in the wrong direction. Past all question they would expect that failure first from Ciaran, half-foundering as he already was. Soon now, very soon.

139

Brother Cadfael was some half-mile back along the ride when he heard the cry, ahead and to the right of the path, loud, wild and desperate. The words were indistinguishable, but the panic in the sound there was no mistaking. In this woodland silence, without even a wind to stir the branches or flutter the leaves, every sound carried clearly. Cadfael spurred ahead in haste, with all too dire a conviction of what he might find when he reached the source of that lamentable cry. All those miles of pursuit, patient and remorseless, half the length of England, might well be ending now, barely a quarter of an hour too soon for him to do anything to prevent. Matthew had overtaken, surely, a Ciaran grown weary of his penitential austerities, now there was no one by to see. He had said truly enough that he did not hate himself so much as to bear his hardships to no purpose. Now that he was alone, had he felt safe in discarding his heavy cross, and would he next have been in search of shoes for his feet? If Matthew had not come upon him thus recreant and disarmed.

The second sound to break the stillness almost passed unnoticed because of the sound of his own progress, but he caught some quiver of the forest's unease, and reined in to listen intently. The rush and crash of something or someone hurtling through thick bushes, fast and arrow-straight, and then, very briefly, a confusion of cries, not loud but sharp and wary, and a man's voice loud and commanding over all. Matthew's voice, not in triumph or terror, rather in short and resolute defiance. There were more than the two of them, there ahead, and not so far ahead now.

He dismounted, and led his horse at an anxious trot as far as he dared along the path, towards the spot from which the sounds had come. Hugh could move very fast when he saw reason, and in Cadfael's bare message he would have found reason enough. He would have left the town by the most direct way, over the western bridge and so by a good road south west, to strike this old path barely two miles back. At this moment he might be little more than a mile behind. Cadfael tethered his horse at the side of the track, for a plain sign that he had found cause to halt here and was somewhere close by.

All was quiet about him now. He quested along the fringe of bushes for a place where he might penetrate without any betraying noise, and began to work his way by instinct and touch towards the place whence the cries had come, and where now all was almost unnaturally silent. In a little while he was aware of the last faint pallor of the afterglow glimmering between the branches. There was a more open glade ahead of him.

He froze and stood motionless, as a shadow passed silently between him and this lingering glimpse of light. Someone tall and lean, slithering snake-like through the bushes. Cadfael waited until the faint pattern of light was restored, and then edged carefully forward until he could see into the clearing.

The great bole of a beech-tree showed in the centre, a solid mass beneath its spread of branches. There was movement there in the dimness. Not one man, but two, stood pressed against the bole. A brief flash of steel caught just light enough to show what it was, a dagger naked and ready. Two at bay here, and surely more than one pinning them thus helpless until they could be safely pulled down. Cadfael stood still to survey the whole of the darkening clearing, and found, as he had expected, another quiver of leaves that hid a man, and then, on the opposite side, yet another. Three, probably all armed, certainly up to no good, thus furtively prowling the woods by night, going nowhere, waiting to make the kill. Three had vanished from the dice school under the bridge at Shrewsbury, and fled in this direction. Three reappeared here in the forest, still doing after their disreputable kind.

Cadfael stood hesitant, pondering how best to deal, whether to steal back to the path and wait and hope for Hugh's coming, or attempt something alone, at least to distract and dismay, to bring about a delay that might afford time for help to come. He had made up his mind to return to his horse, mount, and ride in here with as much noise and turmoil as he could muster, trying to sound like six mounted men instead of one, when with shattering suddenness the decision was taken out of his hands.

One of the three besiegers sprang out of cover with a startling shout, and rushed at the tree on the side where the momentary flash of steel had shown one of the victims, at least, to be armed. A dark figure leaned out from the darkness under the branches to meet the onslaught, and Cadfael knew him then for Matthew. The attacker swerved aside, still out of reach, in a calculated feint, and at the same moment both the other lurking shadows burst out of cover and bore down upon the other side of the tree, falling as one upon the weaker opponent. There was a confusion of violence, and a wild,

141

tormented scream, and Matthew whirled about, slashing round him and stretching a long arm across his companion, pinning him back against the tree. Ciaran hung half-fainting, slipping down between the great, smooth bastions of the bole, and Matthew bestrode him, his dagger sweeping great swathes before them both.

Cadfael saw it, and was held mute and motionless, beholding this devoted enemy. He got his breath only as all three of the predators closed upon their prey together, slashing, mauling, by sheer weight bearing them down under them.

Cadfael filled his lungs full, and bellowed to the shaken night: 'Hold, there! On them, hold them all three. These are our felons!' He was making so much noise that he did not notice or marvel that the echoes, which in his fury he heard but did not heed, came from two directions at once, from the path he had left, and from the opposite point, from the north. Some corner of his mind knew he had roused echoes, but for his part he felt himself quite alone as he kept up his roaring, spread his sleeves like the wings of a bat, and surged headlong into the mêlée about the tree.

Long, long ago he had forsworn arms, but what of it? Barring his two stout fists, still active but somewhat rheumatic now, he was unarmed. He flung himself into the tangle of men and weapons under the beech, laid hands on the back of a dangling capuchon, hauled its wearer bodily backwards, and twisted the cloth to choke the throat that howled rage and venom at him. But his voice had done more than his martial progress. The black huddle of humanity burst into its separate beings. Two sprang clear and looked wildly about them for the source of the alarm, and Cadfael's opponent reached round, gasping, with a long arm and a vicious dagger, and sliced a dangling streamer out of a rusty black sleeve. Cadfael lay on him with all his weight, held him by the hair, and ground his face into the earth, shamelessly exulting. He would do penance for it some day soon, but now he rejoiced, all his crusader blood singing in his veins.

Distantly he was aware that something else was happening, more than he had reckoned on. He heard and felt the unmistakable quiver and thud of the earth reacting to hooves, and heard a peremptory voice shouting orders, the purport of which he did not release his grip to decypher or attend to. The glade was filled with motion as it filled with darkness. The creature under him gathered itself and heaved mightily, rolling

142

him aside. His hold on the folds of the hood relaxed, and Simeon Poer tore himself free and scrambled clear. There was running every way, but none of the fugitives got far.

Last of the three to roll breathless out of hold, Simeon groped about him vengefully in the roots of the tree, touched a cowering body, found the cord of some dangling relic, possibly precious, in his hand, and hauled with all his strength before he gathered himself up and ran for cover. There was a wild scream of pain, and the cord broke, and the thing, whatever it was, came loose in his hand. He got his feet under him, and charged head-down for the nearest bushes, hurtled into them and ran, barely a yard clear of hands that stooped from horse-back to claw at him.

Cadfael opened his eyes and hauled in breath. The whole clearing was boiling with movement, the darkness heaved and trembled, and the violence had ordered itself into purpose and meaning. He sat up, and took his time to look about him. He was sprawled under the great beech, and somewhere before him, towards the path where he had left his horse, someone with flint and dagger and tinder, was striking sparks for a torch, very calmly. The sparks caught, glowed, and were gently blown into flame. The torch, well primed with oil and resin, sucked in the flame and gave birth to a small, shapely flame of its own, that grew and reared, and was used to kindle a second and a third. The clearing took on a small, confined, rounded shape, walled with close growth, roofed with the tree.

Hugh came out of the dark, smiling, and reached a hand to haul him to his feet. Someone else came running light-footed from the other side, and stooped to him a wonderful, torch-lit face, high-boned, lean-cheeked, with eager golden eyes, and blue-black raven wings of hair curving to cup his cheeks.

'Olivier?' said Cadfael, marvelling. 'I thought you were astray on the road to Oswestry. How did you ever find us here?'

'By grace of God and a goat-herd,' said the warm, gay, remembered voice, 'and your bull's bellowing. Come, look round! You have won your field.'

They were gone, Simeon Poer, merchant of Guildford, Walter Bagot, glover, John Shure, tailor, all fled, but with half a dozen of Hugh's men hard on their heels, all to be brought in captive, to answer for more, this time, than a little cheating in the marketplace. Night stooped to enfold a closed arena of torchlight, very quiet now and almost still. Cadfael rose, his torn sleeve dangling awkwardly. The three of them stood in a half-circle about the beech-tree.

The torchlight was stark, plucking light and shadow into sharp relief. Matthew stirred out of his colloquy between life and death very slowly as they watched him, heaved his wide shoulders clear of the tree, and stood forth like a sleeper roused before his time, looking about him as if for something by which he might hold, and take his bearings. Between his feet, as he emerged, the coiled, crumpled form of Ciaran came into view, faintly stirring, his head huddled into his close-folded arms.

'Get up!' said Matthew. He drew back a little from the tree, his naked dagger in his hand, a slow drop gathering at its tip, more drops falling steadily from the hand that held it. His knuckles were sliced raw. 'Get up!' he said. 'You are not harmed.'

Ciaran gathered himself very slowly, and clambered to his knees, lifting to the light a face soiled and leaden, gone beyond exhaustion, beyond fear. He looked neither at Cadfael nor at Hugh, but stared up into Matthew's face with the helpless intensity of despair. Hugh felt the clash of eyes, and stirred to make some decisive movement and break the tension, but Cadfael laid a hand on his arm and held him still. Hugh gave him a sharp sidelong glance, and accepted the caution. Cadfael had his reasons.

There was blood on the torn collar of Ciaran's shirt, a stain that grew sluggishly before their eyes. He put up hands that seemed heavy as lead, and fumbled aside the linen from throat and breast. All round the left side of his neck ran a raw, bleeding slash, thin as a knife-cut. Simeon Poer's last blind clutch for plunder had torn loose the cross to which Ciaran had clung so desperately. He kneeled in the last wretched extreme of submission, baring a throat already symbolically slit.

'Here am I,' he said in a toneless whisper. 'I can run no further, I am forfeit. Now take me!'

Matthew stood motionless, staring at that savage cut the cord had left before it broke. The silence grew too heavy to be bearable, and still he had no word to say, and his face was a blank mask in the flickering light of the torches.

'He says right,' said Cadfael, very softly and reasonably. 'He is yours fairly. The terms of his penance are broken, and his life is forfeit. Take him!'

There was no sign that Matthew so much as heard him, but

for the spasmodic tightening of his lips, as if in pain. He never took his eyes from the wretch kneeling humbly before him.

'You have followed him faithfully, and kept the terms laid down,' Cadfael urged gently. 'You are under vow. Now finish the work!'

He was on safe enough ground, and sure of it now. The act of submission had already finished the work, there was no more to be done. With his enemy at his mercy, and every justification for the act of vengeance, the avenger was helpless, the prisoner of his own nature. There was nothing left in him but a drear sadness, a sick revulsion of disgust, and self-disgust. How could he kill a wretched, broken man, kneeling here unresisting, waiting for his death? Death was no longer relevant.

'It is over, Luc,' said Cadfael softly. 'Do what you must.'

Matthew stood mute a moment longer, and if he had heard his true name spoken, he gave no sign, it was of no importance. After the abandonment of all purpose came the awful sense of loss and emptiness. He opened his blood-stained hand and let the dagger slip from his fingers into the grass. He turned away like a blind man, feeling with a stretched foot for every step, groped his way through the curtain of bushes, and vanished into the darkness.

Olivier drew in breath sharply, and started out of his tranced stillness to catch eagerly at Cadfael's arm. 'Is it true? You have found him out? *He* is Luc Meverel?' He accepted the truth of it without another word said, and sprang ardently towards the place where the bushes still stirred after Luc's passing, and he would have been off in pursuit at a run if Hugh had not caught at his arm to detain him.

'Wait but one moment! You also have a cause here, if Cadfael is right. This is surely the man who murdered your friend. He owes you a death. He is yours if you want him.'

'That is truth,' said Cadfael. 'Ask him! He will tell you.'

Ciaran crouched in the grass, drooping now, bewildered and lost, no longer looking any man in the face, only waiting without hope or understanding for someone to determine whether he was to live or die, and on what abject terms. Olivier cast one wondering glance at him, shook his head in emphatic rejection, and reached for his horse's bridle. 'Who am I,' he said, 'to exact what Luc Meverel has remitted? Let this one go on his way with his own burden. My business is with the other.'

He was away at a run, leading the horse briskly through the

145

screen of bushes, and the rustling of their passage gradually stilled again into silence. Cadfael and Hugh were left regarding each other mutely across the lamentable figure crouched upon the ground.

Gradually the rest of the world flowed back into Cadfael's ken. Three of Hugh's officers stood aloof with the horses and the torches, looking on in silence; and somewhere not far distant sounded a brief scuffle and outcry, as one of the fugitives was overpowered and made prisoner. Simeon Poer had been pulled down barely fifty yards in cover, and stood sullenly under guard now, with his wrists secured to a sergeant's stirrup-leather. The third would not be a free man long. This night's ventures were over. This piece of woodland would be safe even for barefoot and unarmed pilgrims to traverse.

'What is to be done with him?' demanded Hugh openly, looking down upon the wreckage of a man with some distaste.

'Since Luc has waived his claim,' said Cadfael, 'I would not dare meddle. And there is something at least to be said for him, he did not cheat or break his terms voluntarily, even when there was no one by to accuse him. It is a small virtue to have to advance for the defence of a life, but it is something. Who else has the right to foreclose on what Luc has spared?'

Ciaran raised his head, peering doubtfully from one face to the other, still confounded at being so spared, but beginning to believe that he still lived. He was weeping, whether with pain, or relief, or something more durable than either, there was no telling. The blood was blackening into a dark line about his throat.

'Speak up and tell truth,' said Hugh with chill gentleness. 'Was it you who stabbed Bossard?'

Out of the pallid disintegration of Ciaran's face a wavering voice said: 'Yes.'

'Why did you so? Why attack the queen's clerk, who did nothing but deliver his errand faithfully?'

Ciaran's eyes burned for an instant, and a fleeting spark of past pride, intolerance and rage showed like the last glow of a dying fire. 'He came high-handed, shouting down the lord bishop, defying the council. My master was angry and affronted ...'

'Your master,' said Cadfael, 'was the prior of Hyde Mead. Or so you claimed.'

'How could I any longer claim service with one who had

146

discarded me? I lied! The lord bishop himself – I served Bishop
Henry, had his favour. Lost, lost now! I could not brook the
man Christian's insolence to him … he stood against
everything my lord planned and willed. I hated him! I thought
then that I hated him,' said Ciaran, drearily wondering at the
recollection. 'And I thought to please my lord!'

'A calculation that went awry,' said Cadfael, 'for whatever
he may be, Henry of Blois is no murderer. And Rainald
Bossard prevented your mischief, a man of your own party,
held in esteem. Did that make him a traitor in your eyes – that
he should respect an honest opponent? Or did you strike out at
random, and kill without intent?'

'No,' said the level, lame voice, bereft of its brief spark. 'He
thwarted me, I was enraged. I knew what I did. I was glad …
then!' he said, and drew bitter breath.

'And who laid upon you this penitential journey?' asked
Cadfael, 'and to what end? Your life was granted you, upon
terms. What terms? Someone in the highest authority laid that
load upon you.'

'My lord the bishop-legate,' said Ciaran, and wrung
wordlessly for a moment at the pain of an old devotion,
rejected and banished now for ever. 'There was no other soul
knew of it, only to him I told it. He would not give me up to
law, he wanted this thing put by, for fear it should threaten his
plans for the empress's peace. But he would not condone. I am
from the Danish kingdom of Dublin, my other half Welsh. He
offered me passage under his protection to Bangor, to the
bishop there, who would see me to Caergybi in Anglesey, and
have me put aboard a ship for Dublin. But I must go barefoot
all that way, and wear the cross round my neck, and if ever I
broke those terms, even for a moment, my life was his who
cared to take it, without blame or penalty. And I could never
return.' Another fire, of banished love, ruined ambition,
rejected service, flamed through the broken accents for a
moment, and died of despair.

'Yet if this sentence was never made public,' said Hugh,
seizing upon one thing still unexplained, 'how did Luc Meverel
ever come to know of it and follow you?'

'Do I know?' The voice was flat and drear, worn out with
exhaustion. 'All I know is that I set out from Winchester, and
where the roads joined, near Newbury, this man stood and
waited for me, and fell in beside me, and every step of my way
on this journey he has gone on my heels like a demon, and

waited for me to play false to my sentence – for there was no point of it he did not know! – to take my life without guilt, without a qualm, as so he might. He trod after me wherever I trod, he never let me from his sight, he made no secret of his wants, he tempted me to go aside, to put on shoes, to lay by the cross – and sirs, it was deathly heavy! Matthew, he called himself … Luc, you say he is? You know him? I never knew … He said I had killed his lord, whom he loved, and he would follow me to Bangor, to Caergybi, even to Dublin if ever I got aboard ship without putting off the cross or putting on shoes. But he would have me in the end. He had what he lusted for – why did he turn away and spare?' The last words ached with his uncomprehending wonder.

'He did not find you worth the killing,' said Cadfael, as gently and mercifully as he could, but honestly. 'Now he goes in anguish and shame because he spent so much time on you that might have been better spent. It is a matter of values. Study to learn what is worth and what is not, and you may come to understand him.'

'I am a dead man while I live,' said Ciaran, writhing, 'without master, without friends, without a cause …'   .

'All three you may find, if you seek. Go where you were sent, bear what you were condemned to bear, and look for the meaning,' said Cadfael. 'For so must we all.'

He turned away with a sigh. No way of knowing how much good words might do, or the lessons of life, no telling whether any trace of compunction moved in Ciaran's bludgeoned mind, or whether all his feeling was still for himself. Cadfael felt himself suddenly very tired. He looked at Hugh with a somewhat lopsided smile. 'I wish I were home. What now, Hugh? Can we go?'

Hugh stood looking down with a frown at the confessed murderer, sunken in the grass like a broken-backed serpent, submissive, tear-stained, nursing minor injuries. A piteous spectacle, though pity might be misplaced. Yet he was, after all, no more than twenty-five or so years old, able-bodied, well-clothed, strong, his continued journey might be painful and arduous, but it was not beyond his powers, and he had his bishop's ring still, effective wherever law held. These three footpads now tethered fast and under guard would trouble his going no more. Ciaran would surely reach his journey's end safely, however long it might take him. Not the journey's end of his false story, a blessed death in Aberdaron and burial among the saints of Ynys Ennli, but a return to his native place, and a life beginning afresh. He might even be changed. He might well adhere to his hard terms all the way to Caergybi, where Irish ships plied, even as far as Dublin, even to his ransomed life's end. How can you tell?

'Make your own way from here,' said Hugh, 'as well as you may. You need fear nothing now from footpads here, and the border is not far. What you have to fear from God, take up with God.'

He turned his back, with so decisive a movement that his men recognised the sign that all was over, and stirred willingly about the captives and the horses.

'And those two?' asked Hugh. 'Had I not better leave a man behind on the track there, with a spare horse for Luc? He followed his quarry afoot, but no need for him to foot it back. Or ought I to send men after them?'

'No need for that,' said Cadfael with certainty. 'Olivier will manage all. They'll come home together.'

He had no qualms at all, he was beginning to relax into the warmth of content. The evil he had dreaded had been averted, however narrowly, at whatever cost. Olivier would find his stray, bear with him, follow if he tried to avoid, wrung and ravaged as he was, with the sole obsessive purpose of his life for so long ripped away from him, and within him only the aching emptiness where that consuming passion had been. Into that barren void Olivier would win his way, and warm the ravished heart to make it habitable for another love. There was the most comforting of messages to bring from Juliana Bossard, the promise regained of a home and a welcome. There was a future. How had Matthew-Luc seen his future when he emptied his purse of the last coin at the abbey, before taking up the pursuit of his enemy? Surely he had been contemplating the end of the person he had hitherto been, a total ending, beyond which he could not see. Now he was young again, there was a life before him, it needed only a little time to make him whole again.

Olivier would bring him back to the abbey, when the worst desolation was over. For Olivier had promised that he would not leave without spending some time leisurely with Cadfael, and upon Olivier's promise the heart could rest secure.

As for the other ... Cadfael looked back from the saddle, after they had mounted, and saw the last of Ciaran, still on his knees under the tree, where they had left him. His face was

149

turned to them, but his eyes seemed to be closed, and his hands were wrung tightly together before his breast. He might have been praying, he might have been simply experiencing with every particle of his flesh the life that had been left to him. When we are all gone, thought Cadfael, he will fall asleep there where he lies, he can do no other, for he is far gone in something beyond exhaustion. Where he falls asleep, there he will have died. But when he awakes, I trust he may understand that he has been born again.

The slower cortège that would bring the prisoners into the town began to assemble, making the tethering thongs secure, and the torch-bearers crossed the clearing to mount, withdrawing their yellow light from the kneeling figure, so that Ciaran vanished gradually, as though he had been absorbed into the bole of the beech-tree.

Hugh led the way out to the track, and turned homeward. 'Oh, Hugh, I grow old!' said Cadfael, hugely yawning. 'I want my bed.'

Chapter Fifteen

T WAS past midnight when they rode in at the gatehouse, into a great court awash with moonlight, and heard the chanting of Matins within the church. They had made no haste on the way home, and said very little, content to ride companionably together as sometimes before, through summer night or winter day. It would be another hour or more yet before Hugh's officers got their prisoners back to Shrewsbury Castle, since they must keep a foot-pace, but before morning Simeon Poer and his henchmen would be safe in hold, under lock and key.

'I'll wait with you until Lauds is over,' said Hugh, as they dismounted at the gatehouse. 'Father Abbot will want to know how we've sped. Though I hope he won't require the whole tale from us tonight.'

'Come down with me to the stables, then,' said Cadfael, 'and I'll see this fellow unsaddled and tended, while they're still within. I was always taught to care for my beast before seeking my own rest. You never lose the habit.'

In the stable-yard the moonlight was all the light they needed. The quietness of midnight and the stillness of the air carried every note of the office to them softly and clearly. Cadfael unsaddled his horse and saw him settled and provided in his stall, with a light rug against any possible chill, rites he seldom had occasion to perform now. They brought back memories of other mounts and other journeys, and battlefields less happily resolved than the small but desperate skirmish just lost and won.

Hugh stood watching with his back turned to the great court, but his head tilted to follow the chant. Yet it was not any sound of an approaching step that made him look round suddenly, but the slender shadow that stole along the moonlit cobbles beside his feet. And there hesitant in the gateway of the yard stood Melangell, startled and startling, haloed in that pallid sheen.

'Child,' said Cadfael, concerned, 'what are you doing out of your bed at this hour?'

'How could I rest?' she said, but not as one complaining. 'No one misses me, they are all sleeping.' She stood very still and straight, as if she had spent all the hours since he had left her in earnest endeavour to put away for ever any memories he might have of the tear-stained, despairing girl who had sought solitude in his workshop. The great sheaf of her hair was braided and pinned up on her head, her gown was trim, and her face resolutely calm as she asked, 'Did you find him?'

A girl he had left her, a woman he came back to her. 'Yes,' said Cadfael, 'we found them both. There has nothing ill happened to either. The two of them have parted. Ciaran goes on his way alone.'

'And Matthew?' she asked steadily.

'Matthew is with a good friend, and will come to no harm. We two have outridden them, but they will come.' She would have to learn to call him by another name now, but let the man himself tell her that. Nor would the future be altogether easy, for her or for Luc Meverel, two human creatures who might never have been brought within hail of each other but for freakish circumstance. Unless Saint Winifred had had a hand in that, too? On this night Cadfael could believe it, and trust her to bring all to a good end. 'He will come back,' said Cadfael, meeting her candid eyes, that bore no trace of tears now. 'You need not fear. But he has suffered a great turmoil of the mind, and he'll need all your patience and wisdom. Ask him nothing. When the time is right he will tell you everything. Reproach him with nothing –'

'God forbid,' she said, 'that I should ever reproach him. It was I who failed him.'

'No, how could you know? But when he comes, wonder at nothing. Be like one who is thirsty and drinks. And so will he.'

She had turned a little towards him, and the moonlight

152

blanched wonderfully over her face, as if a lamp within her had been newly lighted. 'I will wait,' she said.

'Better go to your bed and sleep, the waiting may be longer than you think, he has been wrung. But he will come.'

But at that she shook her head. 'I'll watch till he comes,' she said, and suddenly smiled at them, pale and lustrous as pearl, and turned and went away swiftly and silently towards the cloister.

'That is the girl you spoke of?' asked Hugh, looking after her with somewhat frowning interest. 'The lame boy's sister? The girl that young man fancies?'

'That is she,' said Cadfael, and closed the half-door of the stall.

'The weaver-woman's niece?'

'That, too. Dowerless and from common stock,' said Cadfael, understanding but untroubled. 'Yes, true! I'm from common stock myself. I doubt if a young fellow who has been torn apart and remade as Luc has tonight will care much about such little things. Though I grant you others may! I hope the lady Juliana has no plans yet for marrying him off to some heiress from a neighbour manor, for I fancy things have gone so far now with these two that she'll be forced to abandon her plans. A manor or a craft – if you take pride in them, and run them well, where's the difference?'

'Your common stock,' said Hugh heartily, 'gave growth to a most uncommon shoot! And I wouldn't say but that young thing would grace a hall better than many a highbred dame I've seen. But listen, they're ending. We'd best present ourselves.'

Abbot Radulfus came from Matins and Lauds with his usual imperturbable stride, and found them waiting for him as he left the cloister. This day of miracles had produced a fittingly glorious night, incredibly lofty and deep, coruscating with stars, washed white with moonlight. Coming from the dimness within, this exuberance of light showed him clearly both the serenity and the weariness on the two faces that confronted him.

'You are back!' he said, and looked beyond them. 'But not all! Messire de Bretagne – you said he had gone by a wrong way. He has not returned here. You have not encountered him?'

'Yes, Father, we have,' said Hugh. 'All is well with him, and he has found the young man he was seeking. They will return

153

here, all in good time.'

'And the evil you feared, Brother Cadfael? You spoke of another death ...'

'Father,' said Cadfael, 'no harm has come tonight to any but the masterless men who escaped into the forest there. They are now safe in hold, and on their way under guard to the castle. The death I dreaded has been averted, no threat remains in that quarter to any man. I said, if the two young men could be overtaken, the better surely for one, and perhaps for both. Father, they were overtaken in time, and better for both it surely must be.'

'Yet there remains,' said Radulfus, pondering, 'the print of blood, which both you and I have seen. You said – you will recall – that, yes, we have entertained a murderer among us. Do you still say so?'

'Yes, Father. Yet not as you suppose. When Olivier de Bretagne and Luc Meverel return, then all can be made plain, for as yet,' said Cadfael, 'there are still certain things we do not know. But we do know,' he said firmly, 'that what has passed this night is the best for which we could have prayed, and we have good need to give thanks for it.'

'So all is well?'

'All is very well, Father.'

'Then the rest may wait for morning. You need rest. But will you not come in with me and take some food and wine, before you sleep?'

'My wife,' said Hugh, gracefully evading, 'will be in some anxiety for me. You are kind, Father, but I would not have her fret longer than she need.'

The abbot eyed them both, and did not press them.

'And God bless you for that!' sighed Cadfael, toiling up the slight slope of the court towards the dortoir stair and the gatehouse where Hugh had hitched his horse. 'For I'm asleep on my feet, and even a good wine could not revive me.'

The moonlight was gone, and there was as yet no sunlight, when Olivier de Bretagne and Luc Meverel rode slowly in at the abbey gatehouse. How far they had wandered in the deep night neither of them knew very clearly, for this was strange country to both. Even when overtaken, and addressed with careful gentleness, Luc had still gone forward blindly, hands hanging slack at his sides or vaguely parting the bushes, saying nothing, hearing nothing, unless some core of feeling within

154

him was aware of this calm, relentless pursuit by a tolerant, incurious kindness, and distantly wondered at it. When he had dropped at last and lain down in the lush grass of a meadow at the edge of the forest, Olivier had tethered his horse a little apart and lain down beside him, not too close, yet so close that the mute man knew he was here, waiting without impatience. Past midnight Luc had fallen asleep. It was his greatest need. He was a man ravished and emptied of every impulse that had held him alive for the past two months, a dead man still walking and unable quite to die. Sleep was his ransom. Then he could truly die to this waste of loss and bitterness, the awful need that had driven him, the corrosive grief that had eaten his heart out for his lord, who had died in his arms, on his shoulder, on his heart. The bloodstain that would not wash out, no matter how he laboured over it, was his witness. He had kept it to keep the fire of his hatred white-hot. Now in sleep he was delivered from all.

And he had awakened in the first mysterious pre-dawn stirring of the earliest summer birds, beginning to call tentatively into the silence, to open his eyes upon a face bending over him, a face he did not know, but remotely desired to know, for it was vivid, friendly and calm, waiting courteously on his will.

'Did I kill him?' Luc had asked, somehow aware that the man who bore this face would know the answer.

'No,' said a voice clear, serene and low. 'There was no need. But he's dead to you. You can forget him.'

He did not understand that, but he accepted it. He sat up in the cool, ripe grass, and his senses began to stir again, and record distantly that the earth smelled sweet, and there were paling stars in the sky over him, caught like stray sparks in the branches of the trees. He stared intently into Olivier's face, and Olivier looked back at him with a slight, serene smile, and was silent.

'Do I know you?' asked Luc wonderingly.

'No. But you will. My name is Olivier de Bretagne, and I serve Laurence d' Angers, just as your lord did. I knew Rainald Bossard well, he was my friend, we came from the Holy Land together in Laurence's train. And I am sent with a message to Luc Meverel, and that, I am sure, is your name.'

'A message to me?' Luc shook his head.

'From your cousin and lady, Juliana Bossard. And the message is that she begs you to come home, for she needs you, and there is no one who can take your place.'

He was slow to believe, still numbed and hollow within; but

155

there was no impulsion for him to go anywhere or do anything now of his own will, and he yielded indifferently to Olivier's promptings. 'Now we should be getting back to the abbey,' said Olivier practically, and rose, and Luc responded, and rose with him. 'You take the horse, and I'll walk,' said Olivier, and Luc did as he was bidden. It was like nursing a simpleton gently along the way he must go, and holding him by the hand at every step.

They found their way back at last to the old track, and there were the two horses Hugh had left behind for them, and the groom fast asleep in the grass beside them. Olivier took back his own horse, and Luc mounted the fresh one, with the lightness and ease of custom, his body's instincts at least reawakening. The yawning groom led the way, knowing the path well. Not until they were halfway back towards the Meole brook and the narrow bridge to the highroad did Luc say a word of his own volition.

'You say she wants me to come back,' he said abruptly, with quickening pain and hope in his voice. 'Is it true? I left her without a word, but what else could I do? What can she think of me now?'

'Why, that you had your reasons for leaving her, as she has hers for wanting you back. Half the length of England I have been asking after you, at her entreaty. What more do you need?'

'I never thought to return,' said Luc, staring back down that long, long road in wonder and doubt.

No, not even to Shrewsbury, much less to his home in the south. Yet here he was, in the cool, soft morning twilight well before Prime, riding beside this young stranger over the wooden bridge that crossed the Meole brook, instead of wading through the shrunken stream to the pease-fields, the way by which he had left the enclave. Round to the highroad, past the mill and the pond, and in at the gatehouse to the great court. There they lighted down, and the groom took himself and his two horses briskly away again towards the town.

Luc stood gazing about him dully, still clouded by the unfamiliarity of everything he beheld, as if his senses were still dazed and clumsy with the effort of coming back to life. At this hour the court was empty. No, not quite empty. There was someone sitting on the stone steps that climbed to the door of the guest-hall, sitting there alone and quite composedly, with her face turned towards the gate, and as he watched she rose and came down the wide steps, and walked towards him with a swift, light step. Then he knew her for Melangell.

In her at least there was nothing unfamiliar. The sight of her brought back colour and form and reality into the very stones of the wall at her back, and the cobbles under her feet. The elusive grey between-light could not blur the outlines of head and hand, or dim the brightness of her hair. Life came flooding back into Luc with a shock of pain, as feeling returns after a numbing wound. She came towards him with hands a little extended and face raised, and the faintest and most anxious of smiles on her lips and in her eyes. Then, as she hesitated for the first time, a few paces from him, he saw the dark stain of the bruise that marred her cheek.

It was the bruise that shattered him. He shook from head to heels in a great convulsion of shame and grief, and blundered forward blindly into her arms, which reached gladly to receive him. On his knees, with his arms wound about her and his face buried in her breast, he burst into a storm of tears, as spontaneous and as healing as Saint Winifred's own miraculous spring.

He was in perfect command of voice and face when they met after chapter in the abbot's parlour, abbot, prior, Brother Cadfael, Hugh Beringar, Olivier and Luc, to set right in all its details the account of Rainald Bossard's death, and all that had followed from it.

'Unwittingly I deceived you, Father,' said Cadfael, harking back to the interview which had sent him forth in such haste. 'When you asked if we had entertained a murderer unawares, I answered truly that I did think so, but that we might yet have time to prevent a second death. I never realised until afterwards how you might interpret that, seeing we had just found the blood-stained shirt. But see, the man who struck the blow might be spattered as to sleeve or collar, but he would not be marked by this great blot that covered breast and shoulder over the heart. No, that was rather the sign of one who had held a wounded man, a man wounded to death, in his arms as he died. Nor would the slayer, if his clothing was blood-stained, have kept and carried it with him, but burned or buried it, or somehow rid himself of it. But this shirt, though washed most carefully, still bore the outline of the stain clear to be seen, and it was carried as a sacred relic is carried, perhaps as a pledge to exact vengeance. So I knew that this same Luc

157

whom we knew as Matthew, and in whose scrip the talisman was found, was not the murderer. But when I recalled all the words I had heard those two young men speak, and all the evidence of devoted attendance, the one on the other, then suddenly I saw that pairing in the utterly opposed way, as a pursuit. And I feared it must be to the death.'

The abbot looked at Luc and asked simply: 'Is that a true reading?'

'Father, it is.' Luc set forth with deliberation the progress of his own obsession, as though he discovered it and understood it only in speaking. 'I was with my lord that night, close to the Old Minster it was, when four or five set on the clerk, and my lord ran, and we with him, to beat them off. And then they fled, but one turned back and struck. I saw it done, and it was done of intent! I had my lord in my arms – he had been good to me, and I loved him,' said Luc with grimly measured moderation and burning eyes as he remembered. 'He was dead in a mere moment, in the twinkling of an eye … And I had seen where the murderer fled, into the passage by the chapter house. I went after him, and I heard their voices in the sacristy – Bishop Henry had come from the chapter house after the council ended for the night, and there Ciaran had found him and fell on his knees to him, blurting out all. I lay in hiding, and heard every word. I think he even hoped for praise,' said Luc with bitter deliberation.

'Is it possible?' wondered Prior Robert, shocked to the heart. 'Bishop Henry could not for one moment connive at or condone an act so evil.'

'No, he did not condone. But neither would he deliver over one of his own intimate servants as a murderer. To do him justice,' said Luc, but with plain distaste, 'his concern was not to cause further anger and quarrelling, but to put away and smooth over everything that threatened the empress's fortunes and the peace he was trying to make. But condone murder – no, that he would not. Therefore I overheard the sentence he laid upon Ciaran – though then I did not know who he was, nor that Ciaran was his name. He banished him back to his Dublin home, for ever, and condemned him to go every step of the way to Bangor and to the ship at Caergybi barefoot, and carrying that heavy cross. And if ever he put on shoes or laid by the cross from round his neck, then his forfeit life was no longer spared, but might be taken by whoever willed, without sin or penalty. But see,' said Luc, merciless in judgement, 'how he cheated! For not only did he give his creature the ring that would ensure him the protection of the church to Bangor, but also, mark, not one word was ever made public of this guilt or this sentence, so how was that forfeit life in danger? No one was to know of it but they two, if God had not prevented and brought there a witness to hear the sentence and take upon himself the vengeance due.'

'As you did,' said the abbot, and his voice was even and calm, avoiding judgement.

'As I did, Father. For as Ciaran swore to keep the terms laid down on pain of death, so did I swear an oath as solemn to follow him the length of the land, and if ever he broke his terms for a moment, to have his life as payment for my lord.'

'And how,' asked Radulfus in the same mild tone, 'did you know what man you were thus to hunt to his death? For you say you did not see his face clearly or know his name then.'

'I knew the way he was bound to go, and the day of his setting out. I waited by the roadside for one walking north, barefoot – and one not used to going barefoot, but very well shod,' said Luc with a brief, wry smile. 'I saw the cross at his neck. I fell in at his side, and I told him, not who I was, but what. I took another name, so that no failure nor shame of mine should ever cast a shadow on my lady or her house. One Evangelist in exchange for another! Step for step with him I went all this way, here to this place, and never let him from my sight and reach, night or day, and never let him forget that I meant to be his death. He could not ask help to rid himself of me, since I could then as easily strip him of his pilgrim holiness and show what he really was. And I could not denounce him – partly for fear of Bishop Henry, partly because neither did I want more feuding between factions – my feud was between two men! – but chiefly because he was mine, mine, and I would not let any other vengeance or danger reach him. So we kept together, he trying to elude me – but he was court-bred and tender and crippled by the miles – and I holding fast to him, and waiting.'

He looked up suddenly and caught the abbot's compassionate but calm eyes upon him, and his own eyes were wide, dark and clear. 'It is not beautiful, I know. Neither was murder beautiful. And this blotch was only mine – my lord went to his grave immaculate, defending one opposed to him.'

It was Olivier, silent until now, who said softly: '*And so did you!*'

The grave, thought Cadfael at the height of the Mass, had closed firmly to deny Luc entrance, but that arm outstretched between his enemy and the knives of three assailants must never be forgotten. Hell had also shut its mouth and refused to devour him. He was young, clean, alive again after a kind of death. Yes, Olivier had uttered truth. His own life ventured, his enemy's life defended, what was there beween Luc and his lord but the accident, the vain and random accident of the death itself?

He recalled also, when he was most diligent in prayer, that these few days while Saint Winifred was manifesting her virtue in disentangling the troubled lives of some half-dozen people in Shrewsbury, were also the vital days when the fates of Englishmen in general were being determined, perhaps with less compassion and wisdom. For by this time the date of the empress's coronation might well be settled, the crown even now placed upon her head. No doubt God and the saints had that consideration in mind, too.

Matthew-Luc came once again to ask audience of the abbot, a little before Vespers. Radulfus had him admitted without question, and sat with him alone, divining his present need.

'Father, will you hear me my confession? For I need absolution from the vow I could not keep. And I do earnestly desire to be clean of the past before I undertake the future.'

'It is a right and a wise desire,' said Radulfus. 'One thing tell me – are you asking absolution for failing to fulfil the oath you swore?'

Luc, already on his knees, raised his head for a moment from the abbot's knee, and showed a face open and clear. 'No, Father, but for ever swearing such an oath. Even grief has its arrogance.'

'Then you have learned, my son, that vengeance belongs only to God?'

'More than that, Father,' said Luc. 'I have learned that in God's hands vengeance is safe. However long delayed, however strangely manifested, the reckoning is sure.'

When it was done, when he had raked out of his heart, with measured voice and long pauses for thought, every drifted grain of rancour and bitterness and impatience that fretted him, and received absolution, he rose with a great sigh, and raised a bright and resolute face.

'Now, Father, if I may pray of you one more grace, let me have one of your priests to join me to a wife before I go from here. Here, where I am made clean and new, I would have love and life begin together.'

Chapter Sixteen

N THE next morning, which was the twenty-fourth
day of June, the general bustle of departure began.
There was packing of belongings, buying and
parcelling of food and drink for the journey, and
much leave-taking from friends newly made and arranging of
company for the road. No doubt the saint would have due
regard for her own reputation, and keep the June sun shining
until all her devotees were safely home, and with a wonderful
tale to tell. Most of them knew only half the wonder, but even
that was wonder enough.

Among the early departures went Brother Adam of
Reading, in no great hurry along the way, for today he would
go no farther than Reading's daughter-house of Leominster,
where there would be letters waiting for him to carry home to
his abbot. He set out with a pouch well filled with seeds of
species his garden did not yet possess, and a scholarly mind still
pondering the miraculous healing he had witnessed from every
theological angle, in order to be able to expound its full
significance when he reached his own monastery. It had been a
most instructive and enlightening festival.

'I'd meant to start for home today, too,' said Mistress
Weaver to her cronies Mistress Glover and the apothecary's
widow, with whom she had formed a strong matronly alliance
during these memorable days, 'but now there's such work
doing, I hardly know whether I'm waking or sleeping, and I
must stay over yet a night or two. Who'd ever have thought

what would come of it, when I told my lad we ought to come and make our prayers here to the good saint, and have faith that she'd be listening? Now it seems I'm to lose the both of them, my poor sister's chicks; for Rhun, God bless him, is set on staying here and taking the cowl, for he says he won't ever leave the blessed girl who healed him. And truly I don't wonder at it, and won't stand in his way, for he's too good for this wicked world outside, so he is! And now comes young Matthew – no, but it seems we must call him Luc, now, and he's well-born, if from a poor landless branch, and will come in for a manor or two in time, by his good kinswoman's taking him in ...'

'Well, and so did you take the boy and girl in,' pointed out the apothecary's widow warmly, 'and gave them a roof and a living. There's good sound justice there.'

'Well, so Matthew, I mean Luc, he comes to me and asks for my girl for his wife, last night it was, and when I answered honestly, for honest I am and always will be, that my Melangell has but a meagre dowry, though the best I can give her I will, what says he? That as at this moment he himself has not one penny to his name in this world, but must go debtor to the young lord's charity that came to find him, and as for the future, if fortune favours him he'll be thankful, and if not, he has hands and a will and can make a way for two to live. Provided the other is my girl, he says, for there's none other for him. So what can I say but God bless them both, and stay to see them wedded?'

'It's a woman's duty,' said Mistress Glover heartily, 'to make sure all's done properly, when she hands over a young girl to a husband. But sure, you'll miss the two of them.'

'So I will,' agreed Dame Alice, shedding a few tears rather of pride and joy than of grief, at the advancement to semi-sainthood and promising matrimony of the charges who had cost her dear enough, and could now be blessed and sped on their respective and respectable ways with a quiet mind. 'So I will! But to see them both set up where they would be ... And good children both, that will take pains for me when I come to need, as I have for them.'

'And they're to marry here, tomorrow?' asked the apothecary's widow, visibly considering putting off her own departure for another day.

'They are indeed, before Mass in the morning. So it seems I'll have none to take home but my sole self,' said Dame Alice,

163

dropping another proud tear or two, and wearing her reflected glory with admirable grace, 'when I take to the road again. But the day after tomorrow there's a sturdy company leaving southward, and with them I'll go.'

'And duty well done, my dear soul,' said Mistress Glover, embracing her friend in a massive arm, 'duty very well done!'

They were married in the privacy of the Lady Chapel, by Brother Paul, who was not only master of the novices, but the chief of their confessors, too, and already had Rhun under his care and instruction, and felt a fatherly interest in him, which the boy's affection very readily extended to embrace the sister. No one else was present but the family and their witnesses, and the bridal pair wore no festal garments, for they had none. Luc was in the serviceable brown cotte and hose he had slept in, out in the fields, and the same crumpled shirt, though newly washed and smoothed. Melangell was neat and modest in her homespun, proudly balancing her coronal of braided, deep-gold hair. They were pale as lilies, bright as stars, and solemn as the grave.

After high and moving events, daily life must still go on. Cadfael went to his work that afternoon well content. With the meadow grasses in ripe seed and the harvest imminent he had preparations to make for two seasonal ailments which could be relied upon to recur every year. There were some who suffered with eruptions on their hands when working in the harvest, and others who took to sneezing and wheezing, with running eyes, and needed lotions to help them.

He was busy bruising fresh leaves of dock and mandrake in a mortar for a soothing ointment, when he heard light, long-striding steps approaching along the gravel of the path, and then half the sunlight from the wide-open door was cut off, as someone hesitated in the doorway. He turned with the mortar hugged to his chest, and the green-stained wooden pestle arrested in his hand, and there stood Olivier, dipping his tall head to evade the hanging bunches of herbs, and asking, in the mellow, confident voice of one assured of the answer, 'May I come in?'

He was in already, smiling, staring about him with a boy's candid curiosity, for he had never been here before. 'I've been a truant, I know, but with two days to wait before Luc's marriage I thought best to get on with my errand to the sheriff of Stafford, being so close, and then come back here. I was back, as I said I'd be, in time to see them wedded. I thought you would have been there.'

'So I would, but I was called out to Saint Giles. Some poor soul of a beggar stumbled in there overnight covered with sores, they were afraid of a contagion, but it's no such matter. If he'd had treatment earlier it would have been an easy matter to cure him, but a week or so resting in the hospital will do him no harm. Our pair of youngsters here had no need of me. I'm a part of what's over and done with for them, you're a part of what's beginning.'

'Melangell told me where I should find you, however, you were missed. And here I am.'

'And as welcome as the day,' said Cadfael, laying his mortar aside. Long, shapely hands gripped both his hands heartily, and Olivier stooped his olive cheek for the greeting kiss, as simply as for the parting kiss when they had separated at Bromfield. 'Come, sit, let me offer you wine – my own making. You knew, then, that those two would marry?'

'I saw them meet, when I brought him back here. Small doubt how it would end. Afterwards he told me his intent. When two are agreed, and know their own minds,' said Olivier blithely, 'everything else will give way. I shall see them both properly provided for the journey home, since I must go by a more roundabout way.'

When two are agreed, and know their own minds! Cadfael remembered confidences now a year and a half past. He poured wine carefully, his hand being a shade less steady than usual, and sat down beside his visitor, the young, wide shoulder firm and vital against his elderly and stiff one, the clear, elegant profile close, and a pleasure to his eyes. 'Tell me,' he said, 'about Ermina,' and was sure of the answer even before Olivier turned on him his sudden blinding smile.

'If I had known my travels would bring me to you, I should have had so many messages to bring you, from both of them. From Yves – and from my wife!'

'Aaaah!' breathed Cadfael, on a deep, delighted sigh. 'So, as I thought, as I hoped! You have made good, then, what you told me, that they would acknowledge your worth and give her to you.' Two, there, who had indeed known their own minds, and been invincibly agreed! 'When was this match made?'

'This Christmas past, in Gloucester. She is there now, so is the boy. He is Laurence's heir – just fifteen now. He wanted to come to Winchester with us, but Laurence wouldn't let him be put in peril. They are safe, I thank God. If ever this chaos is ended,' said Olivier very solemnly, 'I will bring her to you, or you to her. She does not forget you.'

'Nor I her, nor I her! Nor the boy. He rode with me twice, asleep in my arms, I still recall the warmth and the shape and the weight of him. A good boy as ever stepped!'

'He'd be a load for you now,' said Olivier, laughing. 'This year past, he's shot up like a weed, he'll be taller than you.'

'Ah, well, I'm beginning to shrink like a spent weed. And you are happy?' asked Cadfael, thirsting for more blessedness even than he already had. 'You and she both?'

'Beyond what I know how to express,' said Olivier no less gravely. 'How glad I am to have seen you again, and been able to tell you so! Do you remember the last time? When I waited with you in Bromfield to take Ermina and Yves home? And you drew me maps on the floor to show me the ways?'

There is a point at which joy is only just bearable. Cadfael got up to refill the wine-cups, and turn his face away for a moment from a brightness almost too bright. 'Ah, now, if this is to be a contest in "do-you-remembers" we shall be at it until Vespers, for not one detail of that time have I forgotten. So let's have this flask here within reach, and settle down to it in comfort.'

But there was an hour and more left before Vespers when Hugh put an abrupt end to remembering. He came in haste, with a face blazingly alert, and full of news. Even so he was slow to speak, not wishing to exult openly in what must be only shock and dismay to Olivier.

'There's news. A courier rode in from Warwick just now, they're passing the word north by stages as fast as horse can go.' They were both on their feet by then, intent upon his face, and waiting for good or evil, for he contained it well. A good face for keeping secrets, and under strong control now out of courteous consideration. 'I fear,' he said, 'it will not come as gratefully to you, Olivier, as I own it does to me.'

'From the south ...' said Olivier, braced and still. 'From London? The empress?'

'Yes, from London. All is overturned in a day. There'll be no coronation. Yesterday as they sat at dinner in Westminster, the Londoners suddenly rang the tocsin – all the city bells. The entire town came out in arms, and marched on Westminster.

166

They're fled, Olivier, she and all her court, fled in the clothes they wore and with very little else, and the city men have plundered the palace and driven out even the last hangers-on. She never made move to win them, nothing but threats and reproaches and demands for money ever since she entered. She's let the crown slip through her fingers for want of a few soft words and a queen's courtesy. For your part,' said Hugh, with real compunction, 'I'm sorry! For mine, I find it a great deliverance.'

'With that I find no fault,' said Olivier simply. 'Why should you not be glad? But she ... she's safe? They have not taken her?'

'No, according to the messenger she's safely away, with Robert of Gloucester and a few others as loyal, but the rest, it seems, scattered and made off for their own lands, where they'd feel safe. That's the word as he brought it, barely a day old. The city of London was being pressed hard from the south,' said Hugh, somewhat softening the load of folly that lay upon the empress's own shoulders, 'with King Stephen's queen harrying their borders. To get relief their only way was to drive the empress out and let the queen in, and their hearts were on her side, no question, of the two they'd liefer have her.'

'I knew,' said Olivier, 'she was not wise – the Empress Maud. I knew she could not forget grudges, no matter how sorely she needed to close her eyes to them. I have seen her strip a man's dignity from him when he came submissive, offering support ... Better at making enemies than friends. All the more she needs,' he said, 'the few she has. Where is she gone? Did your messenger know?'

'Westward for Oxford. And they'll reach it safely. The Londoners won't follow so far, their part was only to drive her out.'

'And the bishop? Is he gone with her?' The entire enterprise had rested upon the efforts of Henry of Blois, and he had done his best for her, not entirely creditably but understandably and at considerable cost, and his best she herself had undone. Stephen was a prisoner in Bristol, but Stephen was still crowned and anointed king of England. No wonder Hugh's eyes shone.

'Of the bishop I know nothing as yet. But he'll surely join her in Oxford. Unless ...'

'Unless he changes sides again,' Olivier ended for him, and laughed. 'It seems I shall have to leave you in more haste than I

167

expected,' he said with regret. 'One fortune rises, another falls. No sense in quarrelling with the lot.'

'What will you do?' asked Hugh, watching him steadily. 'You know, I think, that whatever you may ask of us here, is yours, and the choice is yours. Your horses are fresh. Your men will not yet have heard the news, they'll be waiting on your word. If you need stores for a journey, take whatever you will. Or if you choose to stay ...'

Olivier shook his blue-black head, and the clasping curves of glossy hair danced on his cheeks. 'I must go. Not north, where I was sent. What use in that, now? South for Oxford. Whatever she may be else, she is my liege lord's liege lady, where she is he will be, and where he is, I go.'

They eyed each other silently for a moment, and Hugh said softly, quoting remembered words: 'To tell you truth, now I've met you I expected nothing less.'

'I'll go and rouse my men, and we'll get to horse. You'll follow to your house, before I go? I must take leave of Lady Beringar.'

'I'll follow you,' said Hugh.

Olivier turned to Brother Cadfael without a word but with the brief golden flash of a smile breaking through his roused gravity for an instant, and again vanishing. 'Brother ... remember me in your prayers!' He stooped his smooth cheek yet again in farewell, and as the elder's kiss was given he embraced Cadfael vehemently, with impulsive grace. 'Until a better time!'

'God go with you!' said Cadfael.

And he was gone, striding rapidly along the gravel path, breaking into a light run, in no way disheartened or down, a match for disaster or for triumph. At the corner of the box hedge he turned in flight to look back, and waved a hand before he vanished.

'I wish to God,' said Hugh, gazing after him, 'he was of our party! There's an odd thing, Cadfael! Will you believe, just then, when he looked round, I thought I saw something of you about him. The set of the head, something ...'

Cadfael, too, was gazing out from the open doorway to where the last sheen of blue had flashed from the burnished hair, and the last echo of the light foot on the gravel died into silence. 'Oh, no,' he said absently, 'he is altogether the image of his mother.'

An unguarded utterance. Unguarded from absence of mind, or design?

The following silence did not trouble him, he continued to gaze, shaking his head gently over the lingering vision, which would stay with him through all his remaining years, and might even, by the grace of God and the saints, be made flesh for him yet a third time. Far beyond his deserts, but miracles are neither weighed nor measured, but as uncalculated as the lightnings.

'I recall,' said Hugh with careful deliberation, perceiving that he was permitted to speculate, and had heard only what he was meant to hear, 'I do recall that he spoke of one for whose sake he held the Benedictine order in reverence … one who had used him like a son …'

Cadfael stirred, and looked round at him, smiling as he met his friend's fixed and thoughtful eyes. 'I always meant to tell you, some day,' he said tranquilly, 'what he does not know, and never will from me. He *is* my son.'

An Excellent Mystery

Chapter One

AUGUST CAME in, that summer of 1141, tawny as a lion and somnolent and purring as a hearthside cat. After the plenteous rains of the spring the weather had settled into angelic calm and sunlight for the feast of Saint Winifred, and preserved the same benign countenance throughout the corn harvest. Lammas came for once strict to its day, the wheat-fields were already gleaned and white, ready for the flocks and herds that would be turned into them to make use of what aftermath the season brought. The loaf-Mass had been celebrated with great contentment, and the early plums in the orchard along the riverside were darkening into ripeness. The abbey barns were full, the well-dried straw bound and stacked, and if there was still no rain to bring on fresh green fodder in the reaped field for the sheep, there were heavy morning dews. When this golden weather broke at last, it might well break in violent storms, but as yet the skies remained bleached and clear, the palest imaginable blue.

'Fat smiles on the faces of the husbandmen,' said Hugh Beringar, fresh from his own harvest in the north of the shire, and burned nut-brown from his work in the fields, 'and chaos among the kings. If they had to grow their own corn, mill their own flour and bake their own bread they might have not time left for all the squabbling and killing. Well, thank God for present mercies, and God keep the killing well away from us here. Not that I rate it the less ill-fortune for being there in the south, but this shire is my field, and my people, mine to keep. I have enough to do to mind my own, and when I see them brown and rosy and fat, with full byres and barns, and a high wool tally in good quality fleeces, I'm content.'

They had met by chance at the corner of the abbey wall, where the Foregate turned right towards Saint Giles, and beside it the great grassy triangle of the horse-fair ground opened, pallid and pockmarked in the sun. The three-day annual fair of Saint Peter was more than a week past, the stalls taken down, the merchants departed. Hugh sat aloft on his raw-boned and cross-grained grey horse, tall enough to carry a heavyweight instead of this light, lean young man whose mastery he tolerated, though he had precious little love for any other human creature. It was no responsibility of the sheriff of Shropshire to see that the fairground was properly vacated and cleared after its three-day occupation, but for all that Hugh liked to view the ground for himself. It was his officers who had to keep order there, and make sure the abbey stewards were neither cheated of their fees nor robbed or otherwise abused in collecting them. That was over now for another year. And here were the signs of it, the dappling of post-holes, the pallid oblongs of the stalls, the green fringes, and the trampled, bald paths between the booths. From sun-starved bleach to lush green, and back to the pallor again, with patches of tough, flat cover surviving in the trodden paths like round green footprints of some strange beast.

'One good shower would put all right,' said Brother Cadfael, eyeing the curious chessboard of blanched and bright with a gardener's eye. 'There's nothing in the world so strong as grass.'

He was on his way from the abbey of Saint Peter and Saint Paul to its chapel and hospital of Saint Giles, half a mile away at the very rim of the town. It was one of his duties to keep the medicine cupboard there well supplied with all the remedies the inmates might require, and he made this journey every couple of weeks, more often in times of increased habitation and need. On this particular early morning in August he had with him young Brother Oswin, who had worked with him among the herbs for more than a year, and was now on his way to put his skills into practice among the most needy. Oswin was sturdy, well-grown, glowing with enthusiasm. Time had been when he had cost plenty in breakages, in pots burned beyond recovery, and deceptive herbs gathered by mistake for others only too like them. Those times were over. All he needed now

174

to be a treasure to the hospital was a cool-headed superior who would know when to curb his zeal. The abbey had the right of appointment, and the lay head they had installed would be more than proof against Brother Oswin's too exuberant energy.

'You had a good fair, after all,' said Hugh.

'Better than ever I expected, with half the south cut off by the trouble in Winchester. They got here from Flanders,' said Cadfael appreciatively. East Anglia was no very peaceful ground just now, but the wool merchants were a tough breed, and would not let a little bloodshed and danger bar them off from a good profit.

'It was a fine wool clip.' Hugh had flocks of his own on his manor of Maesbury, in the north, he knew about the quality of the year's fleeces. There had been good buying in from Wales, too, all along this border. Shrewsbury had ties of blood, sympathy and mutual gain with the Welsh of both Powys and Gwynedd, whatever occasional explosions of racial exuberance might break the guarded peace. In this summer the peace with Gwynedd held firm, under the capable hand of Owain Gwynedd, since they had a shared interest in containing the ambitions of Earl Ranulf of Chester. Powys was less predictable, but had drawn in its horns of late after several times blunting them painfully on Hugh's precautions.

'And the corn harvest the best for years. As for the fruit … It *looks* well,' said Cadfael cautiously, 'if we get some good rains soon to swell it, and no thunderstorms before it's gathered. Well, the corn's in and the straw stacked, and as good a hay crop as we've had since my memory holds. You'll not hear me complain.'

But for all that, he thought, looking back in mild surprise, it had been an unchancy sort of year, overturning the fortunes of kings and empresses not once, but twice, while benignly smiling upon the festivities of the church and the hopeful labours of ordinary men, at least here in the midlands. February had seen King Stephen made prisoner at the disastrous battle of Lincoln, and swept away into close confinement in Bristol castle by his arch-enemy, cousin and rival claimant to the throne of England, the Empress Maud. A good many coats had been changed in haste after that reversal, not least that of Stephen's brother and Maud's cousin, Henry of Blois, Bishop of Winchester and papal legate, who had delicately hedged his wager and come round to the winning

175

side, only to find that he would have done well to drag his feet a little longer. For the fool woman, with the table spread for her at Westminster and the crown all but touching her hair, had seen fit to conduct herself in so arrogant and overbearing a manner towards the citizens of London that they had risen in fury to drive her out in ignominious flight, and let King Stephen's valiant queen into the city in her place.

Not that this last spin of the wheel could set King Stephen free. On the contrary, report said it had caused him to be loaded with chains by way of extra security, he being the one formidable weapon the empress still had in her hand. But it had certainly snatched the crown from Maud's head, most probably for ever, and it had cost her the not inconsiderable support of Bishop Henry, who was not the man to be over-hasty in his alliances twice in one year. Rumour said the lady had sent her half-brother and best champion, Earl Robert of Gloucester, to Winchester to set things right with the bishop and lure him back to her side, but without getting a straight answer. Rumour said also, and probably on good grounds, that Stephen's queen had already forestalled her, at a private meeting with Henry at Guildford, and got rather more sympathy from him than the empress had succeeded in getting. And doubtless Maud had heard of it. For the latest news, brought by latecomers from the south to the abbey fair, was that the empress with a hastily gathered army had marched to Winchester and taken up residence in the royal castle there. What her next move was to be must be a matter of anxious speculation to the bishop, even in his own city.

And meantime, here in Shrewsbury the sun shone, the abbey celebrated its maiden saint with joyous solemnity, the flocks flourished, the harvest whitened and was gathered in exemplary weather, the annual fair took its serene course through the first three days of August, and traders came from far and wide, conducted their brisk business, took their profits, made their shrewd purchases, and scattered again in peace to return to their own homes, as though neither king nor empress existed, or had any power to hamper the movements or threaten the lives of ordinary, sensible men.

'You'll have heard nothing new since the merchants left?' Cadfael asked, scanning the blanched traces their stalls had left behind.

'Nothing yet. It seems they're eyeing each other across the city, each waiting for the other to make a move. Winchester must be holding its breath. The last word is that the empress sent for Bishop Henry to come to her at the castle, and he has sent a soft answer that he is preparing himself for the meeting. But stirred not a foot, so far, to move within reach of her. But for all that,' said Hugh thoughtfully, 'I dare wager he's preparing, sure enough. She has mustered her forces, he'll be calling up his before ever he goes near her – if he does!'

'And while they hold their breath, you may breathe more freely,' said Cadfael shrewdly.

Hugh laughed. 'While my enemies fall out, at least it keeps their minds off me and mine. Even if they come to terms again, and she wins him back, there's at least a few weeks' delay gained for the king's party. If not – why, better they should tear each other than save their arrows for us.'

'Do you think he'll stand out against her?'

'She has treated him as haughtily as she does every man, when he did her good menial service. Now he has half-defied her he may well be reflecting that she takes very unkindly to being thwarted, and that a bishop can be clapped in chains as easily as a king, once she lays hands on him. No, I fancy his lordship is stocking his own castle of Wolvesey to withstand a siege, if it comes to that, and calling up his men in haste. Who bargains with the empress had better bargain from behind an army.'

'The queen's army?' demanded Cadfael, sharp-eyed.

Hugh had begun to wheel his horse back towards the town, but he looked round over a bare brown shoulder with a flashing glint of black eyes. 'That we shall see! I would guess the first courier ever he sent out for aid went to Queen Matilda.'

'Brother Cadfael ...' began Oswin, trotting jauntily beside him as they walked on towards the rim of the town, where the hospital and its chapel rose plain and grey within their long wattle fence.

'Yes, son?'

'Would even the empress really dare lay hands on the Bishop of Winchester? The Holy Father's legate here?'

'Who can tell? But there's not much she will not dare.'

'But ... That there could be fighting between them ...'

Oswin puffed out his round young cheeks in a great breath of wonder and deprecation. Such a thing seemed to him unimaginable. 'Brother, you have been in the world and have experience of wars and battles. And I know that there were

177

bishops and great churchmen went to do battle for the Holy Sepulchre, as you did, but should they be found in arms for any lesser cause?'

Whether they should, thought Cadfael, is for them to take up with their judge in the judgement, but that they are so found, have been aforetime and will be hereafter, is beyond doubt. 'To be charitable,' he said cautiously, 'in this case his lordship may consider his own freedom, safety and life to be a very worthy cause. Some have been called to accept martyrdom meekly, but that should surely be for nothing less than their faith. And a dead bishop could be of little service to his church, and a legate mouldering in prison little profit to the Holy Father.'

Brother Oswin strode beside for some moments judicially mute, digesting that plea and apparently finding it somewhat dubious, or else suspecting that he had not fully comprehended the argument. Then he asked ingenuously: 'Brother, would *you* take arms again? Once having renounced them? For *any* cause?'

'Son,' said Cadfael, 'you have the knack of asking questions which cannot be answered. How do I know what I would do, in extreme need? As a brother of the Order I would wish to keep my hands from violence against any, but for all that, I hope I would not turn my back if I saw innocence or helplessness being abused. Bear in mind even the bishops carry a crook, meant to protect the flock as well as guide it. Let princes and empresses and warriors mind their own duties, you give all your mind to yours, and you'll do well.'

They were nearing the trodden path that led up a grassy slope to the open gate in the wattle fence. The modest turret of the chapel eyed them over the roof of the hospice. Brother Oswin bounded up the slope eagerly, his cherubic face bright with confidence, bound for a new field of endeavour, and certain of mastering it. There was probably no pitfall here he would evade, but none of them would hold him for long, or damp his unquenchable ardour.

'Now remember all I've taught you,' said Cadfael. 'Be obedient to Brother Simon. You will work for a time under him, as he did under Brother Mark. The superior is a layman from the Foregate, but you'll see little of him betwen his occasional visitations and inspections, and he's a good soul and listens to counsel. And I shall be in attendance every now and again, should you ever need me. Come, and I'll show you where everything is.'

Brother Simon was a comfortable, round man in his forties.

178

He came out to meet them at the porch, with a gangling boy of about twelve by the hand. The child's eyes were white with the caul of blindness, but otherwise he was whole and comely, by no means the saddest sight to be found here, where the infected and diseased might find at once a refuge and a prison for their contagion, since they were not permitted to carry it into the streets of the town, among the uncorrupted. There were cripples sunning themselves in the little orchard behind the hospice, old, pox-riddled men, and faded women in the barn plaiting bands for the straw stooks as they were stacked. Those who could work a little were glad to do so for their keep, those who could not were passive in the sun, unless they had skin rashes which the heat only aggravated. These kept under the shade of the fruit-trees, or those most fevered in the chill of the chapel.

'As at present,' said Brother Simon, 'we have eighteen, which is not so ill, for so hot a season. Three are able-bodied, and mending of their sickness, which was not contagious, and they'll be on their way within days now. But there'll be others, young man, there'll always be others. They come and go. Some by the roads, some out of this world's bane. None the worse, I hope, for passing through that door in this place.'

He had a slightly preaching style which caused Cadfael to smile inwardly, remembering Mark's lovely simplicity, but he was a good man, hardworking, compassionate, and very deft with those big hands of his. Oswin would drink in his solemn homilies with reverence and wonder, and go about his work refreshed and unquestioning.

'I'll see the lad round myself, if you'll let me,' said Cadfael, hitching forward the laden scrip at his girdle. 'I've brought you all the medicaments you asked for, and some I thought might be needed, besides. We'll find you when we're done.'

'And the news of Brother Mark?' asked Simon.

'Mark is already deacon. I have but to save my most fearful confession a few more years, then, if need be, I'll depart in peace.'

'According to Mark's word?' wondered Simon, revealing unsuspected depths, and smiling to gloss them over. It was not often he spoke at such a venture.

'Well,' said Cadfael very thoughtfully, 'I've always found Mark's word good enough for me. You may well be right.' And he turned to Oswin, who had followed this exchange with a face dutifully attentive and bewilderedly smiling, earnest to

179

understand what evaded him like thistledown. 'Come on, lad, let's unload these and be rid of the weight first, and then I'll show you all that goes on here at Saint Giles.'

They passed through the hall, which was for eating and for sleeping, except for those too sick to be left among their healthier fellows. There was a large locked cupboard, to which Cadfael had his own key, and its shelves within were full of jars, flasks, bottles, wooden boxes for tablets, ointments, syrups, lotions, all the products of Cadfael's workshop. They unloaded their scrips and filled the gaps along the shelves. Oswin enlarged with the importance of this mystery into which he had been initiated, and which he was now to practise in earnest.

There was a small kitchen garden behind the hospice, and an orchard, and barns for storage. Cadfael conducted his charge round the entire enclave, and by the end of the circuit they had three of the inmates in close and curious attendance, the old man who tended the cabbages and showed off his produce with pride, a lame youth herpling along nimbly enough on two crutches, and the blind child, who had forsaken Brother Simon to attach himself to Cadfael's girdle, knowing the familiar voice.

'This is Warin,' said Cadfael, taking the boy by the hand as they made their way back to Brother Simon's little desk in the porch. 'He sings well in chapel, and knows the office by heart. But you'll soon know them all by name.'

Brother Simon rose from his accounts at sight of them returning. 'He's shown you everything? It's no great household, ours, but it does a great work. You'll soon get used to us.'

Oswin beamed and blushed, and said that he would do his best. It was likely that he was waiting impatiently for his mentor to depart, so that he could begin to exercise his new responsibility without the uneasiness of a pupil performing before his teacher. Cadfael clouted him cheerfully on the shoulder, bade him be good, in the tones of one having no doubts on that score, and turned towards the gate. They had moved out into the sunlight from the dimness of the porch.

'You've heard no fresh news from the south?' The denizens of Saint Giles, being encountered at the very edge of the town, were usually beforehand with news.

'Nothing to signify. And yet a man must wonder and speculate. There was a beggar, able-bodied but getting old, who came in three days ago, and stayed only overnight to rest. He was from the Staceys, near Andover, a queer one, perhaps a mite touched in his wits, who can tell? He gets notions, it seems, that move him on into fresh pastures, and when they come to him he must go. He said he got word in his head that he had best get away northwards while there was time.'

'A man of those parts who had no property to tie him might very well get the same notion now,' said Cadfael ruefully, 'without being in want of his wits. Indeed, it might be his wits that advised him to move on.'

'So it might. But this fellow said – if he did not dream it – that the day he set out he looked back from a hilltop, and saw smoke in clouds over Winchester, and in the night following there was a red glow all above the city, that flickered as if with still quick flames.'

'It could be true,' said Cadfael, and gnawed a considering lip. 'It would come as no great surprise. The last firm news we had was that empress and bishop were holding off cautiously from each other, and shifting for position. A little patience ... But she was never, it seems, a patient woman. I wonder, now, I wonder if she has laid him under siege. How long would your man have been on the road?'

'I fancy he made what haste he could,' said Simon, 'but four days at least, surely. That sets his story a week back, and no word yet to confirm it.'

'There will be, if it's true,' said Cadfael grimly, 'there will be! Of all the reports that fly about the world, ill news is the surest of all to arrive!'

He was still pondering this ominous shadow as he set off back along the Foregate, and his preoccupation was such that his greetings to acquaintances along the way were apt to be belated and absent-minded. It was mid-morning, and the dusty road brisk with traffic, and there were few inhabitants of this parish of Holy Cross outside the town walls that he did not know. He had treated many of them, or their children, at some time in these his cloistered years; even, sometimes, their beasts, for he who learns about the sicknesses of men cannot but pick up, here and there, some knowledge of the sicknesses of their animals, creatures with as great a capacity for suffering as their masters, and much less means of complaining, together with far less inclination to complain. Cadfael had often wished that men would use their beasts better, and tried to show them that it would be good husbandry. The horses of war had been part of that curious, slow process within him that had turned him at length from the trade of arms into the cloister.

Not that all abbots and priors used their mules and stock beasts well, either. But at least the best and wisest of them recognised it for good policy, as well as good Christianity.

But now, what could really be happening in Winchester, to turn the sky over it black by day and red by night? Like the pillars of cloud and fire that marked the passage of the elect through the wilderness, these had signalled and guided the beggar's flight from danger. He saw no reason to doubt the report. The same foreboding must have been on many loftier minds these last weeks, while the hot, dry summer, close cousin of fire, waited with a torch ready. But what a fool that woman must be, to attempt to besiege the bishop in his own castle in his own city, with the queen, every inch her match, no great distance away at the head of a strong army, and the Londoners implacably hostile. And how adamant against her, now, the bishop must be, to venture all by defying her. And both these high personages would remain strongly protected, and survive. But what of the lesser creatures they put in peril? Poor little traders and craftsmen and labourers who had no such fortresses to shelter them!

He had meditated his way from the care of horses and cattle to the tribulations of men, and was startled to hear at his back, at a moment when the traffic of the Foregate was light, the crisp, neat hooves of mules catching up on him at a steady clip. He halted at the corner of the horse-fair ground and looked back, and had not far to look, for they were close.

Two of them, a fine, tall beast almost pure white, fit for an abbot, and a smaller, lighter, fawn-brown creature stepping decorously a pace or two to the rear. But what caused Cadfael to pull up and turn fully towards them, waiting in surprised welcome for them to draw alongside, was the fact that both riders wore the Benedictine black, brothers to each other and to him. Plainly they had noted his own habit trudging before them, and made haste to overtake him, for as soon as he halted and recognised them for his like they eased to a walk, and so came gently alongside him.

'God be with you, brothers!' said Cadfael, eyeing them with interest. 'Do you come to our house here in Shrewsbury?'

'And with you, brother,' said the foremost rider, in a rich voice which yet had a slight, harsh crepitation in it, as though

182

the cave of his breast created a grating echo. Cadfael's ears pricked at the sound. He had heard the breath of many old men, long exposed to harsh outdoor living, rasp and echo in the same way, but this man was not old. 'You belong to this house of Saint Peter and Saint Paul? Yes, we are bound there with letters for the lord abbot. I take this to be his boundary wall beside us? Then it is not far to go now.'

'Very close,' said Cadfael. 'I'll walk beside you, for I'm homeward bound to that same house. Have you come far?'

He was looking up into a face gaunt and drawn, but fine-featured and commanding, with deep-set eyes very dark and tranquil. The cowl was flung back on the stranger's shoulders, and the long, fleshless head wore its rondel of straight black hair like a crown. A tall man, sinewy but emaciated. There was the fading sunburn of hotter lands than England on him, a bronze acquired over more years than one, but turned somewhat dull and sickly now, and though he held himself in the saddle like one born there, there was also a languor upon his movements, and an uncomplaining weariness in his face, a serene resignation which would better have fitted an old man. This man might have been somewhere in his mid-forties, surely not much more.

'Far enough,' he said with a thin, dark smile, 'but today only from Brigge.'

'And bound further? Or will you stay with us for a while? You'll be heartily welcome visitors, you and the young brother here.'

The younger rider hovered silently, a little apart, as a servant might have done in dutiful attendance on his master. He was surely scarcely past twenty, lissome and tall, though his companion would top him by a head if they stood together. He had the oval, smooth, boy's face of his years, but formed and firm for all its suave planes. His cowl was drawn forward over his face, perhaps against the sun's glare. Large, shadowed eyes gazed out from the hood, fixed steadily upon his elder. The one glance they flashed at Cadfael was as quickly averted.

'We look to stay here for some time, if the lord abbot will give us refuge,' said the older man, 'for we have lost one roof, and must beg admittance under another.'

They had begun to move on at a leisurely walk, the dust of the Foregate powder-fine under the hooves of the mules. The young man fell in meekly behind, and let them lead. To the civil greetings that saluted them along the way, where Cadfael

183

was well known, and these his companions matter for friendly curiosity, the older man made quiet, courteous response. The younger said never a word.

The gatehouse and the church loomed, ahead on their left, the high wall beside them reflected heat from its stones. The rider let the reins hang loose on his mule's neck, folded veined hands, long-fingered and brown, and fetched a long sigh. Cadfael held his peace.

'Forgive me that I answer almost churlishly, brother, it is not meant so. After the habit and the daily company of silence, speech comes laboriously. And after a holocaust, and the fires of destruction, the throat is too dry to manage many words. You asked if we had come far. We have been some days on the road, for I cannot ride hard these days. We are come like beggars from the south …'

'From Winchester!' said Cadfael with certainty, recalling the foreboding, the cloud and the fire.

'From what is left of Winchester.' The worn but muscular hands were quite still, leaving it to Cadfael to lead the mule round the west end of the church and in at the arch of the gatehouse. It was not grief or passion that made it hard for the man to speak, he had surely seen worse in his time than he was now recalling. The chords of his voice creaked from under-use, and slowed upon the grating echo. A beautiful voice it must have been in its heyday, before the velvet frayed. 'Is it possible,' he said wonderingly, 'that we come the first? I had thought word would have flown thus far north almost a week ago, but true, escape this way would have been no simple matter. Have we to bring the news, then? The great ones fell out over us. Who am I to complain, who have had my part in the like, elsewhere? The empress laid siege to the bishop in his castle of Wolvesey, in the city, and the bishop rained fire-arrows down upon the roofs rather than upon his enemies. The town is laid waste. A nunnery burned to the ground, churches razed, and my priory of Hyde Mead, that Bishop Henry so desired to take into his own hands, is gone for ever, brought down in flames. We are here, we two, homeless and asking shelter. The brothers are scattered through all the Benedictine houses of the land, wherever they have ties of blood or friendship. There will never be any going home to Hyde.'

So it was true. The finger of God had pointed one poor devil out of the trap, and let him look back from a hill to see the scarlet and the black of fire and smoke devour a city. Bishop Henry's own city, to which his own hand had set light.

'God sort all!' said Cadfael.

'Doubtless he will!' The voice with its honeyed warmth and abrasive echo rang under the archway of the gatehouse. Brother Porter came out, smiling welcome, and a groom came running for the horses, sighting fraternal visitors. The great court opened serene in sunshine, crossed and re-crossed by busy, preoccupied people, brothers, lay brothers, stewards, all about their normal, mastered affairs. The child oblates and schoolboys, let loose from their studies, were tossing a ball, their shrill voices gay and piercing in the still half-hour before noon. Life here made itself heard, felt and seen, as regular as the seasons.

They halted within the gate. Cadfael held the stirrup for the stranger, though there was no need, for he lighted down as naturally as a bird settling and folding its wings; but slowly, with languid grace, and stood to unfold a long, graceful but unfeebled body, well above six feet tall, and lance-straight as it was lance-lean. The young one had leaped from the saddle in an instant, and stood baulked, circling uneasily, jealous of Cadfael's ministering hand. And still made no sound, neither of gratitude nor protest.

'I'll be your herald to Abbot Radulfus,' said Cadfael, 'if you'll permit. What shall I say to him?'

'Say that Brother Humilis and Brother Fidelis, of the sometime priory of Hyde Mead, which is laid waste, ask audience and protection of his goodness, in all submission, and in the name of the Rule.'

This man had surely known little in the past of humility, and little of submission, though he had embraced both now with a whole heart.

'I will say so,' said Cadfael, and turned for a moment to the young brother, expecting his amen. The cowled head inclined modestly, the oval face was hidden in shadow, but there was no voice.

'Hold my young friend excused,' said Brother Humilis, erect by his mule's milky head, 'if he cannot speak his greeting. Brother Fidelis is dumb.'

Chapter Two

RING OUR brothers in to me,' Abbot Radulfus, rising from his desk in surprise and concern when Cadfael had reported to him the arrivals, and the bare bones of their story. He pushed aside parchment and pen and stood erect, dark and tall against the brilliant sunlight through the parlour window. 'That this should ever be! City and church laid waste together! Certainly they are welcome here lifelong, if need be. Bring them hither, Cadfael. And remain with us. You may be their guide afterwards, and bring them to Prior Robert. We must make appropriate places for them in the dortoir.'

Cadfael went on his errand content not to be dismissed, and led the newcomers down the length of the great court to the corner where the abbot's lodging lay sheltered in its small garden. What there was to be learned from the travellers of affairs in the south he was eager to learn, and so would Hugh be, when he knew of their coming. For this time news had been unwontedly slow on the road, and matters might have been moving with considerably greater speed down in Winchester since the unlucky brothers of Hyde dispersed to seek refuge elsewhere.

'Father Abbot, here are Brother Humilis and Brother Fidelis.'

It seemed dark in the little wood-panelled parlour after the radiance without, and the two tall, masterful men stood studying each other intently in the warm, shadowy stillness.

Radulfus himself had drawn forward stools for the newcomers, and with a motion of a long hand invited them to be seated, but the young one drew back deferentially into deeper shadow and remained standing. He could never be the spokesman; that might well be the reason for his self-effacement. But Radulfus, who had yet to learn of the young man's disability, certainly noted the act, and observed it without either approval or disapproval.

'Brothers, you are very welcome in our house, and all we can provide is yours. I hear you have had a long ride, and a sad loss that has driven you forth. I grieve for our brothers of Hyde. But here at least we hope to offer you tranquillity of mind, and a secure shelter. In these lamentable wars we have been fortunate. You, the elder, are Brother Humilis?'

'Yes, Father. Here I present you our prior's letter, commending us both to your kindness.' He had carried it in the breast of his habit, and now drew it forth and laid it on the abbot's desk. 'You will know, Father, that the abbey of Hyde has been an abbey without an abbot for two years now. They say commonly that Bishop Henry had it in mind to bring it into his own hands as an episcopal convent, which the brothers strongly resisted, and denying us a head may well have been a move designed to weaken us and reduce our voice. Now that is of no consequence, for the house of Hyde is gone, razed to the ground and blackened by fire.'

'Is it such entire destruction?' asked Radulfus, frowning over his linked hands.

'Utter destruction. In time to come a new house may be raised there, who knows? But of the old nothing remains.'

'You had best tell me all that you can,' said Radulfus heavily. 'Here we live far from these events, almost in peace. How did this holocaust come about?'

Brother Humilis – what could his proud name have been before he thus calmly claimed for himself humility? – folded his hands in the lap of his habit, and fixed his hollow dark eyes upon the abbot's face. There was a creased scar, long ago healed and pale, marking the left side of his tonsure, Cadfael noted, and knew, the crescent shape of a glancing stroke from a right-handed swordsman. It did not surprise him. No straight western sword, but a Seljuk scimitar. So that was where he had got the bronze that had now faded and sickened into dun.

'The empress entered Winchester towards the end of July, I

do not recall the date, and took up her residence in the royal castle by the west gate. She sent to Bishop Henry in his palace to come to her, but they say he sent back word that he would come, but must a little delay, by what excuse I never heard. He delayed too long, but by what followed he made good use of such days of grace as he had, for by the time the empress lost patience and moved up her forces against him he was safely shut up in his new castle of Wolvesey, in the south-east corner of the city, backed into the wall. And the queen, or so they said in the town, was moving her Flemings up in haste to his aid. Whether or no, he had a great garrison within there, and well supplied. I ask pardon of God and of you, Father,' said Brother Humilis gently, 'that I took such pains to follow these warlike reports, but my training was in arms, and a man cannot altogether forget.'

'God forbid,' said Radulfus, 'that a man should feel he need forget anything that was done in good faith and loyal service. In arms or in the cloister, we have all a score to pay to this country and this people. Closed eyes are of little use to either. Go on! Who struck the first blow?'

For they had been allies only a matter of weeks earlier!

'The empress. She moved to surround Wolvesey as soon as she knew he had shut himself in. Everything they had they used against the castle, even such engines as they were able to raise. And they pulled down any buildings, shops, houses, all that lay too close, to clear the ground. But the bishop had a strong garrison, and his walls are new. He began to build, as I hear, only ten years or so ago. It was his men who first used firebrands. Much of the city within the wall has burned, churches, a nunnery, shops – it might not have been so terrible if the season had not been high summer, and so dry.'

'And Hyde Mead?'

'There's no knowing from which side came the arrows that set us alight. The fighting had spilled outside the city walls by then, and there was looting, as always,' said Brother Humilis. 'We fought the fire as long as we could, but there was none besides to help us, and it was too fierce, we could not bring it under. Our prior ordered that we withdraw into the countryside, and so we did. Somewhat short of our number,' he said. 'There were deaths.'

Always there were deaths, and usually of the innocent and helpless. Radulfus stared with locked brows into the chalice of his linked hands, and thought.

'The prior lived to write letters. Where is he now?'

'Safe, in a manor of a kinsman, some miles from the city. He has ordered our withdrawal, dispersing the brothers wherever they might best find shelter. I asked if I might come to beg asylum here in Shrewsbury, and Brother Fidelis with me. And we are come, and are in your hands.'

'Why?' asked the abbot. 'Welcome indeed you are, I ask only, why here?'

'Father, some mile or two up-river from here, on a manor called Salton, I was born. I had a fancy to see the place again, or at least be near it, before I die.' He smiled, meeting the penetrating eyes beneath the knotted brows. 'It was the only property my father held in this shire. There I was born, as it so happened. A man displaced from his last home may well turn back to his first.'

'You say well. So far as is in us, we will supply that home. And your young brother?' Fidelis put back the cowl from his neck, bent his head reverently, and made a small outward sweep of submissive hands, but no sound.

'Father, he cannot speak for himself, I offer thanks from us both. I have not been altogether in my best health in Hyde, and Brother Fidelis, out of pure kindness, has become my faithful friend and attendant. He has no kinsfolk to whom he can go, he elects to be with me and tend me as before. If you will permit.' He waited for the acknowledging nod and smile before he added: 'Brother Fidelis will serve God here with every faculty he has. I know him, and I answer for him. But one, his voice, he cannot employ. Brother Fidelis is mute.'

'He is no less welcome,' said Radulfus, 'because his prayers must be silent. His silence may be more eloquent than our spoken words.' If he had been taken aback he had mastered the check so quickly as to give no sign. It would not be so often that Abbot Radulfus would be disconcerted. 'After this journey,' he said, 'you must both be weary, and still in some distress of mind until you have again a bed, a place, and work to do. Go now with Brother Cadfael, he will take you to Prior Robert, and show you everything within the enclave, dortoir and frater and gardens and herbarium, where he rules. He will find you refreshment and rest, your first need. And at Vespers you shall join us in worship.'

Word of the arrivals from the south brought Hugh Beringar down hotfoot from the town to confer first with the abbot, and then with Brother Humilis, who repeated freely what he had

189

already once related. When he had gleaned all he could, Hugh
went to find Cadfael in the herb-garden, where he was busy
watering. There was an hour yet before Vespers, the time of
day when all the necessary work had been done, and even a
gardener could relax and sit for a while in the shade. Cadfael
put away his watering-can, leaving the open, sunlit beds until
the cool of the evening, and sat down beside his friend on the
bench against the high south wall.

'Well, you have a breathing-space, at least,' he said. 'They
are at each other's throats, not reaching for yours. Great pity,
though, that townsmen and monastics and poor nuns should be
the sufferers. But so it goes in this world. And the queen and
her Flemings must be in the town by now, or very near. What
happens next? The besiegers may very well find themselves
besieged.'

'It has happened before,' agreed Hugh. 'And the bishop had
fair warning he might have need of a well-stocked larder, but
she may have taken her supplies for granted. If I were the
queen's general, I would take time to cut all the roads into
Winchester first, and make certain no food can get in. Well, we
shall see. And I hear you were the first to have speech with
these two brothers from Hyde.'

'They overtook me in the Foregate. And what do you make
of them, now you've been closeted with them so long?'

'What should I make of them, thus at first sight? A sick man
and a dumb man. More to the purpose, what do your brothers
make of them?' Hugh had a sharp eye on his old friend's face,
which was blunt and sleepy and private in the late afternoon
heat, but was never quite closed against him. 'The elder is
noble, clearly. And he is ill. I guess at a martial past, for I think
he has old wounds. Did you see he goes a little sidewise,
favouring his left flank? Something has never quite healed.
And the young one … I well understand he has fallen under the
spell of a such a man, and idolises him. Lucky for both! He has
a powerful protector, his lord has a devoted nurse. Well?' said
Hugh, challenging judgement with a confident smile.

'You haven't yet divined who our new elder brother is? They
may not have told you all,' admitted Cadfael tolerantly, 'for it
came out almost by chance. A martial past, yes, he avowed it,
though you could have guessed it no less surely. The man is
past forty-five, I judge, and has visible scars. He has said, also,
that he was born here at Salton, then a manor of his father's.
And he has a scar on his head, bared by the tonsure, that was

190

made by a Seljuk scimitar, some years back. A mere slice, readily healed, but left its mark. Salton was held formerly by the Bishop of Chester, and granted to the church of Saint Chad, here within the walls. They let it go many years since to a noble family, the Marescots. There's a local tenant holds it under them.' He opened a levelled brown eye, beneath a bushy brow russet at autumn. 'Brother Humilis is a Marescot. I know of only one Marescot of this man's age who went to the Crusade. Sixteen or seventeen years ago it must be. I was newly monk, then, part of me still hankered, and I had one eye always on the tale of those who took the Cross. As raw and eager as I was, surely, and bound for as bitter a fall, but pure enough in their going. There was a certain Godfrid Marescot who took three score with him from his own lands. He made a notable name for valour.'

'And you think this is he? Thus fallen?'

'Why not? The great ones are open to wounds no less than the simple. All the more,' said Cadfael, 'if they lead from before, and not from behind. They say this one was never later than first.'

He had still the crusader blood quick within him, he could not choose but awake and respond, however the truth had sunk below his dreams and hopes, all those years ago. Others, no less, had believed and trusted, no less to shudder and turn aside from much of what was done in the name of the Faith.

'Prior Robert will be running through the tale of the lords of Salton this moment,' said Cadfael, 'and will not fail to find his man. He knows the pedigree of every lord of a manor in this shire and beyond, for thirty years back and more. Brother Humilis will have no trouble in establishing himself, he sheds lustre upon us by being here, he need do nothing more.'

'As well,' said Hugh wryly, 'for I think there is no more he can do, unless it be to die here, and here be buried. Come, you have a better eye than mine for mortal sickness. The man is on his way out of this world. No haste, but the end is assured.'

'So it is for you and for me,' said Cadfael sharply. 'And as for haste, it's neither you nor I that hold the measure. It will come when it will come. Until then, every day is of consequence, the last no less than the first.'

'So be it!' said Hugh, and smiled, unchidden. 'But he'll come into your hands before many days are out. And what of his youngling – the dumb boy?'

'Nothing of him! Nothing but silence and shrinking into the

191

shadows. Give us time,' said Cadfael, 'and we shall learn to know him better.'

A man who has renounced possessions may move freely from one asylum to another, and be no less at home, make do with nothing as well in Shrewsbury as in Hyde Mead. A man who wears what every other man under the same discipline wears need not be noticeable for more than a day. Brother Humilis and Brother Fidelis resumed here in the midlands the same routine they had kept in the south, and the hours of the day enfolded them no less firmly and serenely. Yet Prior Robert had made a satisfactory end of his cogitations concerning the feudal holdings and family genealogies in the shire, and it was very soon made known to all, through his reliable echo, Brother Jerome, that the abbey had acquired a most distinguished son, a crusader of acknowledged valour, who had made a name for himself in the recent contention against the rising Atabeg Zenghi of Mosul, the latest threat to the Kingdom of Jerusalem. Prior Robert's personal ambitions lay all within the cloister, but for all that he missed never a turn of the fortunes of the world without. Four years since, Jerusalem had been shaken to its foundations by the king's defeat at this Zenghi's hands, but the kingdom had survived through its alliance with the emirate of Damascus. In that unhappy battle, so Robert made known discreetly, Godfrid Marescot had played a heroic part.

'He has observed every office, and worked steadily every hour set aside for work,' said Brother Emund the infirmarer, eyeing the new brother across the court as he trod slowly towards the church for Compline, in the radiant stillness and lingering warmth of evening. 'And he has not asked for any help of yours or mine. But I wish he had a better colour, and a morsel of flesh more on those long bones. That bronze gone dull, with no blood behind it ...'

And there went the faithful shadow after him, young, lissome, with strong, flowing pace, and hand ever advanced a little to prop an elbow, should it flag, or encircle a lean body, should it stagger or fall.

'There goes one who knows it all,' said Cadfael, 'and cannot speak. Nor would if he could, without his lord's permission. A son of one of his tenants, would you say? Something of that kind, surely. The boy is well born and taught. He knows Latin, almost as well as his master.'

192

On reflection it seemed a liberty to speak of a man as anyone's master who called himself Humilis, and had renounced the world.

'I had in mind,' said Edmund, but hesitantly, and with reverence, 'a natural son. I may be far astray, but it is what came to mind. I take him for a man who would love and protect his seed, and the young one might well love and admire him, for that as for all else.'

And it could well be true. The tall man and the tall youth, a certain likeness, even, in the clear features – insofar, thought Cadfael, as anyone had yet looked directly at the features of young Brother Fidelis, who passed so silently and unobtrusively about the enclave, patiently finding his way in this unfamiliar place. He suffered, perhaps, more than his elder companion in the change, having less confidence and experience, and all the anxiety of youth. He clung to his lodestar, and every motion he made was oriented by its light. They had a shared carrel in the scriptorium, for Brother Humilis had need, only too clearly, of a sedentary occupation, and had proved to have a delicate hand with copying, and artistry in illumination. And since he had limited control after a period of work, and his hand was liable to shake in fine detail, Abbot Radulfus had decreed that Brother Fidelis should be present with him to assist whenever he needed relief. The one hand matched the other as if the one had taught the other, though it might have been only emulation and love. Together, they did slow but admirable work.

'I had never considered,' said Edmund, musing aloud, 'how remote and strange a man could be who has no voice, and how hard it is to reach and touch him. I have caught myself talking of him to Brother Humilis, over the lad's head, and been ashamed – as if he had neither hearing nor wits. I blushed before him. Yet how do you touch hands with such a one? I never had practice in it till now, and I am altogether astray.'

'Who is not?' said Cadfael.

It was truth, he had noted it. The silence, or rather the moderation of speech enjoined by the Rule had one quality, the hush that hung about Brother Fidelis quite another. Those who must communicate with him tended to use much gesture and few words, or none, reflecting his silence. As though, truly, he had neither hearing nor wits. But manifestly he had both, quick and delicate senses and sharp hearing, tuned to the least sound. And that was also strange. So often the dumb were dumb because they had never learned of sounds, and therefore made none. And this young man had been well taught in his letters, and knew some Latin, which argued a mind far more agile than most. Unless, thought Cadfael doubtfully, his muteness was a new-come thing in recent years, from some constriction of the cords of the tongue or the sinews of the throat? Or even if he had it from birth, might it not be caused by some strings too tightly drawn under his tongue, that could be eased by exercise or loosed by the knife?

'I meddle too much,' said Cadfael to himself crossly, shaking off the speculation that could lead nowhere. And he went to Compline in an unwontedly penitent mood, and by way of discipline observed silence himself for the rest of the evening.

They gathered the purple-black Lammas plums next day, for they were just on the right edge of ripeness. Some would be eaten at once, fresh as they were, some Brother Petrus would boil down into a preserve thick and dark as cakes of poppy-seed, and some would be laid out on racks in the drying house to wrinkle and crystallise into gummy sweetness. Cadfael had a few trees in a small orchard within the enclave, though most of the fruit-trees were in the main garden of the Gaye, the lush meadow-land along the riverside. The novices and younger brothers picked the fruit, and the oblates and schoolboys were allowed to help; and if everyone knew that a few handfuls went into the breasts of tunics rather than into the baskets, provided the depredations were reasonable Cadfael turned a blind eye.

It was too much to expect silence in such fine weather and such a holiday occupation. The voices of the boys rang merrily in Cadfael's ears as he decanted wine in his workshop, and went back and forth among his plants along the shadowed wall, weeding and watering. A pleasant sound! He could pick out known voices, the children's shrill and light, their elders in a whole range of tones. That warm, clear call, that was Brother Rhun, the youngest of the novices, sixteen years old, only two months since received into probation, and not yet tonsured, lest he should think better of his impulsive resolve to quit a world he had scarcely seen. But Rhun would not repent of his choice. He had come to the abbey for Saint Winifred's festival, a cripple and in pain, and by her grace now he went straight and tall and agile, radiating delight upon everyone who came near him. As now, surely, on whoever was his partner at the nearest of the plum-trees. Cadfael went to the edge of the

194

orchard to see, and there was the sometime lame boy up among the branches, secure and joyous, his slim, deft hands nursing the fruit so lightly his fingers scarcely blurred the bloom, and leaning down to lay them in the basket held up to him by a tall brother whose back was turned, and whose figure was not immediately recognisable, until he moved round, the better to follow Rhun's movements, and showed the face of Brother Fidelis.

It was the first time Cadfael had seen that face so clearly, in sunlight, the cowl slung back. Rhun, it seemed, was one creature at least who found no difficulty in drawing near to the mute brother, but spoke out to him merrily and found no strangeness in his silence. Rhun leaned down laughing, and Fidelis looked up, smiling, one face reflecting the other. Their hands touched on the handle of the basket as Rhun dangled it at the full stretch of his arm while Fidelis plucked a cluster of low-growing fruit pointed out to him from above.

After all, thought Cadfael, it was to be expected that valiant innocence would stride in boldly where most of us hesitate to set foot. And besides, Rhun has gone most of his life with a cruel flaw that set him apart, and taken no bitterness from it, naturally he would advance without fear into another man's isolation. And thank God for him, and for the valour of the children!

He went back to his weeding very thoughtfully, recalling that eased and sunlit glimpse of one who habitually withdrew into shadow. An oval face, firm-featured and by nature grave, with a lofty forehead and strong cheekbones, and clear ivory skin, smooth and youthful. There in the orchard he looked scarcely older than Rhun, though there must surely be a few years between them. The halo of curling hair round his tonsure was an autumn brown, almost fiery-bright, yet not red, and his wide-set eyes, under strong, level brows, were of a luminous grey, at least in that full light. A very comely young man, like a veiled reflection of Rhun's sunlit beauty. Noonday and twilight met together.

The fruit-pickers were still at work, though with most of their harvest already gleaned, when Cadfael put away his hoe and watering-can and went to prepare for Vespers. In the great court there was the usual late-afternoon bustle, brothers returning from their work along the Gaye, the stir of arrival in guest-hall and stable-yard, and in the cloister the sound of Brother Anselm's little portative organ testing out a new

195

chant. The illuminators and copiers would be putting the finishing touches to their afternoon's work, and cleaning their pens and brushes. Brother Humilis must be alone in his carrel, having sent Fidelis out to the joyous labour in the garden, for nothing less would have induced the boy to leave him. Cadfael had intended crossing the open garth to the precentor's workshop, to sit down comfortably with Anselm for a quarter of an hour, until the Vesper bell, and talk and perhaps argue about music. But the memory of the dumb youth, so kindly sent out to his brief pleasure in the orchard among his peers, stirred in him as he entered the cloister, and the gaunt visage of Brother Humilis rose before him, self-contained, uncomplaining, proudly solitary. Or should it be, rather, humbly solitary? That was the quality he had claimed for himself and by which he desired to be accepted. A large claim, for one so celebrated. There was not a soul within here now who did not know his reputation. If he longed to escape it, and be as mute as his servitor, he had been cruelly thwarted.

Cadfael veered from his intent, and turned instead along the north walk of the cloister, where the carrels of the scriptorium basked in the sun, even at this hour. Humilis had been given a study midway, where the light would fall earliest and linger longest. It was quiet there, the soft tones of Anselm's organetto seemed very distant and hushed. The grass of the open garth was blanched and dry, in spite of daily watering.

'Brother Humilis...' said Cadfael softly, at the opening of the carrel.

The leaf of parchment was pushed askew on the desk, a small pot of gold had spilled drops along the paving as it rolled. Brother Humilis lay forward over his desk with his right arm flung up to hold by the wood, and his left hand gripped hard into his groin, the wrist braced to press hard into his side. His head lay with the left cheek on his work, smeared with the blue and the scarlet, and his eyes were shut, but clenched shut, upon the controlled awareness of pain. He had not uttered a sound. If he had, those close by would have heard him. What he had, he had contained. So he would still.

Cadfael took him gently about the body, pinning the sustaining arm where it rested. The blue-veined eyelids lifted in their high vaults, and eyes brilliant and intelligent behind their veils of pain peered up into his face. 'Brother Cadfael ...?'

'Lie still a moment yet,' said Cadfael. 'I'll fetch Edmund – Brother Infirmarer...'

'No! Brother, get me hence ... to my bed ... This will pass ... it is not new. Only softly, softly help me away! I would not be a show...

It was quicker and more private to help him up the night stairs from the church to his own cell in the dortoir, rather than across the great court to the infirmary, and that was what he earnestly desired, that there might be no general alarm and fuss about him. He rose more by strength of will than any physical force, and with Cadfael's sturdy arm about him, and his own arm leaning heavily round Cadfael's shoulders, they passed unnoticed into the cool gloom of the church and slowly climbed the staircase. Stretched on his own bed, Humilis submitted himself with a bleakly patient smile to Cadfael's care, and made no ado when Cadfael stripped him of his habit, and uncovered the oblique stain of mingled blood and pus that slanted across the left hip of his linen drawers and down into the groin.

'It breaks,' said the calm thread of a voice from the pillow. 'Now and then it suppurates – I know. The long ride ... Pardon brother! I know the stench offends...'

'I must bring Edmund,' said Cadfael, unloosing the drawstring and freeing the shirt. He did not yet uncover what lay beneath. 'Brother Infirmarer must know.'

'Yes ... But no other! What need for more?'

'Except Brother Fidelis? Does he know all?'

'Yes, all!' said Humilis, and faintly and fondly smiled. 'We need not fear him, even if he could speak he would not, but there's nothing of what ails me he does not know. Let him rest until Vespers is over.'

Cadfael left him lying with closed eyes, a little eased, for the lines of his face had relaxed from their grimace of pain, and went down to find Brother Edmund, just in time to draw him away from Vespers. The filled baskets of plums lay by the garden hedge, awaiting disposal after the office, and the gatherers were surely already within the church, after hasty ablutions. Just as well! Brother Fidelis might at first be disposed to resent any other undertaking the care of his master. Let him find him recovered and well doctored, and he would accept what had been done. As good a way to his confidence as any.

'I knew we should be needed before long,' said Edmund, leading the way vigorously up the day stairs. 'Old wounds, you

197

think? Your skills will avail more than mine, you have ploughed that field yourself.'

The bell had fallen silent. They heard the first notes of the evening office raised faintly from within the church as they entered the sick man's cell. He opened slow, heavy lids and smiled at them.

'Brothers, I grieve to be a trouble to you …'

The deep eyes were hooded again, but he was aware of all, and submitted meekly to all.

They drew down the linen that hid him from the waist, and uncovered the ruin of his body. A great misshapen map of scar tissue stretched from the left hip, where the bone had survived by miracle, slantwise across his belly and deep, deep into the groin. Its coloration was of limestone pallor and striation below, where he was half disembowelled but stonily healed. But towards the upper part it was reddened and empurpled, the inflamed belly burst into a wet-lipped wound that oozed a foul jelly and a faint smear of blood.

Godfrid Marsecot's crusade had left him maimed beyond repair, yet not beyond survival. The faceless, fingerless lepers who crawl into Saint Giles, thought Cadfael, have not worse to bear. Here ends his line, in a noble plant incapable of seed. But what worth is manhood, if this is not a man?

Chapter Three

DMUND RAN for soft cloths and warm water, Cadfael for draughts and ointments and decoctions from his workshop. Tomorrow he would pick the fresh, juicy water betony, and wintergreen and woundwort, more effective than the creams and waxes he made from them to keep in store. But for tonight these must do. Sanicle, ragwort, moneywort, adder's tongue, all cleansing and astringent, good for old, ulcerated wounds, were all to be found around the hedgerows and the meadows close by, and along the banks of the Meole Brook.

They cleaned the broken wound of its exudations with a lotion of woundwort and sanicle, and dressed it with a paste of the same herbs with betony and the chickweed wintergreen, covered it with clean linen, and swathed the patient's wasted trunk with bandages to keep the dressing in place. Cadfael had brought also a draught to soothe the pain, a syrup of woundwort and Saint John's wort in wine, with a little of the poppy syrup added. Brother Humilis lay passive under their hands, and let them do with him what they would.

'Tomorrow,' said Cadfael, 'I'll gather the same herbs fresh, and bruise them for a green plaster, it works more strongly, it will draw out the evil. This has happened many times since you got the injury?'

'Not many times. But if I'm overworn, yes – it happens,' said the bluish lips, without complaint.

'Then you must not be allowed to overwear. But it has also

healed before, and will again. This woundwort got its name by good right. Be ruled now, and lie still here for two days, or three, until it closes clean, for if you stand and go it will be longer in healing.'

'He should by rights be in the infirmary,' said Edmund anxiously, 'where he could be undisturbed as long as is needful.'

'So he should,' agreed Cadfael, 'but that he's now well bedded here, and the less he stirs the betters. How do you feel yourself now, Brother?'

'At ease,' said Brother Humilis, and faintly smiled.

'In less pain?'

'Scarcely any. Vespers will be over,' said the faint voice, and the high-arched lids rolled back from fixed eyes. 'Don't let Fidelis fret for me ... He has seen worse – let him come.'

'I'll fetch him to you,' said Cadfael, and went at once to do it, for in this concession to the stoic mind there was more value than in anything further he could do here for the ravaged body. Brother Edmund followed him down the stair, anxious at his shoulder.

'Will it heal? Marvel he ever lived for it to heal at all. Did you ever see a man so torn apart, and live?'

'It happens,' said Cadfael, 'though seldom. Yes, it will close again. And open again at the least strain.' Not a word was said between them to enjoin or promise secrecy. The covering Godfrid Marescot had chosen for his ruin was sacred, and would be respected.

Fidelis was standing in the archway of the cloister, watching the brothers as they emerged, and looking with increasing concern for one who did not come.

Late from the orchard, the fruit-gatherers had been in haste for the evening office, and he had not looked then for Humilis, supposing him to be already in the church. But he was looking for him now. The straight, strong brows were drawn together, the long lips taut in anxiety. Cadfael approached him as the last of the brothers passed by, and the young man was turning to watch them go, almost in disbelief.

'Fidelis...' The boy's cowled head swung round to him in quick hope and understanding. It was not good news he was expecting, but any was better than none. It was to be seen in the set of his face. He had experienced all this more than once before.

'Fidelis, Brother Humilis is in his own bed in the dortoir. No

200

call for alarm now, he's resting, his trouble is tended. He's asking for you. Go to him.'

The boy looked quickly from Cadfael to Edmund, and back again, uncertain where authority lay, and already braced to go striding away. If he could ask nothing with his tongue, his eyes were eloquent enough, and Edmund understood them.

'He's easy, and he'll mend. You may go and come as you will in his service, and I will see that you are excused other duties until we're satisfied he does well, and can be left. I will make that good with Prior Robert. Fetch, carry, ask, according to need – if he has a wish, write it and it shall be fulfilled. But as for his dressings, Brother Cadfael will attend to them.'

There was yet a question, more truly a demand, in the ardent eyes. Cadfael answered it in quick reassurance. 'No one else has been witness. No one else need be, but for Father Abbot, who has a right to know what ails all his sons. You may be content with that as Brother Humilis is content.'

Fidelis flushed and brightened for an instant, bowed his head, made that small open gesture of his hands in submission and acceptance, and went from them swift and silent, to climb the day stairs. How many times had he done quiet service at the same sick-bed, alone and unaided? For if he had not grudged them being the first on the scene this time, he had surely lamented it, and been uncertain at first of their discretion.

'I'll go back before Compline,' said Cadfael 'and see if he sleeps, or if he needs another draught. And whether the young one has remembered to take food for himself as well as for Humilis! Now I wonder where that boy can have learned his medicine, if he's been caring for Brother Humilis alone, down there in Hyde?' It was plain the responsibility had not daunted him, nor could he have failed in his endeavours. To have kept any life at all in that valiant wreck was achievement enough.

If the boy had studied in the art of healing, he might make a good assistant in the herbarium, and would be glad to learn more. It would be something in common, a way in through the sealed door of his silence.

Brother Fidelis fetched and carried, fed, washed, shaved his patient, tended to all his bodily needs, apparently in perfect content so to serve day and night, if Humilis had not ordered him away sometimes into the open air, or to rest in his own cell, or to attend the offices of the church on behalf of both of them; as within two days of slow recovery Humilis increasingly did order, and was obeyed. The broken wound was healing, its lips no longer wet and limp, but drawing together gradually under the plasters of freshly-bruised leaves. Fidelis witnessed the slow improvement, and was glad and grateful, and assisted without revulsion as the dressing were changed. This maimed body was no secret from him.

A favoured family servant? A natural son, as Edmund had hazarded? Or simply a devout young brother of the Order who had fallen under the spell of a charm and nobility all the more irresistible because it was dying? Cadfael could not choose but speculate. The young can be wildly generous, giving away their years and their youth for love, without thought of any gain.

'You wonder about him,' said Humilis from his pillow, when Cadfael was changing his dressing in the early morning, and Fidelis had been sent down with the brothers to Prime.

'Yes,' said Cadfael honestly.

'But you don't ask. Neither have I asked anything. My future,' said Humilis reflectively, 'I left in Palestine. What remained of me I gave to God, and I trust the offering was not all worthless. My novitiate, clipped though it was because of my state, was barely ending when he entered Hyde. I have had good cause to thank God for him.'

'No easy matter,' said Cadfael, musing, 'for a dumb man to vouch for himself and make known his vocation. Had he some elder to speak for him?'

'He had written his plea, how his father was old, and would be glad to see his sons settled, and while his elder brother had the lands, he, the younger, wished to choose the cloister. He brought an endowment with him, but it was his fine hand and his scholarship chiefly commended him. I know no more of him,' said Humilis, 'except what I have learned from him in silence, and that is enough. To me he has been all the sons I shall never father.'

'I have wondered,' said Cadfael, drawing the clean linen carefully over the newly-knit wound, 'about his dumbness. Is it possible that it stems only from some malformation in the tongue? For plainly he is not deaf, to blot out speech from his knowledge. He hears keenly. I have usually found the two go together, but not in him. He learns by ear, and is quick to learn. He was taught, as you say, a fine hand. If I had him with me always among the herbs I could teach him all the years have taught me.'

'I ask no questions of him, he asks none of me,' said Humilis. 'God knows I ought to send him away from me, to a better service than nursing and comforting my too early corruption. He's young, he should be in the sun. But I am too craven to do it. If he goes, I will not hold him, but I have not the courage to dismiss him. And while he stays, I never cease to thank God for him.'

August pursued its unshadowed course, without a cloud, and the harvest filled the barns. Brother Rhun missed his new companion from the gardens and the garth, where the roses burst open daily in the noon and faded by night from the heat. The grapes trained along the north wall of the enclosed garden swelled and changed colour. And far south, in ravaged Winchester, the queen's army closed round the sometime besiegers, severed the roads by which supplies might come in, and began to starve the town. But news from the south was sparse, and travellers few, and here the unbiddable fruit was ripening early.

Of all the cheerful workers in that harvest, Rhun was the blithest. Less than three months ago he had been lame and in pain, now he went in joyous vigour, and could not have enough of his own happy body, or put it to sufficient labours to testify to his gratitude. He had no learning as yet, to admit him to the work of copying or study or colouring of manuscripts, he had a pleasant voice but little musical training; the tasks that fell to him were the unskilled and strenuous, and he delighted in them. There was no one who could fail to reflect the same delight in watching him stretch and lift and stride, dig and hew and carry, he who had lately dragged his own light weight along with crippled effort and constant pain. His elders beheld his beauty and vigour with fond admiration, and gave thanks to the saint who had healed him.

Beauty is a perilous gift, but Rhun had never given a thought to his own face, and would have been astonished to be told that he possessed so rare an endowment. Youth is no less vulnerable, by the very quality it has of making the heart ache that beholds and has lost it.

Brother Urien had lost more than his youth, and had not lost his youth long enough to have grown resigned to its passing. He was thirty-seven years old, and had come into the cloister barely a year past, after a ruinous marriage that had left him contorted in mind and spirit. The woman had wrung and left him, and he was not a mild man, but of strong and passionate appetites and imperious will. Desperation had driven him in to the cloister, and there he found no remedy. Deprivation and rage bite just as deeply within as without.

They were working side by side over the first summer apples, at the end of August, up in the dimness of the loft over the barn, laying out the fruit in wooden trays to keep as long as it would. The hot weather had brought on the ripening by at least ten days. The light in there was faintly golden, and heady with motes of dust, they moved as through a shimmering mist. Rhun's flaxen head, as yet unshorn, might have been a fair girl's, the curve of his cheek as he stooped over the shelves was suave as a rose-leaf, and the curling lashes that shadowed his eyes were long and lustrous. Brother Urien watched him sidewise, and his heart turned in him, shrunken and wrung with pain.

Rhun had been thinking of Fidelis, how he would have enjoyed the expedition to the Gaye, and he noticed nothing amiss when his neighbour's hand brushed his as they laid out the apples, or their shoulders touched briefly by chance. But it was not by chance when the outstretched hand, instead of brushing and removing, slid long fingers over his hand and held it, stroking from fingertips to wrist, and there lingering in a palpable caress.

By all the symbols of his innocence he should not have understood, not yet, not until much more had passed. But he did understand. His very candour and purity made him wise. He did not snatch his hand away, but withdrew it very gently and kindly, and turned his fair head to look Urien full in the face with wide, wide-set eyes of the clearest blue-grey, with such comprehension and pity that the wound burned unbearably deep, corrosive with rage and shame. Urien took his hand away and turned aside from him.

Revulsion and shock might have left a morsel of hope that one emotion could yet, with care, be changed gradually into another, since at least he would have known he had made a sharp impression. But this open-eyed understanding and pity repelled him beyond hope. How dared a green, simple virgin, who had never become aware of his body but through his lameness and physical pain, recognise the fire when it scorched him, and respond only with compassion? No fear, no blame, and no uncertainty. Nor would he complain to confessor or superior. Brother Urien went away with grief and desire

204

burning in his bowels, and the remembered face of the woman clear and cruel before his mind's eyes. Prayer was no cure for the memory of her.

Rhun brought away from that encounter, only a moment long and accomplished in silence, his first awareness of the tyranny of the body. Troubles from which he was secure could torture another man. His heart ached a little for Brother Urien, he would mention him in his prayers at Vespers. And so he did, and as Urien beheld still his lost wife's hostile visage, so did Rhun continue to see the dark, tense, handsome face that had winced away from his gaze with burning brow and hooded eyes, bitterly shamed where he, Rhun, had felt no blame, and no bitterness. This was indeed a dark and secret matter.

He said no word to anyone about what had happened. What had happened? Nothing! But he looked at his fellow men with changed eyes, by one dimension enlarged to take in their distresses and open his own being to their needs.

This happened to Rhun two days before he was finally acknowledged as firm in his vocation, and received the tonsure, to become the novice, Brother Rhun.

'So our little saint has made good his resolve,' said Hugh, encountering Cadfael as he came from the ceremony. 'And his cure shows no faltering! I tell you honestly, I go in awe of him. Do you think Winifred had an eye to his comeliness, when she chose to take him for her own? Welshwomen don't baulk their fancy when they see a beautiful youth.'

'You are an unregenerate heathen,' said Cadfael comfortably, 'but the lady should be used to you by now. Never think you'll shock her, there's nothing she has not seen in her time. And had I been in her reliquary I would have drawn that child to me, just as she did. She knew worth when she saw it. Why, he has almost sweetened even Brother Jerome!'

'That will never last!' said Hugh, and laughed. 'He's kept his own name – the boy?'

'It never entered his mind to change it.'

'They do not all so,' said Hugh, growing serious. 'This pair that came from Hyde – Humilis and Fidelis. They made large claims, did they not? Brother Humble we know by his former name, and he needs no other. What do we know of Brother Faithful? And I wonder which name came first?'

'The boy is a younger son,' said Cadfael. 'His elder has the lands, this one chose the cowl. With his burden, who could blame him? Humilis says his own novitiate was not yet completed when the young one came, and they drew together and became fast friends. They may well have been admitted together, and the names ... Who knows which of them chose first?'

They had halted before the gatehouse to look back at the church. Rhun and Fidelis had come forth together, two notably comely creatures with matched steps, not touching, but close and content. Rhun was talking with animation. Fidelis bore the traces of much watching and anxiety, but shone with a responsive glow. Rhun's new tonsure was bared to the sun, the fair hair round it roused like an aureole.

'He frequents them,' said Cadfael, watching. 'No marvel, he reaches out to every soul who has lost a piece of his being, such as a voice.' He said nothing of what the elder of that pair had lost. 'He talks for both. A pity he has small learning yet. There's neither of those two can read to Humilis, the one for want of a voice, the other for want of letters. But he studies, and he'll learn. Brother Paul thinks well of him.'

The two young men had vanished at the archway of the day stairs, plainly bound for the dortoir cell where Brother Humilis was still confined to his bed. Who would not be heartened by the vision of Brother Rhun just radiant from his admission to his heart's desire? And it was fitting, that reticent kinship between two barren bodies, the one virgin unawakened, the other hollowed out and despoiled in its prime. Two whose seed was not of this world.

It was that same afternoon that a young man in a soldier's serviceable riding gear, with rolled cloak at his saddle-bow, came in towards the town by the main London road to Saint Giles, and there asked directions to the abbey of Saint Peter and Saint Paul. He went bare-headed in the sun, and in his shirt-sleeves, with breast bared, and face and breast and naked forearms were brown as from a hotter sun even than here, where the summer did but paint a further copper shade on a hide already gilded. A neatly-made young man, on a good horse, with an easy seat in the saddle and a light hand on the rein, and a bush of wiry dark hair above a bold, blunt-featured face.

Brother Oswin directed him, and with pricking curiosity watched him ride on, wondering for whom he would enquire there. Evidently a fighting man, but from which army, and from whose household troops, to be heading for Shrewsbury abbey so particularly? He had not asked for town or sheriff. His business was not concerned with the warfare in the south. Oswin went back to his work with mild regret at knowing no more, but dutifully.

The rider, assured that he was near his goal, eased to a walk along the Foregate, looking with interest at all he saw, the blanched grass of the horse-fair ground, still thirsty for rain, the leisurely traffic of porter and cart and pony in the street, the gossiping neighbours out at their gates in the sun, the high, long wall of the abbey enclave on his left hand, and the lofty roof and tower of the church looming over it. Now he knew that he was arriving. He rounded the west end of the church, with its great door ajar outside the enclosure for parish use, and turned in under the arch of the gatehouse.

The porter came amiably to greet him and ask his business. Brother Cadfael and Hugh Beringar, still at their leisurely leave-taking close by, turned to examine the newcomer, noted his business-like and well-used harness and leathern coat slung behind, and the sword he wore, and had him accurately docketed in a moment. Hugh stiffened, attentive, for a man in soldier's gear heading in from the south might well have news. Moreover, one who came alone and at ease here through these shires loyal to King Stephen was likely to be of the same complexion. Hugh went forward to join the colloquy, eyeing the horseman up and down with restrained approval of his appearance.

'You're not, by chance, seeking me, friend? Hugh Beringar, at your service.'

'This is the lord sheriff,' said Brother Porter by way of introduction; and to Hugh: 'The traveller is asking for Brother Humilis – though by his former name.'

'I was some years in the service of Godfrid Marescot,' said the horseman, and slid his reins loose and lighted down to stand beside them. He was taller than Hugh by half a head, and strongly made, and his brown countenance was open and cheerful, lit by strikingly blue eyes. 'I've been hunting for him among the brothers dispersed in Winchester after Hyde burned to the ground. They told me he'd chosen to come here. I have some business in the north of the shire, and need his approval for what I intend. To tell the truth,' he said with a wry smile, 'I had clean forgotten the name he took when he entered Hyde. To me he's still my lord Godfrid.'

'So he must be to many,' said Hugh, 'who knew him aforetime. Yes, he's here. Are you from Winchester now?'

'From Andover. Where we've burned the town,' said the young man bluntly, and studied Hugh as attentively as he himself was being studied. It was plain they were of the same party.

'You're with the queen's army?'

'I am. Under FitzRobert.'

'Then you'll have cut the roads to the north. I hold this shire for King Stephen, as you must know. I would not keep you from your lord, but will you ride with me into Shrewsbury and sup at my house before you move on? I'll wait your convenience. You can give me what I'm hungry for, news of what goes forward there in the south. May I know your name? I've given you mine.'

'My name is Nicholas Harnage. And very heartily I'll tell you all I know, my lord, when I've done my errand here. How is it with Godfrid?' he asked earnestly, and looked from Hugh to Cadfael, who stood by watching, listening, and until now silent.

'Not in the best of health,' said Cadfael, 'but neither was he, I suppose, when you last parted from him. He has broken an old wound, but that came, I think, after his long ride here. It is mending well now, in a day or two he'll be up and back to the duties he's chosen. He is well loved, and well tended by a young brother who came here with him from Hyde, and had been his attendant there. If you'll wait but a moment I'll tell Father Prior that Brother Humilis has a visitor, and bring you to him.'

That errand he did very briskly, to leave the pair of them together for a few minutes. Hugh needed tidings, all the firsthand knowledge he could get from that distant and confused battlefield, where two factions of his enemies, by their mutual clawings, had now drawn in the whole formidable array of his friends upon one side. A shifty side at best, seeing the bishop had changed his allegiance now for the third time. But at least it held the empress's forces in a steel girdle now in the city of Winchester, and was tightening the girdle to starve them out. Cadfael's warrior blood, long since abjured, had a way of coming to the boil when he heard steel in the offing. His chief uneasiness was that he could not be truly penitent about it. His king was not of this world, but in this world he could not help having a preference.

Prior Robert was taking his afternoon rest, which was known to others as his hour of study and prayer. A good time, since he was not disposed to rouse himself and come out to view the visitor, or exert himself to be ceremoniously hospitable. Cadfael got what he had counted on, a gracious permission to conduct the guest to Brother Humilis in his cell, and attend him to provide whatever assistance he might require. In addition, of course, to Father Prior's greetings and blessing, sent from his daily retreat into meditation.

They had had time to grow familiar and animated while he had been absent, he saw it in their faces, and the easy turn of both heads, hearing his returning step. They would ride together into the town already more than comrades in arms, potential friends.

'Come with me,' said Cadfael, 'and I'll bring you to Brother Humilis.'

On the day stairs the young, earnest voice at his shoulder said quietly: 'Brother, you have been doctoring my lord since this fit came on. So the lord sheriff told me. He says you have great skills in herbs and medicine and healing.'

'The lord sheriff,' said Cadfael, 'is my good friend for some years, and thinks better of me than I deserve. But, yes, I to tend your lord, and thus far we two do well together. You need not fear he is not valued truly, we do know his worth. See him, and judge for yourself. For you must know what he suffered in the east. You were with him there?'

'Yes. I'm from his own lands, I sailed when he sent for a fresh force, and shipped some elders and wounded for home. And I came back with him, when he knew his usefulness there was ended.'

'Here,' said Cadfael, with his foot on the top stair, 'his usefulness is far from ended. There are young men here who live the brighter by his light – under the light by which we all live, that's understood. You may find two of them with him now. If one of them lingers, let him, he has the right. That's his companion from Hyde.'

They emerged into the corridor that ran the whole length of the dortoir, between the partitioned cells, and stood at the opening of the dim, narrow space allotted to Humilis.

'Go in,' said Cadfael. 'You do not need a herald to be welcome.'

Chapter Four

N THE cell the little lamp for reading was not
lighted, since one of the young attendants could not
read, and the other could not speak, while the
incumbent himself still lay propped up with pillows
in his cot, too weak to nurse a heavy book. But if Rhun could
not read well, he could learn by heart, and recite what he had
learned with feeling and warmth, and he was in the middle of a
prayer of Saint Augustine which Brother Paul had taught him,
when he felt suddenly that he had an audience larger than he
had bargained for, and faltered and fell silent, turning towards
the open end of the cell.

Nicholas Harnage stood hesitant within the doorway, until
his eyes grew accustomed to the dim light. Brother Humilis
had opened his eyes in wonder when Rhun faltered. He beheld
the best-loved and most trusted of his former squires standing
almost timorously at the foot of his bed.

'Nicholas?' he ventured, doubtful and wondering, heaving
himself up to stare more intently.

Brother Fidelis stooped at once to prop and raise him, and
brace the pillows at his back, and then as silently withdrew into
the dark corner of the cell, to leave the field to the visitor.

'Nicholas! It *is* you!'

The young man went forward and fell on his knee to clasp
and kiss the thin hand stretched out to him.

'Nicholas, what are you doing here? You're welcome as the
morning, but I never looked to see you in this place. It was

kind indeed to seek me out in such a distant refuge. Come, sit by me here. Let me see you close!'

Rhun had slipped away silently. From the doorway he made a small reverence before he vanished. Fidelis took a step to follow him, but Humilis laid a hand on his arm to detain him.

'No, stay! Don't leave us! Nicholas, to this young brother I owe more than I can ever repay. He serves me as truly in this field as you did in arms.'

'All who have been your men, like me, will be grateful to him,' said Nicholas fervently, looking up into a face shadowed by the cowl, and as featureless as voiceless in this half-darkness. If he wondered at getting no answer, but only an inclination of the head by way of acknowledgement, he shrugged it off without another thought, for it was of no importance that he should reach a closer acquaintance with one he might never see again. He drew the stool close to the bedside, and sat studying the emaciated face of his lord with deep concern.

'They tell me you are mending well. But I see you leaner and more fallen than when I left you, that time in Hyde, and went to do your errand. I had a long search in Winchester to find your prior, and enquire of him where you were gone. Need you have chosen to ride so far? The bishop would have taken you into the Old Minster, and been glad of you.'

'I doubt if I should have been so glad of the bishop,' said Brother Humilis with a wry smile. 'No, I had my reasons for coming so far north. This shire and this time I knew as a child. A few years only, but they are the years a man remembers later in life. Never trouble for me, Nick, I'm very well here, as well as any other place, and better than most. Let us speak rather of you. How have you fared in your new service, and what has brought you here to my bedside?'

'I've thrived, having your commendation. William of Ypres has mentioned me to the queen, and would have taken me among his officers, but I'd rather stay with FitzRobert's English than go to the Flemings. I have a command. It was you who taught me all I know,' he said, at once glowing and sad, 'you and the mussulmen of Mosul.'

'It was not the Atabeg Zenghi,' said Brother Humilis smiling, 'whose affairs sent you here so far to seek me out. Leave him to the King of Jerusalem, whose noble and perilous business he is. What of Winchester, since I fled from it?'

'The queen's armies have encircled it. Few men get out, and

no food gets in. The empress's men are shut tight in their castle, and their stores must be running very low. We came north to straddle the road by Andover. As yet nothing moves, therefore I got leave to ride north on my own business. But they must attempt to break out soon, or starve where they are.'

'They'll try to reopen one of the roads and bring in supplies, before they abandon Winchester altogether,' said Humilis, frowning thoughtfully over the possibilities. 'If and when they do break, they'll break for Oxford first. Well, if this stalemate has sent you here to me, one good thing has come of it. And what is this business that brought you to Shrewsbury?'

'My lord,' began Nicholas, leaning forward very earnestly, 'you remember how you sent me here to the manor of Lai, three years ago, to take the word to Humphrey Cruce and his daughter that you could not keep your compact to marry her? – that you were entering the cloister at Hyde Mead?'

'It is not a thing to forget,' agreed Humilis drily.

'My lord, neither can I forget the girl! You never saw her but as a child five years old, before you went to the Crusade. But I saw her a grown lady, nearly nineteen. I did your message to her father and to her, and came away glad to have it delivered and done. But now I cannot get her out of my mind. Such grace she had, and bore the severance with such dignity and courtesy. My Lord, if she is still not wed or betrothed, I want to speak for her myself. But I could not go without first asking your blessing and consent.'

'Son,' said Humilis, glowing with astonished pleasure, 'there's nothing could delight me more than to see her happy with you, since I had to fail her. The girl is free to marry whom she will, and I could wish her no better man than you. And if you succeed I shall be relieved of all my guilt towards her, for I shall know she has made a better bargain than ever I should have been to her. Only consider, boy, we who enter the cloister abjure all possessions, how then can we dare lay claim to rights of possession in another creature of God? Go, and may you get her, and my blessing on you both. But come back and tell me how you fare.'

'My lord, with all my heart! How can I fail, if you send me to her?'

He stooped to kiss the hand that held him warmly, and rose blithely from the stool to take his leave. The silent figure in the shadows returned to his consciousness belatedly; it was as if he had been alone with his lord all this time, yet here stood the mute witness. Nicholas turned to him with impulsive warmth.

'Brother, I do thank you for your care of my lord. For this time, farewell. I shall surely see you again on my return.'

It was disconcerting to receive by way of reply only silence, and the courteous inclination of the cowled head.

'Brother Fidelis,' said Humilis gently, 'is dumb. Only his life and works speak for him. But I dare swear his good will goes with you on this quest, like mine.'

There was silence in the cell when the last crisp, light echo had died away on the day stairs. Brother Humilis lay still thinking, it seemed, tranquil and contented thoughts, for he was smiling.

'There are parts of myself I have never given to you,' he said at last, 'things that happened before ever I knew you. There is nothing of myself I would not wish to share with you. Poor girl! What had she to hope for from me, so much her elder, even before I was broken? And I never saw her but once, a little lass with brown hair and a solemn round face. I never felt the want of a wife or children until I was thirty years old, having an elder brother to carry on my father's line after the old man died. I took the Cross, and was fitting out a company to go with me to the east, free as air, when my brother also died, and I was left to balance my vow to God and my duty to my house. I owed it to God to do as I had sworn, and go for ten years to the Holy Land, but also I owed it to my house to marry and breed sons. So I looked for a sturdy, suitable little girl who could well wait all those years for me, and still have all her child-bearing time in its fullness when I returned. Barely six years old she was – Julian Cruce, from a family with manors in the north of this shire, and in Stafford, too.'

He stirred and sighed for the follies of men, and the presumptuous solemnity of the arrangements they made for lives they would never live. The presence beside him drew near, put back the cowl, and sat down on the stool Nicholas had vacated. They looked each other in the eyes gravely and without words, longer than most men can look each other in the eyes and not turn aside.

'God knew better, my son!' said Humilis. 'His plans for me were not as mine. I am what I am now. She is what she is. Julian Cruce ... I am glad she should escape me and go to a better man. I pray she has not yet given herself to any, for this Nicholas of mine would make her a fitting match, one that would set my soul at rest. Only to her do I feel myself a debtor, and forsworn.'

Brother Fidelis shook his head at him, reproachfully smiling, and leaned and laid a finger for an instant over the mouth that spoke heresy.

Cadfael had left Hugh waiting at the gatehouse, and was crossing the court to return to his duties in the herb-garden, when Nicholas Harnage emerged from the arch of the stairway, and recognising him, hailed him loudly and ran to pluck him urgently by the sleeve.

'Brother, a word!'

Cadfael halted and turned to face him. 'How do you find him? The long ride put him to too great a strain, and he did not seek help until his wound was broken and festering, but that's over now. All's clean, wholesome and healing. You need not fear we shall let him founder like that a second time.'

'I believe it, Brother,' said the young man earnestly. 'But I see him now for the first time after three years, and much fallen even from the man he was after he got his injuries. I knew they were grave, the doctors had him in care between life and death a long time, but when he came back to us at least he looked like the man we knew and followed. He made his plans then to come home, I know, but he had served already more years than he had promised, it was time to attend to his lands and his life here at home. I made that voyage with him, he bore it well. Now he has lost flesh, and there's a languor about him when he moves a hand. Tell me the truth of it, how bad is it with him?'

'Where did he ever get such crippling wounds?' asked Cadfael, considering scrupulously how much he could tell, and guessing at how much this boy already knew, or at least hazarded.

'In that last battle with Zenghi and the men of Mosul. He had Syrian doctors after the battle.'

That might very well be why he survived so terrible a maiming, thought Cadfael, who had learned much of his own craft from both Saracen and Syrian physicians. Aloud he asked cautiously: 'You have not seen his wounds? You don't know their whole import?'

Surprisingly, the seasoned crusader was struck silent for a moment, and a slow wave of blood crept up under his golden tan, but he did not lower his eyes, very wide and direct eyes of a profound blue. 'I never saw his body, no more than when I helped him into his harness. But I could not choose but understand what I can't claim I know. It could not be

214

otherwise, or he would never have abandoned the girl he was betrothed to. Why should he do so? A man of his word! He had nothing left to give her but a position and a parcel of dower lands. He chose rather to give her her freedom, and the residue of himself to God.'

'There was a girl?' said Cadfael.

'There *is* a girl. And I am on my way to her now,' said Nicholas, as defiantly as if his right had been challenged. 'I carried the word to her and her father that he was gone into the monastery at Hyde Mead. Now I am going to Lai to ask for her hand myself, and he has given me his consent and blessing. She was a small child when she was affianced to him, she has never seen him since. There is no reason she should not listen to my suit, and none that her kin should reject me.'

'None in the world!' agreed Cadfael heartily. 'Had I a daughter in such a case, I would be glad to see the squire follow in his lord's steps. And if you must report to her of his well-being, you may say with truth that he is doing what he wishes, and enjoys content of mind. And for his body, it is cared for as well as may be. We shall not let him want for anything that can give him aid or comfort.'

'But that does not answer what I need to know,' insisted the young man. 'I have promised to come back and tell him how I've fared. Three or four days, no longer, perhaps not so long. But shall I still find him then?'

'Son,' said Cadfael patiently, 'which of us can answer that for himself or any other man? You want truth, and you deserve it. Yes, Brother Humilis is dying. He got his death-wound long ago in that last battle. Whatever has been done for him, whatever can be done, is staving off an ending. But death is not in such a hurry with him as you fear, and he is in no fear of it. You go and find your girl and bring him back good news, and he'll be here to be glad of it.'

'And so he will,' said Cadfael to Edmund, as they took the air in the garden together before Compline that evening, 'if that young fellow is brisk about his courting, and I fancy he's the kind to go straight for what he wants. But how much longer we can hold our ground with Humilis I dare not guess. This fashion of collapse we can prevent, but the old harm will devour him in the end. As he knows better than any.'

'I marvel how he lived at all,' agreed Edmund, 'let alone bore the journey home, and has survived three years or more since.'

215

They were private together down by the banks of the Meole Brook, or they could not have discussed the matter at all. No doubt by this hour Nicholas Harnage was well on his way to the north-east of the county, if he had not already arrived at his destination. Good weather for riding, he would be in shelter at Lai before dark. And a very well-set-up young fellow like Harnage, in a thriving way in arms by his own efforts, was not an offer to be sneezed at. He had the blessing of his lord, and needed nothing more but the girl's liking, her family's approval, and the sanction of the church.

'I have heard it argued,' said Brother Edmund, 'that when an affianced man enters a monastic order, the betrothed lady is not necessarily free of the compact. But it seems a selfish and greedy thing to try to have both worlds, choose the life you want, but prevent the lady from doing likewise. But I think the question seldom arises but where the man cannot bear to loose his hold of what once he called his, and himself fights to keep her in chains. And here that is not so, Brother Humilis is glad there should be so happy a solution. Though of course she may be married already.'

'The manor of Lai,' mused Cadfael. 'What do you know of it, Edmund? What family would that be?'

'Cruce had it. Humphrey Cruce, if I remember rightly, he might well be the girl's father. They hold several manors up there, Ightfeld, and Harpecote – and Prees, from the Bishop of Chester. Some lands in Staffordshire, too. They made Lai the head of their honour.'

'That's where he's bound. Now if he comes back in triumph,' said Cadfael contentedly, 'he'll have done a good day's work for Humilis. He's already given him a great heave upward by showing his honest brown face, but if he settles the girl's future for her he may have added a year or more to his lord's life, at the same time.'

They went to Compline at the first sound of the bell. The visitor had indeed given Humilis a heft forward towards health, it seemed, for here he came, habited and erect on Fidelis's arm, having asked no permission of his doctors, bent on observing the night office with the rest. But I'll hound him back as soon as the observance is over, thought Cadfael, concerned for his dressing. Let him brandish his banner this once, it speaks well for his spirit, even if his flesh is drawn with effort. And who am I to say what a brother, my equal, may or may not do for his own salvation?

The evenings were already beginning to draw in, the height of the summer was over while its heat continued as if it would never break. In the dimness of the choir what light remained was coloured like irises, and faintly fragrant with the warm, heady scents of harvest and fruit. In this stall the tall, handsome, emaciated man who was old in his middle forties stood proudly, Fidelis on his left hand, and next to Fidelis, Rhun. Their youth and beauty seemed to gather to itself what light there was, so that they shone with a native radiance of their own, like lighted candles.

Across the choir from them Brother Urien stood, kneeled, genuflected and sang, with the full, assured voice of maturity, and never took his eyes from those two young, shining heads, the flaxen and the brown. Day by day those two drew steadily together, the mute one and the eloquent one, matched unfairly, unjustly, to his absolute exclusion, the one as desirable and as inviolable as the other, while his need burned in his bowels day and night, and prayer could not cool it, nor music lull it to sleep, but it ate him from within like the gnawing of wolves.

They had both begun – dreadful sign! – to look to him like the woman. When he gazed at either of these two, the boy's lineaments would dissolve and change subtly, and there would be her face, not recognising, not despising, simply staring through him to behold someone else. His heart ached beyond bearing, while he sang mellifluously in the Compline psalm.

In the twilight of the softer, more open country in the north-east of the shire, where day lingered longer than among the folded hills of the western border, Nicholas Harnage rode between flat, rich fields, unwontedly dried by the heat, into the wattled enclosure of the manor of Lai. Wrapped round on all sides by the enlarged fields of the plain, sparsely tree'd to make way for wide cultivation, the house rose long and low, a stone-built hall and chambers over a broad undercroft, with stables and barns about the interior of the fence. Fat country, good for grain and for roots, with ample grazing for any amount of cattle. The byres were vocal as Nicholas entered at the gate, the mild, contented lowing of well-fed beasts, milked and drowsy.

A groom heard the entering hooves and came forth from the stables, bared to the waist in the warm night. Seeing one young horseman alone, he was quite easy. They had had comparative peace here while Winchester burned and bled.

'Seeking whom, young sir?'

'Seeking the master, your lord, Humphrey Cruce,' said Nicholas, reining in peaceably and shaking the reins free. 'If he still keeps house here?'

'Why, the lord Humphrey's dead, sir, three years ago. His son Reginald is lord here now. Would your errand do as well to him?'

'If he'll admit me, yes, surely to him, then,' said Nicholas, and dismounted. 'Let him know, I was here some three years ago, to speak for Godfrid Marescot. It was his father I saw then, but the son will know of it.'

'Come within,' said the groom placidly, accepting the credentials without question. 'I'll have your beast seen to.'

In the smoky, wood-scented hall they were at meat, or still sitting at ease after the meal was done, but they had heard his step on the stone stairs that led to the open hall door, and Reginald Cruce rose, alert and curious, as the visitor entered. A big, black-haired man of austere features and imperious manner, but well-disposed, it seemed, towards chance travellers. His lady sat aloof and quiet, a pale-haired woman in green, with a boy of about fifteen at her side, and a younger boy and girl about nine or ten, who by their likeness might well be twins. Evidently Reginald Cruce had secured his succession with a well-filled quiver, for by the lady's swelling waist when she rose to muster the hospitality of the house, there was another sibling on the way.

Nicholas made his reverence and offered his name, a little confounded at finding Julian Cruce's brother a man surely turned forty, with a wife and growing children, where he had assumed a young fellow in his twenties, perhaps newly-married since inheriting. But he recalled that Humphrey Cruce had been an old man to have a daughter still so young. Two marriages, surely, the first blessed with an heir, the second undertaken late, when Reginald was a grown man, ready for marriage himself, or even married already to his pale, prolific wife.

'Ah, that!' said Reginald of his guest's former errand to this same house. 'I remember it, though I was not here then. My wife brought me a manor in Staffordshire, we were living there. But I know how it fell out, of course. A strange business altogether. But it happens! Men change their minds. And you were the messenger? Well, but leave it now and take some refreshment. Come to table! There'll be time to talk of all such business afterwards.'

He sat down and kept his visitor company while a servant brought meat and ale, and the lady, having made her grave good night, drove her younger children away to their beds, and the heir sat solemn and silent studying his elders. At last, in the deepening evening, the two men were left alone to their talk.

'So you are the squire who brought that word from Marescot. You'll have noticed there's a generation, as near as need be, between my sister and me – seventeen years. My mother died when I was nine years old, and it was another eight before my father married again. An old man's folly, she brought him nothing, and died when the girl was born, so he had little joy of her.'

At least, thought Nichoals, studying his host dispassionately, there was no second son, to threaten a division of the lands. That would be a source of satisfaction to this man, he was authentically of his class and kind, and land was his lifeblood.

'He may well have had great joy of his daughter, however,' he said firmly, 'for she is a very gracious and beautiful girl, as I well recall.'

'You'll be better informed of that than I,' said Reginald drily, 'if you saw her only three years ago. It must be eighteen or more since I set eyes on her. She was a stumbling infant then, two years old, or three, it might be. I married about that time, and settled on the lands Cecilia brought me. We exchanged couriers now and then, but I never came back here until my father was on his death-bed, and they sent for me to come to him.'

'I didn't know of his death when I set out to come here on this errand of my own,' said Nicholas. 'I heard it only from your groom at the gate. But I may speak as freely with you as I should have done with him. I was so much taken with your sister's grace and dignity that I've thought of her ever since, and I've spoken with my lord Godfrid, and have his full consent to what I'm asking. As for myself,' he thrust on, leaning eagerly across the board, 'I am heir to two good manors from my father, and shall have some lands also after my mother, I stand well in the queen's armies and my lord will speak for me, that I'm in earnest in this matter, and will provide for Julian as truly as any man could, if you will …'

His host was gazing, astonished, smiling at his fervour, and had raised a warning hand to still the flood.

'Did you come all this way to ask me to give you my sister?'

'I did! Is that so strange? I admired her, and I'm come to

219

speak for her. And she might have worse offers,' he added, flushing and stiffening at such a reception.

'I don't doubt it, but, man, man, you should have put in a word to give her due warning then. You come three years too late!'

'Too late?' Nicholas sat back and drew in his hands slowly, stricken. 'Then she's already married?'

'You might call it so!' Reginald hoisted wide shoulders in a helpless gesture. 'But not to any man. And you might have sped well enough if you'd made more haste, for all I know. No, this is quite a different story. There was some discussion, even, about whether she was still bound like a wife to Marescot – a great foolery, but the churchmen have to assert their authority, and my father's chaplain was prim as a virgin – though I suspect, for all that, in private he was none! – and clutched at every point of canon law that gave him power, and he took the extreme line, and would have it she was legally a wife, while the parish priest argued the opposing way, and my father, being a sensible man, took his side and insisted she was free. All this I learned by stages since. I never took part or put my head into the hornets' nest.'

Nicholas was frowning into his cupped hands, feeling the cold heaviness of disappointment drag his heart down. But still this was not a complete answer. He looked up ruefully. 'So how did this end? Why is she not here to use her freedom, if she has not yet given herself to a husband?'

'Ah, but she has! She took her own way. She said that if she was free, then she would make her own choice. And she chose to do as Marescot had done, and took a husband not of this world. She has taken the veil as a Benedictine nun.'

'And they let her?' demanded Nicholas, wrung between rage and pain. 'Then, when she was moved by this broken match, they let her go so easily, throw away her youth so unwisely?'

'They let her, yes. How do I know whether she was wise or no? If it was what she wished, why should she not have it? Since she went I've never had word from her, never has she complained or asked for anything. She must be happy in her choice. You must look elsewhere for a wife, my friend!'

Nicholas sat silent for a time, swallowing a bitterness that burned in his belly like fire. Then he asked, with careful quietness: 'How was it? When did she leave her home? How attended?'

'Very soon after your visit, I judge. It might be a month

220

while they fought out the issue, and she said never a word. But all was done properly. Our father gave her an escort of three men-at-arms and a huntsman who had always been a favourite and made a pet of her, and a good dowry in money, and also some ornaments for her convent, silver candlesticks and a crucifix and such. He was sad to see her go, I know by what he said later, but she wanted it so, and her wants were his commands always.' A very slight chill in his brisk, decisive voice spoke of an old jealousy. The child of Humphrey's age had plainly usurped his whole heart, even though his son would inherit all when that heart no longer beat. 'He lived barely a month longer,' said Reginald. 'Only long enough to see the return of her escort, and know she was safely delivered where she wished to be. He was old and feeble, we knew it. But he should not have dwindled so soon.'

'He might well miss her,' said Nicholas, very low and hesitantly, 'about the place. She had a brightness ... And you did not send for her, when her father died?'

'To what end? What could she do for him, or he for her? No, we let her be. If she was happy there, why trouble her?'

Nicholas gripped his hands together under the board, and wrung them hard, and asked his last question: 'Where was it she chose to go?' His own voice sounded to him hollow and distant.

'She's in the Benedictine abbey of Wherwell, close by Andover.'

So that was the end of it! All this time she had been within hail of him, the house of her refuge encircled now by armies and factions and contention. If only he had spoken out what he felt in his heart at the first sight of her, even hampered as he had been by the knowledge of the blow he was about to deal her, and gagged by that knowledge when for once he might have been eloquent. She might have listened, and at least delayed, even if she could feel nothing for him then. She might have thought again, and waited, and even remembered him. Now it was far too late, she was a bride for the second time, and even more indissolubly.

This time there was no question of argument. The betrothal vows made by or for a small girl might justifiably be dissolved, but the vocational vows of a grown woman, taken in the full knowledge of their meaning, and of her own choice, never could be undone. He had lost her.

221

Nicholas lay all night in the small guest-chamber prepared for him, fretting at the knot and knowing he could not untie it. He slept shallowly and uneasily, and in the morning he took his leave, and set out on the road back to Shrewsbury.

Chapter Five

T SO happened that Brother Cadfael was private
with Humilis in his cell in the dortoir when Nicholas
again rode in at the gatehouse and asked leave to
visit his former lord, as he had promised. Humilis
had risen with the rest that morning, attended Prime and Mass,
and scrupulously performed all the duties of the horarium,
though he was not yet allowed to exert himself by any form of
labour. Fidelis attended him everywhere, ready to support his
steps if need arose, or fetch him whatever he might want, and
had spent the afternoon completing, under his elder's
approving eye, the initial letter which had been smeared and
blotted by his fall. And there they had left the boy to finish the
careful elaboration in gold, while they repaired to the dortoir,
physician and patient together.

'Well closed,' said Cadfael, content with his work, 'and
firming up nicely, clean as ever. You scarcely need the
bandages, but as well keep them a day or two yet, to guard
against rubbing while the new skin is still frail.'

They were grown quite easy together, these two, and if both
of them realised that the mere healing of a broken and festered
wound was no sufficient cure for what ailed Humilis, they were
both courteously silent on the subject, and took their moderate
pleasure in what good they had achieved.

They heard the footsteps on the stone treads of the day
stairs, and knew them for booted feet, not sandalled. But there
was no spring in the steps now, and no hasty eagerness, and it

was a glum young man who appeared, shadowy, in the doorway of the cell. Nor had he been in any hurry on the way back from Lai, since he had nothing but disappointment to report. But he had promised, and he was here.

'Nick!' Humilis greeted him with evident pleasure and affection. 'You're soon back! Welcome as the day, but I had thought ...' There he stopped, even in the dim interior light aware that the brightness was gone from the young man's face. 'So long a visage? I see it did not go as you would have wished.'

'No, my lord.' Nicholas came in slowly, and bent his knee to both his elders. 'I have not sped.'

'I am sorry for it, but no man can always succeed. You know Brother Cadfael? I owe the best of care to him.'

'We spoke together the last time,' said Nicholas, and found a half-hearted smile by way of acknowledgement. 'I count myself also in his debt.'

'Spoke of me, no doubt,' said Humilis, smiling and sighing. 'You trouble too much for me, I am well content here. I have found my way. Now sit down a while, and tell us what went wrong for you.'

Nicholas plumped himself down on the stool beside the bed on which Humilis was sitting, and said what he had to say in commendably few words: 'I hesitated three years too long. Barely a month after you took the cowl at Hyde, Julian Cruce took the veil at Wherwell.'

'Did she so!' said Humilis on a long breath, and sat silent to take in all that his news could mean. 'Now I wonder ... No, why should she do such a thing unless it was truly her wish? It cannot have been because of me! No, she knew nothing of me, she had only once seen me, and must have forgotten me before my back was turned. She may even have been glad ... It may be this is what she always wished, if she could have her way...' He thought for a moment, frowning, perhaps trying to recall what that little girl looked like. 'You told me, Nick, that I do remember, how she took my message. She was not distressed, but altogether calm and courteous, and gave me her grace and pardon freely. You said so!'

'Truth, my lord,' said Nicholas earnestly, 'though she cannot have been glad.'

'Ah, but she may – she may very well have been glad. No blame to her! Willing though she may have been to accept the match made for her, yet it would have tied her to a man more than twenty years her elder, and a stranger. Why should she not be glad, when I offered her her liberty – no, urged it upon her? Surely she must have made of it the use she preferred, perhaps had longed for.'

'She was not forced,' Nicholas admitted, with somewhat reluctant certainty. 'Her brother says it was the girl's own choice, indeed her father was against it, and only gave in because she would have it so.'

'That's well,' agreed Humilis with a relieved sigh. 'Then we can but hope that she may be happy in her choice.'

'But so great a waste!' blurted Nicholas, grieving. 'If you had seen her, my lord, as I did! To shear such hair as she had, and hide such a form under the black habit! They should never have let her go, not so soon. How if she has regretted it long since?'

Humilis smiled, but very gently, eyeing the downcast face and hooded eyes. 'As you described her to me, so gracious and sensible, of such measured and considered speech, I don't think she will have acted without due thought. No, surely she has done what is right for her. But I'm sorry for your loss, Nick. You must bear it as gallantly as she did – if ever I was any loss!'

The Vesper bell had begun to chime. Humilis rose to go down to the church, and Nicholas rose with him, taking the summons as his dismissal.

'It's late to set out now,' suggested Cadfael, emerging from the silence and withdrawal he had observed while these two talked together. 'And it seems there's no great haste, that you need leave tonight. A bed in the guest-hall, and you could set off fresh in the morning, with the whole day before you. And spend an hour or two more with Brother Humilis this evening while you have the chance.'

To which sensible notion they both said yes, and Nicholas recovered a little of his spirits, if nothing could restore the ardour with which he had ridden north from Winchester.

What did somewhat surprise Brother Cadfael was the considerate way in which Fidelis, confronted yet again with this visitant from the time before he had known Humilis and established his own intimacy with him, withdrew himself from sight as he was withdrawn from the possibility of conversation, and left them to their shared memories of travel, Crusade and battle, things so far removed from his own experience. An affection which could so self-effacingly make room for a rival and prior affection was generous indeed.

There was a merchant of Shrewsbury who dealt in fleeces all up
and down the borders, both from Wales and from such fat
sheep-country as the Cotswolds, and had done an interesting
side-trade in information, for Hugh's benefit, in these contrary
times. His active usefulness was naturally confined to this
period of high summer when the wool clip was up for sale, and
many dealers had restricted their movements in these
dangerous times, but he was a determined man, intrepid
enough to venture well south down the border, towards
territory held by the empress. His suppliers had sold to him for
some years, and had sufficient confidence in him to hold their
clip until he made contact. He had good trading relations as far
afield as Bruges in Flanders, and was not at all averse to a large
risk when calculating on a still larger profit. Moreover, he took
his own risks, rather than delegating these unchancy journeys
to his underlings. Possibly he even relished the challenge, for
he was a stubborn and stalwart man.

Now, in early September, he was on his way home with his
purchases, a train of three wagons following from
Buckingham, which was as near as he could reasonably go to
Oxford. For Oxford had become as alert and nervous as a town
itself under siege, every day expecting that the empress must
be forced by starvation to retreat from Winchester. The
merchant had left his men secure on a road relatively peaceful,
to bring up his wagons at leisure, and himself rode ahead at
good speed with his news to report to Hugh Beringar in
Shrewsbury, even before he went home to his wife and family.

'My lord, things move at last. I had it from a man who saw
the end of it, and made good haste away to a safer place. You
know how they were walled up there in their castles in
Winchester, the bishop and the empress, with the queen's
armies closing all round the city and sealing off the roads. No
supplies have gone in through that girdle for four weeks now,
and they say there's starvation in the town, though I doubt if
either empress or bishop is going short.' He was a man who
spoke his mind, and no great respecter of higher personages.
'A very different tale for the poor townsfolk! But it's biting
even the garrison within there at the royal castle, for the queen
has been supplying Wolvesey while she starves out the
opposing side. Well, they came to the point where they must
try to win a way through.'

'I've been expecting it,' said Hugh, intent. 'What did they hit on? They could only hope to move north or west, the queen holds all the south-east.'

'They sent out a force, three or four hundred as I heard it, northwards, to seize on the town of Wherwell, and try to secure a base there to open the Andover road. Whether they were seen on the move, or whether some townsman betrayed them – for they're not loved in Winchester – however it was, William of Ypres and the queen's men closed in on them when they'd barely reached the edge of the town, and cut them to pieces. A great killing! The fellow who told me fled when the houses started to burn, but he saw the remnant of the empress's men put up a desperate fight of it and reach the great nunnery there. And they never scrupled to use it, either, he says. They swarmed into the church itself and turned it into a fortress, although the poor sisters had shut themselves in there for safety. The Flemings threw in firebrands after them. A hellish business it must have been. He could hear from far off as he ran, he said, the women screaming, the flames crackling and the din of fighting within there, until those who remained were forced to come out and surrender, half-scorched as they were. Not a man can have escaped either death or capture.'

'And the women?' demanded Hugh aghast. 'Do you tell me the abbey of Wherwell is burned down, like the convent in the city, like Hyde Mead after it?'

'My man never dallied to see how much was left,' said the messenger drily. 'But certainly the church burned down to the ground, with both men and women in it – the sisters cannot all have come out alive. And as for those who did, God alone knows where they will have found refuge now. Safe places are hard to find in those parts. And for the empress's garrison, I'd say there's no hope for them now but to muster every man they have, and try to burst out by force of numbers through the ring, and run for it. And poor chance for them, even so.'

A poor chance indeed, after this last loss of three or four hundred fighting men, probably hand-picked for the exploit, which must have been a desperate gamble from the first. The year only at early September, and the fortunes of war had changed and changed again, from the disastrous battle of Lincoln which had made the king prisoner and brought the empress within grasp of the crown itself, to this stranglehold drawn round the same proud lady now. Now only give us the empress herself prisoner, thought Hugh, and we shall have

227

stalemate, recover each our sovereign, and begin this whole struggle all over again, for what sense there is in it! And at the cost of the brothers of Hyde Mead and the nuns of Wherwell. Among many others even more defenceless, like the poor of Winchester.

The name of Wherwell, as yet, meant no more to him than any other convent unlucky enough to fall into the field of battle.

'A good year for me, all the same,' said the wool-merchant, rising to make his way home to his own waiting board and bed. 'The clip measures up well, it was worth the journey.'

Hugh took the latest news down to the abbey next morning, immediately after Prime, for whatever of import came to his ears was at once conveyed to Abbot Radulfus, a service the abbot appreciated and reciprocated. The clerical and secular authorities worked well together in Shropshire, and moreover, in this case a Benedictine house had been desecrated and destroyed, and those of the Rule stood together, and helped one another where they could. Even in more peaceful times, nunneries were apt to have much narrower lands and more restricted resources than the houses of the monks, and often had to depend upon brotherly alms, even under good, shrewd government. Now here was total devastation. Bishops and abbots would be called upon to give aid.

He had come from his colloquy with Radulfus in the abbot's parlour with half an hour still before High Mass and, choosing to stay for the celebration since he was here, he did what he habitually did with time to spare within the precinct of the abbey and went looking for Brother Cadfael in his workshop in the herb-garden.

Cadfael had been up since long before Prime, inspected such wines and distillations as he had working, and done a little watering while the soil was in shade and cooled from the night. At this time of year, with the harvest in, there was little work to be done among the herbs, and he had no need as yet to ask for an assistant in place of Brother Oswin.

When Hugh came to look for Cadfael he found him sitting at ease on the bench under the north wall, which at this time of day was pleasantly warm without being too hot, contemplating between admiration and regret the roses that bloomed with such extravagant splendour and wilted so soon. Hugh sat down beside him, rightly interpreting placid silence as welcome.

'Aline says it's high time you came to see how your godson has grown.'

'I know well enough how much he will have grown,' said Giles Beringar's godfather, between complacency and awe of his formidable responsibility. 'Not two years old until Christmas, and too heavy already for an old man.'

Hugh made a derisive noise. When Cadfael claimed to be an old man he must either be up to something, or inclined to be idle, and giving fair warning.

'Every time he sees me he climbs me like a tree,' said Cadfael dreamily. 'You he daren't treat so, you are but a sapling. Give him fifteen more years, and he'll make two of you.'

'So he will,' agreed the fond father, and stretched his lithe, light body pleasurably in the strengthening sun. 'A long lad from birth – do you remember? That was a Christmas indeed, what with my son – and yours ... I wonder where Olivier is now? Do you know?'

'How should I know? With d'Angers in Gloucester, I hope. She can't have drawn them all into Winchester with her, she must leave force enough in the west to hold on to her base there. Why, what made you think of him just now?'

'It did enter my head that he might have been among the empress's chosen at Wherwell.' He had recoiled into grim recollection, and did not at first notice how Cadfael stiffened and turned to stare. 'I pray you're right, and he's well out of it.'

'At Wherwell? Why, what of Wherwell?'

'I forgot,' said Hugh, startled, 'you don't yet know the latest news, for I've only just brought it within here, and I got it only last night. Did I not say they'd have to try to break out – the empress's men? They have tried it, Cadfael, disastrously for them. They sent a picked force to try to seize Wherwell, no doubt hoping to straddle the road and the river there, and open a way to bring in supplies. William of Ypres cut them to pieces outside the town, and the remnant fled into the nunnery and shut themselves into the church. The place burned down over them ... God forgive them for ever violating it, but they were Maud's men who first did it, not ours. The nuns, God help them, had taken refuge there when the fight began...'

Cadfael sat frozen even in the sunlight. 'Do you tell me Wherwell has gone the way of Hyde?'

'Burned to the ground. The church at least. As for the rest ... But in so hot and dry a season...'

229

Cadfael, who had gripped him hard and suddenly by the arm, as abruptly loosed him, leaped from the bench, and began to run, veritably to run, as he had not done since hurtling to get out of range from the rogue castle on Titterstone Clee, two years earlier. He had still a very respectable turn of speed when roused, but his gait was wonderful, legless under the habit, like a black ball rolling, with a slight oscillation from side to side, a seaman's walk become a headlong run. And Hugh, who loved him, and rose to pursue him with a very sharp sense of the urgency behind this flight, nevertheless could not help laughing as he ran. Viewed from behind, a Benedictine in a hurry, and a Benedictine of more than sixty years and built like a barrel, at that, may be formidably impressive to one who knows him, but must be comic.

Cadfael's purposeful flight checked in relief as he emerged into the great court; for they were there still, in no haste with their farewells, though the horse stood by with a groom at his bridle, and Brother Fidelis tightening the straps that held Nicholas Harnage's bundle and rolled cloak behind the saddle. They knew nothing yet of any need for haste. There was a whole sunlit day before the rider.

Fidelis wore the cowl always outdoors, as though to cover a personal shyness that stemmed, surely, from his mute tongue. He who would not open his mind to others shrank from claiming any privileged advance from them. Only Humilis had some manner of silent and eloquent speech with him that needed no voice. Having secured the saddle-roll the young man stepped back modestly to a little distance, and waited.

Cadfael arrived more circumspectly than he had set out from the garden. Hugh had not followed him so closely, but halted in shadow by the wall of the guest-hall.

'There's news,' said Cadfael bluntly. 'You should hear it before you leave us. The empress has made an attack on the town of Wherwell, a disastrous attack. Her force is wiped out by the queen's army. But in the fighting the abbey of Wherwell was fired, the church burned to the ground. I know no more detail, but so much is certain. The sheriff here got the word last night.'

'By a reliable man,' said Hugh, drawing close. 'It's certain.'

Nicholas stood staring, eyes and mouth wide, his golden sunburn dulling to an earthen grey as the blood drained from beneath it. He got out in a creaking whisper: 'Wherwell? They've dared …?'

'No daring,' said Hugh ruefully, 'but plain terror. They were men penned in, the raiding party, they sought any place of hiding they could find, surely, and slammed to the door. But the end was the same, whoever tossed in the firebrands. The abbey's laid waste. Sorry I am to say it.'

'And the women ...? Oh, God ... Julian's there ... Is there any word of the women?'

'They'd taken to the church for sanctuary,' said Hugh. In such civil warfare there were no sanctuaries, not even for women and children. 'The remnant of the raiders surrendered – most may have come out alive. All, I doubt.'

Nicholas turned blindly to grope for his bridle, plucking his sleeve out of the quivering hand Humilis had laid on his arm. 'Let me away! I must go ... I must go there and find her.' He swung back to catch again briefly at the older man's hand and wring it hard. 'I *will* find her! If she lives I'll find her, and see her safe.' He found his stirrup and heaved himself into the saddle.

'If God's with you, send me word,' said Humilis. 'Let me know that she lives and is safe.'

'I will, my lord, surely I will.'

'Don't trouble her, don't speak to her of me. No questions! All I need, all you must ask, is to know that God has preserved her, and that she has the life she wanted. There'll be a place elsewhere for her, with other sisters. If only she still lives!'

Nicholas nodded mutely, shook himself out of his daze with a great heave, wheeled his horse, and was gone, out through the gatehouse without another word or a look behind. They were left gazing after him, as the light dust of his passing shimmered and settled under the arch of the gate, where the cobbles ended, and the beaten earth of the Foregate began.

All that day Humilis seemed to Cadfael to press his own powers to the limit, as though the stress that drove Nicholas headlong south took its toll here in enforced stillness and inaction, where the heart would rather have been riding with the boy, at whatever cost. And all that day Fidelis, turning his back even on Rhun, shadowed Humilis with a special and grievous solicitude, tenderness and anxiety, as though he had just realised that death stood no great distance away, and advanced one gentle step with every hour that passed.

Humilis went to his bed immediately after Compline, and Cadfael, looking in on him ten minutes later, found him already asleep, and left him undisturbed accordingly. It was not a festering wound and a maimed body that troubled Humilis now, but an obscure feeling of guilt towards the girl who might, had he married her, have been safe in some manor far remote from Winchester and Wherwell and the clash of arms, instead of driven by fire and slaughter even out of her chosen cloister. Sleep could do more for his grieving mind than the changing of a dressing could do now for his body. Sleeping, he had the hieratic calm of a figure already carved on a tomb. He was at peace. Cadfael went quietly away and left him, as Fidelis must have left him, to rest the better alone.

In the sweet-scented twilight Cadfael went to pay his usual nightly visit to his workshop, to make sure all was well there, and stir a brew he had standing to cool overnight. Sometimes, when the nights were so fresh after the heat of the day, the skies so full of stars and so infinitely lofty, and every flower and leaf suddenly so imbued with its own lambent colour and light in despite of the light's departure, he felt it to be a great waste of the gifts of God to be going to bed and shutting his eyes to them. There had been illicit nights of venturing abroad in the past – he trusted for good enough reasons, but did not probe too deeply. Hugh had had his part in them, too. Ah, well!

Making his way back with some reluctance, he went in by the church to the night stairs. All the shapes within the vast stone ship showed dimly by the small altar lamps. Cadfael never passed through without stepping for a moment into the choir, to cast a glance and a thought towards Saint Winifred's altar, in affectionate remembrance of their first encounter, and gratitude for her forbearance. He did so now, and checked abruptly before venturing nearer. For there was one of the brothers kneeling at the foot of the altar, and the tiny red glow of the lamp showed him the uplifted face, fast-closed eyes and prayerfully folded hands of Fidelis. Showed him no less clearly, as he drew softly nearer, the tears glittering on the young man's cheeks. A perfectly still face, but for the mute lips moving soundlessly on his prayers, and the tears welling slowly from beneath his closed eyelids and spilling on to his breast. The shocks of the day might well send him here, now his charge was sleeping, to put up fervent prayers for a better ending to the story. But why should his face seem rather that of a penitent than an innocent appellant? And a penitent unsure of absolution!

Cadfael slipped away very quietly to the night stairs and left the boy the entire sheltering space of the church for his inexplicable pain.

The other figure, motionless in the darkest corner of the choir, did not stir until Cadfael had departed, and even then waited long moments before stealing forward by inches, with held breath, over the chilly paving.

A naked foot touched the hem of Fidelis's habit, and as hastily and delicately drew back again from the contact. A hand was outstretched to hover over the oblivious head, longing to touch and yet not daring until the continued silence and stillness gave it courage. Tensed fingers sank into the curling russet that ringed the tonsure, the light touch set the hand quivering, like the pricking of imminent lightning in the air before a storm. If Fidelis also sensed it, he gave no sign. Even when the fingers stirred lovingly in his hair, and stroked down into the nape of his neck within the cowl he did not move but rather froze where he kneeled, and held his breath.

'Fidelis,' whispered a hushed and aching voice close at his shoulder. 'Brother, never grieve alone! Turn to me … I could comfort you, for everything, everything … whatever your need…'

The stroking palm circled his neck, but before it reached his cheek Fidelis had started to his feet in one smooth movement, resolute and unalarmed, and swung out of reach. Without haste, or perhaps unwilling to show his face, even by this dim light, until he had mastered it, he turned to look upon the intruder into his solitude, for whispers have no identity, and he had never before taken any particular notice of Brother Urien. He did so now, with wide and wary grey eyes. A dark, passionate, handsome man, one who should never have shut himself in within these walls, one who burned, and might burn others before ever he grew cool at last. He stared back at Fidelis, and his face was wrung and his outstretched hand quaked, yearning towards Fidelis's sleeve, which was withdrawn from his austerely before he could grasp it.

'I've watched you,' breathed the husky, whispering, 'I know every motion and grace. Waste, waste of youth, waste of beauty … Don't go! No one sees us now…'

Fidelis turned his back steadily, and walked out from the choir towards the night stairs. Silent on the tiled floor, Urien's naked feet followed him, the tormented whisper followed him.

'Why turn your back on loving kindness? You will not

233

always do so. Think of me! I will wait...'

Fidelis began to climb the stairs. The pursuer halted at the foot, too sick with anguish to go where other men might still be wakeful. 'Unkind, unkind ...' wailed the faintest thread of a voice, receding, and then, with barely audible but extreme bitterness: 'If not here, in another place ... If not now, at another time!'

Chapter Six

ICHOLAS COMMANDEERED a change of horses twice on the way south, leaving those he had ridden hard to await the early return he foresaw, with the news he had promised to carry faithfully, whether good or bad. The stench of burning, old and acrid now, met him on the wind some miles from Wherwell, and when he entered what was left of the small town it was to find an almost de-peopled desolation. The few whose houses had survived unlooted and almost undamaged were sorting through their premises and salvaging their goods, but those who had lost their dwellings in the fire held off cautiously as yet from coming back to rebuild. For though the raiding party from Winchester had been either wiped out or made prisoner, and William of Ypres had withdrawn the queen's Flemings to their old positions ringing the city and the region, this place was still within the circle, and might yet be subjected to more violence.

Nicholas made his way with a cramped and anxious heart to the enclave of the nunnery, one of the three greatest in the shire, until this disaster fell upon its buildings and laid the half of them flat and the rest uninhabitable. The shell of the church stood up gaunt and blackened against the cloudless sky, the walls jagged and discoloured like decayed teeth. There were new graves in the nuns' cemetery. As for the survivors, they were gone, there was no home for them here. He looked at the newly-turned earth with a sick heart, and wondered whose daughters lay beneath. There had not yet been time to do more

235

for them than bury them, they were nameless.

He would not let himself even consider that she might be there. He looked for the parish church and sought out the priest, who had gathered two homeless families beneath his roof and in his barn. A careworn, tired man, growing old, in a shabby gown that needed mending.

'The nuns?' he said, stepping out from his low, dark doorway. 'They're scattered, poor souls, we hardly know where. Three of them died in the fire. Three that we know of, but there may well be more, lying under the rubble there still. There was fighting all about the court and the Flemings were dragging their prisoners out of the church, but neither side cared for the women. Some are fled into Winchester, they say, though there's little safety to be found there, but the lord bishop must try to do something for them, their house was allied to the Old Minster. Others ... I don't know! I hear the abbess is fled to a manor near Reading, where she has kin, and some she may have taken with her. But all's confusion – who can tell?'

'Where is this manor?' demanded Nicholas feverishly, and was met by a weary shake of the head.

'It was only a thing I heard – no one said where. It may not even be true.'

'And you do not know, Father, the names of those sisters who died?' He trembled as he asked it.

'Son,' said the priest with infinite resignation, 'what we found could not have a name. And we have yet to seek there for others, when we have found enough food to keep those alive who still live. The empress's men looted our houses first, and after them the Flemings. Those who have, here, must share with those who have nothing. And which of us has very much? God knows not I!'

Nor had he, in material things, only in tired but obstinate compassion. Nicholas had bread and meat in his saddle-bag, brought for provision on the road from his last halt to change horses. He hunted it out and put it into the old man's hands, a meagre drop in a hungry ocean, but the money in his purse could buy nothing here where there was nothing to buy. They would have to milk the countryside to feed their people. He left them to their stubborn labours, and rode slowly through the rubble of Wherwell, asking here and there if anyone had more precise information to impart. Everyone knew the sisters had dispersed, no one could say where. As for one woman's name, it meant nothing, it might not even be the name by which she had entered on her vows. Nevertheless, he continued to utter it wherever he enquired, doggedly proclaiming the irreplaceable uniqueness of Julian Cruce, separate from all other women.

From Wherwell he rode on into Winchester. A soldier of the queen could pass through the iron ring without difficulty, and in the city it was plain that the empress's faction were hard-pressed, and dared not venture far from their tight fortress in the castle. But the nuns of Winchester, themselves earlier endangered and now breathing more easily, could tell him nothing of Julian Cruce. Some sisters from Wherwell they had taken in and cherished, but she was not among them. Nicholas had speech with one of their elder members, who was kind and solicitous, but could not help him.

'Sir, it is a name I do not know. But consider, there is no reason I should know it, for surely this lady may have taken a very different name when she took her vows, and we do not ask our sisters where they came from, nor who they once were, unless they choose to tell us freely. And I had no office that should bring me knowledge of these things. Our abbess would certainly be able to answer you, but we do not know where she is now. Our prioress, also. We are as lost as you. But God will find us, and bring us together again. As he will find for you the one you seek.'

She was a shrewd, agile, withered woman, thin as a gnat but indestructible as scutch grass. She eyed him with mildly amused sympathy, and asked blandly: 'She is kin to you, this Julian?'

'No,' said Nicholas shortly, 'but I would have had her kin, and very close kin, too.'

'And now?'

'I want to know her safe, living, content. There is no more in it. If she is so, God keep her so, and I am satisfied.'

'If I were you,' said the lady, after viewing him closely for some moments in silence, 'I should go on to Romsey. It is far enough removed to be a safer place than here, and it is the greatest of our Benedictine houses in these parts. God knows which of our sisters you may find there, but surely some, and it may be, the highest.'

He was young enough and innocent enough still, for all his travels, to be strongly moved by any evidence of trust and kindness, and he caught and kissed her hand in taking leave, as though she had been his hostess somewhere in hall. She, for her part, was too old and experienced to blush or bridle, but when he was gone she sat smiling a long, quiet while, before she rejoined her sisters. He was a very personable young man.

Nicholas rode the twelve miles or so to Romsey in sobering solemnity, aware he might be drawing near to an answer possibly not to his liking. Once clear of Winchester and on his way further south-west, he was delivered from any threat, for he went through country where the queen's writ ran without challenge. Pleasant, rolling country, well tree'd even before he reached the fringes of the great forest. He came to the abbey gatehouse, in the heart of the small town, in the late evening, and rang the bell at the gate. The portress peered at him through the grille, and asked his business. He stooped entreatingly to the grid, and gazed into a pair of bright, elderly eyes in beds of wrinkles.

'Sister, have you given refuge here to some of the nuns of Wherwell? I am seeking for news of one of them, and could get no answers there.'

The portress eyed him narrowly, and saw a young face soiled and drawn with travel, a young man alone, and in dead earnest, no threat. Even here in Romsey they had learned to be cautious about opening their gates, but the road beyond him was empty and still, and the twilight folded down on the little town peacefully enough.

'The prioress and three sisters reached here,' she said, 'but I doubt if any of them can tell you much of the rest, not yet. But come within, and I'll ask if she will speak with you.'

The wicket clanked open, lock and chain, and he stepped through into the court. 'Who knows?' said the portress kindly, fastening the door again after him. 'One of our three may be the one you're seeking. At least you may try.'

She led him along dim corridors to a small, panelled parlour, lit by a tiny lamp, and there left him. The evening meal would be long over, even Compline past, it was almost time for sleeping. They would want him satisfied, if satisfaction was possible, and out of their precinct before the night.

He could not rest or sit, but was prowling the room like a caged bear when a further door opened, and the prioress of Wherwell came quietly in. A short, round, rosy woman, but with a formidably strong face and exceedingly direct brown eyes, that studied her visitor from head to foot in one piercing

238

glance as he made his reverence to her.

'You asked for me, I am told. I am here. How can I help you?'

'Madam,' said Nicholas, trembling for awe of what might come, 'I was well north, in Shropshire, when I heard of the sack of Wherwell. There was a sister there of whose vocation I had only just learned, and now all I want is to know that she lives and is safe after that outrage. Perhaps to speak with her, and see for myself that she is well, if that can be permitted. I did ask in Wherwell itself, but could get no word of her – I know only the name she had in the world.'

The prioress waved him to a seat, and herself sat down apart, where she could watch his face. 'May I know your own name, sir?'

'My name is Nicholas Harnage. I was squire to Godfrid Marescot until he took the cowl in Hyde Mead. He was formerly betrothed to this lady, and he is anxious now to know that she is safe and well.'

She nodded at that very natural desire, but nevertheless her brows had drawn together in a thoughtful and somewhat puzzled frown. 'That name I know, Hyde was proud of having gained him. But I never recall hearing ... What is the name of this sister you seek?'

'In the world she was Julian Cruce, of a Shropshire family. The sister I spoke with in Wherwell had never heard the name, but it may well be that she chose a very different name when she took the veil. But you will know of her both before and after.'

'Julian Cruce?' she repeated, erect and intent now, her sharp eyes narrowing. 'Young sir, are you not in some mistake? You are sure it was Wherwell she entered? Not some other house?'

'No, certainly, madam, Wherwell,' he said earnestly. 'I had it from her brother himself, he could not be mistaken.'

There was a moment of taut silence, while she considered and shook her head over him, frowning. 'When was it that she entered the Order? It cannot be long ago.'

'Three years, madam. The date I cannot tell, but it was about a month after my lord took the cowl, and that was in the middle of July.' He was frightened now by the strangeness of her reception. She was shaking her head dubiously, and regarding him with mingled sympathy and bewilderment. 'It may be that this was before you held office...'

'Son,' she said ruefully, 'I have been prioress for more than

239

seven years now, there is not a name among our sisters that I
don't know, whether the world's name or the cloistered, not an
entry I have not witnessed. And sorry as I am to say it, and little
as I myself understand it, I cannot choose but tell you, past any
doubt, that no Julian Cruce ever asked for, or received the veil
at Wherwell. It is a name I never heard, and belongs to a woman
of whom I know nothing.'

He could not believe it. He sat staring and passing a dazed
hand once and again over his forehead. 'But ... this is
impossible! She set out from home with an escort, and a dowry
intended for her convent. She declared her intent to come to
Wherwell, all her household knew it, her father knew it and
sanctioned it. About this, I swear to you, madam, there is no
possible mistake. She set out to ride to Wherwell.'

'Then,' said the prioress gravely, 'I fear you have questions to
ask elsewhere, and very serious questions. For believe me, if
you are certain she set out to come to us, I am no less certain that
she never reached us.'

'But what could prevent?' he asked urgently, wrenching at
impossibilities. 'Between her home and Wherwell ...'

'Between her home and Wherwell were many miles,' said the
prioress. 'And many things can prevent the fulfilment of the
plans of men and women in this world. The disorders of war, the
accidents of travels, the malice of other men.'

'But she had an escort to bring her to her journey's end!'

'Then it's of them you should be making enquiries,' she said
gently, 'for they signally failed to do so.'

No point whatever in pressing her further. He sat stunned into
silence, utterly lost. She knew what she was saying, and at least
she had pointed him towards the only lead that remained to him.
What was the use of hunting any further in these parts, until he
had caught at the clue she offered him, and begun to trace that
ride of Julian's from Lai, where it had begun. Three men-at-
arms, Reginald had said, went with her, under a huntsman who
had an affection for her from her childhood. They must still be
there in Reginald's service, there to be questioned, there to be
made to account for the mission that had never been completed.

The prioress had yet one more point to make, even as she rose
to indicate that the interview was over, and the late visitor
dismissed.

'She was carrying, you say, the dowry she intended to bring to
Wherwell? I know nothing of its value, of course, but ... The
roads are not entirely free of evil customs...'

'She had four men to guard her,' cried Nicholas, one last flare in desperation.

'And they knew what she carried? God knows,' said the prioress, 'I should be loth to cast suspicion on any upright man, but we live in a world, alas, where of any four men, one at least may be corruptible.'

He went away into the town still dazed, unable to think or reason, unable to grasp and understand what with all his heavy heart he believed. It was growing dark, and he was too weary to continue now without sleep, besides the care he must have for his horse. He found an alehouse that could provide him a rough bed, and stabling and fodder for his beast, and lay wakeful a long time before his own exhaustion of body and mind overcame him.

He had an answer, but what to make of it he did not know. Certain it was that she had never passed through the gates of Wherwell, and therefore had not died there in the fire. But – three years, and never a word or a sign! Her brother had not troubled himself with a half-sister he scarcely knew, believing her to be settled in life according to her own choice. And never a word had come from her. Who was there to wonder or question? Cloistered women are secure in their own community, have all their sisterhood about them, what need have they of the world, and what should the world expect from them? Three years of silence from those vowed to the cultivation of silence is natural enough; but three years without a word now became an abyss, into which Julian Cruce had fallen as into the ocean, and sunk without trace.

Now there was nothing to be done but hasten back to Shrewsbury, confess his shattering failure in his mission, and go on to Lai to tell the same dismal story to Reginald Cruce. Only there could he again hope to find a thread to follow. He set off early in the morning to ride back into Winchester.

It was mid-morning when he drew near to the city. He had left it, prudently, not by the direct way through the west gate, since the royal castle with its hostile and by this time surely desperate garrison lay so close and had complete command of the gate. But some time before he reached the spot where he should, in the name of caution, turn eastward from the Romsey road and circle round the south of the city to a safer approach, he began to be aware of a constant chaotic murmur of sound ahead, that grew from a murmur to a throbbing

241

clamour, to a steely din of clashing and screaming that could mean nothing but battle, and a close and tangled and desperate battle at that. It seemed to centre to his left front, at some distance from the town, and the air in that direction hung hazy with the glittering dust of struggle and flight.

Nicholas abandoned all thought of turning aside towards the bishop's hospital of Saint Cross or the east gate, and rode on full tilt towards the west gate. And there before him he saw the townsfolk of Winchester boiling out into the open sunlight with shouting and excitement, and the streets within full of people, loud, exultant and fearless, all clamouring for news or imparting news at the tops of their voices, throwing off all the creeping caution that had fettered them for so long.

Nicholas caught at a tall fellow's shoulder and bellowed his own question: 'What is it? What's happened?'

'They're gone! Marched out at dawn, that woman and her royal uncle of Scotland and all her lords! Little they cared about the likes of us starving, but when the wolf bit them it was another story. Out they went, the lot of them – in good order, *then*! Now hark to them! The Flemings at least let them get clear of the town before they struck, and let us alone. There'll be pickings, over there!'

They were only waiting, these vengeful tradesmen and craftsmen of Winchester, hovering here until the din of battle moved away into the distance. There would be gleanings before the night. No man can ride his fastest loaded down with casque and coat of mail. Even their swords they might discard to lighten the weight their horses had to bear. And if they had retained enough optimism to believe they could convey their valuables away with them, there would be rich pickings indeed before the day was out.

So it had come, the expected attempt to break out of the iron circle of the queen's army, and it had come too late to have any hope of success. After the holocaust of Wherwell even the empress must have known she could hold out here no longer.

North-west along the Stockbridge road and wavering over the rising downs, the glittering halo of dust rolled and danced, spreading wider as it receded. Nicholas set off to follow it, as the boldest of the townsmen, or the greediest, or the most vindictive, were also doing afoot. He had far outridden them, and was alone in the undulating uplands, when he saw the first traces of the assault which had broken the empress's army. A single fallen body, a lamed horse straying, a heavy shield

242

hurled aside, the first of many. A mile further on and the ground was littered with arms, pieces of armour torn off and flung aside in flight, helmets, coats of mail, saddle-bags, spilling garments and coins and ornaments of silver, fine gowns, pieces of plate from noble tables, all expendable where mere life was the one thing to be valued. Not all had preserved it, even at this cost. There were bodies, tossed and trampled among the grasses, frightened horses running in circles, some ridden almost to death and gasping on the ground. Not a battle, but a rout, a headlong flight in contagious terror.

He had halted, staring in sick wonder at such a spectacle, while the flight and pursuit span forward into the distance under its shining cloud, towards the Test at Stockbridge. He did not follow it further, but turned and rode back towards the city, wanting no part in that day's work. On his way he met the first of the gleaners, hungry and eager, gathering the spoils of victory.

It was three days later, in the early afternoon, when he rode again into the great court at Shrewsbury abbey, to fulfil the promise he had made. Brother Humilis was in the herb-garden with Cadfael, sitting in the shade while Fidelis chose from among the array of plants a few sprigs and tendrils he wanted for an illuminated border, bryony and centaury and bugloss, and the coiled threads of vetches, infinitely adaptable for framing initial letters. The young man had grown interested in the herbs and their uses, and sometimes helped to make the remedies Cadfael used in the treatment of Humilis, tending them with passionate, still devotion, as though his love could add the final ingredient that would make them sovereign.

The porter, knowing Nicholas well by this time, told him without question where he would find his lord. His horse he left tethered at the gatehouse, intending to ride on at once to Lai, and came striding round the clipped bulk of the tall hedge and along the gravel path to where Humilis was sitting on the stone bench against the south wall. So intent was Nicholas upon Humilis that he brushed past Fidelis with barely a glance, and the young brother, startled by his sudden and silent arrival, turned on him for once a head uncovered and a face open to the sun, but as quickly drew aside in his customary reticent manner, and held aloof from their meeting, deferring to a prior loyalty. He even drew the cowl over his head, and sank silently into its shadow.

243

'My lord,' said Nicholas, bending his knee to Humilis and clasping the two hands that reached to embrace him, 'your sorry servant!'

'No, never that!' said Humilis warmly, and freed his hands to draw the boy up beside him and peer searchingly into his face. 'Well,' he said with a sigh and a small, rueful smile, 'I see you have not the marks of success on you. No fault of yours, I dare swear, and no man can command success. You would not be back so soon if you had found out nothing, but I see it cannot be what you hoped for. You did not find Julian. At least,' he said, peering a little closer, and in a voice careful and low, 'not living...'

'Neither living nor dead,' said Nicholas quickly, warding off the worst assumption. 'No, it's not what you think – it's not what any of us could have dreamed.' Now that it came to the telling, he could only blurt out the whole of it as baldly and honestly as possible, and be done. 'I searched in Wherwell, and in Winchester, until I found the prioress of Wherwell in refuge in Romsey abbey. She has held the office seven years, she knows every sister who has entered there in that time, and none of them is Julian Cruce. Whatever has become of Julian she never reached Wherwell, never took vows there, never lived there – and cannot have died there. A blind ending!'

'She never came there?' Humilis echoed in an astonished whisper, staring with locked brows across the sunny garden.

'She never did! Always,' said Nicholas bitterly, 'I come three years too late. Three years! And where can she have been all that time, with never a word of her here, where she left home and family, nor there, where she should have come to rest? What can have happened to her, between here and Wherwell? That region was not in turmoil then, the roads should have been safe enough. And there were four men with her, well provided.'

'And they came home,' said Humilis keenly. 'Surely they came home, or Cruce would have been wondering and asking long ago. In God's name, what can they have reported when they returned? No evil! None from other men, or there would have been an instant hue and cry, none of their own, or they would not have returned at all. This grows deeper and deeper.'

'I am going on to Lai,' said Nicholas, rising, 'to let Cruce know, and have him hunt out and question those who rode with her. His father's men will be his men now, whether at Lai or on some other of his manors. They can tell us, at least, where they parted from her, if she foolishly dismissed them and rode the last miles alone. I'll not rest until I find her. If she lives, I *will* find her!'

Humilis held him by the sleeve, doubtfully frowning. 'But your command ... You cannot leave your duties for so long, surely?'

'My command,' said Nicholas, 'can do very well without me now for a while. I've left them snug enough, encamped near Andover, living off the land, and my sergeants in charge, old soldiers well able to fill my place, the way things are now. For I have not told you the half. I'm so full of my own affairs, I have no time for kings. Did we not say, last time, that the empress must try to break out from Winchester soon, or starve where she was? She has so tried. After the disaster at Wherwell they must have known they could not hold out longer. Three days ago they marched out westward, towards Stockbridge, and William de Warenne and the Flemings fell on them and broke them to pieces. It was no retreat, it was headlong flight. Everything weighty about them they threw away. If ever they do come safe back to Gloucester it will be half naked. I'll make a stay in the town and let Hugh Beringar know.'

Brother Cadfael, who had gone on with a little desultory weeding between his herb-beds, at a little distance, nevertheless heard all this with stretched ears and kindling blood, and straightened his back now to stare.

'And she – the empress? They have not taken her?' An empress for a king would be fair exchange, and almost inevitable, even if it meant not an ending, but stalemate, and a new beginning over the same exhausted and exhausting ground. Had Stephen been the one to capture the implacable lady, with his mad, endearing, chivalry he would probably have given her a fresh horse and an escort, and sent her safely to Gloucester, to her own stronghold, but the queen was no such magnanimous idiot, and would make better use of a captive enemy.

'No, not Maud, she's safely away. her brother sped her off ahead with Brian FitzCount to watch over her, and stayed to rally the rearguard and hold off the pursuit. No, it's better than Maud! He could have gone on fighting without her, but she'll be hard put to it without him. The Flemings caught them at Stockbridge, trying to ford the river, and rounded up all those who survived. It's the king's match we've taken, the man himself, Robert of Gloucester!'

Chapter Seven

EGINALD CRUCE, whether he had, or indeed could well be expected to have any deep affection for a half-sister so many years distant from him and seldom seen, was not the man to be tolerant of any affront or injury towards any of his house. Whatever touched a Cruce reflected upon him, and roused his hackles like those of a pointing hound. He heard the story out in stoic silence but ever-growing resentment and rage, the more formidable for being under steely control.

'And all this is certain?' he said at length. 'Yes, the woman would know her business, surely. The girl never came there. I was not in this matter at all, I was not here and did not witness either the going or the return, but now we will see! At least I know the names of those who rode with her, for my father spoke of the journey on his death-bed. He sent his closest, men he trusted – who would not, with his daughter? And he doted on her. Wait!'

He bellowed from the hall door for his steward, and in from the fading daylight, cooling now towards dusk, came a grey elder dried and tanned like old leather, but very agile and sinewy. He might have been older than the lord he had lost, and was in no awe of either father or son here, but plainly master of his own duties, and aware of his worth. He spoke as an equal, and easy in the relationship.

'Arnulf, you'll remember,' said Reginald, waving him to a seat at the table with them, as free in acknowledgement of the association as his man, 'when my sister went off to her convent, the lads my father sent off with her – the Saxon brothers, Wulfric and Renfred, and John Bonde, and the other, who was he? He went off with the draft, I know, soon after I came here...'

'Adam Heriet,' said the steward readily, and drew across the board the horn his lord filled for him. 'Yes, what of them?'

'I want them, Arnulf, all of them – here.'

'Now, my lord?' If he was surprised, he took surprises in his stride.

'Now, or as soon as may be. But first, all these were of my father's close household, you knew them better than ever I did. Would you count them trustworthy?'

'Out of question,' said the steward without hesitation, in a voice as dry and tough as his hide. 'Bonde is a simpleton, or little better, but a hard worker and open as the day. The Saxon pair are clever and subtle, but clever enough to know when they have a good lord, and loyal enough to be grateful for him. Why?'

'And the other, Heriet? Him I hardly knew. That was when Earl Waleran demanded my service of men in arms, and I sent him whatever offered, and this Heriet put himself forward. They told me he was restless because my sister was gone from the manor. He was a favourite of hers, so I heard, and fretted for her.'

'That could be true,' said Arnulf the steward. 'Certainly he was never the same after he came back from that journey. Such girl children can worm their way into a man and get at his heart. So she may have done with him. If you've known them from the cradle, they work deep into your marrow.'

Reginald nodded dourly. 'Well, he went. Twenty men my overlord asked of me, and twenty men he got. It was about the time he had that contention of his against the bishops, and needed reinforcements. Well, wherever he may be now, Heriet is out of our reach. But the rest are all here?'

'The Saxon pair are in the stable loft this minute. Bonde should be coming in about this time from the fields.'

'Bring them,' said Reginald. And to Nicholas he said, when the steward had drained his horn and departed down the stone stair into the court as nimbly and rapidly as a youth of twenty: 'Wherever I look among these four, I can see no treachery. Why should they return, if they had somehow betrayed her? And why should they do so, any man of them? Arnulf says

247

right, they knew they had the softest of beds here, my father was of the old, paternal, household kind, easier far than I, and I am not hated.' He was well aware, to judge by the sharp smile and curl of the lip, yellow-outlined in the low lamplight, of all the tensions that still bound and burned between Saxon and Norman, and was too intelligent to strain them too far. In the countryside memories were very long, and loyalties with them, hard to displace, slow to replace.

'Your steward is Saxon,' said Nicholas drily.

'So he is! And content! Or if not content,' said Reginald, at once dour and bright in the intimate light, 'at least aware of worse, worse by far. I have benefited by my father's example, I know when to bend. But where my sister is concerned, I tell you, I feel my spine stiffen.'

So did Nicholas, as stiff as if the marrow there had petrified into stone. And he viewed the three hinds, when they came marshalled sleepily up the steps into the hall, with the same blank, opaque eyes as did their master. Two long, fair fellows surely no more than thirty years old, with all the lean grace of their northern kin and eyes that caught the light in flashes of pale, blinding blue, and a softer, squat, round-faced man perhaps a little older, bearded and brown.

It might be true enough, thought Nicholas, watching them, that they had no hate for their lord, but rather reckoned themselves lucky by comparison with many of their kind, now for the third generation subject to Norman masters. But for all that, they went in awe of Reginald, and any such summons as this, outside the common order of their labouring day, brought them to questioning alert and wary, their faces closed, like a lid shut down over a box of thoughts that might not all be acceptable to authority. But it was different when they understood the subject of their lord's enquiry. The shut faces opened and eased. It was clear to Nicholas that none of these three felt he had any reason for uneasiness concerning that journey, rather they recalled it with pleasure, as well they might, the one carefree pilgrimage, the one holiday of their lives, when they rode instead of going afoot, and went well-provided and in the pride of arms.

Yes, of course they remembered it. No, they had had no trouble by the way. A lady accompanied by two good bowmen and two swordsmen had had nothing to fear. The taller of the Saxon pair, it seemed, used the new long-bow, drawn to the shoulder, while John Bonde carried the short Welsh bow, drawn to the breast, of less range and penetration than the long-bow, but wonderfully fast and agile in use at shorter range. The other brother was a swordsman, and so had the fourth member been, the missing Adam Heriet. A good enough company to travel briskly and safely, at whatever speed the lady could maintain without fatigue.

'Three days on the way, my lord,' said the Saxon bowman, spokesman for all three, and encouraged with vehement nods, 'and then we came into Andover, and because it was already evening, we lay there overnight, meaning to finish the journey the next morning. Adam found lodging for the lady with a merchant's household there, and we lay in the stables. It was but three or four miles more to go, so they told us.'

'And my sister was then in health and spirits? Nothing had gone amiss?'

'No, my lord, we had a good journey. She was glad then to be so close to what she wished. She said so, and thanked us.'

'And in the morning? You brought her on those few miles?'

'Not we, my lord, for she chose to go the rest of the way with only Adam Heriet, and we were to wait in Andover for his return, and so we did as we were ordered. And when he came, then we set out for home.'

To this the other two nodded firm assent, satisfied that their errand had been completed in obedience to the lady's wishes. So it was only one, only her servant and familiar, according to repute, who had gone the rest of the way with Julian Cruce.

'You saw them ride for Wherwell?' demanded Reginald, frowning heavily at every complexity that arose to baulk him. 'She went with him freely, content?'

'Yes, my lord, fresh and early in the morning they went. A fine morning, too. She said farewell to us, and we watched them out of sight.'

No need to doubt it. Only four miles from her goal, and yet she had never reached it. And only one man could know what had become of her in that short distance.

Reginald waved them away irritably. What more could they tell him? To the best of their knowledge she had gone where she had meant to go, and all was well with her. But as the three made for the hall door, glad to be off to their beds, Nicholas said suddenly: 'Wait!' And to his host: 'Two more questions, if I may ask them?'

'Do so, freely.'

'Was it the lady herself who told you it was her wish to go on with only Heriet, and ordered you to remain in Andover and wait for him?'

'No,' said the spokesman, after a moment's thought, 'it was Adam told us.'

'And they set out in the early morning, you said. At what hour did Heriet return?'

'Not until twilight, sir. It was getting dark when he came. Because of that we stayed the night over, to make an early start for home next day.'

'There was another question I might have added,' said Nicholas, when he was alone with his host, and the hall door stood open on the deepening dusk and quiet of the yard, 'but I doubt he would have seen to his own horse, and after a night's rest there'd be no way of judging how far it had been ridden. But see how the time testifies – three or four miles to Wherwell, and he would have had no call to linger, once he had brought her there. Yet he was the whole day away, twelve hours or more. What was he about all that time? Yet he's said to have been her devoted slave from infancy.'

'It got him credit with my father, who also doted,' said Reginald sourly. 'I knew little of him. But there he is at the heart of this, and who else is there? He alone rode with her that last day. And came back here with his fellows, letting it be seen all had gone well, and the matter was finished. But between Andover and Wherwell my sister vanishes. And a month or so later, when our overlord, Earl Waleran, from whom we hold three manors, sends asking for men, who should be first to offer himself but this same man? Why so ready to seize on a way of leaving here? For fear questions should yet be asked, some day? Something untoward come to light, and start the hunt?'

'Would he have come back at all,' wondered Nicholas, 'if he had done her harm or any way betrayed her?'

'If he had wit enough, yes, and wit enough he surely had, for see how he has succeeded! If he had failed to return with the others, there would have been a hue and cry at once. They would have started it before ever they left Andover. As it is, three years are gone without a word or a shadow of doubt, and where is Heriet now?'

He had fastened on the notion now, tearing it with his teeth, savouring the inner rage he felt at any such thing being dared against his house. It was for that he would want revenge, if

250

ever it came to the proof, not for Julian's own injuries. And yet
Nicholas could not but tread the same way with him. Who else
was there, to have wiped out the very image and memory of
that girl committed to his care? Two had ridden from Andover,
one had returned. The other was gone from the face of the
earth, vanished into air. It was hard to go on believing that she
would ever be seen again.

A servant brought in a lamp, and refilled the pitcher of ale
on the table. The lady kept her chamber with her children, and
left the men to confer without interruption. The night came
down almost suddenly, in the brief customary breeze that came
with this hour.

'She is dead!' said Reginald abruptly, and spread a large
hand flat on the table.

'No, that's not certain. And *why* should he do such a thing?
He lost his security here, for he dared not stay, once the chance
of leaving offered. What was there to gain that would outweigh
that? Is a man-at-arms in Waleran of Meulan's service better
off than your trusted people here? I think not!'

'Service for half a year? If he stayed longer it was from
choice, half a year was all that was demanded. And as for
what he had to gain – and by God, he was the only one of the
four who could have known the worth of it – my sister had
three hundred silver marks in her saddle-bags, besides a list of
valuables meant for her convent. I cannot recite you the whole
tally offhand, but they're listed somewhere in the manor
books, the clerk can lay hands on the record. I know there
was a pair of silver candle-holders. And such jewels as she
had from her mother she also took in gift, having no further
use for them herself in this world. Enough to tempt a man –
even if he had to buy in a confederate to put a better face on
the deed.'

And it could be so! A woman carrying her dowry with her,
with a father and household satisfied of her well-being at
home, and no one to wonder at her silence ... But no, that
could not be right, Nicholas caught himself up hopefully, not if
she had already sent word of her coming ahead to Wherwell.
Surely a girl intending to take the veil must advance her plea
and be sure of acceptance before venturing on the journey
south. But if she had done so, then there would have been
wonder at her failure to arrive, and rapid enquiry, and the
prioress, had there ever been letters or a courier from Julian
Cruce, would have known and remembered the name. No, she

251

could not have bargained beforehand. She had taken her dowry and simply gone to knock on the door and ask admittance. He had not the experience in such matters to know if that was very unusual, nor the cynicism to reflect that it would hardly be refused if the portion brought was large enough.

'This man Heriet will have to be found,' said Nicholas, making up his mind. 'If he's still serving with Waleran of Meulan, then I may be able to find him. Waleran is the king's man. If not, he'll be far to seek, but what other choice have we? He's native in this shire, is he? If he has kin, they'll be here?'

'He's second son to a free tenant at Harpecote. Why, what are you thinking?'

'That you'd best have your clerk make two copies of the list of what your sister took with her when she left. The money can't be traced and known, but it may be the valuables can. Have him describe them fully if he can. Plate meant for church use may turn up on sale or be noted somewhere, so may gems. I'll have the list circulated round Winchester – if the bishop's well rid of his empress he may know now where his interest lies! – and try to find Adam Heriet among Meulan's companies, or get word when and how he left them. You do as much here, where if he has kin he may some day visit. Can you think of anything better? Or anything more we can undertake?'

Reginald heaved himself up from the table, making the flame of the lamp gutter. A big, black-avised, affronted man, with a face grimly set. 'That's well reasoned, and we'll do it. Tomorrow I'll have him copy the items – he's a finicky little fellow who has everything at his finger-ends – and I'll ride with you to Shrewsbury and see Hugh Beringar, and have this matter in train before the day's out. If this or any villain has done murder and robbery against my house, I want justice and I want restitution.'

Nicholas rose with his host, and went to the bed prepared for him so weary that he could not fail to sleep. So did he want justice. But what was justice in this matter? He planned and thought as one following a trail. He must pursue it with all his powers, having nothing else left to attempt, but he could not and would not believe in it. What he wanted above everything else in the world was a breath of some fresh breeze, blowing from another quarter, suggesting that she was not dead, that all this coil of suspicion and cupidity and treachery was false, a mere appearance, to be blown away when the morning came. But the morning came, and nothing was new, and nothing changed.

Thus two who had only one quest in common, and nothing besides to make them allies, rode together back into Shrewsbury, armed with two well-scripted copies of the valuables and money Julian Cruce had carried with her as her dowry on entering the cloister.

Hugh had come down from the town to dine with Abbot Radulfus, and acquaint him with the latest developments in the political tangle that was England. The flight of the empress back into her western stronghold, the scattering of a great part of her forces, and the capture of Earl Robert of Gloucester, without whom she was impotent, must transform the whole pattern of events, though its first effect was to freeze them from any action at all. The abbot might not have any interest in factional strife, but he was entitled to the mitre and a place in the great council of the country, and the welfare of people and church was very much his business. They had conferred a long time over the abbot's well-furnished table, and it was mid-afternoon when Hugh came looking for Cadfael in the herb-garden.

'You'll have heard? The word that Nicholas Harnage brought me yesterday? He said he had come here first, to his lord. Robert of Gloucester is penned up in Rochester a prisoner, and everything has halted while both sides think on what comes next – we, how best to make use of him; they, how to survive without him.' Hugh sat down on the stone bench in the shade, and spread his booted feet comfortably. 'Now comes the argument. And she had better order the king loosed from his chains, or Robert may find himself tethered, too.'

'I doubt if she'll see it so,' said Cadfael, pausing to lean on his hoe and pluck out a wisp of weed from between his neat, aromatic beds. 'More than ever, Stephen is her only weapon now. She'll try to exact the highest possible price for him, her brother will scarcely be enough to satisfy her.'

Hugh laughed. 'Robert himself takes the same line, by young Harnage's account. He refuses to consider an exchange for the king, says he's no fair match for a monarch, and to balance it fitly we must turn loose all the rearguard that were taken with him, to make up Stephen's weight in the scale. But wait a while! If the empress argues in the same way now, within a month wiser men will have shown her she can do nothing, nothing at all, without Robert. London will never let her enter again, much less get within reach of the crown, and for all she has Stephen in a dungeon, he is still king.'

'It's Robert they'll have trouble persuading,' Cadfael reasoned.

'Even he will have to see the truth in the end. If she is to continue her fight, it can only be with Robert beside her. They'll convince him. Reluctant as they all may be to loose their hold on him, we shall have Stephen back before the year's end.'

They were still there together in the garden when Nicholas and Reginald Cruce, having enquired in vain for Hugh at the castle, as they entered the town, and again at Hugh's house by Saint Mary's church, as they passed through, followed the directions given by his porter, and came purposefully hunting for him at the abbey. At the sound of their boots on the gravel, and the sight of them rounding the box hedge, Hugh rose alertly to meet them.

'You're back in good time. What news?' And to the second man he said, eyeing him with interest: 'I have not enjoyed your acquaintance until now, sir, but you are surely the lord of Lai. Nicholas here has told me how things stood at Wherwell. You're welcome to whatever service I can offer. And what now?'

'My lord sheriff,' said Cruce loudly and firmly, as one accustomed to setting the pace for others to follow, 'in the matter of my sister there's ground for suspicion of robbery and murder, and I want justice.'

'So do all decent men, and so do I. Sit down here, and let me hear what grounds you have for such suspicions, and where the finger points. I grant you the matter looks ugly enough. Let me know what you've found at home to add to it.'

It was over-hot in the afternoon sun, and even in shirt-sleeves Cruce was sweating freely. They moved back into the shade, and there sat down together, and Cadfael, hospitable in his own domain, and by no means inclined to be ousted from it in the middle of his work, went instead to bring a pitcher of wine from his workshop, and beakers for their use. He served them and went aside, but not so far that he did not hear what passed. All that had gone before he already knew, and on certain points his curiosity was already pricked into

254

wakefulness, and foresaw circumstances in which he might yet be needed. His patient fretted over the girl, and could not afford further fraying away of what little flesh he had. Cadfael clove to his fellow-crusader in a solidarity of shared experience and mutual respect. One of those few, like Guimar de Massard, who came clean and chivalrous out of a very deformed and marred holy war. And however gradually, dying of it. Whatever concerned his welfare, body or soul, Cadfael wanted to know.

'My lord,' said Nicholas earnestly, 'you'll remember all I told you of the men of my lord Cruce's household who escorted his sister to Wherwell. Three of the four we have questioned at Lai, and I am sure they have told us truth. But the fourth ... and he the only one who accompanied her on the last day of her journey, the last few miles – he is no longer there, and him we must find.'

They told the whole story between them, at times in chorus, very vehemently.

'He left with her from Andover early in the morning, and the other three, who had orders to remain there, watched them away.'

'And he did not return until late evening, too late to set out for home that night. Yet Wherwell is but three or four miles from Andover.'

'And he, alone of those four,' said Cruce fiercely, 'was so deep in her confidence from old familiarity that he may well have known, must have known, the dowry she carried with her.'

'And that was?' demanded Hugh sharply. His memory was excellent. There was nothing he needed to be told twice.

'Three hundred marks in coin, and certain valuables for church use. My lord, we have had my clerk, who keeps good accounts, write a list of what she took, and here we have two copies. The one we hold you should circulate in these parts, where the man is native, and so was my sister, and the other Harnage here will carry to make known round Winchester, Wherwell and Andover, where she vanished.'

'Good!' said Hugh heartily. 'The coins can never be certainly traced, but the pieces of church ornaments may.' He took the scroll Nicholas held out to him, and read with lowered and frowning brows: Item, a pair of candlesticks of silver, made in the form of tall sconces entwined with the vine, with snuffers attached by silver chains, also ornamented with grape leaves.

Item, a standing cross a man's hand-length in height, on a silver pedestal of three steps, and studded with semi-precious stones of yellow pebble, amethyst and agate, together with a similar cross of the same metal and stones, a little finger's length, on a thin silver neck-chain for a priest's wear. Item, a silver pyx, small, engraved with ferns. Also certain pieces of jewellery to her belonging, as, a necklet of polished stones from the hills above Pontesbury, a bracelet of silver engraved with tendrils of vetch, and curious ring of silver set with enamels all round, in the form of yellow and blue flowers.' He looked up. 'Surely identifiable if they can be found, almost any of these. Your clerk did well. Yes, I'll have this made known to all officers and tenants of mine here in the shire, but it seems to me that in the south they're more likely to be traced. As for the man, if he's native here he has kin, and may well keep in touch with them. You say he went to do fighting services?'

'Only a matter of weeks after he returned to my father's household, yes. My father was newly dead, and the Earl of Worcester, my overlord, demanded a draft of men, and this Adam Heriet offered himself.'

'How old?' asked Hugh.

'A year or so past fifty. A strong man with sword or bow. He had been forester and huntsman to my father, Waleran would think himself lucky to get him. The rest were younger, but raw.'

'And where did this Heriet hail from? Your father's man must belong to one of your own manors.'

'Born at Harpecote, a younger son of a free man who farmed a yardland there. His elder brother farmed it after him. A nephew has it now. They were not on good terms, or so my father said. But for all that there may be some trace of him to be picked up there.'

'Had they any other kin? And the fellow never took a wife?'

'No, he never did. I know of no others of his family, but there well may be some around Harpecote.'

'Let them be,' said Hugh decidedly. 'It had best be left to me to probe there. Though I doubt if a man with no ties here will have come back to the shire, once having taken to the fighting life. More likely to be found where you're bound for, Nicholas. Do your best!'

'I mean to,' said Nicholas grimly, and rose to be off about the work without delay. The scroll of Julian's possessions he rolled and thrust into the breast of his coat. 'I must say a word first to my lord Godfrid, and let him know I'll not abandon this hunt while there's a grain of hope left. Then I'm on the road!' And he was away at a fast stride that became a light, long-paced run before he was out of sight. Cruce rose in his turn, eyeing Hugh somewhat grudgingly, as if he doubted to find in him a sufficient force of vengeful fury for the undertaking.

'Then I may leave this with you, my lord? And you will pursue it vigorously?'

'I will,' said Hugh drily. 'And you will be at Lai? That I may know where to find you, at need?'

Cruce went away silenced, for the time being, but none too content, and looked back from the turn of the hedge dubiously, as if he felt that the lord sheriff should already have been on horseback, or at least shaping for it, in the cause of Cruce vengeance. Hugh stared him out coolly, and watched him round the thick screen of box and disappear.

'Though I had best move speedily,' he said then, wryly smiling, 'for if that one found the fellow first I would not give much for his chances of escaping a few broken bones, if not a stretched neck. And even if it may come to that in the end, it shall not be at Reginald Cruce's hands, nor without a fair trial.' He clapped Cadfael heartily on the back, and turned to go. 'Well, if it's close season for kings and empresses, at least it gives us time to hunt the smaller creatures.'

Cadfael went to Vespers with an unquiet mind, troubled by imaginings of a girl on horseback, with silver and rough gems and coin in her saddle-bags, parting from her last known companions only a few miles from her goal, and then vanishing like morning mist in the summer sun, as if she had never been. A wisp of vapour over the meadow, and then gone. If those who agonised after her, the old and the young, had known her dead and with God, they, too, could have been at peace. Now there was no peace for any man drawn into this elaborate web of uncertainty.

Among the novices and schoolboys and the child oblates, last of their kind, for Abbot Radulfus would accept no more infants into a cloistered life decreed for them by others, Rhun stood rapt and radiant, smiling as he sang. A virgin by nature and aptitude, as well as by years, untroubled by the bodily agonies that tore most men, but miraculously aware of them and tender towards them, as few are to pains that leave their own flesh unwrung.

Vespers at this time of year shone with filtered summer light, that showed Rhun's flaxen beauty in crystalline pallor, and flashed across into the ranks of the brothers to burn in the sullen, smouldering darkness of Brother Urien, and the dilated brilliance of his black eyes, and cool into discreet shade where Brother Fidelis stood withdrawn into the shadows of the wall, alert at his lord's elbow, with no eyes and no thought for what went on around him, as he had no voice to join in the chant. His shadowed eyes looked nowhere but at Humilis, his slight body stood braced to receive and support at any moment the even frailer form that stood lance-straight beside him.

Well, worship has its own priorities, and a duty once assumed is a duty to the end. God and Saint Benedict would understand and respect that.

Cadfael, whose mind should also have been on higher things, found himself thinking: he dwindles before our eyes. It will be even sooner than I had thought. There is nothing that can prevent, or even greatly delay it now.

Chapter Eight

F ROBERT of Gloucester had not been trapped and captured in the waters of the river Test, and the Empress Maud in headlong flight with the remnant of her army into Gloucester, by way of Ludgershall and Devizes, the hunt for Adam Heriet might have gone on for a much longer time. But the freezing chill of stalemate between the two armies, each with a king in check, had loosed many a serving man, bored with inaction and glad of a change, to stretch his legs and take his leisure elsewhere, while the lull lasted and the politicians argued and bargained. And among them an ageing, experienced practitioner of sword and bow, among the Earl of Worcester's forces.

Hugh was a man of the northern part of the shire himself, but from the Welsh border; and the manors to the north-east, dwindling into the plain of Cheshire, were less familiar to him and less congenial. Over in the tamer country of the hundred of Hodnet the soil was fat and well-farmed, and the gleaned grain-fields full of plump, contented cattle at graze, at once making good use of what aftermath there was in a dry season, and leaving their droppings to feed the following year's tilth. There were abbey tenants here and there in these parts, and abbey stock turned into the fields now the crop was reaped. Their treading and manuring of the ground was almost as valuable as their fleeces.

The manor of Harpecote lay in open plain, with a small coppiced woodland on the windward side, and a low ridge of common land to the south. The house was small and of timber, but the fields were extensive, and the barns and byres that clung within the boundary fence were well-kept, and probably well-filled. Cruce's steward came out into the yard to greet the sheriff and his two sergeants, and direct them to the homestead of Edric Heriet.

It was one of the more substantial cottages of the hamlet, with a kitchen-garden before it and a small orchard behind, where a tousled girl with kilted skirts was hanging out washing on the hedge. Hens ran in the orchard grass, and a she-goat was tethered to graze there. A free man, this Edric was said to be, farming a yardland as a rent-paying tenant of his lord, a dwindling phenomenon in a country where a tiller of the soil was increasingly tied to it by customary services. These Heriets must be good husbandmen and hard workers to continue to hold their land and make it provide them a living. Such families could make good use of younger sons, needing all the hands they could muster. Adam was clearly the self-willed stray who had gone to serve for pay, and cultivated the skills of arms and forestry and hunting instead of the land.

A big, tow-headed, shaggy fellow in a frayed leather coat came ducking out of the low byre as Hugh and his officers halted at the gate. He stared, stiffening, and stood fronting them with a wary face, recognising authority though he did not know the man who wore it.

'You're wanting something here, masters?' Civil but not servile, he eyed them narrowly, and straddled his own gateway like a man on guard.

Hugh gave him good-day with the special amiability he used towards uneasy poor men bitterly aware of their disadvantages. 'You'll be Edric Heriet, I'm told. We're looking for word of where to find one Adam of that name, who should be your uncle. And you're all his kin that we know of, and may be able to tell us where to seek him. And that's the whole of it, friend.'

The big young man, surely no more than thirty years old, and most likely husband to the dishevelled but comely girl in the orchard, and father to the baby that was howling somewhere within the croft, shifted uncertainly from foot to foot, made up his mind, and stood squarely, his face inclined to clear.

'I'm Edric Heriet. What is it you want with this uncle of mine? What has he done?'

Hugh was not displeased with that. There might be small warmth of kinship between them, but this one was not going to open his mouth until he knew what was in the wind. Blood thickened at the hint of offence and danger.

'To the best of my knowledge, nothing amiss. But we need to have out of him as witness what he knows about a matter he had a hand in some years ago, sent by his lord on an errand from Lai. I know he is – or was – in the service of the Earl of Worcester since then, which is why he may be hard to find, the times being what they are. If you've had word from him, or can tell us where to look for him, we'll be thankful to you.'

He was curious now, though still uncertain. 'I have but one uncle, and Adam he's called. Yes, he was huntsman at Lai, and I did hear from my father that he went into arms for his lord's overlord, though I never knew who that might be. But as long as I recall, he never came near us here. I never remember him but from when I was a child shooing the birds off the ploughland. They never got on well, those brothers. Sorry I am, my lord,' he said, and though it was doubtful if he felt much sorrow, it was plain he spoke truth as to his ignorance. 'I have no notion where he may be now, nor where he's been these several years.'

Hugh accepted that, perforce, and considered a moment. 'Two brothers, were they? And no more? Never a sister between them? No tie to fetch him back into the shire?'

'There's an aunt I have, sir, only the one. It was a thin family, ours, my father was hard put to it to work the land after his brother left, until I grew up, and two younger brothers after me. We do well enough now between us. Aunt Elfrid was the youngest of the three, she married a cooper, bastard Norman he was, a little dark fellow from Brigge, called Walter.' He looked up, unaware of indiscretion, at the little dark Norman lord on the tall, raw-boned dapple-grey horse, and wondered at Hugh's blazing smile. 'They're settled in Brigge, I think she has childer. She might know. They were nearer.'

'And no other beside?'

'No, my lord, that was all of them. I think,' he said, hesitant but softening, 'he was godfather to her first. He might take that to heart.'

'So he might,' said Hugh mildly, thinking of his own masterful heir, to whom Cadfael stood godfather, 'so he very well might. I'm obliged to you, friend. At least we'll ask there.' He wheeled his horse, without haste, to the homeward way. 'A good harvest to you!' he said over his shoulder, smiling, and chirruped to the grey and was off, with his sergeants at his heels.

Walter the cooper had a shop in the hilltop town of Brigge, in a narrow alley no great way from the shadow of the castle walls. His booth was a narrow-fronted cave that drove deep within, and backed on an open, well-lit yard smelling of cut timber, and stacked with his finished and half-finished barrels, butts and pails, and the tools and materials of his craft. Over the low wall the ground fell away by steep, grassy terraces to where the Severn coiled, almost as it coiled at Shrewsbury, close about the foot of the town, broad and placid now at low summer water, with sandy shoals breaking its surface, but ready to wake and rage if sudden rains should come.

Hugh left his sergeants in the alley, and himself dismounted and went in through the dark booth to the yard beyond. A freckled boy of about seventeen was stooped over his jointer, busy bevelling a barrel-stave, and another a year or two younger was carefully paring long bands of willow for binding the staves together when the barrel was set up in its truss hoop. Yet a third boy, perhaps ten years old, was energetically sweeping up shavings and cramming them into bags for firing. It seemed that Walter had a full quiver of helpers in his business, for they were all alike, and all plainly sons of one father, and he the small, spry, dark man who straightened up from his shaving-horse, knife in hand.

'Serve you, sir?'

'Master cooper,' said Hugh, 'I'm looking for one Adam Heriet, who I'm told is brother to your wife. They know nothing of his whereabouts at his nephew's croft at Harpecote, but thought you might be in closer touch with him. If you can tell me where he's to be found, I shall be grateful.'

There was a silence, sudden and profound. Walter stood gravely staring, and the hand that held the draw-knife with its curved blade sank quite slowly to hang at his side while he thought. Manual dexterity was natural to him, but thought came with deliberation, and slowly. All three boys stood equally mute and stared as their father stared. The eldest, Hugh supposed, must be Adam's godson, if Edric had the matter aright.

'Sir,' said Walter at length, 'I don't know you. What's your will with my wife's kin?'

262

'You shall know me, Walter,' said Hugh easily. 'My name is Hugh Beringar, I am sheriff of this shire, and my business with Adam Heriet is to ask him some questions concerning a matter three years old now, in which I trust he'll be able to help us do right. If you can bring me to have speech with him, you may be helping him no less than me.'

Even a law-abiding man, in the circumstances, might have his doubts of that, but a law-abiding man with a decent business and a wife and a family to look after would also take a careful look all round the matter before denying the sheriff a fair answer. Walter was no fool. He shuffled his feet thoughtfully in the sawdust and the small shavings his youngest son had missed in his sweeping, and said with every appearance of candour and goodwill: 'Why, my lord, Adam's been away soldiering some years, but now it seems there's almost quiet down in the southern parts, and he's free to take his pleasure for a few days. You come very apt to your time, sir, as it chances, for he's here within the house this minute.'

The eldest boy had made to start forward softly towards the house door by this, but his father plucked him unobtrusively back by the sleeve, and gave him a swift glance that froze him where he stood. 'This lad here is Adam's godson and namesake,' said Walter guilelessly, putting him forward by the hand which had restrained him. 'You show the lord sheriff into the room, boy, and I'll put on my coat and follow.'

It was not what the younger Adam had intended, but he obeyed, whether in awe of his father or trusting him to know best. But his freckled face was glum as he led the way through the door into the large single room that served as hall and sleeping-quarters for his elders. An uncovered window, open over the descent to the river, let in ample light on the centre of the room, but the corners receded into a wood-scented darkness. At a big trestle table sat a solid, brown-bearded, balding man with his elbows spread comfortably on the board, and a beaker of ale before him. He had the weathered look of a man who lives out of doors in all but the bleakest seasons, and an air of untroubled strength about his easy stillness. The woman who had just come in from her cupboard of a kitchen, ladle in hand, was built on the same generous fashion, and had the same rich brown colouring. It was from their father that the boys got their wiry build and dark hair, and the fair skins that dappled in the sun.

'Mother,' said the youth, 'here's the lord sheriff asking after Uncle Adam.'

263

His voice was flat and loud, and he halted a moment, blocking the doorway, before he moved within and let Hugh pass by him. It was the best he could do. The unshuttered window was large enough for an active man, if he had anything on his conscience, to vault through it and make off down the slope to a river he could wade now without wetting his knees. Hugh warmed to the loyal godson, and refrained from letting him see even the trace of a smile. A dreaming soul, evidently, who saw no use in a sheriff but to bring trouble to lesser men. But Adam the elder sat attentive and interested a reasonable moment before he got to his feet and gave amiable greeting.

'My lord, you have your asking. That name and title belongs to me.'

One of Hugh's sergeants would be circling the slope below the window by now, while the other stayed with the horses. But neither the man nor the boy could have known that. Evidently Adam had seen action enough not to be easily startled or affrighted, and here had no reason he could see, so far, to be either.

'Be easy,' he said. 'If it's a matter of some of King Stephen's men quitting their service, no need to look here. I have leave to visit my sister. You may have a few strays running loose, for all I know, but I'm none.'

The woman came to his side slowly and wonderingly, bewildered but not alarmed. She had a round, wholesome, rosy face, and honest eyes.

'My lord, here's my good brother come so far to see me. Surely there's no wrong in that?'

'None in the world,' said Hugh, and went on without preamble, and in the same mild manner: 'I'm seeking news of a lady who vanished three years since. What do you know of Julian Cruce?'

That was sheer blank bewilderment to mother and son, and to Walter, who had just come into the room at Hugh's back, but it was plain enough vernacular to Adam Heriet. He froze where he stood, half-risen from the bench, leaning on the trestle table, and hung there staring into Hugh's face, his own countenance wary and still. He knew the name, it had flung him back through the years, every detail of that journey he was recalling now, threading them frantically through his mind like the beads of a rosary in the hands of a terrified man. But he was not terrified, only alerted to danger, to the pains of memory, to the necessity to think fast, and perhaps select

264

between truth, partial truth and lying. Behind that firm, impenetrable face he might have been thinking anything.

'My lord,' said Adam, stirring slowly out of his stillness, 'yes, of her certainly I know. I rode with her, I and three others from her father's household, when she went to take the veil at Wherwell. And I do know, seeing I serve in those parts, I do know how the nunnery there was burned out. But vanished three years since? How is that possible, seeing it was well known to her kin where she was living? Vanished now – yes, all too certainly, for I've been asking in vain since the fire. If you know more of my lady Julian since then than I, I beg you tell me. I could get no word whether she's living or dead.'

It had all the ring of truth, if he had not so strongly contained himself in those few moments of silence. It might be more than half truth, even so. If he was honest, he would have looked for her there, after the holocaust. If dishonest – well, he knew and could use the recent circumstances.

'You went with her to Wherwell,' said Hugh, answering nothing and volunteering nothing. 'Did you then see her safe within the convent gates there?'

This silence was brief indeed, but pregnant. If he said yes, boldly, he lied. If not, at least he might be telling truth.

'No, my lord, I did not,' said Adam heavily. 'I wish I had, but she would not have it so. We lay the last night at Andover, and then went on with her the last few miles. When we came within a mile – but it was not within sight yet, and there were small woodlands between – she sent me back, and said she would go the end of the way alone. I did what she wished. I had done what she wished since I carried her in my arms, barely a year old,' he said, with the first flash of fire out of his dark composure, like brief lightning out of banked clouds.

'And the other three?' asked Hugh mildly.

'We left them in Andover. When I returned we set out for home all together.'

Hugh said nothing yet about the discrepancy in time. That might well be held in reserve, to be sprung on him when he was away from this family solidarity, and less sure of himself.

'And you know nothing of Julian Cruce since that day?'

'No, my lord, nothing. And if you do, for God's sake let me know of it, worst or best!'

'You were devoted to this lady?'

'I would have died for her. I would die for her now.'

Well, so you may yet, thought Hugh, if you turn out to be

265

the best player of a part that ever put on a false face. He was in two minds about this man, whose brief flashes of passion had all the force of truth, and yet who picked his way among words with a rare subtlety.

Why, if he had nothing to hide?

'You have a horse here, Adam?'

The man lifted upon him a long, calculating stare, from eyes deep-set beneath bushy brows. 'I have, my lord.'

'Then I must ask you to saddle and ride with me.'

It was an asking that could not be refused, and Adam Heriet was well aware of it, but at least it was put in a fashion which enabled him to rise and go with composed dignity. He pushed back the bench and stood clear.

'Ride where, my lord?' And to the freckled boy, watching dubiously from the shadows, he said: 'Go and saddle for me, lad, make yourself useful.'

Adam the younger went, though not willingly, and with a long backward glance over his shoulder, and in a moment or two hooves thudded on the hard-beaten earth of the yard.

'You must know,' said Hugh, 'all the circumstances of the lady's decision to enter a convent. You know she was betrothed as a child to Godfrid Marescot, and that he broke off the match to become a monk at Hyde Mead.'

'Yes, I do know.'

'After the burning of Hyde, Godfrid Marescot came to Shrewsbury in the dispersal that followed. Since the sack of Wherwell, he frets for news of the girl, and whether you can bring him any or no, Adam, I would have you come with me and visit him.' Not a word yet of the small matter of her non-arrival at the refuge she had chosen. Nor was there any way of knowing from this experienced and well-regulated face whether Adam knew of it or no. 'If you cannot shed light,' said Hugh amiably, 'at least you can speak to him of her, share a remembrance heavy enough, as things are now, to carry alone.'

Adam drew a long, slow, cautious breath. 'I will well, my lord. He was a fine man, so everyone reports of him. Old for her, but a fine man. It was a great pity. She used to prattle about him, proud as if he was making a queen of her. Pity such a lass should ever take to the cloister. She would have been his fair match. I knew her. I'll ride with you in goodwill.' And to the husband and wife who stood close together, wondering and distrustful, he said calmly: 'Shrewsbury is not far. You'll see me back again before you know it.'

It was a strange and yet an everyday ride back to Shrewsbury. All the way this hardened and resilient man-at-arms conducted himself as though he did not know he was a prisoner, and suspect of something not yet revealed, while very well knowing that two sergeants rode one at either quarter behind him, in case he should make a break for freedom. He rode well, and had a very decent horse beneath him, and must be a man held in good repute and trusted by his commander to be loosed as he pleased, and thus well provided. Concerning his own situation he asked nothing, and betrayed no anxiety; but three times at least before they came in sight of Saint Giles he asked:

'My lord, did you ever hear word of her at all, after the troubles fell on Winchester?'

'Sir, if you have made enquiries round Wherwell, did you come upon any trace? There must have been many nuns scattered there.'

And last, in abrupt pleading: 'My lord, if you do know, is she living or dead?'

To none of which could he get a direct answer, since there was none to give him. Last, as they passed the low hillock of Saint Giles, with its squat roofs and modest little turret, he said reflectively: 'That must have been a hard journey for a sick and ageing man, all this way from Hyde alone. I marvel how the lord Godfrid bore it.'

'He was not alone,' said Hugh almost absently. 'They were two who came here from Hyde Mead.'

'As well,' said Adam, nodding approval, 'for they said he was a sorely wounded man. He might have foundered on the way, without a helper.' And he drew a slow, cautious breath.

After that he went in silence, perhaps because of the looming shadow of the abbey wall on his left, that cut off the afternoon sun with a sharp black knife-stroke along the dusty road.

They rode in under the arch of the gatehouse to the usual stir of afternoon, following the half-hour or so allowed for the younger brothers to play, and older ones to sleep after dinner. Now they were rousing and going forth to their various occupations, to their desks in the scriptorium, or their labours in the gardens along the Gaye, or at the mill or the hatcheries of the fishponds. Brother Porter came out from his lodge at

267

sight of Hugh's gangling grey horse, observed the attendant officers, and looked with some natural curiosity at the unknown who rode with them.

'Brother Humilis? No, you won't find him in the scriptorium, nor in the dortoir, either. After Mass this morning he swooned, here crossing the court, and though the fall did him no great harm, the young one catching him in his arms and bringing him down gently, it took some time to bring him round afterwards. They've carried him to the infirmary. Brother Cadfael is there with him now.'

'I'm sorry to hear it,' said Hugh, checking in dismayed concern. 'Then I can hardly trouble him now ...' And yet, if this was one more step towards the end which Cadfael said was inevitable and daily drawing nearer, Hugh could not afford to delay any enquiry which might shed light on the fate of Julian Cruce. Humilis himself most urgently desired knowledge.

'Oh, he's come to himself now,' said the porter, 'and as much his own master – under God, the master of us all! – as ever he was. He wants to come back to his own cell in the dortoir, and says he can still fulfil all his duties a while longer here, but they'll keep him where he is. He's in his full wits, and has all his will. If you have word for him of any import, I would at least go and see if they'll let you in to him.'

'They', when it came to authority in the infirmary, meant Brother Edmund and Brother Cadfael, and their judgement would be decisive.

'Wait here!' said Hugh, making up his mind, and swung down from the saddle to stride across the court to its north-western corner, where the infirmary stood withdrawn into the angle of the precinct wall. The two sergeants also dismounted, and stood in close and watchful attendance on their charge, though it seemed that Adam was quite prepared to brazen out whatever there was to be answered, for he sat his horse stolidly for a few moments, and then lit down and freely surrendered his bridle to the groom who had come to see to Hugh's mount. They waited in silence, while Adam looked about the clustered buildings round the court with wary interest.

Hugh encountered Brother Edmund just emerging from the doorway of the infirmary, and put his question to him briskly. 'I hear you have Brother Humilis within. Is he fit to have visitors? I have the one missing man here under guard, with luck we may start something out of him between us, before he

268

has too much time to think out his cover and make it impregnable.'

Edmund blinked at him for a moment, hard put to it to leave his own preoccupations for another man's. Then he said, after some hesitation: 'He grows daily feebler, but he's resting well now, and he has been fretting over this matter of the girl, feeling his own acts brought her to this. His mind is strong and determined. I think he would certainly wish to see you. Cadfael is there with him – his wound broke again when he fell, where it was newly healed, but it's clean. Yes, go in to him.' His face said though his lips did not utter it: 'Who knows how long his time may be? An easy mind could lengthen it.'

Hugh went back to his men. 'Come, we may go in.' And to the two sergeants he said: 'Wait outside the door.'

He heard the familiar tones of Cadfael's voice as soon as he entered the infirmary with Adam docile at his heels. They had not taken Brother Humilis into the open ward, but into one of the small, quiet cells apart, and the door stood open between. A cot, a stool and a small desk to support book or candle were all the furnishings, and wide-open door and small, unshuttered window let in light and air. Brother Fidelis was on his knees by the bed, supporting the sick man in his arm while Cadfael completed the bandaging of hip and groin where the frail new scar tissue had split slightly when Humilis fell. They had stripped him naked, and the cover was drawn back, but Cadfael's solid body blocked the view of the bed from the doorway, and at the sound of feet entering Fidelis quickly drew up the sheet to the patient's waist. So emaciated was the long body that the young man could lift it briefly on one arm, but the gaunt face showed clear and firm as ever, and the hollow eyes were bright. He submitted to being handled with a wry and patient smile, as to a salutary discipline. It was the boy who so jealously reached to conceal the ruined body from uninitiated eyes. Having drawn up the sheet, he turned to take up and shake out the clean linen shirt that lay ready, lifted it over Humilis's head, and very adroitly helped his thin arms into the sleeves, and lifted him to smooth the folds comfortably under him. Only then did he turn and look towards the doorway.

Hugh was known and accepted, even welcomed. Humilis and Fidelis as one looked beyond him to see who followed.

From behind Hugh's shoulder the taller stranger looked quickly from face to face, the mere flicker of a sharp glance that touched and took flight, a lightning assessment by way of taking stock of what he might have to deal with. Brother Cadfael, clearly, belonged here and was no threat, the sick man in the bed was known by repute, but the third brother, who stood close by the cot utterly still, wide eyes gleaming within the shadow of the cowl, was perhaps not so easily placed. Adam Heriet looked last and longest at Fidelis, before he lowered his eyes and composed his face into a closed book.

'Brother Edmund said we might come in,' said Hugh, 'but if we tire you, turn us out. I am sorry to hear you are not so well.'

'It will be the best of medicines,' said Humilis, 'if you have any better news for me. Brother Cadfael will not grudge another doctor having a say. I am not so sick, it was only a faintness – the heat gets ever more oppressive.' His voice was a little less steady than usual, and slower in utterance, but he breathed evenly, and his eyes were clear and calm. 'Who is this you have brought with you?'

'Nicholas will have told you, before he left,' said Hugh, 'that we have already questioned three of the four who rode as escort to the lady Julian when she left for Wherwell. This is the fourth – Adam Heriet, who went the last part of the way with her, leaving his fellows in Andover to wait for his return.'

Brother Humilis stiffened his frail body and sat upright to gaze, and Brother Fidelis kneeled and braced an arm about him, behind the supporting pillow, stooping his head into shadow behind his lord's lean shoulder.

'Is it so? Then we know all those who guarded her now. So you,' said Humilis, urgently studying the stalwart figure and blunt, brow-bent face that stooped a sunburned forehead to him, like a challenged bull, 'you must be that one they said loved her from a child.'

'So I did,' said Adam Heriet firmly.

'Tell him,' said Hugh, 'how and when you last parted from the lady. Speak up, it is your story.'

Heriet drew breath long and deeply, but without any evidence of fear or stress, and told it again as he had told it to Hugh at Brigge. 'She bade me go and leave her. And so I did. She was my lady, to command me as she chose. What she asked of me, that I did.'

'And returned to Andover?' asked Hugh mildly.

'Yes, my lord.'

'Scarcely in haste,' said Hugh with the same deceptive gentleness. 'From Andover to Wherwell is but a few short miles, and you say you were dismissed a mile short of that. Yet you returned to Andover in the dusk, many hours later. Where were you all that time?'

There was no mistaking the icy shock that went through Adam, stopping his breath for an instant. His carefully hooded eyes rolled wide and flashed one wild glance at Hugh, then were again lowered. It took him a brief and perceptible struggle to master voice and thoughts, but he did it with heroic smoothness, and even the pause seemed too brief for the inspired concoction of lies.

'My lord, I had never been so far south before, and reckoned at that time I never should again. She dismissed me, and the city of Winchester was there close. I had heard tell of it, but never thought to see it. I know I had no right so to borrow time, but I did it. I rode into the town, and there I stayed all that day. It was peace there, then, a man could walk abroad, view the great church, eat at an alehouse, all without fear. And so I did, and went back to Andover only late in the evening. If they have told you so, they tell truth. We never set out for home until next morning.'

It was Humilis, who knew the city of Winchester like his own palm, who took up the interrogation there, drily and calmly, eyes and voice again alert and vigorous. 'Who could blame you for taking a few hours to yourself, with your errand done? And what did you see and do in Winchester?'

Adam's wary breathing eased again readily. This was no problem for him. He launched into a very full and detailed account of Bishop Henry's city, from the north gate, where he had entered, to the meadows of St Cross, and from the cathedral and the castle of Wolvesey to the north-western fields of Hyde Mead. He could describe in detail the frontages of the steep High Street, the golden shrine of Saint Swithun, and the magnificent cross presented by Bishop Henry to his predecessor Bishop Walkelin's cathedral. No doubt but he had seen all he claimed to have seen. Humilis exchanged glances with Hugh and assured him of that. Neither Hugh nor Cadfael, who stood a little apart, taking note of all, had ever been in Winchester.

'So that is all you know of Julian Cruce's fate,' said Hugh at length.

'Never word of her, my lord, since we parted that day,' said Adam, with every appearance of truth. 'Unless there is something you can tell me now, as you know I have asked and

271

asked.' But he was asking no longer, even this repetition had lost all its former urgency.

'Something I can and will tell you,' said Hugh abruptly and harshly. 'Julia Cruce never entered Wherwell. The prioress of Wherwell never heard of her. From that day she has vanished, and you were the last ever to see her. What's your answer to that?'

Adam stood mute, staring, a long minute. 'Do you tell me this is true?' he said slowly.

'I do tell you so, though I think there never was any need to tell you, for you knew it, none better. As you are now left, the only one who may, who must, know where she did go, since she never reached Wherwell. Where she went and what befell her, and whether she is now on this earth or under it.'

'I swear to God,' said Adam slowly, 'that when I parted from my lady at her wish, I left her whole and well, and I pray she is now, wherever she may be.'

'You knew, did you not, what valuables she carried with her? Was that enough to tempt you? Did you, I ask you now in due form, did you rob your mistress and do her violence when she was left alone with you, and no witness by?'

Fidelis laid Humilis gently back against his pillows, and stood up tall and straight beside him. The movement drew Adam's gaze, and for a moment held it. He said loudly and clearly: 'So far from that, I would have died for her then, and so I would, gladly, now, rather than she should suffer even one moment's grief.'

'Very well!' said Hugh shortly. 'That's your plea. But I must and will keep you in hold until I know more. For I will know more, Adam, before I let go of this knot.' He went to the door, where his sergeants waited for their orders, and called them in. 'Take this man and lodge him in the castle. Securely!'

Adam went out between them without a word of surprise or protest. He had looked for nothing else, events had hedged him in too closely not to lock the door on him now. It seemed that he was not greatly discomforted or alarmed, either, though he was a stout, practised man who would not betray his thoughts. He did cast one look back from the doorway, a look that embraced them all, but said nothing and conveyed nothing to Hugh, and little enough to Cadfael. A mere spark, too small as yet to cast any light.

Chapter Nine

ROTHER HUMILIS watched the departure of prisoner and guards with a long, unwavering stare, and when they had vanished he sank back on his bed with a deep sigh, and lay gazing up into the low stone vault over him.

'We've tired you out,' said Hugh. 'We'll leave you now to rest.'

'No, wait!' There was a fine dew of sweat breaking on his high forehead. Fidelis leaned and wiped it away, and a preoccupied smile flashed up at him for a moment, and lingered to darken into a frown.

'Son, go out from here, take the sun and the air, you spend too much time caring for me, and you see I am in need of nothing now. It is not right that you should make me your only work here. In a little while I shall sleep.' It was not clear, from the serenity of his voice, weak though it was, whether he spoke of a mere restful slumber on a hot afternoon, or the last sleep of the body at the awakening of the soul. He laid his hand for a moment on the young man's hand, in the most delicate touch possible, austerely short of a caress. 'Yes, go, I wish it. Finish my work for me, your touch is steadier than mine, and the detail – too fine for me now.'

Fidelis looked down at him with a composed face, looked up briefly at the two who watched, and again lowered submissively those clear grey eyes that rang so striking a contrast with the curling bronze ring of his tonsure. He went as he was bidden, perhaps gladly, certainly with a free and rapid step.

'Nicholas never stopped to tell me,' said Humilis, when silence had closed over the last light footstep, 'what these valuables were, that my affianced wife took with her. Were they so distinctive as to be recognisable, should they ever be traced?'

'I doubt if there were any two such,' said Hugh. 'Gold- and silversmiths generally make to their own designs, even when they aim at pairs I wonder if they ever match exactly. These were singular enough. Once known, known for all time.'

'May I know what they were? She had coined money, I understand – that is at the service of whoever takes it. But the rest?'

Hugh, whose memory for words was exact as a mirror, willingly described them: 'A pair of candlesticks of silver, made in the form of tall sconces entwined with the vine, with snuffers attached by silver chains, also ornamented with grapeleaves. A standing cross a man's hand-length in height, on a silver pedestal of three steps, and studded with semi-precious stones of yellow pebble, amethyst and agate, together with a similar cross of the same metal and stones, a little finger's length, on a thin silver neck-chain for a priest's wear. Also some pieces of jewellery, a necklet of polished stones from the hills above Pontesbury, a bracelet of silver engraved with tendrils of vetch, and a curious ring of silver set with enamels all round, in the form of yellow and blue flowers. That's the tally. They must surely all have left this shire. They'll be found, if ever found at all, somewhere in the south, where they and she vanished.'

Humilis lay quiet, his eyelids closed, his lips moving soundlessly on the details of these chattels. 'A very small fortune,' he said in a whisper. 'But not small to some poor wretched souls. Do you truly believe she may have died for these few things?'

'Men, and women too,' said Hugh starkly, 'have died for very much less.'

'Yes, true! A small cross,' said Humilis, lips moving again upon the recollected phrases, 'the length of a little finger, set with yellow stones, and green agate and amethyst ... Fellow to an altar cross of the same, but made for wearing. Yes, a man would know that again.'

The faint dew of weakness was budding again on his

274

forehead, a great drop ran down into the folds of a closed eyelid. Cadfael wiped the corroding drops away, and frowned Hugh before him out at the door.

'I shall sleep ... ' said Humilis, and faintly and fleetingly smiled.

In the large room across the stone passage, where a dozen beds lay spaced in two rows, either side an open corridor, Brother Edmund and another brother, his back turned and his strong, erect figure unidentifiable from behind, were lifting a cot and the lay brother in it, to move them a short way along the wall, and make room for a new pallet and a new patient. The helper set down his end of the bed as Cadfael and Hugh passed by the open doorway. He straightened and turned, brushing his hands together to rub out the dents left by the weight, and showed them the dark, level brows and burning eyes of Brother Urien. In unaccustomed content with himself and the walls and persons about him, he wore a slight, taut smile that curled his lips but never damped the smouldering of his eyes. He watched them pass as if a shadow had passed, and crossed their tracks as soon as they were by, to stack an armful of washed linen in the press that stood in the passage.

In the infirmary, by custom, all doors stood open, so that a call for help might safely reach attentive ears, and help come hurrying. Voices, the chant of the office, even birdsong, circulated freely. Only in times of storm or heavy rain or winter cold were doors closed and shutters secured, never as now, in the heat of summer.

'The man is lying,' said Hugh, pacing beside Cadfael in the great court, and worrying at the texture of truth and deceit. 'But also half the time he is telling the truth, and which half holds the lies? Tell me that!'

'If I could,' said Cadfael mildly, 'I should be more than mortal.'

'He had her trust, he knew what she was worth, he rode alone with her the last few miles, and no trace of her since,' said Hugh, gnawing the evidence savagely. 'And yet, on the road there, he asked me time and again if I knew whether she lived or was dead, and I would have sworn he was honest in asking. But now see him! Halfway through that business, he stands there unmoved as a rock, and never makes protest against being held, nor shows any further trouble over *her* fate. What's to be made of him?'

'Or of any of this,' agreed Cadfael ruefully. 'I'm of your mind, he is certainly lying. He knows what he has not declared. Yet if he has possessed himself of all she had, what has he done with it? It may not be great riches, but it would be worth more to a man than the low pay and danger and sweat of a simple soldier, yet here is he manifestly a simple soldier still, and nothing more.'

'Soldier he may be,' said Hugh wryly, 'but simple he is not. His twists and turns have me baffled. Winchester he knows well – yes, maybe, but wherever he has served the greater part of these three years, since this winter all forces have closed in on Winchester. How could he not know it? And yet I'd have sworn, at first, that he truly did not know, and longed to know, what had become of the girl. Either that, or he's the cunningest mime that ever twisted his face to deceive.'

'He did not seem to me greatly uneasy,' said Cadfael thoughtfully, 'when you brought him in. Wary, yes, and picking his words with care – and that gives them all the more meaning,' he added, brightening. 'I'll be thinking on that. But fearful or anxious, no, I would not say so.'

They had reached the gatehouse, where the groom waited with Hugh's horse. Hugh gathered the reins and set toe in stirrup, and paused there to look over his shoulder at his friend.

'I tell you what, Cadfael, the only sure way out of this tangle is for that girl to turn up somewhere, alive and well. Then we can all be easy. But there, you've had more than your fair share of miracles already this year, not even you dare ask for more.'

'And yet,' said Cadfael, fretting at the disorderly confusion of shards that would not fit together, 'there's something winks at me in the corner of my mind's eye, and is gone when I look towards it. A mere will-o'-wisp – not even a spark…'

'Let it alone,' said Hugh, wheeling his horse towards the gate. 'Never blow on it for fear it may go out altogether. If you breathe the other way, who knows? It may grow into a candle-flame, and bring the moths in to singe their wings.'

Brother Urien lingered long over stacking the laundered linen in its press in the infirmary. He had let Fidelis pass without a sign, his mind still intent upon the three who were left within the sickroom, and the stone walls brought hollow echoes ringing across the passage, through the open doors. Brother Urien's senses were all honed into acute sensitivity by his inward anguish, to the point where his skin crawled and his short hairs stood on end at the torture of sounds which might seem soft and gentle to another ear.

He moved with precision and obedience to fulfil whatever Edmund required of him: a bed to be moved, without disturbing its occupant, who was half-paralysed and very old, a new cot to be installed ready for another sufferer. He turned to watch the departure of sheriff and herbalist brother without conceal, his mind still revolving words sharply remembered. All those artifacts of precious metal and semi-precious stones, vanished with a vanished woman. But a cross made to match, on a silver neck-chain ... Benedictine brothers may not retain the trappings of the person, the fruit of the world, however slight, without special permission, seldom granted. Yet there are brothers who wear chains about the neck – one, at least. He had touched, once, to bitter humiliation, and he knew.

The time, too, spoke aloud, the time and the place. Those who have killed for a desperate venture, for gain, and find themselves hard pressed, may seek refuge wherever it offers. Gains may be hidden until flight is again possible and sage. But why, then, follow that broken crusader here into Shrewsbury? Flight would have been easy after Hyde burned, in that inferno who could count heads?

Yet no one knew better than he how love, or whatever the name for this torment truly is, may be generated, nursed, take tyrannical possession of a man's soul, with far greater fury and intensity here in the cloister than out in the world. If he could be made to suffer it thus, driven blind and mad, why should not another? And how could two such victims not have something to bind them together, if nothing else, their inescapable guilt and pain? And Humilis was a sick man, and could not live long. There would be room for another when he vacated his place, when the void left after him began to ache intolerably. Urien's heart melted in him like wax, thinking what Fidelis might be enduring in his impenetrable silence.

He finished the work to which he had been called in the infirmary, closed the press, glanced once round the open ward, and went out to the court. He had been a body-servant and groom in the world, and was without craft skills, and barely literate until entering the Order. He lent his sinews and strength where they were needed, indoors or out, to any labour. He did not grudge the effort such labour cost him, nor feel his unskilled aid to be menial, for the fuel that fired him

277

within demanded a means of expending itself without, or there could be no sleep for him in his bed, nor ease when he awoke. But whatever he did he could not rid himself of the too well remembered face of the woman who had spurned and left him in his insatiable hunger and thirst. He had seen again her smooth young face, the image of innocence, and her great, lucid grey eyes in the boy Rhun, until those eyes turned on him full and seared him to the bone by their sweetness and pity. But her rich, burning russet hair, not red but brown in its brightness, he had found only in Brother Fidelis, crowning and corroborating those same wide grey eyes, the pure crystals of memory. The woman's voice had been clear, high and bold. This mirror image was voiceless, and therefore could never be harsh or malicious, never condemn, never scarify. And it was male, blessedly not of the woman's cruel and treacherous clan. Once Fidelis might have recoiled from him, startled and affrighted. But he had said and believed then that it would not always be so.

He had achieved the measured monastic pace, but not the tranquillity of mind that should have gone with it. By lowering his eyes and folding his hands before him in his sheltering sleeves he could go anywhere within these walls, and pass for one among many. He went where he knew Fidelis had been sent, and where he would surely go, valuing the bench where he sat by the true tenant who should have been sitting there, and the vellum leaf on the desk before him, and the little pots of colour deployed there, by the work Humilis had begun, and bade him finish.

At the far end of the scriptorium range in the cloister, under the south wall of the church, Brother Anselm the precentor was trying out a chant on his small hand-organ, a sequence of a half-dozen notes repeated over and over, like an inspired bird-call, sweet and sad. One of the boy pupils was there with him, lifting his childish voice unconcernedly, as gifted children will, wondering why the elders make so much fuss about what comes by nature and costs no pain. Urien knew little of music, but felt it acutely, as he felt everything, like arrows piercing his flesh. The boy rang purer and truer than any instrument, and did not know he could wring the heart. He would rather have been playing with his fellow-pupils, out in the Gaye.

The carrels of the scriptorium were deep, and the stone partitions cut off sound. Fidelis had moved his desk so that he could sit half in shade, while the full sunlight lit his leaf. His left side was turned to the sun, so that his hand cast no shadow as he worked, though the coiled tendril which was his model for the decoration of the capital letter M was wilting in the heat. He worked with a steady hand and a very fine brush, twining the delicate curls of the stem and starring them with pale, bright flowers frail as gossamer. When the singing boy, released from his schooling, passed by at a skipping run, Fidelis never raised his head. When Urien cast a long shadow and did not pass by, the hand that held the brush halted for a moment, then resumed its smooth, long strokes, but still Fidelis did not look up. By which token Brother Urien was aware that he was known. For any other this mute painter would have looked up briefly, for many among the brothers he would have smiled. And without looking, how could he know? By a silence as heavy as his own, or by some quickening that flushed his flesh and caused the hairs of his neck to rise when this one man of all men came near?

Urien stepped within the carrel, and stood close at Fidelis's shoulder, looking down at the intricate M that still lacked its touches of gold. Looking down also, with more intense awareness, at the inch or two of thin silver chain that showed within the dropped folds of collar and cowl, threading the short russet hairs on the bent neck. A cross a little finger long, on a neck-chain, and studded with yellow, green and purple stones ... He could have inserted a finger under the chain and plucked it forth, but he did not touch. He had learned that a touch is witchcraft, instant separation, putting cold distance between.

'Fidelis,' said the softest of yearning voices at Fidelis's shoulder, 'you keep from me. Why do you so? I can be the truest friend ever you had, if you will let me. What is there I will not do for you? And you have need of a friend. One who will keep secrets and be as silent as you are. Let me in to you, Fidelis...' He did not say 'brother'. 'Brother' is a title beyond desire, an easy title, no shaker of the mind or spirit. 'Let me in, and I can be to you all you need of love and loyalty. To the death!'

Fidelis laid aside his brush very slowly, and set both hands to the edge of the desk as though bracing himself to rise, and all this with rigid body and held breath. Urien pressed on in hushed haste.

'You need not fear me, I mean you only good. Don't stir, don't draw away! I know what you have done, I know what you have to hide ... No one else will ever hear it from me, if only

279

you'll do your part. Silence deserves a reward … love deserves love!'

Fidelis slid along the polished wood of the bench and stood clear, putting the desk between them. His face was pale and fixed, the dilated grey eyes enormous. He shook his head vehemently, and moved round to push past Urien and quit the carrel, but Urien spread his arms and blocked the way.

'Oh, no, not this time! Not now! That's over. I've asked, I've begged, now I give you to know even asking is over.' His tight control had burned into abrupt and savage anger, his eyes flared redly. 'I have ears, I could be your ruin if I were so minded. You had best be kind to me.' His voice was still very low, no one would hear, and no one passed along the cloister flagstones to see and wonder. He moved closer, driving Fidelis deeper into shadow within the carrel. 'What is it you wear round your neck, under your habit, Fidelis? Will you show it to me? Or shall I tell you what it is? And what it means! There are those who would give a good deal to know. To your cost, Fidelis, unless you grow kind to me.'

He had backed his quarry into the deepest corner, and pinned him there with arms outspread, and a palm flattened against the wall on either side, preventing escape. Still the pale, oval face confronted him icily, even scornfully, and the grey eyes had burned into a slow blaze of anger, utterly rejecting him.

Urien struck like a snake, flashing a hand into the bosom of Fidelis's habit, down within the ample folds, to drag out of hiding the length of the silver chain, and the trophy that hung hidden upon it, warmed by the flesh and the heart beneath. Fidelis uttered a strange, breathy sound, and leaned back hard against the wall, and Urien started back from him one unsteady step, himself appalled, and echoed the gasp. For an instant there was a silence so deep that both seemed to drown in it, then Fidelis gathered up the slack of the chain in his hand, and stowed his treasure away again in its hiding place. For that one moment he had closed his eyes, but instantly he opened them again and kept them fixed with a bleak, unbending stare upon his persecutor.

'Now, more than ever,' said Urien in a whisper, 'now you shall lower those proud eyes of yours, and stoop that stiff neck, and come to me pliantly, or go to whatever fate such an offence as yours brings down on the offender. But no need to threaten, if you will but listen to me. I pledge you my help, oh, yes, faithfully, with my whole heart – you have only to let me in to yours. Why not? And what choice have you, now? You need me, Fidelis, as cruelly as I need you. But we two together – and there need be no cruelty, only tenderness, only love...'

Fidelis burned up abruptly like a candle-flame, and with the hand that was not clutching his profaned treasure to his breast he struck Urien in the mouth and silenced him.

For a moment they hung staring, eye to eye, with never a sound or a breath between them. Then Urien said thickly, in a grating whisper that was barely audible: 'Enough! Now you shall come to me! Now you shall be the beggar. Of your own need and your own will you shall come, and beg me for what you now refuse. Or I will tell all that I know, and what I know is enough to damn you. You shall come to me and plead, and follow me like a little dog at my heels, or else I will destroy you, as now you *know* I can. Three days I give you, Fidelis! If you do not seek me out and give yourself to me by Vespers of the third day from now, *Brother*, I will let loose hell to swallow you, and smile to watch you burn!'

He swung on his heel then, and flew out of the carrel. The long black shadow vanished, the afternoon light came in again placidly. Fidelis leaned in the darkness of his corner a long moment with eyes closed and breast heaving in deep, exhausted rise and fall. Then he groped his way heavily back to his bench and sat down, and took up his brush in a hand too unsteady to be able to use it. Holding it gave him a hold on normality, and presented a fitting picture of an illuminator at work, if anyone should come to witness it. Within, there was a numbed desperation past which he could not see any light or any deliverance.

It was Rhun who came to be a witness. He had met Brother Urien in the garth, and seen the set face and smouldering, wounded eyes. He had not seen from which carrel Urien had issued, but here he sensed, smelled, felt in the prickling of his own flesh where Urien in his rank rage and pain had been.

He said no word of it to Fidelis, nor remarked on the pallor of his friend's face or the strange stiffness of his movements as he greeted him. He sat down beside him on the bench, and talked of the simple matters of the day, and the pattern of the capital letter still unfinished, and took up the fine brush for the gilding and laid in carefully the gold edges of two or three leaves, the tip of his tongue arching at the corner of his mouth, like a child at his letters.

281

When the bell rang for Vespers they went in together, both with calm faces, neither with a quiet heart.

Rhun absented himself from supper, and went instead to the infirmary, and into the small room where Brother Humilis lay sleeping. He sat beside the bed patiently for a long time, but the sick man slept on. And now, in this silence and solitude, Rhun could scan every line of the worn, ageing face, and see how the eyes were sunk deep into the skull, the cheeks fallen into gaunt hollows, and the flesh slack and grey. He was so full of life himself that he recognised with exquisite clarity the approach of another man's death. He abandoned his first purpose. For even if Humilis should awaken, and however ardently he would exert what life was left to him for the sake of Fidelis, Rhun could not now cast any part of this load upon a man already burdened with the spiritual baggage of his own departure. But he sat there still, and waited, and after supper Brother Edmund came to make the rounds of his patients before nightfall.

Rhun approached him in the stone-flagged passage.

'Brother Edmund, I'm anxious about Humilis. I've been sitting with him, and surely he grows weaker before our eyes. I know you keep good care of him always, but I thought – could not a cot be put in with him for Fidelis? It would be much to the comfort of them both. In the dortoir with the rest of us Fidelis will fret, and not sleep. And if Humilis should wake in the night, it would be a grace to see Fidelis close by him, ready to serve as he always is. They went through the fire at Hyde together…' He drew breath, watching Brother Edmund's face. 'They are closer,' he said gravely, 'than ever were father and son.'

Brother Edmund went himself to look at the sleeping man. Breath came shallowly and rapidly. The single light cover lay very flat and lean over the long body.

'It might be well so,' said Edmund. 'There is an empty cot in the anteroom of the chapel, and it would go in here, though the space is a little tight for it. Come and help me to carry it, and then you may tell Brother Fidelis he can come and sleep here this night, if that's his wish.'

'He will be glad,' said Rhun with certainty.

The message was delivered to Fidelis simply as a decision by Brother Edmund, taken for the peace of mind and better care of his patient, which seemed sensible enough. And certainly Fidelis was glad. If he suspected that Rhun had had a hand in procuring the dispensation, that was acknowledged only with a fleeting smile that flashed and faded in his grave face too rapidly to be noticed. He took his breviary and went gratefully across the court, and into the room where Humilis still slept his shallow, old man's sleep, he who was barely forty-seven years old, and had lived at a gallop the foreshortened life that now crept so softly and resignedly towards death. Fidelis kneeled by the bedside to shape the night prayers with his mute lips.

It was the most sultry night of the hot, oppressive summer, a low cloud cover had veiled the stars. Even within stone walls the heat hung too heavy to bear. And here at last there was true privacy, apart from the necessities and duties of brotherhood, not low panelled partitions separating them from their chosen kin, but walls of stone, and the width of the great court, and the suffocating weight of the night. Fidelis stripped off his habit and lay down to sleep in his linen. Between the two narrow cots, on the stand beside the breviary, the little oil lamp burned all night long with a dwindling golden flame.

Chapter Ten

N HIS shallow half-sleep, half-swoon Brother Humilis dreamed that he heard someone weeping, very softly, almost without sound but for the break in the breath, the controlled but extreme weeping of a strong being brought to a desperation from which there was no escape. It so stirred and troubled him that he was lifted gradually out of his dream and into a wakeful reality, but by then there was only silence. He knew that he was not alone in the room, though he had not heard the second cot carried in, nor the coming of the one who was to lie beside him. But even before he turned his head, and saw by the faint glimmer of lamplight the white shape stretched on the pallet, he knew who it was. The presence or absence of this one creature was the pulse of his life now. If Fidelis was by, the beat of his blood was strong and comforting, without him it flagged and weakened.

And therefore it must be Fidelis who had grieved alone in the night, enduring what he could not change, whatever burden of sin or sorrow it was that swelled in him speechless and found no remedy.

Humilis put back the single cover from over him, and sat up, swinging his feet to the stone floor between the two beds. He had no need to stand, only to lift the little lamp carefully and lean towards the sleeper, shielding the light so that it should not fall too sharply upon the young man's face.

Seen thus, aloof and impenetrable, it was a daunting face. Under the ring of curling hair, the colour of ripe chestnuts, the forehead was both lofty and broad, ivory-smooth above level, strong brows darker than the hair. Large, arched eyelids, faintly veined like the petals of a flower, hid the clear grey eyes. An austere face, the jaw sharply outlined and resolute, the mouth fastidious, the cheekbones high and proud. If he had indeed shed tears, they were gone. There was only a fine dew of sweat on his upper lip. Humilis sat studying him steadily for a long time.

The boy had shed his habit in order to sleep in better comfort. He lay on his side, cheek pressed into the pillow, the loose linen shirt open at his throat, and the chain that he wore had slid its link down in a silver coil into the hollow of his neck, and laid bare to view on the pillow the token that hung upon it.

Not a cross studded with semi-precious stones, but a ring, a thin gold finger-ring made in the spiral form of a coiled snake, with two splinters of red for eyes. An old ring, very old, for the finer chasing of head and scales was worn smooth with time, and the coils were wafer-thin.

Humilis sat gazing at this small, significant thing, and could not turn his eyes away. The lamp shook in his hand, and he laid it back on its stand in careful haste, for fear he should spill a drop of hot oil on the naked throat or outflung arm, and startle Fidelis out of what was at least oblivion, if not genuine rest. Now he knew everything, the best and the worst, all there was to know, except how to find a way out of this web. Not for himself – his own way out opened clear before him, and was no long journey. But for this sleeper…

Humilis lay back on his bed, trembling with the knowledge of a great wonder and a great danger, and waited for morning.

Brother Cadfael rose at dawn, long before Prime, and went out into the garden, but even there there was little air to breathe. A leaden stillness hung over the world, under a thin ceiling of cloud, through which the rising sun seemed to burn unimpeded. He went down to the Meole Brook, down the bleached slopes of the pease-fields, from which the haulms had long since been sickled and taken in for stable-bedding, leaving the white stubble to be ploughed into the ground for the next year's crop. Cadfael shed his sandals and waded into the slack, shallow water that was left, and found it warm where he had hoped for a little coolness. This weather, he thought, cannot continue much longer, it must break. Someone will get the brunt of the storm, and if it's thunder, as by the smell in the air and the prickling of my skin it surely will be, Shrewsbury will get its share. Thunder, like commerce, followed the river valleys.

Once out of his bed, he had lost the fine art of being idle. He filled in the time until Prime with some work among the herbs, and some early watering while the sun was still climbing, round and dull gold behind its veil of haze. These functions his hands and eyes could take care of, while his mind was free to fret and speculate over the complicated fortunes of people for whom he had formed a strong affection. No question but Godfrid Marescot – to think of him as an affianced man was to give him his old name – was busy leaving this world at a steady, unflinching walk, and every day he quickened his pace like a man anxious to be gone, and yet every day looked back over his shoulder in case that lost bride of his might be following on his heels rather than waiting for him patiently along the road ahead. And what could any man tell him for his reassurance? And what could afford any comfort to Nicholas Harnage, who had been too slow in prizing her fitly and making his bid for her favour?

A mile from Wherwell, and never seen again. And gone with her, temptation enough for harm, the valuables and the money she carried. And one man only as visible and obvious suspect, Adam Heriet, with everything against him except for Hugh's scrupulous conviction that he had been in genuine desperation to get news to her. He had asked and asked, and never desisted until he reached Shrewsbury. Or had he simply been fishing, not for news of her so much as for a glimpse, any glimpse, into Hugh's mind, any unwary word that would tell him how much the law already knew, and what chance he still had, by silence or lies or any other means, of brazening his way safely through his present peril?

Other inconsequent questions jutted from the obscurity like the untrimmed overgrowths from the hedges of a neglected maze. Why did the girl choose Wherwell in the first place? Certainly she might have preferred it as being far from her home, no bad principle when beginning a new life. Or because it was one of the chief houses of Benedictine nuns in all the south country, with scope for a gifted sister to rise to office and power. And why did she give orders to three of her escort to remain in Andover instead of accompanying her all the way? True, the one she retained was her confidant and willing slave from infancy? If that was indeed true of him? It was reputed of

286

him, yes, but truth and reputation sometimes part company. And if true, why did she dismiss even him short of her goal? Perhaps better phrase that more carefully: *did* she dismiss him short of her goal? Then where did he spent the lost hours before he returned to Andover? Gaping at the wonders of Winchester, as he claimed? Or attending to more sinister business? What became of the treasures she carried? No great fortune, except to a man who lacked any fortune, but to him wealth enough. And always: *What became of her?*

And through the tangle he was beginning to glimpse a possible answer, and that uncertain inkling dismayed and terrified him more than all the rest. For if he was right, there could be no good end to this that he could see, every way he probed thorns closed the path. No way out, without worse ruin. Or a miracle.

He went to Prime at last, prompt to the bell, and prayed earnestly for a beckoning light. The needy and the deserving must surely be known elsewhere even better than here, he thought, who am I to presume to fill a place far too big for me?

Brother Fidelis did not attend Prime, his empty place ached like the soreness left after a pulled tooth. Rhun shone beside his friend's vacant stall, and never once glanced at Brother Urien. Such problems must not be allowed to distract his rapt attention from the office and the liturgy. There would be a time later in the day to give some thought to Urien, whose aggression had not been absolved, but only temporarily prevented. Rhun had no fear of shouldering the responsibility for another man's soul, being still half-child, with a child's certainty and clarity. To go to his confessor and tell what he suspected and knew of Urien would be to deprive Urien of the whole value of the sacrament of confession, and to tell tales upon a comrade in travail; the former was arrogant in Rhun's eyes, a kind of spiritual theft, and the latter was despicable, a schoolboy's treachery. Yet something would have to be done, something more than merely removing Fidelis from the sphere of Urien's torment and greed. Meantime, Rhun prayed and sang and worshipped with a whole happy heart, and trusted his saint to give him guidance.

Cadfael made short work of breakfast, asked leave, and went to visit Humilis. Coming armed with clean linen pad and green healing salve, he found his patient propped up in his bed freshly washed and shaven, already fed, if indeed he had managed to swallow anything, his toilet seen to in devoted

287

privacy, and a cup of wine and water ready to his hand. Fidelis sat on a low stool beside the bed, ready to stir at once in answer even to a guessed-at need, in any look or gesture. When Cadfael entered, Humilis smiled, though the smile was pallidly blue of lip and cheek, translucent as ice. It is true, thought Cadfael, receiving that salutation, he is fast bound out of this world. It cannot be many days. The flesh melts from his bones as you watch, into smoke, into air. His spirit outgrows his body, soon it must burst out and become visible, there is no room for it in this fragile parcel of bones.

Fidelis looked up and echoed his master's smile, and leaned to turn back the single light cover from the shrunken shanks, then rose from the stool to give place to Cadfael, and stood ready to offer a deft, assisting hand. Those menial services he offered with so much love must be called on frequently now. It was a marvel this body could function of itself at all, but there was a will that would not let it surrender its rights – certainly not anything less than love.

'Have you slept?' asked Cadfael, smoothing his new dressing into place.

'I have, and well,' said Humilis. 'The better for having Fidelis by me. I have not deserved such privilege, but I am meek enough to entreat for it to be continued. Will you speak with Father Abbot for me?'

'I would, if there was need,' said Cadfael heartily, 'but he already knows and approves.'

'Then if I'm to have my indulgence,' said Humilis, 'speak for me now to this nurse and confessor and tyrant of mine, that he use a little kindness also to himself. At least he should go now to Mass, since I cannot, and take a turn in the garden for a little while, before he shuts himself here again with me.'

Fidelis heard all this smiling, but with a smile of inexpressible sadness. The boy, thought Cadfael, knows all too well the time cannot be long, and numbers every moment, charging it with meaning. Love in ignorance squanders what love, informed, crowds and overfills with tokens of eternity.

'He says rightly,' said Cadfael. 'You go to Mass, and I'll stay here until you come again. No need to hurry, I fancy you'll find Brother Rhun waiting for you.'

Fidelis accepted what he recognised as his purposeful dismissal, and went out silently, leaving them no less silent until his slight shadow had passed from the threshold of the room and out into the open court.

Humilis lay back in his raised pillows, and drew a great breath that should have floated his diminished body into the air, like thistledown.

'Will Rhun truly be looking for him?'

'He surely will,' said Cadfael.

'That's well! Of such a one he has need. An innocent, of such native power! Oh, Cadfael, for the simplicity and the wisdom of the dove! I wish Fidelis were such a one, but he is the other, the complement, the inward one. I had to send him away, I must talk with you. Cadfael, I am troubled in my mind for Fidelis.'

It was not news. Cadfael honestly nodded, and said nothing.

'Cadfael,' said the patient voice, delivered from stress now that they were alone. 'I've grown to know you a little, in this time you have been tending me. You know as well as I that I am dying. Why should I grieve for that? I owe a death that has been all but claimed of me a hundred times already. It is not for myself I'm troubled, it is for Fidelis. I dread leaving him alone here, trapped in this life without me.'

'He will not be alone,' said Cadfael. 'He is a brother of this house. He will have the service and fellowship of all here.' The sharp, wry smile did not surprise him. 'And mine,' he said, 'if that means anything more to you. Rhun's, certainly. You have said yourself that Rhun's loyalty is not to be despised.'

'No, truly. The saints of simplicity are made of his metal. But you are not simple, Brother Cadfael. You are sometimes of frightening subtlety, and that also has its place. Moreover, I believe you understand me. You understand the nature of the need. Will you take care of Fidelis for me, stand his friend, believe in him, be shield and sword to him if need be, after I am gone?'

'To the best of my power,' said Cadfael, 'yes, I will.' He leaned to wipe away a slow trickle of spittle from the corner of a mouth wearied with speaking and slack at the lip, and Humilis sighed, and let him serve, docile under the brief touch. 'You know,' said Cadfael gently, 'what I only guess at. If I have guessed right, there is here a problem beyond my wit or yours to solve. I promise my endeavour. The ending is not mine, it belongs only to God. But what I can do, I will do.'

'I would happily die,' said Humilis, 'if my death can serve and save Fidelis. But what I dread is that my death, which cannot delay long, may only aggravate his trouble and his suffering. Could I take them with me into the judgement, how

289

gladly would I embrace them and go. God forbid he should ever be brought to shame and punishment for what he has done.'

'If God forbids, man cannot touch him,' said Cadfael. 'I see what needs to be done, but how to achieve it, God knows, I cannot see. Well, God's vision is clearer than mine, he may both see a way out of this tangle and open my eyes to it when the time is ripe. There's a path through every forest, and a safe passage somewhere through every marsh, it needs only the finding.'

A faint grey smile passed slowly over the sick man's face, and left him grave again. 'I am the marsh out of which Fidelis must find safe passage. I should have Englished that name of mine, it would have been more fitting, with more than half my blood Saxon – Godfrid of the Marsh for Godfrid de Marisco. My father and my grandfather thought best to turn fully Norman. Now it's all one, we leave here all by the same gate.' He lay still and silent for a while, visibly gathering his thoughts and such strength as he had. 'There is one other longing I have, before I die. I should like to see again the manor of Salton, where I was born. I should like to take Fidelis there, just once to be with him outside the monastery walls, in the place that saw my beginning. I ought to have asked permission earlier, but there is still time. It's only a few miles up-river from us. Will you speak for me to the lord abbot, and ask this one kindness?'

Cadfael eyed him in doubt and consternation. 'You cannot ride, that's certain. Whatever means we might take to get you there, it would be asking too much of such strength as you have left.'

'No effort on my part can now alter by more than hours what is left of my life, but it would be a happiness to exchange some part of my time remaining for a glimpse of the place where I was a child. Ask it for me, Cadfael.'

'There is the river,' said Cadfael dubiously, 'but such twists and turns, it adds double to the journey. And such low water, you'd need a boatman who knows every shoal and current.'

'You must know of such a one. I remember how we used to swim and fish off our own shore. Shrewsbury lads were watermen from birth, I could swim before I could walk. There must be many such adepts along this riverside.'

And so there were, and Cadfael knew the best of them, whose knowledge of the Severn spanned every islet, every bend and shallow, and who at any season could judge accurately where anything cast into the water would again be cast ashore. Madog of the Dead Boat had earned his title through the many sad services he had rendered in his time to distracted families who had lost sons or brothers into the flood after the melting of the Welsh snows far up-river, or too venturesome infants left unguarded for a moment while their mothers spread the washing on the bushes of the shore, or fishermen fathers putting out in their coracles with too much ale already under their belts. He did not resent his title, though his preferred trade was fishing and ferrying. What he did for the dead someone had to do, in grace, and since he could do it better than any other, why should he not take pride in it? Cadfael had known him many years, an elderly Welshman like himself, and had several times had occasion to seek his help, which was never grudged.

'Even in this low water,' said Cadfael thoughtfully, 'Madog could get a coracle up the brook from the river, but a coracle wouldn't carry you and Fidelis besides. But his light skiff draws very little water, I daresay he could bring it into the mill pond, there's still depth enough that far up the brook, with the mill race fed back into it. We could carry you out by the wicket to the mill, and see you bestowed...'

'That far I could walk,' said Humilis resolutely.

'You'd be wise to save your energy for Salton. Who knows?' marvelled Cadfael, noting the slight flush of blood that warmed the thin grey face at the very prospect of returning to the first remembered home of his childhood – perhaps to end where he began. 'Who knows, it may yet do you a world of good!'

'And you will ask the lord abbot?'

'I will,' said Cadfael. 'When Fidelis returns, I'll go to him.'

'Tell him there may be need for haste,' said Humilis, and smiled.

Abbot Radulfus listened with his usual shrewd gravity, and considered for a while in silence before making any comment. Outside the dim, wood-panelled parlour in his lodging the hot sun climbed, still veiled with a thin haze that turned it copper-colour, and made it seem to burn even more fiercely. The roses budded, flowered and fell all in one day.

'Is he strong enough to bear it?' asked the abbot at length. 'And is it not too great a load to lay upon Brother Fidelis, to bear responsibility for him all that time.'

'It's the passing of his strength that makes him ask so

291

urgently,' said Cadfael. 'If his wish is to be granted at all, it must be now, quickly. And he says rightly, it can make very little difference to the tale of his remaining days, whether they end tomorrow or after another week. But to his peace of mind this visit might make all the difference. As for Brother Fidelis, he has never yet shrunk from any burden laid upon him for love, and will not now. And if Madog takes them, they'll be in the best of hands. No one knows the river as he does. And he is to be trusted utterly.'

'For that I take your word,' said Radulfus equably. 'But it is a desperate enterprise for so frail a man. Granted it is his heart's wish, and he has every right to advance it. But how will you get him to the boat? And at the other end, is he sure of his welcome at Salton? Will there be willing attendants there to care for him?'

'Salton is a part of the honour he has relinquished now to a cousin he hardly knows, Father, but tenant and servants there will remember him. We can make a sling chair for him and carry him down to the mill. The infirmary lies close to the wall there, it's no distance to the mill wicket.'

'Very well,' said the abbot. 'It had better be very soon. If you know where to find this Madog, I give you leave, seek him out today, and if he's willing this journey had better be made tomorrow.'

Cadfael thanked him and departed, well pleased on his own account. He was no longer quite as ready as he would once have been to take leave of absence without asking, unless for a life-or-death reason, but he had no objection to making the very most of official leave when it was given. The prospect of a meal with Hugh and Aline in the town, instead of the hushed austerity of the refectory, and then a leisurely hunt along the waterside for Madog or news of him, and a comradely gossip when he was found, had all the attractions of a feast-day. But he looked in again on Humilis before he left the enclave, and told him how he had fared. Fidelis was again in careful attendance at the bedside, withdrawn and unobtrusive as ever.

'Abbot Radulfus grants your wish,' said Cadfael, 'and gives me leave to go and find Madog for you this very day. If he's agreeable, you can go to Salton tomorrow.'

Hugh's house by Saint Mary's church had an enclosed garden behind it, a small central herber with grassed benches round it, and fruit trees to give shade. There Aline Beringar was sitting

292

on the clipped seat sown with close-growing, fragrant herbs, with her son playing beside her. Not two years old until Christmas, Giles stood tall and sturdy and firm on his feet, made on a bigger scale than either his dark, trim father or his slender, fair mother. He had a rich colouring somewhere between the two, light bronze hair and round brown eyes, and a will of steel inherited, perhaps, from both, but not yet disciplined. He was wearing, in this hot summer, nothing at all, and was brown as a hazel-nut from brow to toes.

He had a pair of cut-out wooden knights, garishly painted and strung by two strings through their middles, their feet weighted with little blobs of lead, their legs and sword-arms jointed so that when the cords were tweaked from both ends they flourished their weapons and danced and slashed at each other in a very bloodthirsty manner. Constance, his willing slave, had forsaken him to go and supervise the preparations for dinner, and he clamoured imperiously for his godfather to supply the vacated place. Cadfael kneeled in the turf, only mildly complaining of the creaks in his joints, and manned the cords doughtily. In these arts he was well practised since the birth of Giles. Moreover, he must be careful not to be seen to give his opponent the better of the exchange by design, or there would be a shriek of knightly outrage. The heir and pride of the Beringars knew when he was being condescended to, and wholeheartedly resented it, convinced he was any man's equal. But he was none too pleased when he was defeated, either. It was necessary to walk a mountebank's tightrope to avoid his displeasure.

'You'll be wanting Hugh,' said Aline serenely through her son's squeals of delight, and drew in her feet to give them full play for their strings. 'He'll be home for dinner in a little while. There's venison – they've started the cull.'

'So have a few other law-abiding citizens of the town, I daresay,' said Cadfael, energetically manipulating the cords to make the twin wooden swords flail like windmills.

'One here and there, what does it matter? Hugh knows how long to turn a blind eye. Good meat, and enough of it – and the king with little use for it, as things are! But it may not be long now,' said Aline, and smiled over her needlework, inclining her pale gold head and fair face above her naked son, sprawled on the grass tugging his strings in two plump brown fists. 'His own friends are beginning to work upon Robert of Gloucester, urging him to agree to the exchange. He knows she can do nothing about him. He must give way.'

Cadfael sat back on his heels, letting the cords fall back. The two wooden warriors fell flat in one embrace, both slain, and Giles tugged indignantly to bring them to life again, and was left to struggle in vain for a while.

'Aline,' said Cadfael earnestly, looking up into her gentle face, 'if ever I should have need of you suddenly, and come to fetch you, or send word to come – would you come? Wherever it was? And bring whatever I asked you to bring?'

'Short of the sun or the moon,' said Aline, smiling, 'whatever you asked, I would bring, and wherever you wanted me, I would come. Why? What's in your mind? Is it secret?'

'As yet,' said Cadfael, ruefully, 'it is. For I'm almost as blind as I must leave you, girl dear, until I see my way, if ever I do. But indeed, some day soon I might need you.'

The imp Giles, distracted from his game and losing interest in the inexplicable conversation of his elders, hoisted his fallen knights, and went off hopefully after the floating savour of his dinner.

Hugh came hungry and in haste from the castle, and listened to Cadfael's account of developments at the abbey with meditative interest, over the venison Aline brought to the board.

'I remember it was said when they came here – was it you who told me so? It might well be! – that Marescot was born at Salton, and had a hankering to see it again. A pity he's brought so low. It seems this matter of the girl may not be solved for him this side of death. Why should he not have what can best make his going pleasant and endurable? It can cost him nothing but a few hours or days of surely burdensome living. But I wish we could have done better for him over the girl.'

'We may yet,' said Cadfael, 'if God wills. You've had no further word from Nicholas in Winchester?'

'Nothing as yet. And small wonder, in a town and a countryside torn to pieces by fire and war. Hard to find anything among the ashes.'

'And how is it with your prisoner? He has not conveniently remembered anything more from his journey to Winchester?'

Hugh laughed. 'Heriet has the good sense to know where he's safe, and sits very contentedly in his cell, well fed, well housed and well bedded. Solitude is no hardship to him. Question him, and he says again what he has already said, and

294

never falls foul of a detail, either, no matter how you try to trip him. Not all the king's lawyers would get anything more out of him. Besides, I took care to let him know that Cruce has been here twice, thirsty for his blood. It may be necessary to put a guard on his prison to keep Cruce out, but certainly not to keep Heriet in. He sits quietly and bides his time, sure we must loose him at last for want of proof.'

'Do you believe he ever harmed the girl?' said Cadfael.

'Do you?'

'No. But he is the one man who knows what did happen to her, and if he but knew it, he would be wise to speak, but to you only. No need for any witness besides. Do you think you could bring him to speak, by giving him to understand it was between you two only?'

'No,' said Hugh simply. 'What cause has he to trust me so far, if he has gone three years without trusting any other and keeps his mouth shut still, even to his own peril? No, I think I know his mettle. He'll continue secret as the grave.'

And indeed, thought Cadfael, there are secrets which should be buried beyond discovery, things, even people, lost beyond finding, for their own sake, for all our sakes..

He took his leave, and went on through the town, and down to the waterside under the western bridge that led out towards Wales, and there was Madog of the Dead Boat working at his usual small enclosure, weaving the rim of a new coracle with intertwined hazel withies, peeled and soaked in the shallows under the bridge. A squat, square, hairy, bandy-legged Welshman of unknown age, though apparently made to last for ever, since no one could remember a time when he had looked any younger, and the turning of the years did not seem to make him look any older. He squinted up at Cadfael from under thick, jutting eyebrows that had turned grey while his hair was still black, and gave leisurely greeting, his brown hands still plaiting at the wands with practised dexterity.

'Well, old friend, you've become almost a stranger this summer. What's the word with you, to bring you here looking for me – for I take it that was your purpose, this side the town? Sit down and be neighbourly for a while.'

Cadfael sat down beside him in the bleached grass, and measured the diminished level of the Severn with a considering eye.

'You'll be saying I never come near but when I want

something of you. But indeed we've had a crowded year, what with one thing and another. How do you find working the water now, in this drought? There must be a deal of tricky shallows upstream, after so long without rain.'

'None that I don't know,' said Madog comfortably. 'True, the fishing's profitless, and I wouldn't say you could get a loaded barge up as far as Pool, but I can get where I want to go. Why? Have you work for me? I could do with a day's pay, easy come by.'

'Easy enough, if you can get yourself and two more up as far as Salton. Lightweights both, for the one's skin and bone, and the other young and slender.'

Madog leaned back from his work, interested, and asked simply: 'When?'

'Tomorrow, if nothing prevents.'

'It would be far shorter to ride,' Madog observed, studying his friend with kindling curiosity.

'Too late for one of these ever to ride again. He's a dying man, and wants to see again the place where he was born.'

'Salton?' Shrewd dark eyes blinked through their thick silver brows. 'That should be a de Marisco. We heard you had the last of them in your house.'

'Marescot, they're calling it now. Of the Marsh, Godfrid says it should better have been, his line being Saxon. Yes, the same. His time is not long. He wants to complete the circle of birth to death before he goes.'

'Tell me,' said Madog simply, and listened with still and serene attention as Cadfael told him the nature of his cargo, and all that was required of him.

'Now,' he said, when all was told, 'I'll tell what I think. This weather will not hold much longer, but for all that, it may still tarry a week or so. If your paladin is as set on his pilgrimage as you say, if he's willing to venture whatever comes, then I'll bring my boat into the mill pool tomorrow after Prime. I'll have something aboard to shelter him if the rain does come. I keep a waxed sheet to cover goods that will as well cover a knight or a brother of the Benedictines at need.'

'Such a cerecloth,' said Brother Cadfael very soberly, 'may be only too fitting for Brother Humilis. And he will not despise it.'

Chapter Eleven

 N THE streets of Winchester the stinking, blackened debris of fire was beginning to give place to the timid sparks of new hope, as those who had fled returned to pick over the remnants of their shops and households, and those who had stayed set to work briskly clearing the wreckage and carting timber to rebuild. The merchant classes of England were a tough and resilient breed, after every reverse they came back with fresh vigour, grimly determined upon restoration and willing to retrench until a profit was again possible. Warehouses were swept clear of what was spoiled, and made ready within to receive new merchandise. Shops collected what was still saleable, cleaned out ravaged rooms and set up temporary stalls. Life resumed, with astonishing speed and energy, its accustomed rhythms, with an additional beat in defiance of misfortune. As often as you fell us, said the tradesmen of the town, we will get up again and take up where we left off, and you will tire of it first.

The armies of the queen, secure in possession here and well to westward, as well as through the south-east, went leisurely about their business, consolidating what they held, and secure in the knowledge that they had only to sit still and wait, and King Stephen must now be restored to them. There must have been a few shrewd captains, both English and Flemish, who saw no great reason to rejoice at the exchange of generals, for however vital Stephen might be as a figurehead to be prized and protected at all costs, and however doughty a fighter, he was no match for his valiant wife as a strategist in war. Still, his release was essential. They sat stolidly on their winnings, and waited for the enemy to surrender him, as sooner or later they must. There was a degree of boredom to be endured, while the negotiators parleyed and wrangled. The end was assured.

Nicholas Harnage, with the list of Julian Cruce's valuables in his pouch, went doggedly about the city of Winchester, enquiring wherever such articles might have surfaced, whether stolen, sold, or given in reverence. And he had begun with the highest, the Holy Father's representative in England, the Prince-Bishop of Winchester, Henry of Blois, just shaking together his violated dignity and emerging with formidable resolution into the field of discussion, as if he had never changed and rechanged his coat, nor been shut up fast in his own castle in his own city, in peril of his life. It took a deal of persistence to get admission to his lordship's presence, but Nicholas, in his present cause, had persistence enough to force his way through even these prickly defences.

'Do you trouble me with such trifles?' Bishop Henry had demanded, after perusing, with blackly frowning countenance, the list Nicholas presented to him. 'I know nothing of any such tawdry trinkets. None of these have I ever seen, none belongs to any house of worship known here to me. What is there here to concern me?'

'My lord, there is a lady's life,' said Nicholas, stung. 'She intended what she never achieved, a life of dedication in the abbey of Wherwell. Before ever reaching there she was lost, and what I intend is to find her, if she lives, and avenge her, if she is dead. And only by these, as you say, tawdry trinkets can I hope to trace her.'

'In that,' said the bishop shortly, 'I cannot help you. I tell you certainly, none of these things ever came into the possession of the Old Minster, nor of any church or convent under my supervision. But you may enquire where you will among other houses in this city, and say that I have sanctioned your search. That is all I can do.'

And with that Nicholas had had to be content, and indeed it did give him a considerable authority, should he be questioned as to what right he had in the matter. However eclipsed for a time, Henry of Blois would rise again like the phoenix, as formidable as ever, and the fire that had all but consumed him could be relied upon to scorch whoever dared his enmity afterwards.

From church to church and priest to priest Nicholas carried his list, and found nothing but shaken heads and helplessly knitted brows everywhere, even where there was manifest goodwill towards him. No house of religion surviving in Winchester knew anything of the twin candlesticks, the stone-studded cross or the silver pyx that had been a part of Julian Cruce's dowry. There was no reason to doubt their word, they had no reason to lie, none even to prevaricate.

There remained the streets, the shops of goldsmiths, silversmiths, even the casual market-traders who would buy and sell whatever came to hand. Nicholas began the systematic examination of them all, and in so rich a city, with so wealthy a clientele of lofty churchmen and rich foundations, they were many.

Thus he came, on the morning of this same day when Brother Humilis entreated passage to the place of his birth, into a small, scarred shop in the High Street, close under the shadow of Saint Maurice's church. The frontage had suffered in the fires, and the silversmith had rigged a shuttered opening like a fairground booth, and drawn his work-bench close to it, to have the full daylight on his work. The raised shutter overhead protected his face from glare, but let in the morning shine to the brooch he was handling, and the fine stones he was setting in it. A man in his prime, probably well-fleshed when times were good, but now somewhat shrunken after the privations of the long siege, for his skin hung on him flaccid and greyish, like a too-large coat on a fasting man. He looked up alertly through a forelock of greying hair, and asked if he could serve the gentleman.

'I begin to think it a thin enough chance,' admitted Nicholas ruefully, 'but at least let's make the assay. I am hunting for word, any word, of certain pieces of church plate and ornaments that went astray in these parts three years ago. Do you handle such things?'

'I handle anything of gold or silver. I have made church plate in my time. But three years is a long while. What is so notable about them? Stolen, you think? I deal in no suspect goods. If there's anything dubious about what's offered, I never touch it.'

'There need not have been anything here to deter you. True enough they might have been stolen, but there need be nothing to tell you so. They belonged to no southern church or convent, they were brought from Shropshire, and most likely

299

made in that region, and to a man like you they'd be recognisable as northern work. The crosses might well be old, and Saxon.'

'And what are these items? Read me your list. My memory is not infallible, but I may recall, even after three years.'

Nicholas went through the list slowly, watching for a gleam of recognition. 'A pair of silver candlesticks with tall sconces entwined with vines, with snuffers attached by silver chains, these also decorated with vine-leaves. Two crosses made to match in silver, the larger a standing cross a man's hand in height, on a three-stepped silver pedestal, the other a small replica on a neck-chain for a priest's wear, both ornamented with semi-precious stones, yellow pebble, agate and amethyst...'

'No,' said the silversmith, shaking his head decidedly, 'those I should not have forgotten. Nor the candlesticks, either.'

'... a small silver pyx engraved with ferns ... '

'No. Sir, I recall none of these. If I had still my books I could look back for you. The clerk who kept them for me was always exact, he could find you every item even after years. But they're gone, every record, in the fire. It was all we could do to rescue the best of my stock, the books are all ash.'

The common fate in Winchester this summer, Nicholas thought resignedly. The most meticulous of book-keepers would abandon his records when his life was at risk, and if he had time to take anything but his life with him, he would certainly snatch up the most precious of his goods, and let the parchments go. It seemed hardly worth listing the small personal things which had belonged to Julian, for they would be less memorable. He was hesitating whether to persist when a narrow door opened and let in light from a yard behind the shop, and a woman came in.

When the outer door was closed behind her she vanished again briefly into the dimness of the interior, but once more emerged into light as she approached her husband's bench and the bright sunlight of the street, and leaned forward to set a beaker of ale ready at the silversmith's right hand. She looked up, as she did so, at Nicholas, with candid and composed interest, a good-looking woman some years younger than her husband. Her face was still shadowed by the awning that protected her husband's eyes, but her hand emerged fully into the sun as she laid the cup down, a pale, shapely hand cut off startlingly at the wrist by the black sleeve.

300

Nicholas stood staring in fascination at that hand, so fixedly that she remained still in wonder, and did not withdraw it from the light. On the little finger, too small, perhaps, to go over the knuckle of any other, was a ring, wider than was common, its edge showing silver, but its surface so closely patterned with coloured enamels that the metal was hidden. The design was of tiny flowers with four spread petals, the florets alternately yellow and blue, spiked between with small green leaves. Nicholas gazed at it in disbelief, as at a miraculous apparition, but it remained clear and unmistakable. There could not be two such. Its value might not be great, but the workmanship and imagination that had created it set it apart from all others.

'I pray your pardon, madam!' he said, stammering as he drew his wits together. 'But that ring ... May I know where it came from?'

Both husband and wife were looking at him intently now, surprised but not troubled.

'It was come by honestly,' she said, and smiled in mild amusement at his gravity. 'It was brought in for sale some years back, and since I liked it, my husband gave it to me.'

'When was this? Believe me, I have good reasons for asking.'

'It *was* three years back,' said the silversmith readily. 'In the summer, but the date ... that I can't be sure of now.'

'But *I* can,' said his wife, and laughed. 'And shame on you for forgetting, for it was my birthday, and that was how I wooed the ring out of you. And my birthday, sir, is the twentieth day of August. Three years I've had this pretty thing. The bailiff's wife wanted my husband to copy it for her once, but I wouldn't have it. This must still be the only one of its kind. Primrose and periwinkle ... such soft colours!' She turned her hand in the sun to admire the glow of the enamels. 'The other pieces that came with it were sold, long ago. But they were not so fine as this.'

'There were other pieces that came with it?' demanded Nicholas.

'A necklace of polished pebbles,' said the smith, 'I remember it now. And a silver bracelet chased with tendrils of pease – or it might have been vetch.'

The ring alone would have been enough; these three together were certainty. The three small items of personal jewellery belonging to Julian Cruce had been brought into this shop for sale on the twentieth of August, three years ago. The first clear echo, and its note was wholly sinister.

'Master silversmith,' said Nicholas, 'I had not completed the

301

tale of all I sought. These three things came south, to my certain knowledge, in the keeping of a lady who was bound for Wherwell, but never reached her destination.'

'Do you tell me so?' The smith had paled, and was gazing warily and doubtfully at his visitor. 'I bought the things honestly, I've done nothing amiss, and know nothing, beyond that some fellow, decent enough to all appearance, brought them in here openly for sale...'

'Oh, no, don't mistake me! I don't doubt your good faith, but see, you are the first I have found that even may help me to discover what is become of the lady. Think back, tell me, who was this man who came? What like was he? What age, what style of man? He was not known to you?'

'Never seen before nor since,' said the silversmith, cautiously relieved, but not sure that telling too much might not somehow implicate him in dangerous business. 'A man much of my years, fifty he might be. Ordinary enough, plain in his dress, I took him for what he claimed, a servant sent on an errand.'

The woman did better. She was much interested by this time, and saw no reason to fear involvement, and some sympathetic cause to help, insofar as she could. She had a sharper eye for a man than had her husband, and was disposed to approve of Nicholas and desire his goodwill.

'A solid, square-made man he was,' she said, 'brown as his leather coat. That was not a hot summer like this, his brown was the everlasting kind that would only yellow a little in winter, the kind that comes with living out of doors year-round – forester or huntsman, perhaps. Brown-bearded, brown-haired but for his crown, he was balding. He had a bold, oaken face on him, and a quick eye. I should never have remembered him so well, but that he was the one who brought my ring. But I tell you what, I fancy he remembered me for a good while. He gave me long enough looks before he left the shop.'

She was used to that, being well aware that she was handsome, and it was one more reason why she had recalled the man so well. Good reason, also, for paying close attention to all she had to say of him.

Nicholas swallowed burning bitterness. It was not the fifty years, nor the beard, nor the bald crown, nor even the weathered hide that identified the man, for Nicholas had never seen Adam Heriet. It was the whole circumstance, possession of the jewellery, the evidence of the date, the fact that the other three had been left in Andover, and in any case Nicholas had seen them for himself, and none of them resembled this description. The fourth man, the devoted servant, the fifty-year-old huntsman and forester, a stout man of his hands, a man Waleran of Meulan would think himself lucky to get … yes, every word Nicholas had heard said of Adam Heriet fitted with what this woman had to say of the man who had sold Julian's jewels.

'I did question possession,' said the silversmith, still uneasy, 'seeing they were clearly a lady's property. I asked how he came by them, and why he was offering them for sale. He said he was simply a servant sent on an errand, his business to do as he was told, and he had too much sense to quibble over it, seeing whoever questioned the orders that man gave might find himself short of his ears, or with a back striped like a tabby cat. I could well believe it, there are many such masters. He was quite easy about it, why should I be less so?'

'Why, indeed!' said Nicholas heavily. 'So you bought, and he departed. Did he argue over the price?'

'No, he said his orders were to sell, he was no valuer and was not expected to be. He took what I gave. It was a fair price.'

With room for a fair profit, no doubt, but why not? Silversmiths were not in the business to dole out charity to chance vendors.

'And was that all? He left you so?'

'He was going, when I did call after him, and asked him what was become of the lady who had worn these things, and had she no further use for them, and he turned back in the doorway and looked at me, and said no, for such she had no further use at all, for that this lady who had owned them was dead.'

The hardness of the answer, its cold force, was there in the silversmith's voice as he repeated it. Remembering had brought it back far more vividly than ever he had dreamed, it shook him as he voiced it. Even more fiercely it stabbed at Nicholas, a knife in the heart, driving the breath out of him. It rang so hideously true, and named Adam Heriet almost beyond doubt. She who had owned them was dead. Ornaments were of no further concern to her.

Out of the chill rage that consumed him he heard the woman, roused now and eager, saying: 'No, but that's not all! For it so chanced I followed the man out when he left, but softly, not to be seen too soon.' Had he given her an appraising

303

look, smiled, flashed an admiring eye, to draw her on a string? No, not if he had anything to hide, no, he would rather have slid away unobtrusively, glad to be rid of his winnings for money. No, she was female, curious, and had time on her hands to spare, she went out to see whatever was to be seen. And what was it she saw? 'He slipped along to the left here,' she said, 'and there was another man, a young fellow, pressed close against the wall there, waiting for him. Whether he gave him the money, all of it or some of it, I could not be sure, but something was handed over. And then the older one looked over his shoulder and saw me, and they slipped away very quickly round the corner into the side street by the market, and that was all I saw of them. And more than I was meant to see,' she reflected, herself surprised now that she came to see more in it than was natural.

'You're sure of that?' asked Nicholas intently. 'There was a second with him, a younger man?' For the three innocents from Lai had been left waiting in Andover. If it had not been true, one or other of them, the simpleton surely, would have given the game away at once.

'I am sure. A young fellow, neat enough but homespun, such as you might see hanging around inns or fairs or markets, the best of them hoping for work, and the worst hoping for a chance to get a hand in some other man's pouch.'

Hoping for work or hoping to thieve! Or both, if the work offered took that shape – yes, even to the point of murder.

'What was he like, this second?'

She furrowed her brow and considered, gnawing a lip. She was in strong earnest, searching her memory, which was proving tenacious and long. 'Tallish but not too tall, much the older one's height when they stood together, but half his bulk. I say young because he was slender and fast when he slipped away, and light on his feet. But I never saw his face, he had the capuchon over his head.'

'I did wonder,' said the silversmith defensively. 'But it was done, I'd paid, and I had the goods. There was no more I could do.'

'No. No, there's no blame. You could not know.' Nicholas looked again at the bright ring on the woman's finger. 'Madam, will you let me buy that ring of you? For double what your husband paid for it? Or if you will not, will you let me borrow it of you for a fee, and my promise to return it when I can? To you,' he said earnestly, 'it is dear as a gift, and prized, but I need it.'

304

She stared back at him wide-eyed and captivated, clasping and turning the ring on her finger. 'Why do you need it? More than I?'

'I need it to confront that man who brought it here, the man who has procured, I do believe, the death of the lady who wore it before you. Put a price on it, and you shall have it.'

She closed her free hand round it defensively, but she was flushed and bright-eyed with excitement, too. She looked at her husband, who had the merchant's calculating, far-off look in his eyes, and was surely about to fix a price that would pay the repairs of his shop for him. She tugged suddenly at the ring, twisted it briskly over her knuckle, and held it out to Nicholas.

'I lend it to you, for no fee. But bring it back to me yourself, when you have done, and tell me how this matter ends. And should you find you are mistaken, and she is still living, and wants her ring, then give it back to her, and pay me for it whatever you think fair.'

The hand she had extended to him with her bounty he caught and kissed. 'Madam, I will! All you bid me, I will! I pledge you my faith!' He had nothing fit to offer her as a return pledge, she had the better of him at all points. Her husband was looking at her indulgently, as one accustomed to the whims of a very handsome wife, and made no demur, at least until the visitor was gone. 'I serve here under FitzRobert,' said Nicholas. 'Should I fail you, or you ever come to suppose that I have so failed you, complain to him, and he will show you justice. But I will not fail you!'

'Are you so ready to say farewell to my gifts?' asked the silversmith, when Nicholas was out of sight. But he sounded amused rather than offended, and had turned back to his close work on the brooch with unperturbed concentration.

'I have not said farewell to it,' she said serenely. 'I trust my judgement. He will be back, and I shall have my ring again.'

'And how if he finds the lady living, and takes you at your word? What then?'

'Why, then,' said his wife, 'I think I may earn enough out of his gratitude to buy myself all the rings I could want. And I know you have the skill to make me a copy of that one, if I so wish. Trust me, whichever way his luck runs – and I wish him better than he expects! – we shall not be the losers.'

Nicholas rode out of Winchester within the hour, in burning

haste, by the north gate towards Hyde, passing close by the blackened ground and broken toothed walls of the ill-fated abbey from which Humilis and Fidelis had fled to Shrewsbury for refuge. These witnesses to tragedy and loss fell behind him unnoticed now. His sights were set far ahead.

The inertia of despair had lasted no longer than the length of the street, and given place to the most implacable fury of rage and vengefulness. Now he had something as good as certain, a small circlet of witness, evidence of the foulest treachery and ingratitude. There could be no doubt whatever that these modest ornaments were the same that Julian had carried with her, no chance could possibly have thrown together for sale three such others. Two witnesses could tell of the disposal of that ill-gotten plunder, one could describe the seller only too well, with even more certainty once she was brought face to face with him, as, by God, she should be before all was done. Moreover, she had seen him meet with his hired assassin in the street, and pay him for his services. There was no possibility of finding the hireling, nameless and faceless as he was, except through the man who had hired him, and such enquiries as Nicholas had set in motion after Adam Heriet had so far failed to trace his present whereabouts. Only one company of Waleran's men remained near Winchester, and Heriet was not with them. But the search should go on until he was found, and when found, he had more now to explain away than a few stolen hours – possession of the lost girl's goods, the disposal of them for money, the sharing of his gains with some furtive unknown. For whatever conceivable purpose, but to pay him for his part in robbery and murder?

Once the principal villain was found, so would his tool be. And the first thing to do now was inform Hugh Beringar, and accelerate the hunt for Adam Heriet in Shropshire as in the south, until he was run to earth at last, and confronted with the ring.

It was barely past noon when Nicholas rode out of the city. By dusk he was near Oxford, secured a remount, and rode on at a steadier and more sparing pace through the night. A hot, sultry night it was, all the more as he went north into the midlands. The sky was clear of cloud, yet without moon or stars, very black. And all about him, in the mid hours of the night, lightnings flared and instantly died again into blackness, conjuring up, for the twinkling of an eye, trees and roofs and distant hills, only to obliterate them again before the eye could truly perceive them. And all in absolute silence, with nowhere any murmur of thunder to break the leaden hush. Forewarnings of the wrath of God, or of His inscrutable mercies.

Chapter Twelve

HE MORNING came bright, veiled and still, the rising sun a disc of copper, the mill pond flat and dull like a pewter dish. The ripples evoked by Madog's oars did no more than heave sluggishly and settle again with an oily heaviness, as he brought his boat in from the river after Prime.

Brother Edmund had fussed and hesitated over the whole enterprise, unhappy at allowing the risk to his patient, but unable to prevent, since the abbot had given his permission. By way of a compromise with his conscience, he saw to it that every possible provision was made for the comfort of Humilis on the journey, but absented himself from the embarkation to busy himself about his other duties. It was Cadfael and Fidelis who carried Humilis in a simple litter out through the wicket in the enclave wall which led directly to the mill, and down to the waterside. For all his long bones, he weighed hardly as much as a half-grown boy. Madog, shorter by head and shoulders, hoisted him bodily in his arms without noticeable effort, and bade Fidelis first take his place on the thwart, so that the sick man could be settled on brychans against the young man's knees, and propped comfortably with pillows. Thus he might travel with as little fatigue as possible. Fidelis drew the thin shoulders gently back to rest against him, the tonsured head, bared to the morning air, pillowed on his knees. The ring of dark hair still showed vigorous and young where all else was enfeebled, drained and old. Only the eyes had kindled to unusual brightness in the excitement of this venture, the fulfilment of a dear wish. After all the great endeavours, all the crossing and recrossing of oceans and continents, all the battles and victories and strivings, adventure at last was a voyage of a few miles up an English river, to revisit a modest manor in a peaceful English shire.

Happiness, thought Cadfael, watching him, consists in small things, not in great. It is the small things we remember, when time and mortality close in, and by small landmarks we may make our way at last humbly into another world.

He drew Madog aside for a moment before he let them go. The two in the boat were already engrossed, the one in the open day, the sky above him, the green and brightness of the land outside the cloister, the other in his beloved charge. Neither was paying attention to anything else.

'Madog,' said Cadfael earnestly, 'if anything untoward should come to your notice – if there should be anything strange, anything to astonish you … for God's sake say no word to any other, only bring it to me.'

Madog looked sideways at him, blinking knowingly through the thorn-bushes of his brows, and said: 'And you, I suppose, will be no way astonished! I know you! I can see as far into a dark night as most men. If there's anything to tell, you shall be the first, and from me the only one to hear it.'

He clapped Cadfael weightily on the shoulder, slipped loose the mooring rope he had twined about a stooping willow stump, and set foot with a boy's agility on the side of the boat, at once pushing it off from the shore and sliding down to the thwart in one movement. The dull sheen of the water heaved and sank lethargically between boat and bank. Madog took the oars, and pulled the boat round easily into the outflowing current, lax and sleepy in the heat like a human creature, but still alive and in languid motion.

Cadfael stood to watch them go. The morning light, hazy though it was, shone on the faces of the two travellers as the boat swung round, the young face and the older face, the one hovering, solicitous and grave, the other upturned and pallidly smiling for pleasure in his chosen day. Both great-eyed, intent, perhaps even a little intimidated by the enterprise they had undertaken. Then the boat came round, the oars dipped, and it was on Madog's squat, capable figure the eastern light fell.

There was a ferryman called Charon, Cadfael recalled from his few forays into the writings of antiquity, who had the care of souls bound out of this world. He, too, took pay from his passengers, indeed he refused them if they had not their fare. But he did not provide rugs and pillows and cerecloth for the soul he ferried across to eternity. Nor had he ever cared to seek and salvage the forlorn bodies of those the river took as its prey. Madog of the Dead Boat was the better man.

There is always a degree of coolness on the water, however sultry the air and sunken the level of the stream. On the still, metallic lustre of the Severn there was at least the illusion of a breeze, and a breath from below that seemed to temper the glow from above, and Humilis could just reach a frail arm over the side and dip his fingers in the familiar waters of the river beside which he had been born. Fidelis nursed him anxiously, his hands braced to steady the pillowed head, so that it lay in a chalice of his cupped palms, quite at rest. Later he might seek to withdraw the touch of his hands, flesh against flesh, for the sake of coolness, but as yet there was no need. He hung above the upturned, dreaming face, delicately shifting his hands as Humilis turned his head from side to side, trying to take in and recall both banks as they slid by. Fidelis felt no cramp, no weariness, almost no grief. He had lived so long with one particular grief that it had settled amicably into his being, a welcome and kindly guest. Here in the boat, thus islanded together, he found also an equally profound and poignant joy.

They had circled the whole of the town in their early passage, for the Severn, upstream from the abbey, made a great moat about the walls, turning the town almost into an island, but for the neck of land covered and protected by the castle. Once under Madog's western bridge, that gave passage to the roads into Wales, the meanderings of the river grew tortuous, and turned first one cheek, then the other, to the climbing, copper sun. Here there was ample water still, though below its common summer level, and the few shoals clung inshore, and Madog was familiar with all of them, and rowed strongly and leisurely, conscious of his mastery.

'All this stretch I remember well,' said Humilis, smiling towards the Frankwell shore, as the great bend north of the town brought them back on their westward course. 'This is pure pleasure to me, friend, but I fear it must be hard labour to you.'

'No,' said Madog, taciturn in English, but able to hold his own, 'no, this water is my living and my life. I go gladly.'

'Even in wintry weather?'

310

'In all weathers,' said Madog, and glanced up briefly at the sky, which continued a brazen vault, cloudless but hazy.

Beyond the suburb of Frankwell, outside the town walls and the loop of the river, they were between wide stretches of water-meadows, still moist enough to be greener than the grass on high ground, and a little coolness came up from the reedy shores, as though the earth breathed here, that elsewhere seemed to hold its breath. For a while the banks rose on either side, and old, tall trees overhung the water, casting a leaden shade. Heavy willows leaned from the banks, half their roots exposed by the erosion of the soil. Then the ground levelled and opened out again on their right hand, while on the left the bank rose in low, sandy terraces below and a slope of grass above, leading up to hillocks of woodland.

'It is not far now,' said Humilis, his eyes fixed eagerly ahead. 'I remember well. Nothing here is changed.'

He had gathered a degree of strength from his pleasure in this expedition, and his voice was clear and calm, but there were beads of sweat on his brow and lip. Fidelis wiped them away, and leaned over him to give him shade without touching.

'I am a child given a holiday,' said Humilis, smiling. 'It's fitting that I should spend it where I was a child. Life is a circle, Fidelis. We go outward from our source for half our time, leave behind our kin and our familiar places, value far countries and new-made friends. But then at the furthest point we begin the roundabout return, drawing in again towards the place from which we came. When the circle joins, there is nowhere beyond to go in this world, and it's time to depart. There is nothing sad in that. It's right and good.'

He made to raise himself a little in the boat to look ahead, and Fidelis lifted and supported him under the arms. 'Yonder, behind the screen of trees, there is the manor. We're home!'

The soil was reddish and sandy here, and provided a long, narrow beach, beyond which a slope of grass climbed, and a trodden path went up through the trees. Madog ran his boat into the sand, shipped his oars, and stepped ashore to haul the boat firmly aground and moor it.

'Bide quiet here a while, and I'll go and tell them at the house.'

The tenant of Salton was a man of fifty-five, and had not forgotten the boy, nine years or so his junior, who had been born to his lord in this manor, and lived the first few years of his life there. He came himself in haste down to the river, with

311

a pair of servants and an improvised chair to carry Godfrid up to the house. It was not the paladin of the Kingdom of Jerusalem he came hurrying to welcome, but the boy he had taught to fish and swim, and lifted on to his first pony at three years old. The early companionship had not lasted many years, and perhaps he had not given it a thought now for thirty years or more, being busy marrying and raising a family of his own, but the memories were readily reawakened. And in spite of Madog's dry warning, he checked in sharp and shocked dismay at sight of the frail spectre that awaited him in the boat. He was quick to recover and run to offer hand and knee and service, but Humilis had seen.

'You find me much changed, Aelred,' he said, fetching the name out of the well of his memory by instinct when it was needed. 'We are none of us the boys we once were. I have not worn well, but never let that trouble you. I'm well content. And glad, most glad, to see you here again on this same soil where I left you so long ago, and looking in such good heart.'

'My lord Godfrid, you do me great honour,' said Aelred. 'All here is at your service. My wife and my sons will be proud.'

He lifted his guest bodily out of the boat, startled by the light weight, and set him carefully in the sling chair. As a boy of twelve, long ago, son of his lord's steward, he had more than once carried the little boy in his arms. The elder brother, Marescot's heir, had scorned, at ten, to play nursemaid to a mere baby. Now the same arms carried the last wisp of a life, and found it scarcely heavier than the child.

'I am not come to put you to any trouble,' said Humilis, 'but only to sit here a while with you, and hear your news, and see how your fields prosper and your children grow. That will be great pleasure. And this is my good friend and helper, Brother Fidelis, who takes such good care of me that I lack nothing.'

Up the green slope and through the windbreak of trees they carried their burden, and there in the fields of the demesne, small but well husbanded, was the manor-house of Salton in its ring fence lined with byres and barns. A low, modest house, no more than a hall and one small chamber over a stone undercroft, and a separate kitchen in the yard. There was a little orchard outside the fence, and a wooden bench in the cool under the apple-trees. There they installed Humilis, with brychans and pillows to ease his sparsely covered bones, and ran busily back and forth in attendance on him with ale, fruit, new-baked bread, every gift they could offer. The wife came, fluttered and shy, dissembling startled pity as well as she could. Two big sons came, the elder about thirty, the younger surely achieved after one or two infant losses, for he was fifteen years younger. The elder son brought a young wife to make her reverence beside him, a dark, elfin girl, already pregnant.

Under the apple-trees Fidelis sat silent in the grass, leaving the bench for host and guest, while Aelred talked with sudden unwonted eloquence of days long past, and recounted all that had happened to him since those times. A quiet, settled, hard-working life, while crusaders roamed the world and came home childless, unfruitful and maimed. And Humilis listened with a faint, contented smile, his own voice used less and less, for he was tiring, and much of the stimulus of excitement was ebbing away. The sun was in the zenith, still a hazed and angry sun, but in the west swags of cloud were gathering and massing.

'Leave us now a little while,' said Humilis, 'for I tire easily, and I would not wear you out, as well. Perhaps I may sleep. Fidelis will watch by me.'

When they were alone he drew breath deep, and was silent a long time, but certainly not sleeping. He reached a lean hand to pluck Fidelis up by the sleeve, and have him sit beside him, in the place Aelred had vacated. A soft, drowsy lowing came to them from the byres, preoccupied as the humming of bees. The bees had had a hectic summer, frenziedly harvesting the flowers that bloomed so lavishly but died so soon. There were three hives at the end of the orchard. There would be honey in store.

'Fidelis...' The voice that had begun to flag and fail him had recovered clarity and calm, only it sounded at a little distance, as though he had already begun to depart. 'My heart, I brought you here to be with you, you only, you of all the world, here where I began. No one but you should hear what I say now. I know you better than I know my own soul. I value you as I value my own soul and my hope of heaven. I love you above any creature on this earth. Oh, hush ... still!'

The arm on which his hand lay so gently had jerked and stiffened, the mute throat had uttered some small sound like a sob.

'God forbid I should cause you any manner of pain, even by speaking too freely, but time is short. We both know it. And I have things to say while there's time. Fidelis ... your sweet companionship has been the blessing, the bliss, the joy and comfort of these last years of mine. There is no way I can recompense you but by loving you as you have loved me. And so I do. There can be nothing beyond that. Remember it, when I am gone, and remember that I go exulting, knowing you now as you know me, and loving as you have loved me.'

Beside him Fidelis sat still and mute as stone, but stones do not weep, and Fidelis was weeping, for when Humilis stooped and kissed his cheek he tasted tears.

That was all that passed. And shortly thereafter Madog stood before them, saying practically that there was a possible storm brewing, and they had better either make up their minds to stay where they were, or else get aboard at once and make their way briskly down with what current there was in this slack water, back to Shrewsbury.

The day belonged to Humilis, and so did the decision, and Humilis looked up at the western sky, darkening into an ominous twilight, looked at his companion, who sat like one straining to prolong a dream, remote and passive, and said, smiling, that they should go.

Aelred's sons carried him down to the shore, Aelred lifted him to his place in the bottom of the boat on his bed of rugs, with Fidelis to prop and cherish him. The east was still sullenly bright, they launched towards the light. Behind them the looming clouds multiplied with black and ominous speed, dangling like overfull udders of venomous milk. Under that darkness, Wales had vanished, distance became a matter of three miles or four. Somewhere there to westward there had already been torrential rain. The first turgid impulse of storm-water, creeping insidiously, began to muddy the Severn under them, and push them purposefully downstream.

They were well down the first reach between the water-meadows when the east suddenly darkened, almost instantly, to reflect back the purple-black frown of the west, and suddenly the light died into dimness, and the rumblings of thunder began, coming from the west at speed, like rolls of drums following them, or peals of deep-mouthed hounds on their trail in a hunt by demi-gods. Madog, untroubled but ready, rested on his oars to unfold the waxed cloth he used for covering goods in passage, and spread it over Humilis and across the body of the boat, making a canopy for his head, which Fidelis held over spread hands to prevent it from impeding the sick man's breathing.

Then the rain began, first great, heavy, single drops striking the stretched cloth loud as stones, then the heavens opened and let fall all the drowning accumulation of water of which the bleached earth was creditor, a downpour that set the Severn seething as if it boiled, and spat abrupt fountains of sand and soil from the banks. Fidelis covered his head, and bent to sustain the cover over Humilis. Madog made out into the centre of the stream, for the lightning, though it followed the course of the river, would strike first and most readily at whatever stood tallest along the banks.

Already soaked, he shook off water merrily as a fish, as much at home in it as beside it. He had been out in storms quite as sudden and drastic as this, and furious though it might be, he was assured it would not last very long.

But somewhere far upstream they had received this baptism several hours ago, for flood-water was coming down by this time in a great, foul brown wave, sweeping them before it. Madog ran with it, using his oars only to keep his boat well out in midstream. And steadily and viciously the torrent of rain fell, and the rolls and peals and slashes of thunder hounded them down towards Shrewsbury, and the lightnings, hot on the heels of the thunder, flashed and flamed and criss-crossed their path, the only light in a howling darkness. They could barely see either bank except when the lightning flared and vanished, and the blindness after its passing made the succeeding blaze even more blinding.

Wet and streaming as a seal, Fidelis shook off water on either side, and held the cover over Humilis with braced and aching forearms. His eyes were tight-shut against the deluge of the rain, he opened them only by burdened glimpses, peering through the downpour. He did not know where they were, except by flaming visions that forced light through his very eyelids, and caused him to blink the torment away. Such a flare showed him trees leaning, gaunt and sinister, magnified by the lurid light before they were swallowed in the darkness. So they were already past the open water-meadows, surely by now morasses dimpled and pitted with heavy rain. They were being driven fast between the trees, not far now from possible shelter in Frankwell.

In spite of the covering cloth they were awash. Water swirled in the bottom of the boat, cold and sluggish, a discomfort, but not a danger. They ran with the current, fouled and littered with leaves and the debris of branches, muddied and turgid and curling in perverse eddies. But very soon now they could come ashore in Frankwell and take cover in the nearest dwelling, hardly the worse for all this turmoil and violence.

The thunder gathered and shrieked, one ear-bursting bellow. The lightning struck in time with it, a blinding glare. Fidelis opened his drowned eyes in shock at the blow, in time to see the thickest, oldest, most misshapen willow on the left bank leap, split asunder in flame, wrench out half its root from the slithering, sodden shore, and burst into a tremendous blossom of fire, hurled into midstream over them, and blazing as it fell.

Madog flung himself forward over Humilis in the shell of the boat. Like a bolt from a mangonel the shattered tree crashed down upon the bow of the skiff, smashed through its sides and split it apart like a cracked egg. Trunk and boat and cargo went down deep together into the murky waters. The fire died in an immense hissing. Everything was dark, everything suddenly cold and in motion and heavier than lead, dragging body and soul down among the weed and debris of storm, turning and turning and drifting fast, drawn irresistibly towards the ease and languor of death.

Fidelis fought and kicked his way upward with bursting heart, against the comforting persuasion of despair, the cramping, crippling weight of his habit, and the swirling and battering of drifting branches and tangling weeds. He came to the surface and drew deep breath, clutching at leaves that slid through his fingers, and fastening greedily on a branch that held fast, and supported him with his head above water. Gasping, he shook off water and opened his eyes upon howling darkness. A cage of shattered branches surrounded and held him. Torn but still tenacious roots anchored the willow, heaving and plunging, against the surging current. A brychan from the boat wound itself about his arm like a snake, and almost tore him from his hold. He dragged himself along the branch, peering and straining after any glimpse of a floating hand, a pale face, phantom-like in all that chaotic gloom.

A fold of black cloth coiled past, driven through the threshing leaves. The end of a sleeve surfaced, a pallid hand trailed by and went under again. Fidelis loosed his hold, and launched himself after it, clear of the tree, diving beneath the trammelling branches. The hem of the habit slid through his fingers, but he got a grip on the billowing folds of the cowl, and struck out towards the Frankwell shore to escape the trailing wreckage of the willow. Clinging desperately, he shifted to a better hold, holding the lax body of Humilis above him. Once they went down together. Then Madog was beside them, hoisting the weight of the unconscious body from arms that could not have sustained it longer.

Fidelis drifted for a moment on the edge of acceptance, in an exhaustion which rendered the idea of death perilously attractive. Better by far to let go, abandon struggle, go wherever the current might take him.

And the current took him and stranded him quite gently in the muddied grass of the shore, and laid him face-down beside the body of Brother Humilis, over which Madog of the Dead Boat was labouring all in vain.

The rain slackened suddenly, briefly; the wind, which had the whistle of anguish on its driving breath, subsided for an instant; and the demons of thunder rolled and rumbled away downstream, leaving a breath of utter silence and almost stillness, between frenzies. And piercing through the lull, a great scream of deprivation and loss and grief shrilled aloft over the Severn, startling the hunched and silent birds out of the bushes, and echoing down the flood in a long ululation from bank to bank, crying a bereavement beyond remedy.

Chapter Thirteen

ICHOLAS WAS approaching Shrewsbury when the sky began to darken ominously, and he quickened his pace in the hope of reaching shelter in the town before the storm broke. But the first heavy drops fell as he reached the Foregate, and before his eyes the street was emptied of life, all its inhabitants going to ground within their houses, and closing doors and shutters against the rage to come. By the time he rode past the gatehouse of the abbey, abandoning the thought of waiting out the storm there, since he was now so close, the sky had opened, in a downpour so opaque and blinding that he found himself veering from side to side as he crossed the bridge, unable to steer a straight course. It seemed he was the only man left in a depopulated town in an empty world, for there was not another soul stirring.

Under the arch of the town gate he halted to draw breath and clear his eyes, shaking off the weight of the rain. The whole width of Shrewsbury lay between him and the castle, but Hugh's house by Saint Mary's was no great distance, only up the curve of the Wyle and the level street beyond. Hugh was as likely to be there as at the castle. At least he could call in and ask, on his way through to the High Cross, and the descent to the castle gatehouse. He could hardly get wetter than he already was. He set off up the hill. Saner folk peered out through the chinks in their shuttered windows, and watched him scurrying head-down through the deluge. Overhead the thunder rolled and rattled round a sky dark as midnight, and lightnings flickered, drawing the peals ever closer after them. The horse was unhappy but well-trained, and pressed on obedient but quivering with fear.

The gates of Hugh's courtyard stood open, there was a degree of shelter under the lee of the house, and as soon as hooves were heard on the cobbles the hall door opened, and a groom came haring across from the stables to take the horse to cover. Aline stood peering anxiously out into the murky gloom, and beckoned the traveller in.

'Before you drown, sir,' she said, all concern, as Nicholas plunged into the shelter of the doorway and let fall his streaming cloak, to avoid bringing it within. They stood looking earnestly at each other, for the light was too dim for instant recognition. Then she tilted her head, recaptured a memory, and smiled. 'You are Nicholas Harnage! You came here with Hugh, when first you came to Shrewsbury. I remember now. Forgive such a slow welcome back, but I am not used to midnight in the afternoon. Come within, and let me find you some dry clothes – though I fear Hugh's will be a tight fit for you.'

He was warmed by her candour and kindness, but it could not divert him from the black intensity of his purpose here. He looked beyond her, where Constance hovered, clutching her tyrant Giles firmly by the hand, for fear he should mistake the deluge for a new amusement, and dart out into it.

'The lord sheriff is not here? I must see him as soon as may be. I bring grim news.'

'Hugh is at the castle, but he'll come by evening. Can it not wait? At least until this storm blows by. It cannot last long.'

No, he could not wait. He would go on the rest of the way, fair or foul. He thanked her, almost ungraciously in his preoccupation, swung the wet cloak about him again, took back his horse from the groom, and was off again at a trot towards the High Cross. Aline sighed, shrugged, and went in, closing the door on the chaos without. Grim news! What could that mean? Something to do with King Stephen and Robert of Gloucester? Had the attempts at an exchange foundered? Or was it something to do with that young man's personal quest? Aline knew the bare bones of the story, and felt a mild, rueful interest – a girl set free by her affianced husband, a favoured squire sent to tell her so, and too modest or too sensitive to pursue at once the attraction he felt towards her on his own account. Was the girl alive or dead? Better to know, once for all, than to go on tormented by uncertainty. But surely 'grim news' could only mean the worst.

Nicholas reached the High Cross, spectral through the streaming rain, and turned down the slight slope towards the castle, and the broad ramp to the gatehouse. Water lay ankle-deep in the outer ward, draining off far too slowly to keep pace with the flood. A sergeant leaned out from the guard-room, and called the stranger within.

'The lord sheriff? He's in the hall. If you bear round into the inner ward close to the wall you'll escape the worst. I'll have your horse stabled. Or wait a while here in the dry, if you choose, for this can't last for ever...'

But no, he could not wait. The ring burned in his pouch, and the acid bitterness in his mind. He must get his tale at once to the ears of authority, and his teeth into the throat of Adam Heriet. He dared not stop hating, or the remaining grief became more than he could stand. He bore down on Hugh in the huge dark hall with the briefest of greetings and the most abrupt of challenges, an unkempt apparition, his wet brown hair plastered to forehead and temples, and water streaking his face.

'My lord, I'm back from Winchester, with plain proof Julian is dead and her goods made away with long ago. And we must leave all else and turn every man you have here and I can raise in the south, to hunt down Adam Heriet. It was his doing – Heriet and his hired murderer, some footpad paid for his work with the price of Julian's jewellery. Once we lay hands on him, he won't be able to deny it. I have proof, I have witnesses that he said himself she was dead!'

'Come, now!' said Hugh, his eyes rounding. 'That's a large enough claim. You've been a busy man in the south, I see, but so have we here. Come, sit, and let's have the full story. But first, let's have those wet clothes off you, and find you a man who matches, before you catch your death.' He shouted for the servants, and sent them running for towels and coats and hose.

'No matter for me,' protested Nicholas feverishly, catching at his arm. 'What matters is the proof I have, that fits only one man, to my mind, and he going free, and God knows where ... '

'Ah, but Nicholas, if it's Adam Heriet you're after, then you need fret no longer. Adam Heriet is safe behind a locked door here in the castle, and has been for a matter of days.'

'You have him? You found Heriet? He's taken?' Nicholas drew deep and vengeful breath, and heaved a great sigh.

'We have him, and he'll keep. He has a sister married to a

craftsman in Brigge, and was visiting his kin like an honest man. Now he's the sheriff's guest, and stays so until we have the rights of it, so no more sweat for him.'

'And have you got any part of it out of him? What has he said?'

'Nothing to the purpose. Nothing an honest man might not have said in his place.'

'That shall change,' said Nicholas grimly, and allowed himself to notice his own sudden condition for the first time, and to accept the use of the small chamber provided him, and the clothes put at his disposal. But he was half into his tale before he had dried his face and his tousled hair and shrugged his way into dry garments.

'... never a trace anywhere of the church ornaments, which should be the most notable if ever they were marketed. And I was in two minds whether it was worth enquiring further, when the man's wife came in, and I knew the ring she was wearing for Julian's. No, that's to press it too far, I know – say rather I saw that it fitted only too well the description we had of Julian's. You remember? Enamelled all round with flowers in yellow and blue...'

'I have the whole register by heart,' said Hugh drily.

'Then you'll see why I was so sure. I asked where she got it, and she said it was brought into the shop for sale along with two other pieces of jewellery, by a man about fifty years old. Three years back, on the twentieth day of August, for that was the day of her birth, and she asked the ring as a present, and got it from her husband. And the other two pieces, both sold since, they described to me as a necklace of polished stones and a silver bracelet engraved with sprays of vetch or pease. Three such, and all together! They could only be Julian's.'

Hugh nodded emphatic agreement to that. 'And the man?'

'The description the woman gave me fits what little I have been told of Adam Heriet, for till now I have not seen him. Fifty years old, tanned from living outdoor like forester or huntsman... You have seen him, you know more. Brown-bearded, she said, and balding, a face of oak ... Is that in tune?'

'To the letter and the note.'

'And the ring I have. Here, see! I asked it of the woman for this need, and she trusted me with it, though she valued it and would not sell, and I must give it back – when its work is done! Could this be mistaken?'

'It could not. Cruce and all his household will confirm it, but truth, we hardly need them. Is there more?'

'There is! For the jeweller questioned the ownership, seeing these were all a woman's things, and asked if the lady who owned them had no further use for them. And the man said, as for the lady who had owned them, no, she had no further use for them, seeing she was dead!'

'He said so? Thus baldly?'

'He did. Wait, there's more! The woman was a little curious about him, and followed him out of the shop when he left. And she saw him meet with a young fellow who was lurking by the wall outside, and give something over to him – a part of the money or the whole, or so she thought. And when they were aware of her watching, they slipped away round the corner out of sight, very quickly.'

'All this she will testify to?'

'I am sure she will. And a good witness, careful and clear.'

'So it seems,' said Hugh, and shut his fingers decisively over the ring. 'Nicholas, you must take some food and wine now, while this downpour continues – for why should you drown a second time when we have our quarry already in safe hold? But as soon as it stops, you and I will go and confront Master Heriet with this pretty thing, and see if we cannot prise more out of him this time than a child's tale of gaping at the wonders of Winchester.'

Ever since dinner Brother Cadfael had been dividing his time between the mill and the gatehouse, forewarned of possible trouble by the massing of the clouds long before the rain began. When the storm broke he took refuge in the mill, from which vantage-point he could keep an eye on both the pond and its outlet to the brook, and the road from the town, in case Madog should have found it advisable to land his charges for shelter in Frankwell, rather than completing the long circuit of the town, in which case he would come afoot to report as much.

The mill's busy season was over, it was quiet and dim within, no sound but the monotonous dull drumming of the rain. It was there that Madog found him, a drowned rat of a Madog, alone. He had come by the path outside the abbey enclave, by which the town customers approached with their grain to be milled, rather than enter at the gatehouse. He loomed shadowy against the open doorway, and stood mute, dangling long, helpless arms. No man's strength could fight off the powers of weather and storm and thunder. Even his long endurance had its limits.

'Well?' said Cadfael, chilled with foreboding.

'Not well, but very ill.' Madog came slowly within, and what light there was showed the dour set of his face. 'Anything to astonish me, you said! I have had my fill of astonishment, and I bring it straight to you, as you wished. God knows,' he said, wringing out beard and hair, and shaking rivulets of rain from his shoulders, 'I'm at a loss to know what to do about it. If you had foreknowledge, you may be able to see a way forward – I'm blind!' He drew deep breath, and told it all in words blunt and brief. 'The rain alone would not have troubled us. The lightning struck a tree, heaved it at us as we passed, and split us asunder. The boat's gone piecemeal down the river, where the shreds will fetch up there's no guessing. And those two brothers of yours...'

'*Drowned?*' said Cadfael in a stunned whisper.

'The older one, Marescot, yes ... Dead, at any rate. I got him out, the young one helping, though him I had to loose, I could not grapple with both. But I could get no breath back into Marescot. There was barely time for him to drown, the shock more likely stopped his heart, frail as he was – the cold, even the noise of the thunder. However it was, he's dead. There's an end. As for the other – what is there I could tell you of the other, that you do not know?' He was searching Cadfael's face with close and wondering attention. 'No, there's no astonishment in it for you, is there? You knew it all before. Now what do we do?'

Cadfael stirred out of his stillness, gnawed a cautious lip, and stared out into the rain. The worst had passed, the sky was growing lighter. Far along the river valley the diminishing rolls of thunder followed the foul brown flood-water downstream.

'Where have you left them?'

'On the far side of Frankwell, not a mile from the bridge, there's a hut on the bank, the fishermen use it. We fetched up close by, and I got them into cover there. We'll need a litter to bring Marescot home, but what of the other?'

'Nothing of the other! The other's gone, drowned, the Severn has taken him. And no alarm, no litter, not yet. Bear with me, Madog, for this is a desperate business, but if we tread carefully now we may come through it unscathed. Go back to them, and wait for me there. I'm coming with you as far as the town, then you go on to the hut, and I'll come to you there as soon as I can. And never a word of this, never to any, for the sake of us all.'

The rain had stopped by the time Cadfael turned in at the gate of Hugh's house. Every roof glistened, every guter streamed, as the grey remnants of cloud cleared from a sun now bright and benevolent, all its coppery malignancy gone down-river with the storm.

'Hugh is still at the castle,' said Aline, surprised and pleased as she rose to meet him. 'He has a visitor with him there – Nicholas Harnage is come back, he says with grim news, but he did not stay to confide it to me.'

'He? He's back?' Cadfael was momentarily distracted, even alarmed. 'What can he have found, I wonder? And how wide will he have spread it already?' He shook the speculation away from him. 'Well, that makes my business all the more urgent. Girl dear, it's you I want! Had Hugh been here, I would have begged the loan of you of your lord in a proper civil fashion, but as things are … I need you for an hour or two. Will you ride with me in a good cause? We'll need horses – one for you to go and return, and one for me to go further still – one of Hugh's big fellows that can carry two at a pinch. Will you be my advocate, and see me back into good odour if I borrow such a horse? Trust me, the need is urgent.'

'Hugh's stables have always been open to you,' said Aline, 'since ever we got to know you. And I'll lend myself for any enterprise you tell me is urgent. How far have we to go?'

'Not far. Over the western bridge and across Frankwell. I must ask the loan of some of your possessions, too,' said Cadfael.

'Tell me what you want, and then you go and saddle the horses – Jehan is there, tell him you have my leave. And you can tell me what all this means and what I'm needed for on the way.'

Adam Heriet looked up sharply and alertly when the door of his prison was opened at an unexpected hour of the early evening. He drew himself together with composure and caution when he saw who entered. He was practised and prepared in all the questions with which he had so far had to contend, but this promised or threatened something new. The bold oaken face the jeweller's wife had so shrewdly observed

324

served him well. He rose civilly in the presence of his betters, but with a formal stiffness and a blank countenance which suggested that he did not feel himself to be in any way inferior. The door closed behind them, though the key was not turned. There was no need, there would be a guard outside.

'Sit, Adam! We have been showing some interest in your movements in Winchester, at the time you know of,' said Hugh mildly. 'Would you care to add anything to what you've already told us? Or to change anything?'

'No, my lord. I have told you what I did and where I went. There is no more to tell.'

'Your memory may be faulty. All men are fallible. Can we not remind you, for instance, of a silversmith's shop in the High Street? Where you sold three small things of value – not your property?'

Adam's face remained stonily stoical, but his eyes flickered briefly from one face to the other. 'I never sold anything in Winchester. If anyone says so, they have mistaken me for some other man.'

'You lie!' said Nicholas, flaring. 'Who else would be carrying these very three things? A necklace of polished stones, an engraved silver bracelet – and *this*!'

The ring lay in his open palm, thrust close under Adam's nose, its enamels shining with a delicate lustre, a small work of art so singular that there could not be a second like it. And he had known the girl from infancy, and must have been familiar with her trinkets long before that journey south. If he denied this, he proclaimed himself a liar, for there were plenty of others who could swear to it.

He did not deny it. He even stared at it with a well-assumed wonder and surprise, and said at once: 'That is Julian's! Where did you get it?'

'From the silversmith's wife. She kept it for her own, and she remembered very well the man who brought it, and painted as good a picture of him as the law will need to put your name to him. Yes, this is Julian's!' said Nicholas, hoarse with passion. 'That is what you did with her goods. *What did you do with her?*'

'I've told you! I parted from her a mile or more from Wherwell, at her orders, and I never saw her again.'

'You lie in your teeth! You destroyed her.'

Hugh laid a hand on the young man's arm, which started and quivered at the touch, like a pointing hound distracted from his aim.

325

'Adam, you waste your lying, which is worse. Here is a ring you acknowledge for your mistress's property, sold, according to two good witnesses, on the twentieth of August three years ago, in a Winchester shop, by a man whose description fits you better than your own clothes … '

'Then it could fit many a man of my age,' protested Adam stoutly. 'What is there singular about me? The woman has not pointed the finger at *me*, she has not seen me...'

'She will, Adam, she will. We can bring her, and her husband, too, to accuse you to your face. As I accuse you,' said Hugh firmly. 'This is too much to be passed off as a children's tale, or a curious chance. We need no better case against you than this ring and those two witnesses provide – for robbery, if not for murder. Yes, murder! How else did you get possession of her jewellery? And if you did not connive at her death, then where is she now? She never reached Wherwell, nor was she expected there, it was quite safe to put her out of the world, her kin here believing her safe in a nunnery, the nunnery undisturbed by her never arriving, for she had given no forewarning. So where is she, Adam? On the earth or under it?'

'I know no more than I've told you,' said Adam, setting his teeth.

'Ah, but you do! You know how much you got from the silversmith – and how much of it you paid over to your hired assassin, outside the shop. Who was he, Adam?' demanded Hugh softly. 'The woman saw you meet him, pay him, slither away round the corner with him when you saw her standing at the door. Who was he?'

'I know nothing of any such man. It was not I who went there, I tell you.' His voice was still firm, but a shade hurried now, and had risen a tone, and he was beginning to sweat.

'The woman has described him, too. A young fellow about twenty, slender, and kept his capuchon over his head. Give him a name, Adam, and it may somewhat lighten your load. If you know a name for him? Where did you find him? In the market? Or was he bespoken well before for the work?'

'I never entered such a shop. If all this happened, it happened to other men, not to me. I was not there.'

'But Julian's possessions were, Adam! That's certain. And brought by someone who much resembled you. When the woman sees you in the flesh, then I may say, brought by *you*. Better to tell us, Adam. Spare yourself a long uncovering, make your confession of your own will, and be done. Spare the silversmith's wife a long journey. For she *will* point the finger, Adam. This, she will say when she sets eyes on you, *this* is the man.'

'I have nothing to confess. I've done no wrong.'

'Why did you choose that particular shop, Adam?'

'I was never in the shop. I had nothing to sell. I was not there...'

'But this ring was, Adam. How did it get there? And with a necklace and bracelet, too? Chance? How far can chance stretch?'

'I left her a mile from Wherwell...'

'Dead, Adam?'

'I parted from her living, I swear it!'

'Yet you told the silversmith that the lady who had owned these gems was dead. Why did you so?'

'I told you, it was not I, I was never in the shop.'

'Some other man, was it? A stranger, and yet he had those ornaments, all three, and he resembled you, and he knew and said that the lady was dead. Here are so many miraculous chances, Adam, how do you account for them?'

The prisoner let his head fall back against the wall. His face was grey. 'I never laid hand on her. I loved her!'

'And this is not her ring?'

'It *is* her ring. Anyone at Lai will tell you so.'

'Yes, they will, Adam, they will! They will tell the court so, when your time comes. But only you can tell us how it came into your possession, unless by murder. Who was the man you paid?'

'There was none. I was not there. It was not I...'

The pace had steadily increased, the questions coming thick as arrows and as deadly. Round and round, over and over the same ground, and the man was tiring at last. If he was breakable at all, he must break soon.

They were so intent, and strung so taut, like overtuned instruments, that they all three started violently when there was a knock at the door of the cell, and a sergeant put his head in, visibly agape with sensational news. 'My lord, pardon, but they thought you should know at once ... There's word in town that a boat sank today in the storm. Two brothers from the abbey drowned in the Severn, they're saying, and Madog's boat smashed to flinders by a tree the lightning fetched down. They're searching downstream for one of the pair...'

327

Hugh was on his feet, aghast. '*Madog*'s boat? That must be the hiring Cadfael told me of ... Drowned? Are they sure of their tale? Madog never lost man nor cargo till now.'

'My lord, who can argue with lightning? The tree crashed full on them. Someone in Frankwell saw the bolt fall. The lord abbot may not even know of it yet, but they're all in the same story in the town.'

'I'll come!' said Hugh, and swung hurriedly on Nicholas. 'God knows I'm sorry, Nick, if this is true. Brother Humilis – your Godfrid – had a longing to see his birthplace at Salton again, and set out with Madog this morning, or so he intended – he and Fidelis. Come with me! We'd best go find out the truth of it. Pray God they've made much of little, as usual, and they've come by nothing worse than a ducking ... Madog can outswim most fish. But let's go and make sure.'

Nicholas had risen with him, startled and slow to take it in. 'My lord? And he so sick? Oh, God, he could not live through such a shock. Yes, I'll come ... I must know!'

And they were away, abandoning their prisoner. The door closed briskly between, and the key turned in the lock. No one had given another look or thought to Adam Heriet, who sank back slowly on his hard bed, and bowed himself into his cupped hands, a demoralised hulk of a man, worn out and emptied at heart. Gradually slow tears began to seep between his braced fingers and fall upon his pillow, but there was no one there to see and wonder, and no one to interpret.

They took horse in haste through the town, through streets astonishingly drying out already in the gentle warmth after the deluge. It was still broad day and late sunlight, and the roofs and walls and roads steamed, so that the horses waded a shallow, frail sea of vapour. They passed by Hugh's house without halting. As well, for they would have found no Aline there to greet them.

People were emerging into the streets again wherever they passed, gathering in twos and threes, heads together and chins earnestly wagging. The word of tragedy had gone round rapidly, once it was whispered. Nor was it any false alarm this time. Out through the eastern gate and crossing the bridge towards the abbey, Hugh and Nicholas drew rein at sight of a small, melancholy procession crossing ahead of them. Four men carried an improvised litter, an outhouse door taken from its hinges in some Frankwell householder's yard, and draped decently with rugs to carry the corpse of one victim, at least, of the storm. One only, for it was a narrow door, and the four bearers handled it as if the weight was light, though the swathed body lay long and large-boned on its bier.

They fell in reverently behind, as many of the townsfolk afoot were also doing, swelling the solemn progress like a funeral cortège. Nicholas stared and strained ahead, measuring the mute and motionless body. So long and yet so light, fallen away into age before age was due, this could be no other but Godfrid Marescot, the maimed and dwindling flesh at last shed by its immaculate spirit. He stared through a mist, trying impatiently to clear his eyes.

'That is this Madog, that man who leads them?'

Hugh nodded silently, yes. No doubt but Madog had recruited friends from the suburb, part Welsh, as he was wholly Welsh, to help him bring the dead man home. He commanded his helpers decorously, dolorously, with great dignity.

'The other one – Fidelis?' wondered Nicholas, recalling the retiring anonymous figure forever shrinking into shadow, yet instant in service. He felt a pang of self-reproach that he grieved so much for Godfrid, and so little for the young man who had made himself a willing slave to Godfrid's nobility.

Hugh shook his head. There was but one here.

They were across the bridge and moving along the approach to the Foregate, between the Gaye on the left hand and the mill and mill-pool on the right, and so to the gatehouse of the abbey. There the bearers turned in to the right with their burden, under the arch, into the great court, where a silent, solemn assembly had massed to wait for them, and there they set down their charge, and stood in silent attendance.

The news had reached the abbey as the brothers came from Vespers. They gathered in a stunned circle, abbot, prior, obedientiaries, monks and novices, brought thus abruptly to the contemplation of mortality. The townspeople who had followed the procession to its destination hovered within the gate, somewhat apart, and gazed in awed silence.

Madog approached the abbot with the Welshman's unservile readiness to accept all men as equals, and told his story simply. Radulfus acknowledged the will of God and the helplessness of man with an absolving motion of his hand, and stood looking down at the swathed body a long moment, before he stooped and drew back the covering from the face.

Humilis in dying had shed all but his proper years. Death could not restore the lost and fallen flesh, but it had relaxed the sharp, gaunt lines, and smoothed away the engraved hollows of pain. Hugh and Nicholas, standing aloof at the corner of the cloister, caught a brief glimpse of Humilis translated, removed into superhuman serenity and repose, before Radulfus lowered the cloth again, blessed the bier and the bearers, and motioned to his obedientiaries to take up the body and carry it into the mortuary chapel.

Only then, when Brother Edmund, reminded of old reticences those two lost brothers had shared, and manifestly deprived of Fidelis, looked round for the one other man who was in the intimate secrets of Humilis's broken body, and failed to find him – only then did Hugh realise that Brother Cadfael was the one man missing from this gathering. He, who of all men should have been ready and dutiful in whatever concerned Humilis, to be elsewhere at this moment! The dereliction stuck fast in Hugh's mind, until he made sense of it later. It was, after all, possible that a dead man should have urgent unfinished business elsewhere, even more dear to him than the last devotions paid to his body.

They extended their respects and condolences to Abbot Radulfus, with the promise that search should be made downstream for the body of Brother Fidelis, as long as any hope remained of finding him, and then they rode back at a walking pace into the town, host and guest together. The dusk was closing gently in, the sky clear, bland, innocent of evil, the air suddenly cool and kind. Aline was waiting with the evening meal ready to be served, and welcomed two men returning as graciously as one. And if there was still a horse missing from the stables, Hugh did not linger to discover it, but left the horses to the grooms, and devoted his own attention to Nicholas.

'You must stay with us,' he said over supper, 'until his burial. I'll send word to Cruce, he'll want to pay the last honours to one who once meant to become his brother by law, and he has a right to know how things stand now with Heriet.'

That caused Aline to prick up her ears. 'And how do things stand now with Heriet? So much has happened today, I seem to have missed at least the half of it. Nicholas did say he brought grim news, but even the downpour couldn't delay him long enough to say more. What has happened?'

330

They told her, between them, all that had passed, from the dogged search in Winchester to the point where news of Madog's disaster had interrupted the questioning of Adam Heriet, and sent them out in consternation to find out the truth of the report. Aline listened with a slight, anxious frown.

'He burst in crying that two brothers from the abbey were dead, drowned in the river? Named names, did he? There in the cell, in front of your prisoner?'

'I think it was I who named names,' said Hugh. 'It came at the right moment for Heriet, I fancy he was nearing the end of his tether. Now he can draw breath for the next bout, though I doubt if it will save him.'

Aline said no more on that score until Nicholas, short of sleep after his long ride and the shocks of this day, took himself off to his bed. When he was gone, she laid by the embroidery on which she had been working, and went and sat down beside Hugh on the cushioned bench beside the empty hearth, and wound a persuasive arm about his neck.

'Hugh, love – there's something you must hear – and Nicholas must *not* hear, not yet, not until all's over and safe and calm. It might be best if he never does hear it, though perhaps he'll divine at least half of it for himself in the end. But *you* we need now.'

'*We?*' said Hugh, not too greatly surprised, and turned to wind an arm comfortably about her waist and draw her closer to his side.

'Cadfael and I. Who else?'

'So I supposed,' said Hugh, sighing and smiling. 'I did wonder at his abandoning the disastrous end of a venture he himself helped to launch.'

'But he did not abandon it, he's about resolving it this moment. And if you should hear someone about the stables, a little later, no need for alarm, it will only be Cadfael bringing back your horse, and you know he can be trusted to see to his horse's comfort before he gives a thought to his own.'

'I foresee a long story,' said Hugh. 'It had better be interesting.' Her fair hair was soft and sweet against his cheek. He turned to touch his lips to hers, very softly and briefly.

'It is. As any matter of life and death must be. You'll see! And since it was blurted out in front of poor Adam Heriet that two brothers have drowned, you ought to pay him a visit as soon as you can, tomorrow, and tell him he need not fret, that things are not always what they seem.'

331

'Then tell me,' said Hugh, 'what they really are.'

She settled herself warmly into the circle of his arm, and very gravely told him.

The search for the body of Brother Fidelis was pursued diligently from both banks of the river, at every spot where floating debris commonly came ashore, for more than two days, but all that came to light was one of his sandals, torn from his foot by the river and cast up in the sandy shoals near Atcham. Most bodies that went into the Severn were also put ashore by the Severn, sooner or later. This one never would be. Shrewsbury and the world had seen the last of Brother Fidelis.

Chapter Fourteen

HE BURIAL of Brother Humilis brought together
in the abbey guest-hall representatives of all the
small nobility of the shire, and most of the
Benedictine foundations within the region. Sheriff
and town provost would certainly attend and so would many of
the elders and merchants of Shrewsbury, more by reason of the
dramatic and tragic nature of the dead man's departure than
for any real knowledge they had had of him in his short sojourn
in the town. Most had never seen him, but knew his reputation
before he took the cowl, and felt that his birth and death here
in the midst gave them some title in him. It would be a great
occasion, befitting an entombment within the church itself, a
rare honour.

Reginald Cruce came down from Lai a day in advance of the
ceremony, malevolently gratified at all that Nicholas had to
report, and taking vengeful pleasure in having the miscreant
who had dared do violence to a member of the Cruce family
securely in prison and tacitly acknowledged as guilty, even if
trial had to await the legal formalities. Hugh did nothing to cast
doubts on his satisfaction.

Reginald held the enamelled ring in a broad palm, and
studied the intricate decoration with interest. 'Yes, I
remember it. Strange it should be this small thing that
condemns him. She had another ring, I recall, that she valued,
perhaps all the more because it was given to her as a child,
when her fingers were far too small to retain it. Marescot sent it

to her when the contract of betrothal was concluded, it was old, one that had been handed down bride to bride in his family. She used to wear it on a chain round her neck because it was too big for her fingers. I'm sure she would not leave that behind.'

'This was the only ring listed in the valuables she took with her,' said Nicholas, taking back the little jewel. 'I'm pledged to return it to the silversmith's wife in Winchester.'

'The list was of the things intended for her dowry. The ring Marescot sent her she probably meant to keep. It was gold, a snake with red eyes making two coils about the finger. Very old, the scales were worn smooth. I wonder,' said Reginald, 'where it is now. There are no more Marescots left, not of that branch, to give it to their brides.'

No more Marescots, thought Nicholas, and no more Julians. A double, grievous loss, for which revenge, now that he seemed to have it securely in his hands, was no compensation at all. 'Should you be mistaken, and she is still living,' the silversmith's wife had said, 'and wants her ring, then give it back to her, and pay me for it whatever you think fair.' If I had more gold than king and empress put together, thought Nicholas, nursing the ache he carried within him, it would not be enough to pay for so inexpressible a blessing.

Brother Cadfael had behaved himself extremely modestly and circumspectly these last days, strict to every scruple of the horarium, prompt in every service, trying, he admitted to himself ruefully, to deserve success, and disarm whatever disapproval the heavens might be harbouring against him. The end in view, he was certain, was not only good but vitally necessary, for the sake of the abbey and the church, and the peace of mind of all those whose fate it was to live on now that Humilis was delivered out of the body, and safe for ever. But the means – he was less certain that the means were above reproach. But what can a man do, or a woman either, but use what comes to hand?

He rose early on the funeral day, to have a little time for his private and vehement prayers before Prime. Much depended on this day, he had good reason to be uneasy, and to turn to Saint Winifred for indulgence, pardon and aid. She had forgiven him, before this, for very irregular means towards desirable ends, and shown him humouring kindness when sterner patrons might have frowned.

334

But this morning she had another petitioner before him. Someone was crouched almost prostrate on the three steps leading up to her altar. The rigid lines of body and limbs, the convulsive knot of the linked hands contorted on the highest step, spoke of a need at least as extreme as his own. Cadfael drew back silently into shadow, and waited, and after what seemed a long anguished time the petitioner gathered himself stiffly and slowly, like a man crippled, rose from his knees, and slipped away towards the south door into the cloister. It came as a surprise and a wonder that Brother Urien should be tearing out his heart thus alone in the early morning. Cadfael had never paid, perhaps, sufficient attention to Brother Urien. Who did? Who talked with him, who was familiar with him? The man elected himself into solitude.

Cadfael made his prayers. He had done what seemed best, he had had loyal and ingenious helpers, now he could only plump the whole matter confidingly into Saint Winifred's tolerant Welsh arms, remind her he was her distant kin, and leave the rest to her.

In the morning of a mild, clear day, with all due ceremony and every honour, Brother Humilis, Godfrid Marescot, was buried in the transept of the abbey church of Saint Peter and Saint Paul.

Cadfael had been looking in vain for one particular mourner, and had not found her, but having rested his case with the saint he left the church not greatly troubled. And as the brothers emerged into the great court, Abbot Radulfus leading, there she was, neat and competent and comely as ever, waiting near the gatehouse to advance to meet the concourse, like a lone knight venturing undeterred against an army. She had a gift for timing, she had conjured up for herself a great cloud of witnesses. Let the revelation be public and wonderful.

Sister Magdalen, of the Benedictine cell of Godric's Ford, a few miles distant towards the Welsh border, had been both beautiful and worldly in her youth, a baron's mistress by choice, and honest and loyal to her bargain at that. True to her word and bond then, so she was now in her new vocation. If she had brought as escort some of her devoted army of countrymen from the western forests on this occasion, she had discreetly removed them from sight at this moment. She had the field to herself.

A plump, rosy, middle-aged lady, bright-eyed and brisk, the

335

remnant of her beauty wisely tempered by the austere whiteness of her wimple and blackness of her habit into something homely and comfortable, at least until her indomitable dimple plunged dazzlingly in her cheek, like the twinkling dive of a small golden fish, and again smoothed out as rapidly and demurely as the water of a stream resuming its sunny level. Cadfael had known her for a few years now, and had had occasion to rely on her more than once in complex matters. His trust in her was absolute.

She advanced decorously upon the abbot, glanced aside and veered slightly towards Hugh, and succeeded in halting them both, arresting sacred and secular authority together. All the remaining mourners, monks and laymen, flooded out from the church and stood waiting respectfully for the nobility to disperse unimpeded.

'My lords,' said Sister Magdalen, dividing a reverence between church and state, 'I pray your pardon that I come so late, but the recent rains have flooded some parts of the way, and I did not allow enough time for the delays. *Mea culpa!* I shall make my prayers for our brothers in private, and hope to attend the Mass for them here, to make amends for today's failing.'

'Late or early, sister, you have a welcome assured,' said the abbot. 'You should stay a day or two, until the ways are clear again. And certainly you must be my guest at dinner now you are here.'

'You are very gracious, Father,' she said. 'Having failed of my time, I would not have ventured to trouble you now, but that I am the bearer of a letter, to the lord sheriff.' She turned and looked full at Hugh, very gravely. She had the rolled and sealed parchment leaf in her hand. 'I must tell you how this came to Godric's Ford. Mother Mariana regularly receives letters from the prioress of our mother house at Polesworth. In the most recent, which came only yesterday, this other letter was enclosed, from a lady just arrived with a company of other travellers, and now resting after her journey. It is superscribed to the lord sheriff of Shropshire, and sealed with the seal of Polesworth. I brought it with me at this opportunity, seeing it may be important. With your leave, Father, here I deliver it.'

How it was done remained her secret, but she had a way of holding people so that they felt they might miss some prodigy if they went away from her. No one had moved, no one had slipped into casual talk, all the movement there was in the

336

court was of those still making their way out to join the press, and sliding softly round the periphery to find a place where they might see and hear better. There was only the softest rustling of garments and shuffling of feet as Hugh took the scroll. The seal would be immaculate, for it was also the seal of Polesworth's daughter cell at Godric's Ford.

'Have I your leave, Father? It may well be something of importance.'

'By all means, read,' said the abbot.

Hugh broke the seal and unrolled the leaf. He read with brows drawn close in fixed attention. Round the great court men held their breath, or drew it very softly and cautiously. There was tension in the air, after all that had passed.

'Father,' said Hugh, looking up abruptly, 'there is matter here that concerns more than me. Others here have much more to do in this, and deserve and need to know at once what is set down here. It is a marvel! O such weight, I should have had to issue its purport as a public proclamation. With your leave I'll do so here and now, before all this company.'

There was no need to raise his voice, every ear was strained to attend on every word as he read clearly:

' "My lord Sheriff,
It is come to my ears, to my great dismay, that in my own shire I am rumoured to be dead, robbed and done to death for gain. Wherefore I send in haste this present witness that I am not so wronged, but declare myself alive and well, here arrived into the hospitality of the house of sisters at Polesworth. I repent me that lives and honours may have been put in peril mistakenly on my account, some, perhaps, who have been good friends and servants to me. And I ask pardon if I have been the means of disruption and distress to any, unknown to me but through my silence. There shall be amends made.

' "As to my living heretofore, I confess with all humility that I came to doubt whether I had the nun's true vocation before ever I reached my goal, and therefore I have been living retired and serviceable, but have taken no vows as a nun. At Sopwell Priory by Saint Albans a devout woman may live a life of holiness and service short of the veil, through the charity of Prior Geoffrey. Now, being advised I am sought as one dead, I desire to show myself to all those who know me, that no one may go any longer in

337

grief of peril because of me.

' "I entreat you, my lord, make this known to my good brother and all my kin, and send some trustworthy man to bring me safe to Shrewsbury, and I shall rest your lordship's grateful debtor.

Julian Cruce." '

Long before he had reached the end there had begun a stirring, a murmur, an eddy that shook its way like a sudden rising wind through the ranks of the listeners, and then a roused humming like bees in swarm, and suddenly Reginald's stunned silence broke in a bellow of wonder, bewilderment and delight all mingled:

'My sister *living*? She's alive! By God, we have been wildly astray ... '

'Alive!' echoed Nicholas in a dazed whisper. 'Julian is alive ... alive and well ... '

The murmur grew to a throbbing chorus of wonder and excitement, and above it the voice of Abbot Radulfus soared exultantly: 'God's mercies are infinite. Out of the shadow of death he demonstrates his miraculous goodness.'

'We have wronged an honest man!' cried Reginald, as vehement in amends as in accusation. 'He was as truly her man as ever he claimed! Now it comes clear to me – all that he sold he sold for her, surely for her! Only those woman's trinkets that were hers in the world – she had the right to what they would fetch ... '

'I'll bring her from Polesworth myself, along with you,' said Hugh, 'and Adam Heriet shall be hauled out of his prison a free man, and go along with us. Who has a better right?'

The burial of Brother Humilis had become in a moment the resurrection of Julian Cruce, from a mourning into a celebration, from Good Friday to Easter. 'A life taken from us and a life restored,' said Abbot Radulfus, 'is perfect balance, that we may fear neither living nor dying.'

Brother Rhun came from the refectory with his mind full of a strange blend of pleasure and sorrow, and took them with him into the quietness and solitude of the abbey orchards along the Gaye. There would be no one there at this hour of this season if he left the kitchen garden and the fields behind, and went on to the very edge of abbey ground. Beyond, trees came right down to the waterside, overhanging the river. There he halted, and stood gazing downstream, where Fidelis was gone.

The water was still turgid and dark, but the level had subsided slightly, though it still lay in silvery shallows over hollows in the water-meadows on the far shore. Rhun thought of his friend's body being swept down beneath that opaque surface, lost beyond recovery. The mourning had seen a woman supposed dead restored to life, and there was gladness in that, but it did not balance the grief he felt over the loss of Fidelis. He missed him with an aching intensity, though he had said no word of his pain to anyone, nor responded when others found the words he could not find to give expression to sorrow.

He crossed the boundary of abbey land, and threaded a way through the belt of trees, to have a view down the next long reach. And there suddenly he stopped and drew back a pace, for someone else was there before him, some creature even more unhappy than himself. Brother Urien sat huddled in the muddy grass among the bushes at the edge of the water, and stared at the rapid eddies as they coiled and sped by. Downstream from here the dull mirrors of water dappling the far meadows had been fed, since the storm, by two nights of gentler rain, and once filled could not drain away, they could only dry up slowly. Their stillness and tranquillity, reflecting back the pale blue of sky and fleeting white of clouds, made the demonic speed of the main stream seem more than a mere aspect of nature, rather a live, malignant force that gulped down men.

Rhun had made no noise in his approach, yet Urien grew aware that he was not alone, and turned a defensive face, hollow-eyed and hostile.

'You, too?' he said dully. 'Why you? It was I destroyed Fidelis.'

'No, you did no such thing!' protested Rhun, and came out of the bushes to stand beside him. 'You must not say or think it.'

'Fool, you know what I did, why deny it? You know it, you did what you could to undo it,' said Urien bleakly. 'I drove, I threatened – I destroyed Fidelis. If I had the courage I would go after him by the same way, but I have not the courage.'

Rhun sat down beside him in the grass, close but not touching him, and earnestly studied the drawn and embittered face. 'You have not slept,' he said gently.

'How should I sleep, knowing what I know? Not slept, no, nor eaten, either, but it takes a long time to die of not eating.

339

A man can go on water alone for many weeks. And I am neither patient nor brave. There's only one way for me, and that is full confession. Oh, not for absolution, no – for retribution. I have been sitting here preparing for it. Soon I will go and get it over.'

'No!' said Rhun, with sudden, fierce authority. 'That you must not do.' He was not entirely clear himself why this was so urgent a matter, but there was something pricking at his mind, some truth deep within him that he could glimpse only by sidelong flashes, out of the corner of his mind's eye. When he turned to pursue it directly, it vanished. Life and death were both mysteries. A life taken from us and a life restored, Abbot Radulfus had said, is perfect balance. A life taken, and a life restored, almost in the same moment ...

He had it, then. Light opened brilliantly before him, the load on his heart was lifted away. A perfect balance, yes! He sat entranced, so filled and overfilled with enlightenment that all his senses were turned inward to the glow, like cold hands spread blissfully at a bright fire, and he scarcely heard Urien saying savagely: 'That I must and will do. How can I bear this longer alone?'

Rhun stirred and awakened from his trance of bliss. 'You need not be alone,' he said. 'You are not alone now. I am here. Say what you choose to me, but never to any other. Even the confessional might not be secret enough. Then you would indeed have destroyed all that Fidelis was, all that Fidelis did, fouled and muddied it into a byword, a scandal that would cast a shadow on us all, on the Order, most of all on his memory...' He caught himself up there, smiling. 'See how strong is habit! But I do know – I know now what you could tell, and for the sake of Fidelis it must never be told. Surely you see that, as clearly as I now see it. Do no more harm! Bear what you have to bear, and be as silent as Fidelis was.'

Urien's stony face quivered and melted suddenly like wax. He clenched his arms fiercely over his eyes and bowed himself into the long, wet grass, and shook with a terrible storm of dry and silent sobbing. Rhun leaned down and confidently embraced the heaving shoulders. At the touch a great, soft groan passed through Urien's body and ebbed out of him, leaving him limp and still. Once it had been Urien who touched, and Rhun who looked him mildly in the eyes and filled him with rage and shame. Now Rhun touched Urien, laid an arm about him and let it lie quiet there, and all the rage and

340

shame sighed out of him and left him clean.

'Keep the secret. You must, if you loved him.'

'Yes – yes,' said Urien brokenly out of his sheltering arms.

'For his sake…' This time Rhun turned back, smiling, to set right what he had said. 'For her sake!'

'Yes, yes – to the grave. Stay with me!'

'I'm here. When we go, we'll go together. Who knows? Even the harm already done may not be incurable.'

'Can the dead live again?' demanded Urien bitterly.

'If God pleases!' said Rhun, who had his own good reasons for believing in miracles.

Julian Cruce arrived at the abbey of Saint Peter and Saint Paul just in time to attend the Mass for the souls of Brother Humilis and Brother Fidelis, drowned together in the great storm. It was the second day after the burial of Humilis, a fresh, cool day of soft blue sky and soft green earth, the gloss of summer briefly restored. By that time every soul in and around Shrewsbury had heard the story of the woman come back from the dead, and everyone was curious to witness her return. There was a great crowd in the court to watch her ride in, her brother at her side and Hugh Beringar and Adam Heriet following. Within the gates they dismounted, and the horses were led away. Reginald took his sister by the hand, and brought her between the eager watchers to the church door.

Cadfael had had some qualms about this moment, and had taken his stand close beside Nicholas Harnage, where he could pluck at his sleeve in sharp warning should he be startled into some indiscreet utterance. It might have been better to warn him beforehand, and forestall the danger. But on the other hand, it must be gain if the young man never did make the connection, and it seemed worth taking the risk. If he was never forced to consider how formidable a rival was gone before him, and how indelible must be the memory of a devotion unlikely ever to be matched, there would be less of a barrier to his own courtship. If he approached her in innocence he came with strong advantages, having had the trust and affection of Godfrid Marescot, as well as amply proving his concern for the girl herself. There was every ground for kindness there. If he recognised her, and saw in a moment the whole pattern of events, he might be too discouraged ever to approach her at all, for who could follow Humilis and not be diminished? But he might – it was just possible – he might even

341

be large enough to accept all the disadvantages, hold his tongue, and still put his fortune to the test. There was promise in him. Still, Cadfael stood alerted and anxious, his hand hovering at the young man's elbow.

She came through the crowd on her brother's arm, no great beauty, simply a tall girl in a dark cloak and gown, with a grave oval face austerely framed in a white wimple and a dark blue hood. Sister Magdalen and Aline between them had done well by her. The general mourning forbade bright colours, but Aline had carefully avoided providing anything that could recall the rusty monastic black. They were of much the same build, tall and slender, the gown fitted well. The tonsure would take some time to grow out, but hiding the ring of chestnut hair completely and covering half the lofty brow did much to change the shape of the serious face. She had darkened her lashes, which gave a changed value and an iris shade to the clear grey of her eyes. She held up her head and walked slowly past men who had lived side by side with Brother Fidelis for many weeks now, and they saw no one but Julian Cruce, nothing to do with the abbey of Shrewsbury, simply a nine days' wonder from the outer world, interesting now but soon to be forgotten.

Nicholas watched her draw near, and was filled with deep, glowing gratitude, simply that she was alive. Her life might have no place for him, but at least it was hers, all the years he had thought stolen from her by a cruel crime, while here, it seemed, was no crime at all. He could, he would, make the assay, but not yet. Let her have time to know him, for she knew nothing of him yet, and he had no claim on her, unless, perhaps, Hugh Beringar had told her of his part in the search for her. Even that gave him no rights. Those he would have to earn.

But as she drew level with him she turned her head and looked him in the eyes. An instant only, but it was enough.

Cadfael saw him start and quiver, saw him open his lips, perhaps to cry out in the sheer shock of recognition. But he made no sound, after all. Cadfael had gripped him by the arm, but released him at once, for there had been no need. Nicholas turned on him a face of starry brightness, dazzled and dazzling, and said in a rapid whisper: 'Never fret! I am the dumb one now!'

So quick and agile a mind, thought Cadfael approvingly, would not be put off by difficulties. And the girl was still barely twenty-three. They had time. Why should a girl who had had the devoted company of one fine man therefore fail to appreciate the value of a second? I wonder, he thought, what Humilis said to her at Salton that last day? Did he know, in the end, what and who she was? I hope he did. Certainly he knew the candlesticks and the cross, once Hugh described them to him, for of course she took them with her into Hyde, and with Hyde they must have gone to dust. But then, I think, he was in two minds, half afraid his Fidelis had been mixed up in Julian's death, half wondering ... By the end, however the light came, surely he knew the truth.

In his chosen stall next to Brother Urien, Rhun leaned close to whisper: 'Look! Look at the lady! This is she who should have been wife to Brother Humilis.'

Urien looked, but with listless eyes that saw only what they expected to see. He shook his head.

'You know her,' said Rhun. 'Look again!'

He looked again, and he knew her. The load of guilt and grief and penitence lifted from him like a lark rising. He ceased to sing, for his throat was constricted and his tongue mute. He stood lost between knowledge and wonder, the inheritor of her silence.

Julian emerged from the church into the temperate sunlight with the blankness of wonder, endurance and loss still in her face. Watching her from the shadow of the cloister, Nicholas abandoned all thought of approaching her yet. Now that he understood at last the magnitude of what she had done, it became impossible to offer her an ordinary marriage and a customary love. Not yet, not for a long while yet. But he could bide his time, keep touch with her brother, make his way to her by delicate degrees, open his heart to her only when hers was reconciled and at peace.

She had halted, looking about her, withdrawing her hand from her brother's as if she sought someone to whom recognition was due. The palest of smiles touched her face. She came towards Nicholas with hand extended. About the middle finger the little golden serpent twined in a double coil, he caught the tiny glitter of its ruby eyes.

'Sir,' said Julian, in a voice pitched almost childishly high, but very soft and sweet, 'the lord sheriff has told me of all the pains you have been spending for me. I am sorry I have caused

343

you and others so much needless trouble and care. Thanks are poor recompense for so much kindness.'

Her hand lay firm and cool in his. Her smile was still faint and remote, acknowledging nothing of any other identity but that of Julian Cruce. He might have thought she was denying her other self, but for the clear, straight gaze of her grey eyes, opened wide to admit him into a shared knowledge where words were unnecessary. Nothing need ever be said where everything was known and understood.

'Madam,' said Nicholas, 'to see you here alive and well is all the recompense I need or want.'

'But I hope you will come soon to visit us at Lai,' she said. 'It would be a kindness. I should like to make better amends.'

And that was all. He kissed the hand he held, and she turned and went away from him. And surely this was nothing more than paying a due of gratitude, as she paid all her dues, to the last scruple of pain, devotion and love. But she had asked, and she was not one of those women who ask without meaning. And he would go to Lai, soon, yes, very soon. To make do with the touch of her hand and her pale smile and the undoubted trust she had just placed in him, until it was fair and honourable to hope for more.

They sat in Cadfael's workshop in the herb-garden, in the after-dinner hush, Sister Magdalen, Hugh Beringar and Cadfael together. It was all over, the curious all gone home, the brothers innocent of all ill except the loss of two of their number, and two who had been with them only a short time, and somewhat withdrawn from the common view, at that. They would soon become but very dim figures, to be remembered by name in prayer while their faces faded from memory.

'There could still be some awkward questions asked,' admitted Cadfael, 'if anyone went to the trouble to probe deeper, but now no one ever will. The Order can breathe again. There'll be no scandal, no aspersions cast on either Hyde or Shrewsbury, no legatine muck-raking, no ballad-makers running off dirty rhymes about monks and their women, and hawking them round the markets, no bishops bearing down on us with damning visitations, no carping white monks fulminating about the laxity and lechery of the Benedictines ... And no foul blight clinging round that poor girl's name and blackening her for life. Thank God!' he concluded fervently.

He had broached one of his best flasks of wine. He felt they deserved it as much as they needed it.

'Adam was in her confidence throughout,' said Hugh. 'It was he who got her the clothes to turn her into a young man, he who cut her hair, and sold for her the few things she considered her own, to pay her lodging until she presented herself at Hyde. When he said she was dead, he spoke in the bitterness of his heart, for she was indeed dead to the world, by her own choice. And when I brought him from Brigge, he was frantic to get news of her, for he'd given her up for lost after Hyde burned, but when I told him there was a second brother come from Hyde with Godfrid, then he was easy, for he knew who the second must be. He would have died rather than betray her. He knew the ugliness of which men are capable, as well as we.'

'And she, I hope and think,' said Cadfael, 'must know the loyalty and devotion of which one man, at least, was capable. She should, seeing it is the mirror of her own. No, there was no other solution possible but for Fidelis to die and vanish without trace, before Julian could come back to life. But I never thought the chance would come as it did...'

'You took it nimbly enough,' said Hugh.

'It was then or never. It would have come out else. Madog would never have said anything, but she had stopped caring when Humilis died.' He had had her in his arms, herself half-dead, on that ride to Godric's Ford to commit her to Sister Magdalen's care, the russet tonsure wet and draggled on his shoulder, the pale, soiled face stricken into ice, the grey eyes wide open, seeing nothing. 'It was as much as we could do to get him out of her arms. Without Aline we should have been lost. I almost feared we might lose the girl as well as the man. But Sister Magdalen is a powerful physician.'

'That letter I composed for her,' said Sister Magdalen, looking back on it with a critical but satisfied eye, 'was the hardest ever I had to write. And not a lie from start to finish! Not one in the whole of it. A little mild deception, but no lies. That was important, you understand. Do you know why she chose to be mute? Well, there is the matter of her voice, of course, a woman's if ever there was. The face – it's a good face, clear and strong and delicate, one that could as well belong to a boy as to a girl, but not the voice. But beyond that,' said Sister Magdalen, 'she had two good reasons for being dumb. First,

345

she was resolute she would never ask anything of him, never make any woman's appeal, for she held he owed her nothing, no privilege, no consideration. What she got of him she had to earn. And second, she was absolute she would never lie to him. Who cannot speak cannot plead or cajole, and cannot lie.'

'So he owed her nothing, and she owed him all,' said Hugh, shaking his head over the unfathomable strangeness of women.

'Ah, but she also had her due,' said Cadfael. 'What she wanted and held to be hers she took, the whole of it, to the end, to the last moment. His company, the care of him, the secrets of his body, as intimate as ever was marriage – his love, far beyond the common claims of marriage. No use any man telling her she was free, when she *knew* she was a wife. I wonder is she free even now.'

'Not yet, but she will be,' Sister Magdalen assured them. 'She has too much courage to give over living. And if that young man who fancies her has courage enough not to give over loving, he may do very well in the end. He starts with a strong advantage, having loved the same idol. Besides,' she added, viewing a future that held a certain promise even for some who felt just now that they had only a past, 'I doubt if that household of her brother's, with a wife in possession, and three children, not to speak of another on the way – no, I doubt if an unwed sister's part in Lai will have much lasting attraction for a woman like Julian Cruce.'

The half-hour of rest after dinner had passed, the brothers stirred again to their work, and so did Cadfael, parting from his friends at the turn of the box hedge. Sister Magdalen and her two stout woodsmen would be off back to Godric's Ford by the westward track, and Hugh was heading thankfully for home. Cadfael passed through the herb-garden into the small plot where he had a couple of apple trees and a pear tree of his own growing, just old enough to crop. He surveyed the scene with deep content. Everything was greening afresh where it had been pale as straw. The Meole Brook had still a few visible shoals, but was no longer a mere sad, sluggish network of rivulets struggling through pebble and sand. September was again September, mellowed and fruitful after the summer heat and drought. Much of the abundant weight of fruit had fallen unplumped by reason of the dryness, but even so there would still be harvest enough for thanksgiving. After every extreme the seasons righted themselves, and won back the half at least of what was lost. So might the seasons of men right themselves, with a little help by way of rain from heaven.

*   *   *

O God, who has consecrated the state of Matrimony to such an excellent mystery ... Look mercifully upon these thy servants.
from 'The form of Solemnization of Matrimony'
in *The Book of Common Prayer*

The Raven in the Foregate

Chapter One

BBOT RADULFUS came to chapter, on this first day of December, with a preoccupied and frowning face, and made short work of the various trivialities brought up by his obedientiaries. Though a man of few words himself, he was disposed, as a rule, to allow plenty of scope to those who were rambling and loquacious about their requests and suggestions, but on this day, plainly, he had more urgent matters on his mind.

'I must tell you,' he said, when he had swept the last trifle satisfactorily into its place, 'that I shall be leaving you for some days to the care of Father Prior, to whom, I expect and require, you shall be as obedient and helpful as you are to me. I am summoned to a council to be held at Westminster on the seventh day of this month, by the Holy Father's legate, Henry of Blois, bishop of Winchester. I shall return as soon as I can, but in my absence I desire you will make your prayers for a spirit of wisdom and reconciliation in this meeting of prelates, for the sake of the peace of this land.'

His voice was dry and calm to the point of resignation. For the past four years there had been precious little inclination to reconciliation in England between the warring rivals for the crown, and no very considerable wisdom shown on either side. But it was the business of the Church to continue to strive, and if possible to hope, even when the affairs of the land seemed to have reverted to the very same point where the civil war had begun, to repeat the whole unprofitable cycle all over again.

'I am well aware there are matters outstanding here,' said the abbot, 'which equally require our attention, but they must wait for my return. In particular there is the question of a successor to Father Adam, lately vicar of this parish of Holy Cross, whose loss we are still lamenting. The advowson rests with this house. Father Adam has been for many years a much valued associate with us here in the worship of God and the cure of souls, and his replacement is a matter for both thought and prayer. Until my return, Father Prior will direct the parish services as he thinks fit, and all of you will be at his bidding.'

He swept one long, dark glance round the chapter house, accepted the general silence as understanding and consent, and rose.

'This chapter is concluded.'

'Well, at least if he leaves tomorrow he has good weather for the ride,' said Hugh Beringar, looking out from the open door of Brother Cadfael's workshop in the herb garden over grass still green, and a few surviving roses, grown tall and spindly by now but still budding bravely. December of this year of Our Lord 1141 had come in with soft-stepping care, gentle winds and lightly veiled skies, treading on tiptoe. 'Like all those shifting souls who turned to the Empress when she was in her glory,' said Hugh, grinning, 'and are now put to it to keep well out of sight while they turn again. There must be a good many holding their breath and making themselves small just now.'

'Bad luck for his reverence the papal legate,' said Cadfael, 'who cannot make himself small or go unregarded, whatever he does. His turning has to be done in broad daylight, with every eye on him. And twice in one year is too much to ask of any man.'

'Ah, but in the name of the Church, Cadfael, in the name of the Church! It's not the man who turns, it's the representative of Pope and Church, who must preserve the infallibility of both at all costs.'

Twice in one year, indeed, had Henry of Blois summoned his bishops and abbots to a legatine council, once in Winchester on the seventh of April to justify his endorsement of the Empress Maud as ruler, when she was in the ascendant and had her rival King Stephen securely in prison in Bristol, and now at Westminster on the seventh of December to justify his swing back to Stephen, now that the King was free again, and the city of London had put a decisive end to Maud's bid to establish herself in the capital, and get her hands at last on the crown.

'If his head is not going round by now, it should be,' said Cadfael, shaking his own grizzled brown tonsure in mingled admiration and deprecation. 'How many spins does this make? First he swore allegiance to the lady, when her father died without a male heir, then he accepted his brother Stephen's seizure of power in her absence, thirdly, when Stephen's star is darkened he makes his peace – a peace of sorts, at any rate! – with the lady, and justifies it by saying that Stephen has flouted and aggrieved Holy Church … Now must he turn the same argument about, and accuse the Empress, or has he something new in his scrip?'

'What is there new to be said?' asked Hugh, shrugging. 'No, he'll wring the last drop from his stewardship of Holy Church, and make the best of it that every soul there will have heard it all before, no longer ago than last April. And it will convince Stephen no more than it did Maud, but he'll let it pass with only a mild snarl or two, since he can no more afford to reject the backing of Henry of Blois than could Maud in her day. And the bishop will grit his teeth and stare his clerics in the eyes, and swallow his gall with a brazen face.'

'It may well be the last time he has to turn about-face,' said Cadfael, feeding his brazier with a few judiciously placed turves, to keep it burning with a slow and tempered heat. 'She has thrown away what's likely to be her only chance.'

A strange woman she had proved, King Henry's royal daughter. Married in childhood to the Holy Roman Emperor Henry V, she had so firmly ingratiated herself with her husband's people in Germany that when she was recalled to England, after his death, the populace had risen in consternation and grief to plead with her to stay. Yet here at home, when fate threw her enemy into her hands and held the crown suspended over her head, she had behaved with such vengeful arrogance, and exacted such penalties for past affronts, that the men of her capital city had risen just as indignantly, not to appeal to her to remain, but to drive her out and put a violent end to her hopes of ever becoming their ruler. And it was common knowledge that though she could turn even upon her own best allies with venom, yet she could also retain the love and loyalty of the best of the baronage. There was not a man of the first rank on Stephen's side to match the quality of her half-brother, Earl Robert of Gloucester, or her champion and reputed lover, Brian FitzCount, her east-ernmost paladin in his fortress at Wallingford. But it would take more than a couple of heroes to redeem her cause now. She had been forced to surrender her royal prisoner in exchange for her half-brother, without whom she could not hope to achieve anything. And here was England back to the beginning, with all to do again. For if she could not win, neither could she give up.

'From here where I stand now,' said Cadfael, pondering, 'these things seem strangely distant and unreal. If I had not been forty years in the world and among the armies myself, I doubt if I could believe in the times we live in but as a disturbed dream.'

'They are not so to Abbot Radulfus,' said Hugh with unwonted gravity. He turned his back upon the mild, moist prospect of the garden, sinking gently into its winter sleep, and sat down on the wooden bench against the timber wall. The small glow of the brazier, damped under the turf, burned on the bold, slender bones of his cheeks and jaw and brows, conjuring them out of deep shadows, and sparkling briefly in his black eyes before the lids and dark lashes quenched the sparks. 'That man would make a better adviser to kings than most that cluster round Stephen now he's free again. But he would not tell them what they want to hear, and they'd all stop their ears.'

'What's the news of King Stephen now? How has he borne this year of captivity? Is he likely to come out of it fighting, or has it dimmed his ardour? What is he likely to do next?'

'That I may be better able to answer after Christmas,' said Hugh. 'They say he's in good health. But she put him in chains, and that even he is not likely to forgive too readily. He's come out leaner and hungrier than he went in, and a gnaw in the belly may well serve to concentrate the mind. He was ever a man to begin a campaign or siege all fire the first day, weary of it if he got no gain by the third, and go off after another prey by the fifth. Maybe now he's learned to keep an unwavering eye fixed on one target until he fetches it down. Sometimes I wonder why we follow him, and never look round, then I see him roaring into personal battle as he did at Lincoln, and I know the reason well enough. Even when he has the woman as good as in his hands, as when she first landed at Arundel, and gives her an escort to her brother's fortress instead of having the good sense to seize her, I curse him for a fool, but I love

354

him while I'm cursing him. What monumental folly of mistaken chivalry he'll commit next, only God knows. But I'll welcome the chance to see him again, and try to guess at his mind. For I'm bidden forth, Cadfael, like the abbot. King Stephen means to keep Christmas at Canterbury this year, and put on his crown again, for all to see which of two heads is the anointed monarch here. And he's called all his sheriffs to attend him and render account of their shires. Me among the rest, seeing we have here no properly appointed sheriff to render account.'

He looked up with a dark, sidelong smile into Cadfael's attentive and thoughtful face. 'A very sound move. He needs to know what measure of loyalty he has to rely on, after a year in prison, or close on a year. But there's no denying it may bring me a fall.'

For Cadfael it was a new and jolting thought. Hugh had stepped into the office of sheriff perforce, when his superior, Gilbert Prestcote, had died of his battle wounds and the act of a desperate man, at a time when the King was already a prisoner in Bristol castle, with no power to appoint or to demote any officer in any shire. And Hugh had served him and maintained his peace here without authority, and deserved well of him. But now that he was free to make and break again, would Stephen confirm so young and so minor a nobleman in office, or use the appointment to flatter and bind to himself some baron of the march?

'Folly!' said Cadfael firmly. 'The man is a fool only towards himself. He made you deputy to his man out of nowhere, when he saw your mettle. What does Aline say of it?'

Hugh could not hear his wife's name spoken without a wild, warm softening of his sharp, subtle face, nor could Cadfael speak it without relaxing every solemnity into a smile. He had witnessed their courtship and their marriage, and was godfather to their son, two years old this coming Christmastide. Aline's girlish, flaxen gentleness had grown into a golden, matronly calm to which they both turned in every need.

'Aline says that she has no great confidence in the gratitude of princes, but that Stephen has the right to choose his own officers, wisely or foolishly.'

'And you?' said Cadfael.

'Why, if he gives me his countenance and writ I'll go on keeping all his borders for him, and if not, then I'll go back to

Maesbury and keep the north, at least, against Chester, if the earl tries again to enlarge his palatinate. And Stephen's man must take charge of west, east and south. And you, old friend, must pay a visit or two over Christmas, while I'm away, and keep Aline company.'

'Of all of us,' said Cadfael piously, 'that makes me the best blessed at this coming feast. I'll pray good joy to my abbot in his mission, and to you in yours. My joy is assured.'

They had buried old Father Adam, seventeen years vicar of the parish of Holy Cross in the Foregate of Shrewsbury, only one week before Abbot Radulfus was summoned to the legatine council at Westminster. The advowson of the living was vested in the abbey, and the great church of Saint Peter and Saint Paul was equally the parish church of Holy Cross, the nave open to the people living here outside the town gates, in this growing suburb which almost considered itself a borough like the borough within the walls. The reeve of the Foregate, Erwald the wheelwright, publicly if unofficially used the title of provost, and abbey, church and town humoured his harmless flourish, for the Monks' Foregate was a relatively law-abiding, respectable district, and gave barely any trouble to the properly constituted authorities of the town itself. An occasional squabble between seculars and abbey, a brief tangle between the high-spirited young of Foregate and town, what was there in that to worry anyone beyond the day?

Father Adam had been there so long that all the young had grown up under his easy-going shadow, and all the old had known him as one of themselves, hardly set apart by his office. He had lived alone in his little house up a narrow alley opposite the church, looking after himself, with only an elderly freeman to take care of his glebe and his strip fields in the country part of the parish, for Holy Cross spread wide outside the main street of the Foregate. A big parish, a population made up equally of the craftsmen and merchants of the suburb and the cottars and villagers in the countryside. It was a matter of importance to them all what manner of priest they got in succession to Father Adam. The old man himself, from whatever gentle purgatory now contained him, would be keeping an anxious eye on his own.

Abbot Radulfus had presided at Adam's funeral, and Prior Robert at his most dignified and elegiac, tall and silvery and consciously patrician, had pronounced his eulogy, perhaps with a slight touch of condescension, for Adam had been barely literate, and a man of humble origins and no pretensions. But it was Cynric, the verger of Holy Cross, who had been with the priest through most of his years of office, who had best spoken his epitaph, and that privately, over the trimming of the candles on the parish altar, to Brother Cadfael, who had halted in passing through to say a word of personal sympathy to the man who would surely miss the dead most deeply.

'A sad, kind man,' said Cynric, his deep-sunk eyes narrowed on the wick he was trimming, and his low voice as grainy and grudging as ever, 'a tired man, with a soft spot for sinners.'

It was rare enough for Cynric to utter thirteen words together, except by way of the responses learned by heart in the holy office. Thirteen words of his own had the force of prophecy. A sad man, because he had been listening to and bearing with the perpetual failures of humankind for seventeen years, a tired man because endless consoling and chiding and forgiving takes it out of any man by the time he's sixty, especially one with neither malice nor anger in his own make-up. A kind man, because he had somehow managed to preserve compassion and hope even against the tide of human fallibility. Yes, Cynric had known him better than anyone. He had absorbed, in the years of his service, something of the same qualities without the authority.

'You'll feel the want of him,' said Cadfael. 'So shall we all.'

'He'll not be far,' said Cynric, and snipped the dead wick with thumb and finger.

The verger was a man past fifty, but there was no knowing by how many years, for he himself did not know the exact year of his birth, though he knew the day and month. He was dark of hair and eyes, and sallow-skinned, and went in a rusty black gown somewhat frayed at the hems from long years of wear, and he lived in the tiny upper room over the north porch where Father Adam robed and kept his church furnishings. A taciturn, grave, durable man, built upon long, strong bones, but very meagre in flesh, as much by reason of the hermit's forgetfulness as any want of means. He came of a country family of free folk, and had a brother somewhere north of the town with a grown family, and very occasionally at feast or holiday he visited there, but that happened very rarely now, his whole life being centred here in the great church and the small upper room. So spare, silent and dark a form and face might

357

have aroused awe and avoidance, but did not, since what the darkness and the silence covered was known to all, even the mischievous boys of the Foregate, and inspired no fear or revulsion at all. A good man, with his own preferences and peculiarities, and certainly no talker, but if you needed him, he was there, and like his master, would not send you away empty.

Those who could not be easy with his mute company at least respected him, and those who could included the most innocent and guileless. Children and dogs would sit companionably on the steps of the north porch with him in summer weather, and do all the talking necessary to such a friendship, after their own fashion, while he listened. Many a mother in the Foregate, content to see her young consorting so familiarly with a respectable churchman, had wondered why Cynric had never married and had children of his own, since plainly he had an affinity for them. It could not be because of his office of verger, for there were still plenty of married priests scattered through the parishes of the shire, and no one thought any wrong of them. The new order of clerics without women was only just beginning to make headway here, no one, not even bishops, had yet begun to look sidewise at those of the old school who did not conform. Monks were monks, and had made their choice, but surely the secular clergy could still be secular without reproach.

'He had no living kin?' asked Cadfael. For of all men remaining behind, Cynric would know.

'None.'

'He was newly priest here,' said Cadfael, 'when I came first from Woodstock with Abbot Heribert – Prior Heribert he was then, for Abbot Godefrid was still alive. You came, as I remember, a year or two later. You're a younger man than I. You and I between us could put together a history of cowl and cassock here in the Foregate all this long while. It would make a very handsome memorial to Father Adam. No falling out, no falling off. He had his everlasting penitents, but that was his glory, that they always came back. They could not do without him. And he kept his thread that drew them back, whether they would or no.'

'So he did,' said Cynric, and clipped the last blackened wick with a snap of his finger-nails, and straightened the candle-sticks on the parish altar, standing back a pace with narrowed lids to check that they stood correct as soldiers on guard.

His throat creaked, forcing unwilling chords to flex, when he used more words. The strings protested now. 'Is there a man in mind?'

'No,' said Cadfael, 'or Father Abbot would have told you. He goes south by forced rides tomorrow to the legate's council in Westminster, and this presentation must wait his return, but he's promised haste. He knows the need. You may well get Brother Jerome now and again until the abbot returns, but never doubt that Radulfus has the parish very much at heart.'

To that Cynric nodded silent assent, for the relations between cloister and parish here had been harmonious under three abbots in succession, all the years of Father Adam's incumbency, whereas in some churches thus shared, as everyone knew, there was constant friction, the monastics grudging the commonalty room in their enclave and entry to their privileged buildings, and the secular priest putting up a fight for his rights to avoid being elbowed out. Not so here. Perhaps it was the modest goodness of Father Adam that had done the lion's share in keeping the peace, and making the relationship easy.

'He liked a sup now and again,' said Cadfael meditatively. 'I still have some of a wine he liked – distilled with herbs, good for the blood and heart. Come and take a cup with me in the garden, some afternoon, Cynric, and we'll drink to him.'

'I will so,' said Cynric, and relaxed for one moment into his rare, indulgent smile, the same by which children and dogs found him out and approached him with confidence.

They crossed the chill tiles of the nave together, and Cynric went out by the north porch, and up to his little dark room above. Cadfael looked after him until the door had closed between. All these years they had been within arm's reach of each other, and on the best of terms, yet never familiar. Who had ever been familiar with Cynric? Since the ties with his mother loosened, and he turned his back on home, whatever and wherever that home had been, perhaps only Father Adam had truly drawn near to him. Two solitaries together make a very special matched pair, two in one. Yes, of all the mourners for Father Adam, and they must be many, Cynric must now be the most painfully bereaved.

They had lighted the fire in the warming room for the first time when December came in, and in the relaxed half-hour between Collations and Compline, when tongues were allowed considerable licence, there was far more talk and speculation about the parish cure than about the legate's council in Westminster, to which Abbot Radulfus had just set out. Prior Robert had withdrawn into the abbot's lodging, as representing that dignitary in his absence, which gave further freedom to the talkative, but his chaplain and shadow, Brother Jerome, in his turn took upon himself the duty and privilege of representing the prior, and Brother Richard, the sub-prior, was too easy-going, not to say indolent, to assert himself with any vigour.

A meagre man in the flesh was Brother Jerome, but he made up for it in zeal, though there were those who found that zeal too narrowly channelled, and somewhat dehydrated of the milk of human tolerance. Which rendered it understandable that he should consider Father Adam to have been rather over-supplied with that commodity.

'Certainly a man of virtue himself,' said Jerome, 'I would not for a moment take that from him, we all know he served devotedly. But somewhat loose upon others who did offend. His discipline was too slack, and his penances too light and too indulgently given. Who spares the sinner condones the sin.'

'There's been good order and neighbourliness in his parish the length of his life here,' said Brother Ambrose the almoner, whose office brought him into contact with the poorest of the poor throughout the Foregate. 'I know how they speak of him. He left a cure ready and fit for another to step into, with the general goodwill open to whoever comes, because the general goodwill was there to speed the one departed.'

'Children will always be glad of a weak master who never uses the rod,' said Jerome sagely, 'and a rascal of a judge who lets them off lightly. But the payment that falls due later will be fearful. Better they should be brought up harshly against the wages of sin now, and lay up safety for their souls hereafter.'

Brother Paul, master of the novices and the boys, who very rarely laid a hand upon his pupils, and certainly only when they had well deserved it, smiled and held his peace.

'In too much mercy is too little kindness,' pronounced Jerome, conscious of his own eloquence, and mindful of his reputation as a preacher. 'The Rule itself decrees that where the child offends he must be beaten, and these folk of the Foregate, what are they but children?'

They were called by the bell to Compline at that moment, but in any case it was unlikely that any of them would have troubled to argue with Jerome, whose much noise and small effect hardly challenged notice. No doubt he would preach stern sermons at the parish Mass, on the two days allotted to him, but there would be very few of the regular attenders there to listen to him, and even those who did attend would let his homily in at one ear and out at the other, knowing his office here could last but a few days.

For all that, Cadfael went up to his bed that night very thoughtful, and though he heard a few whispered exchanges in the dortoir, himself kept silence, mindful of the rule that the words of Compline, the completion, the perfecting of the day's worship, should be the last words uttered before sleep, that the mind should not be distracted from the '*Opus Dei*'. Nor was it. For the words lingered with him between sleep and waking, the same words over and over, faintly returning. By chance the psalm was the sixth. He took it with him into slumber.

'*Domine, ne in furore* – O Lord, rebuke me not in thine anger, neither chasten me in thy displeasure ... Have mercy upon me, O Lord, for I am weak ...'

Chapter Two

N THE tenth day of December, Abbot Radulfus returned, riding in at the gatehouse just as the daylight was fading, and the brethren were within at Vespers. Thus the porter was the only witness of his arrival, and of the embellished entourage he brought back with him, and not until the next day at chapter did the brothers hear all that he had to tell, or as much of it as concerned the abbey itself. But Brother Porter, the soul of discretion when required, could also be the best-informed gossip in the enclave to his special friends, and Cadfael learned something of what was toward that same night, in one of the carrels in the cloister, immediately after Vespers.

'He's brought back with him a priest, a fine tall fellow – not above thirty-five years or so I'd guess him to be. He's bedded now in the guest hall, they rode hard today to get home before dark. Not a word has Father Abbot said to me, beyond giving me my orders to let Brother Denis know he has a guest for the night, and to take care of the other two. For there's a woman come with the priest, a decent soul going grey and very modestly conducted, that I take to be some sort of aunt or housekeeper to the priest, for I was bidden get one of the lay grooms to show her the way to Father Adam's cottage, and that I did. And not the woman alone, there's another young servant lad with her, that waits on the pair of them and does their errands. A widow and her son they could be, in the priest's service. Off he goes with only Brother Vitalis, as always, and comes back with three more, and two extra horses. The young lad brought the woman pillion behind him. And what do you make of all that?'

'Why, there's but one way of it,' said Cadfael, after giving the matter serious thought. 'The lord abbot has brought back a priest for Holy Cross from the southlands, and his household with him. The man himself is made comfortable in the guest hall overnight, while his domestics go to open up the empty house and get a good fire going for him, and food in store, and the place warmed and ready. And tomorrow at chapter, no doubt, we shall hear how the abbot came by him, and which of all the bishops gathered there recommended him to the benefice.'

'It's what I myself was thinking,' agreed the porter, 'though it would have been more to the general mind, I fancy, if a local man had been advanced to the vacancy. Still, it's what a man is that counts, not his name nor where he came from. No doubt the lord abbot knows his business best.' And he went off briskly, probably to whisper the news into one or two other discreet ears before Compline. Certainly several of the brothers came to the next morning's chapter already forewarned and expectant, alertly waiting for the new man to be first heralded, and then produced for inspection. For though it was very unlikely that anyone would raise objections to a man chosen by Abbot Radulfus, yet the whole chapter had rights in the presentation to the living, and Radulfus was not the man to infringe its privileges.

'I have made all possible haste to return to you,' the abbot began, when the normal routine matters had been quickly dealt with. 'In brief, I must report to you of the legatine council held at Westminster, that the discussions and decisions there have brought the Church back into full allegiance to King Stephen. The King himself was present to confirm the establishment of this relationship, and the legate to declare him blessed by the countenance of the Apostolic See, and the followers of the Empress, if they remain recalcitrant, as enemies of King and Church. There is no need,' said the abbot, somewhat drily, 'to go into further detail here.'

None, thought Cadfael, attentive in his chosen stall, conveniently sheltered behind a pillar in case he nodded off when material matters became tiresome. No need for us to hear the spiral manipulations by which the legate extricated himself from all his difficulties. But beyond doubt, Hugh would get a full account of all.

'What does more nearly concern this house,' said Radulfus, 'is certain conference I had with Bishop Henry of Winchester in private. Knowing of the cure left vacant here at Holy Cross, he recommended to me a priest of his own following, at present waiting for a benefice. I have talked with the man in question, and found him in every way able, scholarly and fitted for advancement. His personal life is austere and simple, his scholarship I have myself tested.'

It was a point powerful enough, by contrast with Father Adam's want of learning, though it would count for more with the brothers here than with the folk of the Foregate.

'Father Ailnoth is thirty-six years of age,' said the abbot, 'and comes rather late to a parish by reason of having served as a clerk to Bishop Henry, loyally and efficiently, for four years, and the bishop desires to reward his diligence now by seeing him settled in a cure. For my part, I am satisfied that he is both suitable and deserving. But if you will bear with me so far, brothers, I will have him called in to give account of himself, and answer whatever you may wish to ask him.'

A stir of interest, consent and curiosity went round the chapter house, and Prior Robert, surveying the heads nodding in anticipation and obeying the abbot's glance, went out to summon the candidate.

Ailnoth, thought Cadfael, a Saxon name, and reported as a fine, tall fellow. Well, better than some Norman hanger-on from the fringes of the court. And he formed a mental picture of a big young man with fresh, ruddy skin and fair hair, but dismissed it in a breath when Father Ailnoth came in on Prior Robert's heels, and took his stand with composed grace in the middle of the chapter house, where he could be seen by all.

He was indeed a fine, tall fellow, wide-shouldered, muscular, fluent and rapid in gait, erect and very still when he had taken his stand. And a very comely man, too, in his own fashion, but so far from Saxon pallor that he was blacker of hair and eye than Hugh Beringar himself. He had a long, patrician countenance, olive-skinned and with no warmer flush of red in his well-shaven cheeks. The black hair that ringed his tonsure was straight as wire, and thick, and clipped with such precision that it looked almost as if it had been applied with black paint. He made an austere obeisance to the abbot, folded his hands, which were large and powerful, at the waist of his black gown, and waited to be catechized.

'I present to this assembly Father Ailnoth,' said Radulfus,

'whom I propose we should prefer to the cure of Holy Cross. Examine him of his own wishes in this matter, his attainments and his past service, and he will answer freely.'

And freely indeed he did answer, launched by a first gracious word of welcome from Prior Robert, who clearly found his appearance pleasing. He answered questions briefly and fluently, like one who never has had and never expects to have any lack of confidence or any time to waste, and his voice, pitched a shade higher than Cadfael had expected from so big a man and so broad a chest, rang with an assured authority. He accounted for himself forcefully, declared his intent to pursue his duty with energy and integrity, and awaited the verdict upon himself with steely confidence. He had excellent Latin, some Greek, and was versed in accountancy, which promised well for his church management. His acceptance was assured.

'If I may make one request, Father Abbot,' he said finally, 'I should be greatly thankful if you could find some work here among your lay servants for the young man who has travelled here with me. He is the nephew and only kin of my housekeeper, the widow Hammet, and she entreated me to let him come here with her and find some employment locally. He is landless and without fortune. My lord abbot, you have seen that he is healthy and sturdy and not afraid of hard work, and he has been willing and serviceable to us all on the journey. He has, I believe, some inclination to the cloistered life, though as yet he is undecided. If you could give him work for a while it might settle his mind.'

'Ah, yes, the young man Benet,' said the abbot. 'He seems a well-conditioned youth, I agree. Certainly he may come, upon probation, no doubt work can be found for him. There must be a deal of things to be done about the grange court, or in the gardens ...'

'Indeed there is, Father,' Cadfael spoke up heartily. 'I could make good use of a younger pair of hands, there's much of the rough digging for the winter still to be done, some of the ground in the kitchen garden has only now been cleared. And the pruning in the orchard – heavy work. With the winter coming on, short days, and Brother Oswin gone to Saint Giles, to the hospice, I shall be needing a helper. I should shortly have been asking for another brother to come and work with me, as is usual, though through the summer I've managed well enough.'

'True! And some of the ploughing in the Gaye remains to be

done, and around Christmas, or soon after, the lambing will begin in the hill granges, if the young man is no longer needed here. Yes, by all means send Benet to us. Should he later find other employment more to his advantage, he may take it with our goodwill. In the meantime hard labour here for us will do him no harm.'

'I will tell him so,' said Ailnoth, 'and he will be as thankful to you as I am. His aunt would have been sad at leaving him behind, seeing he is the only younger kinsman she has, to be helpful to her. Shall I send him here today?'

'Do so, and tell him he may ask at the gatehouse for Brother Cadfael. Leave us now to confer, Father,' said the abbot, 'but wait in the cloister, and Father Prior will bring you word of our decision.'

Ailnoth bowed his head with measured reverence, withdrew a respectful pace or two backwards from the abbot's presence, and strode out of the chapter house, his black, handsome head erect and confident. His gown swung like half-spread wings to the vigour of his stride. He was already sure, as was everyone present, that the cure of Holy Cross was his.

'It went much as you have probably supposed,' said Abbot Radulfus, somewhat later in the day, in the parlour of his own lodging, with a modest fire burning on the chimney stone, and Hugh Beringar seated opposite him across the glow. The abbot's face was still a little drawn and grey with tiredness, his deep-set eyes a little hollow. The two knew each other very well by this time, and had grown accustomed to sharing with complete confidence, for the sake of order and England, whatever they gathered of events and tendencies, without ever questioning whether they shared the same opinions. Their disciplines were separate and very different, but their acceptance of service was one, and mutually recognized.

'The bishop had little choice,' said Hugh simply. 'Virtually none, now the King is again free, and the Empress again driven into the west, with little foothold in the rest of England. I would not have wished myself in his shoes, nor do I know how I would have handled his difficulties. Let him who is certain of his own valour cast blame, I cannot.'

'Nor I. But for all that can be said, the spectacle is not edifying. There are, after all, some who have never wavered, whether fortune favoured or flayed them. But it is truth that the legate had received the Pope's letter, which he read out to us in conference, reproving him for not enforcing the release of the King, and urging him to insist upon it above all else. And who dare wonder if he made the most of it? And besides, the King came there himself. He entered the hall and made formal complaint against all those who had sworn fealty to him, and then suffered him to lie in prison, and come near to slaying him.'

'But then sat back and let his brother use his eloquence to worm his way out of the reproach,' said Hugh, and smiled. 'He has the advantage of his cousin and rival, he knows when to mellow and forget. She neither forgets nor forgives.'

'Well, true. But it was not a happy thing to hear. Bishop Henry made his defence, frankly owning he had had no choice open to him but to accept the fortune as it fell, and receive the Empress. He said he had done what seemed the best and only thing, but that she had broken all her pledges, outraged all her subjects, and made war against his own life. And to conclude, he pledged the Church again to King Stephen, and urged all men of consequence and goodwill to serve him. He took some credit,' said Abbot Radulfus with sad deliberation, 'for the liberation of the King to himself. And outlawed from the Church all those who continued to oppose him.'

'And mentioned the Empress, or so I've heard,' said Hugh equally drily, 'as the countess of Anjou.' It was a title the Empress detested, as belittling both her birth and her rank by her first marriage, a king's daughter and the widow of an emperor, now reduced to a title borrowed from her none-too-loved and none-too-loving second husband, Geoffrey of Anjou, her inferior in every particular but talent, common sense and efficiency. All he had ever done for Maud was give her a son. Of the love she bore to the boy Henry there was no doubt at all.

'No one raised a voice against what was said,' the abbot mentioned almost absently. 'Except an envoy from the lady, who fared no better than the one who spoke, last time, for King Stephen's queen. Though this one, at least, was not set upon by assassins in the street.'*

Inevitably those two legatine councils, one in April, one in December, had been exact and chilling mirror-images, fortune turning her face now to one faction, now to the other, and taking back with the left hand what she had given with the

* *The Pilgrim of Hate.*

right. There might yet be as many further reversals before ever there was an end in sight.

'We are back where we began,' said the abbot, 'and nothing to show for months of misery. And what will the King do now?'

'That I shall hope to find out during the Christmas feast,' said Hugh, rising to take his leave. 'For I'm summoned to my lord, Father, like you. King Stephen wants all his sheriffs about him at his court at Canterbury, where he keeps the feast, to render account of our stewardships. Me among them, as his sheriff here for want of a better. What he'll do with his freedom remains to be seen. They say he's in good health and resolute spirits, if that means anything. As for what he means to do with me – well, that, no doubt, I shall discover, in due time.'

'My son, I trust he'll have the good sense to leave well alone. For here,' said Radulfus, 'we have at least preserved what good we can, and by the present measure in this unhappy realm, it *is* well with this shire. But I doubt whatever he does else can only mean more fighting and more wretchedness for England. And you and I can do nothing to prevent or better it.'

'Well, if we cannot give England peace,' said Hugh, smiling somewhat wryly, 'at least let's see what you and I can do between us for Shrewsbury.'

After dinner in the refectory Brother Cadfael made his way across the great court, rounded the thick, dark mass of the box hedge – grown straggly now, he noted, and ripe for a final clipping before growth ceased in the cold – and entered the moist flower gardens, where leggy roses balanced at a man's height on their thin, leafless stems, and still glowed with invincible light and life. Beyond lay his herb garden, walled and silent, all its small, square beds already falling asleep, naked spears of mint left standing stiff as wire, cushions of thyme flattened to the ground, crouching to protect their remaining leaves, yet over all a faint surviving fragrance of the summer's spices. Partly a memory, perhaps, partly drifting out from the open door of his workshop, where bunches of dried herbs swung from the eaves and the beams within, but surely, also, still emanating from these drowsy minor manifestations of God, grown old and tired now only to grow young and vigorous again with the spring. Green phoenixes every one, visible proof, if any were needed, of perpetual life.

Within the wall it was mild and still, a sanctuary within a

sanctuary. Cadfael sat down on the bench in his workshop, facing the open door, and composed himself at ease to employ his half-hour of permitted repose in meditation rather than sleep. The morning had provided plenty of food for thought, and he did his best thinking alone here in his own small kingdom.

So that, he thought, is the new priest of Holy Cross. Now why did Bishop Henry take the trouble to bestow on us one of his own household clerks, and one he valued, at that? One who either was born with or has acquired by reverent imitation what I take to be his overlord's notable qualities? Is it possible that two masterful, confident, proud men had become one too many for comfort, and Henry was glad to part with him? Or is the legate, after the humiliation of publicly eating his own words twice in one year, and the damage that may well have done to his prestige – after all that, has he been taking this opportunity of courting all his bishops and abbots by taking a fatherly interest in all their wants and needs? Flattering them by his attentions to prop up what might be stumbling allegiance? That is also possible, and he might be willing to sacrifice even a valued clerk to feel certain of a man like Radulfus. But one thing is sure, Cadfael concluded firmly, our abbot would not have been a party to such an appointment if he had not been convinced he was getting a man fit for the work.

He had closed his eyes, to think the better, and braced his back comfortably against the timber wall, sandalled feet crossed before him, hands folded in the sleeves of his habit, so still that to the young man approaching along the gravel path he seemed asleep. Others, unused to such complete stillness in a waking man, had sometimes made that mistake with Brother Cadfael. Cadfael heard the footsteps, wary and soft as they were. Not a brother, and the lay servants were few in number, and seldom had occasion to come here. Nor would they approach so cautiously if they had some errand here. Not sandals, these, but old, well-worn shoes, and their wearer imagined they trod silently, and indeed they came close to it, if Cadfael had not had the hearing of a wild creature. Outside the open door the steps halted, and for a long moment the silence became complete. He studies me, thought Cadfael. Well, I know what he sees, if I don't know what he makes of it: a man past sixty, in robust health, bar the occasional stiffness in the joints proper to his age, squarely made, blunt-featured, with wiry brown hair laced with grey, and in need of a trim, come to think of it! – round a shaven crown that's been out in all weathers for many a year. He weighs me, he measures me, and takes his time about it.

He opened his eyes. 'I may look a mastiff,' he said amiably, 'but it's years now since I bit anyone. Step in, and never hesitate.'

So brisk and unexpected a greeting, so far from drawing the visitor within, caused him to take a startled pace backwards, so that he stood full in the soft noon light of the day, to be seen clearly. A young fellow surely not above twenty, of the middle height but very well put together, dressed in wrinkled cloth hose of an indeterminate drab colour, scuffed leather shoes very down at heel, a dark brown cotte rubbed slightly paler where the sleeves chafed the flanks, and belted with a frayed rope girdle, and a short, caped capuchon thrown back on his shoulders. The coarse linen of his shirt showed at the neck, unlaced, and the sleeves of the cotte were short on him, showing a length of paler wrist above good brown hands. A compact, stout pillar of young manhood stood sturdily to be appraised, and once the immediate check had passed, even a long and silent appraisal seemed to reassure him rather than to make him uneasy, for a distinct spark lit in his eye, and an irrepressible grin hovered about his mouth as he said very respectfully: 'They told me at the gatehouse to come here. I'm looking for a brother named Cadfael.'

He had a pleasant voice, pitched agreeably low but with a fine, blithe ring to it, and just now practising a meekness which did not seem altogether at home on his tongue. Cadfael continued to study him with quickening interest. A mop of shaggy light-brown curls capped a shapely head poised on an elegant neck, and the face that took such pains to play the rustic innocent abashed before his betters was youthfully rounded of cheek and chin, but very adequately supplied with bone, too, and shaven clean as the schoolboy it aimed at presenting. A guileless face, but for the suppressed smoulder of mischief in the wide hazel eyes, changeable and fluid like peat water flowing over sunlit pebbles of delectable, autumnal greens and browns. There was nothing he could do about that merry sparkle. Asleep, the angelic simpleton might achieve conviction, but not with those eyes open.

'Then you have found him,' said Cadfael. 'That name belongs to me. And you, I take it, must be the young fellow

370

who came here with the priest, and wants work with us for a while.' He rose, gathering himself without haste. Their eyes came virtually on a level. Dancing, brook-water eyes the boy had, scintillating with winter sunlight. 'What was the name they gave you, son?'

'N ... name?' The stammer was a surprise, and the sudden nervous flickering of long brown lashes that briefly veiled the lively eyes was the first sign of unease Cadfael had detected in him. 'Benet – my name's Benet. My Aunt Diota is widow to a decent man, John Hammet, who was a groom in the lord bishop's service, so when he died Bishop Henry found a place for her with Father Ailnoth. That's how we came here. They're used to each other now for three years and more. And I begged to come here along with them to see could I find work near to her. I'm not skilled, but what I don't know I can learn.'

Very voluble now, all at once, and no more stammering, either, and he had stepped within, into shadow from the midday light, quenching somewhat of his perilous brightness. 'He said you could make use of me here,' said the vibrant voice, meekly muted. 'Tell me what to do, and I'll do it.'

'And a very proper attitude to work,' allowed Cadfael. 'You'll be sharing the life here within the enclave, so I'm told. Where have they lodged you? Among the lay servants?'

'Nowhere yet,' said the boy, his voice cautiously recovering its spring and resonance. 'But I'm promised a bed here within. I'd just as soon be out of the priest's house. There's a parish fellow looks after his glebe, they tell me, so there's no need for me there.'

'Well, there's need enough here,' said Cadfael heartily, 'for what with one thing and another I'm behind with the rough digging that ought to be done before the frosts come, and I've half a dozen fruit trees here in the small orchard that need pruning about Christmas time. Brother Bernard will be wanting to borrow you to help with the ploughing in the Gaye, where our main gardens are – you'll scarcely be familiar with the lie of the land yet, but you'll soon get used to it. I'll see you're not snatched away until I've had the worth of you here. Come, then, and see what we have for you within the walls.'

Benet had come a few paces more into the hut, and was looking about him with curiosity and mild awe at the array of bottles, jars and flagons that furnished Brother Cadfael's shelves, the rustling bunches of herbs that sighed overhead in the faint stirrings of air from the open door, the small brass scales, the three mortars, the single gently bubbling wine-jar, the little wooden bowls of medicinal roots, and a batch of small white lozenges drying on a marble slab. His round-eyed, open-mouthed stare spoke for him. Cadfael half-expected him to cross himself defensively against such ominous mysteries, but Benet stopped short of that. Just as well, thought Cadfael, alerted and amused, for I should not quite have believed in it.

'This, too, you can learn, if you put your mind to it diligently enough,' he said drily, 'but it will take you some years. Mere medicines – God made every ingredient that goes into them, there's no other magic. But let's begin with what's needed most. There's a good acre of vegetable garden beds to rough-dig, and a small mountain of well-weathered stable muck to cart and spread on the main butts and the rose beds. And the sooner we get down to it, the sooner it will be done. Come and see!'

The boy followed him willingly enough, his light, lovely eyes scanning everything with interest. Beyond the fish ponds, in the two pease fields that ran down the slope to the Meole Brook, the western boundary of the enclave, the haulms had long since been cut close and dried for stable bedding, and the roots ploughed back into the soil, but there would be a heavy and dirty job there spreading much of the ripened and tempered manure from the stable yard and the byres. There were the few fruit trees in the small orchard to be pruned, but such growth as remained in the grass, in this mild opening of the month, was cropped neatly by two yearling lambs. The flower beds wore their usual somewhat ragged autumn look, but would do with one last weeding, if time served, before all growth ceased in the cold. The kitchen garden, cleared of its crops, lay weedy and trampled, waiting for the spade, a dauntingly large expanse. But it seemed that nothing could daunt Benet.

'A goodish stretch,' he said cheerfully, eyeing the long main butt with no sign of discouragement. 'Where will I find the tools?'

Cadfael showed him the low shed where they were to be found, and was interested to note that the young man looked round him among the assembly with a slightly doubtful face, though he soon selected the iron-shod wooden spade appropriate to the job in hand, and even viewed the length of the ground ahead and started his first row with judgement and energy, if not with very much skill.

'Wait!' said Cadfael, noting the thin, worn shoes the boy wore. 'If you thrust like that in such wear you'll have a swollen foot before long. I have wooden pattens in my hut that you can strap under your feet and shove as hard as you please. But no need to rush at it, or you'll be in a muck sweat before you've done a dozen rows. What you must do is set an even pace, get a rhythm into it, and you can go on all day, the spade will keep time for you. Sing to it if you have breath enough, or hum with it and save your breath. You'll be surprised how the rows will multiply.' He caught himself up there, somewhat belatedly aware that he was giving away too much of what he had already observed. 'Your work's been mainly with horses, as I heard,' he said blandly. 'There's an art in every labour.' And he went to fetch the wooden pattens he had himself carved out to shoe his own feet against either harsh digging or deep mire, before Benet could bridle in self-defence.

Thus shod and advised, Benet began very circumspectly, and Cadfael stayed only to see him launched into a good, steady action before he took himself off into his workshop, to be about his ordinary business of pounding up green herbs for an ointment of his own concoction, good against the chapped hands that would surely make their usual January appearance among the copyists and illuminators in the scriptorium. There would be coughs and colds, too, no doubt, later on, and now was the right time to prepare such of his medicines as would keep through the winter.

When it was almost time to clear away his impedimenta and prepare for Vespers he went out to see how his acolyte was faring. No one likes to be watched at his work, especially if he comes raw to the practice, and maybe a thought sensitive about his lack of skill and experience. Cadfael was impressed by the great surge the young man had made down the formidable butt of ground. His rows were straight, clearly he had a good eye. His cut appeared to be deep, by the rich black of the upturned tilth. True, he had somewhat sprayed soil over the border paths, but he had also ferreted out a twig broom from the shed, and was busy brushing back the spilled earth to where it belonged. He looked up a little defensively at Cadfael, flicking a glance towards the spade he had left lying.

'I've blunted the iron edge against a stone,' he said, and dropped his broom to up-end the spade and run his fingers gingerly along the metal rim that bound the wood. 'I'll hammer it out fine before I leave it. There's a hammer in the shed there, and your water trough has a good wide rim to the stone. Though I was aiming at two rows more before the light goes.'

'Son,' said Cadfael heartily, 'you've already done more than ever I expected of you. As for the spade, that edge has been replaced three times at least since the tool was made, and I know well enough it's due for a fourth sheathing very soon. If you think it will do yet a while, at least to finish this task, then beat it out again by all means, but then put it away, and wash, and come to Vespers.'

Benet looked up from the dented edge, suddenly aware of cautious praise, and broke into the broadest and most unguarded grin Cadfael could ever recall seeing, and the speckled, limpid light blazed up in his trout-stream eyes.

'I'll do, then?' he said, between simple pleasure and subtle impudence, flushed and exhilarated with his own energy; and added with unwary honesty: 'I've hardly had a spade in my hands before.'

'Now that,' said Cadfael, straight faced, and eyeing with interest the form and trim of the hands that jutted a little too far from the outgrown sleeves, 'that I never would have suspected.'

'I've worked mostly with –' Benet began in slight haste.

'... with horses. Yes, I know! Well, you match today's effort tomorrow, and tomorrow's the next day, and yes, you'll do.'

Cadfael went to Vespers with his mind's eye full of the jaunty figure of his new labourer, striding away to beat out the dented iron edge of the spade into even sharpness, and his ears were still stretched to catch the whistled tune, certainly not liturgical in character, to which Benet's large young feet in their scuffed shoes and borrowed pattens kept time.

'Father Ailnoth was installed in his cure this morning,' said Cadfael, coming fresh from the induction on the second day. 'You didn't want to attend?'

'I?' Benet straightened up over his spade in ingenuous surprise. 'No, why should I? I've got my work here, he can take care of his without any help from me. I hardly knew the man until we set off to come here. Why, did all go well?'

'Yes – oh, yes, all went well. His sermon was perhaps a little harsh on poor sinners,' said Cadfael, doubtfully pondering. 'No doubt he wanted to begin by showing his zeal at the outset. The rein can always be slackened later, when priest and people come to know each other better, and know where they stand.

It's never easy for a younger man and a stranger to follow one old and accustomed. The old shoe comforts, the new pinches. But given time enough, the new comes to be the old, and fits as gently.'

It seemed that Benet had very quickly developed the ability to read between lines where his new master was concerned. He stood gazing earnestly at Cadfael with a slight frown, his curly head on one side, his smooth brown forehead creased in unaccustomed gravity, as if he had been brought up without warning against some unforeseen question, and was suddenly aware that he ought to have been giving thought to it long ago, if he had not been totally preoccupied with some other enterprise of his own.

'Aunt Diota has been with him over three years,' he said consideringly, 'and she's never made any complaint of him, as far as I know. I only rubbed shoulders with him on the way here, and I was thankful to him for bringing me. Not a man a servant like me could be easy with, but I minded my tongue and did what he bade me, and he was fair enough in his dealings with me.' Benet's buoyancy returned like a gust of the western wind, blowing doubts away. 'Ah, here is he as raw in his new work as I am in mine, but he sets out to cudgel his way through, and I have the good sense to worm my way in gently. Let him alone, and he'll get his feet to the ground.'

He was right, of course, a new man comes unmeasured and uneasy into a place not yet mellowed to him, and must be given time to breathe, and listen to the breathing of others. But Cadfael went to his own work with fretting memories of a homily half frenetic dream, half judgement day, eloquently phrased, beginning with the pure air of a scarcely accessible heaven, and ending with the anatomy of a far-too-visual hell.

'... that hell which is an island, for ever circled by four seas, the guardian dragons of the condemned. The sea of bitterness, whose every wave burns more white-hot than the mainland fires of hell itself; the sea of rebellion, which at every stroke of swimmer or rower casts the fugitive back into the fire; the sea of despair, in which every barque founders, and every swimmer sinks like a stone. And last, the sea of penitence, composed of all the tears of all the damned, by which alone, for the very few, escape is possible, since a single tear of Our Lord over sinners once fell into the fiery flood, and permeated, cooled and calmed the entire ocean for such as reach the perfection of remorse ...'

375

A narrow and terrifying mercy, thought Cadfael, stirring a balsam for the chests of the old, imperfect men in the infirmary, human and fallible like himself, and not long for this world. Hardly mercy at all!

Chapter Three

HE FIRST small cloud that showed in the serene sky of the Foregate came when Aelgar, who had always worked the field strips of the priest's glebe, and cared for the parish bull and the parish boar, came with a grievance to Erwald the wheelwright, who was provost of the Foregate, rather in anxiety than in any spirit of rebellion, complaining that his new master had raised doubts about whether his servant was free or villein. For there was one strip in the more distant fields which was in mild dispute at the time of Father Adam's death, and the tenure had not been agreed between priest and man when Adam died. Had he lived there would have been an amicable arrangement, since Adam certainly had no greed in his make-up, and there was a fair claim on Aelgar's part through his mother. But Father Ailnoth, unswervingly exact, had insisted rather that the case should come to court, and further, had said outright that in the King's court Aelgar would have no standing, since he was not free, but villein.

'And everyone knows,' said Aelgar, fretting, 'that I'm a free man and always have been, but he says I have villein kin, for my uncle and my cousin have a yardland in the manor of Worthin, and hold it by customary services, and that's the proof. And true enough, for my father's younger brother, being landless, took the yardland gladly when it fell vacant, and agreed to do service for it, but for all that he was born free, like all my kin. It's not that I grudge him or the church that strip, if it's justly his, but how if he bring case to prove me a villein and no free man?'

'He'll not do that,' said Erwald comfortably, 'for it would never stand if he did. And why should he want to do you wrong? He's a stickler for the letter of the law, you'll find, but nothing more than that. Why, every soul in the parish would testify. I'll tell him so, and he'll hear reason.'

But the tale had gone round before nightfall.

The second small blot in the clear sky was an urchin with a broken head, who admitted, between sniffs and sobs, that he and a few more of his age had been playing a somewhat rumbustious ball game against the wall of the priest's house, a clear, windowless wall well suited for the purpose, and that they had naturally made a certain amount of noise in the process. But so they had many times before, and Father Adam had never done worse than shake a tolerant fist at them, and grin, and finally shoo them away like chickens. This time a tall black figure had surged out of the house crying anathema at them and brandishing a great long staff, and even their startled speed had not been enough to bring them off without damage. Two or three had bad bruises to show for it, and this unfortunate had taken a blow on the head that all but stunned him, and left him with a broken wound that bled alarmingly for a while, as head wounds do.

'I know they can be imps of Satan,' said Erwald to Brother Cadfael, when the child had been soothed and bandaged and lugged away by an indignant mother, 'and many a time I expect you and I have clouted a backside or boxed an ear, but not with a great walking-staff like that one he carries.'

'That could well have been an unlucky stroke that was never meant to land,' said Cadfael. 'But I wouldn't say he'll ever be as easy on the scamps as Father Adam was. They'd best learn to stay out of his way, or mind their manners within reach of him.'

It was soon plain that the boys thought so, too, for there were no more noisy games outside the small house at the end of the alley, and when the tall, black-clad figure was seen stalking down the Foregate, cloak flying like a crow's wings in time to his impetuous stride, the children melted away to safe distances, even when they were about blameless business.

It certainly could not be said that Father Ailnoth neglected his duties. He was meticulous in observing the hours, and let nothing interrupt his saying of the office, he preached somewhat stern sermons, conducted his services reverently, visited the sick, exhorted the backsliding. His comfort to the ailing was austere, even chilling, and his penances heavier than those to which his flock was accustomed, but he did all that his cure required of him. He also took jealous care of all the perquisites of his office, tithe and tilth, to the extent that one of his neighbours in the fields was complaining of having half his headland ploughed up, and Aelgar was protesting that he had been ordered to plough more closely, for the waste of ground was blameworthy.

The few boys who had been learning a smattering of letters from Father Adam, and had continued their lessons under his successor, grew less and less willing to attend, and muttered to their parents that they were beaten now for the least error, let alone a real offence.

'It was a mistake,' said Brother Jerome loftily, 'ever to let them run wild, as Father Adam did. They feel a proper curb now as affliction, instead of fair usage. What says the Rule on this head? That boys or youths who cannot yet understand how great a punishment excommunication is, must be punished for their offences either by fasting, or by sharp stripes, for their own good. The priest does very properly by them.'

'I cannot regard a simple mistake in letters,' retorted Brother Paul, up in arms for lads no older than his own charges, 'as an offence. Offence argues a will to offend, and these children answer as best they know, having no will but to do well.'

'The offence,' said Jerome pompously, 'is in the neglect and inattention which caused them to be imperfect in answering. Those who attend diligently will be able to answer without fault.'

'Not when they are already afraid,' snapped Brother Paul, and fled the argument for fear of his own temper. Jerome had a way of presenting his pious face as a target, and Paul, who like most big, powerful men could be astonishingly gentle and tender with the helpless, like his youngest pupils, was only too well aware of what his fists could do to an opponent of his own size, let alone a puny creature like Jerome.

It was more than a week before the matter came to the notice of Abbot Radulfus, and even then it was a relatively minor complaint that set the affair in motion. For Father Ailnoth had publicly accused Jordan Achard, the Foregate baker, of delivering short-weight loaves, and Jordan, rightly pricked in his professional pride, meant to rebut the charge at all costs.

'And a lucky man he is,' said Erwald the provost heartily, 'that he's charged with the one thing every soul in the Foregate will swear is false, for he gives just measure and always has, if he does nothing else justly in his life. If he'd been charged with fathering one or two of the recent bastards in these parts, he'd have had good cause to sing very low. But he bakes good bread, and never cheats on the weight. And how the priest came by this error is a mystery, but Jordan wants blood for it, and he has a fluent mouth on him that might well speak up usefully for others less bold.'

So it was that the provost of the Foregate, backed by Jordan the baker and one or two more of the notables of the parish, came to ask audience of Abbot Radulfus in chapter on the eighteenth day of December.

'I have asked you here into private with me,' said the abbot, when they had withdrawn at his request into the parlour in his lodging, 'so that the daily duties of the brothers may not be disrupted. For I see that you have much to discuss, and I would like you to speak freely. Now we have time enough. Master Provost, you have my attention. I desire the prosperity and happiness of the Foregate, as you do.'

His very use of the courtesy title, to which Erwald had no official right, was meant as an invitation, and as such accepted.

'Father Abbot,' began Erwald earnestly, 'we are come to you thus because we are not altogether easy at the rule of our new priest. Father Ailnoth has his duties in the church, and performs them faithfully, and there we have no complaint of him. But where he moves among us in the parish we are not happy with his dealings. He has called into question whether Aelgar, who works for him, is villein or free, and has not asked of us, who know very well he is a free man. He has also caused Aelgar to plough up a part of the headland of his neighbour Eadwin, without Eadwin's knowledge or leave. He has accused Master Jordan, here, of giving short weight, while all of us here know that is false. Jordan is known for good bread and good measure.'

'That is truth,' said Jordan emphatically. 'I rent my bakery ovens from the abbey, it is on your land I work, you have known me for years, that I take pride in my bread.'

'You have that right,' agreed Radulfus, 'it is good bread. Go on, Master Provost, there is more to tell.'

'My lord, there is,' said Erwald, very gravely now. 'You may

380

have heard with what strict dealing Father Ailnoth keeps his school. The same severity he uses towards the boys of the parish, wherever he sees them gathered, if they put a foot aside – and you know that the young are liable to folly. He is too free with his blows, he has done violence where it was not called for, not by our measure. The children are afraid of him. That is not good, though not everyone has patience with children. But the women are frightened, too. He preaches such dire things, they are afraid of hell.'

'There is no need to fear,' said the abbot, 'unless by reason of a consciousness of sin. I do not think we have here in the parish such great sinners.'

'No, my lord, but women are tender and easily frightened. They look within for sins they may have committed, unknowing. They are no longer sure what is sin and what is not, so they dare not breathe without wondering if they do wrong. But there is more still.'

'I am listening,' said the abbot.

'My lord, there's a decent poor man of this parish, Centwin, whose wife Elen bore a very weakly child, a boy, four days ago. It was about Sext when the baby was born, and it was so small and feeble, they were sure it must die, and Centwin ran quickly to the priest's house, and begged him to come and baptize the boy before he died, that his soul might be saved. And Father Ailnoth sent out word that he was at his devotions, and could not come until he had completed the office. Centwin begged him, but he would not interrupt his prayers. And when he did go, Father, the baby was dead.'

The small, chill silence seemed to bring down a looming darkness on the panelled room.

'Father, he would not give the child Christian burial, because it was not baptized. He said it could not come within the hallowed ground, though he would say what prayers he could at its burial – which was in a grave outside the pale. The place I can show.'

Abbot Radulfus said with infinite heaviness: 'He was within his rights.'

'His rights! What of the child's rights? It might have been christen soul if he had come when he was called for.'

'He was within his rights,' said Radulfus again, inexorably but with deep detestation. 'The office is sacrosanct.'

'So is the newborn soul,' said Erwald, remorselessly eloquent.

381

'You say well. And God hears us both. There can and shall be dispensation. If you have more to tell, go on, tell me all.'

'My lord, there was a girl of this parish – Eluned – very beautiful. Not like other girls, wild as a hare. Everyone knew her. God knows she never harmed a soul but herself, the creature! My lord, she could not say no to men. Time and again she went with this one or that, but always she came back, as wild returning as going, in tears, and made her confession, and swore amendment. And meant it! But she never could keep it, a lad would look at her and sigh … Father Adam always took her back, confessed her, gave her penance, and afterwards absolution. He knew she could not help it. And she as kind a creature to man or child or beast as ever breathed – too kind!'

The abbot sat still and silent, foreseeing what was to come.

'Last month she bore a child. When she was delivered and recovered she came, as she always came, mad with shame, to make her confession. He refused her countenance. He told her she had broken every promise of amendment, and so she had, but still … He would not give her penance, because he would not take her word, and so he refused her absolution. And when she came humbly to enter the church and hear Mass, he turned her away, and shut the door against her. Publicly and loudly he did it, in front of all.'

There was a long and deep silence before the abbot asked, perforce: 'What became of her?' For clearly she was already in the past, an outcast shade.

'They took her out of the mill-pond, my lord. By good fortune she had drifted down to the brook, and those who drew her out were from the town, and did not know her, so they took her with them back to their own parish, and the priest of Saint Chad's has buried her. It was not clear how she came to drown, it was taken for accident.'

Though of course everyone knew it was none. That was clear in look and voice. Despair is deadly sin. Then what of the record of those who deal out despair?

'Leave all this in my hands,' said Abbot Radulfus. 'I will speak to Father Ailnoth.'

There was no trace of guilt, trepidation or want of assurance in the long, austere, handsome face that confronted Abbot Radulfus across the desk in his parlour, after Mass. The man stood quite erect and still, with hands folded at ease and face invincibly calm.

'Father Abbot, if I may speak freely, the souls of my cure had been long neglected, to their own ruin. The garden is full of weeds, they starve and strangle the good grain. I am pledged to do whatever is needed to bring a clean crop, and so I must and will endeavour. I can do no other. The child spared will be the man spoiled. As for the matter of Eadwin's headland, it has been shown me that I have removed his boundary stone. That was in error, and the error has been made good. I have replaced the stone and drawn my own bounds short of it. I would not possess myself of one hand's breadth of land that belonged to another man.'

And that was surely truth. Not a hand's breadth of land nor a penny in money. Nor let go of one or the other that belonged to him. The bare razor of justice was his measure.

'I am less concerned for a yard of headland,' said the abbot drily, 'than for matters that touch a man's being even more nearly. Your man Aelgar was born free, is free man now, and so are his uncle and cousin, and if they take steps to assert it there will be no man query it hereafter. They assume such customary duties as they do by way of payment for a piece of land, there is no disfranchisement, no more than when a man pays in money.'

'So I have found by enquiry,' said Ailnoth imperturbably, 'and have said as much to him.'

'Then that was properly done. But it would have been better to enquire first and accuse afterwards.'

'My lord, no just man should resent the appeal to justice. I am new among these people, I heard of the kinsmen's land, that it was held by villein service. It was my duty to find out the truth, and it was honest to speak first to the man himself.'

Which was true enough, if not kindly, and it seemed he had acknowledged the truth against himself, once established, with the same steely integrity. But what is to be done with such a man, among the common, fallible run of humanity? Radulfus went on to graver matters.

'The child that was born to the man Centwin and his wife, and lived barely an hour ... The man came to you, urging haste, since the baby was very feeble and likely to die. You did not go with him to give it Christian baptism, and since your ministration came too late, as I hear, you denied the infant burial in consecrated ground. Why did you not go at once when you were called, and with all haste?'

'Because I had but just begun the office. My lord, I never

have broken off my devotions according to my vows, and never will, for any cause, though it were my own death. Until I had completed the act of worship I could not go. As soon as it was ended, I did go. I could not know the child would die so soon. But if I had known, still I could not have cut short the worship I owe.'

'There are other obligations you owe no less,' said Radulfus with some asperity. 'There are times when it is needful to make a choice between duties, and yours, I think, is first to the souls of those within your care. You chose rather the perfection of your own personal worship, and consigned the child to a grave outside the pale. Was that well done?'

'My lord,' said Ailnoth, unflinching, and with the high and smouldering gleam of self-justification in his black eyes, 'as I hold, it was. I will not go aside from the least iota of my service where the sacred office is concerned. My own soul and all others must bow to that.'

'Even the soul of the most innocent, new come into the world, the most defenceless of God's creatures?'

'My lord, you know well that the letter of divine law does not permit the burial of unchristened creatures within the pale. I keep the rules by which I am bound. I can do no other. God will know where to find Centwin's babe, if his mercy extends to him, in holy ground or base.'

After its merciless fashion it was a good answer. The abbot pondered, eyeing the stony, assured face.

'The letter of the rule is much, I grant you, but the spirit is more. And you might well have jeopardized your own soul to ensure that of a newborn child. An office interrupted can be completed without sin, if the cause be urgent enough. And there is also the matter of the girl Eluned, who went to her death after – I say after, mark, I do not say because! – you turned her away from the church. It is a grave thing to refuse confessions and penance even to the greatest sinner.'

'Father Abbot,' said Ailnoth, with the first hot spurt of passion, immovable in righteousness, 'where there is no penitence there can be neither penance nor absolution. The woman had pleaded penitence and vowed amendment time after time, and never kept her word. I have heard from others all her reputation, and it is past amendment. I could not in conscience confess her, for I could not take her word. If there is no truth in the act of contrition, there is no merit in confession, and to absolve her would have been deadly sin. A

384

whore past recovery! I do not repent me, whether she died or no. I would do again what I did. There is no compromise with the pledges by which I am bound.'

'There will be no compromise with the answer you must make for two deaths,' said Radulfus solemnly, 'if God should take a view different from yours. I bid you recall, Father Ailnoth, that you are summoned to call not the righteous, but sinners to repentance, the weak, the fallible, those who go in fear and ignorance, and have not your pure advantage. Temper your demands to their abilities, and be less severe on those who cannot match your perfection.' He paused there, for it was meant as irony, to bite, but the proud, impervious face never winced, accepting the accolade. 'And be slow to lay your hand upon the children,' he said, 'unless they offend of malicious intent. To error we are all liable, even you.'

'I study to do right,' said Ailnoth, 'as I have always, and always shall.' And he went away with the same confident step, vehement and firm, the skirts of his gown billowing like wings in the wind of his going.

'A man abstemious, rigidly upright, inflexibly honest, ferociously chaste,' said Radulfus in private to Prior Robert. 'A man with every virtue, except humility and human kindness. That is what I have brought upon the Foregate, Robert. And now what are we to do about him?'

Dame Diota Hammet came on the twenty-second day of December to the gatehouse of the abbey with a covered basket, and asked meekly for her nephew Benet, for whom she had brought a cake for his Christmas, and a few honey buns from her festival baking. The porter, knowing her for the parish priest's housekeeper, directed her through to the garden, where Benet was busy clipping the last straggly growth from the box hedges.

Hearing their voices, Cadfael looked out from his workshop, and divining who this matronly woman must be, was about to return to his mortar when he was caught by some delicate shade in their greeting. A matter-of-fact affection, easy-going and undemonstrative, was natural between aunt and nephew, and what he beheld here hardly went beyond that, but there was a gloss of tenderness and almost deference in the woman's bearing towards her young kinsman, and an unexpected, childish grace in the warmth with which he embraced her. True, he was already known for a young man who did nothing by halves, but here were certainly aunt and nephew who did not take each other for granted.

Cadfael withdrew to his work again and left them their privacy. A comely, well-kept woman was Mistress Hammet, with decent black clothing befitting a priest's housekeeper, and a dark shawl over her neat, greying hair. Her oval face, mildly sad in repose, brightened vividly in greeting the boy, and then she looked no more than forty years old, and perhaps, indeed, she was no more. Benet's mother's sister? wondered Cadfael. If so, he took after his father, for there was very little resemblance here. Well, it was none of his business!

Benet came bounding into the workshop to empty the basket of its good things, spreading them out on the wooden bench. 'We're in luck, Brother Cadfael, for she's as good a cook as you'd find in the King's own kitchen. You and I can eat like princes.'

And he was off again as blithely to restore the empty basket. Cadfael looked out after him through the open door, and saw him hand over, besides the basket, some small thing he drew from the breast of his cotte. She took it, nodding earnestly, unsmiling, and the boy stooped and kissed her cheek. She smiled then. He had a way with him, no question. She turned and went away, and left him looking after her for a long moment, before he also turned, and came back to the workshop. The engaging grin came back readily to his face.

' "On no account," ' quoted Cadfael, straight-faced, ' "may a monk accept small presents of any kind, from his parents or anyone else, without the abbot's permission." That, sweet son, is in the Rule.'

'Lucky you, then, and lucky I,' said the boy gaily, 'that I've taken no vows. She makes the best honey cakes ever I tasted.' And he sank even white teeth into one of them, and reached to offer another to Cadfael.

' "... nor may the brethren exchange them, one with another," ' intoned Cadfael, and accepted the offering. 'Lucky, indeed! Though I transgress in accepting, you go sinless in offering. Have you quite abandoned your inclination to the cloistered life, then?'

'Me?' said the youth, startled out of his busy munching, and open-mouthed. 'When did I ever profess any?'

'Not you, lad, but your sponsor on your account, when he asked work for you here.'

'Did he say that of me?'

'He did. Not positively promising it, mark you, but holding out the hope that you might settle to it one day. I grant you I've never seen much sign of it.'

Benet thought that over for a moment, while he finished his cake and licked the sticky crumbs from his fingers. 'No doubt he was anxious to get rid of me, and thought it might make me more welcome here. My face was never in any great favour with him – too much given to smiling, maybe. No, not even you will pen me in here for very long, Cadfael. When the time comes I'll be on my way. But while I'm here,' he said, breaking into the bountiful smile that might well strike an ascetic as far too frivolous, 'I'll do my fair share of the work.'

And he was off back to his box hedge, swinging the shears in one large, easy hand, and leaving Cadfael gazing after him with a very thoughtful face.

Chapter Four

AME DIOTA Hammet presented herself later that afternoon at a house near Saint Chad's church, and asked timidly for the lord Ralph Giffard. The servant who opened the door to her looked her up and down and hesitated, never having seen her before.

'What's your business with him, mistress? Who sends you?'

'I'm to bring him this letter,' said Diota submissively, and held out a small rolled leaf fastened with a seal. 'And to wait for an answer, if my lord will be so good.'

He was in two minds about taking it from her hand. It was a small and irregularly shaped slip of parchment, with good reason, since it was one of the discarded edges from a leaf Brother Anselm had trimmed to shape and size for a piece of music, two days since. But the seal argued matter of possible importance, even on so insignificant a missive. The servant was still hesitating when a girl came out into the porch at his back, and seeing a woman unknown but clearly respectable, stayed to enquire curiously what was to do. She accepted the scroll readily enough, and knew the seal. She looked up with startled, intent blue eyes into Diota's face, and abruptly handed the scroll back to her.

'Come in, and deliver this yourself. I'll bring you to my step-father.'

The master of the house was sitting by a comfortable fire in a small solar, with wine at his elbow and a deerhound coiled about his feet. A big, ruddy, sinewy man of fifty, balding and bearded, very spruce in his dress and only just beginning to put on a little extra flesh after an active life, he looked what he was, the lord of two or three country manors and this town house, where he preferred to spend his Christmas in comfort. He looked up at Diota, when the girl presented her, with complete incomprehension, but he comprehended all too well when he looked at the seal that fastened the parchment. He asked no questions, but sent the girl for his clerk, and listened intently as the content was read to him, in so low a voice that it was plain the clerk understood how dangerous its import could be. He was a small, withered man, grown old in Giffard's service, and utterly trustworthy. He made an end, and watched his master's face anxiously.

'My lord, send nothing in writing! Word of mouth is safer, if you want to reply. Words said can be denied, to write them would be folly.'

Ralph sat pondering for a while in silence, and eyeing the unlikely messenger, who stood patiently and uneasily waiting.

'Tell him,' he said at last, 'that I have received and understood his message.'

She hesitated, and ventured at last to ask: 'Is that all, my lord?'

'It's enough! The less said the better, for him and for me.'

The girl, who had remained unobtrusive but attentive in a corner of the room, followed Diota out to the shadow of the porch, with doors closed behind them.

'Mistress,' she said softly in Diota's ear, 'where is he to be found – this man who sent you?'

By the brief, blank silence and the doubtful face of the older woman she understood her fears, and made impatient haste to allay them, her voice low and vehement. 'I mean him no harm, God knows! My father was of the same party – did you not see how well I knew the seal? You can trust me, I won't say word to any, nor to him, either, but I want to know how I may know him, where I may find him, in case of need.'

'At the abbey,' said Diota as softly and hurriedly, making up her mind. 'He's working in the garden, by the name of Benet, under the herbalist brother.'

'Oh, Brother Cadfael – I know him!' said the girl, breathing satisfaction. 'He treated me once for a bad fever, when I was ten years old, and he came to help my mother, three Christmases ago, when she fell into her last illness. Good, I know where his herbarium is. Go now, quickly!'

She watched Diota scurry hastily out of the small courtyard, and then closed the door and went back to the solar, where Giffard was sitting sunk in anxious consideration, heavy-browed and sombre.

'Shall you go to this meeting?'

He had the letter still in his hand. Once already he had made an impulsive motion towards the fire, to thrust the parchment into it and be rid of it, but then had drawn back again, rolled it carefully and hid it in the breast of his cotte. She took that for a sign favourable to the sender, and was pleased. It was no surprise that he did not give her a direct answer. This was a serious business and needed thought, and in any case he never paid any great heed to his step-daughter, either to confide in her or to regulate her actions. He was indulgent rather out of tolerant indifference than out of affection.

'Say no word of this to anyone,' he said. 'What have I to gain by keeping such an appointment? And everything to lose! Have not your family and mine lost enough already by loyalty to that cause? How if he should be followed to the mill?'

'Why should he be? No one has any suspicion of him. He's accepted at the abbey as a labourer in the gardens, calling himself Benet. He's vouched for. Christmas Eve, and by night, there'll be no one abroad but those already in the church. Where's the risk? It was a good time to choose. And he needs help.'

'Well ...' said Ralph, and drummed his fingers irresolutely on the small cylinder in the breast of his cotte. 'We have two days yet, we'll watch and wait until the times comes.'

Benet was sweeping up the brushings from the hedge, and whistling merrily over the work, when he heard brisk, light steps stirring the moist gravel on the path behind him, and turned to behold a young woman in a dark cloak and hood advancing upon him from the great court. A small, slender girl of erect and confident bearing, the outline of her swathed form softened and blurred by the faint mist of a still day, and the hovering approach of dusk. Not until she was quite near to him and he had stepped deferentially aside to give her passage could he see clearly the rosy, youthful face within the shadow of the hood, a rounded face with apple-blossom skin, a resolute chin, and a mouth full and firm in its generosity of line, and coloured like half-open roses. Then what light remained gathered into the harebell blue of her wide-set eyes, at once soft and brilliant, and he lost sight of everything else. And though he had made way for her to pass him by, and ducked his head to her in a properly servantlike reverence, she did not pass by, but lingered, studying him closely and candidly, with the fearless, innocent stare of a cat. Indeed there was something of the kitten about the whole face, wider at the brow and eyes than its length from brow to chin, tapered and tilted imperiously, as a kitten confronts the world, never having experienced fear. She looked him up and down gravely, and took her time about it, in a solemn inspection that might have been insolent if it had not implied a very serious purpose. Though what interest some noble young woman of the county or well-to-do merchant daughter of the town could have in him was more than Benet could imagine.

Only when she was satisifed of whatever had been in question in her mind did she ask, in a clear, firm voice: 'Are you Brother Cadfael's new helper here?'

'Yes, my lady,' said the dutiful labourer bashfully, shuffling his feet and somehow even contriving a blush that sat rather oddly on so positive and cheerful a countenance.

She looked at the trimmed hedge and the newly weeded and manured flower beds, and again at him, and for a dazzling instant he thought she smiled, but in the flicker of an eyelash she was solemn again.

'I came to ask Brother Cadfael for some herbs for my kitchen forcemeats. Do you know where I shall find him?'

'He's in his workshop within,' said Benet. 'Please to walk through into the walled garden there.'

'I remember the way,' she said, and inclined her head to him graciously, as noble to simple, and swept away from him through the open gate into the walled enclosure of the herbarium.

It was almost time for Vespers, and Benet could well have quit his labours and gone to make himself ready, but he prolonged his sweeping quite unnecessarily, gathering the brushings into a pile of supererogatory neatness, scattering them a little and massing them again, in order to get another close glimpse of her when she came back with a bunch of dried herbs loosely wrapped in a cloth and carried carefully in her hands. She passed him this time without a glance, or seemed to do so, but still he had the feeling that those wide and wide-set eyes with their startling blueness took him in methodically in passing. The hood had slipped back a little from her head, and showed him a coiled braid of hair of an indefinable spring colour, like the young fronds of bracken when they are just unfolding, a soft light brown with tones of green in the shadows. Or hazel withies, perhaps! Hazel eyes are no great rarity, but how many women can boast of hazel hair?

She was gone, the hem of her cloak whisking round the box hedge and out of his sight. Benet forsook his broom in haste, left his pile of brushings lying, and went to pick Brother Cadfael's brains.

'Who was that lady?' he asked, point-blank.

'Is that a proper question for a postulant like you to be asking?' said Cadfael placidly, and went on cleaning and putting away his pestle and mortar.

Benet made a derisive noise, and interposed his sturdy person to confront Cadfael eye to eye, with no pretence whatsoever to notions of celibacy. 'Come, you know her, or at least she knows you. Who is she?'

'She spoke to you?' Cadfael wondered, interested.

'Only to ask me where she would find you. Yes, she spoke to me!' he said, elated. 'Yes, she stopped and looked me up and down, the creature, as though she found herself in need of a page, and thought I might do, given a little polishing. Would I do for a lady's page, Cadfael?'

'What's certain,' said Cadfael tolerantly, 'is that you'll never do for a monk. But no, I wouldn't say a lady's service is your right place, either.' He did not add: 'Unless on level terms!' but that was what was in his mind. At this moment the boy had shed all pretence of being a poor widow's penniless kinsman, untutored and awkward. That was no great surprise. There had been little effort spent on the imposture here in the garden for a week past, though the boy could reassume it at a moment's notice with others, and was still the rustic simpleton in Prior Robert's patronizing presence.

'Cadfael ...' Benet took him cajolingly by the shoulders and held him, tilting his curly head coaxingly, with a wilfully engaging intimacy. Given the occasion, he was well aware he could charm the birds from the trees. Nor did he have any difficulty in weighing up elder sympathizers who must once have shared much the same propensities. 'Cadfael, I may never speak to her again, I may never see her again – but I can *try*! Who is she?'

'Her name,' said Cadfael, capitulating rather from policy than from compulsion, 'is Sanan Bernières. Her father held a manor in the north-east of the shire, which was confiscated when he fought for his overlord FitzAlan and the Empress at the siege here, and died for it. Her mother married another vassal of FitzAlan, who had suffered his losses, too – the faction holds together, though they're all singing very small and lying very low here now. Giffard spends his winters mainly in his house in Shrewsbury, and since her mother died he brings his step-daughter to preside at his table-head. That's the lady you've seen pass by.'

'And had better let pass by?' said Benet, ruefully smiling in acknowledgement of a plain warning. 'Not for me?' He burst into the glowing grin to which Cadfael was becoming accustomed, and which sometimes gave him such qualms on behalf of his protégé, who was far too rash in the indulgence of his flashing moods. Benet laughed, and flung his arms about his mentor in a bear's hug. 'What will you wager?'

Cadfael freed an arm, without much ado, and held off his boisterous aggressor by a fistful of his thick curls.

'Where you're concerned, you madcap, I would not risk a hair that's left me. But watch your gait, you move out of your part. There are others here have keen eyes.'

'I do know,' said Benet, brought up short and sharp, his smile sobered into gravity. 'I do take care.'

How had they come by this secret and barely expressed understanding? Cadfael wondered as he went to Vespers. A kind of tacit agreement had been achieved, with never a word said of doubt, suspicion or plain, reckless trust. But the changed relationship existed, and was a factor to be reckoned with.

Hugh was gone, riding south for Canterbury in uncustomary state, well escorted and in his finery. He laughed at himself, but would not abate one degree of the dignity that was his due. 'If I come back deposed,' he said, 'at least I'll make a grand departure, and if I come back sheriff still, I'll do honour to the office.'

After his going Christmas seemed already on the doorstep, and there were great preparations to be made for the long night vigil and the proper celebration of the Nativity, and it was past Vespers on Christmas Eve before Cadfael had time to make a brief visit to the town, to spend at least an hour with Aline, and take a gift to his two-year-old godson, a little wooden horse that Martin Bellecote the master-carpenter had made for him, with gaily coloured harness and trappings fit for a knight, made out of scraps of felt and cloth and leather by Cadfael himself.

A soft, sleety rain had fallen earlier, but by that hour in the evening it was growing very cold, and there was frost in the air. The low, moist sky had cleared and grown infinitely tall, there were stars snapping out in it almost audibly, tiny but brilliant. By the morning the roads would be treacherous, and the frozen ruts a peril to wrenched ankles and unwary steps. There were still people abroad in the Foregate, most of them hurrying home by now, either to stoke up the fire and toast their feet, or to make ready for the long night in church. And as Cadfael crossed the bridge towards the town gate, the river in full, silent dark motion below, there was just enough light left to put names to those he met, coming from their shopping laden and in haste to get their purchases home. They exchanged greetings with him as they passed, for he was well known by his shape and his rolling gait even in so dim a light. The voices had the ring of frost about them, echoing like the chime of glass.

And here, striding across the bridge towards the Foregate, just within the compass of the torches burning under the town gate, came Ralph Giffard, on foot. Without the sidelong fall of the torchlight he would not have been recognized, but thus illuminated he was unmistakable. And where could Giffard be going at this time of the evening, and out of the town? Unless he meant to celebrate Christmas at the church of Holy Cross instead of in his own parish of Saint Chad. That was possible, though if so he was over-early. A good number of the wealthier townsfolk would also be making for the abbey this night.

Cadfael went on up the long curve of the Wyle, between the sparkling celestial darkness and the red, warm, earthy torchlight, to Hugh's house close by Saint Mary's church, and in through the courtyard to the hall door. No sooner had he set foot within than the excited imp Giles bore down upon him, yelling, and embraced him cripplingly round the thighs, which was as high as he could reach. To detach him was easy enough. As soon as the small, cloth-wrapped parcel was lowered into his sight he held up his arms for it gleefully, and plumped down in the rushes of the hall floor to unwrap it with cries of delight. But he did not forget, once the first transports were over, to make a rush for his godfather again, and clamber into his lap by the fireside to present him with a moist but fervent kiss in thanks. He had Hugh's self-reliant nature, but something also of his mother's instinctive sweetness.

'I can stay no more than an hour,' said Cadfael, as the boy scrambled down again to play with his new toy. 'I must be back for Compline, and very soon after that begins Matins, and we shall be up all the night until Prime and the dawn Mass.'

'Then at least rest an hour, and take food with me, and stay until Constance fetches my demon there away to his bed. Will you believe,' said Aline, smiling indulgently upon her offspring, 'what he says of this house without Hugh? Though it was Hugh told him what to say. He says he is the man of the house now, and asks how long his father will be away. He's too proud of himself to miss Hugh. It pleases his lordship to be taking his father's place.'

'You'd find his face fall if you told him longer than three or four days,' said Cadfael shrewdly. 'Tell him he's gone for a week, and there'll be tears. But three days? I daresay his pride will last out that long.'

At that moment the boy had no attention to spare for his dignity as lord of the household or his responsibilities as its protector in his father's absence. He was wholly taken up with galloping his new steed through the open plain of rushes, on some heroic adventure with an imaginary rider. Cadfael was left at liberty to sit with Aline, take meat and wine with her, and think and talk about Hugh, his possible reception at Canterbury, and his future, now hanging in the balance.

'He has deserved well of Stephen,' said Cadfael firmly, 'and Stephen is not quite a fool, he's seen too many change their coats, and change them back again when the wind turned. He'll know how to value one who never changed.'

When he noted the sand in the glass and rose to take his leave, he went out from the hall into the bright glitter of frost, and a vault of stars now three times larger than when first they appeared, and crackling with brilliance. The first real frost of the winter. As he made his way cautiously down the Wyle and out at the town gate he was thinking of the hard winter two years earlier, when the boy had been born, and hoping that this winter there would be no such mountainous snows and ferocious winds to drive it.* This night, the eve of the Nativity, hung about the town utterly still and silent, not a breath to temper the bite of the frost. Even the movements of such men as were abroad seemed hushed and almost stealthy, afraid to

* *The Virgin in the Ice.*

shake the wonder.

The bridge had a sheen of silver upon it after the earlier fine rain. The river ran dark and still, with too strong a flow for frost to have any hold. A few voices gave him good night as he passed. In the rutted road of the Foregate he began to hurry, fearing he had lingered a little too long. The trees that sheltered the long riverside level of the Gaye loomed like the dark fur of the earth's winter pelt on his left hand, the flat, pale sheen of the mill-pond opened out on his right, beyond the six little abbey houses of grace, three on either side the near end of the water, a narrow path slipping away from the road to serve each modest row. Silver and dark fell behind, he saw the torchlight glow from the gatehouse golden before him.

Still some twenty paces short of the gate he glimpsed a tall black figure sweeping towards him with long, rapid, fierce strides. The sidelong torchlight snatched it into momentary brightness as it strode past, the darkness took it again as it swept by Cadfael without pause or glance, long staff ringing against the frosty ruts, wide black garments flying, head and shoulders thrusting forward hungrily, long pale oval of face fixed and grim, and for one instant a vagrant light from the opened door of the nearest house by the pool plucked two crimson sparks of fire from the dark pits of the eyes.

Cadfael called a greeting that was neither heeded nor heard. Father Ailnoth swept by, engendering round him the only turbulence in the night's stillness, and was lost in the dark. Like an avenging fury, Cadfael thought later, like a scavenging raven swooping through the Foregate to hunt out little venial sins, and consign the sinners to damnation.

In the church of Saint Chad, Ralph Giffard bent the knee with a satisfactory feeling of a duty done and fences securely mended. He had lost one manor through loyalty to the cause of his overlord FitzAlan and his sovereign, the Empress Maud, and it had taken him a good deal of cautious treading and quiet submission to achieve the successful retention of what remained. He had but one cause that mattered to him now, and that was to preserve his own situation and leave his remaining estate intact to his son. His life had never been threatened, he had not been so deeply involved as to invite death. But possessions are possessions, and he was an ageing man, by no means minded to abandon his lands and flee either abroad, to Normandy or Anjou, where he had no status, or to

396

Gloucester, to take up arms for the liege lady who had already cost him dear. No, better far to sit still, shun every tempter, and forget old allegiance. Only so could he ensure that young Ralph, busy this Christmas happily playing lord of the manor at home, should survive this long conflict for the crown without loss, no matter which of the two claimants finally triumphed.

Ralph welcomed midnight with deep and genuine gratitude for the mercies shown forth upon men, and not least upon Ralph Giffard.

Benet slipped into the abbey church by the parish door, and made his way softly forward towards a spot where he could look through into the choir, and see the monks in their stalls, faintly lit by the yellow sheen of candles and the red glow of the altar lamps. The chanting of psalms came out into the nave muted and mild. Here the lighting was dim, and the cloaked assembly of the Foregate laity shifted and stirred, kneeled and rose again, every man nameless. There was a little while yet to wait before Matins began at the midnight hour, the celebration of God made flesh, virgin-born and wonderful. Why should not the Holy Spirit engender, as fire kindles fire and light light, the necessary instrument of flesh no more than the fuel that renders its substance to provide warmth and enlightenment? He who questions has already denied himself any answer. Benet did not question. He was breathing hard with haste and excitement, and even elation, for risk was meat to him. But once within here, in the obscurity that was at once peopled and isolated, he lost himself in awe, like the child he would never quite outgrow. He found himself a pillar, rather to brace himself by than to hide behind, and laid a hand to the cold stone, and waited, listening. The matched voices, soft as they were, expanded to fill the vault. The stone above, warmed by the music, reflected its arching radiance to the stone below.

He could see Brother Cadfael in his stall, and moved a little to have him more clearly in view. Perhaps he had chosen this spot purely to have in his sights the person most near to him in this place, a man already compromised, already tolerant, and all without any intent, on either part, to invade another's peace of mind. Only a little while, thought Benet, and you shall be free of me. Will you regret it, now and then, if you never again hear of me? And he wondered if he ought to say something clearly, something to be remembered, while there was still time.

A soft voice, just avoiding the sibilance of a whisper, breathed in his ear: 'He did not come?'

Benet turned his head very slowly, entranced and afraid, for surely it could not be the same voice, heard only once before, and briefly, but still causing the strings of his being to vibrate. And she was there, close at his right shoulder, the veritable, the unforgettable she. A dim, reflected light conjured her features out of the dark hood, broad brow, wide-set eyes, deeply blue. 'No,' she said. 'He didn't come!' And having answered herself, she heaved a great sigh. 'I never thought he would. Don't move – don't look round at me.'

He turned his face obediently towards the parish altar again. The soft breath fanned his cheek as she leaned close. 'You don't know who I am, but I know you.'

'I do know you,' said Benet as softly. Nothing more, and even that was uttered like a man in a dream.

Silence for a moment; then she said: 'Brother Cadfael told you?'

'I asked ...'

Silence again, with some soft implication of a smile in it, as though he had said something to please her, even distract her for a moment from whatever purpose had brought her here to his side.

'I know you, too. If Giffard is afraid, I am not. If he won't help you, I will. When can we two talk?'

'Now!' he said, suddenly wide awake and grasping with both hands at an opportunity for which he had never dared to hope. 'After Matins some people will be leaving, so may we. All the brothers will be here until dawn. As good a time as any!'

He felt her warm at his back, and knew when she shook softly with silent, excited laughter. 'Where?'

'Brother Cadfael's workshop.' It was the place he knew best as a possible solitude, while its proprietor kept the Christmas vigil here in the church. The brazier in the hut was turfed down to burn slowly through the night, he could easily blow it into life again to keep her warm. Clearly he could not take advantage of this delicate young being's partisan loyalty so far as to put her in peril, but at least this once he could speak with her alone, feast his eyes on her grave, ardent face, share with her the confidences of allies. Something to remember lifelong, if he never saw her again.

'By the south door, through the cloisters,' he said. 'No one will be there to see us tonight.'

398

The soft, warm breath in his ear said: 'Need we wait? I could slip into the porch now. Matins will be so long tonight. Will you follow?'

And she was away, not waiting for an answer, stealing silently and reverently across the tiles of the nave, and taking station for a few moments where she could be seen to be gazing devoutly in towards the high altar, beyond the chanting in the choir, in case anyone should be taking note of her movements. By that time he would have followed her wherever she chose to lead him. It hurt even to wait patiently the many minutes she delayed, before she chose her moment to withdraw into the darkness of the south porch. When he followed her, by cautious stages, reaching the darkness of the closed doorway with a great heaved breath of relief, he found her waiting with the heavy latch in her hand, motionless against the door. There they waited, close and quivering, for the first jubilant antiphon of Matins, and the triumphant answering cry:

'Christ is born unto us!'

'Oh, come, let us worship!'

Benet set his hand over hers on the massive latch, and lifted it softly as the hymn began. Outside, the night's darkness matched the darkness within. Who was to pay any attention now to two young creatures slipping through the chink of the door into the cold of the night, and cautiously letting the latch slide back into place? There was no one in the cloister, no one in the great court as they crossed it. Whether it was Benet who reached for her hand, or she for his, they rounded the corner of the thick box hedge in the garden hand in hand, and slowed to a walk there, panting and smiling, palms tightly clasped together, their breath a faint silver mist. The vast inverted bowl of sky, dark blue almost to blackness but polished bright and scintillating with stars, poured down upon them a still coldness they did not feel.

Brother Cadfael's timbered hut, solid and squat in the sheltered enclosure, never quite lost its warmth. Benet closed the door gently behind them, and groped along the little shelf he knew now almost as well as did Cadfael himself, where the tinder box and lamp lay ready to hand. It took him two or three attempts before the charred linen caught at the spark, and let him blow it carefully into a glow. The wick of the lamp put up a tiny, wavering flame that grew into a steady flare, and stood up tall and erect. The leather bellows lay by the brazier, he had only to shift a turf or two and spend a minute industriously pumping, and the charcoal glowed brightly, and accepted a feeding of split wood to burn into a warm hearth.

'He'll know someone has been here,' said the girl, but very tranquilly.

'He'll know I was here,' said Benet, getting up lithely from his knees, his bold, boy's face conjured into summer bronze by the glow from the brazier. 'I doubt if he'll say so. But he may wonder why. And with whom!'

'You've brought other women here?' She tilted her head at him in challenge, abruptly displeased.

'Never any, till now. Never any, hereafter. Unless you so pleasure me a second time,' he said, and stared her down with fiery solemnity.

Some resinous knot in the new wood caught and hissed, sending up a clear, white flame for a moment between them. Across its pale, pure gold the two young faces sprang into mysterious brightness, lit from below, lips parted, eyes rounded in astonished gravity. Each of them stared into a mirror, matched and mated, and could not look away from the unexpected image of love.

Chapter Five

PRIME WAS said at an early hour, after a very short interlude for sleep, and the dawn Mass followed with first light. Almost all the people of the Foregate had long since gone home, and the brothers, dazed with long standing and strung taut with the tensions of music and wonder, filed a little unsteadily up the night stairs to rest briefly before preparing for the day.

Brother Cadfael, stiff with being still for so long a time, felt himself in need rather of movement than of rest. Solitary in the lavatorium, he made unusually leisurely ablutions, shaved with care, and went out into the great court, just in time to see Dame Diota Hammet come hurrying in through the wicket in the gate, stumbling and slipping on the glazed cobbles, clutching her dark cloak about her, and gazing round in evident agitation. A furry fringe of hoar frost had formed on the collar of her cloak from her breath. Every outline of wall or bush or branch was silvered with the same glittering whiteness.

The porter had come out to greet her and ask her business, but she had observed Prior Robert emerging from the cloisters, and made for him like a homing bird, making him so low and unwary a reverence that she almost fell on her knees.

'Father Prior, my master – Father Ailnoth – has he been all night in the church with you?'

'I have not seen him,' said Robert, startled, and put out a hand in haste to help her keep her feet, for the rounded stones were wickedly treacherous. He held on to the arm he had grasped, and peered concernedly into her face. 'What is amiss? Surely he has his own Mass to take care of soon. By this time he should be robing. I should not interrupt him now, unless for some very grave reason. What is your need?'

'He is not there,' she said abruptly. 'I have been up to see, Cynric is there waiting, ready, but my master has not come.'

Prior Robert had begun to frown, certain that this silly woman was troubling him for no good reason, and yet made uneasy by her agitation. 'When did you see him last? You must know when he left his house.'

'Last evening, before Compline,' she said bleakly.

'What? And has not been back since then?'

'No, Father. He never came home all night. I thought he might have come to take part in your night offices, but no one has seen him even here. And as you say, by now he should be robing for his own Mass. But he is not there!'

Halted at the foot of the day stairs, Cadfael could not choose but overhear, and having overheard, inevitably recalled the ominous black-winged bird swooping along the Foregate towards the bridge at very much the same hour, according to Diota, when Ailnoth had left his own house. On what punitive errand? Cadfael wondered. And where could those raven wings have carried him, to cause him to fail of his duty on such a festal day?

'Father,' he said, coming forward with unwary haste, slithering on the frosty cobbles, 'I met the priest last night as I was coming back from the town to be in time for Compline. Not fifty paces from the gatehouse here, going towards the bridge, and in a hurry.'

Prior Robert looked round, frowning, at this unsolicited witness, and gnawed a lip in doubt how to proceed. 'He did not speak to you? You don't know where he was bound in such haste?'

'No. I spoke to him,' said Cadfael drily, 'but he was too intent to mark me. No, I have no notion where he was bound. But it was he. I saw him pass the light of the torches under the gate. No mistaking him.'

The woman was staring at him now with bruised, hollow eyes and still face, and the hood had slipped back from her forehead unnoticed, and showed a great leaden bruise on her left temple, broken at the centre by a wavering line of dried blood.

'You're hurt!' said Cadfael, asking no leave, and put back

402

the folds of cloth from her head and turned her face to the dawning light. 'This is a bad blow you've suffered, it needs tending. How did you come by it?'

She shrank a little from his touch, and then submitted with a resigned sigh. 'I came out in the night, anxious about him, to see if there was anyone stirring, or any sign of him. The doorstone was frozen, I fell and struck my head. I've washed it well, it's nothing.'

Cadfael took her hand and turned up to view a palm rasped raw in three or four grazes, took up its fellow and found it marked almost as brutally. 'Well, perhaps you saved yourself worse by putting out these hands. But you must let me dress them for you, and your brow, too.'

Prior Robert stood gazing beyond them, pondering what it was best to do. 'Truly I wonder … If Father Ailnoth went out at that hour, and in such haste, may not he also have fallen, somewhere, and so injured himself that he's lying helpless? The frost was already setting in …'

'It was,' said Cadfael, remembering the glassy sheen on the steep slope of the Wyle, and the icy ring of his own steps on the bridge. 'And sharply! And I would not say he was minding his steps when I saw him.'

'Some charitable errand …' murmured Robert anxiously. 'He would not spare himself …'

No, neither himself nor any other soul! But true enough, those hasty steps might well have lunged into slippery places.

'If he has lain all night helpless in the cold,' said Robert, 'he may have caught his death. Brother Cadfael, do you tend to this lady, do whatever is needful, and I will go and speak to Father Abbot. For I think we had best call all the brothers and lay brothers together, and set in hand a hunt for Father Ailnoth, wherever he may be.'

In the dim, quiet shelter of the workshop in the garden Cadfael sat his charge down on the bench against the wall, and turned to his brazier, to uncover it for the day. All the winter he kept it thus turfed overnight, to be ready at short notice if needed, the rest of the year he let it out, since it could easily be rekindled. None of his brews within here required positive warmth, but there were many among them that would not take kindly to frost.

The thick turves now damping it down were almost fresh, though neatly placed, and the fire beneath them live and comforting. Someone had been here during the night, and someone who knew how to lay his hand on the lamp and the tinder without disturbing anything else, and how to tend the fire to leave it much as he had found it. Young Benet had left few traces, but enough to set his signature to the nocturnal invasion. Even by night, it seemed, he practised very little dissembling where Cadfael was concerned, he was intent rather on leaving everything in order than on concealing his intrusion.

Cadfael warmed water in a pan, and diluted a lotion of betony, comfrey and daisy to cleanse the broken bruise on her forehead and the scored grazes in both palms, scratches that ran obliquely from the wrist to the root of the forefinger and thumb, torn by the frozen and rutted ground. She submitted to his ministrations with resigned dignity, her eyes veiled.

'That's a heavy fall you had,' said Cadfael, wiping away the dried line of blood from her temple.

'I was not minding myself,' she said, so simply that he knew it for plain truth. 'I am not of any importance.'

Her face, seen thus below him as he fingered her forehead, was a long oval, with fine, elongated features. Large, arched eyelids hid her eyes, her mouth was well shaped and generous but drooping with weariness. She braided her greying hair severely and coiled it behind her head. Now that she had told what she had come to tell, and laid it in other hands, she was calm and still under his handling.

'You'll need to get some rest now,' said Cadfael, 'if you've been fretting all night, and after this blow. Whatever needs to be done Father Abbot will do. There! I'll not cover it, better to have it open to the air, but as soon as you're dismissed go home and keep from the frost. Frost can fester.' He made a leisurely business of putting away such things as he had used, to give her time to think and breathe. 'Your nephew works here with me. But of course you know that. I remember you visited him here in the garden a few days ago. A good lad, your Benet.'

After a brief, deep silence she said: 'So I have always found him.' And for the first time, though pallidly and briefly, she smiled.

'Hard-working and willing! I shall miss him if he goes, but he's worth a more testing employment.'

She said nothing to that. Her silence was marked, as though words hovered behind it ready for spilling, and were strongly held back. She said no more, barring a sedate word of thanks, when he led her back to the great court, where a buzzing murmur of voices like a disturbed hive met them before ever they rounded the hedge. Abbot Radulfus was there, and had the brothers already mustering about him, bright and quivering with curiosity, their sleepiness almost forgotten.

'We have cause to fear,' said Radulfus, wasting no words, 'that some accident has befallen Father Ailnoth. He went out from his house towards the town last night, before Compline, and no one has any word of him since. He has not been home, nor did he attend with us in church overnight. He may have suffered a fall on the ice, and lain either senseless, or unable to walk, through the night. It is my order that those of you who did not serve throughout the night in the choir should take some food quickly, and go out to search for him. The last we know of him is that he had passed our gate before Compline, hurrying towards the town. From that point we must consider and attempt every path he may have taken, for who knows upon what parish errand he was called forth? Those of you who have been wakeful all night long, take food and then sleep, and you are excused attendance from the office, so that you may be fit to take up the search when your fellows return. Robert, see to it! Brother Cadfael will show where Father Ailnoth was last seen. The searchers had best go forth in pairs or more, for two at least may be needed if he is found injured. But I pray he may be found in reasonable case, and quickly,'

Brother Cadfael intercepted a startled and solemn Benet at the edge of the dispersing crowd. The boy had a distracted look about him, between mild guilt and deep bewilderment. He jutted a dubious underlip at Cadfael, and shook his head vehemently, as if to shake off some clinging illusion that made no sense, and yet would not be ignored.

'You won't need me today. I'd best go with them.'

'No,' said Cadfael decidedly. 'You stay here and look after Mistress Hammet. Take her home if she'll go, or find her a warm corner in the gatehouse and stay with her. I know where I met with the priest, and I'll see the hunt started. If anyone wants me, you can answer for me that I'll be back as soon as may be.'

'But you've been up the better part of the night,' protested Benet, hesitating.

'And you?' said Cadfael, and made off towards the gatehouse before Benet could reply.

Ailnoth had passed by in the evening like a black arrow from a war-bow, so blind, so deaf that he had neither seen Brother Cadfael nor heard his greeting, called clearly into a brazen frost that rang like bells. At that point in the Foregate he could have been making for the bridge, in which case his urgent business was with someone in the town itself, or for any of the paths which diverged from the Foregate beyond this point. Of these there were four, one to the right, down into the riverside level of the Gaye, where the abbey's main gardens spread for almost half a mile in plots, fields and orchards, and gave place at last to woodland, and a few scattered homesteads; three to the left, a first path turning in on the near side of the mill-pond, to serve the mill and the three small houses fringing the water there, the second performing the same function for the three on the opposite side. Each of these paths was prolonged alongside the water, but to end blindly at the obstacle of the Meole Brook. The third was the narrow but well-used road that turned left just short of the Severn bridge, crossed the Meole Brook by a wooden foot-bridge where it emptied into the river, and continued south-west into woodland country leading towards the Welsh border.

And why should Father Ailnoth be hurtling like the wrath of God towards any one of these paths? The town had seemed a likelier aim, but others were taking care of enquiries there, whether the watch at the gate had seen him, whether he had stopped to enquire for anyone, whether a black, menacing shadow had passed by under the gatehouse torches. Cadfael turned his attention to the more devious ways, and halted to consider, on the very spot, so far as he could judge, where Ailnoth had passed him by.

The Foregate parish of Holy Cross embraced both sides of the road, on the right stretching well into the scattered hamlets beyond the suburb, on the left as far as the brook. Had Ailnoth been bent upon visiting someone in a country croft, he would have started directly eastward from his house in the alley opposite the abbey gatehouse, and never entered the Foregate highway at all, unless his goal was one of the few dwellings beyond the Gaye. Small ground to cover there. Cadfael deployed two parties in that direction, and turned his attention towards the west. Three paths here, one that became a regular road and would take time, two that were near, short and could

406

surely be cleared up with little delay. And in any case, what would Ailnoth be doing at that late hour, setting out on a longer journey? No, he was on his way to some place or person close by, for what purpose only he knew.

The path on the near side of the mill-pond left the road as a decent cart track, since it had to carry the local corn to the mill, and bring the flour homeward again. It passed by the three small houses that crowded close to the highway, between their doors and the boundary wall of the abbey, reached the small plateau by the mill, where a wooden bridge crossed the head-race, and thence wandered on as a mere footpath in rough meadow grass by the edge of the water, where several pollarded willows leaned crookedly from the high bank. The first and second cottages were occupied by elderly people who had purchased bed and board for life by the grant of their own property to the abbey. The third belonged to the miller, who had been in the church throughout the night offices, to Cadfael's knowledge, and was here among the searchers now in mid morning. A devout man, as well as sedulous in preserving the favour he enjoyed with the Benedictines, and the security of his employment.

'Not a soul did I see along the waterside,' said the miller, shaking his head, 'when I came out last night to go to church, and that must have been much the same time as Brother Cadfael met with Father Ailnoth on the road. But I went straight through the wicket into the great court, not along the track, so he could have been bound this way only a matter of minutes later, for all I know. The old dame in the house next mine is house-bound once the frosts begin, she'd be home.'

'And deaf as a stone,' said Brother Ambrose flatly. 'Any man who called for help outside her door, no matter how loudly, would call in vain.'

'I meant, rather,' said the miller, 'that Father Ailnoth may have set out to visit her, knowing she dared not stir out even as far as the church. It's his duty to visit the aged and infirm, for their comfort ...'

The face Cadfael had glimpsed in the frosty night, flaring and fading as it surged past the torches, had not looked to him as if its errand was one of comfort, but he did not say so. Even the miller, charitably advancing the possibility, had sounded dubious.

'But even if he did not,' he said, rallying stoutly, 'the maidservant who looks after the old dame has sharp enough ears, and may have heard or seen him if he did pass this way.'

407

They separated into two parties, to comb the paths on either side the water, Brother Ambrose taking the far side, where it was but a narrow, beaten footpath serving the three little houses and continuing along the waterside under their sloping gardens; Cadfael the cart track that led to the mill, and there dwindled into a footpath in its turn. On both the white sheen of frost was dimpled and darkened by a few footprints, but those belonged all to the morning. The rime had silvered and concealed any that might have been made by night.

The elderly couple living retired in the first house had not been out of their door since the previous day, and had heard nothing of the priest being missing. Such sensational news had them gaping in an excitement partly pleasurable, and set their tongues wagging in exclamation and lamentation, but elicited no information at all. They had shuttered their window and barred their door early, made up a steady fire, and slept undisturbed. The man, once a forester in the abbey's portion of the forest of Eyton, went in haste to pull on his boots and wrap himself in a sacking cape, and join the hunt.

At the second house the door was opened to them by a pretty slattern of about eighteen, with a mane of dark hair and bold, inquisitive eyes. The tenant was merely a high, querulous voice from the inner room, demanding why the door stood open to let in the cold. The girl whisked away for a moment to reassure her, speaking in a loud screech and perhaps with much gesture, for the complaint sank to a satisfied mumble. The girl came back to them, swathing a shawl about her and closing the door behind her to forestall further complaint.

'No,' she said, shaking her dark mane vigorously, 'not a soul that I know of came along here in the night, why should they? Never a sound did I hear after dark, and she was in her bed as soon as the daylight went, and she'd sleep through the trump of doom. But I was awake until later, and there was nothing to hear or see.'

They left her standing on the doorstone, curious and eager, gazing after them along the track as they passed the third house and came to the tall bulk of the mill. Here, with no houses in between, the still surface of the mill-pond opened on their right hand, dull silver, widening and shallowing into a round pool towards the road from which they had come, tapering gradually before them into the stream that carried the water back to the Meole Brook and the river. Rimy grass overhung the high bank, undercut here by the strength of the tail-race.

And still no sign of any black form anywhere in the wintry pallor. The frost had done no more than form a thin frill of ice in the shallows, where the reed beds thickened and helped to hold it. The track reached the mill and became a narrow path, winding between the steep-roofed building and the precinct wall, and crossing the head-race by a little wooden bridge with a single hand-rail. The wheel was still, the sluice above it closed, and the overflow discharging its steady stream aside into the tail-race deep below, and so out into the pool, a silent force perceptible only as a shudder along the surface, which otherwise lay so still.

'Even if he came here,' said the miller, shaking his head, 'he would not go further. There's nothing beyond.'

No, nothing beyond but the path ambling along the grassy plain of the narrow meadow, to dwindle into nothing above the junction of brook and outflow. Fishermen came there sometimes, in season, children played there in the summer, lovers walked there in the twilight, perhaps, but who would walk that way on a frosty night? None the less, Cadfael walked on a little way. Here a few willows grew, leaning out over the water at a drunken angle by reason of the current which was gnawing under the bank. The younger ones had never yet been trimmed, but there were also two or three pollarded trunks, and one cut right down to a stump and bristling with a circle of new wands fine and springy as hairs on a giant, tonsured head. Cadfael passed by the first trees, and stood in the tufted wintry grass on the very edge of the high bank.

The motion of the tail-race, flowing out into the centre of the pool, continued its rippling path through the leaden stillness. Its influence, diminished but present, caused the faintest tremor under the bank on either side for a matter of perhaps ten paces, dying into the metallic lustre just beneath where Cadfael stood. It was that last barely perceptible shimmer that first drew his eyes down, but it was the dull fold of underlying darkness, barely stirring, that held his gaze. An edge of dark cloth, sluggishly swaying beneath the jutting grass of the bank. He went on his knees in the lingering rime, parting the grass to lean over and peer into the water. Black cloth, massed against the naked soils and the eroded willow roots, where the thrust of the tail-race had pushed it aside and tidied it out of the way, and almost out of sight. Twin pallors swayed gently, articulated like strange fish Cadfael had once seen drawn in a traveller's book. Open and empty, Father Ailnoth's hands appealed to a

409

clearing sky, while a fold of his cloak half-covered his face.

Cadfael rose to his feet, and turned a sombre face upon his companions, who were standing by the plank bridge, gazing across the open water to where the other party was just appearing below the gardens of the townward cottages.

'He is here,' said Cadfael. 'We have found him.'

It was no small labour to get him out, even when Brother Ambrose and his fellows, hailed from their own fruitless hunt by the miller's bull's bellow and excited waving, came hurrying round from the road to lend a hand in the work. The high, undercut bank, with deep water beneath it, made it impossible to reach down and get a hold on his clothing, even when the lankiest of them lay flat on his face and stretched long arms down, to grope still short of the surface. The miller brought a boat hook from among his store of tools, and with care they guided the obdurate body along to the edge of the tail-race, where they could descend to water level and grasp the folds of his garments.

The black, ominous bird had become an improbable fish. He lay in the grass, when they had carried him up to level ground, streaming pond-water from wiry black hair and sodden black garments, his uncovered face turned up to the chill winter light marbled blue and grey, with lips parted and eyes half-open, the muscles of cheeks and jaw and neck drawn tight with a painful suggestion of struggle and terror. A cold, cold, lonely death in the dark, and mysteriously his corpse bore the marks of it even when the combat was over. They looked down at him in awe, and no one had anything to say. What they did they did practically, without fuss, in blank silence.

They took a door from its hinges in the mill, and laid him on it, and carried him away through the wicket in the wall into the great court, and thence to the mortuary chapel. They dispersed then about their various businesses, as soon as Abbot Radulfus and Prior Robert had been apprised of their return, and what they brought with them. They were glad to go, to be off to the living, and to the festival the living were still keeping, glad to have the sanction of the season to feel happiness and have a great thing to celebrate.

The word went round the Foregate almost furtively, whispered from ear to ear, without exclaim, without many words, taking its time to reach the outer fringes of the parish, but by nightfall it was known to all. The thanksgiving made no

410

noise, no one acknowledged it or mentioned it, no one visibly exulted. Nevertheless, the parishioners of the Foregate kept Christmas with the heartfelt fervour of a people from whom an oppressive shadow had been lifted overnight. In the mortuary chapel, where even at this end of the year no warmth could be employed, those gathered about the bier shivered and blew into their bunched fingers, wringing the rough, fingerless mittens to set the chill blood flowing and work off the numbness. Father Ailnoth, colder than them all, nevertheless lay indifferent to the gathering frost even in his nakedness, and on his bed of stone.

'We must, then, conclude,' said Abbot Radulfus heavily, 'that he fell into the pool and drowned. But why was he there at such an hour, and on the eve of the Nativity?'

There was no one prepared to answer that. To reach the place where he had been found he must have passed by every near habitation without word or sign, to end in a barren, unpeopled solitude.

'He drowned, certainly,' said Cadfael.

'Is it known,' wondered Prior Robert, 'whether he could swim?'

Cadfael shook his head. 'I've no knowledge of that, I doubt if anyone here knows. But it might not be of much importance whether he could or no. Certainly he drowned. It is less certain, I fear, that he simply fell into the water. See here – the back of his head ...'

He raised the dead man's head with one hand, and propped head and shoulders with the right arm, and Brother Edmund, who had already viewed this corpse with him before ever Abbot Radulfus and Prior Robert were summoned, held a candle to show the nape and the thick circlet of wiry black hair. A broken wound, with edges of skin grazed loose round it and a bleached, moist middle now only faintly discoloured with blood after its soaking in the pool, began just at the rim of the tonsure, and scraped down raggedly through the circle of hair, to end where the inward curve of the nape began.

'He suffered a blow on the head here, before ever he entered the water,' said Cadfael.

'Struck from behind him,' said the abbot, without fastidious disdain, and peered closer. 'You are sure he drowned? This blow could not have killed him? For what you are saying is that this was no accident, but a deliberate assault. Or could he have come by this innocently? Is it possible? The track there is

411

rutted, and it was icy. Could he have fallen and injured himself thus?'

'I doubt it. If a man's feet go from under him he may sit down heavily, even sprawl back on his shoulders, but he seldom goes full-length so violently as to hit his head forcibly on the rough ground, only on smooth sheet ice. And mark, this is not on the round of his head, which would have taken such a shock, but lower, even moving into the curve of his neck, and lacerated, as if he was struck with something rough and jagged. And you saw the shoes he was wearing, felted beneath the sole. I think he went safer from a fall, last night, than most men.'

'Certainly, then, a blow,' said Radulfus. 'Could it have killed?'

'No, impossible! His skull is not broken. Not enough to kill, nor even to do him much lasting harm. But he might well have been stunned for a while, or so dazed that he was helpless when he fell into the water. Fell,' said Cadfael with deliberation, but ruefully, 'or was pushed in.'

'And of those two,' said the abbot with cold composure, 'which is the more likely?'

'In darkness,' said Cadfael, 'any man may step too near a sloping edge and misjudge his footing where a bank overhangs water. But whatever his reason for going along that path, why should he persist beyond the last dwelling? But this broken head I do not believe he got by any natural fall, and he got it before he went into the water. Some other hand, some other person, was there with him, and party to this death.'

'There is nothing in the wound, no fragment to show what manner of weapon it was that struck him?' ventured Brother Edmund, who had worked with Brother Cadfael in similar cases, and found good reason to require his judgement even in the minutest details. But he did not sound hopeful.

'How could there be?' said Cadfael simply. 'He has lain in the water all through the night, everything about him is bleached and sodden. If there had ever been soil or grass in his grazes, it would have soaked away long ago. But I do not think there was. He cannot alone have staggered far after that blow was struck, and he was just past the tail-race, or it would have drifted him the opposing way. Nor would anyone have carried or dragged him far if he was stunned, he being a big, heavy man, and the blow being only briefly disabling, not killing. Not ten paces from where we found him, I judge, he went into the

412

pool. And close by that same stretch he got this blow. On top of all, there he was on grass unrutted by wheels, being past the mill – only rough and tufted, as winter turf is. If he had slipped and fallen, the ground there might have half-stunned him, but it would not have broken his head and fetched blood. I have told you all I can tell from this poor body,' he said wearily. 'Make what you can of it.'

'Murder!' said Prior Robert, rigid with indignation and horror. 'Murder is what I make of it. Father Abbot, what is now to be done?'

Radulfus brooded for some minutes over the indifferent corpse which had been Father Ailnoth, and never before so still and quiet, so tolerant of the views of others. Then he said, with measured regret: 'I am afraid, Robert, we have no choice but to inform the lord sheriff's deputy, since Hugh Beringar himself is elsewhere about his own duties.' And with his eyes still upon the livid face on the stone slab he said, with bleak wonder: 'I knew he had not made himself loved. I had not realized that in so short a time he could make himself so hated.'

Chapter Six

OUNG ALAN Herbard, who was Hugh's deputy in his absence, came down hot-foot from the castle with the most experienced of his sergeants, William Warden, and two other officers in his train. Even if Herbard had not been well acquainted with the Foregate and its people, Will Warden certainly was, and went in no misapprehension concerning the degree of love the congregation of Holy Cross had for its new priest.

'There'll be very little mourning for him hereabouts,' he said bluntly, viewing the dead man without emotion. 'He made a thorough job of turning every soul in the parish against him. A poor end, though, for any man. A poor, cold end!'

They examined the head wound, noted the account rendered by every man who had taken part in the search, and listened to the careful opinions put forward by Brother Edmund and Brother Cadfael, and to everything Dame Diota had to say of her master's evening departure, and the anxious night she had spent worrying about his failure to return.

She had refused to depart, and waited all this time to repeat her story, which she did with a drained but steady composure, now that the matter and the mystery were out of her hands. Benet was beside her, attentive and solicitous, a very sombre Benet, with creased brows and hazel eyes clouded by something between anxiety on her account and sheer puzzlement on his own.

'If you'll give me leave,' said the boy, as soon as the officers

414

had withdrawn from the precinct to go in search of the provost of the Foregate, who knew his people as well as any man could, 'I'll take my aunt back to the house now, and see her settled with a good fire. She needs to rest.' And he added, appealing to Cadfael: 'I won't stay long. I may be wanted here.'

'Stay as long as is needful,' said Cadfael readily. 'I'll answer for you if there should be any questions. But what could you have to tell? I know you were in the church well before Matins began.' And knew, moreover, where the boy had been later on, and probably not alone, but he said nothing about that. 'Has anything been said about making provision for Mistress Hammet's future? This leaves her very solitary, but for you, and still almost a stranger here. But I'm sure Abbot Radulfus will see to it she's not left friendless.'

'He came himself to speak to her,' said Benet, a faint flush and gleam of his usual brightness appearing for a moment, in appreciation of such considerate usage. 'He says she need not be troubled at all, for she came here in good faith to serve the church in her proper station, and the church will see to it that she is provided for. Dwell in the house and care for it, he said, until a new priest is preferred to the benefice, and then we'll see. But in no case shall she be cast away.'

'Good! Then you and she can rest with easy minds. Terrible this may be, but it's no fault of yours or hers, and you should not brood on it.' They were both looking at him then with still, shocked faces that expressed nothing of grief or reassurance, but only stunned acceptance. 'Stay and sleep there, if you see fit,' he said to Benet. 'She may be glad of having you close by, tonight.'

Benet said neither yes nor no to that, nor did the woman. They went out silently from the ante-room of the gatehouse, where they had sat out the long uncertainty of the morning together, and crossing the wide highway of the Foregate, vanished into the narrow mouth of the alley opposite, still silvered with hoar-frost between its enclosing walls.

Cadfael felt no great surprise when Benet was back within the hour, instead of taking advantage of the permission to absent himself overnight. He came looking for Cadfael in the garden, and found him, for once, virtually idle in his workshop, sitting by the glowing brazier. The boy sat down silently beside him, and heaved a glum sigh.

'Agreed!' said Cadfael, stirring out of his thoughts at the sound. 'We're none of us quite ourselves today, small wonder.

But no need for you to rack your conscience, surely. Have you left your aunt all alone?'

'No,' said Benet. 'There's a neighbour with her, though I doubt if she's all that glad of the kind attention. There'll be more of them, I daresay, before long, bursting with curiosity and worming the whole story out of her. Not for grief, either, to judge by the one I left with her. They'll be chattering like starlings all over the parish, and never stop until night falls.'

'They'll stop fast enough, you'll find,' said Cadfael drily, 'as soon as Alan Herbard or one of his sergeant puts a word in. Let one officer show his face, and silence will fall. There's not a soul in the Foregate will own to knowing anything about anything once the questions begin.'

Benet shifted uneasily on the wooden bench, as though his bones rather than his conscience felt uncomfortable. 'I never understood that he was quite so blackly disliked. Do you truly think they'll hang together so close, and never betray even if they know who brought him to his death?'

'Yes, I do think it. For there's hardly a soul but will feel it might as easily have been his own act, but for God's grace. But it need not fret you, one way or the other. Unless it was you who broke his head?' said Cadfael mildly. 'Was it?'

'No,' said Benet as simply, staring down into his linked hands; and the next moment looked up with sharp curiosity: 'But what makes *you* so sure of it?'

'Well, firstly, I saw you in church well before it was time for Matins, and though there's no certainty just when Ailnoth went into the pool, I should judge it was probably after that time. Secondly, I know of no reason why you should bear him any grudge, and you said yourself it comes as a surprise to you he was so hated. But thirdly and best, from what I know of you, lad, if you took such dire offence as to up and hit a man, it would not be from behind, but face to face.'

'Well, thank you for that!' said Benet, briefly recovering his blazing smile. 'But, Cadfael, what *do* you think happened? It was you saw him last, alive, at least as far as is known. Was there any other soul about there? Did you see anyone else? Anyone, as it might be, following him?'

'Never a creature beyond the gatehouse here. There were folk from the Foregate just coming in for the service, but none going on towards the town. Any others who may have seen Ailnoth can only have seen him before ever I did, and with nothing to show where he was bound. Unless someone had speech with him. But by the way he went scurrying past me, I doubt if he had halted for any other.'

Benet considered that in silence for a long moment, and then said, rather to himself than to Cadfael: 'And from his house it's so short a way. He'd come into the Foregate just opposite the gatehouse. Small chance of being seen or stopped in that distance.'

'Leave it to the King's officers to scratch their heads over the how and why,' Cadfael advised. 'They'll find no lack of folk who'll pretend no sorrow at seeing the last of Ailnoth, but I doubt if they'll get much information out of anyone, man, woman or child. No blinking it, the man generated grudges wherever he stepped. He may well have made the most perfect of clerks, where he had to deal only with documents, charters and accounts, but he had no notion how to coax and counsel and comfort common human sinners. And what else is a parish priest for?'

The frost continued that night, harder than ever, freezing over the reedy shallows in the mill-pond, and fringing the townward shore with a white shelf of ice, but not yet sealing over the deeper water or the tremulous path of the tail-race, so that the little boys who went hopefully to examine the ice in the early morning returned disappointed. No point as yet in trying to break the iron ground for Father Ailnoth's grave, even if Herbard would have permitted an early burial, but at least the clear cold made delay acceptable.

In the Foregate a kind of breathless hush brooded. People talked much but in low voices and only among trusted friends, and yet everywhere there was a feeling of suppressed and superstitious gladness, as if a great cloud had been lifted from the parish. Even those who did not confide in one another in words did so in silent glances. The relief was everywhere, and palpable.

But so was the fear. For someone, it seemed, had rid the Foregate of its blight, and all those who had wished it away felt a morsel of the guilt sticking to their fingers. They could not but speculate on the identity of their deliverer, even while they shut their mouths and their eyes, and put away all knowledge of their own suspicions, for fear of betraying them to the law.

All through the routine of the day Cadfael pursued his own thoughts, and they centred, inevitably, on Ailnoth's death. No one would tell Alan Herbard about Eadwin's headland or

417

Aelgar's grievance, of the unconsecrated grave of Centwin's son, or any of the dozen or more other wounds that had made Ailnoth a hated man, but there would be no need. Will Warden would know them all already, and maybe other, lesser offences of which even the abbot had not been told. Every one of those thus aggrieved would be examined as to his movements on the eve of the Nativity, and Will would know where to look for confirmation. And much as the Foregate might sympathize with whoever had killed Ailnoth, and loyally as they would close round him and cover him, it was nevertheless vital that the truth should be known, for there would be no real peace of mind for anyone until it was discovered. That was the first reason why Cadfael, almost against his will, wished for a solution. The second was for the sake of Abbot Radulfus, who carried, in his own mind, a double guilt, for bringing to the fold so ill-fitted a shepherd, and for suffering him to be done to death by some enraged ram among the flock. Bitter though it may be to many, Cadfael concluded, there is no substitute for truth, in this or any case.

Meantime, in occasional reversions to the day's labours, he was thankful that Benet had completed the winter digging just in time, before the hard frost came, and attacked the final thin crop of weeds in all the flower beds so vigorously that now the earth could sleep snugly under the rime, and the whole enclosed garden looked neat and clean, and content as a hedge-pig curled up an arm's length down under leaves and grass and dry herbage until the spring.

A good worker, the boy Benet, cheerful and ungrudging, and good company. Somewhat clouded by the death of this man who had brought him here, and at least never done him any harm, but his natural buoyancy would keep breaking through. Not much was left, now, of the candidate for the cloister. Had that been the one sign of human frailty in Father Ailnoth, that he had deliberately represented his groom on the journey north as desirous of the monastic life, though still a little hesitant to take the final step? A lie to get the boy off his hands? Benet was firm that he had never given voice to any such wish, and Benet, in Cadfael's considered opinion, would make a very poor liar. Come to think of it, not very much left, either, of the wide-eyed, innocent, unlettered bumpkin Benet had first affected, at least not here in the solitude of the garden. He could still slip it on like a glove if for any reason the prior accosted him. Either he thinks me blind, said Cadfael to himself, or he does not care at all to pretend with me. And I am very sure he does not think me blind!

Well, a day or two more, and surely Hugh would be back. As soon as he was released from attendance on the King he would be making his way home by forced marches. Aline and Giles between them would take care of that. God send he would come home with the right answer!

And it seemed that Hugh had indeed made all haste to get home to his wife and son, for he rode into Shrewsbury late in the evening of the twenty-seventh, to hear from a relieved Alan Herbard of the turmoil that awaited solution, the death that came rather as blessing than disaster to the people of the Foregate, but must none the less be taken very seriously by the King's officers. He came down immediately after Prime next morning, to get the most authoritative account from the abbot, and confer with him over the whole troublesome matter of the priest's relationship with his flock. He had also another grave matter of his own to confide.

Cadfael knew nothing of Hugh's return until mid morning, when his friend sought him out in the workshop. The broken-glass grating of boots on the frozen gravel made Cadfael turn from his mortar, knowing the step but hardly believing in it.

'Well, well!' he said, delighted. 'I hadn't thought to clap eyes on you for a day or two yet. Glad I am to see you, and I hope I read the signs aright?' He broke free from Hugh's embrace to hold him off at arm's length and study his face anxiously. 'Yes, you have the look of success about you. Do I see you confirmed in office?'

'You do, old friend, you do! And kicked out promptly to my shire to be about my master's business. Trust me, Cadfael, he's come back to us lean and hungry and with the iron-marks on him, and he wants action, and vengeance, and blood. If he could but keep up this fury of energy, he could finish this contention within the year. But it won't last,' said Hugh philosophically, 'it never does. God, but I'm still stiff with all the riding I've done. Have you got a cup of wine about you, and half an hour to sit and waste with me?'

He flung himself down gratefully on the wooden bench and stretched out his feet to the warmth of the brazier, and Cadfael brought cups and a flagon, and sat down beside him, taking pleasure in viewing the slight figure and thin, eloquent face

419

that brought in with them the whole savour of the outside world, fresh from the court, ratified in office, a man whose energy did not flag as Stephen's did, who did not abandon one enterprise to go off after another, as Stephen did. Or were those days now over? Perhaps the King's privations and grievances in prison in Bristol had put an end to all half-hearted proceedings in the future. But plainly Hugh did not think him capable of sustaining so great a change.

'He wore his crown again at the Christmas feast, and a sumptuous affair it was. Give him his due, there's no man living could look more of a king than Stephen. He questioned me closely in private as to how things shape in these parts, and I gave him a full account of how we stand with the earl of Chester, and the solid ally Owain Gwynedd has been to us there in the north of the shire. He seemed content enough with me – at least he clouted me hard on the back – a fist like a shovel, Cadfael! – and gave me his authority to get on with the work as sheriff confirmed. He even recalled how I ever came to get his countenance as Prestcote's deputy. I fancy that's a rare touch in kings, part of the reason why we cling to Stephen even when he maddens us. So I got not only his sanction, but a great shove to get back on the road and back to my duty. I think he means to make a visit north when the worst of the winter's over, to buckle a few more of the waverers to him again. Lucky I'd thought to get a change of horses four times on the way south,' said Hugh thankfully, 'thinking I might be in haste coming back. I'd left my grey in Oxford, going down. And here I am, glad to be home.'

'And Alan Herbard will be glad to see you home,' said Cadfael, 'for he's been dropped into deep water while you've been away. Not that he shrinks from it, though he can hardly have welcomed it. He'll have told you what's happened here? On the very Nativity! A bad business!'

'He's told me. I've just come from the abbot, to get his view of it. I saw but little of the man, but I've heard enough from others. A man well hated, and in so short a time. Is their view of him justified? I could hardly ask Abbot Radulfus to cry his candidate down, but I would not say he had any great regard for him.'

'A man without charity or humility,' said Cadfael simply. 'Salted with those, he might have been a decent fellow, but both were left out of him. He came down over the parish like a cloud of blight, suddenly.'

420

'And you're sure it was murder? I've seen his body, I know of the head wound. Hard to see, I grant you, how he could have come by that by accident, or alone.'

'You'll have to pursue it,' said Cadfael, 'whatever poor angry soul struck the blow. But you'll get no help from the Foregate folk. Their hearts will be with whoever rid them of the shadow.'

'So Alan says, too,' said Hugh, briefly smiling. 'He knows these people pretty shrewdly, young as he is. And he'd rather I should harry them than he. And inasmuch as I must, I will. I'm warned off charity and humility myself,' said Hugh ruefully, 'on the King's affairs. He wants his enemies hunted down without remorse, and is giving orders right and left to that effect. And I have a charge to be the hunter here in my shire, for one of them.'

'Once before, as I recall,' said Cadfael, refilling his friend's cup, 'he gave you a task to do that you did in your own way, which certainly was not his when he gave the order. He never questioned your way, after. He may as well repent of his, later, and be glad if you shuffle your feet somewhat in the hunt. Not that I need to tell you as much, since you know it all before.'

'I can make a goodly show,' agreed Hugh, grinning, 'and still bear in mind that he might not be grateful for overmuch zeal, once he gets over his grudges. I never knew him bear malice for long. He did his worst here in Shrewsbury, and dislikes to be reminded of it now. The thing is this, Cadfael. Back in the summer, when it seemed the Empress had crown and sceptre and all in her hands, FitzAlan in Normandy is known to have sent over a couple of scouts of his following, to sound out the extent of her support, and see if the time was ripe to bring a fresh force over to add to her strength. How they were discovered I haven't heard, but when her fortunes were reversed, and the Queen brought her army up into London and beyond, these two venturers were cut off from return, and have been one leap ahead of capture ever since. One of them is thought to have got off successfully from Dunwich, but the other is still loose somewhere, and since he's been hunted without result in the south, the cry is now that he's made his way north to get out of range, and try to make contact with sympathizers of Anjou for help. So all the King's sheriffs are ordered to keep a strict watch for him. After his rough treatment, Stephen's in no mind to forgive and forget. I'm obliged to make a show of zeal, and that means making the

421

matter public by proclamation, and so I shall. For my part, I'm glad to know that one of them has slipped overseas again safely, back to his wife. Nor would I be sorry if I heard that the second had followed him. Two bold boys venturing over here alone, putting their skins at risk for a cause – why should I have anything against them? Nor will Stephen, when he comes to himself.'

'You use very exact terms,' said Cadfael curiously. 'How do you know they are mere boys? And how do you know that the one who's fled back to Normandy has a wife?'

'Because, my Cadfael, it's known who they are, the pair of them, youngsters very close to FitzAlan. The hart we're still hunting is one Ninian Bachiler. And the lad who's escaped us, happily, is a certain young fellow named Torold Blund, whom both you and I have good cause to remember.' He laughed, seeing how Cadfael's face brightened in astonished pleasure. 'Yes, the same long lad you hid in the old mill along the Gaye, some years back. And now reported as son-in-law to FitzAlan's closest friend and ally, Fulke Adeney. Yes, Godith got her way!'

Good cause to remember, indeed! Cadfael sat warmed through by the recollection of Godith Adeney, for a short time his garden boy Godric to the outer world, and the young man she had helped him to succour and send away safely into Wales. Man and wife now, it seemed. Yes, Godith had got her way!

'To think,' said Hugh, 'that I might have married her! If my father had lived longer, if I'd never come to Shrewsbury to put my newly inherited manors at Stephen's disposal, and never set eyes on Aline, I might well have married Godith. No regrets, I fancy, on either side. She got a good lad, and I got Aline.'

'And you're sure he's slipped away safely out of England, back to her?'

'So it's reported. And so may his fellow slip away, with my goodwill,' said Hugh heartily, 'if he's Torold's match, and can oblige me by keeping well out of my way. Should you happen on him, Cadfael – you have a way of happening on the unexpected – keep him out of sight. I'm in no mind to clap a good lad into prison for being loyal to a cause which isn't mine.'

'You have a good excuse for setting his case aside,' Cadfael suggested thoughtfully, 'seeing you're come home to find a slain man on the doorstep, and a priest at that.'

'True, I could argue that as the prior case,' agreed Hugh, setting his empty cup aside and rising to take his leave. 'All the more as this affair is indeed laid right at my door, and for all I know young Bachiler may be a hundred miles away or more. A small show of zeal, however, won't come amiss, or do any harm.'

Cadfael went out into the garden with him. Benet was just coming up over the far rim of the rose garden, where the ground sloped away to the pease fields and the brook. He was whistling jauntily as he came, and swinging an axe lightly in one hand, for a little earlier he had been breaking the ice on the fish ponds, to let air through to the denizens below.

'What did you say, Hugh, was the christened name of this young man Bachiler you're supposed to be hunting?'

'Ninian, or so he's reported.'

'Ah, yes!' said Cadfael. 'That was it – Ninian.'

Benet came back into the garden after his dinner with the lay servants, and looked about him somewhat doubtfully, kicking at the hard-frozen ground he had recently dug, and viewing the clipped hedges now silvered with rime that lasted day-long and increased by a fresh frilling of white every night. Every branch that stirred tinkled like glass. Every clod was solid as stone,

'What is there for me to do?' he demanded, tramping into Cadfael's workshop. 'This frost halts everything. No man could plough or dig, a day like this. Let alone copy letters,' he added, round eyed at the thought of the numb fingers in the scriptorium trying to line in a capital with precious gold-leaf, or even write an unshaken line. 'They're still at it, poor wretches. At least there's some warmth in handling a spade or an axe. Can I split you some wood for the brazier? Lucky for us you need the fire for your brews, or we should be as blue and stiff as the scribes.'

'They'll have lighted the fire in the warming room early, a day like this,' said Cadfael placidly, 'and when they can no longer hold pen or brush steady they have leave to stop work. You've done all the digging within the walls here, and the pruning's finished, no need to feel guilty if you sit idle for once. Or you can take a turn at these mysteries of mine if you care to. Nothing learned is ever quite wasted.'

Benet was ready enough to try his hand at anything. He came close, to peer curiously at what Cadfael was stirring in a stone pot on a grid on the side of the brazier. Here in their

423

shared solitude he was quite easy, and had lost the passing disquiet and dismay that had dimmed his brightness on Christmas Day. Men die, and thinking men see a morsel of their own death in every one that draws close to them, but the young soon recover. And what was Father Ailnoth to Benet, after all? If he had done him a kindness in letting him come here with his aunt, the priest had none the less had the benefit of the boy's willing service on the journey, a fair exchange.

'Did you visit Mistress Hammet last evening?' asked Cadfael, recalling another possible source of concern. 'How is she now?'

'Still bruised and shaken,' said Benet, 'but she has a stout spirit, she'll do well enough.'

'She hasn't been greatly worried by the sergeants? Hugh Beringar is home now, and he'll want to hear everything from her own lips, but she need not trouble for that. Hugh has been told how it was, she need only repeat it to him.'

'They've been civility itself with her,' said Benet. 'What is this you're making?'

It was a large pot, and a goodly quantity of aromatic brown syrup bubbling gently in it. 'A mixture for coughs and colds,' said Cadfael. 'We shall be needing it any day now, and plenty of it, too.'

'What goes into it?'

'A great many things. Bay and mint, coltsfoot, hore-hound, mullein, mustard, poppy – good for the throat and the chest – and a small draught of the strong liquor I distil does no harm in such cases, either. But if you want work, here, lift out that big mortar ... yes, there! Those frost-gnawed hands you were pitying, we'll make something for those.'

The chilblains of winter were always a seasonal enemy, and an extra batch of ointment for treating them could not come amiss. He began to issue orders briskly, pointing out the herbs he wanted, making Benet climb for some, and move hastily up and down the hanging bunches for others. The boy took pleasure in this novel entertainment, and jumped to obey every crisp command.

'The small scale, there, at the back of the shelf – fetch that out, and while you're in the corner there, the little weights are in the box beside. Oh, and, Ninian ...' said Cadfael, sweet and calm and guileless as ever.

The boy, interested and off his guard, halted and swung about in response to his name, waiting with a willing smile to hear what next he should bring. And on the instant he froze where he stood, the serene brightness still visible on a face turned to marble, the smile fixed and empty. For a long moment they contemplated each other eye to eye, Cadfael also smiling, then warm blood flushed into Benet's face and he stirred out of his stillness, and the smile, wary as it was, became live and young again. The silence endured longer, but it was the boy who broke it at last.

'Now what should happen? Am I supposed to overturn the brazier, set the hut on fire, rush out and bar the door on you, and run for my life?'

'Hardly,' said Cadfael, 'unless that's what you want. It would scarcely suit me. It would become you better to put that scale down on the level slab there, and pay attention to what you and I are about. And while you're at it, that jar by the shutter is hog's fat, bring that out, too.'

Benet did so, with admirable calm now, and turned a wryly smiling face. 'How did you know? How did you know even my name?' He was making no further pretence at secrecy, he had even relaxed into a measure of perverse enjoyment.

'Son, the story of your invasion of this realm, along with another mad-head as reckless as yourself, seems to be common currency by this time, and the whole land knows you are supposed to have fled northwards from regions where you were far too hotly hunted for comfort. Hugh Beringar got his orders to keep an eye open for you, at the feast in Canterbury. King Stephen's blood is up, and until it cools your liberty is not worth a penny if his officers catch up with you. For I take it,' he said mildly, 'that you *are* Ninian Bachiler?'

'I am. But how did you know?'

'Why, once I heard that there was a certain Ninian lost somewhere in these midland counties, it was not so hard. Once you all but told me yourself. "What's your name?" I asked you, and you began to say "Ninian", and then caught yourself up and changed it to a clownish echo of the question, before you got out "Benet". And oh, my child, how soon you gave over pretending with me that you were a simple country groom. Never had a spade in your hand before! No, I swear you never had, though I grant you you learn very quickly. And your speech, and your hands – No, never blush or look mortified, it was not so obvious, it simply added together grain by grain. And besides, you stopped counting me as someone to be deceived. You may as well admit it.'

425

'It seemed unworthy,' said the boy, and scowled briefly at the beaten earth floor. 'Or useless, perhaps! I don't know! What are you going to do with me now? If you try to give me up, I warn you I'll do all I can to break away. But I won't do it by laying hard on you. We've been friendly together.'

'As well for both you and me,' said Cadfael, smiling, 'for you might find you'd met your match. And who said I had any notion of giving you up? I am neither King Stephen's partisan nor the Empress Maud's, and whoever serves either of them honestly and at risk to himself may go about his business freely for me. But you may as well tell me what that business is. Without implicating any other, of course. I take it, for instance, that Mistress Hammet is not your aunt?'

'No,' said Ninian slowly, his eyes intent and earnest on Cadfael's face. 'You will respect her part in this? She was in my mother's service before she married the bishop's groom. She was my nurse when I was a child. When I was in flight I went to her for help. It was thoughtless, and I wish it could be undone, but believe it, whatever she has done has been done in pure affection for me, and what I've been about is nothing to do with her. She got me these clothes I wear – mine had been living rough in the woods and in and out of rivers, but they still marked me for what I am. And it was of her own will that she asked leave to bring me here with her as her nephew, when Father Ailnoth got this preferment. To get me away from the hunters. She had asked and been given his leave before ever I knew of it, I could not avoid. And it did come as a blessing to me, I own it.'

'What was your intent when you came over from Normandy?' asked Cadfael.

'Why, to make contact with any friends of the Empress who might be lying very low in the south and east, where she's least loved, and urge them to be ready to rise if FitzAlan should think the time ripe for a return. It looked well for her chances then. But when the wind changed, someone – God knows which of those we'd spoken with – took fright and covered himself by betraying us. You know we were two?'

'I know it,' said Cadfael. 'Indeed I know the second. He was of FitzAlan's household here in Shrewsbury before the town fell to the King. He got off safely from an eastern port, as I heard. You were not so lucky.'

'Is Torold clean away? Oh, you do me good!' cried Ninian, flushed with joy. 'We were separated when they almost

426

cornered us near Bury. I feared for him! Oh, if he's safe home ...' He caught himself up there, wincing at the thought of calling Normandy home. 'For myself, I can deal! Even if I do end in the King's prison – but I won't! Fending for one is not so hard as fretting for two. And Torold's a married man!'

'And the word is, he's gone, back to his wife. And what,' wondered Cadfael, 'is your intention now? Plainly the one you came with is a lost cause. What now?'

'Now,' said the boy with emphatic gravity, 'I mean to get across the border into Wales, and make my way down to join the Empress's army at Gloucester. I can't bring her FitzAlan's army, but I can bring her one able-bodied man to fight for her – and not a bad hand with sword or lance, though I do say it myself.'

By the lift of his voice and the sparkle in his eyes he meant it ardently, and it was a course much more congenial to him than acting as agent to reluctant allies. And why should he not succeed? The Welsh border was not so far, though the journey to Gloucester through the ill-disciplined wilds of Powys might be long and perilous. Cadfael considered his companion thoughtfully, and beheld a young man somewhat lightly clad for winter travelling afoot, without weapons, without a horse, without wealth to grease his journeying. None of which considerations appeared to discourage Ninian.

'An honest enough purpose,' said Cadfael, 'and I see nothing against it. We have a few adherents of your faction even in these parts, though they keep very quiet these days. Could not one of them be of use to you now?'

The bait was not taken. The boy closed his lips firmly, and stared Cadfael out with impregnable composure. If he had indeed attempted to contact one of the Empress's partisans here, he was never going to admit it. With his own confidences he might favour his too perceptive mentor, but he was not going to implicate any other man.

'Well,' said Cadfael comfortably, 'it seems that you are not being hunted here with any great zeal, and your position with us is well established, no reason why Benet should not continue to do his work here quietly and modestly, and never be noticed. And if this iron frost goes on as it's begun, your work will be here among the medicines, so we may as well go on with your lesson. Look lively, now, and pay attention to what I show you.'

The boy burst into a soft, half-smothered peal of laughter in sheer relief and pleasure, like a child, and bounded to Cadfael's elbow at the mortar like a hound puppy excited by a fresh scent.

'Good, then tell me what to do, and I'll do it. I'll be half an apothecary before I leave you. Nothing learned,' said Ninian, with an impudently accurate imitation of Cadfael's more didactic style, 'is ever quite wasted.'

'True, true!' agreed Cadfael sententiously. 'Nothing observed, either. You never know where it may fit into a larger vision.'

Exactly as certain details were beginning to fit together and elaborate for him the picture he had of this venturesome, light-hearted, likeable young man. A destitute young man, urgently in need of the means to make his way undetected to Gloucester, one who had come to England, no doubt, with a memorized list of names that should prove sympathetic to the Empress's cause, a few of them even here in Shropshire. A devoted woman all anxiety for her nurseling, bringing honey cakes and carrying away a small token thing that slipped easily into the breast of her gown, from the breast of Benet's cotte. And shortly thereafter, the lady Sanan Bernières, daughter of a father dispossessed for his adherence to Maud, and step-daughter to another lord of the same party, paying a brief visit from Giffard's house near Saint Chad's to buy herbs for her Christmas kitchen, and pausing in the garden to speak to the labouring boy, and look him up and down, as though, as the boy himself had reported, she were in need of a page, 'and thought I might do, given a little polishing'.

Well, well! So far everything in harmony. But why, then, was the boy still here at all, if aid had been asked and given?

Upon this incomplete picture the sudden death of Father Ailnoth intruded like a black blot in a half-written page, complicating everything, relating, apparently, to nothing, a bird of as ill omen dead as alive.

Chapter Seven

HE HUNT for Ninian Bachiler, as a proscribed
agent of the Empress Maud at large in Stephen's
territory, was duly proclaimed in Shrewsbury, and
the word went round in voluble gossip, all the more
exuberantly as a relief from the former sensation of Ailnoth's
death, concerning which no one in the Foregate had been
voluble, unless in privacy. It was good to have a topic of
conversation which departed at so marked a tangent from what
really preoccupied the parishioners of Holy Cross. Since none
of the gossips cared a pin how many dissident agents were at
large in the county, none of the talk was any threat to the
fugitive, much less to Mistress Hammet's dutiful nephew
Benet, who came and went freely between abbey and
parsonage.

In the afternoon of the twenty-ninth of December, Cadfael
was called out to the first sufferers from coughs and colds in the
Foregate, and extended his visits to one elderly merchant in
the town itself, a regular chest patient of his in the winter. He
had left Ninian sawing and splitting wood from the pruning of
the trees, and keeping cautious watch on a pot of herbs in oil of
almonds, which had to warm on the edge of the brazier without
simmering, to make a lotion for the frost-nipped hands too
tender to endure the hog's-fat base of the ointment. The boy
could be trusted to abide by his instructions, and whatever he
did he did with his might.

Cadfael's errands had taken him rather less time than he had

429

expected, and the weather was not such as to encourage him to linger. He re-entered at the gatehouse with more than an hour still in hand before Vespers, and made his way across the great court and out into the garden, rounding the box hedge into the alley that led to his herbarium. In the frost he had wrapped woollen cloths about his boots to give him a grip on the icy roads, and the same sensible precaution made his steps silent on the path. So it happened that he heard the voices before he himself was heard, rapid and soft and vehement from within his workshop. And one of the voices was Ninian's, a tone above its usual pitch by reason of some fierce but subdued excitement. And the other was a girl's, insistent and agitated. Curious that she, too, should convey this same foolhardy sense of enjoyment in the experience of danger and dread. A good match! And what other girl had had to do with this place and this youth, but Sanan Bernières?

'Oh, but he would!' she was saying emphatically. 'He's there by now, he'll tell them everything, where to find you, how you sent to him – all! You must come now, quickly, before they come to take you.'

'Impossible by the gatehouse,' said Ninian, 'we should run into their arms. But I can't believe – why should he betray me? Surely he knows I'd never mention his name?'

'He's been in dread,' said the girl impatiently, 'ever since your message came, but now you're cried publicly as a wanted man, he'll do anything to shake off his own danger. He's not evil – he does as other men do, protects his own life and lands, and his son's, too – he lost enough before ...'

'So he did,' said Ninian, penitent. 'I never should have drawn him in. Wait, I must lift this aside, I can't leave it to boil. Cadfael ...'

The shameless listener, who at least had heard one motion of consideration towards him and his art, in that last utterance, suddenly came to his senses, and to the awareness that in a matter of seconds these two would be issuing forth from the hut and taking to flight, by whatever road this resourceful girl had devised. Just as soon as Ninian had lifted the soothing oil from the heat and laid it carefully in a secure spot. Bless the boy, he deserved to reach Gloucester in safety! Cadfael made haste to dart round behind the barrier of the box hedge, and freeze into stillness there. He had not time to withdraw completely, but it is not certain, in any case, that he would have done so.

They burst out of the workshop hand in hand, she leading, for she knew by what route she had entered here unobserved. Through the garden she drew him, over the rim of the slope, and down towards the Meole Brook. A dark little figure swathed in a cloak, she vanished first, dwindling rapidly out of sight down the field; Ninian followed. They were gone, along the edge of the newly ploughed and manured pease fields and out of sight. So the brook was frozen over, and so must the mill-pond be. That way she had come, straight to where she knew he would be. Yet she might, just as easily, have found Cadfael there as well. Which meant, surely, that she had had converse with Ninian since he had confided in Cadfael, and saw no reason to fear the encounter, when the need was great.

Well, they were gone. No sound came up from the hollow of the brook, and there were trees quite close on the further side for cover, and all they had to do after that was wait for the right moment, cross the brook again by the bridge that carried the westward road, and make their way discreetly to whatever hiding place she had devised for her hostage, whether in the town or out of it. If out of it, surely to the west, since that was the way he desired, at last, to go. But would Ninian consent to depart until he knew that Dame Diota was safe and suspect of nothing in connection with his own expedition? If his cover was stripped from him, then she was also exposed to question. He would not leave her so. Cadfael had begun to know this young man well enough to be certain of that.

It had grown profoundly quiet, as if the very air waited for the next and inevitable alarm. Cadfael spared a moment to peer into his workshop, saw his pot of oil placed carefully on the stone cooling slab close to the brazier, and withdrew again in some haste to the great court, and across it into the cloister, but hovering anxiously where he could watch for any invasion at the gatehouse, without himself being immediately observed.

They were longer in coming than he had expected, and for that he was grateful. Moreover, a sudden flurry of fine snow had begun to fall, and that would soon cover up the footsteps crossing the brook, and in the rising wind of evening even disguise any tracks left in the garden. Until this moment he had not had time to consider the implications of what he had overheard. Clearly Ninian's appeal had gone to Ralph Giffard, who had turned a deaf ear, all too conscious of his own danger if he responded. But the girl, born into another family no less devoted to the Empress's cause, had taken up the charge and

431

made it her own. And now, affrighted by the public crying of an enemy spy, Giffard had thought it best to ensure his own position by carrying the whole story to Hugh Beringar. Who would not be grateful for the attention, but would be forced to act upon it, or at least to put up a fair show of doing so.

All of which left one curious point at issue: Where had Ralph Giffard been going in such purposeful haste on Christmas Eve, striding across the bridge towards the Foregate almost as impetuously as Father Ailnoth had been hastening in the opposite direction an hour or so later? The two intent figures began to look like mirror images of the same man. Giffard, perhaps, the more afraid, Ailnoth the more malevolent. There was a link somewhere there, though the join was missing.

And here they came, in at the gatehouse arch, all of them on foot, Hugh with Ralph Giffard hard and erect at his elbow, Will Warden and a couple of young officers in arms following. No need here for mounted men, they were in search of a youngster horseless and penniless, labouring in the abbey gardens, and the prison that waited for him was only walking distance away.

Cadfael took his time about appearing. Others were there first, and so much the better. Brother Jerome did not love the cold, but kept a watchful eye on the outer world whenever he hopped into the warming room on such frosty days, ready to appear at any moment, dutiful and devout. Moreover, he always knew where to find Prior Robert at need. By the time Cadfael emerged innocently from the cloister they were both there, confronting the visitors from the secular world, and a few other brethren had noted the gathering, and halted within earshot in pure human curiosity, forgetting their chilled hands and feet.

'The boy Benet?' Prior Robert was saying in tones of astonishment and disdain as Cadfael approached. 'Father Ailnoth's groom? The good father himself asked employment for this young man. What absurdity is this? The boy is scarcely better than a simpleton, a mere country lad! I have often spoken with him, I know him for an innocent. My lord sheriff, I fear this gentleman wastes your time in a mistake. This cannot be true.'

'Father Prior, by your leave,' Ralph Giffard spoke up firmly, 'it is only too true, the fellow is not what he seems. I received a message, written in a fair hand, from this same simpleton, sealed with the seal of the traitor and outlaw FitzAlan, the Empress's man who is now in France, and asking me for help in FitzAlan's name – an appeal I rightly left unanswered. I have kept the leaf, the lord sheriff has seen it for himself. He was here, he said, come with the new priest, and he needed help, news and a horse, and laid claim to my aid to get what he wanted. He begged me to meet him at the mill an hour short of midnight on Christmas Eve, when all good folk would be making ready for church. I did not go, I would not touch such treason against our lord the King. But the proof I've given to the sheriff here, and there is not nor cannot be any mistake. Your labourer Benet is FitzAlan's agent Ninian Bachiler, for so he signed himself with his own hand.'

'I fear it's true enough, Father Prior,' said Hugh briskly. 'There are questions to be asked later, but now I must ask your leave at once to seek out this Benet, and he must answer for himself. There need be no disturbance for the brothers, I am asking access only to the garden.'

It was at this point that Cadfael ambled forward out of the cloister, secure across the glazed cobbles, since his feet were still swathed in wool. He came with ears benignly pricked and countenance open as the air. The snow was still falling, in an idle, neglectful fashion, but every flake froze where it fell.

'Benet?' said Cadfael guilelessly. 'You're looking for my labouring boy? I left him not a quarter of an hour since in my workshop. What do you want with him?'

He went with them, all concern and astonishment, as they proceeded into the garden, and threw open the workshop door upon the soft glow of the brazier, the pot of herbal oil drawn close on its stone slab, and the aromatic emptiness, and from that went on to quarter the whole of the garden and the fields down to the brook, where the helpful snow had obliterated every footprint. He was as mystified as the best of them. And if Hugh avoided giving him a single sidelong look, that did not mean he had not observed every facet of this vain pursuit, rather that he had, and was in little doubt as to the purveyor of mystification. There was usually a reason for Brother Cadfael's willing non-cooperation. Moreover, there were other points to be pursued before the search was taken further.

'You tell me,' said Hugh, turning to Giffard, 'that you received this appeal for your help a day or so before Christmas Eve, when a meeting at the mill was requested, somewhat before midnight. Why did you not pass it on at once to my deputy? Something might have been done about it then. Plainly he had wind of us now, since he's fled.'

If Giffard was uneasy at this dereliction of a loyal subject's duty, he gave no sign of it, but stared Hugh fully and firmly in the face. 'Because he was merely your deputy, my lord. Had you been here ... You got your office first after the siege of Shrewsbury, you know how we who had taken the oath to the Empress fared then, you know of my losses. Since then I have submitted to King Stephen, and held by my submission faithfully. But a young man like Herbard, new here, left in charge and liable to stand on his dignity and status – one ignorant of the past, and what it cost me ... I was afraid of being held still as one attained, even if I told honestly all that I knew. And recollect, we had then heard nothing about this Bachiler being hunted in the south, the name meant nothing to me. I thought him probably of no importance, and with no prospect of any success in whipping up support for a lost cause. So I held my peace, in spite of FitzAlan's seal. There were several of his knights held such seals in his name. Do me justice, as soon as you made public the hue and cry, and I understood what was afoot, I came to you and told you the truth.'

'I grant you did,' said Hugh, 'and I understand your doubts, though it's no part of my office to hound any man for what's past and done.'

'But now, my lord ...' Giffard had more to say, and had plainly taken great encouragement from his own eloquence and Hugh's acquiescence, for he had burned into sudden hopeful fervour. 'Now I see more in this than either you or I have thought. For I have not quite told you all, there has hardly been time to think of everything. For see, it was this young man who came here under the protection of Father Ailnoth, vilely deceiving the priest in the pretence that he was a harmless youth seeking work, and kin to the woman who kept the priest's household. And is not Father Ailnoth, who brought him here in all innocence, now done to death and waiting for burial? Who is more likely to stand guilty of his murder than the man who took wicked advantage of his goodness, and made him an unwitting accomplice in treason?'

He knew very well what manner of bolt he was hurling into the circle of listeners, he had even drawn back a pace or two to observe the shock and to distance himself from it. There was

434

no length to which he would not go, now, to prove his own loyal integrity, to keep what he still had, if he must eternally grudge and lament what he had lost by his former allegiance. Perhaps he was secretly relieved that the boy he traduced was well away, and need never answer, but what most troubled him was his own inviolability.

'You're accusing him of the priest's murder?' said Hugh, eyeing him narrowly. 'That's going far. On what grounds do you make such a charge?'

'The very fact that he is fled points to him.'

'That might be valid enough, but not – mark me! – not unless the priest had got wind of the deception practised on him. To the best we know there was no quarrel between them, nothing had arisen to set them at odds. Unless the priest had found out how he had been abused, there could be no ground for any hostility between them.'

'He did know,' said Giffard.

'Go on,' said Hugh after a brief, profound silence. 'You cannot stop there. How do you know the priest had found him out?'

'For the best reason. I told him! I said there was still more that I had not yet told you. On the eve of the Nativity I came down here to his house, and told him how he was cheated and abused by one he had helped. I had given it anxious thought, and though I did not go to your deputy, I felt it only right to warn Father Ailnoth how he had harboured an enemy unawares. Those of the Empress's party are threatened with excommunication now, as you, my lord sheriff, are witness. The priest had been shamefully imposed upon, and so I told him.'

So that was the way of it! That was where he had been bound in such determined haste before Compline. And that was why Father Ailnoth had rushed away vengefully to keep the nocturnal tryst and confront in person the youth who had imposed upon him. Give him his due, he was no coward, he would not run first to the sergeants and get a bodyguard, he would storm forth by the mill-pool to challenge his opponent face to face, denounce, possibly even attempt to overpower him with his own hands, certainly cry him outlaw to the abbot and to the castle if he could not himself hale him to judgement. But things had gone very differently, for Ninian had come unharmed to church, and Ailnoth had ended in the pool with a broken head. And who could avoid making the simple

435

connection now? Who that had not spent so many days in Ninian's blithe company as had Cadfael, and got to know him so well?

'And after you had left him,' said Hugh, eyeing Giffard steadily, 'he knew the time and place appointed for you to meet with Bachiler, and the invitation you had rejected you think he went to accept? But without an acceptance from you, would Bachiler keep the appointment?'

'I made no answer. I had not rejected it outright. He was asking for help, for news, for a horse. He would come! He could not afford not to come.'

And he would meet with a very formidable and very angry enemy, bent on betraying him to the law, a man who verily held himself to be the instrument of the wrath of God. Yes, death could well come of such a meeting.

'Will,' said Hugh, turning abruptly to his sergeant, 'get back to the castle and bring down more men. We'll get the lord abbot's permission to search the gardens here, and the stables and the barns, grange court, storehouses, all. Begin with the mill, and have a watch on the bridge and the highway. If this youngster was in the hut here not half an hour ago, as Cadfael says, he cannot be far. And whether he has killed or no is still open, but the first need is to lay hands on him and have him safe in hold.'

'You will not forget,' said Cadfael, alone with Hugh in the workshop later, 'that there are others, many others, who had as good reason as Ninian, and better, to wish Ailnoth dead?'

'I don't forget it. Far too many others,' agreed Hugh ruefully. 'And all you tell me of this boy – not that I'm dull enough, mind, to suppose you've told me all you could! – shows him as one who might very well hit out boldly in his own defence, but scarcely from behind. Yet he might, in the heat of conflict. Who knows what any of us might do, in extremes? And by what I hear of the priest, he would lash out with all his might and with whatever weapon came to hand. It's the lad's vanishing now that suggests the worst.'

'He had good reason to vanish,' pointed out Cadfael, 'if he heard that Giffard was on his way to the castle to betray him. You'd have had to clap him into prison, guilty or innocent of the priest's death. Your hand's forced. Of course he'd run.'

'*If* someone warned him,' agreed Hugh with a wry smile. 'You, for instance?'

'No, not I,' said Cadfael virtuously. 'I knew nothing about Gifford's errand, or I might have dropped a word in the boy's ear. But no, certainly not I. I do know that Benet – Ninian we must call him now, I suppose! – was in the church some time before midnight on Christmas Eve. If he went to the mill at all, he went early for the meeting, and left early, also.'

'So you told me, and I believe it. But so, by your own account, did Ailnoth go early to the meeting place, perhaps to hide himself and spring out on Bachiler by surprise. There was still time for them to clash and one to die.'

'The boy had not the marks of any agitation or dismay upon him in the church. A little excitement, perhaps, but pleasurable, I would say. And how much have you managed to worm out of the parish folk about this business? There are a number who had justifiable grudges against Ailnoth, what have they to say for themselves?'

'In general, as you'd expect, as little as possible. One or two make no secret of their gratitude that the man's gone, none at all. Eadwin, the one whose boundary stone he moved, he's neither forgotten nor forgiven, even if the stone was replaced afterwards. His wife and children swear he never left the house that night – but so do they all, and so, of course, they would. Jordan Achard, the baker, now there's a man who might kill in a rage. He has a real grievance. His bread is his pride, and there was never any amends made for that insult. It hurt far more than if the priest had denounced him for a notorious lecher, which would at least have had the merit of being true. There are some give him the credit for being the father of that poor girl's baby, the lass who drowned herself, but from all I hear it could as well have been half the other men in the parish, for she couldn't say no to any of them. Our Jordan says he was home and sober every moment of Christmas Eve, and his wife bears him out, but she's a poor, subdued creature who wouldn't dare cross him. But from all accounts it's few nights he does spend in his own bed, and to judge by his wife's sidelong looks and wary answers he may well have been sleeping abroad that night. But we shall never get her to say so. She's both afraid of him and loyal to him.'

'The rest of his women may be less so,' said Cadfael. 'But I hardly see Jordan as a man of violence.'

'Perhaps not. But I do see Father Ailnoth as a man of violence, whether bodily or spiritual. And consider, Cadfael, how he might behave if he happened on one of his flock

437

sneaking into the wrong bed. If not a violent man, Jordan is a big and strong one, and by no means meek enough to suffer assault tamely. He might end the fight another man began, without ever meaning to. But Jordan is one among many, and not the most likely.'

'Your men have been diligent,' said Cadfael with a sigh.

'They have. Alan was on his mettle, and determined to deserve his place. There's a decent poor soul called Centwin, who lives along the Foregate towards the horse-fair ground. You'll have heard his story. It was new to me until I heard it from Alan. The babe that died unchristened because Ailnoth could not interrupt his prayers. That sticks in the craw of every man in the parish, worse than all.'

'You cannot have found out anything black against Centwin?' protested Cadfael. 'As quiet a creature as breathes, never a trouble to any.'

'Never with occasion until now. But this goes deep. And Centwin, quiet as he may be, is also deep. He keeps his own counsel, and broods over his own grievances. I've spoken with him. We questioned the watch on the town gate, Christmas Eve,' said Hugh. 'They saw you go out, and you best know the time that was, and where you met the priest. They also saw Centwin go out not many minutes after you, on his way home, he said, from visiting a friend in the town to whom he owed a small debt. True enough, for the tanner he paid has confirmed it. He wanted, he said, to have all his affairs clear and all dues paid before he went to Matins, as indeed he did go, and left before Lauds for home. But you see how the time fits. One coming a few minutes behind you may also have met with Ailnoth, may have seen him turn from the Foregate along the path to the mill. There in darkness and loneliness, think, might not even a mild, submissive man with that wound burning in his belly have seen suddenly an opportunity to pay off yet another and a more bitter debt? And there was the time between then and Matins for two men to clash in the darkness, and one to die.'

'No,' said Cadfael, 'I do not believe it!'

'Because it would be one cruelty piled upon another? But such things happen. No, take heart, Cadfael, neither do I quite believe it, but it is *possible*. There are too many by far who are not vouched for, or whose guarantors cannot be trusted, too many who hated him. And there is still Ninian Bachiler. Whatever the truth of him, you do understand that I must do my best to find him?'

He looked down at his friend with a dark, private smile that was more eloquent than the words. It was not the first time they had agreed, with considerate courtesy and no need of many words, to pursue each what he held to be his own duty, and bear no malice if the two crossed like swords.

'Oh, yes!' said Cadfael. 'Yes, that I fully understand.'

Chapter Eight

ADFAEL HAD returned to the church after Prime to replenish the perfumed oil in the lamp on Saint Winifred's altar. The inquisitive skills which might have been frowned upon if they had been employed to make scents for women's vanity became permissible and even praiseworthy when used as an act of worship, and he took pleasure in trying out all manner of fragrant herbs and flowers in many different combinations, plying the sweets of rose and lily, violet and clover against the searching aromatic riches of rue and sage and wormwood. It pleased him to think that the lady must take delight in being so served, for virgin saint though she might be, she was a woman, and in her youth had been a beautiful and desirable one.

Cynric the verger came in from the north porch with the twig broom in his hand, from brushing away the night's sprinkling of fine snow from porch and steps, and went to open the great service-book on the reading desk, and trim the candles on the parish altar ready for the communal Mass, and set two new ones on the prickets of the wall brackets on either side. Cadfael gave him good day as he came back into the nave, and got the usual tranquil but brief acknowledgement.

'Freezing as hard as ever,' said Cadfael. 'There'll be no breaking the ground for Ailnoth today.' For it would be Cynric who had to dig the grave, in the green enclosure east of the church, where priests and abbots and brothers were laid to rest.

440

Cynric sniffed the air and considered, his deep eyes veiled. 'A change by tomorrow, maybe. I smell a thaw coming.'

It could be true. He lived on close, if neutral, terms with the elements, tolerating them as they seemed to refrain from harming him, for it must be deathly cold in that small, stony room over the porch.

'The ground's chosen for him?' asked Cadfael, catching the taciturn habit.

'Close under the wall.'

'Not next to Father Adam, then? I thought Prior Robert would have wanted to put him there.'

'He did,' said Cynric shortly. 'I said the earth there was not yet settled, and must have time to bed down.'

'A pity the hard frost came now. A dead man still lying among us unburied makes the young ones uneasy.'

'Ay,' said Cynric. 'The sooner he's in the ground the better for all. Now that he's gone.' He straightened the second thick candle on its spike, stepped back to make sure it stood erect and would not gutter, and brushed the clinging feel of tallow from his hands, for the first time turning his eyes in their hollow caverns upon Cadfael, and lighting up his lantern countenance with the smile of singular if rueful sweetness that brought the children to him with such serene confidence. 'Do you go into the Foregate this morning? I heard there's a few folk having trouble with the cold.'

'No wonder they should!' said Cadfael. 'I'm away to have a look at one or two of the children, but there's no great harm yet. Why, do you know of someone who needs me? I have leave, I can as well make one more visit. Who is sick?'

'It's the little wooden hovel on the left, along the back lane from the horse-fair, the widow Nest. She's caring for her grandchild, the poor worm, Eluned's baby, and she's fretted for it.' Cynric, perforce, was unusually loquacious in explaining. 'Won't take its milk, and cries with the wind in its belly.'

'It was born a healthy child?' asked Cadfael. For it could not be many weeks old, and motherless, deprived of its best food. He had not forgotten the shock and anger that had swept through the Foregate, when they lost their favourite whore. If indeed Eluned had ever been a whore. She never asked payment; if men gave her things, it was of their own will. She, it seemed; had done nothing but give, however unwisely.

'A bonny girl, big and lusty, so Nest said.'

'Then she'll have it in her, infant though she may be, to fight her way into life,' said Cadfael comfortably. 'I must go get the right cordial for an infant's inside. I'll make it fresh. Who sings Mass for you today?'

'Brother Anselm.'

'Well for you!' said Brother Cadfael, making for the south porch and his quickest way to the garden and his workshop. 'It might as easily have been Brother Jerome.'

The house was low and narrow, but sturdy, and the dark passage in which it stood braced against a taller dwelling looked crisp and clean in the hard frost, though in moist, mild weather it might have been an odorous hole. Cadfael rapped at the door, and for immediate reassurance called out loudly: 'Brother Cadfael from the abbey, mistress. Cynric said you need me for the child.'

Whether it was his own name or Cynric's that made him welcome there was no knowing, but instantly there was a stir of movement within, a baby howled fretfully, probably at being laid down in haste, and then the door was opened wide, and from half-darkness a woman beckoned him within, and made haste to close the door after him against the cold.

This one small room was all the house, and its only inlet for light or outlet for smoke was a vent in the roof. In clement weather the door would always be open from dawn to dusk, but frost had closed it, and the dwelling was lit only by a small oil lamp and the dim but steady glow of a fire penned in an iron cage on a flat stone under the vent. But blessedly someone had supplied charcoal for the widow's needs, and there was a mild fume in the nostrils here but little smoke. Furnishings were few, a low bench-bed in a corner, a few pots on the firestone, a rough, small table. Cadfael took a little time to accustom his eyes to the dim light, and the shapes of things emerged gradually. The woman stood by him, waiting, and like all else here, grew steadily out of the gloom, a perceptible human being. The cradle, the central concern of this house, was placed in the most sheltered corner, where the warmth of the fire could come, but not the draught from door or vent. And the child within was wailing indignantly within its wrappings, half-asleep but unable by reason of discomfort to fall deeper into peace.

'I brought an end of candle with me,' said Cadfael, taking in everything about him without haste. 'I thought we might need

442

more light. With your leave!' He took it out from his scrip, tilted the wick into the small flame of the lamp in its clay saucer, and stood the stump upon the corner of the table, where it shed light closely upon the cradle. It was a broad-based candle discarded from one of the prickets in the wall brackets of the church, he found them useful for carrying on his errands because they would stand solidly on any flat surface, and run no risk of being overturned. Among flimsy wooden cottages there was need of such care. This dwelling, poor as it was, had been more solidly built than many.

'They keep you in charcoal?' asked Cadfael, turning to the woman, who stood quite still, gazing at him with fixed and illusionless eyes.

'My man who's dead was a forester in Eyton. The abbey's man there remembers me. He brings me wood, as well, the dead twigs and small chippings for kindling.'

'That's well,' said Cadfael. 'So young a babe needs to be kept warm. Now you tell me, what's her trouble?'

She was telling him herself, in small, fretful wails from her cradle, but she was well wrapped and clean, and had a healthy, well-nourished voice with which to complain.

'Three days now she's sickened on her milk, and cries with the wind inside. But I've kept her warm, and she's taken no chill. If my poor girl had lived this chit would have been at her breast, not sipping from a spoon or my fingers, but she's gone, and left this one to me, all I have now, and I'll do anything to keep her safe.'

'She's been feeding well enough, by the look of her,' said Cadfael, stooping over the whimpering child. 'How old is she now? Six weeks is it, or seven? She's big and bonny for that age.'

The small, contorted face, all wailing mouth and tightshut eyes screwed up with annoyance, was round and clear-skinned, though red now with exertion and anger. She had abundant, fine hair of a bright autumn brown, and inclined to curl.

'Feed well, yes, indeed she did, until this upset. A greedy-gut, even, I was proud of her.'

And kept plying her too long, thought Cadfael, and she without the sense yet to know when she had enough. No great mystery here.

'That's a part of her trouble, you'll find. Give her only a little at a time, and often, and put in the milk a few drops of the cordial I'll leave with you. Three or four drops will be enough.

Get me a small spoon, and she shall have a proper dose of it now to soothe her.'

The widow brought him a little horn spoon, and he unstoppered the glass bottle he had brought, moistened the tip of a finger at its lip, and touched it to the lower lip of the baby's angry mouth. In an instant the howling broke off short, and the contorted countenance resumed a human shape, and even a human expression of wonder and surprise. The mouth closed, small moist lips folding on an unexpected sweetness; and miraculously this became a mouth too shapely and delicate for a baby of seven weeks, with a distant promise of beauty. The angry red faded slowly to leave the round cheeks flushed with rose, and Eluned's daughter opened great eyes of a blue almost as dark as the night sky, and smiled an aware, responsive smile, too old for her few weeks of life. True, she wrinkled her face and uttered a warning wail the next moment, but the far-off vision of loveliness remained.

'The creature!' said her grandmother, ruefully fond. 'She likes it!'

Cadfael half-filled the little spoon, touched it gently to the baby's lower lip, and instantly her mouth opened, willing to suck in the offering. It went down fairly tidily, leaving only a gloss upon the relaxed lips. She gazed upward in silence for a moment, from those eyes that devoured half her face under the rounded brow and fluff of auburn hair. Then she turned her cheek a little into the flat pillow under her, belched resoundingly, and lay quiescent with lids half-closed, her infinitesimal fingers curled into small, easy fists under her chin.

'Nothing amiss with her that need cause you any worry,' said Cadfael, re-stoppering the bottle. 'If she wakes and cries in the night, and is again in pain, you can give her a little of this in the spoon, as I did. But I think she'll sleep. Give her somewhat less food at a time than you've been giving, and put three or four drops of this in the milk, and we'll see how she fares in a few days more.'

'What is in it?' asked the widow, looking curiously at the bottle in her hand.

'There's dill, fennel, mint, just a morsel of poppy-juice ... and honey to make it agreeable to the taste. Put it somewhere safe and use it as I've said. If she's again troubled this way, give her the dose you saw me give. If she does well enough without it, then spare it but for the drop or two in her food. Medicines are of most effect if used only when there's need.'

444

He blew out the end of candle he had brought, leaving it to cool and congeal, for it had still an hour or so of burning left in it, and could serve again in the same office. On the instant he was sorry he had diminished the light in the room so soon, for only now had he leisure to look at the woman. This was the widowed mother of the girl who had been shut out of the church as an irredeemable sinner, whose very penitence and confession were not to be trusted, and therefore could justifiably be rejected. Out of this small, dark dwelling that disordered beauty had blossomed, borne fruit, and died.

The mother must herself have been comely, some years ago, she had still fine features, though worn and lined now in shapes of discouragement, and her greying hair, drawn back austerely from her face, was still abundant, and bore the shadowy richness of its former red-brown colouring. There was no saying whether the dark, hollow eyes that studied her grandchild with such a bitter burden of love were dark blue, but they well might have been. She was probably barely forty. Cadfael had seen her about the Foregate now and then, but never before paid close attention to her.

'A fine babe you have there,' said Cadfael. 'She may well grow into a beautiful child.'

'Better she should be plain as any drab,' said the widow with abrupt passion, 'than take after her mother's beauty, and go the same way. You do know whose child she is? Everyone knows it!'

'No fault of this little one she left behind,' said Cadfael. 'I hope the world will treat her better than it treated her mother.'

'It was not the world that cast her off,' said Nest, 'but the church. She could have lived under the world's malice, but not when the priest shut her out of the church.'

'Did her worship truly mean so much to her,' asked Cadfael gravely, 'that she could not live excommunicate?'

'Truly it did. You never knew her! As wild and rash as she was beautiful, but such a bright, kind, warm creature to have about the house, and for all her wildness she was easily hurt. She who never could bear to wound any other creature was open to wounds herself. But for the thing she could not help, no one could have been a better and sweeter daughter to me. You can't know how it was! She could not refuse to anyone whatever he asked of her, if it was in her power to give it. And the men found it out, and having no shame – for sin was something she spoke of without understanding – she could not

445

say no to men, either. She would go with a man because he was melancholy, or because he begged her, or because he had been blamed or beaten unjustly and was aggrieved at the world. And then it would come over her that this might indeed be sin, as Father Adam had told her, though she could not see why. And then she went flying to confession, in tears, and promised amendment, and meant it, too. Father Adam was gentle with her, seeing she was not like other young women. He always spoke her kindly and fair, and gave her light penance, and never refused her absolution. Always she promised to amend, but then she forgot for some boy's light tongue or dark eyes, and sinned again, and again confessed and was shriven. She couldn't keep from men, but neither could she live without the blessing and comfort of the church. When the door was shut in her face she went solitary away, and solitary she died. And for all she was a torment to me, living, she was a joy, too, and now I have only torment, and no joy – but for this fearful joy here in the cradle. Look, she's asleep!'

'Do you know,' asked Cadfael, brooding, 'who fathered her child?'

Nest shook her head, and a faint, dry smile plucked at her lips. 'No. As soon as she understood it might bring blame on him, whoever he was, she kept him a secret even from me. If, indeed, she knew herself which one of them had quickened her! Yet I think she did know. She was neither mad nor dull of understanding. She was brighter than most, but for the part of caution that was left out of her. She might have confronted the man to his face, but she would never betray him to the black priest. Oh, he asked her! He threatened her, he raged at her, but she said that for her sins she would answer and do penance, but another man's sins were his own, and so must his confession be.'

A good answer! Cadfael acknowledged it with a nod and a sigh.

The candle was cold and set. He restored it to his scrip, and turned to take his leave. 'Well, if she's fretful again and you need me, let me know of it by Cynric, or leave word at the gatehouse, and I'll come. But I think you'll find the cordial will serve your turn.' He looked back for a second with his hand on the latch of the door. 'What have you named her? Eluned, for her mother?'

'No,' said the widow. 'It was Eluned chose her name. Praise God, it was Father Adam who christened her, before he fell ill

446

and died. She's called Winifred.'

Cadfael walked back along the Foregate with that last echo still ringing in his mind. The daughter of the outcast and excommunicate, it seemed, was named for the town's own saint, witness enough to the truth of Eluned's undisciplined devotion. And doubtless Saint Winifred would know where to find and watch over both the living child and the dead mother, whom the parish of Saint Chad, more prodigally merciful than Father Ailnoth, had buried decently, observing a benevolent Christian doubt concerning the circumstances of her unwitnessed death. A strong strain, these Welsh women married into Shropshire families. He knew nothing of the English forester who had been husband to the widow Nest, but surely it must be she who had handed on to her self-doomed child the fierce beauty that had been her downfall, and the same face, in prophetic vision, waited for the infant Winifred in her cradle. Perhaps the choice of her venerated name had been a brave gesture to protect a creature otherwise orphaned and unprotected, a waif in an alien world where too prodigal a union of beauty and generosity brought only grief.

Now there, in the cottage he had left behind, was one being who had the best of all reasons to hate Ailnoth, and might have killed him if a thought could have done it, but was hardly likely to follow him through the winter night and strike him down from behind, much less roll him, stunned, into the pool. She had too powerful a lodestone to keep her watchful and protective at home. But the vengeful fire in her might drive a man to do it for her sake, if she had so close and resolute a friend. Among all those men who had taken comfort from the world's spite in Eluned's arms, might there not be more than one ready and willing? And in particular, if he knew what seed he had sown, the father of the infant Winifred.

At this rate, thought Cadfael, mildly irritated with his own preoccupation, I shall be looking sidewise at every comely man I see, to try if I can find in his face any resemblance to a murderer. I'd best concern myself with my own duties, and leave official retribution to Hugh – not that he'll be grateful for it!

He was approaching the gatehouse, and had just come to the entrance to the twisting alley that led to the priest's house. He halted there, suddenly aware that the heavy covering cloud had lifted, and a faint gleam of sun showed through. Not brilliantly

447

and icily out of a pale, cold sky, but timidly and grudgingly through untidy, wallowing shreds of cloud. The glitter coruscating from icicles and swags of frozen snow along the eaves had acquired a softer, moist brightness. There was even a drip here and there from a gable end where the timorous sun fell. Cynric might be right in his prediction, and a thaw on the way by nightfall. Then they could at least put Ailnoth out of the chapel and under the ground, though his baleful shadow would still be with them.

There was no haste to return to the abbey and his workshop, half an hour more would not do any harm. Cadfael turned into the alley and walked along to the priest's house. He was none too sure of his own motives in paying this visit. Certainly it was his legitimate business to make sure that Mistress Hammet's injuries had healed properly, and she had taken no lingering harm from the blow to her head, but pure curiosity had a part in what prompted him, too. Here was another woman whose attitude to Father Ailnoth might be exceedingly ambivalent, torn between gratitude for a patronage which had given her status and security, and desperation at his raging resentment of the deception practised on him, if she knew how he had found it out, and his all too probable intent to see her nurseling unmasked and thrown into prison. Cadfael's judgement of Diota was that she went in considerable awe and fear of her master, but also that she would dare much for the boy she had nursed. But any suspicion of her was quickly tempered by his recollection of her state on Christmas morning. Almost certainly, whatever her fears after a night of waiting in vain, she had not known that Ailnoth was dead until the searchers returned with his body. As often as Cadfael told himself he could be deceived in believing that, his own memory rejected the doubt.

Just beyond the priest's house the narrow alley opened out into a small grassy space, now a circle of trampled rime, but with the green of grass peeping through by small, indomitable tufts here and there. To this confined playground the house presented its fine, unbroken wall, the one that attracted the players of ball games and the like, to their peril. There were half a dozen urchins of the Foregate playing there now, rolling snowballs and hurling them from an ambitiously remote mark at a target set up on an abandoned fence-post at the corner of the green. A round black cap, with a fluttering end of torn braid quivering in the light wind. A skull cap, such as a priest

448

would wear, or a monk, to cover his tonsure from cold when the cowl was inconvenient.

One small possession of Ailnoth's which had not been recovered with him, nor missed. Cadfael stood and gazed, remembering sharply the clear image of the priest's set and formidable face as he passed the gatehouse torches, unshadowed by any cowl, and capped, yes, certainly capped in black, this meagre circle that cast no shadows, but left his apocalyptic rage plain to view.

One of the marksmen, luckier or more adroit, had knocked the target flying into the grass. The victor, without great interest now, having prevailed, went to pick it up, and stood dangling it in one hand, while the rest of the band, capricious as children can be, burst into a spirited argument as to what they should do next, and like a wisp of snipe rising, suddenly took off across the grass towards the open field beyond.

The marksman made to follow them, but with no haste, knowing they would settle as abruptly as they had taken flight, and he could be up with them whenever he willed. Cadfael went a few paces to intercept his passage, and the boy halted readily enough, knowing him. A bright boy, ten years old, the reeve's sister's son. He had a charming, inscrutable smile.

'What's that you have there, Eddi?' asked Cadfael, nodding at the dangling cap. 'May I see it?'

It was handed over willingly, indifferently. No doubt they had played various games with it for several days now, and were weary of it. Some other brief foundling toy would take its place, and it would never be missed. Cadfael turned it in his hands, and marked how the braid that bound its rim was ripped clear on one side, and dangled the loose end. When he drew it into place there was still a strand missing, perhaps the length of his little finger, and the stitching of two of the segments that made up the circle had been frayed apart with the lost shred. Good black cloth, carefully made, the braid hand-plaited wool.

'Where did you find this, Eddi?'

'In the mill-pond,' said the boy readily. 'Someone threw it away because it was torn. We went down early in the morning to see if the pond was frozen, but it wasn't. But we found this.'

'Which morning was that?' asked Cadfael.

'Christmas Day. It was only just getting light.' The boy was grave, demure of countenance, impenetrable as clever children can be.

'Where in the mill-pond? On the mill side?'

'No, we went along the other path, where it's shallow. That's where it freezes first. The tail-race keeps it open the other side.'

So it did, the movement enough to preserve an open channel until all froze over, and the same stream of moving water would carry a light thing, like this cap, over to lodge in the shallows.

'This was caught among the reeds there?'

The boy said yes, serenely.

'You know whose this is, do you, Eddi?'

'No, sir,' said Eddi, and smiled a brief, guileless smile. He was, Cadfael recalled, one of those unfortunate children who had been learning their letters with Father Adam, and had fallen into less tolerant hands after his death. And wronged and injured children are not themselves merciful to their tyrants.

'No matter, son. Are you done with it? Will you leave it with me? I'll bring you a few apples to your father's, a fair exchange. And you may forget it.'

'Yes, sir,' said the boy, and turned and skipped away without another glance, rid of his prize and his burden.

Cadfael stood looking down at the small, drab thing in his hands, damp now and darkening from the comparative warmth of being handled, but fringed with rime and still stiff. How unlike Father Ailnoth to be seen wearing a cap with a tattered braid and a seam beginning to lose its stitches! If, indeed, it had been in this condition when he put it on? It had been tossed around at random since Christmas Day, and might have come by its dilapidations at any time since it was plucked out of the frosty reeds, where the drift of the tail-race had carried it, while the heavier body from which it had been flung was gradually edged aside under the leaning bank.

And was there not something else that had been forgotten, as this cap had been forgotten? Something else they should have looked for, and had never thought of? Something nagging at the back of Cadfael's mind but refusing to show itself?

He thrust the cap into his scrip, and turned back to rap at the door of the priest's house. It was opened to him by Diota, prim and composed in her customary black. She stepped back readily, unsmiling but hospitable, and beckoned him at once into a small, warm room dimly lit by a brownish light from two small windows, into the shutters of which thin sheets of horn had been set. A bright wood fire burned on the clay hearth in the centre of the room, and in the cushioned bench beside it a young woman was sitting, alert and silent, and to one entering from broad daylight not immediately recognizable.

'I came only to ask how you are,' said Cadfael as the door was closed behind him, 'and to see if you need anything more for your grazes.'

Diota came round to face him and let herself be seen, the palest of smiles visiting a face habitually grave and anxious. 'That was kind of you, Brother Cadfael. I am well, I thank you, quite well. You see the wound is healed.'

She turned her injured temple docilely to the best of the light at the urging of his hand, and let him study what had faded now to a yellow bruise and a small dry scar.

'Yes, that's well, there'll be no mark left to show for it. But I should go on using the ointment for a few days yet, in this frost the skin dries and abrades easily. And you've had no headaches?'

'No, none.'

'Good! Then I'll be off back to my work, and not take up your time, for I see you have a visitor.'

'Oh, no,' said the visitor, rising briskly from the bench, 'I was about to take my leave.' She stepped forward, raising to the light a round young face, broad at the brow and tapering gently to a resolute chin. Challenging harebell-blue eyes, set very wide apart, confronted Cadfael with a direct and searching stare. 'If you must really go so soon,' said Sanan Bernières, with the serene confidence of a masterful child, 'I'll walk with you. I've been waiting to find a right time to talk to you.'

There was no gainsaying such a girl. Diota did not venture to try and detain her, and Brother Cadfael, even if he had wished, would have hesitated before denying her. Law itself, he thought with amused admiration, might come off the loser if it collided with the will of Sanan Bernières. In view of all that had happened, that was a distinct if as yet distant possibility, but she would not let the prospect deter her.

'That will be great pleasure for me,' said Cadfael. 'The walk is very short – but perhaps you'll be needing some more herbs for your kitchen? I have ample supplies, you may come in and take what you wish.'

She did give him a very sharp glance for that, and as suddenly dimpled, and to hide laughter turned to embrace Diota, kissing her thin cheek like a daughter. Then she drew her cloak about her and led the way out into the alley, and together they walked the greater part of the way out into the Foregate in silence.

'Do you know,' she said then, 'why I went to see Mistress Hammet?'

'Out of womanly sympathy, surely,' said Cadfael, 'with her loss. Loss and loneliness – still a virtual stranger here …'

'Oh, come!' said Sanan bluntly. 'She worked for the priest, I suppose it was a secure life for a widow woman, but loss …? Lonely she may well be.'

'I was not speaking of Father Ailnoth,' said Cadfael.

She gave him another straight glance of her startling blue eyes, and heaved a thoughtful sigh. 'Yes, you've worked with him, you know him. He told you, didn't he, that she was his nurse, no blood kin? She never had children in her own marriage, he's as dear as a son to her. I … have talked with him, too – by chance. You know he sent a message to my step-father. Everyone knows that now. I was curious to see this young man, that's all.'

They had reached the abbey gatehouse. She stood hesitant, frowning at the ground.

'Now everyone is saying that he – this Ninian Bachiler – killed Father Ailnoth, because the priest was going to betray him to the sheriff. I knew she must have heard it. I knew she would be alone, afraid for him, now he's fled, and hunted for his life – for it *is* his life, now!'

'So you came to bear her company,' said Cadfael, 'and reassure her. Come through into the garden, and if you have all the pot-herbs you want, I daresay we can find another good reason. You won't be any the worse for having something by you to cure the cough that may be coming along in a week or two.'

She looked up with a flashing smile. 'The same remedy you gave me when I was ten? I've changed so much you can hardly have known me again. Such excellent health I have, I need you only once every seven or eight years.'

'If you need me now,' said Cadfael simply, leading the way across the great court towards the gardens, 'that's enough.'

She followed demurely, lowering her eyes modestly in this male seclusion, and in the safe solitude of the workshop she allowed herself to be installed comfortably with her small feet towards the brazier before she drew breath again and went on talking, now more freely, having left all other ears outside the door.

'I came to see Mistress Hammet because I was afraid that, now that he is so threatened, she might do something foolish. She is devoted to Ninian, in desperation she might do anything – *anything!* – to ensure that he goes free. She might even come forward with some mad story about being to blame herself. She would, I am sure, for him! If she thought it would clear him of all guilt, she would confess to murder.'

'So you came,' said Cadfael, moving about his private world quietly to leave her the illusion that she was not closely observed, 'to urge her to hold her peace and wait calmly, for he's still at liberty and in no immediate danger. Is that it?'

'Yes. And if you go to see her again, or she comes to you, please urge the same upon her. Don't let her do anything to harm herself.'

'Did he send you, to see her and tell her this?' asked Cadfael directly.

She was not yet quite ready to be drawn into the open, though fleetingly she smiled. 'It's simply that I know, I understand, how anxious he must be now about her. He would be glad if he knew I had talked to her.'

As he will know, before many hours are out, thought Cadfael. Now I wonder where she has hidden him. There could well be old retainers of her own father here in Shrewsbury, or close by, men who would do a great deal for Bernières's daughter.

'I know,' said Sanan with slow solemnity, following Cadfael's movements with intent eyes, 'that you discovered Ninian before ever my step-father betrayed him. I know he told you freely who he is and what he's about, and you said you had nothing against any honest man of either party, and would do nothing to harm him. And you've kept his secret until now, when it's no longer a secret. He trusts you, and I am resolved to trust you.'

'No,' said Cadfael hastily, 'tell me nothing! If I don't know where the boy is now, no one can get it out of me, and I can declare my ignorance with a good conscience. I like a gallant lad, even if he is too rash for his own good. He tells me his whole aim now is to reach the Empress, at whatever cost, and offer her his services. He has a right to dispose of his own efforts as he pleases, and I wish him a safe arrival and long life. Such a madcap deserves to have luck on his side.'

'I know,' she said, flushing and smiling, 'he is not very discreet ...'

453

'Discreet? I doubt if he knows the meaning of the word! To write and send such a letter, open as the day, signed with his own name and telling where and under what pretence he's to be found! No, never tell me where he is now, but wherever you've hidden him, keep a weather eye on him, for there's no knowing what breathless foolishness he'll be up to next.' He had been busy filling a small flask, to provide her with a respectable reason for emerging from his herbarium. He sealed it with a wooden stopper and tied it down at the neck under a wisp of thin parchment before wrapping it in a piece of linen and putting it into her hands. 'There, madam, is your permit to be here. And my advice is, get him away as soon as you can.'

'But he won't go,' she said, sighing, but with pride rather than exasperation, 'not while this matter is unresolved. He won't budge until he knows Diota is safe. And there are preparations to make – means to provide ...' She shook herself bracingly, tossed her brown head, and made briskly for the door.

'His first need,' said Cadfael thoughtfully after her, 'will be a good horse.'

She turned about abruptly in the doorway, and gave him a blazing smile, throwing aside all reservations.

'Two horses!' she said in a soft, triumphant whisper. 'I am of the Empress's party, too. I am going with him!'

Chapter Nine

ADFAEL WAS uneasy in his mind all that day, plagued on the one hand by misgivings about Sanan's revelation, and on the other by the elusive gnat that sang in the back of his consciousness, telling him persistently that he had failed to notice the loss of one item that should have been sought with Ailnoth, and might very well have missed another. There was certainly something he should have thought of, something that might shed light, if only he could discover what it was, and go, belatedly, to look for it.

In the meantime, he pursued the round of his duties through Vespers and supper in the refectory, and tried in vain to concentrate upon the psalms for this thirtieth day of December, the sixth day in the octave of Christmas.

Cynric had been right about the thaw. It came furtively and grudgingly, but it was certainly on its way by mid afternoon. The trees were shedding their tinkling filigree of frozen rime and standing starkly black against a low sky. Drips perforated the whiteness under the eaves with small dark pockmarks, and the black of the road and the green of grass were beginning to show through the covering of snow. By morning it might even be possible to break the ground, in that chosen spot sheltered under the precinct wall, and dig Father Ailnoth's grave.

Cadfael had examined the skull-cap closely, and could make no great sense of it. Yet it fretted him simply because he had failed to think of it when the body was found. As for the damage to it, that suggested a connection with the blow to the head, and yet at the same time contradicted that connection, since in the event the cap would surely have fallen on land, when the blow was struck. True, the assailant might very well have thrown it into the water after the priest, but in the dark would he have noticed or thought of it, and if he had, would he necessarily have been able to find it? A small black thing in tufted grass not yet white with rime – not easy to see, and unlikely to be remembered as too dangerous to leave, when murder had been committed. Who was going to grope around in the dark in rough grass, when he had just killed a man? His one thought would be to get well away from the scene as quickly as possible.

Well, if Cadfael had missed this one thing, he might have missed – his demon was nagging at him that he *had* missed! – another as important. And if he had, it was still there by the mill, either along the bank or in the water, or even within the mill itself. No use looking for it elsewhere.

There was half an hour left before Compline, and most of the brothers, very sensibly, were in the warming room, getting the chill out of their bones. It was folly to think of going near the mill at this hour, in the dark, but for all that Cadfael could not keep away, his mind so dwelt upon the place, as though the very ambience of the pool, the mill and the solitary night might reproduce the events of Christmas Eve, and prod his memory into recapturing the lost factor. He crossed the great court to the retired corner by the infirmary, where the wicket in the precinct wall led through directly to the mill.

Outside, with no moon and only ragged glimpses of stars, he stood until his eyes grew accustomed to the night, and the shapes of things grew out of obscurity. The rough grass of the field, the dark bulk of the mill to his right, with the little wooden bridge at the corner of the building immediately before him, crossing the head-race to the overhanging bank of the pool. He crossed, his feet making a small, clear, hollow sound on the planks, and walked across the narrow strip of grass to the bank. The expanse of the water opened beneath him, pale, leaden-still, dappled with patches of open water, rimmed round with half-thawed ice.

Nothing moved here but himself, there was nothing to be heard, nor even a breath of wind stirring in the lissome naked shoots of the pollarded willows at his left hand along the bank. A few yards along there, just past the nearest stump, cut down to hip-height and bristling with wands like hair on the giant head of a terrified man, they had drawn Ailnoth's body laboriously along under the eroded bank, and brought him to shore where the meadow sloped down more gently to the outflow of the tail-race.

In his recollection of the morning every detail stood sharply defined, but shed no light at all on what had happened in the night. He turned from the high bank and walked back across the bridge, and for no good reason that he could see continued round the mill, and down the sloping bank to the big doors where the grain was carried in. Only an outer bar fastened the door, and that, he saw dimly by the faint reflection from bleached timber, was drawn back from its socket. There was a small door on the higher level, giving quick access to the wicket in the precinct wall. That could be fastened within. But why should this heavy bar be drawn back unless someone had made entry from without?

Cadfael set his hand to the closed but unbarred door, eased it open by a hand's breadth, and stiffened to listen with an ear to the chink. Nothing but silence from within. He opened it a little wider, slid quietly through, and eased the door back again behind him. The warm scents of flour and grain tickled his nostrils. He had a nose sharp as fox or hound, and trusted to it in the dark, and there was another scent here, very faint, utterly familiar. In his own workshop he was unaware of it from long and constant acquaintance, but in any other place it pricked his consciousness with a particular insistence, as of a stolen possession of his own, and a valued one, that had no business to stray. A man cannot be in and out of a workshop saturated with years of harvesting herbs, and not carry the scent of them about in his garments. Cadfael froze with his back against the closed door, and waited.

The faintest stir reached his ears, as of a foot carefully placed in dust and husk that could not choose but rustle, however cautiously trodden. Somewhere above him, on the upper floor. So the hatch was open, and someone was leaning there, carefully shifting his stance to drop through. Cadfael moved obligingly in that direction, to give him encouragement. Next moment a body dropped neatly behind him, and an arm clamped about his neck, bracing him back against his assailant, while its fellow embraced him about chest and arms, pinning him close. He stood slack within the double grip, and continued to breathe easily, and with wind to spare.

'Not badly done,' he said with mild approval. 'But you have

457

no nose, son. What are four senses, without the fifth?'

'Have I not?' breathed Ninian's voice in his ear, shaken by a quaver of suppressed laughter. 'You came in at the door so like a waft of wind through your eaves, I was back there with that oil I had to abandon. I hope it took no harm.' Hard and vehement young arms hugged Cadfael close, let him loose gently, and turned him about at arm's length, as though to view him, where there was no light to see more than a shape, a shadow. 'I owed you a fright. You had the wits scared out of me when you eased the door ajar,' said Ninian reproachfully.

'I was none too easy in my own mind,' said Cadfael, 'when I found the bar out of its socket. Lad, you take far too many chances. For God's sake and Sanan's, what are you doing here?'

'I could as well ask you that,' said Ninian. 'And might get the same answer, too. I ventured here to see if there was anything more to be found, though after so many days, heaven knows why there should be. But how can any of us be easy until we know? *I* know I never laid hands on the man, but what comfort is that when everyone else lays it at my door? I should be loth to leave here until it's shown I'm no murderer, even if there were nothing more in it than that, but there is. There's Diota! Wanting the chance to get at me, how long before they begin to turn on her, if not for murder, then for treason in helping me to escape the hunt in the south, and cover my guilt here?'

'If you think Hugh Beringar has any ill intent against Mistress Hammet, or will suffer anyone else to make her a victim,' said Cadfael firmly, 'you may put that out of your mind at once. Well, now since we're both here, and the time and place as good as any, we may as well sit down somewhere in the warmest corner we can find, and put together whatever we have to share. Two heads may make more of it than my one has been able to do. There should be plenty of sacks here somewhere – better than nothing …'

Evidently Ninian had been here long enough to know his way about, for he took Cadfael by the arm, and drew him confidently into a corner where a pile of clean, coarse bags was folded and stacked against the timber wall. They settled themselves close there, flank by flank for warmth, and Ninian drew round them both a thick cloak which had certainly never been in Benet's possession.

'Now,' said Cadfael briskly, 'I should first tell you that this very morning I've spoken with Sanan, and I know what you and she are planning. Probably she's told you as much. I'm half in and half out of your confidence and hers, and if I'm to be of any help to you in putting an end to this vexatious business that holds you here, you had better let me in fully. I do *not* believe you guilty of the priest's death, and I have no reason in the world to stand in your way. But I do believe that you know more of what happened here that night than you have told. Tell the rest, and let me know where we really stand. You did come here to the mill, did you not?'

Ninian blew out a gusty, rueful breath that warmed Cadfael's leaning cheek for a moment. 'I did. I had to. I got no more answer from Giffard than that he'd received and understood the message I sent. I'd no means of knowing whether he meant to come or not. But I came very early, to view the place and find a corner to hide in until I saw what came of it. I stayed there in the doorway in the abbey wall, with the wicket ajar, so that I could watch for whoever came. I had to make haste round the corner of the infirmary, I can tell you, when the miller came bustling through on his way to church, but I had the place to myself after that, to keep watch on the path.'

'And it was Ailnoth who came?' said Cadfael.

'Storming along the path like a bolt from God. Dark as it was, there was no mistaking him, he had a gait all his own. There was no possible reason he should be there at such an hour, unless he'd got wind of what I was up to, and meant all manner of mischief. He was striding up and down and round the mill and along the bank, thumping the ground like a cat lashing its tail. And I'd perhaps got another man into the mud with me, and must make some shift to get him, at least, out of it, even if I was still stuck in the mire.'

'So what did you do?'

'It was still early. I couldn't leave Giffard to come to the meeting all unsuspecting, could I? I didn't know if he meant to come at all, but still he might, I couldn't take the risk. I hared away back through the court and out at the gatehouse, and went to earth among the bushes close by the end of the bridge. If he came at all, he had to come that way from the town. And I didn't even know what the man looked like, though I knew his name and his allegiance from others. But I thought there'd be very few men coming out from the town at that hour, and I could risk accosting any who looked of his age and quality.'

'Ralph Giffard had already come over the bridge,' said

459

Cadfael, 'a good hour earlier, to visit the priest and send him hot-foot to confront you at the mill, but you could hardly know that. I fancy he was already back in his own house while you were watching for him in the bushes. Did you see any others pass by you there?'

'Only one, and he was too young, and too poor and simple in his person and gear to be Giffard. He went straight along the Foregate, and turned in at the church.'

Centwin, perhaps, thought Cadfael, coming from paying his debt, to have his mind free and at peace, owing no man, as he went to celebrate the birth of Christ. Well for him if it proved that Ninian could speak for him, and show clearly that his own bitter debt had gone unreclaimed.

'And you?'

'I waited until I was sure he was not coming – it was past the time. So I made haste back to be in time for Matins.'

'Where you met with Sanan.' Cadfael's smile was invisible in the dark, but perceptible in his voice. 'She was not so foolish as to go to the mill, for like you, she could not be quite sure her step-father would not keep the tryst. But she knew where to find you, and she was determined to respond to the appeal Giffard had preferred to reject. Indeed, as I recall, she had already taken steps to get a good look at you, as you yourself told me. Maybe you'll do for a lady's page, after all. With a little polishing!'

Within the muffling folds of the cloak he heard Ninian laughing softly. 'I never believed, that first day, that anything would really come of it. And now see – everything I owe to her. She would not be put off … You've seen her, you've talked to her, you know how splendid she is … Cadfael, I must tell you – she's coming with me to Gloucester, she's promised herself to me in marriage.' His voice was low and solemn now, as though he had already come to the altar. It was the first time Cadfael had known him in awe of anything or anyone.

'She is a very valiant lady,' said Cadfael slowly, 'and knows her own mind very well, and I, for my part, wouldn't say a word against her choice. But, lad, is it right to let her do this for you? Is she not abandoning property, family, everything? Have you considered that?'

'I have, and urged her to consider it, too. How much do you know, Cadfael, of her situation? She has no land to abandon. Her father's manor was taken from him after the siege here, because he supported FitzAlan and the Empress. Her mother

460

is dead. Her step-father – she has no complaint of him, he has always cared for her in duty bound, but not gladly. He has a son by his first marriage to inherit from him, he will be only too pleased to have an estate undivided, and to escape providing her a dowry. But from her mother she has a good provision in jewels, undeniably her own. She says she loses nothing by coming with me, and gains what she most wants in the world. I do love her!' said Ninian with abrupt and moving gravity. 'I will make a fit place for her. I can! I will!'

Yes, thought Cadfael on reflection, on balance she may be getting none so bad a bargain. Giffard himself lost certain lands for his adherence to the Empress, no wonder he wants all he has left to go to his son. It may even be more for his son's sake than his own that he has so ruthlessly severed himself now from any lingering devotion to his former overlord, and even sought to buy his own security with this boy's freedom. Men do things far out of their nature when deformed by circumstances. And the girl knew a good lad when she saw one, she'll be his fair match.

'Well, I wish you a fortunate journey through Wales, with all my heart,' he said. 'You'll need horses for the journey, is that already arranged?'

'We have them, she procured them. They're stabled where I'm in hiding,' said Ninian, candid and thoughtless, 'out by –'

Cadfael clapped a hand hastily over the boy's mouth, fumbling in the dark but effectively silencing him out of sheer surprise. 'No, hush, tell me nothing! Better I know nothing of where you are, or where you got your horses. What I don't know I can't even be expected to tell.'

'But I can't go,' said Ninian firmly, 'while there's a shadow hanging over me. I won't be remembered, here or anywhere, as a fugitive murderer. Still less can I go while there's such a shadow hanging over Diota. I owe her more already than I know how to repay, I must see her secure and protected before I go.'

'The more credit to you, and we must try by any means we have for a resolution. As it seems we've both been doing tonight, though with very sorry success. But now, had you not best be getting back to your hiding place? How if Sanan should send to you, and you not there?'

'And you?' retorted Ninian. 'How if Prior Robert should make a round of the dortoir, and you not there?'

They rose together, and unwound the cloak from about them, drawing in breath sharply at the invading cold.

'You haven't told me,' said Ninian, opening the heavy door

461

on the comparative light outside, 'just what thought brought you here tonight – though I'm glad it did. I was not happy at leaving you without a word. But you can hardly have been hunting for me! What were you hoping to find?'

'I wish I knew. This morning I found a gaggle of goslings playing in the snow with a black skull-cap that surely belonged to Ailnoth, for the boys had found it here in the shallows of the pool, among the reeds. And I had seen him wearing it that evening, and clean forgotten so small a thing. And it's been nagging at me all day long since then that there was something else I had noted about him, and likewise never missed and never looked for afterwards. I don't know that I came here with any great expectation of finding anything. Perhaps I simply hoped that being here might bring the thing back to mind. Did ever you get up to do something, and then clean forget what it was?' wondered Cadfael. 'And have to go back to where you first thought of it, to bring it back to mind? No, surely not, you're too young, for you to think of doing a thing is to do it. But ask the elders like me, they'll all admit to it.'

'And it still hasn't come back to you?' asked Ninian, delicately sympathetic towards the old and forgetful.

'It has not. Not even here. Have you fared any better?'

'It was a thin hope to find what I came for,' said Ninian ruefully, 'though I did risk coming before the light was quite gone. But at least I know what I came looking for. I was there with Diota when you brought him back on Christmas Day, and I never thought what was missing until later. After all, it's a thing that could well go astray, not like the clothes he was wearing. But I knew he had it with him when he came stamping along the path and stabbing at the ground. Coming all this way through England in his company, I got to know it very well. That great staff he was always so lungeous with – ebony, tall as his elbow, with a stag's-horn handle – that's what I came to look for. And somewhere here it must still be.'

They had emerged on to the low shore, dappled now with moist dark patches of grass breaking through the tattered snow. The dull, pale level of the water stretched away to the dark slope of the further bank. Cadfael had stopped abruptly, staring over the shield of pallor in startled enlightenment.

'So it must!' he said devoutly. 'So it must! Child, that's the will-o'-the-wisp I've been chasing all this day. You get back to your refuge and keep snug within, and leave this search to me now. You've read my riddle for me.'

*

By morning half the snow had melted and vanished, and the Foregate was like a coil of tattered and threadbare lace. The cobbles of the great court shone moist and dark, and in the graveyard east of the church Cynric had broken the turf for Father Ailnoth's grave.

Cadfael came from the last chapter of the year with a strong feeling that more things than the year were ending. No word had yet been said of who was to succeed to the living of Holy Cross, no word would be said until Ailnoth was safely under the ground, with every proper rite and as much mourning as brotherhood and parish could muster between them. The next day, the birth of another year, would see the burial of a brief tyranny that would soon be gratefully forgotten. God send us, thought Cadfael, a humble soul who thinks himself as fallible as his flock, and labours modestly to keep both from falling. If two hold fast together they stand steadily, but if one holds aloof the other may find his feet betraying him in slippery places. Better a limping prop than a solid rock for ever out of reach of the stretched hand.

Cadfael made for the wicket in the wall, and went through to the shores of the mill-pond. He stood on the edge of the overhanging bank between the pollarded willows, at the spot where he had found Ailnoth's body, the pool widening and shallowing on his right hand into the reed beds below the highway, and on his left gradually narrowing to the deeper stream that carried the water back to the brook, and shortly thereafter to the Severn. The body had entered the water probably a few yards to the right, and been nudged aside here under the bank by the tail-race. The skull-cap had been found in the reeds, somewhere accessible from the path on the opposite side. A small, light thing, it would go with the current until reeds or branch or debris in the water arrested it. But where would a heavy ebony staff be carried, whether it flew from his hand as he was struck down, or whether it was thrown in after him, from this spot? It would either be drifted aside in the same direction as the body, in which case it might be sunk deep somewhere in the narrowing channel, or else, if it fell on the other side of the main force of the tail-race, edged away like the skull-cap into the far shore. At least there was no harm in circling the shallow bowl and looking for it.

He re-crossed the little bridge over the head-race, circled the mill and went down to the edge of the water. There was no real path here, the gardens of the three small houses came almost to the lip of the bank, where a narrow strip of open grass just allowed of passage. For some way the path was still raised above water level, and somewhat hollowed out beneath, then it dropped gradually into the first growth of reeds, and he walked in tufted grass, with moisture welling round every step he took. Under the miller's house and garden, under the house where the deaf old woman lived with her pretty slattern of a maidservant, and then he was bearing somewhat away from the final house, round the rim of the broad shallows. Silver of water gleamed through the blanched, pallid green of winter reeds, but though an accumulation of leaves, dead twigs and branches had drifted and lodged here, he saw no sign of an ebony walking-staff. Other cast-offs, however, showed themselves, broken crockery, discarded shards and a holed pot, too far gone to be worth mending.

He went on, round the broad end of the pool, to the trickle of water that came down from the conduit under the highway, stepped over that, and on beneath the gardens of the second trio of abbey houses. Somewhere here the boys had found the cap, but he could not believe he would find the staff here. Either he had missed it, or, if it had been flung well out over the drift of the tail-race, he must look for it on the far side of the channel opposite where the body had been found. The water was still fairly wide there, but what fell beyond its centre might well fetch up on this far side.

He halted to consider, glad he had put on boots to wade about this thawing quagmire. His friend and fellow Welshman, Madog of the Dead Boat, who knew everything there was to be known about water and its properties, given an idea of the thing sought, could have told him exactly where to seek it. But Madog was not here, and time was precious, and he must manage on his own. Ebony was heavy and solid, but still it was wood, and would float. Nor would it float evenly, having a stag's-horn handle, a tip should break the surface, wherever it lodged, and he did not believe it would be carried so far as the brook and the river. Doggedly he went on, and on this side the water there was a trodden path, which gradually lifted out of the boggy ground, and carried him dry-shod a little above the surface of the pool.

He drew level with the mill opposite, and was past the sloping strips of garden on this side the water. The stunted willow stump, defiantly sprouting its head of startled hair, matched his progress and held his eye. Just beyond that the body had lain, nuzzling the undercut bank.

Three paces more, and he found what he was seeking. Barely visible through the fringe of rotting ice and the protruding ends of grass, only its tip emerging, Ailnoth's staff lay at his feet. He took it gingerly by its tapered end, and plucked it out of the water. No mistaking it, once found, there could hardly be two exactly alike. Black and long, with a metal-shod tip and a grooved horn handle, banded to the shaft by a worn silver band embossed in some pattern worn very smooth with age. Whether flying out of the victim's hand or thrown in afterwards, it must have fallen into the water on this side of the current's main flow, and so been cast up here into the encroaching border of grass.

Melting snow dripped from the handle and ran down the shaft. Carrying it by the middle of the shaft, Cadfael turned back on his tracks, and circled the reedy shallows back to the mill. He was not yet ready to share his prize with anyone, not even Hugh, until he had had a close look at it, and extracted from it whatever it had to tell him. His hopes were not high, but he could not afford to let any hint slip through his fingers. He hurried through the wicket in the precinct wall, and across the great court, and went to earth in his own workshop. He left the door open for the sake of light, but also lit a wooden spill at the brazier and kindled his little lamp to make a close examination of the trophy.

The hand-long piece of horn, pale brown furrowed with wavy ruts of darker brown, was heavy and polished from years of use, and its slight curve fitted well into the hand. The band of silver was a thumb-joint wide, and the half-eroded vine leaves with which it was engraved reflected the yellow light of the lamp from worn highlights as Cadfael carefully dabbed off the moisture and held it close to the flame. The silver had worn thin as gauze, and grown so pliant to every touch that both rims had frayed up into rough edges here and there, sharp as knife blades. Cadfael had scratched a finger in drying the metal before he realized the danger.

This was the formidable weapon with which Father Ailnoth had lashed out at the vexatious urchins who played games against the wall of his house, and no doubt prodded the ribs or thumped the shoulders of the unlucky pupils who were less than perfect in their lessons. Cadfael turned it slowly in his

465

hands in the close light of the lamp, and shook his head over the sins of the virtuous. It was while he was so turning it that his eye was caught by the brief, passing gleam of a drop of moisture, spinning past an inch or more from the rim of silver. Hastily he checked, and turned the staff counterwise, and the bead of brightness reappeared. A single minute drop, clinging not to the metal, but to a fine thread held by the metal, something that appeared and vanished in a silvery curve. He uncoiled on his finger-end a long, greying hair, drawing it forth until it resisted, caught in a sharp edge of silver. Not one hair only, for now a second was partly drawn forth with it, and a third made a small, tight ring, stuck fast in the same tiny nick.

It took him some little time to detach them all from the notch in the lower rim of the band, five of them in all, as well as a few tangled ends. The five were all of fine hair, some brown, some greying to silver, and long, too long for any tonsure, too long for a man, unless he wore his hair neglected and untrimmed. If there had ever been any further mark, of blood, or grazed skin, or thread from a cloth, the water had soaked it away, but these hairs, caught fast in the worn metal, had held their place, to give up their testimony at last.

Cadfael ran a careful hand up the shaft of the staff, and felt the needle-stabs of three or four rough points in the silver. In the deepest of these five precious hairs had been dragged by violence from a head. A woman's head!

Diota opened the door to him, and on recognizing her visitor seemed to hesitate whether to open it wider and step aside to let him in, or hold her ground and discourage any lengthy conversation by keeping him on the doorstep. Her face was guarded and still, and her greeting resigned rather than welcoming. But the hesitation was only momentary. Submissively she stepped back into the room, and Cadfael followed her within and closed the door upon the world. It was early afternoon, the light as good as it would be this day, and the fire in the clay hearth bright and clear, almost without smoke.

'Mistress Hammet,' said Cadfael, with no more than a yard of dim, warm air between their faces, 'I must talk with you, and what I have to say concerns also the welfare of Ninian Bachiler, whom I know you value. I am in his confidence, if that helps me to yours. Now sit, and listen to me, and believe in my goodwill, as you have nothing on your conscience but the heart's affection. Which God saw clearly, before ever I held a key to it.'

466

She turned from him abruptly, but with a suggestion rather of balance and resolution than shock and dread, and sat down on the bench where Sanan had been sitting on his former visit. She sat erect, drawn up with elbows tight at her sides and feet firmly planted.

'Do you know where he is?' she asked in a low voice.

'I do not, though he made to tell me. Rest easy, I talked with him only last night, I know he is well. What I have to say has to do with you, and what happened on the eve of the Nativity, when Father Ailnoth died, and you … had a fall on the ice.'

She was already certain that he had knowledge she had hoped to keep from the light, but she did not know what it was. She kept silence, her eyes lifted steadily to his face, and left it to him to continue.

'A fall – yes! You won't have forgotten. You fell on the icy road and struck your head on the doorstone. I dressed the wound then, I saw it again yesterday, and it has healed over, but it still shows the bruise, and the scar where the skin was broken. Now hear what I have found this morning, in the mill-pond. Father Ailnoth's staff, drifted across to the far shore, and caught in the worn silver band, where the thin edges have turned, and are rough and sharp, five long hairs, the like of yours. Yours I saw closely, when I bathed your wound, I know there were broken ends there. I have the means to match them now.'

She had sunk her head into her hands, the long, workworn fingers clutched cheek and temple hard.

'Why should you hide your face?' he said temperately. 'That was not your sin.'

In a little while she raised a tearless face, blanched and wary, and peered at him steadily between her supporting hands. 'I was here,' she said slowly, 'when the nobleman came. I knew him again, I knew why he was here. Why else should he come?'

'Why, indeed! And when he was gone, the priest turned upon you. Reviled you, perhaps cursed you, for an accomplice in treason, for a liar and deceiver … We have learned to know him well enough to know that he would not be merciful, nor listen to excuse or pleading. Did he threaten you? Tell you how he would crush your nurseling first, and discard you with ignominy afterwards?'

Her back stiffened. She said with dignity: 'I nursed my lamb at this breast after my own child was born dead. He had a sickly mother, poor sweet lady. When he came to me, it was as

467

if a son of my own had come home in need. Do you think I cared what he – my master – might do against me?'

'No, I believe you,' said Cadfael. 'Your thought was all of Ninian when you went out after Father Ailnoth that night, to try to turn him from his purpose of challenge and betrayal. For you did follow him, did you not? You must have followed him. How else have I teased your hairs out of the worn band of his staff? You followed and pleaded with him, and he struck you. Clubbed his staff and struck out at your head.'

'I clung to him,' she said, with stony calm now, 'fell on my knees in the frosty grass there by the mill, and clung to the skirts of his gown to hold him, and would not let go. I prayed him, I pleaded, I begged him for mercy, but he had none. Yes, he struck me. He could not endure to be so held and crossed, it enraged him, he might well have killed me. Or so I dreaded then. I tried to fend off his blows, but I knew he would strike again if he could not rid himself of me. So I loosed hold and got to my feet, God knows how, and ran from him. And that was the last I ever saw of him living.'

'And you neither saw nor heard any other creature there? You left him whole, and alone?'

'I tell you truth,' she said, shaking her head, 'I neither heard nor saw any other soul, not even when I reached the Foregate. But neither my eyes nor my ears were clear, my head so rang, and I was in such sick despair. The first I was truly aware of was blood running down my forehead, and then I was in this house, crouched on the floor by the hearth, and shivering with the cold of fear, with no notion how I got here. I ran like an animal to its den, and that was all I knew. Only I am sure I met no one on the way, because if I had I should have had to master myself, walk like a woman in her senses, even give a greeting. And when you have to, you can. No, I know nothing more after I fled from him. All night I waited in fear of his return, knowing he would not spare me, and dreading he had already done his worst against Ninian. I was sure then that we were both lost – that everything was lost.'

'But he did not come,' said Cadfael.

'No, he did not come. I bathed my head, and stanched the blood, and waited without hope, but he never came. It was no help to me. Fear of him turned about into fear for him, for what could he be doing, out in the frost all night long? Even if he had gone up to the castle and called the guard there, still it could not have kept him so long. But he didn't come. Think for

468

yourself what manner of night I spent, sleepless in his house, waiting.'

'There was also, perhaps worst of all,' said Cadfael gently, 'your fear that he had indeed met with Ninian at the mill after you fled, and come to grief at Ninian's hands.'

She said, 'Yes,' in a dry whisper, and shivered. 'It could have been so. A boy of such spirit, challenged, accused, perhaps attacked … It could have been so. Thanks be to God, it was not so!'

'And in the morning? You could not leave it longer or leave it to others to raise an alarm. So you came to the church.'

'And told half a story,' she said with a brief, twisted smile, like a contortion of pain. 'What else could I do?'

'And while we went searching for the priest, Ninian stayed with you, and told you, doubtless, how he had spent the night, knowing nothing at all of what had happened after he left the mill. As doubtless you told him the rest of your story. But neither of you could shed light on the man's death.'

'That is true,' said Diota, 'I swear it. Neither then nor now. And now what do you intend for me?'

'Why, simply that you should do what Abbot Radulfus charged you, continue here and keep this house in readiness for another priest, and trust his word that you shall not be abandoned, since the church brought you here. I must be free to make use of what I know, but it shall be done with as little harm to you as possible, and only when I have understood more than now I understand. I wish you could have helped me one more step on the road, but never mind, truth is there to be found, and there must be a way to it. There were three people, besides Ailnoth, went to the mill that night,' said Cadfael, pausing at the door. 'Ninian was the first, you were the second. I wonder – I wonder! – who was the third?'

469

Chapter Ten

ADFAEL HAD been back in his workshop no more than half an hour, and the light was only just beginning to dim towards the Vesper office, when Hugh came seeking him, as he usually did if shire affairs brought him to confer with the abbot. He brought in with him a gust of moist, chill air and the quiver of a rising breeze that might bring more snow, now that the hard frost had eased, or might blow away the heavy cloud and clear the sky for the morrow.

'I've been with Father Abbot,' said Hugh, and sat down on the familiar bench by the wall and spread his feet appreciatively towards the brazier. 'Tomorrow, I hear, you're burying the priest. Cynric has the grave dug for him so deep you'd think he feared the man might break out of it without six feet of earth on top of him to hold him down. Well, he's going to his funeral unavenged, for we're no nearer knowing who killed him. You said from the first that the entire Foregate would turn blind, deaf and dumb. A man would think the whole parish had been depeopled on Christmas Eve, no one will admit to having been out of his own house but to hurry to church, and not a man of them set eyes on any other living being in the streets that night. It took a stranger to let fall even one little word of furtive comings and goings at an ungodly hour, and I place no great credence in that. And how have you been faring?'

Cadfael had been wondering the same thing in his own mind

ever since leaving Diota, and could see no possibility of keeping back from Hugh what he had learned. He had not promised secrecy, only discretion, and he owed help to Hugh as surely as to the woman caught in the trap of her own devotion.

'Better, perhaps, than I deserve,' he said sombrely, and put aside the tray of tablets he had just set out to dry, and went to sit beside his friend. 'If you had not come to me, Hugh, I should have had to come to you. Last night it was brought back to me what I had seen in Ailnoth's possession that night, and had not found nor thought to look for again the next day, when we brought him back here dead. Two things, indeed, though the first I did not find myself, but got it from the little boys who went down hopefully to the pool on Christmas morning, thinking it might be frozen over. Wait a moment, I'll bring both, and you shall hear.'

He brought them, and carried the lamp closer, to show the detail that might mean so much or so little.

'This cap the children found among the reeds of the shallows. You see how the stitches are started in the one seam, and the binding ripped loose. And this staff – this I found only this morning, almost opposite the place where we found Ailnoth.' He told that story simply and truthfully, but for omitting any mention of Ninian, though that, too, might have to come. 'You see how the silver band is worn into a mere wafer from age, and crumpled at the edges, being so thin. This notch here ...' He set a finger-tip to the razor-sharp points. 'From this I wormed out *these!*'

He had dabbed a tiny spot of grease into one of his clay saucers for selecting seed, and anchored the rescued hairs to the congealed fat, so that no chance draught should blow them away. In the close yellow light of the lamp they showed clearly. Cadfael drew out one of them to its full length.

'A metal edge fissured like this might pick up a stray hair almost anywhere,' said Hugh, but not with any great conviction.

'So it might, but here are five, captured at the same mis-stroke. Which makes this a different matter. Well?'

Hugh likewise laid a finger to the glistening threads and said deliberately: 'A woman's. Not young.'

'Whether you yet know it or no,' said Cadfael, 'there are but two women in all this coil, and one of them is young, and will not be grey, please God, for many years yet.'

471

'I think,' said Hugh, eyeing him with a faint, wise smile, 'you had better tell me. You were here from the beginning, I came late, and brought with me another matter warranted to confuse the first. I am not interested in preventing young Bachiler from making clean away to Gloucester to fight for his Empress, if he has nothing on his conscience that chances to be more particularly my business. But I *am* interested in burying the ugly fact of murder along with Ailnoth tomorrow, if by any means I can. I want the town and the Foregate going about their day's work with a quiet mind, and the way cleared for another priest, and let's hope one easier to live with. Now, what I make of these hairs is that they came from the head of Dame Diota Hammet. I have not even seen the woman in a good light, to know if this colouring is hers, but even there indoors the bruise on her brow was plain to be seen. She had a fall on the icy step – so I had been told, and so she told me. I think you are saying she came by that injury in a very different manner.'

'She came by it,' said Cadfael, 'by the mill that night, when she followed the priest in desperation, to plead with him to let well alone and turn a blind eye to the boy's deception, instead of confronting him like an avenging demon and fetching your sergeants down on him to throw him into prison. She was Ninian's nurse, she would dare almost anything for his sake. She clung about Ailnoth's skirts and begged him to let be, and because he could not shake her off, he clubbed this staff of his and struck her on the head, and would have struck again if she had not loosed him and scrambled away half-stunned, and run for her life back to the house.'

He told the whole of it as he had had it from Diota herself, and Hugh listened with a grave face but the hint of the smile lingering thoughtfully in his eyes. 'You believe this,' he said at the end of it; not a question, but a fact, and relevant to his own thinking.

'I do believe it. Entirely.'

'And she can add nothing more, to point us to any other person. Or would she, even if she could?' wondered Hugh. 'She may very well feel with the Foregate, and prefer to keep her own counsel.'

'So she might, I won't deny, but for all that, I think she knows no more. She ran from him dazed and in terror. I think there's no more to be got from her.'

'Nor from your boy Benet?' said Hugh slyly, and laughed at

472

seeing Cadfael turn a sharp glance on him and bridle for a moment. 'Oh, come now, I do accept that it was not you who warned the boy to make himself scarce when Giffard brought the law down on him. But only because someone else had already spared you the trouble. You were very well aware that he was gone, when you so helpfully led us all round the garden here hunting for him. I'll even believe that you *had* seen him here not half an hour before. You have a way of telling simple truths which is anything but simple. And when did you ever have a young fellow in trouble under your eye, and not wind your way into his confidence? Of course he'll have opened his mind to you. I daresay you know where he is this very moment. Though I'm not asking!' he added hastily.

'No,' said Cadfael, well satisfied with the way that was phrased, 'no, that I don't know, so you may ask, for I can't tell you.'

'Having gone to some trouble not to find out or be told,' agreed Hugh, grinning. 'Well, I did tell you to keep him out of sight if you should happen on him. I might even turn a blind eye myself, once this other matter is cleared up.'

'As to that,' said Cadfael candidly, 'he's of the same mind as you, for until he knows that all's made plain, and Dame Hammet safe and respected, he won't budge. Much as he wants to get to honest service in Gloucester, here he stays while she's in trouble. Which is only fair, seeing the risks she has taken for him. But once this is over, he'll be away, out of your territory. And not alone!' said Cadfael, meeting Hugh's quizzical glance with a complacent countenance. 'Is it possible I still know something you do not know?'

Hugh furrowed his brow and considered this riddle at leisure. 'Not Giffard, that's certain! He could not get himself out of the trap fast enough. Two women in the affair, you said, one of them young ... Do you tell me this young venturer has found himself a wife in these parts? Already? These imps of Anjou work briskly, I grant them that! Let's see, then ...' He pondered, drumming his fingers thoughtfully on the rim of the clay saucer. 'He had got himself into a monastery, where women do not abound, and I think you will have got your due of work out of him, he had small opportunity to go wooing among the townswomen. And as far as I know, he made no approach to any other of the local lordlings. I'm left with Giffard's household, where the boy's embassage may have been a none too well-kept secret, and where there's a very pleasing young woman, of the Empress's faction by blood, and bold and determined enough to choose differently from her step-father. Why, pure curiosity would have brought her to have a close look at such a paladin of romance, come in peril of his liberty and life from over the sea. Sanan Bernières? Is he truly wanting to take her with him?'

'Sanan it is. But I think it was she who made the decision. They have horses hidden away ready for departure, and she has her own small estate in jewels from her mother, easily carried. No doubt she's provided him sword and dagger, too. She'll not let him come before the Empress or Robert of Gloucester shabby, or without arms and horse.'

'They mean this earnestly?' wondered Hugh, frowning over a private doubt as to what his own course ought to be in such a case.

'They mean it. Both of them. I doubt if Giffard will mind much, though he's done his duty by her fairly enough. It saves him a dowry. And the man's had his losses, and is ambitious for his son.'

'And what,' demanded Hugh, 'does she get out of it?'

'She gets her own way. She gets what she wants, and the man she's chosen for herself. She gets Ninian. I think it may not be a bad bargain.'

Hugh sat silent for a brooding while, weighing the rights and wrongs of allowing such a flight, and recalling, perhaps, his own determined pursuit of Aline, not so long past. After a while his brow smoothed, and the private gleam of mischief quickened in his black eyes and twitched at the corner of his mouth. An eloquent eyebrow tilted above a covert glance at Cadfael.

'Well, I can as easily put a stop to that as cross the court here, yes, and bring the lad flying out of hiding into my arms, if I choose. You've taught me the way to flush him out of cover. All I need do is arrest Mistress Hammet, or even put it abroad that I'm about to, and he'll come running to defend her. If I accused her of murder, as like as not he'd go so far as to confess to an act he never committed, to see her free and vindicated.'

'You could do it,' Cadfael admitted, without any great concern, 'but you won't. You are as convinced as I am that neither he nor Dame Diota ever laid hand on Ailnoth, and you certainly won't pretend otherwise.'

'I might, however,' said Hugh, grinning, 'try the same trick

474

with another victim, and see if the man who did drown Ailnoth will be as honest and chivalrous as your lad would be. For I came here today with a small item of news you will not yet have heard, concerning one of Ailnoth's flock who'll be none the worse for a salutary shock. Who knows, there are plenty of rough and ready fellows who would kill lightly enough, but not stand by and let another man be hanged for it. It would be worth the trial, to hook a murderer, and even if it failed, the bait would come to no lasting harm.'

'I would not do it to a dog!' said Cadfael.

'Neither would I, dogs are hones, worthy creatures that fight fair and bear no grudges. When they set out to kill, they do it openly in broad daylight, and never care how many witnesses there may be. I have less scruples about some men. This one – ah, he's none so bad, but a fright won't hurt him, and may do a very sound turn for his poor drab of a wife.'

'You have lost me,' said Cadfael.

'Let me find you again! This morning Alan Herbard brought me a man he'd happened on by chance, a country kinsman of Erwald's who came to spend Christmas with the provost and his family here in the Foregate. The man's a shepherd by calling, and Erwald had a couple of ewes too early in lamb, penned in his shed out beyond the Gaye, and one of them threatened to cast her lamb too soon. So his cousin the shepherd went to the shed after Matins and Lauds on Christmas morning, to take a look at them, and brought off the threatened lamb safely, too, and was on his way back, just coming up from the Gaye and along to the Foregate at first light. And who do you suppose he saw sneaking very furtively up from the path to the mill and heading for home, but Jordan Achard, rumpled and bleared from sleep and hardly expecting to be seen at that hour. By chance one of the few people our man would have known by sight and name here, being the baker from whose oven he'd fetched his cousin's bread the day before. It came out in purest gossip, in all innocence. The countryman knew Jordan's reputation, and thought it a harmless joke to have seen him making for home from some strange bed.'

'Along that path?' said Cadfael, staring.

'Along that path. It was well trodden that night, it seems.'

'Ninian was the first,' said Cadfael slowly. 'I never told you that, but he went there early, not being sure of Giffard. He took himself off smartly when he saw Ailnoth come raging to the meeting, and nothing more did he know of it until morning, when Diota came crying the priest was lost. She was there, as I've told you. I said there must be a third. But Jordan? And blundering homeward at first light? It's hard to believe he had so much durable malice in him as to carry his grudge so long. A big, spoiled babe, I should have said, but for being an excellent baker.'

'So should I. But he was there, no question. Who's abroad at first light on Christmas morning, after a long night's worship? Barring, of course, a shepherd anxious about an ailing ewe! That was very ill luck for Jordan. But it goes further, Cadfael. I went myself to talk to Jordan's wife, while he was busy at his ovens. I told her what news we had of his moves, and made her understand it was proven beyond doubt where he'd been. I think she was ready to break like a branch over-fruited. Do you know how many children she's borne, poor soul? Eleven, and only two of them living. And how he managed to engender so many, considering how seldom he lies at home, only the recording angel can tell. Not a bad-looking woman, if she were not so worn and harried. And still fond of him!'

'And this time,' said Cadfael, awed, 'she really told you truth?'

'Of course she did, she was rightly afraid for him. Yes, she told truth. Yes, he was out all that night, it was nothing new. But not murdering anyone! No, on that she was insistent, he would not hurt a fly. He's done his worst by a poor wretch of a wife, however! All he'd been about, she said, was bedding his latest fancy girl, and that was the bold little bitch who's maidservant to the old woman who lives next to the miller, by the pool.'

'Ah, now that's a far more likely thing,' said Cadfael, enlightened. 'That rings true! We talked to her,' he recalled, fascinated, 'next morning, when we were looking for Ailnoth.' A pretty slut of about eighteen, with a mane of dark hair and bold, inquisitive eyes, saying: 'Not a soul that I know of came along here in the night, why should they?' No, she had not been lying. She had never thought of her covert lover as counting among the furtive visitors to the mill in the darkness. His errand was known, and if not innocent, entirely natural and harmless. She spoke according to her understanding.

'And she never said word of Jordan! No, why should she? She knew what he'd been up to, it was not about him you were asking. Oh, no, I've nothing against the girl. But I would stake much that she knows nothing of time, and has no notion exactly when he came or when he left, except by the beginning of light. He could have killed a man before ever he whispered at the deaf woman's door, for ears that were forewarned and sharp enough.'

'I doubt if he did,' said Cadfael.

'So do I. But see how beautiful a case I can make against him! His wife has admitted that he went there. The shepherd saw him leaving. We know that Father Ailnoth went along that same path. After Mistress Hammet had fled from him, still he waited for his prey. And how if he saw a parishioner of his, already in dispute with him, and whose reputation he may well have heard before then, whispering his way furtively into a strange house, and being let in by a young woman? How then? His nose was expert at detecting sinners, he might well be distracted from his first purpose to flush out an evil-doer on the spot. The old woman is stone deaf. The girl, if she witnessed such a collision, and saw its end, would hold her tongue and tell a good story. In such a case, Cadfael, old friend, the priest might well have started too hot a hare, and got the worst of it, ending in the pool.'

'The blow to Ailnoth's head,' said Cadfael, jolted, 'was deep to the back. Men in conflict go face to face.'

'True, but one may easily be spun aside and involuntarily turn his back for an instant. But you know how the wound lay, and I know. But do the commons know?'

'And you will really do this?' marvelled Cadfael.

'Most publicly, my friend, I will do it. Tomorrow morning, at Ailnoth's funeral – even those who most hated him will be there to make sure he's safely underground, what better occasion could there be? If it bears fruit, then we have our answer, and the town can be at peace, once the turmoil's over. If not, Jordan will be none the worse for a short-lived fright, and a few nights, perhaps,' pondered Hugh, gleaming mischief, 'on a harder bed than usual with him, and lying alone. He may even learn that his own bed is the safest from this on.'

'And how if no man speaks up to deliver him,' said Cadfael with mild malice, 'and the thing happened just as you have pictured it to me a minute ago, and Jordan really is your man? What then? If he keep his head and deny all, and the girl bears witness for him, you'll have trailed your bait in vain.'

'Ah, you know the man better than that,' said Hugh,

undisturbed. 'Big-boned and hearty, but no great stiffening in his back. If he did it, deny it as loudly as he may when he's first accused, a couple of nights on stone and he'll be blabbing out everything, how he did no more than defend himself, how it was mere accident, and he could not haul the priest out of the water, and took fright, and dared not speak, knowing that the bad blood between them was common knowledge. A couple of nights in a cell won't hurt him. And if he holds out stoutly any longer than that,' said Hugh, rising, 'then he deserves to get away with it. The parish will think so.'

'You are a devious creature,' said Cadfael, in a tone uncertain between reproach and admiration. 'I wonder why I bear with you?'

Hugh turned in the doorway to give him a flashing glance over his shoulder. 'Like calling to like, I daresay!' he suggested, and went striding away along the gravel path, to disappear into the gathering dusk.

At Vespers the psalms had a penitential solemnity, and at Collations in the chapter house after supper the readings were also of a funereal colouring. The shadow of Father Ailnoth hung over the death of the year, and it seemed that the year of Our Lord 1142 would be born, not at midnight, but only after the burial service was over, and the grave filled in. The morrow might, according to the Church's calendar, be the octave of the Nativity and the celebration of the Circumcision of Our Lord, but to the people of the Foregate it was rather the propitiatory office that would lift their incubus from them. A wretched departure for any man, let alone a priest.

'On the morrow,' said Prior Robert, before dismissing them to the warming room for the blessed last half-hour of ease before Compline, 'the funeral office for Father Ailnoth will follow immediately after the parish Mass, and I myself shall preside. But the homily will be delivered by Father Abbot, at his desire.' The prior's incisive and well-modulated voice made this statement with a somewhat ambiguous emphasis, as if in doubt whether to welcome the abbot's decision as a devout compliment to the dead, or to regret and perhaps even resent it as depriving him of an opportunity to exercise his own undoubted eloquence. 'Matins and Lauds will be said according to the Office of the Dead.'

That meant that they would be long, and prudent brothers would be wise to make straight for their beds after Compline.

Cadfael had already turfed down his brazier to burn slowly through the night, and keep lotions and medicines from freezing and bottles from bursting, should a hard frost set in again in the small hours. But the air was certainly not cold enough yet for frost, and he thought by the slight wind and lightly overcast sky that they would get through the night safely. He went thankfully to the warming room with his brothers, and settled down to half an hour of pleasant idleness.

This was the hour when even the taciturn relaxed into speech, and not even the prior frowned upon a degree of loquacity. And inevitably the subject of their exchanges tonight was the brief rule of Father Ailnoth, his grim death, and the coming ceremonial of his burial.

'So Father Abbot means to pronounce the eulogy himself, does he?' said Brother Anselm in Cadfael's ear. 'That will make interesting listening.' Anselm's business was the music of the Divine Office, and he had not quite the same regard for the spoken word, but he appreciated its power and influence. 'I had thought he'd be only too glad to leave it to Robert. *Nil nisi bonum* ... Or do you suppose he looks upon it as a fitting penance for bringing the man here in the first place?'

'There may be something in that,' admitted Cadfael. 'But more, I think, in a resolve that only truth shall be told. Robert would be carried away into paeans of praise. Radulfus intends clarity and honesty.'

'No easy task,' said Anselm. 'Well for me no one expects words from me. There's been no hint yet of who's to follow in the parish. They'll be praying for a man they know, whether he has any Latin or not. Even a man they did not much like would be welcomed, if he belongs here, and knows them. You can deal with the devil you know.'

'No harm in hoping for better than that,' said Cadfael, sighing. 'A very ordinary man, more than a little lower than the angels, and well aware of his own shortcomings, would do very nicely for the Foregate. A pity these few weeks were wasted, wanting him.'

In the big stone hearth the fire of logs burned steadily, sinking down now into a hot core of ash, nicely timed to last the evening out, and die down with little waste when the bell rang for Compline. Faces pinched with cold and outdoor labour during the day flushed into rosy content, and chapped hands smoothed gratefully at the ointment doled out from Cadfael's store. Friends foregathered in their own chosen

479

groups, voices decorously low blended into a contented murmur like a hive of bees. Some of the healthy young, who had been out in the air most of the day, had much ado to keep their eyelids open in the warmth. Compline would be wisely brief tonight, as Matins would be long and sombre.

'Another year tomorrow,' said Brother Edmund the infirmarer, 'and a new beginning.'

Some said: 'Amen!' whether from habit or conviction, but Cadfael stuck fast at the word. 'Amen' belongs rather to an ending, a resolution, an acceptance into peace, and as yet they were within reach of none of these things.

A mile to the west of Cadfael's bed in his narrow cell in the dortoir, Ninian lay in the plenteous hay of a well-stocked loft, rolled in the cloak Sanan had brought for him, and with the heartening warmth of her still in his arms, though she had been gone two hours and more, in time to have her pony back in the town stable before her step-father returned from the night office at Saint Chad's church. Ninian had been urgent with her that she should not venture alone by night, but as yet he had no authority over her, and she would do what she would do, having been born into the world apparently without fear. This byre and loft on the edge of the forest belonged to the Giffards, who had grazing along the open meadow that rimmed the trees, but the elderly hind who kept the cattle was from Sanan's own household, and her willing and devoted slave. The two good horses she had bought and stabled here were his joy, and his privity to Sanan's marriage plans would keep him proud and glad to the day of his death.

She had come, and she had lain with Ninian in the loft, the two rolled in one cloak and anchored with embracing arms, not yet for the body's delight but rather for its survival and comfort. Snug like dormice in their winter sleep, alive and awake enough to be aware of profound pleasure, they had talked together almost an hour, and now that she had left him he hugged the remembrance of her and got warmth from it to keep him glowing through the night. Some day, some night, please God soon, she would not have to rise and leave him, he would not have to open reluctant arms and let her go, and the night would be perfect, a lovely, starry dark shot through with flame. But now he lay alone, and ached a little, and fretted about her, about the morrow, about his own debts, which seemed to him so inadequately paid.

With her hair adrift against his cheek, and her breath warm in the hollow of his throat, she had told him everything that had happened during these last days of the old year, how Brother Cadfael had found the ebony staff, how he had visited Diota and got her story out of her, how Father Ailnoth's funeral was to take place next day after the parish Mass. And when he started up in anxiety for Diota, she had drawn him down to her again with her arms wreathed about his neck, and told him he need have no uneasiness, for she had promised to go with Diota to the priest's funeral Mass, and take as great care of her as he himself could have done, and deal with any threat that might arise against her as valiantly as even he would have dealt with it. And she had forbidden him to stir from where he lay hidden until she should come to him again. But just as she was a lady not lightly to be disobeyed, so he was a man not lightly to be forbidden.

All the same, she had got a promise out of him that he would wait, as she insisted, unless something unforeseen should arise to make action imperative. And with that she had had to be content, and they had kissed on it, and put away present anxieties to whisper about the future. How many miles to the Welsh border? Ten? Certainly not much more. And Powys might be a wild land, but it had no quarrel with a soldier of the Empress more than with an officer of King Stephen, and would by instinct take the part of the hunted rather than the forces of English law. Moreover, Sanan had claims to a distant kinship there, through a Welsh grandmother, who had bequeathed her her un-English name. And should they encounter masterless men in the forests, Ninian was a good man of his hands, and there was a good sword and a long dagger hidden away in the hay, arms once carried by John Bernières at the siege of Shrewsbury, where he had met his death. They would do well enough on the journey, they would reach Gloucester and marry there, openly and honourably.

Except that they could not go, not yet, not until he was satisfied that all danger to Diota was past, and her living secure under the abbot's protection. And now that he lay alone, Ninian could see no present end to that difficulty. The morrow would lay Ailnoth's body to rest, but not the ugly shadow of his death. Even if the day passed without threat to Diota, that would not solve anything for the days yet to come.

Ninian lay wakeful until past midnight, fretting at the threads that would not untangle for him. Over the watershed between the old year and the new he drifted at last into an uneasy sleep, and dreamed of fighting his way through interminable forest tracks overgrown with bramble and thorn towards a Sanan forever withdrawn from him, and leaving behind for him only a sweet, aromatic scent of herbs.

Under the vast inverted keel of the choir, dimly lit for Matins, the solemn words of the Office of the Dead echoed and re-echoed as sounds never seemed to do by day, and the fine, sonorous voice of Brother Benedict the sacristan was magnified to fill the whole vault as he read the lessons in between the spoken psalms, and at every ending came the insistent versicle and response:

'*Requiem aeternam dona eis, Domine ...*'
'*Et lux perpetua luceat eis ...*'

And Brother Benedict, deep and splendid: ' "My soul is very weary of my life ... I will speak in the bitterness of my soul, I will say unto God, Do not condemn me, show me wherefore thou contendest with me ..." '

Not much comfort in the book of Job, thought Cadfael, listening intently in his stall, but a great deal of fine poetry – could not that in itself be a kind of comfort, after all? Making even discomfort, degradation and death, everything Job complained of, a magnificent defiance?

' "O that thou wouldst hide me in the grave, that thou wouldst keep me secret until thy wrath be past ...

' "My breath is corrupt, my days are extinct, the grave is ready for me ... I have made my bed in the darkness, I have said to corruption, Thou art my father, to the worm, Thou art my mother. And where is now my hope?

' "Cease, then, and let me alone, that I may take comfort a little, before I go whence I shall not return, even to the land of darkness and the shadow of death ... land without order, where even the light is as darkness ..." '

Yet in the end the entreaty that was itself a reassurance rose again, one step advanced beyond hope towards certainty:

'*Rest eternal grant unto them, O Lord ...*'
'*And let light perpetual shine upon them ...*'

Stumbling up the night stairs back to bed after Lauds, half asleep, Cadfael still had that persistent appeal echoing in his mind, and by the time he slept again it had become almost a triumphant claim reaching up to take what it pleaded for. Rest eternal and light perpetual ... even for Ailnoth.

Not only for Ailnoth, but for most of us, thought Cadfael, subsiding into sleep, it will be a long journey through purgatory, but no doubt even the most winding way gets there in the end.

Chapter Eleven

HE FIRST day of the New Year, 1142, dawned grey
and moist, but with a veiled light that suggested the
sun might come through slowly, and abide for an
hour or so in the middle of the day, before mist again
closed in towards nightfall. Cadfael, who was often up well
before Prime, awakened this morning only when the bell
sounded, and made his way down the night stairs with the
others still drowsy from so short a rest. After Prime he went to
make sure that all was well in the workshop, and brought away
with him fresh oil for the altar lamps. Cynric had already
trimmed the candles, and gone out through the cloister to the
graveyard, to see all neat and ready where the open grave
waited under the precinct wall, covered decorously with
planks. The body in its wooden coffin rested on a bier before
the parish altar, decently draped. After the Mass it would be
carried in procession from the north door, along the Foregate,
and in at the great double gate just round the corner from the
horse-fair ground, where the laity had access, instead of
through the monastic court. A certain separateness must be
preserved, for the sake of the quietude necessary to the Rule.

There was a subdued bustle about the great court well before
the hour for Mass, brothers hurrying to get their work ready
for the rest of the day, or finish small things left undone the
previous day. And the people of the Foregate began to gather
outside the great west door of the church, or hover about the
gatehouse waiting for friends before entering. They came with

faces closed and shuttered, dutifully grave and ceremonious, but with quick and careful eyes watching from ambush, uncertain still whether they were really out of the shadow of that resented presence. Perhaps after today they would draw breath and come out of hiding, no longer wary of speaking openly to their neighbours. Perhaps! But what if Hugh should spring his trap in vain?

Cadfael was uneasy about the entire enterprise, but even more dismayed at the thought of this uncertainty continuing for ever, until distrust and fear died at last only from attrition and forgetfulness. Better to have it out into the light, deal with it, and be done. Then at least all but one could be at peace. No – he, too! He most of all!

The notabilities of the Foregate had begun to appear, Erwald the reeve, sombre-faced and aware of his dignity, as befitted and almost justified his use of the title of provost. The smith from his forge, Rhys ab Owain the Welsh farrier – several of the craftsmen of the Foregate were Welsh – Erwald's shepherd kinsman, and Jordan Achard the baker, big and burly and well fleshed, wooden-faced like the rest but nevertheless with a sort of glossy content about him, having survived to bury his detractor. And the little people, too. Aelgar who had worked for the priest and been affronted by the doubt whether he was villein or free, Eadwin whose boundary stone had been shifted by Ailnoth's too-close ploughing, Centwin whose child had been buried in unblessed ground and abandoned as lost, the fathers of boys who had learned the hard way to stay out of range of the ebony staff, and shivered in their shoes at having to attend Ailnoth's lessons. The boys themselves gathered at a little distance from their elders, whispering, shuffling, shifting to get a view within but never entering, and sometimes their wary faces showed a sudden fleeting grin here and there, and sometimes their whispering turned briefly to sniggering, half from bravado and half from involuntary awe. The Foregate dogs, sensing the general excitement and unease, ran about between the crowding watchers, snapped edgily at the hooves of passing horses, and loosed volleys of high-pitched barking at every sudden noise.

The women, for the most part, had been left at home. No doubt Jordan's wife was looking after his bakery, raking out the ashes from the early morning firing, and making ready for the second batch, the loaves already shaped and waiting. Just

485

as well for her to be at a safe distance from what was to come, though surely Hugh would not involve the poor soul, when she had only admitted her husband's sleeping abroad in order to save him from this worse accusation. Well, that must be left to Hugh, and Hugh was usually adroit about his manipulations of people and events. But some of the women were here, the elders, the matrons, the widows of solid craftsmen, those who upheld the church even when others became backsliders. The stalwarts at all the least timely services, attending doggedly even at the monastic Vespers as well as the parish Mass, were mostly these sturdy she-elders in their decent black, like lay members of the community itself. They would not miss the ceremonies of this day.

Cadfael was watching the arrivals with a half-attentive gaze and his mind elsewhere, when he saw Diota Hammet come in at the gate, with Sanan's hand solicitous at her elbow. It came both as an anxious reminder and a pleasant refreshment to his eyes, two comely women thus linked in a carefully groomed and perhaps brittle dignity, very calm and stiff with resolution. Autumn and spring came gallantly supporting each other. Ninian in his banishment and solitude would require a full account, and never have an easy moment until he got it. Two hours more and the thing would be done, one way or the other.

They had come in through the gate to the court, and were looking about them, clearly seeking someone. It was Sanan who saw him first, and brightened as she turned to speak quickly into Diota's ear. The widow turned to look, and at once started towards him. He went to meet them, since it seemed he must be the one they were seeking.

'I'm glad to have found you thus before the service,' said the widow. 'The ointment you gave me – there's the half of it left, and you see I don't need it any more. It would be a shame to waste it, you must have a deal of call for it in this wintry weather.' She had it put away safely in the little bag slung from her girdle, and had to fumble under her cloak to get it out. A small, rough pottery jar, with a wooden lid stoppered tightly into the neck to seal it. She held it out to him on her open palm, and offered him with it a pale but steady smile. 'All my grazes are gone, this can still serve someone else. Take it, with my thanks.'

The last of her grazes, faded now almost to invisibility, hair-fine threads of white, showed elusively round the jar in her palm. The mark on her temple was merely a hyacinth oval, the

486

bruise all but gone.

'You could have kept it against future need, with all my goodwill,' said Cadfael, accepting the offering.

'Well, should I ever have need again, I hope I shall still be here, and able to send to you,' said Diota.

She made him a small, dignified reverence, and turned back towards the church. Over her shoulder Cadfael caught Sanan's confiding blue gaze, harebell-soft and sky-bright, almost as intimate as a signal between conspirators. Then she, too, turned, taking the older woman's arm, and the two of them walked away from him, across the court to the gate, and in at the west door of the church.

Ninian awoke when it was full daylight, thick-headed and slow to collect his wits from having lain half the night wakeful, and then fallen into too profound a slumber. He rose, and swung himself down from the loft without using the ladder, and went out into the fresh, chill, moist morning to shake off the lingering cobwebs. The stalls below were empty. Sanan's man Sweyn had been here already from his own cottage nearer the town, and turned out the two horses into the fenced paddock. They needed a little space for exercise, after the harder frosts when they had been kept indoors, and they were making good use of their freedom, glad of the air and the light. Young and high-spirited and short of work, they would not easily let themselves be caught and bridled, but it was unlikely they would be needed this day.

The cattle byre was still peopled, they would not be let out to the grazing along the riverside until Sweyn was near to keep an eye on them. The byre and stable stood in a large clearing between slopes of woodland, with an open side only to the river, pleasantly private, and under the western stand of trees a little stream ran down to the Severn. Ninian made for it sleepily, stripped off coat and shirt, shivering a little, and plunged head and arms into the water, flinching and drawing in hissing breath at the instant coldness, but taking pleasure in feeling his wits start into warm wakefulness. Shaking off drops from his face and wringing his hands through his thick thatch of curls, he ran a couple of circuits of the open grass at full gallop, caught up his discarded clothes and ran back with them into the shelter of the stable, to scrub himself vigorously with a clean sack until he glowed, and dress himself to face the day. Which might be long and lonely and full of anxieties, but at this

487

moment felt bracing and hopeful.

He had combed his hair into such order as his fingers could command, and was sitting on a bale of straw eating a hunk of bread and an apple from the store Sanan had provided, when he heard the herdsman come along the rough path towards the door. Or was this some other man, and not Sweyn at all? Ninian stiffened to listen, with his cheek bulging with apple, and his jaws motionless. No whistling, and Sweyn always whistled, and these feet came in unusual haste, clearly audible in the rough grass and small stones. Ninian was up in still greater haste, and swung himself up into the loft and hung silent over the hatch, ready for whoever should come.

'Young master ...' called a voice in the open doorway, without any suggestion of caution. Sweyn, after all, but a Sweyn who had been hurrying, was a little out of breath, and had no thought to spare for whistling this morning. 'Lad, where are you? Come down!'

Ninian let out his breath in a great gust, and slid back through the hatch to hang at arm's length and drop beside the herdsman. 'God's love, Sweyn, you had me reaching for a knife then! I never thought it was you. I thought I had you by heart, by this time, but you came like a stranger. What is it?' He flung an arm about his friend and ally boisterously in his relief, and as quickly held him off to look him up and down from head to foot. 'Lord, lord, in your best, too! In whose honour?'

Sweyn was a thickset, grizzled man of middle age, with a ragged brown beard and a twinkling glance. Whatever warm clothing he put on against the winter he must have put on underneath, for he had but the one stout pair of cloth hose, and Ninian had never yet seen him in any coat but the much-mended drab brown, but evidently he possessed another, for this morning he had on a green coat, unpatched, and a dark brown capuchon protecting head and shoulders.

'I've been into Shrewsbury,' he said shortly, 'fetching a pair of shoes my wife left to be clouted at Provost Corviser's. I was here at first light and let out the horses, they've been penned long enough, and then I went back to fettle myself for the town, and I've had no time to put on my working gear again. There's word going round the town, master, that the sheriff means to attend the Foregate priest's funeral, and fetch a murderer away with him. I thought I'd best bring you word as fast as I could. For it may be true.'

488

Ninian stood gaping at him aghast for a moment in stricken silence. 'No! He's going to take her? Is that the word? Oh, God, not Diota! And she there to be seized, all unsuspecting. And I not there!' He clutched earnestly at Sweyn's arm. 'Is this certain?'

'It's the common talk about the town. Folks are all agog, there'll be a stream of them making haste over the bridge to see it done. They don't say who – leastways, they guess at it, two or three ways, but they all agree it's coming, be the poor wretch who he may.'

Ninian flung away the apple he had still been holding, and beat his fists together in frantic thought. 'I must go! The parish Mass won't be until ten, there's still time …'

'You can't go. The young mistress said –'

'I know what she said, but this is my business now. I must and will get Diota out of it. Who else can it be the sheriff means to accuse? But he shan't have her! I won't suffer it!'

'You'll be known! It may not be your woman he has in mind, how then? He may have the rights of it, and know well what he's doing. And you'll have thrown yourself away for nothing,' urged the herdsman reasonably.

'No, I needn't be known. One in a crowd – and only the people of the abbey and a few in the Foregate know me well by sight. In any case,' said Ninian grimly, 'let anyone lay a hand on her and I *will* be known, and with a vengeance, too. But I can be lost among a crowd, why not? Lend me that coat and capuchon, Sweyn, who's to know me under a hood? And they've never seen me but in this gear, yours is far too fine for the Benet they've seen about the place …'

'Take the horse,' said Sweyn, stripping off his capuchon without protest, and hoisting the loose cotte over his head.

Ninian did cast one glance out into the field where the two horses kicked up their heels, happy to be at large. 'No, no time! I can do it as fast afoot. And I'd be more noticeable, mounted. How many horsemen will there be about Ailnoth's funeral?' He thrust his way into the over-ample garment already warmed for him, and emerged ruffled and flushed. 'I daren't show a sword. But the dagger I can hide about me.' He was up into the loft to fetch it, and fasten it safely out of sight under his coat, secure in the belt of his hose.

At the doorway, poised to run, he was stricken with another qualm, and turned to clutch again at the herdsman's arm. 'Sweyn, if I'm taken – Sanan will see you shan't be the loser.

Your good clothes – I've no right ...'

'Ah, go on with you!' said Sweyn, half-affronted, and gave him a shove out into the field and towards the trees. 'I can go in sacking if needs must. You bring yourself back safe, or the young mistress will have my head for it. And put up your hood, fool boy, before you come near the road!'

Ninian ran, across the meadow and into the slope of trees, heading for the track that would bring him, within a mile or so, to the Meole Brook, and across it into the Foregate, close by the bridge into the town.

Word of the fat rumour that was running round Shrewsbury reached Ralph Giffard some time later, none of his household having been abroad in the town before nine o'clock, when a maidservant went out to fetch a pitcher of milk, and was a long time about it by reason of the juicy gossip she learned on her errand. Even when she returned to the house the news took some time to be carried from the kitchen to the clerk, who had come to see what all the chatter was about, and thence to Giffard himself, who was at that moment reflecting whether it was not time to leave the town house to the caretaker and make for his chief manor in the north-east. It was pleasant to prolong the comfortable stay here, and he had taken pleasure in falling in with his young son's wish to practise the skills of managing a manor for himself, unsupervised. The boy was sixteen, two years younger than his step-sister, and somewhat jealous of her show of maturity and responsibility in running the distaff side of the household. He was already affianced, a good match with a neighbour's daughter, and naturally he was eager to try his wings. And no doubt he would be doing well enough, and proud of his prowess, but still a father would be only prudent to keep an eye on affairs. There was no bad blood between boy and girl, but for all that, young Ralph would not be sorry to have Sanan safely married and out of the house. If only her marriage did not threaten to cost so much!

'My lord,' said the old clerk, coming in upon his ponderings towards mid morning, 'I think you are rid of your incubus this day, or soon will be. It seems it's all round the town, being bandied across every counter and every doorstep, that Beringar has his murderer known and proved, and means to take him at the priest's burial. And who can it be but that youngster of FitzAlan's? He may have made his escape once, but it seems they've run him to earth this time.'

490

He brought it as good news, and as such Giffard received it. Once the troublesome fellow was safely in hold, and his own part in the matter as clearly decorous and loyal, he could be at ease. While the rogue ran loose, there might still be unpleasant echoes for any man who had had to do with him.

'So I did well to uncover him,' he said, breathing deeply. 'I might still have been suspect else, when they lay hands on him. Well, well! So the thing's as good as over, and no harm done.'

The thought was very satisfying, even though he would have been just as pleased if it could have been achieved without the act of betrayal with which a lingering scruple in his own mind still reproached him. But now, if it was to be proven that the young fellow really had murdered the priest, then there was no longer need to feel any qualms on his behalf, for he had his deserts.

It was some last superstition that something might yet go wrong, added to a contradictory desire to see the successful consummation in person, that made him think again, and make up his mind, somewhat belatedly, to be in at the death. To make sure, and to wring the fullest savour out of his own preservation.

'After the parish Mass, this was to be? They'll be well into the abbot's sermon by now. I think I'll ride down and see the end of it.' And he was out of his chair and shouting across the yard for the groom to saddle his horse.

Abbot Radulfus had been speaking for some time, slowly, with the high, withdrawn voice of intense thought, every word measured. In the choir it was always dim, a parable of the life of man, a small, lighted space arched over by a vast shadowy darkness, for even in the darkness there are degrees of shadow. The crowded nave was lighter, and with so many people in attendance not even notably cold. When choir monks and secular congregation met for worship together, the separation between them seemed accentuated rather than softened. We here, you out there, thought Brother Cadfael, and yet we are all like flesh, and our souls subject to the same final judgement.

'The company of the saints,' said Abbot Radulfus, his head raised so that he looked rather into the vault than at those he addressed, 'is not to be determined by any measure within our understanding. It cannot be made up of those without sin, for who that ever wore flesh, except one, can make so high a

491

claim? Surely there is room within it for those who have set before themselves lofty aims, and done their best to reach them, and so, we believe, did our brother and shepherd here dead. Yes, even though they fail of attaining their aims, more, even though those aims may have been too narrow, the mind that conceived them being blinded by prejudice and pride, and channelled too greedily towards a personal excellence. For even the pursuit of perfection may be sin, if it infringes the rights and needs of another soul. Better to fail a little, by turning aside to lift up another, than to pass by him in haste to reach our own reward, and leave him to solitude and despair. Better to labour in lameness, in fallibility, but holding up others who falter, than to stride forward alone.

'Again, it is not enough to abstain from evil, there must also be an outgoing goodness. The company of the blessed may extend justifiably to embrace even men who have been great sinners, yet also great lovers of their fellow men, such as have never turned away their eyes from other men's needs, but have done them such good as they might, and as little harm as they must. For in that they saw a neighbour's need, they saw God's need, as he himself has shown us, and inasmuch as they saw a neighbour's face more clearly than their own, so also they saw God's face.

'Further, I show you certainly that all such as are born into this world and die untainted by personal sin partake of the martyred purity of the Holy Innocents, and die for Our Lord, who also will embrace them and quicken them living, where they shall no more partake of death. And if they died without name here, yet their name is written in his book, and no other need know it, until the day come.

'But we, all we who share the burden of sin, it behoves us not to question or fret concerning the measure dealt out to us, or try to calculate our own merit and deserving, for we have not the tools by which to measure values concerning the soul. That is God's business. Rather it behoves us to live every day as though it were our last, to the full of such truth and kindness as is within us, and to lie down every night as though the next day were to be our first, and a new and pure beginning. The day will come when all will be made plain. Then shall we know, as now we trust. And in that trust we commit our pastor here to the care of the shepherd of shepherds, in the sure hope of the resurrection.'

He uttered the blessing with his face lowered at last to those who listened. Probably he wondered how many had understood, and how many, indeed, had need of understanding.

It was over here, people stirred stealthily in the nave, sliding towards the north door to be first out and secure a good place ahead of the procession. In the choir the three ministering priests, abbot, prior and sub-prior, descended to the bier, and the brothers formed silent file, two by two, after them. The party of bearers took up the burden, and made towards the open north doorway into the Foregate. How is it, thought Cadfael, watching, and glad of a distraction, however sinful at such a moment, how is it that there is always one out of step, or just a little too short in height and stride to match the others? Is it so that we should not fall into the error of taking even death too seriously?

It was no great surprise to find the Foregate crowded when the procession issued from the north porch and turned to the right along the precinct wall, but at first glance it did come as a surprise to find half the townspeople among the starers, as well as the men of the parish. Then Cadfael understood the reason. Hugh had had discreet whispers of his plans leaked within the town walls, too late for them to be carried out here to the folk most concerned, and give warning, but in time to bring the worthies of Shrewsbury – or perhaps even more surely the unworthies, who had time to waste on curiosity – hurrying here to be witnesses of the ending.

Cadfael was still wondering what that ending was to be. Hugh's device might provoke some man's conscience and make him speak out, to deliver a neighbour mistakenly accused, but equally it might come as an immense relief to the guilty, and be accepted as a gift – certainly not from heaven, rather from the other place! At every step along the Foregate he fretted at the tangle of details churning in his mind, and found no coherence among them. Not until the little jar of ointment he had thrust into the breast of his habit nodded against his middle as his foot slid in a muddy rut. The touch was like an impatient nudge at his mind. He saw it again, resting in the palm of a shapely but work-worn hand, as Diota held it out to him. A hand seamed with the lines proper to the human palm, graven deep with lifelong use, but also bearing thread-like white lines that crossed these, fanning from wrist to fingers, barely visible now, soon to vanish altogether.

An icy night, certainly, he had trodden cautiously through it himself, he knew. And a woman slipping as she turned to step back on to the frozen doorstone of a house, and falling forward, naturally puts out her hands to save herself, and her hands take the rough force of the fall, even though they may not quite save her head. Except that Diota had not fallen. Her head injury was sustained in quite a different way. She had fallen on her knees that night, yes, but of desperate intent, with hands clutching not at frozen ground, but at the skirts of Ailnoth's cassock and cloak. So how did she get those scored grazes in both palms?

In innocence she had told him but half a story, believing she told him all. And here was he helpless now, he must hold his place in this funeral procession, and she must hold hers, and he could not get to her, to probe the corners of memory which had eluded her then. Not until this solemn rite was over and done would he be able to speak again with Diota. No, but there were other witnesses, mute by their nature but possibly eloquent in what they might be able to demonstrate. He walked on perforce, keeping pace with Brother Henry along the Foregate and round the corner by the horse-fair ground, unable to break the decorum of burial. Not yet! But perhaps within? For there would be no procession through the street afterwards, not for the brethren. They would be already within their chosen enclave, to disperse severally to their ablutions and their dinner in the refectory. Once within, why should he be missed if he slipped quietly away?

The broad double doors in the precinct wall stood wide open to let the mourning column into the wide prospect of the cemetery garth, giving place on the left to kitchen gardens, and beyond, the long roof of the abbot's lodging, and the small enclosed flower garden round it. The brothers were buried close under the east end of the church, the vicars of the parish a little removed from them, but in the same area. The number of graves as yet was not large, the foundation being no more than fifty-eight years old, and though the parish was older, it had been served by the small wooden church Earl Roger had replaced in stone and given to the newly founded abbey. There were trees here, and grass, and meadow flowers in the summer, a pleasant enough place. Only the dark, raw hole close to the wall marred the green enclosure. Cynric had placed trestles to receive the coffin before it was lowered into the grave, and he was stooped over the planks he had just removed, stacking them tidily against the wall.

Half the Foregate and a good number of the inhabitants of the town came thronging through the open doors after the brothers, crowding close to see all there was to be seen. Cadfael drew back from his place in the ranks, and contrived to be swallowed up by their inquisitive numbers. No doubt Brother Henry would eventually miss him from his side, but in the circumstances he would say no word. By the time Prior Robert had got out the first sonorous phrases of the committal, Cadfael was round the corner of the chapter house and scurrying across the great court towards the wicket by the infirmary, that led through to the mill.

Hugh had brought down with him from the castle two sergeants and two of the young men of the garrison, all mounted, though they had left their horses tethered at the abbey gatehouse, and allowed the funeral procession to make its way along the Foregate to the cemetery before they showed themselves. While all eyes were on the prior and the coffin Hugh posted two men outside the open doors, to make a show of preventing any departures, while he and the sergeants went within, and made their way unobtrusively forward through the press. The very discretion with which they advanced, and the respectful silence they preserved when they had drawn close to the bier, which should have kept them inconspicuous, perversely drew every eye, so that by the time they were where Hugh had designed they should be, himself almost facing the prior across the coffin, the sergeants a pace or two behind Jordan Achard, one on either side, many a furtive glance had turned on them, and there was a wary shifting and staring and stealthy shuffling of feet on all sides. But Hugh held his hand until all was over.

Cynric and his helpers hoisted the coffin, and fitted the slings to lower it into the grave. Earth fell dully. The last prayer was said. There was the inevitable stillness and hush, before everyone would sigh and stir, and very slowly begin to move away. The sigh came like a sudden gust of wind, it fell from so many throats. The stir followed like the rustle of leaves in the gust. And Hugh said loudly and clearly, in a voice calculated to arrest any movement on the instant:

'My lord abbot, Father Prior ... I must ask your pardon for having placed a guard at your gate – outside your walls, but even so I beg your indulgence. No one must leave here until I've made known my purpose. Hold me excused that I must come at such a time, but there's no help for it. I am here in the name of the King's law, and in pursuit of a murderer. I am here to take into charge a felon suspected of the slaying of Father Ailnoth.'

Chapter Twelve

HERE WAS not very much to be found, but there was enough. Cadfael stood on the rim of the high bank where Ailnoth's body had bobbed and nestled, held fast there by the slight side impulse from the tail-race of the mill. The stump of the felled willow, no more than hip-high, bristled with its whips of blanched green hair. Some broken shoots among them, at the rim of the barren, dead surface, dried and cracked with time and jagged from the axe. And a finger length of black thread fluttering, one end securely held in the frayed ridge of dead wood. A finger length of unravelled woollen braid, just enough to complete the binding of a black skull-cap. Frost and thaw had come and gone, whitened and moistened and changed and obliterated whatever else had once been there to be found, a smear of blood, perhaps, some minute fragments of torn skin. Nothing left but a fluttering black roving, clawed loose when the cap flew wide and went with the current into the reeds.

Cadfael went back in haste with the infinitesimal scrap of wool in his hand. Halfway across the great court he heard the clamour of voices howling protest, excitement and confusion, and slackened his pace, for clearly there was no more need for haste. The trap was sprung, and must hold whatever it caught. Too late to prevent, at least he could undo whatever harm came of it, and if none came, so much the better. What he had to say and to show would keep.

497

Ninian reached the open track and the bridge over the Meole Brook in a glow from running most of the way, and remembered to slow to a walk before he reached the highway, close to the end of the bridge into Shrewsbury, and to haul up the hood of Sweyn's capuchon to shadow his face. At the turning into the Foregate he first checked in mild alarm, and then realized his luck and took heart, for so many people were still hurrying out of the town towards the abbey that it was very simple to mingle with them and be lost. He went with the stream, ears pricked for every word uttered around him, and heard his own name bandied back and forth with anticipatory relish. So that was the arrest some of these were expecting, though it could hardly be what Hugh Beringar had in mind, since he had lost the scent some days ago, and had no reason to suppose that he would recover it today. But others spoke of the woman, the priest's servant, not even knowing a name by which to call her. Others again were speculating wildly between two or three names unknown to Ninian, but who had evidently suffered under Ailnoth's unbending severities.

It seemed he had come only in time to join the stragglers in the traffic from the town, those who had been late in hearing the gossip, for the Foregate from the gatehouse of the abbey on was already crowded. Just as Ninian reached the gatehouse the clergy were emerging from the north door, and after them the coffin, and all the brothers in solemn procession. This was the one danger he must avoid, at least until he knew whether he had to face the worst, and deliver himself up of his own will. These were the men, any one of whom might know him on sight if he caught a clear glimpse of his face, indeed might be able to place him even by his build and gait. He withdrew hastily, weaving between the curious watchers to the far side of the street, and slipped into the mouth of the narrow alley until the monks had all passed by. After them came those of the parish worthies whose dignity had forbidden them to scurry first out of the church and secure a favourable place in the cemetery garth. And after them streamed the watchers in the Foregate, intent and avid as children and dogs after a travelling tumbler, though not so candidly loud in their anticipation of wonders.

To be the last and alone would be as bad as thrusting himself to the fore. Ninian slid out of concealment in time to join the rear guard, and hung just within the fringes as the cortège made its way along the Foregate to the corner by the horse-fair, and rounded it to the cemetery doors, which stood wide open.

There were a few besides himself, it seemed, who wanted to see everything there was to be seen, without making themselves conspicuous, and likewise preferred to hang upon the fringes of the crowd outside the gates, peering within. And that might be because two men of the castle garrison stood one on either side the entrance, very casually, not interfering with those who went in, but nevertheless to be eyed with caution.

Ninian halted in the wide opening, neither in nor out, and peered forward, craning to see between the massed heads, and reach the group gathered about the grave. Both abbot and prior were more than commonly tall, he could see them clearly above the rest, and hear the prayers of the committal ring aloud in Prior Robert's consciously mellifluous tones, to reach every ear. The prior had a genuinely splendid voice, and loved to exercise it in all the highly dramatic possibilities of the liturgy.

Edging a step or two to one side, Ninian caught a glimpse of Diota's face, a pale oval under her black hood. She stood close beside the bier, her due as the only member of the priest's household. The curve of a shoulder pressed close to hers, the arm linked in her arm, could only belong to Sanan, though no matter how he craned to one side and the other, he could not get a view of the beloved face, taller heads moved always between.

There was a ripple of movement as the priests advanced to the grave-side, the crowd swinging that way with them. The coffin was being lowered, the last dismissal spoken. Under the high precinct wall the first clods of earth fell on Father Ailnoth's coffin. It was almost over, and nothing had broken the decorum of the occasion. The first shuffle and rustle and stir passed through the assembly, acknowledging an ending. Ninian's heart settled in him, cautiously hoping, and as suddenly seemed to heave over in his breast as another voice, raised to carry clearly, spoke up from the grave-side.

'My lord abbot, Father Prior … I must ask your pardon for having placed a guard at your gate …'

For the beating of the blood in his ears Ninian missed what came next, but he knew the voice must belong to the sheriff, for who else bore such authority even here, within the enclave?

And the end he heard all too clearly: 'I am here to take into charge a felon suspected of the slaying of Father Ailnoth.'

So the worst had fallen on them, after all, just as rumour had foretold. There was a sudden stunned silence, and then a great buzz of confusion and excitement that shook the crowd like a gale of wind. The next words were lost, though Ninian held his breath and strained to hear. Some of those standing with him outside the gate had pressed forward, to miss nothing of this sensation, and no one had any ears for the clatter of hooves coming briskly round the corner by the horse-fair, and heading towards them at a trot. Within the walls there came a sudden wild outcry, a babel of voices exclaiming and protesting, bombarding those before them with questions, passing back probably inaccurate answers to those behind. Ninian braced himself to plunge in and shoulder his way through to where his womenfolk stood embattled and defenceless. For it was over, his liberty was forfeit, if not his life. He drew breath deep, and laid his hand on the shoulder of the nearest body that barred his way, for the curious had abandoned caution and filled up the open gateway.

The bellow of dismay and indignation that suddenly rose from under the precinct wall stopped him in his tracks and hurled him back almost physically from the doorway. A man's voice, howling protests, calling heaven to witness his innocence. Not Diota! Not Diota, but a man!

'My lord, I swear to you I know nothing of it … I never saw hide or hair of him that day or that night. I was fast at home, my wife will tell you so! I never harmed any man, much less a priest … Someone has lied about me, lied! My lord abbot, as God sees me …'

The name was borne back to Ninian's ears rank by rank through the crowd. 'Jordan Achard … it was Jordan Achard … They're seizing Jordan Achard …'

Ninian stood trembling, weak with reaction, and so neglectful of his own situation that he had let the hood of Sweyn's capuchon slip back from his head and lie in folds on his shoulders. Behind him the hooves had halted, shifting lightly in the thin mud of the thaw.

'Hey, you, fellow!'

The butt of a whip jabbed him sharply in the back, and he swung about, startled, to look up directly into the face of a rider who leaned down to him from the saddle of a fine roan horse. A big, ruddy, sinewy man in his fifties, perhaps, very

500

spruce in his own gear and the accoutrements of his mount, and with the nobleman's authority in his voice and face. A handsome face, bearded and strong-featured, now just beginning to run to flesh and lose its taut, clear lines, but still memorable. The brief moment they spent staring closely at each other was terminated by a second impatient but good-natured prod of the whip's butt against Ninian's shoulder, and the brisk order:

'Yes, you, lad! Hold my horse while I'm within, and you shan't be the loser. What's afoot in there, do you know? Someone's making a fine noise about it.'

In the exuberance of relief from his terror for Diota, Ninian rebounded into impudent glee, knuckled his forehead obsequiously, and reached willingly for the bridle, once again the penniless peasant groom Benet to the life. 'I don't rightly know, master,' he said, 'but there's some in there saying a man's been taken up for killing the priest ...' He smoothed a hand over the horse's silken forehead and between the pricked ears, and the roan tossed his head, turned a soft, inquisitive muzzle to breathe warmth at him, and accepted the caress graciously. 'A lovely beast, my lord! I'll mind him well.'

'So the murderer's taken, is he? Rumour told truth for once.' The rider was down in a moment, and off through the quivering crowd like a sickle cutting grass, a brusque, hard shoulder forward and a masterful tongue ready to demand passage. Ninian was left with his cheek against a glossy shoulder, and a tangle of feelings boiling within him, laughter and gratitude, and the joyful anticipation of a journey now free from all regrets and reservations, but also a small, bitter jet of sadness that one man was dead untimely, and another now accused of his murder. It took him some little time to remember to pull the hood over his head again, and well forward to shadow his face, but luckily all attention was fixed avidly upon the hubbub within the cemetery garth, and no one was paying any heed to a hind holding his master's horse in the street. The horse was excellent cover, but it did prevent him from advancing again into the wide-open doorway, and even by straining his ears he could make little sense out of the babel from within. The clamour of terrified protest went on for some time, that was plain enough, and the shrill commentary from the bystanders made a criss-cross of conflicting sounds around it. If there were saner voices speaking, Hugh Beringar's or the abbot's, they were drowned in the general chaos.

501

Ninian leaned his forehead against the warm hide that quivered gently under his touch, and offered devout thanks for so timely a deliverance.

In the heart of the tumult Abbot Radulfus raised a voice that seldom found it necessary to thunder, and thundered to instant effect.

'Silence! You bring shame on yourselves and desecrate this holy place. Silence, I say!'

And there was silence, sudden and profound, though it might as easily break out in fresh chaos if the rein was not tightened.

'So, and keep silence, all you who have nothing here to plead or deny. Let those speak and be heard who have. Now, my lord sheriff, you accuse this man Jordan Achard of murder. On what evidence?'

'On the evidence,' said Hugh, 'of a witness who has said and will say again that he lies in saying he spent that night at home. Why, if he has nothing to hide, should he find it necessary to lie? On the evidence also of a witness who saw him creeping out from the mill path and making for his home at earliest light on Christmas morning. It is enough to hold him upon suspicion,' said Hugh crisply, and motioned to the two sergeants, who grasped the terrified Jordan almost tenderly by the arms. 'That he had a grievance against Father Ailnoth is known to everyone.'

'My lord abbot,' babbled Jordan, quaking, 'on my soul I swear I never touched the priest. I never saw him, I was not there ... it's false ... they lie about me ...'

'It seems there are those,' said Radulfus, 'who will equally swear that you were there.'

'It was I who told that I'd seen him,' spoke up the reeve's shepherd cousin, worried and shaken by the result he had achieved. 'I could say no other, for I did see him, and it was barely light, and all I've told is truth. But I never intended mischief, and I never thought any harm but that he was at his games, for I knew what's said of him ...'

'And what is said of you, Jordan?' asked Hugh mildly.

Jordan swallowed and writhed, agonized between shame at owning where he had spent his night, and terror of holding out and risking worse. Sweating and wriggling, he blurted: 'No evil, I'm a man well respected ... If I was there, it was for no wrong purpose. I ... I had business there early, charitable

502

business there early – with the old Widow Warren who lives along there ...'

'Or late, with her slut of a maidservant,' called a voice from the safe anonymity of the crowd, and a great ripple of laughter went round, hastily suppressed under the abbot's flashing glare.

'Was that the truth of it? And by chance under Father Ailnoth's eye?' demanded Hugh. 'He would look very gravely upon such depravity, from all accounts. Did he catch you sneaking into the house, Jordan? I hear he was apt to reprove sin on the spot, and harshly. Is that how you came to kill him and leave him in the pool?'

'I never did!' howled Jordan. 'I swear I never had ado with him. If I did fall into sin with the girl, that was all I did. I never went past the house. Ask her, she'll tell you! I was there all night long ...'

And all this time Cynric had gone on patiently and steadily filling in the grave, without haste, without apparently paying any great attention to all the tumult at his back. During this last exchange he had straightened up creakily, and stretched until his joints cracked. Now he turned to thrust his way into the centre of the circle, the iron-shod spade still dangling in his hand.

So strange an intrusion from so solitary and withdrawn a man silenced all voices and drew all eyes.

'Let him be, my lord,' said Cynric. 'Jordan had nought to do with the man's death.' He turned his greying head and long, sombre, deep-eyed face from Hugh to the abbot, and back again. 'There's none but I,' he said simply, 'knows how Ailnoth came by his end.'

Then there was utter silence, beyond what the abbot's authority had been able to invoke, a silence deep enough to drown in, as Ailnoth had drowned. The verger stood tall and dignified in his rusty black, waiting to be questioned further, without fear or regret, seeing nothing strange in what he had said, and no reason why he should have said more or said it earlier, but willing to bear with those who demanded explanations.

'You know?' said the abbot, after long and astonished contemplation of the man before him. 'And you have not spoken before?'

'I saw no need. There was no other soul put in peril, not till now. The thing was done, best leave well alone.'

'Are you saying,' demanded Radulfus doubtfully, 'that you were there, that you witnessed it? ... Was it *you* ...?'

'No,' said Cynric with a slow shake of his long, grizzled head. 'I did not touch him.' His voice was patient and gentle, as it would have been to questioning children. 'I was there, I witnessed it. But I did not touch him.'

'Then tell us now,' said Hugh quietly. 'Who killed him?'

'No one killed him,' said Cynric. 'Those who do violence die by the same. It's only just.'

'Tell us,' said Hugh again as softly. 'Tell us how this befell. Let us all know, and be at peace again. You are saying his death was an accident?'

'No accident,' said Cynric, and his eyes burned in their deep sockets. 'A judgement.'

He moistened his lips, and lifted his head to stare into the wall of the Lady Chapel, above their heads, as if he, who was illiterate, could read there the words he had to say, he who was a man of few words by nature.

'I went out that night to the pool. I have often walked there by night, when there has been no moon, and none awake to see. Between the willow trees there, beyond the mill, where she went into the water ... Eluned, Nest's girl ... because Ailnoth refused her confession and the uses of the church, denounced her before all the parish and shut the door in her face. He could as well have stabbed her to the heart, it would have been kinder. All that brightness and beauty taken from us ... I knew her well, she came so often for comfort while Father Adam lived, and he never failed her. And when she was not fretting over her sins she was like a bird, like a flower, a joy to see. There are not so many things of beauty in the world that a man should destroy one of them, and make no amends. And when she fell into remorse she was like a child ... she *was* a child, it was a child he cast out ...'

He fell silent for a moment, as though the words had become hard to read by reason of the blindness of grief, and furrowed his high forehead to decipher them the better, but no one ventured to speak.

'There I was standing, where Eluned went into the pool, when he came along the path. I did not know who it was, he did not come as far as where I stood – but someone, a man stamping and muttering, there by the mill. A man in a rage, or so it sounded. Then a woman came stumbling after him, I heard her cry out to him, she went on her knees to him,

504

weeping, and he was trying to shake her off, and she would not let go of him. He struck her – I heard the blow. She made no more than a moan, but then I did go towards them, thinking there could be murder done, and therefore I saw – dimly, but I had my night eyes, and I did see – how he swung his stick at her again, and she clung with both hands to the head of it to save herself, and how he tugged at it with all his strength and tore it out of her hands ... The woman ran from him, I heard her stumbling away along the path, but I doubt she ever heard what I heard, or knows what I know. I heard him reel backwards and crash into the stump of the willow. I heard the withies lash and break. I heard the splash – it was not a great sound – as he went into the water.'

There was another silence, long and deep, while he thought, and laboured to remember with precision, since that was required of him. Brother Cadfael, coming up quietly behind the ranks of the awestruck brothers, had heard only the latter part of Cynric's story, but he had the poor draggled proof of it in his hand as he listened. Hugh's trap had caught nothing, rather it had set everyone free. He looked across the mute circle to where Diota stood, with Sanan's arm about her. Both women had drawn their hoods close round their faces. One of the hands torn by the sharp edges of the silver band held the folds of Diota's cloak together.

'I went towards the place,' said Cynric, 'and looked into the water. It was only then I knew him certainly for Ailnoth. He drifted at my feet, stunned or dazed ... I knew his face. His eyes were open ... And I turned my back and walked away from him, as he turned his back on her and walked away from her, shutting the door on her tears as he struck at this other woman's tears ... If God had willed him to live, he would have lived. Why else should it happen there, in that very place? And who am I, to usurp the privilege of God?'

All this he delivered in the same reasonable voice with which he would have rendered account of the number of candles bought for the parish altar, though the words came slowly and with effort and thought, studying to make all plain now that plainness was needed. But to Abbot Radulfus it had some distant echo of the voice of prophecy. Even if the man had wished to save, could he have saved? Might not the priest have been already past saving? And there in the dark, alone, with no time to summon help, since everyone was preparing for the night office, and with that undercut bank to contend with, and

505

the dead weight of a big man to handle – could any man, singly, have saved? Better to suppose that the thing had been impossible, and accept what to Cynric was the will of God!

'And now with your leave, my lord abbot,' said Cynric, having waited courteously but vainly for some comment or question, 'if you've no more need of me I'll be getting on with filling in the grave, for I'll need the most of the daylight to make a good job of it.'

'Do so,' said the abbot, and looked at him for a moment, eye to eye, with no shadow of blame, and saw no shadow of doubt. 'Do so, and come to me for your fee when it is done.'

Cynric went as he had come, back to his work, and those who watched him in awe-stricken silence saw no change in his long-legged walk, or in the quiet, steady rhythm with which he plied his spade.

Radulfus looked at Hugh, and then to Jordan Achard, mute and wilting with relief from terror between his guards. For a brief instant the abbot's austere face was shaken by the merest fleeting shadow of a smile. 'My lord sheriff, I think your charge against this man is already answered. What other offences he may have on his conscience,' said the abbot, fixing the demoralized Jordan with a severe eye, 'I recommend him to bring to confession. And to avoid henceforward! He may well reflect on the dangers into which such a manner of life has led him, and take this day as a warning.'

'For my part, I'm glad to know the truth and find that none of us here has the guilt of murder on his soul,' said Hugh. 'Master Achard, take yourself home and be glad you have a loyal and dutiful wife. Lucky for you there was one here to speak for you, for there was a strong case against you had there been no such witness. Loose him!' he said to his sergeants. 'Let him be about his business. By rights he owes a gift to the parish altar, by way of thanks for a good deliverance.'

Jordan all but sagged to the ground when the two officers took their hands from him, and Will Warden was moved in good humour to lend him a supporting hand again under one arm until he got his legs to stand solid under him. And now at last it was truly over, but that every soul there was so petrified with wonder that it took another benediction by way of dismissal to start them moving.

'Go now, good people,' said the abbot, somewhat brusquely accepting the need. 'Make your prayers for the soul of Father Ailnoth, and bear in mind that our neighbour's failings should but make us mindful rather of our own. Go, and trust to us who have the grant of this parish to bestow, to consider your needs above all in whatever we determine.' And he blessed them departing, with a vigour and brevity that actually set them in motion. Silent as yet, even as they melted like snow and began to move away, but soon they would be voluble enough. Town and Foregate would ring with the many and contradictory accounts of this morning's events, to be transmuted at last into myth, a folk memory of momentous things witnessed, once, long ago.

'And you, brothers,' said Radulfus shortly, turning to his own flock, doves with fluttered feathers now and disrupted cooing, 'go now to your daily duties, and make ready for dinner.'

They broke ranks almost fearfully, and drifted apart as the rest were doing, apparently aimlessly at first, then making slowly for the places where now they should be. Like sparks from a fire, or dust scattered on a wind, they disseminated, still half-dazed with revelation. The only one who went about his business with purpose and method was Cynric, busy with his spade under the wall.

Brother Jerome, deeply disturbed by proceedings which in no way fitted in with his conception of the rule and routine of the Benedictine order, went about rounding up some of his strayed chicks towards the lavatorium and the frater, and shooing some of the lingering parishioners out of the abbey's confines. In so doing he drew near to the wide-open doors upon the Foregate, and became aware of a young man standing in the street outside, holding the bridle of a horse, and casting an occasional brief glance over those emerging, but from within a close-drawn capuchon, so that his face was not clearly visible. But there was something about him that held Jerome's sharp eyes. Something not quite recognized, since the coat and capuchon were strange, and the face obstinately averted, and yet something reminiscent of a certain young fellow known for a while to the brethren, and later vanished in strange circumstances. If only the fellow would once turn his face fully!

Cadfael, lingering to watch Sanan and Diota depart, saw them instead draw back into the shadow of the chapel wall, and wait there until the greater part of the throng had moved towards the Foregate. The impulse came from Sanan, he saw her restraining hand laid upon the older woman's arm, and wondered why she should delay. Had she seen someone among

the crowd whom she was anxious not to encounter? In search
of such a person, he scanned the retreating backs, and saw one
at least whose presence there would certainly not be too
welcome to her. And had she not, like Diota, drawn the hood
of her cloak closely round her face, during the time that
Cadfael himself had been absent, as if to avoid being noticed
and recognized by someone?

Now the two women began to move after the rest, but with
cautious slowness, and Sanan's eyes were intent upon the back
of the tall man who had almost reached the open doorway.
Thus both Sanan and Cadfael at the same moment also saw
Brother Jerome, hovering hesitant for a moment, and then
making purposefully for the street. And following the
converging courses of these two very dissimilar backs, the one
erect and confident, the other meagre and stooped, inevitably
lighted upon the horse waiting in the Foregate, and the young
man holding his bridle.

Brother Jerome was still not quite sure, though he was bent
on making sure, even if it meant leaving the precinct without
due reason or permission. It would be counted due reason
enough if he succeeded in raising a righteous alarm, and
handing over a fugitive enemy of the King to the King's justice.
A guard outside the gates, the sheriff had said. He had but to
halloo the soldiers on to their quarry, who stood within arm's
reach, believing himself safe. If, of course, *if* this really was the
youngster once known as Benet?

But if Jerome was not yet certain, Sanan was, and Cadfael
was. Who, in these parts, had known that figure and stance and
carriage as well as they? And there was Jerome bearing down
upon him with plainly malevolent intent, before their eyes, and
they had no way of preventing the disaster.

Sanan dropped Diota's arm and started forward. Cadfael,
approaching from another angle, bellowed: '*Brother!*' per-
emptorily after Jerome, in a self-righteous and scandalized
voice of which Jerome himself need not have been ashamed, in
the hope of diverting his attention, but vainly. Jerome
nose-down on the trail of a malefactor was almost as
undeflectable as Father Ailnoth himself. It was left to someone
else to turn the trick.

Ninian's horseman, long-legged and striding briskly away
from a field which left him unthreatened and well satisfied,
arrived at the doorway only a pace or two ahead of Jerome,
indeed he brushed past him into the Foregate. Not the ending

he had expected, but on the whole he was glad of it. As long as he was neither suspect of disloyalty nor threatened with loss of lands or status, he bore no grudge now against the rash young man who had caused him so much anxiety. Let him get away unscathed, provided he never came back here to make trouble for others.

Ninian had glanced round to see his patron approaching, and saw at the same time, very belatedly, the ferret countenance of Brother Jerome, all too clearly making for him with no kindly intent. There was no time to evade, he had no choice but to stand his ground. Blessedly the horseman reached him barely ahead of the hunter, and blessedly he was well content with whatever he had witnessed within, for he clapped his horse-boy on the shoulder as the bridle was surrendered into his hand. Ninian made haste to stoop to the stirrup, and hold it for the rider to mount.

It was enough! Jerome stopped so abruptly in the gateway that Erwald, coming behind, collided with him, and put him aside good-naturedly with one large hand as he passed. And by that time the horseman had dropped a careless word of thanks into Ninian's ear and a silver penny into his hand, and set off back along the Foregate at a leisurely trot, to vanish round the corner by the horse-fair ground, with his supposed groom loping behind him on foot.

A lucky escape, thought Ninian, dropping into a walk as soon as he was round the corner of the high wall and out of sight. And he span delightedly in his hand the silver penny a satisfied and lavish patron had tossed to him as he rode away. God bless the man, whoever he may be, he's saved my life, or at least my hide! A man of consequence, and evidently well known here. Just as well for me his grooms are not equally well known, and all over fifty and bearded, or I should have been a lost man.

A lucky escape, thought Cadfael, heaving a great sigh of relief, and turning back to where Hugh still stood in earnest talk with Abbot Radulfus, under the great east window of the Lady Chapel. Salvation comes from strange places and unexpected friends. And a very apt ending, too!

A lucky escape, thought Sanan, shaking with dismay and fear suddenly transmuted into triumphant laughter. And he has no idea what has just happened! Neither of them has! Oh, to see Ninian's face when I tell him!

A lucky escape, thought Jerome, scurrying thankfully back

to his proper duties. I should have made a sorry fool of myself if I had challenged him. A mere chance resemblance in figure and bearing, after all, nothing more. What a blessing for me that his master brushed by in time to acknowledge him as his, and warn me of my error.

For of course, Ralph Giffard, of all people, could scarcely be harbouring in his own service the very man he himself had so properly denounced to the law!

Chapter Thirteen

'THERE IS one question,' said the abbot, 'which not only has not been answered, it has not yet been asked.'

He had waited until the table was cleared, and his guest supplied with the final cup of wine. Radulfus never allowed business of any kind to be discussed during a meal. The pleasures of the table were something he used sparingly, but respected.

'What is that?' asked Hugh.

'Has he told all the truth?'

Hugh looked up sharply across the table. 'Cynric? Who can say of any man that he never lies? But general report of Cynric says that he never speaks at all unless he must, and then to the point. It is why he said nothing until Jordan was accused. Words come very hard to Cynric. I doubt if he ever in his life used as many in one day as we heard from him in a handful of moments this morning. I doubt if he would waste breath on lying, when even necessary truth costs him such labour.'

'He was eloquent enough today,' said Radulfus with a wry smile. 'But I should be glad if we had some sure sign to confirm what he told us. He may very well have done no more than turn and walk away, and leave the issue of life and death to God, or whatever force he regards as the arbiter of justice in such a strange case. Or he may have struck the blow himself. Or he may have seen the thing happen, much as he says, but helped the priest into the water while he was stunned. Granted

I do not think Cynric would be very ingenious at making up plausible tales to cover the event, yet we cannot *know*. Nor do I think him at all a man of violence, even where he found much to provoke it, but again we cannot *know*. And even if we have the entire truth from him, what should be done about such a man? How proceed with him?'

'For my part,' said Hugh firmly, 'nothing can or will be done. There is no law he has broken. It may be a sin to allow a death to take place, it is not a crime. I hold fast to my own writ. Sinners are in your province, not mine.' He did not add that there was some accounting due from the man who had brought Ailnoth, a stranger scarcely known, to assume the pastoral care of a bereaved flock that had no voice in the choosing of their new shepherd. But he suspected that the thought was in the abbot's mind, and had been ever since the first complaints were brought to his ears. He was not a man to shut his eyes to his own errors, or shirk his own responsibilities.

'This I can tell you,' said Hugh. 'What he said of the woman who followed Ailnoth and was struck down by him is certainly true. Mistress Hammet claimed then that she had fallen on the icy ground. That was a lie. The priest did that to her, she has owned it since to Brother Cadfael, who treated her injuries. And since I have now brought Cadfael into this, I think you would do well, my lord, to send for him. I have had no chance to speak with him since the events of this morning, and it's in my mind that he may have something further to say in this matter. He was missing from the ranks of the brothers in the cemetery when I came, for I looked for him and couldn't find him. He came later, not from the Foregate but from within the court. He would not have absented himself but for good reason. If he has things to tell me, I cannot afford to neglect them.'

'Neither, it seems, can I,' said Radulfus, and reached for the little bell that lay on his desk. The small silver chime brought in his secretary from the ante-room. 'Brother Vitalis, will you find Brother Cadfael, and ask him to come here to us?'

When the door had closed again the abbot sat silent for a while, considering. 'I know now, of course,' he said at last, 'that Father Ailnoth was indeed grossly deceived, and that is some extenuation for him. But the woman – I gather she is no kin to the youth she sheltered, the one we knew as Benet? – she had been an exemplary servant to her master for three years, her only offence was in protecting the young man, an

512

offence which sprang only from affection. There shall be no penalty visited upon her, never by my authority. She shall have quiet living here, since it was I who brought her here. If we get a new priest who has neither mother nor sister to mind his dwelling, then she may serve him as she did Ailnoth, and I hope there may never be reason for her to kneel to him but in the confessional, and none ever for him to strike her. And as for the boy ...' He looked back with a resigned and tolerant eye, and shook his head a little, smiling. 'I remember we gave him to Cadfael to do the rough work before the winter freeze. I saw him once in the garden, digging the long butt. At least he gave honest value. FitzAlan's squire was not afraid to dig, nor ashamed.' He looked up, head tilted, into Hugh's face. 'You don't, by any chance, know ...?'

'I have been rather careful not to know,' said Hugh.

'Well ... I am glad he never fouled his hands with murder. I saw them black enough with soil, from plucking out the weeds too gross to be dug in,' said Radulfus, and smiled distantly, looking out of the window at a pearl-grey, low-hanging sky. 'I expect he'll do well enough. Pity of all pities there should be one such young man in arms against another in this land, but at least let the steel be bared only in the open field, not privily in the dark.'

Cadfael laid out on the abbot's desk the remaining relics of Father Ailnoth, the ebony staff, the draggled black skull-cap with its torn binding, and the unravelled woollen remnant of braid that completed the circle.

'Cynric told simple truth, and here are the proofs of it. Only this morning when I saw Mistress Hammet's open hand once again, and remembered the grazes I had dressed, did I understand how she got those injuries. Not from a fall – there was no fall. The wound on her head was dealt by this staff, for I found several long hairs of her greying light-brown colour here, caught in the frayed edges of this silver band. You see it's worn wafer-thin, and the edges turned and cracking.'

Radulfus ran a long, lean finger round the crumpled, razor-sharp rim, and nodded grimly. 'Yes, I see. And from this same band she got the grazes to her hands. He swung his staff at her a second time, so Cynric said, and she caught and clung to it, to save her head ...'

'... and he tugged at it with all his strength, and tore it by main force out of her hands,' said Hugh, 'to his own undoing.'

513

'They could not have been many paces past the mill,' said Cadfael, 'for Cynric was some way beyond, among the willows. On the side of that first stump that overhangs the pool I found a few broken withies, and this black ravelling of wool braid snagged in the cracked, dead wood of the stump. The priest went stunned or dazed into the water, the cap flew from his head, leaving this scrap held fast in the tree, as the silver band held her torn hairs. The staff was flung from his hand. The winter turf is tufted and rough there, no wonder if he caught his heel, as he reeled backwards when she loosed her hold. He crashed into the stump. The axe that felled it, long ago, left it uneven, the jagged edge took him low at the back of the head. Father, you saw the wound. So did the sheriff.'

'I saw it,' said Radulfus. 'And the woman knew nothing from the time she ran from him?'

'She barely knows how she got home. Certainly she waited out the night in dread, expecting him to finish what he intended against the boy, and return to his house to denounce and cast her out. But he never came.'

'Could he have been saved?' wondered the abbot, grieving as much for the roused and resentful flock as for the dead shepherd.

'In the dark,' said Cadfael, 'I doubt if any one man could have got him from under that bank, however he laboured at it. Even had there been help within reach, I think he would have drowned before ever they got him out.'

'At the risk of falling into sin,' said Radulfus, with a smile that began sourly and ended in resignation, 'I find that comforting. We have not a murderer among us, at any rate.'

'Talk of falling into sin,' said Cadfael later, when he and Hugh were sitting easy together in the workshop in the herb garden, 'forces me to examine my own conscience. I enjoy some privileges, by reason of being called on to attend sick people outside the enclave, and also by virtue of having a godson to visit. But I ought not to take advantage of that permission for my own ends. Which I have done shamelessly on three or four occasions since Christmas. Indeed, Father Abbot must be well aware that I went out from the precinct this very morning without leave, but he's said no word about it.'

'No doubt he takes it for granted you'll be making proper confession voluntarily, at chapter tomorrow,' said Hugh, straight-faced.

'That I doubt! He'd hardly welcome it. I should have to explain the reason, and I know his mind by now. There are old hawks like Radulfus and myself in here, who can stand the gales, but there are also innocents who will not benefit by too stormy a wind blowing through the dovecote. He's fretted enough about Ailnoth's influence, now he wants it put by and soon forgotten. And I prophesy, Hugh, that the Foregate will soon have a new priest, and one who is known and welcome not only to us who have the bestowing of the benefice, but to those who are likely to reap the results. No better way of burying Ailnoth.'

'In all fairness,' said Hugh thoughtfully, 'it would have been a very delicate matter to reject a priest recommended by the papal legate, even for a man of your abbot's stature. And the fellow was impressive to the eye and the ear, and had scholarship ... No wonder Radulfus thought he was bringing you a treasure. God send you a decent, humble, common man next time.'

'Amen! Whether he has Latin or not! And here am I the well-wisher, if not the accomplice, of an enemy of the King, criminal as well as sinner! Did I say I was being obliged to search my conscience? But not too diligently – that always leads to trouble.'

'I wonder,' said Hugh, smiling indulgently into the glow of the brazier, 'if they'll have set out yet?'

'Not until dark, I fancy. Overnight they'll be gone. I hope she has somehow left word for Ralph Giffard,' said Cadfael, considering. 'He's no bad man, only driven, as so many are now, and mainly for his son. She had no complaint of him, except that he had compounded with fortune, and given up his hopes for the Empress. Being more than thirty years short of his age, she finds that incomprehensible. But you and I, Hugh, can comprehend it all too well. Let the young ones go their own gait, and find their own way.'

He sat smiling, thinking of the pair of them, but chiefly of Ninian, lively and bold and impudent, and a stout performer with the spade, even though he had never had one in his hand before, and had to learn the craft quickly. 'I never had such a stout-hearted labourer under me here since Brother John – that must be nearly five years now! The one who stayed in Gwytherin, and married the smith's niece. He'll have made a doughty smith himself by now. Benet reminded me of him, some ways ... all or nothing, and ready for every venture.'

'Ninian,' said Hugh, correcting him almost absently.

'True, Ninian we must call him now, but I tend to forget. But I haven't told you,' said Cadfael, kindling joyfully to the recollection, 'the very best of the ending. In the middle of so much aggravation and suspicion and death, a joke is no bad thing.'

'I wouldn't say no to that,' agreed Hugh, leaning forward to mend the fire with a few judiciously placed pieces of charcoal, with the calculated pleasure of one for whom such things are usually done by others. 'But I saw very little sign of one today. Where did you find it?'

'Why, you were kept busy talking with Father Abbot, close by the grave, while the rest were dispersing. You had no chance to observe it. But I was loose, and so was Brother Jerome, with his nose twitching for officious mischief, as usual. Sanan saw it,' said Cadfael, with fond recollection. 'It scared the wits out of her for a moment or two, but then it was all resolved. You know, Hugh, how wide those double doors of ours are, in the wall ...'

'I came that way,' said Hugh patiently, a little sleepy with relief from care, the fumes of the brazier, and the early start to a day now subsiding into a dim and misty evening. 'I know!'

'There was a young fellow holding a horse, out there in the Foregate. Who was to notice him until everyone began screaming out by that way? Jerome was running like a sheep-dog about the fringes, hustling them out, he was bound to take a frequent look out there to the streets. He saw a man he thought he recognized, and went closer to view, all panting with fervour and zeal – you know him!'

'Every uncoverer of evil acquires merit,' said Hugh, taking idle pleasure in the mild satire upon Brother Jerome. 'What merit could there be for him there, in a lad holding a horse?'

'Why, one Benet, or Ninian, hunted as recreant to our lord King Stephen, and denounced to our lord sheriff – saving your presence, Hugh, but you know you were just confirmed in office, you mean more now to Brother Jerome than ever before! – by Ralph Giffard, no less. That is what Jerome saw, barring that the malefactor did seem to be wearing clothes never seen on him before.'

'Now you do surprise me,' said Hugh, turning a gleaming and amused face upon his friend. 'And this really was the said Benet or Ninian?'

'It was indeed. I knew him, and so did Sanan when she looked ahead, where Jerome was looking, and saw him there. The lad himself, Hugh, bold as ever to plunge his head into

516

whatever snare. Come to make sure himself where the blame was flying, and see that none of it fell upon his nurse. God knows what he would have done, if you had not carolled aloud your preference for Jordan. After all, what did he know of all that happened after he came panting into the church, that night? It could have been Jordan, for all he knew. No doubt he believed it was, once you bayed the quarry.'

'I have a fine, bell-mouthed bay,' acknowledged Hugh, grinning. 'And just as well Father Abbot kept me talking and would have me stay and dine with him, or I might have run my nose full into this madcap lad of yours, and just as Jerome plucked him by the hood. So how did all this end? I heard no foray in the Foregate.'

'There was none,' agreed Cadfael complacently. 'Ralph Giffard was there among the crowd, did you never see him? He's tall enough to top most of the Foregate folk. But there, you were held fast in the middle, no time to look about you. He was there. At the end he turned to go, not worst pleased, I fancy, that you had no hold on the lad he'd felt obliged to hand to you earlier. It was good to see, Hugh! He shouldered past Jerome, having legs so much longer, just as our most eager hound had his nose down on a hot scent. And he took the bridle from the lad's hand, and even smiled at him, eye to eye, and the lad held his stirrup for him and steadied him astride, as good a groom as ever you saw. And Jerome baulked like a hound at a loss, and came scuttling back, aghast that he'd as good as howled accusation at Giffard's own groom, waiting honestly for his master. That was when I saw Sanan shudder into such laughter as might almost have broken her apart, but that she's very sturdily made, that lady! And Giffard rode away, back along the Foregate, and the groom that was no groom of his went trotting after him afoot, out of sight and away.'

'And this verily happened?' demanded Hugh,

'Son, I saw it. I shall cherish it. Off they went and Ralph Giffard threw a silver penny to young Ninian, and Ninian caught it and went on his way round the corner and out of sight, before he stopped for breath. And still does not know, I suppose,' said Cadfael, peering through the doorway into a late afternoon light that still lacked an hour or so to Vespers, 'still does not know to whom he owes his salvation. How I would love to be by, when Sanan tells him to whom he owes his fat pay for less than an hour of holding a horse! I wager that lad

517

will never part with that penny, he'll have it pierced for his neck or for hers. There are now many such keepsakes,' said Cadfael smugly, 'in one lifetime.'

'Are you telling me,' said Hugh, delighted, 'that those two met so and parted so, in mutual service, and had no notion with whom they dealt?'

'No notion in the world! They had exchanged messages, they were allies, adversaries, friends, enemies, what you please, in the most intimate degree,' said Cadfael, with deep and grateful contentment, 'but neither of them had the least idea what the other one looked like. They had never once set eyes on each other.'